The Spirit Shield Saga Collection

Susan Faw

Soul Survivor

Seer of Souls

Soul Sanctuary

Soul Sacrifice

Cover Design by Greg Simanson
Edited by Pam Elise Harris

This is a work of fiction. Names, characters, places, brands, media, and incidents are either the product of the author's imagination or are used fictitiously. Any resemblance to similarly named places or to persons living or deceased is unintentional.

Soul Survivor

"Artio, the moon godling, slumped to the horizon, blood red. Helga found her oozing a bloody light across the heavens.
Convinced that her sister was dying, Helga carried her into the bowels of the earth.
The darkness stilled Artio's light.
Helga believed Artio would be reborn as the rest of the mortals of the earth were, but the godling had no one to care for her rebirth and was forever lost.
Caerwyn and Alfreda banished Helga to the depths of the underworld, never to return, for the crime of slaying a godling.

So began the Battle of Daimon Ford."

Excerpt from the Tome of Salvation, Sixth Scribed Copy, Royal Library of Cathair

Chapter 1

Caerwyn

CAERWYN STRODE THROUGH the palatial gardens of Cathair, a royal purple, autumn oak leaf embroidered cape billowing over his rune-enhanced armour plate. The segmented chest sections clicked in time to his hurried stride while his manservant sidestepped and hopped striving to keep up.

The manservant tugged at the flapping leather straps of Caerwyn's metal-studded leather greaves, struggling to tighten them onto his swinging arm, all the while casting anxious glances at his footing. He juggled the king's helmet in the crook of his right elbow and his sword belt over the left.

"One moment, my king!" he puffed. "If you will pause for just a moment, I can complete your battle armour."

Caerwyn growled in response and did not pause until he reached the cool shade created by the towering outer curtain wall. Stone steps led to the battlements at the end of the curving stone walkway that hugged the curtain. Horns blared overhead, long and low, warning of the approach of an enemy force.

"Be about it quickly, Hud." Caerwyn held his arms out at his side, his impatience evident in the tightening of his jaw. Hud swiftly fastened the greaves and swung the sheath of Caerwyn's sword around his waist, buckling it into place before he bowed over the king's helm, an intricately carved metal bowl with large wings decorating both sides and a long nose plate, dividing his face in half.

Caerwyn bent his neck, and Hud slid it onto his head.

Straightening, Caerwyn met Hud's eyes creased with worry. He placed his hand on Hud's shoulder and squeezed gently. "Let us pray it is good news approaching our gates this day for the tidings have been ill as of late." Caerwyn turned and strode away to the stairs, taking them two at a time, his guard of hand-picked Kingsmen hurrying to keep up in his wake.

Hud, pensive and preoccupied, watched the god-king mount the stairs until he vanished from view. With a sigh, he hobbled back in the direction of the armoury. He massaged his hip as he limped across the stony clearing, attempting to ease the annoyingly painful twinges.

Battle is for the young, thought the salt and pepper-haired Hud, but it was an empty thought. He longed for nothing more than to be able to raise his sword in battle once again to defend his king and god.

Hud's sword arm was strong and true, but he could no longer sit a saddle or ride a Pegasus, a requirement of active service in the Kingsmen. Now in retirement, Hud tended the king directly, for even though he could not fly, his skill with a sword and his knowledge of battle had not dimmed. In addition to his duties to his sire, he put whetstone to blade in the armoury and oversaw the care of the winged mounts of the royal stables.

He grabbed the large circular pull on the heavy oak armoury door and pulled, his hip squealing in protest, a personal echo of the rusted hinges. He gritted his teeth then hobbled into the dim interior as the door swung and creaked behind him.

Rows and rows of swords hanging by their hilts on wooden racks met his eyes, glinting in the light streaming from high narrow windows set into the drystone walls. The smell of oil and polishing paste blended with the scent of cedar. He inhaled deeply, and limping over the workbench in the corner, eased himself onto it then took up where he had left off, polishing the flat of a fine curved blade. At least this much of his day was the same. He set to work, and the repetitive action relaxed him and the pain in his hip eased.

He placed the finished sword on the rack beside him then bent to pick up his third sword, laying it on the table and dipped the cloth into the pot of hot oil, when the castle warning bells rang out in alarm.

*   *   *

Caerwyn cleared the lip of the staircase, pulling his sword as he ran to the battlement to peer down at the approaching army.

A billowing cloud of dust created by the feet of many mounts partially obscured their numbers but was easily spotted by the watchtowers, and the battlement was consequently crowded four deep with fully armed Kingsmen, who parted their ranks for the king as he made his way to his Captain General.

Captain Brennan focused his one good eye on the king, shouldering his way to the front lines, frowning at the king as he strode up to Brennan. Despite his armour-clad form, the king screamed royalty, his purple cape fastened at the throat by an eagle pin.

"Might as well pin a flaming bullseye on your chest," Captain Brennan grumbled audibly. "Who told you weak-willed curs to stand aside?" he bellowed "It's just the flaming king! Back to your positions!" he roared, his drooping mustache quivering.

Caerwyn chuckled as the men attempted to regain their positions without actually touching his royal person. He was by far the tallest man in the contingent and easily peered over their helms as they shifted in front of him.

"Report, Brennan."

Brennan passed the spyglass to Caerwyn, and he placed the narrow tube against his eye. The dust cloud resolved into a multitude of large hairy brown beasts with great curving tusks and legs as large as tree trunks. They were fully plated in armour, including the weak spot located between the eyes. One strike by something as small as a stone would kill them instantly, so they were armoured at all times.

On the back of each beast was a saddle carrying three to four people. They were still a fair distance away, and Caerwyn was unable to determine if the riders were male or female.

"A Primordial host, my lord. They come with their battering mammoths. And there," he pointed off to the left, "are the sabretooths." Caerwyn leaned forward to catch a glimpse of the great cats as they padded around a small hill.

"Have you located Alfreda yet? She must be with the most forward guard."

"Not yet, my lord."

"Well then, I am going out to greet them." Caerwyn turned to head back down the staircase when the warning bells of the watchtowers began to peal.

Surprised, he turned back, just as a large boulder soared over the wall, crashing into the wall of the upper story and knocking a hole straight through the stonework. Crumbling masonry rained down on the Kingsmen and cries rang out, some in pain, some in warning. Caerwyn found himself instantly crushed to the stone surface as the Kingsmen around him threw their bodies at him to physically shield him from the attack.

"Find out where that attack came from!" bellowed Brennan, just as a second boulder soared over the wall, this time striking the base of one of the watchtowers. The impact sent a shudder through the walkway, and then the tower crumbled with a trickle of mortar, quickly joined by a cascade of stone. The tower trembled and with a sharp crack, it toppled, crushing the Kingsmen scrambling to clear the area in time.

Down below, similar projectiles were falling amongst the Primordial ranks, crushing man and beast alike.

Brennan jerked himself upright as he spied more massive stones tumbling from the sky.

"Get the king below. *Now!*"

Brennan hauled the men off of Caerwyn then dragged the king upright by an arm and onto his feet. Caerwyn, spying the confusion and panic of the Primordial forces now trapped outside the castle walls shrugged off the hands of the Kingsmen and grabbed Brennan by his sleeve. "Get the Primordial inside the walls. *Now!*"

Brennan turned and bellowed an order to be carried to the gates. "Open the gates! Open the gates! Sound the horns for sanctuary! Hurry!"

The runners set off, calling out as they ran. The horns on the walls sounded three short blasts followed by a long wail, the universal sounding of sanctuary. The gates shivered then parted, sliding slowly over the gravelly surface. The Primordials on the plain, hearing the call, galloped their mounts toward the safety of the castle walls while the deadly missiles continued to fall all around them.

The gates clanked and ground their way wide open as the Primordial warriors swept across the threshold, following the great cats, who slunk close to the ground, yellow eyes angry, yowling and spitting their displeasure, while the lumbering mammoths bellowed angrily, snorting fire at any that came too close. They swung their great horned heads, creating islands of calm around then while the ground buzzed with warriors.

Caerwyn reached the commons just as the last of the Primordial crossed into the crowded green. His eyes frantically scanned the convulsing crowd, seeking the face of his sister, Alfreda.

Caerwyn pushed his way into the milling mass, giving his guard apoplectic fits as they tried to shield him from all angles in the midst of the panicked crowd. He dodged the gouts of fire that blasted across his path, causing the Kingsman on his right to swear, frantically patting down the flames ignited on his tunic. It was then that he spied her.

She stood unperturbed beside a sabretooth, stroking the cat's sleek head and murmuring to it, her eyes also scanning the milieu. As her beautiful head turned, the sun turned her normally black hair to purple. It curled to her shoulders and one side was tucked behind her tiny ear. Their eyes met across the crowd, and they crinkled into a smile of greeting. Caerwyn rushed over and swung his twin into his arms, whirled her around, and hugged her tight to his chest.

Alfreda hugged him back and as her feet touched the ground once more, her smile faded.

"We must talk," she murmured "Right now and in private."

"Agreed." The bombardment had ceased as soon as the Primordial people reached the sanctuary of the castle. Caerwyn snapped his fingers and a Kingsman stepped forward, saluting. "Find Hud, and bring him to the library." He made to turn away but Caerwyn's hand on his arm halted him. "And I want to know the count of the injured."

"Yes, sir!" He snapped another sharp salute then set off at a jog for the armory.

"This way." Caerwyn took his sister by the elbow, turning her in the proper direction.

"I remember the way, Caerwyn," she said with a tilt of her chin and plunged into the throng.

Chapter 2

Alfreda

ALFREDA WAS SHORT IN STATURE, which was not to say she was diminished. What she lacked in height, she made up for in bearing. She rose only to the tip of Caerwyn's shoulder, yet she parted the crowd by sheer presence. Her people calmed as she passed and bowed low, hands over hearts, a queen amongst her subjects.

Caerwyn bobbled along in his sister's wake, appearing to be little more than her manservant rather than her brother. The only thing destroying this image was his royal armour, but to the Primordial people, it had no more value than the true servant who fell in behind them silently carrying her bags. Alfreda was the mother goddess and the sum total of all things regal and worthy of worship, in the eyes of a Primordial. No other being could come close.

Once clear of the press of people and animals, Caerwyn moved up alongside her and steered her not toward the residences, but toward a round building visible only by the conical shape of the metal-plated roof set back behind a private wall of the garden reserved for royals. Caerwyn produced a large key and let them in through a small garden door set into the limestone wall.

Alfreda's guard and Caerwyn's guard jointly crowded their way through the garden gate and Caerwyn glared at them, frustrated by all the fussing. The kingsmen pointedly avoided meeting his eyes.

He retraced the route he had taken earlier that day, their guards bobbing in their wake like a raft of ducklings. Reaching the library door, Caerwyn halted them with a raised hand. "No one is to enter except Hud, on our command." The dual contingent of guards strung themselves out around the building, reminiscent of a string of festival lanterns but without the gaiety. Caerwyn mounted the steps, Alfreda matching him stride for stride then he slammed the door shut behind them, shutting them away from the crowd.

"You should not treat them so," said Alfreda, her eyes twinkling. "They are protecting you the only way they know how."

"I would have no quibble over it except that I do not need protection. And neither do you."

"From mortal men, yes. But from the gods? That might be different."

"And what, pray tell, are they going to be able to do to shield me from a god's wrath?"

"A distraction perhaps or a lie? They are quite adept at it when they choose to be." Alfreda wandered over to her favourite chair under the tall stained glass windows and curled into the high-backed, overstuffed seat. She tucked her feet under her, disappearing into the tapestry folds of the chair. "I hate to think that our people would betray us, but events are outpacing our knowledge of them. I fear the people no longer pray to the gods." She lifted the lid of the tea pot sitting by her elbow and seeing that it was empty, commanded *"Tea!"* It filled with a hiss and an aromatic citrusy scent filled the air, steam rising from its spout. She tipped the hot brew into her cup, then reached over and filled one for Caerwyn.

Caerwyn's forehead creased into a frown as he sat down heavily, legs splayed, elbows resting on knees. With a deep sigh, he reached over and picked up the waiting cup.

"How many were hurt or killed today? The Kingsmen run around trying to protect me when it should be the other way around. I should be protecting them." He took a sip then put the cup back down with a rattle and grunted. "We are their caretakers, not the other way around. I hate seeing lives wasted, prematurely ended for no good reason. Those deaths out there today should not have happened. Their souls are now our responsibility. It is our fault."

"It is not our fault, and you know it. What *is our problem* and potentially our fault is the escalating problem with Helga. That is why I came to see you," said Alfreda.

"You are closer to her than I am. What is she experimenting with?" Caerwyn asked. "Is she responsible for this? Is it something she and Artio are doing together? I asked Helga outright, and she laughed at me and told me to mind my own business."

Alfreda set her cup down, picked up the pot of tea, and refilled it to the brim.

"Artio is up to something. As the caretaker of the heavens, she is responsible for safeguarding the movements of the stars and planets. It is her domain and her charge. But lately I have noticed that the timing of the planetary movements is off. It is the tiniest of increments, true, but there should be no variation at all. It's almost as though she is absent," she said thoughtfully, shaking her head. "Maybe she is taking a vacation? Absurd as it sounds, she has not been seen for months."

"Well she does like to work undisturbed" said Caerwyn "If something was really wrong, and she was really missing, it wouldn't be a slight problem. It would be catastrophic."

Alfreyda nodded, lips pressed together in puzzlement. "I first noticed it one night when the stars dimmed, as though a haze covered the sky, the moon's timing slightly off. I might not have noticed at all if were not for the butterflies. They are sensitive to the slightest change in the world and are the first to suffer when their environment changes. She frowned. "I think the moon's slippage is creating a disturbance in their internal equilibrium."

Caerwyn grimaced and took another sip of tea, as though to wash away a sour taste. "It's another sign. Artio plays with the planets like she is plucking toadstools in the forest. While they are hers to command, she forgets that she can cause harm to the mortals around her, both animal and human. If she causes their deaths, and then their souls become *our responsibility*. I've begun to notice an influx of human souls beyond the normal. I can only imagine what Helga is doing, shut away in her home under the mountain. Do they not understand that their interference with the natural world is causing calamitous results? People are dying!"

"I know. It's not just people." Alfreda plucked a loose thread in the tapestry of the chair. "I came across a meadow as we travelled this way" she said softly. "It was littered with thousands and thousands of dead butterflies; so many that they carpeted the grass. I wept at the sight. So many fey lives *lost*. Crushed out of existence!" Tears welled and one escaped, sliding down her cheek. "I was not in time to save them."

Caerwyn stood and strode around the room, boots clicking on the tiled floor, restless with the need to act. At that moment, the door opened and Caerwyn paused, turning to see who had entered. Hud limped inside, hugging an object wrapped in cloth to his chest.

"My lady, sire." He bowed at the waist and then approached them, pausing beside the table.

"Hud. Thank you for coming so quickly."

"Of course, sire. How may I assist you?"

"I need your help. Do you remember the patrol three months ago to the base of the Highland Spine at the ford of the river Erinn?"

"How could I forget, sire?" Hud resisted the urge to massage his bad leg, twinging sympathetically at the memory. "It ended my career as a Kingsman."

Caerwyn frowned at the shared memory. "This time, we must penetrate the spells cast around that mountain. Something stirs in its black depths. We must know what it is, if mortal existence is to be preserved."

Hud's grim smile met Alfreda's clear gaze. He bowed deeply to her. "My lady, you will be our guide?"

Alfreda nodded her head in acceptance and turned back to her brother. "I will assist in your search and offer what protection I can. The creatures of the mountain's slopes are yours to command if they may be of assistance," she replied.

"Then may I suggest you make use of this?" Hud placed the wrapped bundle on the table. Caerwyn watched while Alfreda bent over and unwound the parcel.

As the wrappings fell away, a box was revealed. Midnight blue, it was so dark that it absorbed all light surrounding it, making it difficult to define the edges. Magic leaked from the box, peeking out the sides of the lid as though it strove to push back the cover and expand the darkness held at bay. It gave off a faint hum that set Caerwyn's teeth on edge.

"A balance box! Where ever did you find it?" asked Alfreda. "Our father used to speak of them. I thought they were all destroyed."

"This box has been in my family for generations," said Hud. "It has been passed down from father to son for as long as anyone can remember. And now it is my son, Mordecai's. He is the keeper of the box. He has the magic to control it."

Caerwyn backed away from the humming box, unnerved by the power emanating from it. "Why have we not heard of this before?" he asked harshly, his tone sharper than he had intended. "Bring your son to us that we may speak to him of it."

"Of course, sire. I will be but a moment." He bowed, then turned and limped back to the carved door, disappearing through it. It closed with a thud behind him.

"I do not like that box," said Caerwyn. "It is a god-killer." The box shuddered and rattled. It whispered to him, so low that he could not catch its words, but the words shivered and stroked at his soul.

Alfreda ran her hands briskly over her arms in an attempt to smooth the goosebumps pebbling her skin. "Nor do I, but if what stirs in the mountain is what we fear, this may be the only hope we have. We will keep it safe and secure with Hud's son. He must be a wizard if he is able to handle the box. He will be able to control its powers. It is but one challenge we face."

Alfreda stood up and took over Caerwyn's pacing, while he sank into the chair opposite the box and stared at it, refusing to take his eyes from it as though it were a wild beast about to spring.

"The truth is, I believe Artio and Helga are behind the disruptions in the natural world we see around us," said Alfreda. "It might not be intentional, but the effect is the same. The last time I spoke to Artio, she was running off to experiment with the moon, chasing a wild theory of her own making." She paused by the window, eyes caught on the nearly full moon that shone palely in the noon sky. "She believed that slowing its progress would give longer growing days as it exerts gravity on the earth. And Helga, well she never looks much beyond the rock beneath her feet, preoccupied as she is with her tending to the condemned. She never considers the living world. What could possibly bring them together

I cannot imagine…if they are indeed working together. We don't actually know that is the case."

Caerwyn stood up and walked over to Alfreda, gripping her shoulder with his left hand and squeezing it in comfort. "We will figure this out before it's too late, you and I together."

They both turned to the sound of the door reopening. Hud limped back into view and at first it appeared he had come alone. Then he shifted slightly. A young child trailed in his wake, brown hair falling in curls to his shoulders around a cherubic face. "This is my son, Mordecai."

The child appeared to be no more than seven summers in age. A big smile wreathed his face at the sight of the king. He ran over and climbed up into the chair beside Alfreda. "I'm hungry!" He settled into the oversized chair then grinned over at a bemused Caerwyn. "Can we have lunch, now, sire?"

Chapter 3

Helga

HELGA STRODE ALONG THE NARROW PATH that ran along the sheer cliff face with an ease of long practice. The midday sun shone directly down, and she pulled the hood of her cloak forward on her head to cut the glare.

She hated the sun. It blinded her to all that moved and made the shadowy reaches of her sanctuary retreat beneath the blazing onslaught. *If I had my way, I would never leave my home.* But Artio had begged her to come see her latest experiment with the moon. *Acch! Who cares about planetary bodies? Cold and remote and eternally boring, like the gods who formed them. For that matter, what good was their useless father, outcast of the gods?* She had long since stopped praying to them.

And then there were the useless twins, the honoured siblings. Favoured by their outcast father and useless mother and pampered by the gods, they were the "golden children" who could do no wrong, at least in their father's eyes. Even in banishment, Morpheus had seen fit to give them the prime real estate on the earth. They were given dominion over the living. But she? She was stuck with the dead, those unredeemable souls, the castaways. She was also cast out for the smallest of crimes. What was the loss when the transformed soul had been banished in the first place? When thousands had been dumped at her rocky doorstep to rot?

She was ashamed of their father, if truth be known. *How could a god lower himself to rut with a mortal woman? Was he insane? I would have banished him too.* She skirted a large bolder and then swerved off to a descending path that led into the shade of some scrubby pines with half their branches missing. Thinking of their father wound her up, her anger bubbling to the surface of her skin and blistering the stone she trod on, leaving a blackened outline of her boot where she stepped.

Flame leapt to her fingertips and the trailing grasses ignited with the heat of her anger. The smell of fresh burn made her withdraw from her introspection and she tamped down her hatred, realizing she was leaving a literal blazing trail of her passing.

Helga glanced at the blue sky overhead, peaking through the tree tops. She could just make out the pale shadow of the moon in the sky. Somewhere beyond it, in the celestial realm, was the home of the gods. Their home wandered across the sky, the nightly reminder of their presence now obscured by the brightness of daylight. *The home of the gods.* Helga snorted. *The gods never visit. They ignore us, their half-mortal half-immortal children, preferring to keep themselves pure and untouched by the bastard offspring of one of their own.* Helga tossed a wet blanket over her thoughts, her temperature rising once again.

Now is not the time to dwell on family history, she thought. *But there will come a time. Oh yes.*

She left the scrubby pines behind her and followed the winding path to where it parted the stunted brush, barren of green growth in the early spring cold that still clung to this side of her mountain home. The bushes ended, and she paused out of long habit to take in her surroundings.

The glen was a flattish field, flush with new shoots of growth, the fuzzy sprouts the first signs of the emerging spring. It was nondescript yet stirred like a kicked anthill. At regular intervals, deep holes sank into the ground beside mounds of freshly turned earth and beside each of these breeches lay grey stones of mammoth size. Helga spotted large groups of men, hauling wooden sleds on runners that slowly inched the stones toward the lip of the pits.

A man stood in the center of the activity, directing the stone's placement. The man was as close to a god as humanity could produce. He stood in the exact center of the maelstrom, a calm epicentre in the yelling, grunting, sweating ring of humanity struggling to tip the stones into their final resting places.

Helga studied him. Even though it was early morning and the dew was not yet gone, he had discarded his overcoat and wore a sleeveless linen shirt tied loosely at the front. Dark chest hair curled through the drawstrings, and his heavy shoulders bulged as he lifted a corded arm to illustrate a shouted instruction. His chin was square and shadowed by a trimmed beard that travelled down his throat. His nose was sharp as an eagle's beak, but it only added to his stature, accenting piercing chestnut eyes, framed by jet black lashes and hair that curled thickly to the nape of his neck.

Genii spotted her standing at the mouth of the glade and waved, motioning to her to come down, flashing a huge smile full of white teeth in her direction. Helga mouth twitched into a semblance of a smile in acknowledgement.

Artio, who she had not noticed until now, rose from the side of one of the stones where she had been instructing the worker on an adjustment to the slip of the sled, brushing dirt from her knees and hands. She wore her favorite sleeveless leather vest and pleated skirt studded with tiger eye cabochon over a chestnut tunic. Her matching lace up boots ran to mid-thigh and fit like a second skin. Tawny brown and sun streaked, her hair tumbled to her mid-back and a long fringe fell over her green eyes. She shoved it back out of her youthful face as she stood up, checking the progress of the other stones. She was the epitome of a young godling, strong and proud and free. She turned toward Genii. Seeing his gaze focused on a point at the entrance to the bowl, she turned and spotted Helga. Artio's smile was as broad as Genii's. With brisk strides, she climbed the short hill to meet Helga.

"What do you think?" Artio yelled over the din of the hammers and the grunts of men, bodies straining to move the fingers of stone.

Helga's eyes strayed back to Genii. *Marvelous form. Quite delicious, really.*

"What is all this?" Helga flicked a hand in the general direction of the glade. "Another temple to the gods?" Derision seeped through in her tone.

Artio did not seem to hear it, for she gushed on, "It's a focus, a radiant focus. It will harness the moon's rays and harvest the latent energy, allowing for the moon's rays to be transformed into a pulled power stream that…"

Helga's eyes glazed over as her mind drifted away from Artio's explanation and back onto Genii. He had left the epicenter, and his long muscular legs carried him over to a slip that was caught up on a rock impeding its forward motion. The runner had dug deep into the soft soil and churned up a large rock just beneath the surface, which was now jammed up against another stone.

He is the epitome of the poetry of the gods. I really must have him for myself.

Genii bent down and, with the strength of three men and the assistance of two, lifted the skid over the offending stone and placed it back down on the clear path where it shot forward by several inches as it was suddenly freed.

Genii walked to the other side of the stone across the landing pit and pulled an instrument from his pocket, checking the alignment of the rock. When he was satisfied, he checked the other eight's bearings. He went from group to group and stopped their work as the stones' alignment was verified. The seventy-odd men who'd toiled the morning to pull the stones into place put down their ropes and slumped wearily, grateful for the rest.

Artio, noticing Helga's glassy-eyed vacant stare, turned back to the valley and with exclamation of "Oh, never mind!" ran back down to Genii.

Genii watched her come, an even wider smile on his patrician face, eyes crinkled with caring. Artio skidded to a halt in front of him and grabbed his muscular arm to stop her slide, and Genii's hand grasped her waist to stop her motion. He held her for a moment and his gaze was so tender, *so smitten*, it was impossible to miss.

Jealousy and a pure white rage spiked within Helga's chest. She carefully masked the emotions and, pasting a smile on her face, regally descended into the glade.

She approached the couple and they broke apart, oblivious to her jealousy. "It's time to set the stones. Come look!" Artio grabbed Helga's hand and tugged her over to examine a large stone lying on its side. At least twenty feet tall, the massive stone was freshly chiseled with likenesses of the gods, the elements, and the living creatures inhabiting the earth.

Artio chatted away about the various methods the stones would harvest and channel the moon's energies. "See this picture?" She placed a hand on a carving of a bear. "This image rune can bring forth the spirit bear! The spirit bear is my favourite! I wish I could be a spirit bear. They are so regal and intelligent. Did you know…?" Helga's eyes glazed over once again, distracted by the form of Genii who had unfurled a parchment and was now consulting the schematic, his arms holding the papyrus at an angle to compare the drawings against the current configuration of stones.

"…and when all the stones are perfectly aligned, they will be able to heal anything within the circle. It's a medicine wheel, see? But this one is powered by the celestial bodies, the moon specifically. Did you hear me, Helga?"

Helga started and then turned back to Artio. "Yes, medicine wheel. Very nice," she said in a bored voice that dripped sarcasm. She spun around and walked back to the path.

"Where are you going?" shouted Artio.

"I have matters to attend to," said Helga with a lazy wave over her shoulder. "I do not want to keep you from your building."

"But I want you to see how it works!" yelled Artio.

"Call me when you have it working, and I will come back for a demonstration." The words drifted back into the vale as Helga disappeared into the brambles. As she entered the overhang of the scraggly pines, a thought surfaced. *The only way I will return to this vale, is if there is something in it for me…or someone. What a bloody waste of time.*

Chapter 4

Artio

THEY LABOURED LONG INTO the afternoon after an hour's rest to eat and drink. As the final stones slipped into their berths, the evening's western rays settled on the clearing. The remaining workers raked the last of the freshly churned soil around the base of the freestanding stones, tamping it into place.

Artio peered at the angle of the sun and smiled. So many times, she had come to this spot with Papa because of the magical way the sun's rays lanced through the valley between the mountain peaks. The precision of it thrilled her, and her medicine wheel playset had performed every bit as well as the real thing.

Artio smiled, remembering the tiny dead sparrow she'd placed at the convergence of the rays, its neck broken. The setting sun triggered the runes on the tiny stones. A liquid flame shot around the circle of little pillars and then converged on the stiff bird. A small tremor quivered under her feet and two stones toppled, but when the flash of light faded and the blinking spots in her vision passed, there sat the sparrow, wings quivering. Then with a squawk, it flashed up into the trees.

It was then that Artio knew that she would return and build the medicine wheel but on a much grander scale with full granite monoliths that would withstand the test of time. To be able to bring such a gift to humanity made her heart sing with joy. A tiny frown creased her brow. Helga just didn't understand. Artio believed that life should be lived to the fullest, and one should die with the fullness of days, not in an accident or due to sickness or ill health.

She shoved the thought aside and ran over to Genii, slipping her hand into his. His eyes crinkled into a smile in return, his smile a wordless caress to match the feeling of warmth at her touch. He drew her to the side to watch the workers sprawled in the center of the ring. Exhausted from the day's toil and with various aches and pains from the journey called life, they stood amidst the circle of their own free will, wanting to test the effect of what their labour had wrought.

The sun settled into its final resting place until its rebirth in the eastern morning sky. The rays touched the guardians perched at the top of the wheel of stone and the deeply carved images glowed, first with the light striking their exterior but then the surface flush faded and an inner light flared in the eyes of the guardians. The columns shuddered and a wave of light spread down lighting the runes internally then flashed around the circle. The ground shook with mighty tremors yet nothing toppled. Outside the circle, nothing stirred.

With the last gasp of light from the setting sun, the healing light of the medicine wheel whitened and disappeared. Blinking back the light streaks in her eyes, Artio could see the workers peering hesitantly around at each other and then running hands over their bodies, examining hands and old scars and missing appendages which had suddenly reformed. Cries of shock and joy erupted from the circle, but those were not what attracted Artio's eyes.

The ghostly forms of animals rose from the meadow, restored to their spirit form from deaths that should not have been. Artio was sure the others could not see them, but they were there nonetheless. She frowned. *Someone has been hunting and slaying the animals of the Primordial forests but to what purpose? What could be important enough to deny them their rebirth? I will speak to Alfreda about this. This is her area of expertise.*

"Wonderful!" Artio clapped her hands together, celebrating the healing of the workers, who surged forward to show her that their fingers had regrown straight and youthful, that their scars had vanished, and eyesight had strengthened. "Go share your joy with your families. Remember that the medicine wheel will only work during this moon cycle each year with the alignment of the spring solstice. Remember the gods and honour their spirits for giving you this great gift!"

The workers bowed and scraped and then vanished out of the glade, eager to return to their kin to share the joyous news.

Artio turned back to the circle of rock eyes running over their towering forms. They were quiet and still, as they had been when erected "Now the real work begins, Genii. Help me fine tune the alignment. We have a week before the full moon arrives. We must be ready by then, if we hope to capture this phase of it." She gathered his hands in hers, running her thumbs over his calloused palms, and then peered up into the warm depths of his eyes. "Then and only then can we truly be one for all eternity."

Genii kissed her, a gentle kiss full of shared hope and longing, mixed with awe and trepidation. Although Artio acted as any normal human female, she was not a human, or at least fully human. That fact alone would have terrified any normal mortal, but Genii wasn't a normal human male. He was a bastard who happened to be a wizard.

Chapter 5

Caerwyn

MORDECAI SAT MUNCHING on a ham and cheese sandwich from a rapidly emptying tray brought in by a servant. He alternated bites between a tottering stack of sandwiches and an equally large pile of crunchy pickles, fresh from the pickle vat of the kitchens. Caerwyn pulled Hud to the side of the room by his shirt sleeve while Alfreda distracted the child with tales of the woods that were her home when she lived amongst the Primordials. Occasionally, she snuck a pickle from Mordecai's stack. Mordecai's eyes followed the stolen pickle, as though missing one would cause him to go hungry.

Across the room, an argument in hushed tones was being carried out.

"…You suggest that we give control of this box *to a child?* Hud, even a full grown wizard would struggle to control the danger of this box," muttered Caerwyn. "It contains a great evil. If it were to be activated or even worse seized by the wrong company, they could destroy the world. There is no room for failure in this. He is too young!"

"Sire, you speak as if magic is something that is learned. I assure you, it is not. You are either gifted with it by the gods or you are not. Did you have to learn to be a godling? No. You simply *are* a godling. It is a part of your very being, the fabric of your existence. He is the same. Mordecai could do things before he could speak. He does not need to be taught how to control the box. He is controlling it right now."

Caerwyn looked over at the box and the boy, alarmed, and Hud grinned. "It has been part of him since birth. No one understands its working better than Mordecai. If there is a great evil to be fought, he is the boy for the job."

"He is but a child!" Caerwyn protested. "He cannot go to battle!"

His father shook his head. "He may be a child in years, but there is an old man tucked away inside, at times I see it in his eyes, a wisdom and experience far beyond his years. I believe he was put here to help you." Hud's eyes glazed over as he thought about his words.

Caerwyn sighed and turned back to Alfreda, who was now laughing at something the child had said, her eyes sparkling. Mordecai met Caerwyn's eyes and his eyes beckoned to Caerwyn in invitation. He slowly walked back to the table, studying the child as he drew closer then knelt down next to Mordecai's chair, bringing his eyes on level with the boy. Mordecai's sparkling blue eyes twinkled, and he placed his hand on Caerwyn's shoulder.

"Do not be afraid, sire. I understand the box. I know how it works. I can help you." Mordecai picked up the box and wrapped it back up in the soft cloth hiding it from view. It did not seem to affect him as it did them. Mordecai looked up and smiled at the bemusement in their gazes as he handled the box without harm.

Caerwyn smiled back at him and patted his knee. "Thank you, Mordecai, I accept your offer of assistance. Mind if I steal one of those sandwiches?"

Chapter 6

Alfreda

THE CASUALTIES FROM THE BOMBARDMENT were not as severe as originally thought. Two dead, their souls passing into Caerwyn's care, and fifteen injured and now being treated in the hospital wing of the castle.

Alfreda visited each Kingsmen or Primordial in the infirmary, murmuring a kind word of thanks for their service.

On exiting the infirmary, she joined Caerwyn and they climbed to the outer wall to examine the massive stone still sitting on the wall where it had landed. They were surrounded by guards, which made the upper wall extremely crowded and, to Caerwyn's mind, advertised their presence to the enemy if indeed the attack had been targeted.

The massive stone was as polar opposite to the limestone blocks forming the castle walls as it was possible to be. It was roughly a comet in shape, as though it had been formed by the wind passing over it. The surface was greyed and bubbled. Small fissures and craters pockmarked the surface. Alfreda bent down and picked up a chunk of stone that had fractured off the main rock with the impact. Inside, a smooth, tar-coloured glass was revealed. She turned it over in her hands, frowning.

She turned back to Caerwyn and handed him the chunk. "This is the evidence we needed. Look at the composition of this rock. This is obsidian, part of a lava flow. This was not an attack but an eruption."

She walked over to the wall and gazed down at the approach. Great stones dotted the hillside, some large enough to leave large gouges of overturned earth as they skidded and bounced to their final resting places. The sizes ranged from massive rocks like the one beside them to stones no bigger than a human head.

"But the question is what is causing the eruptions? And where are they coming from? What do you think of the angle of the impacts?" She lifted her arm and pointed in a northwesterly direction. "I think they have come from there."

Caerwyn followed the line of sight produced by her outstretched arm. "That would put it in the Highland Needle, near the pass, possibly just above the ford of the River Erinn."

"Yes, that is what I was thinking too, very near to Helga's home at the edge of her domain, her *protected* domain." Alfreda leaned on the wall, studying the patterns. "What could she possibly be up to that would cause breaches in the mountain? Or is this a natural phenomenon of some sort? Do you think Artio is visiting her right now?"

"It's possible."

"Then I will return and see if I can talk to Helga. She is on my doorstep. Perhaps she does not know of the eruption," Alfreda shook her head slowly from side to side, "but I do not see how that is possible. The mountain must rumble with the building pressure. Earthquakes would be a natural side effect of such a breach."

"I do not like the idea of you confronting her alone." Caerwyn took his sister's elbow and steered her toward a door set in the wall that lead to an interior corridor of the castle. The sweep of guards followed. "If you will give me a few days, I will gather my Kingsmen and then we can present a unified front to Helga. The last visit to her realm did not go well and several of my Kingsmen were injured trying to reach Helga to chat. She has put up defences against unwanted visitors and it seems we head that list. It would have been nice if she had warned us and the fact she did not," he grimaced, "means she did not care who came to visit. That, of and by itself, is alarming. She has become reclusive as of late."

"Agreed." Alfreda paused just inside as she crossed the threshold into the castle's interior, allowing her eyes to adjust to the dim interior. "All right, I will stay until you are prepared and we will leave together. We will make her see reason. I would like a word with my clansmen, so that we may prepare a plan of action."

"Your normal suites have been prepared for you and your chiefs. I will leave you to your discussions and we can meet again for dinner in the grand hall."

Alfreda hugged Caerwyn and with a smile, she walked off down the right hallway, gathering her guard as she disappeared down the tiled floor, her steps sure and confident, a queen amongst her people.

Chapter 7

Hud

MORDECAI SKIPPED ALONG beside his father, holding his hand and chatting about how nice the king and the Primordial queen were and that they made about the best sandwiches in the world. Hud carried the blanket-wrapped balance box under his arm and matched his steps to his son's as he retraced the familiar path back to their lodgings, tucked into a corner of the castle wall part way between the door to the kitchens and the large stable that housed the horses.

Reaching the front door, Mordecai waved his hand and the door swung open on silent hinges before he could place a hand on the latch. For Mordecai, the things he could do were as natural as breathing, things that made others stop and stare.

The box had been handed down to his family for safekeeping longer than anyone could remember. Hud had no magical ability, but his mother had been a witch of immeasurable ability. Somehow it had skipped him, though. When she died, he had despaired that the ability had been lost. It was after her death that he and his wife conceived and gave birth to Mordecai, who was now the end of the line.

Hud's wife had died giving Mordecai life, as was often the case where magic was involved. The birth of magic often demanded a life for a life. It was a reason that magic was dying out in the realm, and matches were hard to find, as no one would consciously give their daughter's hand only to find that they died due to the magic coursing through the child's veins. Consequently, the few wizards to exist in the world were often born to whores and lived a rough life on the streets, often falling to a knife or to disease before reaching an age where they could take conscious control of their magic. They were a dying breed on the cusp of extinction.

Mordecai, on the other hand, flourished within the castle walls. Protected physically by their impenetrability, his mind nourished by the best library in the kingdom, he studied the history of the lands and people, both mortal and mythical that abided within it. By the tender age of five, he had mastered the ancient language of the gods and could read the ancient texts without assistance. Now, at the age of seven, he carried the knowledge of a man ten times as his years. What he lacked was experience.

Yet that lack of experience did not hold him back, just as Hud had told Caerwyn. Hud stopped in front of the cabinet built into the wall of the kitchen beside the fireplace and reaching around the side of it, found the hidden latch and pulled. There was a click and he tugged on the front of the cabinet, which swung open on giant hinge, revealing a hidden closet. It was here that the box had been stored for millennia, safe and secure within the stone wall. At the back of the closet was a trap door embedded into the floor that led to a set of tunnels running under the castle.

Hud placed the box on a shelf and then pushed the cabinet door closed. Once it clicked into place, there was no telling that it was anything other than what it appeared to be, a functional kitchen cupboard.

Mordecai was still chattering away but as his father stopped in front of him, he paused long enough to look up at his whiskered face.

"I know. It's time for me to study…uh, father?" Mordecai asked his face hopeful.

"What is it?"

"Can I go with you this time? When the king goes to meet his other sisters?"

Hud studied his son for a moment and then nodded.

"Yippee!" shouted Mordecai, and he clambered onto his chair and pulled the books forward. "This time, I get to see the real thing. This time I get to see the gods up close."

"And why are you so anxious to see them up close?" asked his father.

"Because of this!" Mordecai pulled a skinny book from the pile and shoved it at his father. It was entitled *Prophetic Musings: The War of the Gods.* He did not need to read further to know who had written it. The last witch or wizard with prophetic ability had died years ago. It was written by Hud's mother.

Chapter 8

Artio

THE FOLLOWING MORNING dawned grey and overcast. The rain, hinted at by the pink clouds of the previous evening's setting sun, had settled in, obscuring the top of the ash-filled clouds ringing the peak of the smoking mountain. Fog had sunk onto the clearing floor, so that the monolithic stones appeared to be floating in the sky. Only erected for a day, they nevertheless gave an impression of great age and exuded air of mystery.

Artio witnessed none of these things as she'd left the meadow in the predawn hours, travelling deep into the Primordial forest, Genii at her side. In order for the bonding of the moon to work, there were certain elements that had to be gathered from the misty woods, elements only found there.

The plan had been Genii's from the beginning. Of course, Artio had agreed to the plan as soon as he had proposed it. They were in love, weren't they? The only thing keeping them from being together was his mortality. He had lived longer than most humans due to the magic coursing through his veins, but he would still succumb to old age in time and die, something Artio could not fathom or accept.

So they'd hatched the plan and what could be more eternal than the moon? Tying his life force to the celestial would ensure that his aging was tied directly to the moon's aging and would be so slow as to be unnoticeable. Still not immortal in the true sense, but close enough as to not matter.

Locating the binding agents, now that was the true challenge. For the magic to work, Genii's blood must be bound to the light cast on a full moon, and not just any full moon, but the master moon of the spring equinox. The equinox was the time for rebirth when the sun and moon are equal partners in the sky. The balance of the celestial bodies of moon and world, mimicking the relationship between lovers, would make the magic possible.

Artio pushed through the dense underbrush, the wet leaves slapping against her legs. The object of their search was not far ahead. They had watched the trajectory carefully and had set out as soon as it hit the atmosphere.

The chunk of moon rock came into view, the crush of vegetation an arrow pointing to its final resting place.

"Finally, we have found it! It tumbled further than we figured." Genii took the cape from around his shoulders and gave it a shake to dislodge the moisture dripping from its oiled surface.

"But we have found it, finally," said Artio, quickening her steps. "Please let there be enough," she prayed out loud.

Genii took her hand and knelt on the ground beside a tree trunk with scorch marks on its bark. He parted the ferns and there it was a chunk of moon rock the size of his fist. The colour of ash, it was jagged on all exposures, some protrusions sharp and spiky and some smoothed. To Artio, it looked more like a cockle burr than a rock.

She dropped Genii's hand then pulled out a cloth from her satchel, draping it over the stone. She picked it up and wrapped the cloth securely around the moon rock, careful not to touch it with her bare flesh and then tucked it away deep in her satchel.

Artio stood up, beaming. "We've got it!" She flung her arms around him and kissed him full on the lips, and he snugged her close, kissing her back.

"You are my joy, shade of my heart. Whatever did I do to deserve you for eternity?" he rumbled against her hair. "The day you found me on the streets my life changed. I can never repay you for your love, for your kindness. I love you, Artio, and will love you till the moon crashes into the sea."

"As street urchins go, you were adorable." Drawing back, she swept the fringe of hair off his forehead and smiled, remembering the small boy. "My heart was lost the moment I saw you." She stroked his cheek, eyes alive with the tenderness of love returned. "But the adult man is so much more. You are worthy of a goddess's love."

"You saved me." His eyes darkened slightly with memory. "I would be dead by now, if you had not taken me in."

"Yes, but even then I knew you were special," she said, "that you were unique. We were meant to be together. It is a blessing of the gods."

"And so we shall be together forever." He lowered his forehead to touch hers and kissed the bridge of her nose. "Together...always."

Chapter 9

Caerwyn

THE KINGSMEN BARRACKS were located on the western side of Cathair, outside the castle walls and tucked up tight against the outer ring wall where it joined with the castle itself. A postern gate allowed for the pasturing of the horse herds in a Y formed by the tributary of Cathair Lake to the south and the crumbling ancient stone wall of the old town pastures. They were overgrown with grasses and lichen, the roots sinking deep into the dirt of time's passing. These walls remembered when the god, Morpheus had made Cathair his home, not just his descendants.

Morpheus' creation of humanity was initially considered trivial, a curiosity to the other Gods. Almost on a dare, he formed the people of the world from the native elements: purest air provided by the abundant plant life, virginal waters of mountain streams fed from the snow-capped mountain tops, and the physical essence of the planet – soils so fertile that the planet exploded with life. Morpheus mixed fire and spirit into this raw mould and then breathed the breath of a God into his creation.

The result was miraculous.

He'd created not one, but two unique life forms and then watched as the first people multiplied until they filled every corner of the world. The other Gods applauded his ingenuity, smiling down on the little planet. Amused with the scurrying creatures, they indulged Morpheus, congratulating him on creating a new life form that thrived in the primitive climate. The Gods began to visit the planet and *played* with the people, as though they were pets. They set up palaces in the most beautiful of locations and the world became a vacation paradise for the bored immortals.

Impressed, they asked Morpheus to repeat the process and create life on other worlds. That is, until Morpheus fell in love with one of his creation, a mortal woman, and took her for wife.

When they learned of the union, the Gods were horrified, for they saw the people as little more than animals. Morpheus debased himself in their eyes and in a unanimous decision it was decreed that he must give up his mortal wife.

Morpheus refused. For what he had done, Morpheus was cast down to the earth and his return to the gods barred for as long as he kept his mortal wife. The Gods were forbidden to visit the planet and the planet was decreed off limits for all immortals.

When they abandoned the people of the world, their palaces fell in ruin, but two were preserved; the primordial temple in Faylea and a large castle built on the present day site of Cathair. The others were angrily smashed by the gods, grinding the pieces to dust until only broken jagged pieces of the original foundation stones could be found. Even these had been swallowed by time, and reclaimed by the earth. Never again were the Gods seen in Cathair, nor was it said that the gods protected Cathair. They turned their backs on the people of the world. Out of this rubble, the current castle was built by the people for the heir to Cathair, for the Spirit Shield guardian, the sole son of Morpheus. So it was that the current-day Castle Cathair was formed.

Caerwyn enjoyed walking along the top of the remnant of the ancient walls, for he felt closer to his father during these strolls. He balanced his footing on the slippery moss-covered rocks, hopping from one to the next, while his ever-present guard trailed along behind him, amused at his antics.

He reached a corner of the wall, where a platform stood mostly intact, and climbed up the structure, despite the shouted warnings and appeals for caution. Balancing on the flattish rock, he peered out toward the Spine examining the clouds that gathered around its peak. Despite the watery sun currently washing the field, he could see that real rain was falling at its base.

It would be a journey of three days, maybe four if the weather turned foul, and both man and beast would be slowed by the accompanying slick mud. That many feet and hooves and paws would churn the roads into a malaise of clinging clay that became heavier by the step. The most direct route was a twisting path that swung perilously close to the swamps to the northwest. Although normally a faster route, the delays along the main road would become substantially longer if their equipment became stuck in the mud slick roads. At least the swamps had solid paths that drained well, but there were other hazards to an army along the edges of the swamps.

In the end, it was decided to divide the armies as this would also allow them to approach the mountain from two directions and hopefully surprise what might be waiting for them when they arrived, if anything stirred in the area.

Caerwyn's horse-backed Kingsmen would take the swamp route and Alfreda would take her people along the Cathair Road with the plan to meet up again at the River Erinn ford where the shallow waters afforded a safe crossing. On the other side, a well-travelled trail led into the high passes, the gateway into the Primordial lands to the north. This plan also had the optical advantage of a people returning home, rather than a people coming to invade, as would be the case if he moved the Kingsmen across too soon.

Caerwyn wondered if Helga would even care to note the difference. She did not own the passes, but as they came very close to her home, both human and Primordial skirted the area, fearful of upsetting a descendent of the gods.

He climbed back down to ground level. As he straightened came eye to eye with his general, Captain Brennan. His one good eye glared at Caerwyn. Even though his lips did not move, he could hear the accusation all the same. He held up his hand to ward off the impending lecture and instead asked "How soon will we be ready to move out?"

"As soon as my liege returns to the castle. Your Pegasus is saddled and awaits you."

"Excellent! What are we waiting for?" Caerwyn strode off across the field and away from his general's angry stare.

He entered through the open gate. As soon as he stepped through, a cacophony of sound assailed his ears. Trumpets blared from the top of the walls at his appearance and the various animals and soldiers stirred with the announcement. Caerwyn spotted Alfreda, already mounted on a sabretooth, leaning forward to scratch the great cat behind its ear.

Caerwyn's favorite Pegasus was an ebony winged creature named Brimstone, fiery-eyed and fierce. Brimstone stamped his hooves impatiently, anxious to be in the air. The rest of the Kingsmen rode ordinary horses, but they were the best breeding stock to be found, deep-chested and long-legged. They could handle any terrain and battle on the flats as well.

With a cheer from the watching crowd, Caerwyn mounted Brimstone and took off into the air soaring in slow circles over Cathair. The main gates swung open and the legion of Kingsmen spilled out into the streets, heading for the open spaces beyond the village of Upper Cathair.

From the sky, Caerwyn could see the entire town below, laid out within the circles of confusion. Semi-concentric ring walls converged on a common focal point within the castle perched on the edge of cliffs falling to the ocean below. A natural barrier, it had yet to be breeched and made an impenetrable defense on the southernmost tip of the peninsula.

The main branch of the combined army snaked through the wall the way they had entered via the broad approach that spilled from the hills on the eastern flank. They skirted the main town and rejoined the central road, a twisting trail clearly visible from the air.

They journeyed together for several hours, the descent a lazy sloping to the great plains.

Brimstone could move faster than the armies, and Caerwyn settled the Pegasus at the agreed location, which was a bend in the river that slowed the waters and afforded a natural watering hole for a large quantity of beasts. Here, he would cross with the Kingsmen. The swamp lay a few miles to the west and already he could feel the muggy air that enveloped the place. It was said to be the birthplace of magic for those few who still possessed the ability.

He was anxious to see what Hud's son made of the place. Many a twisted beast was said to live in the swamps, the imperfect experiments of the gods or the dabbling of wizards and witches gone wrong. None of them were mythical beings like his Pegasus. Everyone knew the mythical were those reborn from a mortal animal's existence.

The mythical creatures were Alfreda's charge, not his. His was the protection of the souls of humanity. That was his to command, his to protect.

But the swamp creatures fell under no one's mandate and were generally left alone, not protected, but not challenged either. Some rudimentary villages had sprung up in the swamp, most of the unsavory kind. They paid neither taxes nor homage but kept to themselves and ignored the world at large.

Caerwyn leaned forward in his saddle, studying the approaching Primordial army, three thousand strong. They crested the hill and spilled over the rise, like so many pebbles sliding down a rock slide.

Chapter 10

Helga

HELGA STROLLED THROUGH the infested village, her nose wrinkling in disgust at the putrid smells of rotting fish and vegetation that clung to simply everything. It did not matter which set of the suspended bridges one chose. They all crossed the same fetid swamp. Swinging rope bridges barely cleared the thick, black waters. A deck of reeds, slick with damp, made the passage treacherous underfoot, even without the swaying movement inherent to its construction. Occasionally, she glimpsed a long snakelike body, rolling just under the surface, smooth and sleek and way too long for her liking.

If she had had her choice, she would not have been there at all. Yet the person she was searching for called the Village of Morass-Fen home, so she traversed the quagmire to a hut perched like a squat tree house at the end of a swing bridge. The leaves of a nearby swamp belly fern shaded it from view, so that the house appeared at first to be only a door with a string of small desiccated skulls hanging on a knotted cord as a door knocker. Helga lifted the skull necklace and let it drop. It made a tinkling sound as the skulls struck the hollow reeds behind them.

The door slowly opened of its own accord in invitation, and Helga ducked through the low entrance, straightening as she cleared the threshold.

A woman sat in a low chair by a flickering fireplace of cedar and stone, the flame warming and providing a low-level lighting to the shadowed interior. Helga was instantly at home in the room, the shadows pleasing to her. She took a step and then halted as she bumped into an invisible barrier.

"Calleigh granted you entry, but she did not invite you to sit." The woman shifted and the firelight bounced off a face full of crags and wrinkles. "Only welcomed guests are to sit."

Helga frowned but quickly smoothed her face and stepped back from the barrier. "Many pardons, madam. I did not mean to barge into your home. I came to the village to seek your assistance."

"Calleigh is not a fairy godmother granting the wishes of strangers or foolish young women…or even foolish young godlings. Calleigh's skills are sought by both the high and the low and by those who seek a magic beyond their own or that they simply cannot perform. Which do you seek today, godling?"

Helga's eyes widened, surprised by her words. She was positive that her disguise was impenetrable. She appeared to be a young woman of perhaps twenty with dark red hair and dressed in the peasant clothing of a local farm wife. The ties of her neckline dangled, and a deep V displayed more cleavage than Helga had intended. The clinging moisture of the swamp beaded on her skin and rolled down the convenient channel on her chest.

"I do not know what you mean, madam," she stuttered, attempting to sound contrite and shy at the same time.

The witch laughed, her eyes reflective as a cat's in the bright firelight. "Calleigh would know Helga even if she dressed like a harlot of the swamp. There is no mistaking a daughter of Morpheus." She looked her up and down. "Even if she *is* dressed like a harlot."

Helga blushed and made to step forward, forgetting the shield, and once again was rebuffed. "Fine, if you insist." The deception dissolved and her normal features returned, and a black dress of fine silk molded to her form. Her rough cloak morphed into a fur-lined cape with a deep hood. "Is this more to your liking, madam?"

"It is a truthful image, even if the reasons for the journey are less than honest." She grabbed the handle of a cane resting against her chair and pulled herself to her feet, hobbling over to the transparent wall that held Helga at the door. As Calleigh wobbled into the firelight, what Helga had thought was a cane was revealed to be the thigh bone of a beast, the upper joint carved into a handle.

"You may enter, but you may not leave until Calleigh grants it. While in my home, you are my guest. The minute you leave, we are once again…less than friends. You may take only what Calleigh gives to you willingly. To take anything not freely given will trigger a curse you will not survive. Do you understand and agree to these terms?"

Helga nodded curtly, curbing her annoyance at the restrictions.

I am no common thief, she thought, *but I am an uncannily good one when I choose to be.* Helga stood regally by the door as the old crone hobbled closer to the doorway and touched a talisman hanging on the pole. The restriction vanished and she turned and hobbled back to her chair, lowering herself painfully into the blanket-covered seat.

"Why does a daughter of Morpheus pay Calleigh a visit?" she asked, settling the blankets back over her knees. She invited Helga to sit with a flick of her hand, directing her to a straight-backed chair set to the right of the fireplace.

"I have need of a potion," Helga said as she settled onto the proffered chair, "and I have heard that you are particularly adept at the blending of potions and elixirs. The potion I seek will bind the will of a foe to me, one born of myth and magic."

Calleigh's watery blue eyes studied the godling but did not ask questions. "Calleigh may have a rendering that would suit your desires but, as with all things, there is a cost. Are you willing to pay this? The price of an enslaving elixir is steep, even for a godling."

Helga's eyes narrowed. "What is this cost?"

"In order for the potion to bind properly, the one who is creating the binding link is also bound in return. It is a symbiotic relationship. The souls of the two individuals are merged at their core. Think of it as Siamese twins, but rather than a physical connection, a shared heart or arm or leg, it is a spiritual one. Sever the bond and you both will die. So Calleigh asks once again. Is this a price that you, godling Helga, are willing to pay?"

Helga stared into the shimmering eyes of the witch, weighing her options. "And what, exactly, is the price *you demand*? You must have a price."

"Calleigh's price is simple. Protect my son Genii. I feel an ill breeze on the air. A foul storm rapidly approaches. I fear for my child, that I will not be able to save him from the approaching calamity, a calamity that is somehow associated with you. A great darkness swirls around him when he visits." She grimaced, as though the taste of the bargain was sour in her mouth. "My price is fair. Do not allow harm to come to him. Swear that you will forfeit your eternity before his. Do this and you shall have the potion you so greatly desire."

Helga was silent while she considered the terms. *Without the elixir, everything I have put into play will fail. I need that elixir before the full moon…but there is more than one way to interpret the deal. They are but words.*

"The deal is struck. I will pay your price, and I swear with my eternal soul that Genii will not die for all eternity. The deal is struck!" she intoned.

"The deal is struck," Calleigh repeated then clapped her wrinkled hands together. A gong sounded sealing the pact. "Let us begin."

A double bind. Genii will be protected for all eternity now. Thank you, daughters of Morpheus.

Calleigh smiled grimly to herself as she prepared the potion.

Chapter 11

Mordecai

MORDECAI BOUNCED ALONG on the seat of the wagon beside his father, as the wheel hit a deep rut along the roadside at the little used fork of the road. He twisted in his seat to watch the Primordial warriors and their fantastic beasts disappear over the crest of the hill behind him then leaned back in his seat as far as he could for as long as he could to keep them in sight. A copse of trees swallowed the view. He gave up and turned back to facing forward.

"I wish I could have a sabretooth," he moaned for the fifth time since leaving Cathair.

Hud grinned at his son. "You can have one when you are grown, if you learn how to take care of one. They are highly intelligent, you know. Do not be fooled into seeing a sabretooth as a pet."

Mordecai frowned at his father and kicked the wooden slat at the front of the wagon with his boot. "I know that, Father. I spoke to Cinda, the one that Alfreda is riding. She is really nice!" he grinned, revealing a missing tooth in his gaping smile. "She let me scratch her behind her ears and everything!"

They bounced along in silence again for a while. Then, with a glance at the creaking leather seat beside him on which sat the cloth bundle containing the box, Mordecai said, "The box is humming."

"Humming? What do you mean, by humming?" This time Hud did look directly at his son.

"It's vibrating and I can hear it." He frowned at the wrapped parcel sitting between them on the seat. "It has a voice, but it is not strong enough for me to understand it yet. But it is getting stronger and louder. Where ever we are going, it likes it."

"That is a lot to gather from a vibrating parcel."

"It's not the box, Papa. It is what's inside the box that is humming."

"Something is inside the box?" Hud asked sharply.

"Oh yes!" said Mordecai happily. "There is something alive inside the box."

Hud's frown deepened. He would bring this up with Caerwyn when they stopped. Perhaps it was not wise to leave his son in sole possession of the box, and perhaps he was the only one it was safe to leave in possession of it. Was the entity in the box evil or benign or neutral? Was it even alive? Mordecai seemed to think so, and he had found his son to be extremely accurate in matters of magic.

"Keep it close to you, Son, but do not open it for any reason. I am serious about this request. Understand?"

"I won't open it. I don't need to. I can talk to it without opening the box."

"It may ask you to, though. Do not do what it asks unless you speak to me or Caerwyn first. This is not a request. It is a command. This is not a game."

Mordecai looked up from where his hand rested on the top of the box, meeting his father's serious eyes and nodded. "I will not open the box unless you say that I can."

Hud reached over and ruffled Mordecai's curls. "You are a good boy."

Mordecai's eyes drifted closed as he tried to sort through the humming to find the words buried in the buzz. It wasn't clear enough yet, but it *was* getting stronger.

They bounced along the dried rutted track for the better part of the day, munching on biscuits, but as they came closer to the village of Morass-Fen the hard ruts softened and smoothed and the humidity rose until Mordecai shed his tan coat. The flies thickened and were joined by bog bugs, which buzzed his ears and tried to land on his exposed skin. His father swatted any that got too close but still by the time the sun sunk toward the horizon, he had several itchy welts to occupy his hands.

As the village jounced into sight, Mordecai's jaw dropped. The entire village *dangled*, impossibly suspended from ropes that disappeared into the canopy overhead. Large mangrove trees with roots running in every direction dotted the dark waters as if they were out for a stroll on a spring evening. The source of the swarms of pests was revealed to be a burping swamp, the surface of which was rarely still. Creatures large and small snapped at the feast of flying annoyances that flitted over the bubbling surface. The coats abandoned earlier were dragged back over bare flesh in an attempt to ward off the bloodsucking insects.

The main body of Kingsmen hung back from the village as all approaches had to be on foot. Caerwyn, Mordecai, Hud, and several Kingsmen guards continued on and stepped onto the boardwalk, which swayed and creaked as their weight settled on the first of the bridges. Hollowed gourds chuckled as they walked, announcing their presence to any who listened.

Mordecai's head swiveled side to side taking everything in. He slipped his hand into his father's, unsure of what the village was about. Mordecai could feel the magic in the air, a rough form to his way of thinking yet the swamp teemed with the essence of magic. He peered that the oozing sludge below the rocking wagon, uncertain as to why they had come to this place. Hud squeezed his hand back reassuring him. He carried the balance box with his right arm, hugged tight against his chest.

Halfway across the first bridge, shadows detached themselves from the huts strung along the intersections and stood, waiting for the party to join them on the landing. A raven cawed from the treetop and a monkey chattered a high pitched babble that announced their arrival as succinctly as a herald's trumpet.

A tall man stepped forward and gestured with one hand to a large communal hut on the far side of the swamp at the end of a curving boardwalk. "She is waiting for you, sire. Please follow me."

He turned and led them through the thickening swarms of bugs toward the entrance draped with a cloth woven with images of birds and snakes and fish. He drew aside the curtain and held it for them while they ducked through the opening.

Calleigh sat in a dark red chair of woven vines as thick as a thumb. The chair's twisted form was suspended from a looped chain of living vines that exited the hut through a hole in the roof. It looked to Mordecai like a child's swing in many ways and swayed gently as she leaned forward to see who approached from the doorway. Her eyes took in the men filing in the doorway and then she focused on Mordecai. She held out a gnarled hand. "Come to Calleigh, boy."

Mordecai approached Calleigh and took the proffered hand, hopping up onto her lap with a grin. She rocked the swing while the others watched. Hud took a half step but was stopped by the sharp look cast by Calleigh.

Caerwyn nodded his head in respect, as equals, but did not attempt to approach closer.

"So, child, what do you bring to Calleigh today?"

Mordecai shook the blanket-covered box and grinned. "It's a balance box, Calleigh, and I know how it works!" he said proudly, puffing out his chest.

"Do you? Well aren't you a brilliant one! Tell Calleigh. What does it do?"

"It balances the forces of good and evil at a spiritual level. It brings the world into harmony by restricting what will not balance, both good and evil."

"Very good!" she said, clapping her hands together, a big smile crinkling her cheeks. "And what happens if one tries to exert their will on the box?"

"It will entrap them within the box."

"Correct. So what was the original purpose of the box? Why was it created?"

"To heal the land and the people. To give them a way to correct the imbalances caused by greed in the world. It is also to give the mortal rulers a place to come and create peace between peoples. The box will right an imbalance both physically and spiritually."

"You are very wise for one so young, Mordecai. Calleigh is pleased. The king is wise to trust you with it." She raised her head to look Caerwyn directly in the eye.

"Step forward and petition Calleigh, son of Morpheus."

Caerwyn strode forward and bowed to the witch and then straightened.

"What is it you wish to ask of Calleigh? Speak the truth in your heart, as has this child."

Caerwyn cleared his throat then met her eyes once again.

"I come to ask your assistance and guidance. Your foresight is legendary. I ask that you to look into the future and what it holds. There is an ill breeze blowing. You must have felt it too? Alfreda and her people rode to the very gates of Cathair to bring warning of the trouble brewing along the border between my realm and the Primordial lands. It centers on the Highland Spine, and a foul smoke that stings the eyes and clogs the throat is rising from the peaks. If I am to be successful in curbing the unrest I need to know what is causing the smoke. Scouting parties return and report that mountain is erupting where volcanos never existed and periodic earthquakes shake the earth. Alfreda's people are being hurt, and some have died as a result of the eruptions."

Calleigh shifted in her chair, her wandering right eye struggling to focus on Caerwyn. "Calleigh can see the truth of the matter, but it may not help you, son of Morpheus."

Caerwyn frowned. "The truth is always useful. How can it not help? The Primordial are a superstitious people. They see signs and portends in the mountain's activity. They are rightly nervous and suspicious and interpret the eruptions as a sign of the god's displeasure."

Meanwhile, in Cathair, despite our assurances, the people of the kingdom spread rumours of Primordial tribes sneaking through the hills, snatching the unwary and performing rituals that are known only to their societies. Alfreda refuses to speak of the religious factions within the Primordial tribes, as the sacred rituals are not for outsiders to know or witness. Rumours and fear are fracturing the fragile peace between our peoples. Events are spiralling out of our control. We are on the verge of outright war. Alfreda swears that her people are not behind it, but I need to know the truth of the matter."

Calleigh closed her eyes, and silence descended. A lone tear leaked from the corner of her eye, tracing a bumpy path over the careworn wrinkles of her cheek. Mordecai reached up and softly wiped the tear away.

When she opened her mouth to speak it was barely a whisper, as though she were afraid to speak the words aloud. Softly, she murmured, "Calleigh knows that the answer is within you, Caerwyn. The people are both right and wrong. A terrible cataclysm is set to erupt and the godlings are central to it. Calleigh's Seeing Eye sees two paths set before you.

"On one path, world is swallowed by a terrible darkness and shadow spreads across the earth. On this path is the end of all mortal life within three generations of this vision.

"On the other path, the gods cease to exist and so do the godlings. The magical world dies and passes into myth. The world is inhabited by mortal beings, and mortal beings alone with no chance of rebirth.

"You must choose. Calleigh does not know which path is the right one or if you will be successful, regardless of which path you choose. Calleigh does know that if you do not choose a path, the world will be plunged into chaos and wars will ravage it until all life is eradicated, both mortal and immortal. The land will be salted until no life can exist. Calleigh's, yours, theirs, all life will be eliminated for all time.

Caerwyn stepped back in shock, and swallowed heavily. "All life?" His hands shook and he struggled to control the trembling of his limbs. "Surely there is some other path? Something other than an either-or proposition? There must be something that can be done to preserve all the life forms that live on this world?"

Her eyes opened, glistening bright but steady and bored into him, weighing, judging. "The answer is within you," she whispered softly, "and you must find it. Calleigh can see nothing more than what she has told you. Calleigh gives you these words of her own free will, at no cost. They are Calleigh's gift in the hope that you will recognize the way when it is placed before you."

She straightened in her chair and then set Mordecai on his feet. He gave Calleigh a hug then patted her shoulder, before running back to his father. Calleigh's eyes followed his progress. "The child can help you. Of that, Calleigh is certain. But it is all I know. Go now, you do not have much time."

Chapter 12

Artio

THE CLEARING WAS EXACTLY as they had left it. The fog had cleared, and in its place a steady drizzle of rain soaked the freshly churned earth. Already new growth sprung from the settled ground, a fuzzy green carpet of soft grass.

Hand in hand Artio and Genii entered the clearing and paused at the lip, eyes roving over their creation. Three years they had worked on it, planning the cutting of the rock from the mountain side. For the three years prior to that, they had searched for the precise materials, as Calleigh had been very precise in the recipe to make such a thing happen.

She had given Genii into Artio's care, allowing the godling to take her precious son from the swamp. His life had been in danger, so she had struck a bargain for his care for all time.

Initially, Artio had been looking for a companion that could help her with her care of the celestial bodies, as it was a lonely vigil, but the humans around her were too short lived. When she'd found the young wizard, it had seemed like the perfect solution.

Of course, Calleigh was reluctant to let her son go and had to be persuaded that the odds of him achieving adulthood were slim. Most wizards and witches did not survive a journey past edge of the swamp, falling prey to the swamp's hold on their magic.

Their magic was bound to the swamp, and it was a rare wizard or witch that could leave it with their magic intact. Without their magic, they were physically and mentally weakened and susceptible to a magical cancer which infested the hollows where their magic had been, destroying any residual ability until senility crept into their minds and they surrendered and died.

But Artio had surrounded Genii's magic within her eternal sphere of influence and had been able to shield him from the effects of being isolated from the swamp. They had been together ever since. What she had not counted on was falling in love with the young man as he grew. He soon caught up with her, in mental age if not in exact years, and she planned to increase his life span, as they appeared to be exactly the same age and would be forever more.

So Artio had visited Calleigh once more, when Genii was sixteen, and this time, with him in tow, to receive her blessing and her assistance in not only preserving his life but in making him as close to immortal as it was possible for a human to be.

And now, seven years later, they stood on the cusp of the fulfillment of that dream, to bind their souls to each other for all eternity.

Artio ran down the slope, her cape flapping around her shoulders, to the very center of the clearing. A broad whitish disc sat in the center of the circle of stones, and in its center a shallow basin was scooped out. Around the bowl, partially completed carvings were etched, runes of magic and spirit, taught to them by Calleigh. She had made them practice over and over and over, until they could carve them precisely. There could not be a line out of place.

The first set had allowed for the healing of the people. They had triggered the medicine wheel of the stones, a vital function, as the transformation to a near god would bring Genii to the edge of death. Without the healing of the medicine wheel, the absorption of the moon's energy would sear him to a crisp before he could be transformed by the moon. A careful balance between healing and absorption, aided by the potion, must be maintained or all would be for naught...and the runes were the trigger.

Genii joined her, and despite the rain, they set to work. Genii withdrew a leather-wrapped pouch from inside his cloak and flipped it open, extracting two chisels and two small hammers. He handed one set to Artio and he took the other and they set to work, chiselling the hard stone until the grey light failed them. As they worked, Genii's magic flowed into the stone and the lines glowed as they chiseled, the flow of magic sealing itself into the figure. The rock warmed and the light rain made a hissing sound as it evaporated on the heated surface.

As night descended, the ability to see accurately lessened. Fearful of making a mistake, they quit for the evening, retiring to the shelter of a crystal cave located through a rift of rock at the far end of the meadow. The cave had been their temporary home for the last year, and they had been overseeing the construction of the circle from it.

They lit the fireplace set against one wall and pulled provisions from a hollow shelf in the rock wall to eat. A kettle of water was placed on the hook over the fire, and Artio tossed some tea leaves into the water. They did not speak, content to enjoy the peace of their surroundings and weary from the day's work. As they sat near the warming fire, the light reflected off several thin glass vials, perched on a high shelf. A shimmer of magic surrounded the potions.

Three days. They had three days to complete the runes. Three days.

Chapter 13

Alfreda

THE PERSISTENT RAIN chased them down the Cathair road, the great cat that was Alfreda's mount yowling with displeasure about the mud clinging to her paws.

The battering mammoths, on the other hand, placidly plodded along the grassy roadsides, the divisions of their toes splayed like toes to counterbalance the slip and slide of the soil beneath their enormous feet. They left large flat discs behind them, which would dry to stepping stones of clay once warmed by the sun. Occasionally, they dipped their heads, dragging a tusk through the grasses and snagging a mouthful of the tender shoots, munching as they lumbered along.

Alfreda pulled her hood up higher and spread the cloak over her knees and down the back of the sabretooth to help keep him dry. The cat disliked travelling in any form of rain but did so at her command.

As she raised her head from the adjustment of her clothing, she saw a scout riding swiftly toward her. The captain of her forces peeled away from the head of one column and rode back toward her, intercepting the scout. Then, together they rode toward her position.

The scout's horse was lathered with sweat from the hard ride, despite the rain, nostrils flared wide as it sucked in air. It tossed its head as it was pulled to a halt in front of the great cat. The sabretooth paused, tail flicking, eyes narrowed at the snorting beast. The horse noticed the cat at the last minute and shied, nearly unseating its rider.

"My lady!" the scout said, recovering his balance. "I bring you grave news. There is a large Primordial force about twenty miles ahead. The flesh clans are on the move! They look to be headed toward Cathair."

"Toward Cathair?" she said sharply. "Are you sure?"

"Yes, my lady! I would put their numbers at two thousand strong, and they have a high priest with them!"

"High priest? Which one?" The scout shrugged, and Alfreda's frown turned into a scowl. "How dare they move onto this soil without my express permission! Return and bring this high priest to me, immediately! This is my command and so it shall be."

Captain Enyeto cleared his throat. Alfreda's eyes slid over to meet his grey ones. "You have something to add, Captain?"

He nodded. "The location of such a parley should be neutral. It is too great a risk to bring the two clans in close proximity. May I suggest we pick a location and invite them to meet with us? There is a good place about a day's ride from here, a natural amphitheatre. Command that they bring no more than three Primordial, including the high priest, and we do the same. Any accompanying guards must be left behind half a league from the meeting location."

"Excellent suggestion." Alfreda turned back to the scout. "Take these words to the high priest." As he made to turn away, she grabbed the scout's sleeve "Tell them, that if they fail to appear, I will be *sorely displeased.*"

The scout nodded and raced away.

Captain Enyeto tugged on his reins and dropped in beside Alfreda. His hand wandered to his mustache and he smoothed it with two fingers, a nervous habit of his especially when he feared his words were bound to be contentious.

He cleared his throat. With a rumbling catch in his voice, he said, "They can be here for only one reason, my lady. They are here to appease the silence of the gods. They are here to find a sacrifice."

"Ridiculous. I have forbidden it." She tightened her knees, squeezing harder than she intended and the cat quickened his pace, so that Alfreda jumped ahead of the captain.

He urged his mount forward and parallel to hers once again. "They cannot be allowed to roam the land. It would be an act of war against Cathair, and especially if they start taking human sacrifices."

Alfreda scowled at her captain but did not answer.

"Negotiation will fail, and every step they take into the country will escalate the tensions. There is only one solution. They must join their will to ours and submit their high priest as a token of peace."

"They will refuse to give up their high priest! He is sacrosanct. No one may touch a priest."

"Exactly…that is why we must take him while he sleeps."

"What do you propose?"

"We kidnap him. If we control the priest, we control the army."

She shook her head "It's too dangerous. He will be heavily guarded."

"Then he must be assassinated."

"*What?*"

"If he is dead, the reason for coming here is gone."

"Temporarily, yes, but at what cost? Do you really think they will not seek revenge?"

"Pardon, my lady, but isn't it part of the ritual of the high priests to have their people drink of the blood of the sacrifice to bind them to the priest?"

She nodded, staring straight ahead.

"Then you must strike the snake in the head to kill the body. Anything else is giving license. My lady." He ducked his head in respect.

They rode in silence for a while, the persistent drizzle obscuring her view of the battering mammoths by the roadside. Alfreda sighed and adjusted her hood when a drip splashed onto her nose. She sighed again, and then the hood turned slightly.

"Set it up. I do not want to know the details." The hood straightened, and she nudged her cat into a lope, leaving her captain behind.

Chapter 14

Helga

HELGA SKIRTED AROUND the splashing waters of Thunder Falls, anxious to get away from the cold mist rolling off the surface of the pool at its base. She clutched the satchel with the precious potion to her breast, afraid that she might drop it in a sudden slip on the damp path.

The mouth of her cave, disguised by a ribbon of water from the falls, parted as she approached. She passed through the waters untouched and into her fortress home.

She had chosen the location deliberately, as the falls masked the sounds of her experiments and other than the occasional Primordial pilgrim no one came to the remote location. She was able, therefore, to conduct her research without needing to constantly fend off intruders.

And now as she entered the cave, an unnatural heat met her. She smiled as the warm air enveloped her, chasing away the chill. The damp and musty cave smells of living underground also faded away. She placed the palm of her hand on a rune, cast into stone just inside the entrance, and a glowing strip of light as bright as a window to the outside world appeared down the center of the ceiling. A tunnel resembling a hallway was revealed. She walked down the smoothed stone floor following its natural twists and turns until it emptied into a cavern, open to the sky.

A railing of chiseled stone steered to the left to a stone staircase that clung to the side of the cavern, spiralling down on a gentle incline around the circumference of the walls until it spilled out onto the cavern floor. The walls faded from grey to a glossy black, the pumice stone giving way to smoothed obsidian.

Great curls of smoke twisted and rose from a deep pit that glowed ruby with the reflected light of lava, flowing at great speed past the breach, a great underground river of flame.

Helga glided down the curving staircase, intent on her destination. As she entered the lower half of her descent, her image danced across the dark mirror and she studied her reflection out of the corner of her eye as it slid across the glassy surface. Tall and slender of build, she knew that she was by far the most beautiful of the godling sisters. *My radiance should not be dimmed. Soon the world will acknowledge me as the supreme godling, or they will perish. I will have their obedience in life or their souls in death. Either way, they are mine. My dear brother, Caerwyn, will kneel to me before the solstice is finished or he will die, forever.*

At the base of the cavern, she walked across the pitted surface, her destination a tunnel in the far wall. Before she reached the dark smudge, the smudge moved and hooded figures detached themselves from the wall, sliding forward to hover a few paces from the wall. The Charun bowed its head in acknowledgement of its mistress and then glided over to her side.

"What is your command, my mistress?" it hissed, the sound of its voice the rasp of a file. The sound raised a shiver along Helga's spine, a delicious shiver of anticipation. A second Charun slid out from a crack and followed the first. As Helga reached the opening, three more joined the first two, drifting along impossibly above the floor.

The Charun looked identical, except for the one who spoke. A circle glowed in the middle of its forehead. Tattooed between its eyes was a rune, the image a golden sickle blade on a sea of blood. The circle dripped between the deep ridges as the Charun's face crinkled the leathery grey reptilian skin reptilian of its brow.

"Time grows short. The solstice approaches and Artio has erected healing stones. This will undo all our hard work. The animal souls we have been enslaving may be snatched away from us before we can complete the circle. Come!" she snapped "We must make final preparations."

She entered the tunnel and with a snap of her fingers, a compressed ball of flame flickered to life to float over her outstretched palm, lighting the path for her feet. She strode along at a pace just short of a run, skipping down the stairs with light steps. The staircase wound down and around and twisted this way and that but finally leveled out and into the rock. After about a half hour of walking, it spilled out into a long cave split down the middle by a giant fissure. A ribbon of lava slipped along its course, flowing swiftly by and tumbled in molten splashes down into a widening pool at the end, which eventually breached into a waterfall of lava. Intense heat and foul fumes rolled and twisted against the ceiling, which stretched so far above that it could not be seen. Yet Helga knew that a thin crack carried the roiling smoke into the cavern above and eventually out a natural chimney to the mountaintop.

At the edge of the lava pool several more Charun lined up by the razor sharp edge, dipping ladles into the river of molten rock and then carrying them, one by one, to a raised platform. A mould stood three stories high with scaffolding and ramps allowing the Charun to float up the ramps unimpeded to the lip of the mould.

The mould resembled a large bull seated on its haunches. The nose was pierced with a golden ring and long horns ending in barbed points curled from its massive face. In its front hooves, it held a large golden scythe, the flickering light of the lava flashing across the surface of the blade. The mouth was open in a frozen snarl, its eyes glimmering sky blue as though alive. The darting eyes followed the movements of the Charun and then flickered over Helga's approach. She shivered at the intelligence reflected in those eyes, the soulful depths swimming in the rounded orbs.

Of course, there is intelligence. How could there not be? Even the lowest beasts have some form of intelligence. Trapped intelligence. Stolen souls enslaved to my will...and now they will become my greatest weapon.

She climbed the ramp and circled around until she could look down into the seemingly bottomless vessel, craning her neck to see over the rim. She reached inside her cloak and pulled out the precious vial of potion. She unstoppered the bottle, staring at the shimmering liquid. Then, with a flick of the wrist, swallowed half of the contents. The other half she tipped into the vessel where, it hissed upon meeting the lava. The bluish haze writhed and twisted in the potions vapour and a keening wail echoed up from the depths and then faded away.

Helga turned and started down the ramp but then stumbled as a piercing cramp rippled across her abdomen, doubling her over in pain. She sucked in a breath, forcing herself to straighten, her hand gripping the stone wall. The Charun by her side flicked its forked tongue across its teeth, sensing her weakness, tasting the air.

Helga pushed off the wall and walked forward, back straight and head held high. She dared not show any weakness around the Charun.

Her vision blurred and she swiped the back of her quivering hand across her eyes, attempting to clear them, to no avail. The fog obscured her vision, and a cold sweat broke out on her upper lip. She ran a hand along the inner wall of the scaffolding, feeling her way to the base, blinking frantically to clear her vision.

The potion…the binding goes both ways. I…must…dominate!

*"You **will** submit your will to mine! I am the master!"* she thundered silently.

Mentally, she stiffened her mind, forcing the mist to obey. She bore down on the silent collective, pressing her will against the hundreds of souls battering against the walls of her mind and slowly melded them, merging them into the core of her own soul.

She lifted her head, eyes clearing, to find a Charun reaching for her, slimy hands stretching for her throat.

Helga lifted a hand and out shot a brilliant white torch of flame that encompassed the Charun. It screamed a high keening wail that rose in pitch as the flames encompassed it, head to hem. With a burst of stars, the Charun exploded and vanished as if it never existed.

Helga whirled, ready to cast another comet of light at the other Charun, but they retreated into the shadows, melting away into the darkness, until hers was the only living soul remaining in the hot cavern. She knew they would return; they were bonded to this task.

Unsteadily, she left the cavern. *I will rest and assimilate the bond. I must be ready. Time is already too short.*

Chapter 15

Artio

"I THINK YOU SHOULD ask Helga."

Genii shook his head, negating the idea, crossing muscular arms across his chest in emphasis. "I don't think Helga would be interested. You saw her the other day. She left as soon as she could. She has no interest in the healing circle or how it works. She certainly doesn't wish to assist."

The medicine wheel, while not technically a wheel, still functioned as one. The wheel that best illustrated its operation was actually a spinning wheel. As it wove the spirit of the gods into a thread of healing, a godling could then take that thread and make a blanket of healing for all those within the circle. No form of healing was too complex. The wheel simply wove the right cloth for the healing required.

Medicine wheels were tricky to create and a gift of the gods. A large percentage of the wheel's operations directly tied in to the flow of spirit that came from the gods, which had been dwindling lately due to the decrease in prayers being offered to them. It was rare for a human to possess the kind of faith needed to power a medicine wheel. The Primordial high priests and high priestesses came close, but even they struggled to maintain a constant flow of spirit through the wheel.

The conversation was a sore spot between them. Genii was firmly of the belief that the further they stayed away from Helga, the better the eventual outcome would be. Something about Artio's sister made him uneasy, and he was reluctant to ignore what made him uneasy. It had kept him alive in the swamp and in the world since leaving the place of his birth.

"We do not need Helga's help. The focus is precisely set." He held up his hands as Artio opened her mouth to speak, halting her response. "Listen, the tremors will stop. The mountain always quiets in time. What could she possibly do that could stop it? Volcanoes are a part of nature."

"Yes, but these are not *natural*. You know this, as well as I do, Genii! You were the first one to note the pattern of the fire fall. She must have some idea of why the eruptions are increasing."

"There is no time. The solstice is tomorrow. By tomorrow evening, we must have the stones perfectly aligned. There is only time left to align them, not to research the why of their shifting. If we go chasing off after Helga right now, we will miss our window." He stepped up to Artio and enfolded her in his arms. "I do not want anything to spoil our plans. The alignment must be right. Perfect. Supreme." He bent his head and kissed her, silencing her protests. The sweetness of the kiss erased all complaint and discussion and when he lifted his head, she sighed and laid her ear over his beating heart. She would go along with his plans, but still the thought niggled in the back of her mind, that they were missing something…something important.

The disk in the center of the circle was now surrounded by a broader circle of crushed willow bark. Foxglove bloomed in tall stalks, and monkshood and mugwart was interspaced here and there. Surrounding it all was a wall of faceted amethyst crystals a full span high, fencing in the herbs which had been carefully gathered from the surrounding meadow to focus the plant energies within the medicine wheel.

All was prepared, except for the final adjustments.

They broke apart and returned to fine tuning of the stones. Genii took new measurements and with levers of stone, shifted the monoliths by fractional increments, so tiny as to be not visible to the naked eye. Genii and Artio worked long into the night, aligning the stones with the stars, the pale moon's reflection sliding over the creamy disk, a near perfect reflection on the smooth stone surface.

Tomorrow night, the moon would be full and perfectly aligned. All was ready.

They stepped back to admire their work. A slight breeze blew up the valley, smelling of sulphur. Genii shivered, but it was not from the cold of the breeze. The smell of an open grave rode the wind. He was being watched and his gaze was drawn to the tree line. A shrub shifted slightly, then stilled. He squinted at the brush, but nothing moved in the dark.

Chapter 16

Alfreda

ALFREDA APPROACHED THE ARRANGED meeting point above the amphitheatre, sliding off her great cat and scratching it behind her tufted ears. With a rumbling purr, the cat sank to the ground and cleaned her paws, great tongue rasping against the pads between her toes.

Two of Alfreda's captains stepped up beside her, short swords in both hands, drawn from harnesses strapped across their chests. They peered warily around at the surrounding tall grasses, but there was no hint that anyone had crossed this portion of land recently. The stalks were tall and unbroken, waving lazily as they passed.

The main body of warriors remained on the main road and three of them crossed the grassy plain. Flat and level, not a tree broke the horizon so they were on top of the dip of land before they saw it. The amphitheatre was a large natural depression in the plain, as though the gods had scooped up a large handful of clay for some purpose known only in celestial circles.

They had been preceded by the assassins sent ahead by Captain Enyeto. Alfreda sucked in a nervous breath as the rim of the bowl dropped away.

At their appearance, a great cloud of ravens burst from the floor of the amphitheatre, flapping and cawing and circling their prey. Captain Enyeto pulled an arrow from his quiver. With an economy of movement, he stroked the arrow to string and loosed. The first arrow was followed by another and another, falling amongst the birds and never missing a shot. Wounded birds flapped and cawed and were set upon by the other ravens, pecking and slashing with razor sharp beaks. In between the flapping and cawing, Alfreda glimpsed the bodies of the assassins, bloodied and unidentifiable except by the remnants of the clothing they wore. Of the high priest, she saw no sign.

Alfreda backed away from the rim and swallowed heavily, striving to not vomit at the smells now wafting out of the bowl on the stirred air. She hurried back to her cat and buried her face in its soft fur.

Captain Enyeto continued to kill the ravens until most were dead and the balance decided that the meal could wait and winged away over the plain with indignant squawks. Several long minutes passed while the Captains went down into the bowl to inspect the scene.

"They died quickly as far as we can tell." Captain Enyeto kept his eyes averted from her grief, not wanting to intrude on her privacy.

Alfreda gave a start at the sound of his voice and lifted her head from the great cat. She could taste the despair on the air, a tugging at her soul that told the real story, at least from the viewpoint of the deceased. Surprise and denial, pain and fear swirled through the air. Assassins they may have been for this particular venture, but at heart, they were Primordial souls and not evil in nature. Although normally this was Caerwyn's duty, she gathered their scattered essence and sent them on their way to her brother's care.

"What of the priest?" Alfreda asked, her voice harsher than she intended.

"I am sorry, my lady, but she appears to have disappeared."

"She? A high priestess? How do you know?" Alfreda asked sharply. Frowning, she reached out with her senses, searching for the woman and the path she had taken away from the meeting location. She could not sense her presence in the area.

"They were killed with this." Captain Enyeto opened his gloved hand to display an empty vial. "They were poisoned, my lady, and that is a woman's method. Men are much more brutal." Alfreda reached over and plucked the vial from his hand. "Be careful, my lady!" he protested "We do not know what kind of poison it is. It could be absorbed through the skin."

Alfreda grimaced and dropped the vial back onto his outstretched palm. "I do not remember the flesh clans having a high priestess. They have always worked with the male lineage. Why would they suddenly appoint a high priestess to this task? It makes no sense. They have always sent a male to the temple for the choosing."

"Yes, but has a male ever been chosen?" he asked.

"No, not as a temple priest. This has been a major part of the discontent between the two clan factions." Alfreda paced the floor with short strides, considering the puzzle. "They have not been silent regarding their displeasure, but there can be no accommodation for the sacrificial rituals they practice under the guise of appeasement of the gods. They refuse all requests from the spirit clan chiefs to attend their ceremonies, zealously guarding their secrets. Rare is the opportunity to observe or participate in their ceremonies. They are very much a closed society, and the only people who are allowed to enter their realm are those who have partaken in their ceremonies and become one of the tribe."

"I have heard that the joining ceremony involves the consumption of human flesh and blood?" Captain Enyeto grimaced at the horrid image, unconsciously gripping the hilt of his sword as though by pulling it out, he could slay the offending thought.

"Yes." Alfreda walked in a widening circle around them questing with her mind, searching once again for the illusive high priestess. She rubbed at a mosquito bite on her arm, smearing a little blood in the process. Frustrated, she hurried back to her mount and climbed back into her saddle. The great cat stretched and stood, tail twitching, and sniffed the air head swinging to the right to stare and then back in the direction of the amphitheatre. The ravens circled overhead and dived low and disappeared into the bowl with their departure.

"Let's rejoin our forces. We will march through the night. I want to join with the Kingsmen by dawn. I sense that Caerwyn is in danger. I must catch up with him quickly."

They galloped off towards the waiting Primordial hoard and reaching the head of the column, set a brisk pace for Daimon Ford.

Dark eyes watched their hurried departure, cloaked in robes that absorbed the background image and bent the light so that the eye slid right past. Standing close enough to hear every word, the cloaked figure chuckled. The narrowed eyes followed Alfreda, then dropped to the hand in front of its face and smiled. It was holding a needle and the needle was dripping with blood.

Alfreda's blood.

Chapter 17

Caerwyn

THE JOURNEY OUT OF THE SWAMP was a long and arduous one, filled with buzzing insects and biting flies, but worst of all, were the tall broad-leafed plants that blocked their passage. Every branch was covered with fine, transparent hairs that hung from the stems like moss, but it was unlike any moss Caerwyn had ever seen.

The fragile strands drifted in the currents of air. Caerwyn swore they were hunting living beings. Attracted to motion, they would wind their tendrils around any creature that crossed their path, twisting in the breeze to float down onto an unsuspecting arm, softly wrapping itself around and around. Microscopic barbs set against the tug as the victim moved on, unaware of the plant's activities. The stinging vegetation went out of their way to slap up against flesh, and Caerwyn swore one plant was actually following them as they finally reached the edge of the swamp.

He did not need to encourage his men to keep going; they had no desire to linger within the confines of the swamp.

Three days and nights after their exit from the swamp brought the Kingsmen to the crest of a ridge. The River Erinn came into view, a ribbon of dark in a flattish flood plain, dotted with willow trees.

The last gasp of night faded before the blush of the predawn sun.

Caerwyn sat his Pegasus at the head of the assembled army, watching the approach of the warriors under Alfreda's watch. The spirit clan warriors moved with the precision of clockwork. Even the battering mammoths swaying gait kept rhythm with the marching clansmen.

Caerwyn could only see them from his vantage point because of the flickering torches held by the lead warriors. They crept out of the darkness of the southern plain, the moon long since set. It would be the better part of the day before they were able to merge their two forces and march on the mountain.

Caerwyn turned Brimstone back to face the mountain. A never-ceasing glow could be seen flickering on the side of the mountain near the summit. Smoke curled and twisted into the air, forming a dense mushroom-shaped cloud with a pink underbelly. Lightning flashed within the roiling smoke, and occasionally a bolt would stab down toward the rocky base.

Helga had planned her distraction well, for between himself and the fiery ledge, a Primordial host stood, watching their approach. He grimaced with distaste. Civil war…he had never wanted it to come to this.

He dug his heels into Brimstone's side and launched into the air.

* * *

From the banks of the ford of the River Erinn, the Primordial clan chief of the flesh tribes watched as the horizon resolved into a skyline thick with mounted Kingsmen. Vertical pikes broke the sky like the sharpened pole fences of a wooden fortress, stretching the entire width of the valley, from river to treeline. The Kingsmen were set six men deep with archers and swordsmen filling in the last two files. Heavy armour plate glinted off the bodies of the horses, reflecting the first rays of morning, refracting over the curvature of the earth.

A Kingsmen rode back and forth in front of the men, a long thin trumpet strung with the sky blue flag of the Royal house of Cathair along its length. Caerwyn lifted the trumpet and blew a long shivering blast on the horn as he galloped past the orderly rows. The front row snapped a salute as he passed, a sea of arms like the curl of a cresting wave.

The flesh clan chief, Akecheta, a necklace of neck bones decorating the front of his skins, sat astride his black and white paint, stroking its muscular neck, comforting the high-strung mountain-bred stallion. It snorted, catching the scent of the other horses across the valley, and whinnied with excitement.

The Primordial warriors, their barebacked mounts snorting and shuffling, crowded in around the clan chief and gestured toward the approaching army jabbering excitedly to one another.

"Enough!" Caerwyn roared, "Do you wish the enemy to see you flapping around like chickens with a fox in their midst? Do you want them to see us as *afraid*?" His dark glare made heads drop in shame, avoiding his hawkish gaze. "Daimon be praised," he spat. "Cease this babbling! Rein in your mounts!"

The milling warriors stilled their horses, forming a loose row facing the intruders and the murmuring ceased. The clan chief rode in front then circled behind the outnumbered clansmen, his stallion snapping at the other horses as he passed. He scanned their heavily painted faces, searching for any trace of fear. No warrior would admit to it. Fear was for the weak, and the penalty was death. Painted onto the skin of some were crude depictions of creatures thought to reside in the underworld. Others wore Daimon masks decorated with glowing charcoal eyes that granted a flickering life to the fierce images. Every warrior brought their spirit guardian to battle; none would dare fight without their protection this day. Today they would face Kingsmen and kin, cousins who called the traitorous spirit tribes home.

A gust of wind roared down the mountainside and gusted out onto the plain, hot and sulphur-scented. It burned the nostrils and coughing broke out in the ranks. It sped past the flesh clan warriors and eyes watered in its wake. Akecheta wheeled around to stare at the mountain, scowling at the source of the offending wind. The mountain rumbled and the cloud of smoke flashed as an eruption of rock and lava spewed from the rent in its side. Boulders of rock shot into the air and sailed in a slow arch past his warriors and out into the plain. The mounted Kingsmen shouted a warning, and their lines were abruptly broken as men and horses dodged the flaming missiles landing amongst their ranks.

Cheers rose from the Primordial warriors and shouts of glee as the mountain continued to spew its fiery belly skyward. Small fires sprung up, burning across the grassy plain, and smoke drifted across the parched surface, spreading quickly. A wall of fire created a barrier between the enemy armies.

"Daimon be praised!" shouted the flesh clan fighters. "Our guardians go before us!"

"The Gods are pleased!" shouted another.

"Victory will be ours!"

"Honour to the high priests! They show us the will of the Gods!"

There was no fear in their eyes now; their faith renewed, they faced the enemy boldly. Assurance that victory would be theirs gleamed in every painted face.

*   *   *

Caerwyn felt the shock wave from the explosion before he heard it, but it was the projectiles of pumice and ash that drew his eyes as balls of fire roared out from the missing face of the mountain crater.

Brimstone screamed and attempted to dodge the flaming bullets but several tore into his wing, puncturing it, others burning along hip and flank. Caerwyn struggled to steer his panicking mount to the west, but the fiery debris rained down on them as the mountain continued to belch. His eyes watered with the acrid smoke. As he cleared his vision, he spied a hollow tucked in against the base of the mountain. Brimstone tumbled toward the surface, and Caerwyn sawed on the reins to steer him toward what was the only sanctuary in sight. The ground rushed up toward him, and at this speed, even he could be killed if he were to make impact with the ground. Caerwyn kicked his feet free of the stirrups and slid further back on his saddle, readying himself to jump at the last second.

A sizzling pellet sliced across Brimstone's cheek and tore through the main muscle of the wing, which folded under the combined weight of Brimstone and Caerwyn. The Pegasus spun around and around, a maple leaf tossed in the wind. With a crash, the Pegasus struck the ground and rolled, a tangle of wings and mane and tail, tossing Caerwyn over his back. He flew through the air and his head smacked hard against an upright grey stone pillar. Bright stars popped across his vision, and he knew no more.

Chapter 18

Mordecai

MORDECAI STOOD UP on the seat of the wagon, peering toward the mountain. Great plumes of smoke rose from its crest, and fiery breaches could be seen in the stone façade despite the dark that clung to the mountainside in the late afternoon sun. It wasn't the roaring mountain that drew his eye. Below the summit, partway down the mountainside a nimbus glowed, a flattish blue aura that was neither cloud nor smoke. Brighter than the rock face, it throbbed with light and life.

"Father, what is that place?" he asked.

Hud followed his son's pointed finger, but his eyes were not as keen as Mordecai's. *Or what he is looking at, is magical,* he thought.

"What is it you see? I see the mountain erupting and lots of clouds and smoke."

"Do you see that blue disk? It sits there, just above that outcropping of pinkish rock." He stared at the spot his lips pursed, hand still pointing in the direction of his gaze.

Hud shook his head. "I'm sorry Son, but I cannot see it. Why do you ask?"

"Because that is where I need to be. Can you take me there?"

"It is behind the Primordial lines. How do you expect us to get there?"

"We can fly. The king brought extra Pegasus." Mordecai pointed to a snowy white Pegasus grazing alongside three other Pegasus at the rear of the Kingsmen. "Her name is Moonbeam. That is her true name. She told me." He grinned and pushed the blanket-covered box to the edge of the floor before hopping down from the wagon. Grabbing the box, Mordecai ran over to the Pegasus. "She told me I could ride her."

Hud jumped down from the wagon and followed his son over to the Pegasus. Moonbeam lifted her slim head and chewed a mouth full of grass, eyeing their approach. She snorted and flapped her wings then settled them against her sides and went back to grazing.

Behind Moonbeam, a great cat bounded through the grass, a woman on her back. Hud raised his hand in greeting. "My lady!" he said and bowed low.

"Cinda!" cried Mordecai, as Alfreda rode up to the pair of them. She halted the cat short of the Pegasus and slid to the ground then hurried over to the pair of them.

"Where is Caerwyn?" she said anxiously, eyes searching the area for her brother.

"He is in the air with Brimstone," Hud said, alarmed at the frantic look on her face. "Why? Is something wrong?"

"Yes, he is in danger, and I cannot reach him. He is not answering my summons. Something is definitely wrong!"

"We must search for him then. The only ones who could find Brimstone are the Pegasuses. We were going to take Moonbeam here and go check out an area by the mountain that has caught Mordecai's attention."

"I will join you then." Alfreda turned around and spied a third, toffee-coloured Pegasus. "I will ride Sandstorm."

"Somehow, it seems appropriate to ride a Sandstorm and Moonbeam to search for elusive Brimstone. It could get hot before we are finished." Hud flashed a crooked smile, amused.

Alfreda gave him a weak smiled in return. Cinda nudged Alfreda's arm, and she yowled, complaining about the change in plans. Her tail twitched and her golden eyes narrowed at the commotion around her, ears twitching. "Not this time, Cinda. I must fly!" Cinda rubbed up against Alfreda and then rolled onto her side, begging a bell scratch. Smiling weakly, Alfreda scratched her soft belly, and straightened.

Mordecai was already scrambling onto the back of Moonbeam. "So what are you waiting for?" he called "Let's get going!"

Hud pulled himself up behind his son and Alfreda caught up Sandstorm and swung onto his back. With a heel to flank, the Pegasuses launched into the air, wings sweeping quick beats to carry them skyward. The ground shrank away and the men shrank to the size of wooden toys. With swift strokes, the Pegasus pulled higher into the sky then leveled off to coast on an updraft from the mountain. The wind was thick with a foul stench that made their eyes water and made them tuck their faces in against their sleeves.

With a roar, the mountain exploded and great chunks of flaming debris arced across the sky, raining down on the troops below. Kingsmen fell like dominos, dodging the deadly missiles.

Hud was suddenly thankful for the height that the Pegasus had climbed to, as they now flew above the debris field, but the wind became white hot, the erupting mountain super-heating the air. Whirlwinds of flame created violent updrafts and downdrafts that sucked at the Pegasus, who struggled to not be pulled into the flaming trailers in the sky.

Mordecai pulled ahead of Alfreda on Moonbeam, intent on the location only he could see. She put Sandstorm nose to tail with Moonbeam, and together they swept toward the bubbling mountainside.

As they crossed over the Primordial forces, faces turned upward and arms pointed and an arrow or two was loosed in their direction, but they fell short and tumbled back to earth. Alfreda looked back over her shoulder, searching the clan for the high priest...or high priestess if that was who was truly in charge...but she could not pick out anyone to fit that description in the crowd of clansmen.

They crossed the River Erinn. Once on the north side of the river, the buffeting winds ceased and they were able to descend through the caustic smoke, coughing and holding their sleeves over their noses through the dense vapours. The heat tore at their throats and scorched the exposed skin on their faces.

The hair on Hud's skull rose. *I wonder if it will burst into flame.*

They passed through the cloud.

"There it is!" shouted Mordecai. He urged Moonbeam on toward what now appeared to be a crater on the mountainside. A blue aura hung over the tree-lined clearing. In the center, large upright stones formed a circle from which the blue mist emanated.

The Pegasuses dropped lower, and one by one they landed in the far end of the clearing, knee-deep in the meadow grass. A whicker came from the long shadows reaching half way across with the setting of the sun. Brimstone stepped forward from the shadow, limping, wings dragging on the ground.

With a gasp, Alfreda slid from Sandstorm's back and ran over to the injured Pegasus.

"Where is Caerwyn, Brimstone?" She edged around Brimstone, careful to not touch the deep burns running across his chest and flank. Brimstone rolled his eyes and bared his teeth in warning.

"Mordecai, Hud, go into the forest and gather some witch hazel. Quickly!"

"But, Alfreda, you need to know..." Mordecai broke off as gave him a push towards the woods. Hud grabbed Mordecai's hand and tugged him along behind him. They ran off up the path past the stones and disappeared into the woods.

Alfreda turned back to Brimstone. "Where is Caerwyn? Where is he, boy?" Alfreda opened her mind, searching for her brother. *Caerwyn, can you hear me?* Her mind quested, searching the link of the bond they shared, but was as if he had disappeared. A stone cold wall was the only sensation where normally there would be a tangled web of emotions.

Alfreda turned on the spot, eyes searching the strange clearing. The stone placement was of recent date, the stone freshly quarried, and the soils around it showing recent activity. In the broad circle, several rings narrowed to focus on a white disk. She frowned and took a step toward the rune-covered stones. *Artio, this is your handiwork, isn't it?*

At that moment, a shout echoed from the woods. "My lady, Alfreda, come quickly!" A shiver of apprehension slide down her back, but she did not need any further calls from Hud, Caerwyn's silence was all the excuse she needed. She hiked up her skirts and ran for the path into the trees.

Alfreda pushed through the scrub brush and into the forest, following Hud's call, but the forest was dark with the descent of night. She stumbled down the path. As she leapt over a thick root, slimy hands grabbed her arms. A cloth was shoved over her face, smelling strongly of petrol. She struggled to get it off her face, but her consciousness faded and she sagged limply in the Charun's hands. They turned as one and floated away into the woods.

Hud kept a hand clamped tightly over his son's mouth, the other arm around his waist, keeping him still and silent.

After several moments of silence, he relaxed his hold.

"The Queen!" Mordecai whimpered, and a big tear rolled down his cheek.

"You knew this was coming, Mordecai. You were the one who told me." His father wiped the tear off his cheek and pulled him onto his lap.

"Yes, but I didn't *want* it to happen. I wish the box had been wrong." Another tear leaked out from under eyes squeezed tight.

"Caerwyn will understand. So will Alfreda. You must trust them." Mordecai nodded then buried his face in his father's chest and sobbed.

Chapter 19

Artio

ARTIO EXITED THE CAVE at the end of the meadow. As she straightened, she stopped so abruptly that Genii plowed into the back of her. He grabbed her around the waist to keep them both from toppling over.

"Pegasuses!" she breathed, watching the winged mounts. "Caerwyn is here somewhere." Her eyes scanned the clearing, but nothing stirred other than the Pegasus gorging on the lush grass.

The mountain rumbled, and her eyes were drawn to the summit towering above them. "The mountain grows restless. Whatever is happening inside that mountain is giving it a belly ache. I fear we will live to regret what that is."

"Come. The light fades. We must prepare."

Genii reached back inside the cave and pulled out a rucksack and slung it over his shoulder and followed Artio down the sloping pasture to the great circle of rock. The sun was already hidden behind the treetops and long fingers of shadow stretched to cover more than half of the clearing. Artio took the sack from Genii's hands and loosened the drawstrings and then reached inside to pull out the two lumps of moon rock. She handed them to Genii before reaching back inside and pulling out the collection of vials.

The first vial contained tiny grains of crushed diamond that sparkled in the low light. Artio crossed into the circle and knelt on the white circle then pulled the stopper and emptied the contents of the vial into the bowl. Genii then placed the two chunks of meteorite in the center of the diamonds.

Returning to the satchel, Artio removed the remaining two vials, both of them containing the purple elixir provided to them by Calleigh. A catalyst, she had called it, to enhance the spells cast.

Artio returned to Genii and gave him one of the vials. She sat on one side of the circle and he sat down opposite her, cross-legged, facing Artio, knees touching. The sun faded and the light of the day waned. As the clearing darkened, the bowl of diamond twinkled, seemingly lit from within. But the source of the light was the moonstones, which initially pulsed weakly but gained strength as the light faded.

Artio pulled the cork on her potion and drank it down in one and Genii copied her, tossing the empty vial away. He reached across to capture Artio's hands in his.

"Do not let go, no matter what happens, Genii," Artio instructed. "You should start to feel numb and may even doze off, but do not let go." Genii nodded, and Artio could already see his face slacken. "I will be here with you the entire time. Do not be afraid, my love." Genii's eyes drooped, but he did not slump. Rather, he seemed frozen, his knees and back locked in place, rigid.

Artio dropped her eyes to the moonstones and chanted an incantation of her own devising. The moonstone's pulsing quickened and so did Artio's heartbeats, excitement and the potion racing through her veins. Her eyes blurred and she entered a trance, continuing to spell the moon, pulling it to her, commanding it to obey her will. Her soul lifted from her body and entered the moonstone, her body locking just as rigidly as Genii's. The clearing, the ring of rune-rock, the moon circle all faded from conscious thought. There was nothing but the moon.

Chapter 20

Captains Collide

CAPTAIN ENYETO DIPPED HIS HEAD and pushed his way into the tent of Captain Brennan, followed closely by his Kingsmen guards, who looked appalled at the Primordial captain's boldness. They knew he was of Alfreda's clan, but even so, all Primordial looked the same to them.

Captain Brennan stood as Enyeto entered then waved his guards away. They bowed and exited the tent.

"Captain." Brennan nodded his head toward a makeshift bench placed on one side of a low table, inviting him to sit across from him.

As Enyeto lowered himself onto the bench, Brennan growled "Alfreda is missing too, I take it?"

"Yes, she left about four hours ago and has not returned. Night is falling. I fear they will not return this evening. I fear for their safety."

Brennan strode back and forth in the small confines of the tent, worrying the familiar groove in the carpet, a result of prior campaign pacing. "I am planning a night attack on the Primordial barring our way. Are your clansmen willing to go up against kin? I would prefer to negotiate, but such offerings have met deaf ears in the past and I see no reason for this to be any different. Nevertheless, I intend to send out a scout under a white truce flag to parley."

"My clansmen are as anxious as the Kingsmen to recover their queen. You would have to fight them also, to keep them from accompanying you. When will the truce flag be sent out?"

"He should be there now. Come let's see what kind of a reception he receives."

Brennan strode out of the tent, Enyeto on his heels. They strode past the infirmary tents where the wounded were being tended to. The moans of men in pain followed them as they passed by. "How many were injured?" Enyeto asked.

"About ten percent of my force. Twenty dead. It could have been worse."

Enyeto grimaced at the numbers.

A few minutes' brisk walk brought them to the closest lookout point. Grabbing a pair of looking glasses from the closest scouts, he climbed the rise, handing one to Enyeto.

The distant rider sprang close as they put the glass to eye, his flag whipping over his head from a pole set in a pocket by his stirrup. He was about one hundred paces from the lead row of Primordial clansmen when a hail of arrows arched out. Multiple arrows pierced his chest, and he fell sideways, dead before he hit the ground. His foot twisted in its stirrup and did not dislodge. His panicked mount snorted and wheeled around, racing back toward them, but a second hail made the horse stumble as arrows pierced its legs, and a final arrow in the neck severed the jugular and it collapsed in a skidding heap. When the dust settled neither rider nor horse moved a muscle.

Brennan swore loudly. "Well, that would be your answer, bloody Primordial heathens!"

Enyeto raised an angry fist and put it down on his thigh. "You will have to race me to the bastards, Captain. We will have first blood!" he snapped and wheeling around marched away toward his waiting escort. Five Primordial horsemen peeled away to race back to the spirit clan warriors. "Meet me on the field of battle in ten minutes."

"*To horse!*" roared Brennan and the scouts took off running to spread the word. His face darkened and all who saw him coming knew it was time. They would cross the River Erinn at Damion Ford or die trying.

Men spilled out of tents and doused cook fires, grabbing armour and belting it over tunics, stamping feet into boots. Within minutes, they were mounted and formed into their units, which peeled off to join up with similar stirrings of the spirit clan forces. They raced toward each other, then both armies curved to ride side by side, Kingsmen's horses matching the horses and great battering mammoth's pace for pace, stride for stride. The battering mammoths sensed the coming battle and bellowed a piercing blast so loud the riders to clap hands over their ears. The ground shook from the combined pounding of thousands of hooves, creating their own mini-earthquake, flattening the grass and churning the soil.

The flesh clans fanned out to face the oncoming rush screaming insults and waving fists clenching blades and wickedly curved scythes on long poles. Their leader rode down the long line in front of them, screaming wildly and carrying a pole from which dangled the head of a man, dripping blood as he passed by. The head swayed side to side and as he turned once again, the face flashed to the oncoming Kingsmen. The head of the scout who had fallen in the field not ten minutes ago. The flesh clans screamed in blood lust, eyes crazed behind devilish masks and as one, they surged out to meet the oncoming rush.

The gap closed swiftly and the battle commenced.

Overhead, a vulture circled lazily. It was quickly joined by others.

Chapter 21

Godlings

CAERWYN'S EYES FLUTTERED SLOWLY as he attempted to crawl out from under the fog of pain. His head thrummed as though stone masons were chipping away at his skull, the throb as sharp as a chisel. He clawed himself awake. As his eyes opened, his first sight was a ceiling of hand-hewn stone. The chamber danced with firelight. He turned his head and a wave of dizziness made the firelight jiggle, in a nauseating way.

He closed his eyes briefly. When he opened them again, he found himself face to face with a robed figure, eyes glowing within a deep hood and skeletal hands folded inside its sleeves. It floated above the surface of the floor.

Caerwyn made to sit up but found his hands were tied behind his back and a chain rattled on the ground. No matter. There was not a rope in the kingdom or in the world that could hold him. He tensed his muscles, straining to shred the bonds, but all that happened was a rattling of the chain as his muscles flexed. Surprised, he bent his head to look at what held him, but this brought another wave of dizziness on so intense that he barely resisted the urge to vomit.

The Charun hissed at him, "Be still. The mistress says you are to lay still."

Caerwyn rested his head back on the cold stone floor to cool his fevered brow. "Who is your mistress?" he asked, but he thought he knew. Only one person would choose to live here and only one could devise a way to restrain him. That knowledge was restricted to those with similar powers.

"She comes. She comes." The creature floated back, and from a doorway Caerwyn could not see before stepped Helga.

She paused in the doorway, silhouetted by a back lighting of her own making. "Hello, dear brother. So nice of you to drop in, but I must admit, you have slept far too long and unfortunately have overstayed your welcome." She descended the last step and strode over to stand in front of him, crossing her arms under her breasts.

"But now that you are here, what to do with you? You see, you really should ask permission before dropping in on me. I could be…busy."

"Helga, untie me, enough of this foolishness!"

"I am afraid I can't do that, not yet. I have plans for this evening. Until I am ready to leave, you will stay right here." She laughed as Caerwyn struggled with his bonds. "Don't worry. I will invite you to the party. Oh yes, I wouldn't want my sibling to miss the fun! Where is our lovely sister, Alfreda? She must be with you. You would think you two were twins, the way you copy each other. Never mind. I am sure she will make an appearance shortly. Either way, she does not have long to live. She seems to have run afoul of poison."

"Helga! Are you mad? Untie me!" She continued to ignore Caerwyn's struggles and he ceased trying to free himself, as the blackened ropes tightened painfully. Instead he demanded, "What is this all about? Are you behind the eruptions?"

Helga smiled, but it did not reach her eyes. "Alas, an unfortunate side effect, but I have made adjustments for it."

"Adjustments? To what?" He stared at her and a chill washed over him. "Helga, you haven't been drilling into the core of the earth, have you?"

Helga's smile widened, and she chuckled at the shock and fear that flashed through Caerwyn's eyes.

"Just a tiny experiment, Caerwyn. You would not understand. This is my realm." Her gaze hardened. "The time has come. I will not be sent the dribbles of humanity to rule. I will have my piece of the world…with or without you." She smiled at his expression. "Don't worry. You will get a front row seat, I promise!"

She spun on her heel and headed deeper into the cave. Caerwyn's eyes followed Helga, and it was then that he saw they were not alone. Hundreds of Charun crowded the cave. What he had originally taken for firelight was revealed to be a river of lava that split the cavern in two. About a dozen of the creatures milled around a tall something, carting containers of lava up a sloping ramp to the top and dumping it over the side. When the last of the Charun descended, the scaffolding collapsed to the ground with an ear-splitting clatter. A two-story tall idol was revealed, the casing glowing with the heat of the lava, but that was not what drew Caerwyn's gaze. The eyes glowed *blue* with intelligence. The idol had a *living soul* trapped within it, perhaps more than one. *Where did Helga find living souls? These souls are mine to care for. They should have returned to me!*

With a grunt, he was roughly rolled over and a canvas sack was pulled over his head. Hands pulled the rough chain from the loops on the floor, and he was dragged by his arms upright, his shoulders screaming in protest. Shoved from behind to get his feet going the desired direction, he stumbled on the rough surface. The same slimy hands lifted him to his feet, bony fingers wrapping around each bicep and Caerwyn felt the presence of death in their grasp.

The death of a godling was never contemplated, the thought foreign to him, but suddenly he knew it to be a real possibility.

Surely Helga would not go so far? Caerwyn thought, but he was unsure of anything anymore. The Charun did not let go of him, but held him tightly between them, his feet dangling in space as they floated him up the passageway.

By the change in temperature, Caerwyn knew they had risen above the level of the lava and into the natural coolness of a cave. Then, a freshening breeze announced the exit to the outside world. A waterfall met Caerwyn's ears and flora slapped against his feet as he floated along between the Charun. They did not speak but carried him silently along, to where he did not know.

Eventually they halted, lowering him to the ground. A pole bumped his back and the chain was dragged through another ring with a rattle, binding him to the pole. The canvas hood was not removed. Silence descended, unbroken by cricket or frog. Caerwyn attempted to scrub the hood off of his head, rubbing it up and down on the pole and it inched up a bit at a time until the sack was over his ears at the back. His head flopped forward and the sack fell off into his lap.

He raised his head and his mouth dropped open at the sight before him. He was tied to a pole at the base of a mammoth stone pillar, over two stories high. A circle of stone created a ring from which a fiery light flickered. In the center of the circle around a flat disk sat his sister, Artio and a man, both frozen in a trance, moonlight circling their still forms in ribbons of streaking light. Directly across the circle from him was Alfreda tied in a similar fashion to one the grey pillars of rock.

The Charun who had carried him to the stones melted away back up the path, and they were left completely alone. Silence fell, complete except for a faint hum at the center of the circle.

Weakly, Alfreda stared at Caerwyn across the expanse and their gazes locked. She was similarly bound, slumped against the pole. She shifted her position, and pain shot up her arm as she straightened. It was as if a poison raced through her veins. She could not feel the connection to her world anymore. Her talents were fading. *I'm sorry,* whispered Alfreda to Caerwyn's mind. *I failed to rescue you.*

It's not your fault. I was knocked out of the sky and hit my head. It knocked me unconscious. Helga captured me that way. What is this place? What is wrong? You look horrible! he messaged.

It is a medicine wheel. I recognized it as soon as we landed in the clearing. I think it is Artio's construct, although I do not understand all of that, she nodded to the circle of light, *or what she is up to. What could she possibly intend to heal?*

Well, when that moon has fully risen, it will dump enough energy into this circle kill everyone within it, including you and me. Look at the runes, Alfreda. This is not good. What are we going to do?

Hud and Mordecai are with me. They fled when Helga attacked, and we were separated. They are still out there, somewhere. Mordecai is a smart boy. He will come up with something to save us.

Suddenly, a distant voice echoed in Caerwyn's ears, advice he had recently received and only now understood.

The answer is within you, she whispered softly, *and you must find it. Calleigh can see nothing more than what she has told you. Calleigh gives you these words of her own free will, at no cost. They are Calleigh's gift in the hope that you will recognize the way when it is placed before you.*

Caerwyn searched with his mind and found the boy huddled with his father in the shrubbery at the edge of the clearing. He pulled their consciences into the web of thought with his sister and spoke to the pair of them.

Mordecai, what is your plan? Do you have the balance box with you?

Chapter 22

Mordecai

THE BRUSH PARTED as Mordecai and Hud squeezed their hands between the branches, creating a small hole through which they could peer at the clearing before them.

The Charun slid past them, sweeping up the path at a much faster pace than they had gone down it, with Caerwyn suspended between them. Helga's summons of the Charun was paramount. Her command they instantly obeyed, and they left the clearing with no more regard for the prisoners than cattle in a feed lot.

Mordecai was glad for the Charun departing. They made his skin crawl. The magic needed to create them was highly sensitive and volatile, and their presence made his skin itch as though he had fallen in stinging nettle.

Suddenly, Mordecai felt the brush of a mind against his, a familiar touch. It was as if he prayed, his mind opening to the presence of God. His father gasped beside him as he felt a similar sensation, and then a voice filled their minds.

Mordecai, with the curiosity of a child and the knowledge of a wizard, easily replicated the form of contact, solidifying the connection.

I have my balance box right here beside me, sire. Mordecai's hand twitched to the box.

I know you have been working on its secrets, and I believe you have figured out how it works.

I have, sire. The box told me.

Caerwyn looked over at Alfreda and grimaced. "Time is short. Either you must free us immediately, and we take our chances on stopping whatever is going on here with no idea of what is about to happen, or we sit here and try to ride out the coming storm and attempt to fight from within. I believe either path spells disaster for the world. Calleigh's warning rings strongly in my ears."

"There is no time to come up with a third plan. Not by me, anyways, but I believe you have the third answer, that you have held it all along."

Caerwyn's head swivelled until he was looking directly at where the small boy hid. "Come to me, Mordecai," he commanded, and Mordecai and his father slid out from the brush and came down into the clearing. They approached the king, both kneeling before him on the grass, heads bowed. Once they were standing before him, Caerwyn spoke.

"Tell us why you have brought the balance box?"

Mordecai stared at his toes poking out of his dusty sandals. The silence stretched.

"Mordecai?" Alfreda's voice drifted across the space. "Do not be afraid. We will not be angry. Tell us what you know."

A fat tear slid down his cheek and it was soon followed by others. Hud hugged him close. "You both must die," he croaked. "It is the only way to stop them."

Silence greeted his words.

"Mordecai, come here, and you too, Hud," commanded Caerwyn.

"I cannot undo these bonds. They are magically forged. But I need to touch you. Help me to stand."

Hud put a hand under Caerwyn's elbow and helped him to his feet, sliding up the pole.

"Now, I want both of you to kneel behind me, under my hands."

They did as they were bidden. Caerwyn placed his hands on either side of Hud's head.

He closed his eyes and drew on his godling spirit and a blue flame sprang to light and enveloped Hud's head in its glow.

"From this day forward, you will be branded with the oak leaf, the royal seal of Cathair. You and your descendants, going forward, will be the royal house of Cathair. You are my heir and my chosen successor. From this day forward, you will be king." The cool blue flame pulsed and a tattoo of an oak leaf appeared briefly on Hud's cheeks and a permanent tattoo appeared on the inside of his right arm.

Caerwyn shifted his hands to Mordecai's small head and the blue flame flickered around him, brightening as it mixed with his wizard's magic. "Mordecai, you are hereby charged with the care of our souls, should the fate of the world demand the sacrifice. You shall hold our souls in your care for all eternity. You are commanded to guard the souls of all humanity and provide for their care in our absence. We place our very existence in your hands. You will be responsible for maintaining the balance of the world, and you will be the counterstroke to Helga's evil for all eternity. So I have commanded, so it shall be done!" Caerwyn shouted.

"So you have commanded, so it shall be done!" shouted Alfreda in confirmation.

The glow faded and Caerwyn slumped back to the ground, the spell tiring him.

Hud and Mordecai stood and came back around in front of Caerwyn and bowed to him. Caerwyn shook his head. "You do not bow to me, my friends. We are now equals."

Mordecai ran up and hugged him tight and then turned away and approached the circle where Artio and Genii sat frozen in time. The moonlight swirled, wisps of fog-like trails fading into the dark. Mordecai crept up to them, careful to not touch the fingers of moonlight, slid the balance box under the orb of light until it rested directly over the heart of circle. He backed carefully away and then ran over to Alfreda and hugged her tightly. She laid her cheek against his soft brown hair, murmuring softly to him.

Mordecai raised his head. The true moon glow increased swiftly as it slowly crested the edge of the clearing. The humming at the center of the stones rose in pitch.

"You must go now. Hurry! Remove yourself from this area. Stay clear of the danger. The future depends on you staying safe. Go, my friends, *go!*" yelled Alfreda.

Hud, with an anguished look at his former king, ran to Mordecai, grabbed his outstretched hand, and bolted for the

Pegasus. They climbed onto Moonbeam's back and launched skyward out of the clearing.

The moon's rays struck the stones and the humming became a roar, as the beams activated the medicine wheel. White hot light flashed around the tops of the column, faster and faster, becoming a ring of lightning, blue forks sparking out of the circle.

The moon continued its climb and as it rose, the lightning sank lower down the column, striking runes which came alive, dancing with an inner life, as the stone changed from grey to a crystalized white. As each layer of rune activated, creatures of the forest entered the clearing, unicorns and fey folk and thunderbirds and sabretooth, every animal or being with a touch of magic in their blood. They were drawn like moths to a flame, unable to resist the pull of the moonlight.

Alfreda watched, open-mouthed, and tried to warn the creatures away, but they could not hear her, for her spiritual connection with them had been broken by the runes and the racing fever in her blood. She could not summon the bond. They were deaf to her call.

As the moonlight reached the bottom, the final course of runes flashed and light swept the circle, striking Caerwyn, Alfreda, Genii, and Artio. Lightning erupted in a bright white beam, which shot out from the circle and struck the moon with a thunderclap that flattened the trees on the edge of the clearing.

Caerwyn jerked as the full force of the moonbeam's bolt caught him full in the chest. His soul was torn from him and the agony was beyond his ability to comprehend. His mouth opened in a scream that was echoed by Alfreda's across the circle. They thrashed in their bonds, bodies shaking and jerking in the force of the lightning. Artio also shrieked and Genii lifted bodily into the air, jerking like a piñata struck by multiple sticks.

An earthquake rocked the ground and with the clap of a metal gong, the mountain above them exploded. The clearing shook, stones vibrating violently and suddenly a huge rent opened up directly below the white disk. The disk melted and oozed, flowing into the opening while ash and lava shot into the air.

From the middle of the blinding inferno, a figure of lava rose, its shape molded and formed by the cooling rock spewing from the flaming sinkhole. It rose, ever higher, until it climbed from the abyss on a swell of bubbling lava that carried it to the surface of the circle. As its feet cleared the lip, it took two steps onto solid ground. Two stories tall, the beast straightened, stretching its craggy body and lifted its massive head. A flat face with a wide forehead ended in a narrow snout with flaring nostrils. It snorted and flames shot from its nose. Long curling horns of flame curved away from either side of its head. A thick mat of fur covered its upper torso, and muscular arms ended in curled human fists. The legs of the beast ended in hoofs, and rippling across its skin was an ever-present flame. Its eyes were also flame, bright pools of lava that switched from orange to yellow to red, ever-changing.

The Daimon lifted its head and roared and then picked up a great scoop of lava and flung it into the stream of moonlight connecting the beam to the great orb of the moon, full on the horizon.

With a howl, the moon absorbed the steady flow of lava and from one moment to the next the pearly white surface bled, streaked with angry red colour. It swelled with the flow of lava and the moonlight changed to orange and the clearing burst into flame.

The touch of flame triggered the lid on the balance box, which sprang open with a click.

The box hummed and a cloud of blue mist rose into the air and encircled the Daimon, ice on fire. With a hiss at their touch, the Daimon flung lava at the mist, snarling when the mist parted, unharmed. Small fires ignited as the lava lurched through the air and fell to the ground.

With a roar, the Daimon twisted around frantic to escape the cooling touch of the spirits. Everywhere they touched the Daimon, his skin froze. The pain was so intense that it began to stamp around within the circle of stones, coming perilously close to trampling the unconscious occupants.

At that moment, Helga appeared at the head of the path screaming in fury. She flung out her hand and pointed it at the circle. As if thrown, the swirling shadows encircling her body launched themselves into the clearing. The Charun disturbed nothing as they swept between the monoliths, encircling the blue mists now shrouding the Daimon.

"Curse you, Caerwyn! How are you controlling the spirits yet? You cannot shield them from me, not any longer!" She stormed down to the edge of the stones, but she dared not enter the circle. The powers she had unleashed raged out of control, and Calleigh's potion provided only so much resistance. And there was something else...something more in the circle...a discordant resonance that hummed, disrupting the rebirth, both staccato and random at the same time.

The Daimon roared, swatting at the mists, ringing the circle with individual fires as it flung its muscular arms around and around. The Charun touched the antithesis of their being and the blue mists darkened as their souls were absorbed into the bottomless soul sucking void of darkness that is a Charun.

Mordecai, with his eyes squeezed shut, sat cross-legged on the cool grass on the opposite side of the valley from Helga. He clutched a smooth milky crystal in his hand. The crystal glowed bright blue, the light spilling out between his fingers. It flashed and trembled in his hands. Tears slid down his cheeks as he murmured to the crystal. He was hidden from Helga's eyes by the brush, but he sat perfectly still. His father lay flat and still by his side, his knuckles white with the tightness of his grip on his sword.

Mordecai's lips moved and the glow in his hand brightened to the intensity of a small sun until Hud worried that Helga would see light. Mordecai raised his head and as he gazed at the clearing, the blue mists of the spirits of the dead swirled brighter around the Daimon, spinning faster and faster, cooling its shell, freezing its hot blood. Slowly the Daimon darkened until with a final gasp, it began to shrink in size, collapsing inward smaller and smaller, drawn by the blue mists back to the balance box. With a snap, the lid sprang close. The beast vanished as though it had never existed.

Silence descended on the clearing.

*   *   *

A lone figure stirred on the ground. Genii woke, face down on the crystalized circle, rolling over and pushed up to a sitting position with one arm. The other arm was missing, and he blinked before the shock of the moment suspended, resolved into an agony of sensation. His arm was sitting a few feet from him on the ground. His scream echoed around the clearing as his body shook with reaction, the pain of severed nerves and sinews. His eyes slid away from the arm, staring around in disbelief. Artio's broken body sat at the edge of their circle, and he could see two other bodies by the stones, slumped over and still. He crawled across the space to Artio's side and pulled her bloody body to his with his remaining arm then collapsed down beside her, stroking her hair with his remaining hand. Genii howled, but this pain was of the heart. He wanted nothing more than to join her in death. He would die with her in his arms.

A foot appeared by his head and he looked up, eyes straining to focus. A shimmering form stood before him. *I am dying* he thought and somehow couldn't muster the strength to care. His eyes closed and his breathing slowed.

*   *   *

Helga's face twisted with anger. She bent down and placed her hands on Genii's head, and he howled with pain, back arching. A blue mist rose from his body which Helga ignored. When her hands lifted, he stared at her, glassy-eyed. His arm had been reattached (he did not know when). At Helga's silent command, he lifted Artio's broken body into his arms and silently followed his new mistress out of the clearing.

Helga did not even glance at the corpses of her brother and other sister. As she stepped from the clearing, their bodies crumbled and turned to dust. They were no more.

Epilogue

MORDECAI BEN-MOSES was a brilliant wizard. Raised in the rich kingdom of Cathair and housed in the royal household, he had the best of everything. Fine robes and fine chambers, and an endless supply of books to study and entertain him were mere bonuses to his true purpose in life.

Mordecai Ben-Moses was also reclusive. He was happy to spend his time studying, honing his skills and preparing for the future. He was eldest of the royal children, but as the son of the king before he was made king, he was ineligible to take the throne. Not that he had an interest in doing so.

As a half-brother he downplayed his semi-royal heritage.

It was also centuries ago. No one remembered those days. He was the last of that line, blessed with long life due to the magic running through his veins. Instead, he took on the role of counsellor, and prepared the later princes and kings in their duties as the royal Spirit Shields of Cathair, teaching them the sanctity of their role and its gravity.

It did not bother Mordecai, for he had known his duty since the age of seven. Teaching the princes kept him close to the castle, permitting him free access to the most sensitive of areas. He was able to wander the castle grounds and the hidden passages below, monitoring the sacred trust placed in him by Caerwyn and Alfreda.

Only he knew where their souls resided. His time would come. The spirits demanded it. The fate of the world hung in the balance. He would be called on, before the end of his days, to restore the true king.

He placed his hand on the balance box, and it murmured to him…as always.

Seer of Souls

Prologue

THE BABY GAVE a feeble, barely discernable kick. Its twin had ceased movement but not with the natural stillness of slumber. Poison moved through their premature bodies, oozing along their tiny veins, a burning acid in their blood.

Mordecai lifted his hand from the woman's sweaty forehead. Gwen's panicked eyes locked onto his sad grey ones. She clutched her distended belly as another wave of pain ripped through her.

"It must be poison! This is more than simple birthing pangs." She coughed and the motion made bile rise in her throat. Gwen clutched at Mordecai's left hand, gripping it so tight the knuckles of her hand whitened. "It's reaching the babies! Mordecai, what do we do?"

Straightening his lanky frame, he released her hand and wandered over to the tall mullioned window of the bartizan room. His sweeping brows pinched together in a frown as he gazed unseeingly at the silent courtyard below him. Purple wisteria climbed the ashlar walls of the castle, revealing their stark outlines. A fresh breeze stirred the heavy tapestry curtains as lightning flashed, highlighting the roiling clouds, puffing in eager anticipation of the storm breaking over the castle.

Her seclusion was for her protection. Gwen's grief over Prince Alexander's failure to return from his most recent patrol with the Kingsmen twisted in her gut, accentuating the pain of the poison. The prince and all of the Kingsmen in his unit had been slaughtered by Primordials in a sudden vicious attack. This sorrowful news had arrived on the heels of the king's death from a heart attack a week prior. The kingdom was reeling from the double disaster. *And now it's my turn. I am the target,* she thought.

Gwen coughed and froth formed in her mouth, drowning her thoughts. Her lungs attempted to fill but failed. Intense pressure gripped her chest as though a large man with a booted foot stood on it compressing it. She pushed aside her discomfort and staggered over to join the wizard at the window. She clutched a handful of his grey robe sleeve, partly to gain his attention and partly to keep from sinking to the floor.

"Please, Mordecai, I must save my babies! What can I do? There has to be a way to help them. Between your magic and my heritage, there *must* be a way."

Mordecai's mouth drooped beneath his long white beard. "I can only think of one solution, Gwen" he said gently. "You must pass the mother bond to me." Tears sparked in her almond-shaped eyes as he locked his to hers. "I think we both know that you cannot survive this poison." He squeezed her hands. "We need to convince Alcina the babes have died with you."

Gwen's liquid green eyes searched and found steely resolve reflected in his grey ones. She nodded once and unconsciously rubbed one hand across her protruding belly, where the foot of the lone stirring child pushed against the thin protection of her skin.

"We need to do this quickly, Gwen. The birth will take most of your remaining strength, and they must be born alive in order to pass the bond."

She groaned again as a hard contraction took her. The twisting pain of a poison-filled cramp left her gasping for air as she sank to her knees beside the wizard. She raised her head, panting. "I do not think that is a problem, Mordecai."

Mordecai gently eased her onto her back, on the cold stone floor. Reaching inside his pocket, he took out a clear crystal stone and placed it between her cold hands, clasping them with in his own. Together, they began to chant.

*   *   *

The late-day sun streamed through the garden-view windows of the bartizan room. Dust motes stirred in a breeze heavy with the smell of damp earth and wisteria. A few trailing clouds scuttled across the sky in an attempt to catch the storm moving off to the east, low rumbles fading softly into the distance.

With a groan, Mordecai sank back to his knees on the polished floor beside the princess. Gwen's sweat-soaked brown hair curled damply over her curiously shaped ears. Dark circles shadowed her eyes; eyes that stared back at him from a deathly pale face.

She lay on the floor, her bloodstained gown bunched to one side. Beside her, wrapped in cotton swaddling, were two newborn infants, a boy and a girl.

Both children were dead.

A tiny red birthmark, resembling the shape of an oak leaf, adorned the right side of each smooth cheek. The tattoos faded away before his eyes. Mordecai smiled a grim smile and trailed a thin finger down the soft cheeks where the tattoos had appeared so briefly, sensing the residue of magic under the skin.

Gwen lifted her hand and caressed the cheeks of her two babes. A hot tear trickled out of the corner of her eye. She would never know them, nor they her.

Mordecai lifted the children and placed them in her arms. She hugged them and wept silently, tears streaming down onto the cherubic face of the closest child.

Gwen's mournful eyes lifted to the man standing beside her.

"Are they truly safe now, Mordecai?" Her weak voice shook with supressed emotion.

"They are as safe as we can make them, Gwen."

She touched his sleeve. "Thank you," she murmured weakly. "You have been a true friend." She stiffened, sucking in a hard breath that ended abruptly. Her eyes widened as the soul in their emerald depths faded away. Her hand slipped from his sleeve and thudded to the floor.

Mordecai gently closed her eyes, squeezing his own shut to dam the tears sliding down his whiskered face.

"Sleep well, Gwen, and welcome the peaceful embrace of the Mother."

He staggered to a chair by the open window. Leaning out over the stone ledge, he saw a dead eagle on the stones below. He dropped back into the chair beside the window and gazed out at the setting sun. The last of the storm clouds faded into the distance. Little did they know that they carried the hopes and dreams of the world in their midst.

Pain stabbed into Mordecai's chest and he sucked in a deep breath. If his calculations were correct, he had little more than a half hour left. The poison was completing its job.

Well, his task was finished. What would be would be. Eyes opened wide, he watched the sun creep toward the horizon. The rays of the setting sun blazed through the retreating clouds, glowing pink and orange. His lips curved with satisfaction. It was done.

*   *   *

The tall, regal woman burst into the room, cruel eyes sweeping the creeping shadows. Her contingent of guards with lanterns held aloft quickly encircled her and then spread out along the sides of the room.

She gazed around at the scene before her. "Search the room for others. Check to see that no one is alive," she snapped at the guards.

She marched up to the woman lying on the floor cuddling her two babes. Frowning, she stepped around the bodies and moved over to the man in the chair.

He sat staring glassy-eyed out the window. She felt for a pulse in his neck and located a faint pulse under the curve of his chin.

"The wizard still lives!" she screamed. "Find the mage. Hurry!"

She snapped her fingers, calling the two guards standing closest. "Pick him up, and move him to the lower dungeon. Secure him with two guards on the door at all times. His head is to be shaven before he awakes and it must remain shaven or his powers will return."

She grabbed Mordecai's whiskered jaw in her long-nailed hand and shook his slack face. "Poor bald wizard," she murmured to him. "You hoped to be dead before I arrived, didn't you? Soon, you will tell me all your secrets, starting with this room. I will know the truth of this before you die." She released his face. "Take him away!"

Whirling around, she barked to the other guards crowding the room. "Burn the bodies—immediately! There will be no Remembrance

Eulogy for them. They are unworthy of the honour. It is reserved for true royalty"—she nudged Gwen's body with her toe—"and she is not royalty! Filthy heathen!"

Furious, she stormed from the room, her black silk skirts snapping in her wake.

Chapter 1

ZIONA ASPENWOOD STOOD at the edge of the glade in the shadow of an ancient oak tree watching the blond-haired young man. Dressed in rough woolen pants and a bleached linen shirt, he sat on a rocky outcropping, whittling a length of wood.

He paused to examine his work, holding it up to his right eye and peering down the long shaft and then turned it over in his hands, running his fingers along the hollows he had carved into the body of the wood.

Satisfied, he picked up a long narrow awl, a useful leather tool that now doubled as a whittling knife, and with deft movements tunnelled into the shaft of wood, starting at one end then working from the other until a tube formed through its length.

He shook his hand and shavings fell to the grass at his feet. He blew into one end and peered down the tube once again. Grunting his satisfaction, he smoothed the center of the piece with the sharp awl.

Suddenly he glanced up, his piercing green eyes staring directly at Ziona. They pinned her to the spot. She flinched back to take cover even though she knew human eyes were not as sharp as a Primordial. Still, his focused concentration made her believe he had spotted her hiding place amongst the trees.

He stared at her like a deer scenting danger for a moment and then picked up his project once again, deciding the danger had passed.

Ziona drew back into the gloom of the woods and joined her companion. Sharisha Fernfell was dark-skinned for a Primordial with brown eyes bordering on black. Her sharp cheekbones and permanent frown provided a stark contrast to Ziona's leafy green eyes, set in a heart-shaped face and framed by sun-kissed hair.

"Did he spot you?" Sharisha crossed her arms over her chest, annoyed by the lingering of her younger companion.

"No, I don't believe so," said Ziona, shaking her head. "I thought he caught my scent, but there is no possibility of that, is there? Perhaps one of his sheep alerted him to our presence."

"We need to be careful," Sharisha huffed. "The escalation of the war has made it unsafe for Primordials to be seen in human lands. Surely you know this, Ziona!'"

"Yes. There is no need to remind me, Sharisha," snapped Ziona.

Sharisha frowned at the younger woman and instead asked, "So…what do you think? Is he the one we seek?"

Ziona was silent for a moment, thinking. Was it possible he was the one? He seemed to fit the parameters, but, on the other hand, he seemed so simple…so common…not at all what she had anticipated.

They had been watching him and his sister on and off for a week now. Other than an affinity for nature, they had not exhibited any skills or talents out of the ordinary.

"I don't know, Sharisha. I just don't know. The elders speak of an undeniable sign that will show them true. I guess we should continue to watch him. If he is the one then eventually he will show us proof of his true nature. The spring equinox is almost here. If a sign is to come, it will be then, when the Goddess returns to bless the land. I think we should wait until then."

"Agreed," said Sharisha. "We will wait and watch."

Sharisha led the way back through the woods to their campsite deep in the forest. She moved without a sound on soft moccasin-shod feet. Ziona followed, slipping into the shadows.

* * *

Cayden Tiernan glanced up from his whittling, staring at a flash of something in the oak grove at the far end of the clifftop pasture.

He stared at the spot, focusing his senses on the spot, searching for anything out of the ordinary. He thought he sensed a presence beneath the ancient oak tree, which stood tall and proud where the field of tall grass ended. He smelled a fresh calming scent, reminiscent of his sister. Someone or something was definitely watching him.

He whittled without focus, his senses attuned to the spot. There. The movement was as graceful as a doe in the trees, so fleeting that the average person would miss it.

Now, the presence was gone.

Who are they? What do they want with that particular spot?

Cayden pocketed his flute and affected a casual stroll toward the ancient oak. As he entered the shadowy circle formed by the canopy of the tree, the lower branch quivered and a slender figure dropped onto his back. He staggered sideways, not as a result of the negligible weight but from the arm that snaked around his skull in a squeezing headlock that blocked his eyes and made spots swim behind his eyelids. His foot caught on a thick tree root that rounded out of the soil. The combination was too much and he tumbled to the earth with a thump that dislodged his attacker, tossing her over his shoulder and rolling away.

Cayden winced at the sharp spear of pain in his knee and looked up to see his twin sister, Avery, lying flat on her stomach, head twisted to the side. Her arms were sprawled to either side and she jerked spasmodically. Alarmed, he lurched to his feet, one hand soothing the friction burn on his face and the other brushing stones from his knee, as he stumbled to her side. Sinking onto his uninjured knee he grabbed her shoulder and flipped her over. Fear tightened his throat and he croaked, "Avery! Are you OK?" His shout trailed away as her face was revealed. Avery was laughing so hard that her shoulders shook and she swiped at the tears streaming from her eyes. A full-bellied laugh burst from her lungs and she rolled onto her side, curling into a ball and hugging her middle.

"I have a stitch in my side," she hiccupped and continued to laugh and hiccup in an alternating pattern that eerily echoed the tune that had just been playing in Cayden's mind.

Miffed, Cayden stood up and stalked away. *She is always doing that, trying to scare me.* His hands drifted into his pockets, checking that his flutes were intact as his eyes quickly scanned the surrounding forest, but whatever had caught his attention earlier was long gone.

Cayden rolled his shoulders, easing the tension there and also relaxing the sore point where Avery's knee had impacted. He turned back and offered her a hand up. "If you are quite through...?"

Avery accepted his hand and he hauled her hiccupping to her feet. She brushed grass and leaves off her tan pants and picked a twig out of the turndown at the top of her boot.

"What were you doing there, Cayden?" She poked at his pocket. "Carving another flute?"

"Shh!" Cayden put a finger to his lips, hushing her question, with an involuntary glance at the suspect shrubbery. He strode to the area that had caught his eye and searched the underbrush for telltale signs of a human presence but found no evidence of anyone having stood there.

Cayden walked back to the ancient oak tree, Avery trailing in his wake. Kneeling at the base Cayden pulled back the pile of oak leaves nestled in the crook between two large surface roots, exposing a small, hollow crevice under the tree. He reached inside and pulled out a deerskin bag, loosening the drawstring. Inside were ten carved flutes.

So the strangers were not here for my flutes, he mused.

Cayden tightened the drawstrings and slid the bag back into the hollow at the base of the tree, deep in the crevice. He replaced the leaves in and over the hole, obscuring it from view and then erased his tracks by covering them with more fallen leaves. He studied his handiwork for a moment and satisfied that their hiding place was perfectly concealed, he perched on his favourite outcropping of rock in the pasture once again.

Avery watched her brother's actions, a bemused expression playing across her features. She followed him to the rock and climbed up beside him, flopping down on her stomach on its warm smooth surface.

"What do you plan to do with all those flutes?" she asked, chin propped in her hand, watching him work with the slim stick of wood.

Cayden didn't answer. The truth was that he didn't know why he carved them. Avery was the only person who knew they existed. Magic in any form was banned, and his flutes would be perceived as magical. Of that he had no doubt. Avery was the only person who knew of his magic, and he knew she also harbored similar magical talents, although hers were more easily hidden.

The warm late day sun made the slab of granite a very pleasant perch for watching the sheep. His bow rested against the base of the rock, a quiver of arrows within easy reach.

Taking out his partially completed flute, Cayden examined it again. A bubble of excitement welled up inside him. He had been working on this flute for the last three days and it was near completion. Each one he had made was slightly different than the one before. Some were longer, some shorter, some fatter, some thinner, some slightly curved. All were decorated with spirals or lines carved into the surface.

He was not sure why he decorated them so, other than it seemed to change the sound and pitch of the tones produced. And the end result? It was completely unpredictable.

Cayden studied the flute in his hands and inspiration struck. Picking up the awl, he deftly carved sinuous lines lengthwise along the shaft of the flute. At the base, he carved his signature mark, a towering oak tree. He always carved in sight of the tree. It seemed magical to him. It gave him the wood to carve and so he wished for it to witness the creation he made with its gift. The oak tree limbs swayed slightly in silent acknowledgement. It was not the first time they had done so.

"Cayden? Do you think it's true, what they say about the war?" Avery's question broke through his concentration.

Cayden grunted and glanced quickly at her before returning his attention to the flute. "What are they saying? I have heard so many different rumours that it's difficult to know what to believe."

"Well do you believe that the Primordials are invading?" Avery frowned at him. "The queen's criers are saying that the Primordial clans plan to come across the Highland Needle and raid the farms. They say that travellers are being snatched and are never seen again. They say that strange creatures have been spotted, dark monsters that suck the soul from people. They say that the Primordials are cursing the sheep that graze closest to the pass, and lambs are being born with two heads. Two heads! How strange is that?" Her words tumbled to a halt.

Cayden snorted. "Do you really think any creature can survive with two heads? It sounds like stories made for telling around a solstice fire."

Avery frowned at Cayden's response. "Well it can't all be stories. What about the McKinnons? They had that two-headed calf born last spring, remember? It actually lived for a few days."

Cayden grimaced and nodded. Curious, he had gone to see it, before it died. He had snuck into the barn just before dark and there it was, in the stall beside the cow which had given birth to it, complete with two heads, one larger than the other. The heads had competed with each other to nurse first and within a few days it had starved itself to death. He shivered involuntarily; the memory was creepy.

"They burned the calf body," Cayden said, picking up the story, "and the McKinnons moved away. The queen's guards were going to arrest them for witchcraft, Pa said so."

It was Avery's turn to nod. "Cayden, I am afraid of anyone learning of our magic." She fidgeted with a few stalks of tall grass as she spoke, braiding them together. "We must be very careful, with the legions on the move."

"They wouldn't want us! We are shepherds. I don't think they even know where Sanctuary-by-the-Sea is located." He waved the flute in her direction. "Here, take a look at this one."

Avery scooted over the rock to his side and peered over his shoulder at the flute in his hands. Pleased with the result, Cayden took a soft cloth and a small container of linseed oil from his pocket. He opened the lid and dipped a folded corner of cloth into the pot, then wiped it onto the flute, working the oil into the raw wood surface. It glowed as the oil was absorbed into the body.

He put the lid back on the container then stowed both the cloth and the pot of oil back in his pocket. His eyes searched the field one more time checking that they were alone, and then he placed the flute to his lips.

A hauntingly soft but reedy sound came from the flute. He tried a couple of other notes, up and down the pipe. Settling his back against the rock outcropping, he played the tune that had been bouncing around in his brain, eyes wandering lazily over to an ewe and newborn lamb, cropping the short grasses a foot or two away. His eyes drifted closed while he played, listening to the tone of the flute. The melody lingered in the air when he finished.

He opened his eyes to find snakes crawling out of rocky dens where they had been hibernating. They crawled toward them and gathered beside him on the rock, seemingly bewitched by the sounds coming from the flute.

He was not surprised, and neither was Avery. Strange things happened around Cayden's flutes, usually involving some creature or another. The only surprise left was what kind of animal the flutes would summon.

He continued to play and the snakes swayed in time to the music. Cayden counted fifty snakes around him of every type known in the area from poisonous black adders to common garden snakes. None showed any aggression toward him at all.

He stopped playing and the snakes slithered up beside him, coiling on the rocks. Their gentle hisses were not words, but he grasped their meaning. He sensed they meant him no harm. His talent was sufficiently strange that to outsiders, especially those who rigidly followed the queen's edicts, it would appear that magic or witchcraft was being practiced. Cayden agreed; the way the music of the flutes attracted creatures to him did seem magical. Magic had been outlawed as long as he had been alive and the queen sent regular patrols to scour the kingdom for signs of its use.

The older men of the village, however, loved to recount tall tales of a time when magic permeated every corner of the world, of the Old Gods and Goddesses, of a time when magic ruled supreme; a time before the Falling; a time before the War of the Gods. It was all very thrilling, the orators' voices rising and waning, the spooky quality heightened by the flickering light of the roaring bonfire, which marked the close of the festival to welcome spring.

The flute he had carved last week had summoned several packs of wolves, the appearance of which panicked the sheep causing them to bolt away, bleating their terror and scattering into the trees. The wolves paid the sheep no attention at all, instead coming to sit right at the base of the rock, their heads cocked to one side listening, expressions of extreme intelligence on their faces. Tongues lolling out of their mouths, they had stayed until Cayden had stopped playing and then slowly faded back into the trees.

Cayden had spent two extra hours gathering up all the sheep, which, of course, had made him late for dinner that day. The lie that he had fallen asleep in the warm sun did not convince his father, earning him a stern lecture and extra chores.

Even stranger still, after each of these encounters with the animals called by the flutes, Cayden felt a bond with them, as though an echo of the song still played in his head. They became a large extended family that never left his side, yet no one ever saw.

Scooping up ten garden snakes, Cayden placed them in the pouch at his waist. They writhed and wiggled and squirmed in the bag.

"Come on, Avery. We need to get back to the farm. Father will be waiting for this flock to come in. The faster we finish dousing the sheep, the sooner we can head into town and check out the festival."

Avery slid off the rock and whistled for the sheep. "I can't wait to check out the decorations. Let's hurry!" She ran off into the pasture, gathered the sheep into a loose bunch and began herding them toward the lane. Grinning, Cayden whistled to gather the few stragglers and headed for home. He had a plan for these snakes.

Chapter 2

AVERY TIERNAN TOOK A DEEP BREATH. She sat cross-legged on the ground out back of the chicken coop, eyes closed, hands resting on her knees, palms up. Exhaling slowly, she let every part of her body relax.

She drew another deep breath, this time holding it until it seemed her lungs would burst with the need to exhale. Spots floated before her eyes, but her senses sharpened and she focused on those smells that came in the deepest of relaxed states.

It made no sense to her, how she could smell so acutely when she wasn't breathing at all, but somehow she knew it wasn't an actual smell she smelled. It was more like an impression of a smell, a memory of a smell. Often it wasn't even a scent she had ever smelled before.

She had discovered this ability quite by accident one day. About six months ago, she had taken a fall from her horse (*of course, it was the horse's fault; she had been perfectly balanced standing on the back of the horse!*) and landed quite painfully on her back, knocking the air from her lungs in a great whoosh. She lay there for several seconds, gasping for a breath that wouldn't come. Like an overturned turtle, she'd lain there, staring at the canopy overhead. Verdant leaves vibrated with every colour and hue, and the rarified air trembled and danced in her vision.

She smelled the scent of an earthworm, wriggling on the soil of the overturned rock that had caused the horse to stumble in the first place. But even more impressive to her, she could sense her horse's surprise and waning fear of falling. Avery watched as her horse,

Sunny, wandered back to nudge her with her nose, snorting. She understood Sunny's thoughts simply from the horse's smell…or what she called a smell.

Sitting up slowly, Avery had patted her mare's nose in comfort.

The smell today was nothing she had ever smelled before. It was the sweet aroma of a wildflower that grew only in the sacred lands to the north of the mountain ranges in the land of the Primordial. How she knew this she did not understand, but she knew it to be true.

She sensed the land knew it too; the trees whispered of the flower and its powers to heal and to soothe. Avery thought the flower had the ability to heal mortal wounds if administered in time.

She shook her head at her crazy thoughts. She knew she was right, though. She would be branded a lunatic and a heretic if she were ever to speak those words out loud. By the queen's decree, she would be declared a witch and the queen would certainly have her burned at the stake were she to even voice the thought. So she kept her dawning abilities to herself and practiced when she had quiet moments alone.

A twig snapped.

Avery's eyes flew open. With her enhanced senses humming, she pinpointed the location, and spied two figures standing about one hundred paces away. They froze and then melted back into the trees and were lost from view.

* * *

Ziona allowed the branches of the dogwood to relax back to their natural position, cutting off her view of the curly haired young woman. Sharisha continued to watch her, a slight frown creasing her brow.

"Did you see an aura around her while she was meditating? It pulsed like a living thing! I have never seen such strength of spirit before. She was glowing blue as a midsummer's sky! Look, it's pulsing from her in waves. She is the one, Sharisha, I know she is!"

Sharisha studied Avery, as Ziona walked deeper into the trees. "It is one of the signs. The boy, her brother, must be the other one, even though we did not witness his spirit yesterday." Sharisha silently withdrew from her place of concealment and allowed a rare smile to soften the rigid set of her lips as she caught up to her companion. "We need to keep a close watch on the pair of them."

"So now we split up." Ziona matched her strides to Sharisha's. "I will keep watch over the boy and you can aid the girl as we planned."

"You must not interfere with the boy, Ziona." Sharisha frowned at the younger woman. Ziona bounced along at her side, her excitement evidenced by the way she thrust a low-hanging branch to the side. "He must come to know his powers on his own. We cannot interfere in his trials."

"I know we cannot interfere, unless it is a life-threatening situation." Ziona shrugged her shoulders. "But it doesn't mean I can't talk to him. He will never know who I am or what I do until it is necessary."

"Remember, Ziona." Sharisha gripped Ziona's arm, halting her in mid stride. "The prophecies of the Elder Scrolls make it very clear that the Goddess will give aid when the time is right. They must come to know the strength of their magic by their own hand, not ours."

"Yes, yes. I understand the plan." Frustrated, Ziona changed the topic slightly. "She saw us. Her eyes are much sharper than the boy's."

"Perhaps."

They arrived at their camp, tucked under a slab of granite fallen millennia ago from the mountain soaring above their heads. The edges were worn smooth with time and a perfect cave had formed that protected any inhabitants sheltering there from the weather on three sides. A crack in the rock provided a natural chimney through which the smoke of their campfire escaped.

They kept their fire small, using some thin sticks and a nest of last year's grasses as kindling. A meal of dried berries, nuts, and flatbread was washed down with spring water from a waterskin.

Dinner complete, Ziona picked up a brush and braided Sharisha's waist-length hair, winding it around her head to cover the tips of her pointed ears and then secured it with wooden carved combs from their packs. Sharisha did the same for Ziona.

Next, they focused on their faces. Human faces often had slanted eyes, but not the sharp angular eyebrows of their heritage. Picking up a knife from their meal kit, Sharisha carefully shaped Ziona's brows to a more human curve.

Finally, they took out clothing they had purchased a few villages back and changed into the style of clothing appropriate to a good wife or a merchant of the area. Skirts of woven wools (green for Ziona and brown for Sharisha) topped with white blouses of good cotton and cloaks of wool. Sturdy walking shoes completed the ensembles.

They unfolded their bedrolls and crawled under the coverings. Humming a Primordial melody of rest, they drifted off to sleep.

Chapter 3

ALCINA CURSETAG ENTERED THE GRAND HALL, ignoring the ripples of movement from her personal attendants as she marched across the tiled expanse to the balcony doors at the far end of the room. Heads bobbed on the men and women curtsied low, but for Alcina they might as well not have existed. Her elite guard trailed along in her wake, trotting to keep up with her long strides. She pushed open the heavy glass doors and stepped out onto the stone balustrade, which overlooked the ceremonial parade grounds below.

It was swollen with rank upon rank of soldiers, jammed shoulder to shoulder between the stone walls of the compound. All stood rigidly at attention, even though the hour was early and the wait had been a long one. They stamped feet in an attempt to keep the cold from seeping into their boots.

Their captains, lords of the land all, restlessly shifted position, having been roused from warm beds and stoked fires out into the crisp morning air. Puffs of frozen breath drifted above the assembled men.

The queen's legions were made up of men recruited from across the kingdom. The original guard of Cathair had contained fifteen hundred men. That number had now swollen to close to ten thousand—some barely old enough to shave and then only once a week—due to the queen's decree commanding the conscription of able-bodied youths sixteen years of age and older.

Alcina surveyed the assembled men, her expression haughty and cold.

A young man, a youth really, near the front of the line of men caught sight of her and nudged the soldier next to him. Both straightened their postures, eager to impress the regal woman above them.

"These would be new recruits," said Alcina to the lord general of her personal guard standing at her shoulder. She gestured toward the young men with a flick of her hand. "So fresh and eager to see battle. Well, I should not disappoint them, I think. Wouldn't you agree, Cyrus?"

Cyrus clasped his hands behind his back and glanced at her out of the corner of his eye, speculation on his face. "What did you have in mind, my queen? The eastern campaign?" he rumbled in his deep-timbral voice.

"All those peasants have been escaping their duty for far too long, hiding on their little farms in the hills by the sea. You may send a small contingent to the area. But I have better plans for these troops. How many legions have you called here today?"

"The First and Third Footmen and the Sixth Cavalry Elite, my queen. They are a full five thousand strong. While there are many new recruits amongst the regular soldiers, these are mostly volunteers and not the usual scum we find with the conscription services. Their commanders are the best we have in the field."

"Is that so? Well then, they should have no difficulty with this assignment."

She held up her bejeweled hands to quiet the men. When silence fell, she raised her voice to carry over the crowd.

"Brave men and soldiers of the realm, a great honour is to be granted to you this day. You have been chosen as the elite of the realm to serve your queen. Honour and glory such as men have only dreamed of are to be yours for never in the history of the world has an army been blessed with such a quest.

"The time has come to avenge the people of this great land against the Primordial infidels plaguing this world. They hide and cower on the other side of the Highland Needle, practicing their pagan beliefs and customs, which all know are an abomination to the true faith. It is time to wipe out these heretics once and for all."

A murmur rose from the helmeted men below at these words. The seasoned soldiers shook their heads, knowing this task was nigh impossible.

Alcina raised her voice, drowning out the grumbling. "I do not need to tell you this will be perilous. These he- and she-devils practice magic and other foul rituals in order to corrupt the nature of the divine. Has not our mage said it is so?"

More murmurs rose to her ears. Soldiers butted their spears on the ground, a rhythmic pounding to show their approval of her words. The sound swelled in the confined space. The hooded mage to her right bobbed his head in acknowledgement, his rheumy eyes peering out at the crowd.

"Ours is a righteous battle!" Alcina shouted, and her eyes gleamed in the firelight of the wall torches. "We will triumph! It is the will of the gods! I have seen it! In a glorious dream, the Great Goddess came to me and commanded me to not leave these heathens to pollute the land. The land cries to be cleansed, to be bathed in righteousness. If it must first be bathed in blood, your sacrifice paves the path to freedom for all lands and all peoples. Are you hungry to serve the Great Goddess? Or are you to be counted with the cowards and the heathens?"

A roar accompanied her words as the soldiers thundered their solidarity. Alcina painted a shallow smile on her face and then raised her hands to touch her forehead then her lips, and then pressed her open palms over her heart, the ritual blessing of soldiers. The mage joined in and together they blessed the assembled men. He spoke for the first time, in a squeaky, high-pitched voice. "Go forth! Know the Great Goddess guides your swords. Be proud of your calling. Be proud of your destiny! Her glory is yours! Kill the infidels!"

Alcina dropped her hands. "Attend me, Cyrus." The mage bowed to her as she departed.

She stepped off the balustrade and into a side meeting room of the Great Hall. The room was warmed by a vigorous fire dancing in a stone fireplace on the far wall. Cyrus pulled closed the gilded double doors behind her. Alcina placed her lacquered-fingered hand on his face, tapping his cheek. His eyes found her pitiless ones.

"My queen, our spies have located the primary Primordial force. They are camped at the pass to the Primordial lands on the north side of the switchback trail that leads to the highland village of Sanctuary-by-the-Sea. They lay in wait for our armies."

She dropped her hand and poured herself a cup of blueberry tea from a tall copper flask beaded with moisture and then gestured to Cyrus to help himself.

"I hope the mage's foreseeing is correct. This battle should eliminate the usurper of the throne forever. We must find him before he can begin to gather a following. Cursed prophesies. " Her mouth twisted in an ugly grimace. "The mage believes the prophesied one was born near the lands of the Primordials. We will never gain entry to search the Primordial lands as they guard the mountain passes and our spies have not located him yet outside of those lands." She paced in front of the fieldstone fireplace, and it cast a distorted shadow that flickered like the Ancient Ones of the Dark.

"Of course, I would prefer to face the insolent pup myself, but so far he has eluded my conscription ranks. We know from the mage's foreseeing that he is of an age to be recruited, and we also know from prophecy that he will be reluctant to kill another being. If we can pull him into the ranks of the legion, he should be easy to identify. Recruit all boys his age, I commanded. Scoop him up with the recruiter's net, and yet my legions fail me in this one, simple task; FIND THE BOY AND BRING HIM TO ME. It is a simple request."

Frustrated, she slammed her cup down on the table as she paced past it.

"Fools and children of fools! How I want to be the one to locate him!" She paused in front of the window to the balcony, arms folded across her chest, back rigid, and then she sighed and dropped her arms. "But I must rise above such petty self-indulgences. I expect you, Cyrus, to bring me the head of this saviour. I would have it as a trophy, stuffed and mounted in my throne room for all to see."

"It shall be as you say, my queen." Cyrus bowed to her stiff form then left the room, leaving the queen contemplating her plans.

Chapter 4

CAYDEN SLIPPED BEHIND a couple of quenching barrels, tucked into the shade at the rear of the blacksmith's shop, ducking low and running crouched to avoid detection. He spied his best friend Ryder, through the open casement window, as he draped the neck strap of his smithy apron on the wooden peg at the rear of the shop.

Clearing the window undetected, Cayden stopped at the rear door and placed the squirming bag on the ground. The bag writhed and flopped as the snakes squirmed over each other, seeking an escape from their confinement.

Cayden lifted the lid off the washing barrel, picked up the scoop for dipping and hung it off the side of the barrel rim by the curved handle. He placed the lid back down on the barrel. Loosening the drawstrings, he placed the bag of snakes upside down inside the bowl of the scoop and quickly stepped back behind a container of rough iron ingots and waited.

The door opened and out stepped Ryder. A huge yawn cracked his jaw as he stretched, then he bent down and picked up the lid to the water barrel. With his other hand, he reached over to pick up the water scoop. Noticing the bag resting in the scoop, he pulled it away from the bowl. Ten tiny green wiggling snakes dropped out of the bag. Some fell back into the spoon, the rest spilling over the sides to the ground below. All hissed in warning.

With a yell, Ryder threw the scoop at the wall and fell backward to the ground, doing a swift crab crawl on all fours away from the snakes.

Cayden burst into laughter as he watched his six-foot-two muscular friend scramble away from the tiny snakes, a high-pitched girly scream echoing down the alley. Cayden snorted and gasped for breath as he tried to stop laughing. He felt twinges of his earlier pains from Avery's prank, he was laughing so hard.

"If you could see your face," he wheezed. His cheeks hurt from grinning so hard. His chest hurt from holding in his mirth. "It's priceless!" He barely got the words out between snorts of laughter.

Ryder hesitated for only a moment and then punched him in the stomach. Cayden's eyes bulged and his laughter cut off abruptly as he doubled over, gasping for air in truth this time.

"Good Goddess, Cayden, you scared the life out of me! I should hand-feed you to those snakes bit by bit! What are you trying to do, frighten me to death?"

Still gasping for air, Cayden straightened up and grinned weakly. "Man, you sure can punch hard, Ryder. Remind me to never get on your bad side, eh?"

Ryder grinned back. "Where did you find so many snakes? Why are they out of their dens at this time of year? It's way too early."

Cayden pretended to be searching for escaping snakes, reluctant to meet Ryder's gaze. He couldn't tell Ryder about what happened with his flutes. He decided on a piece of the truth. Reaching into his pocket, Cayden pulled out the flute of carved oak he made earlier in the day. He handed it to Ryder.

"I was sitting on the rocks playing my flute when suddenly I noticed some snakes. Maybe they were disturbed by my playing?" His mouth twitched into a smile. "Maybe I was too loud?"

Ryder inspected the flute. It was about seven inches long, shaped and rounded to fit comfortably in the hand. The holes were saucer shaped and smooth, the right size for Cayden's hands but much too large for his sausage shaped fingers. A small oak tree was carved into the bell-shaped end of the flute. He handed it back to Cayden.

"They were sunning themselves, curled up and still as rocks." *And listening to me*, he thought to himself. He shrugged his shoulders sheepishly. "I know, it sounds weird, eh? Well, I decided I couldn't leave them all there, so I brought you some. I know how much you like snakes."

Ryder grinned. "I loathe snakes." He could not stop himself from checking that all the snakes had slithered away.

"Some dashing knight you will make," said Cayden. "You will throw your horse, before the horse can throw you, the first time you spy a snake out on patrol!" He ducked as his friend made to grab him in a headlock.

Laughing, Cayden nodded his head in the direction of the inn. "Fancy grabbing a pint before we head home? I saw strangers in town earlier. They must be here for the festival."

"OK. Let me wash up first. You don't have any more snakes hiding around here do you?" Ryder's suspicious eyes raked the area around him.

"No, that was it," Cayden chuckled. "Hurry up. I'm thirsty!"

Stripping off his shirt, Ryder quickly dunked his head into the barrel and poured water over his muscular chest and neck. Grabbing a towel, he dried off and then donned his shirt before joining his friend.

***

Avery lifted her long skirts and carefully placed her booted feet on drier patches of ground as she crossed the street. The spring air dampened her dark ringlets and they glistened around her fine features. Stepping up onto the boardwalk, she opened the door and entered the baker's shop, setting a bell to tinkling. The smell of baking bread filled the air. Sniffing appreciatively, she approached the display counter.

"Good morning, young miss!" said the portly owner of the shop. "What can I get for you this fine day?"

"Six of your honeyed sticky buns, Master Hampton, and a loaf of raisin braid bread."

He wrapped the goods in brown paper and handed them over the counter. She tucked the items into her bag. Placing the proper payment in his waiting hand, she thanked the baker and left the shop.

Preparations for the spring festival were well underway. The village square was buzzing with people setting up a large central stage in the round for the traditional resurrection plays. Large striped canvas booths were being erected along the sides of the square for games and challenges. At the far end, a strong man erected a tall pole. Brightly striped in green and red, the strong man's pole contained multiple weights suspended by ropes and run through a series of pulleys on a cross arm. These ropes were guided through and secured to sets of metal eyes that were grasped by the hands of the contestants.

A silly pastime, she mused, but one the men of the village seemed to eagerly anticipate almost as much as the archery competition which was set up in the open field behind the blacksmith's building.

She drew the hood of her cloak up around her head and continued on toward the inn.

Her ears registered the sound of horse hooves ringing on the occasional paving stone of the street. She drew back into the entranceway of a building and watched as the procession approached. Men on horseback, clad in dark red metal breastplates and matching helmets, rounded the corner and entered the square.

They were riding three abreast and five rows deep. A man to the right of the central figure carried a flag, red background with a white circle in the middle. A black hand clutching a golden sceptre was centered in the disk.

Behind the riders came several rows of men on foot, all wearing leather vests dyed dark red and sporting matching leather caps. An arrow quiver was visible on each of their backs and unstrung bows were held in their hands. Behind them came a similar group of men, but these carried broad shields and two swords were strapped to each of their backs in crisscrossed scabbards.

Surprised, Avery withdrew even further into the shadows of the doorway. Something smelled wrong about these men. The very air around them brought to mind a festering swamp full of leeches and rotting vegetation. She shuddered and raised a sleeve to cover her nose. She didn't think it was the actual odour of the men, but more a sensation of decay that crept along with them, causing the hair to rise on the skin of her arms. They seemed to be an abomination to her soul, an offense to her very being. Gagging, she slipped into the alley between the buildings to either side. She kept to the shade in order to avoid detection.

The central horseman of the front row was dressed similar to his men; however, he also wore a dark red cape lined with black silk held in place by a silver clasp over his armour. The same symbol as on the flag was embroidered on the left breast of the cape. Steel gauntlets covered his forearms and his lower shins were also encased in armour.

As he strode past, his head swung in her direction. For a brief moment, she felt his eyes rest on her. She sensed open hatred in the gaze. The cold of a murderer stalking his victim assaulted her senses. His gaze roved over the inn and fixed on an object in his line of vision.

Turning her head to follow the direction of his gaze, she saw her brother Cayden about to enter the inn on the other side of the green with his friend Ryder. Cayden glanced up and their eyes met. He grinned, waved to her, and continued on into the inn. A blue glow emanated from his skin. The glow brightened, growing stronger to her eyes as she watched. She first noticed it about six months ago. No one else seemed to be able to see it except for her.

She slipped out the back end of the alley and ran back toward the direction she had entered town. She recognized the flag carried by the bearer to be the Queen's Guard, and there was only one reason for them to be in town. They were there to recruit.

Hiking up her skirts, she ran.

Chapter 5

CAYDEN AND HIS SISTER'S EYES MET, worry shadowing them. He saw a blue glow surrounding her. *Does she know she glows like that?* No one else seemed to notice but he.

He followed Ryder into the inn. As he did so, he saw the riders entering the village square. *Military men, the Queen's Guard for sure,* Cayden thought. He pushed Ryder in ahead of him and entered the inn.

Eyes followed Cayden, he was sure of it. He felt the intense gaze of the man at the head of the column. Cayden glanced back and found himself pinned by the man's hawk-like gaze. A sudden fury rose in him and he glared back in challenge.

The door swung shut behind them, shutting off the noises and view of the street. Cayden tried to shrug off the feeling of foreboding that followed him into the room. Ryder was also looking apprehensively over his shoulder.

"Did you see those guys? They're legionnaires, without a doubt," Cayden said.

Ryder nodded and quickened his pace, heading for the bar at the end of the hall. "They are probably heading here for a meal and a drink. First village they would have seen for days, right? I bet that is all it is." He shrugged, as though not convinced of his own words.

"What will it be, boys?" The sweaty innkeeper, Hans, was mopping his brow on a soiled apron tied to his generous waist.

The inn was busy with the usual dinner crowd and swollen with the addition of merchants and tradesmen recently arrived for the festival. It was the only reputable inn in the village. The only other place to stay was old Molly Bechard's boarding house if you needed to rent a room, complete with bedbugs to keep you company at night.

"Two pints, if you please." Cayden set the coppers on the counter in exchange for the beverages and then picked up the pints and settled into a booth near the rear door of the common room. "Hey, why don't we have a bit of fun with them tonight?"

Ryder paused with his mug of ale halfway to his lips. "What did you have in mind?"

"Well, it would be fun to check out their camp. See what it is like. I have never seen a soldiers' camp before, have you? And they can't all stay here. The inn is too full. I'll bet only the officers stay at the inn and the true soldiers set up camp in Geordie Frenchman's hayfield out on the south end of town. It's the closest cleared ground to the creek. It's a natural spot to set up camp." Cayden took a hefty swig from his pint and set the beaded mug back on the table.

Ryder scratched at his five o'clock shadow, considering. Grinning, he leaned in closer. "Well, what if we made off with a couple of their swords? Or better yet, a couple of their horses?"

Cayden frowned. "That would be stealing."

"No, it wouldn't!" Ryder waved vaguely in the direction of the next town. "They stole it from some farmer further up the road along with all their food supplies and metals for melting down into more swords. The merchants tell stories of what happens when one of these legions come through. They take everything of value. We would be giving them back a taste of their own."

Cayden nodded in agreement. He had heard the stories. But Ryder had lived them.

Ryder burned with hatred and longed for a chance to set right the wrongs being carried out in the name of the queen. He had lost his parents to such a raid when he was five years old and had been sent to this village, Sanctuary-by-the-Sea, to be raised by his aunt. Ryder still remembered the smell of the smoke, the stench of burning flesh and blood spilled, and the cries of his friends as they were burned alive.

The soldiers had descended on the town on an afternoon not dissimilar to this one. The mayor had stepped out to greet the strangers, and before he could do more than say "Greetings, my fine fellows, how may we help you?" the lead soldier had run him through with a sword from horseback. While the mayor lay bleeding to death on the ground, the remaining soldiers spread out through the town, rounding up all the citizens they could locate and herding them to the central square. There, they were held and selectively questioned about their beliefs and if there were any witches or healers in the town. When the townsfolk failed to produce a witch for burning, the soldiers separated out all the young men who appeared to be of military age, between sixteen and twenty-five and took them off down the road. The rest of the people, women, children, and men over the age of twenty-five, they forced into the village inn and barricaded them inside. Then, they had set fire to the building.

He had witnessed it all from the spot where he had hid when the slaughter had begun. Ryder had been running some errands for his father, the smithy, and had been sent down into the basement storage under the floor to fetch a small file for his father when he heard the commotion start. The door to the shop banged open as though someone had shoved it, hard. His father shouted out and began to argue with some heavily booted men and then scuffling erupted, the men crashing into a barrel. It either toppled over or was moved onto the trap door Ryder had gone down. In retrospect, he thought his dad shifted the barrel during the fight in order to hide the entrance from the men who were confronting him. His father was attacked and eventually dragged out into the square, but not before he had taken out two of the soldiers himself with his bare hands. It had taken three men to hold him, even while beating him.

Ryder had watched everything through a ventilation hole carved out of the framing under the porch steps. His father was the first used as an example of the cost of resistance. His throat had been slit in front of Ryder's eyes. Ryder had screamed and screamed, but no one could hear him. Eventually he fell asleep, having screamed himself into exhaustion, curling up on the straw-covered floor in an old work shirt of his father's, burying himself in a cocoon of his father's scent. It was a full day later before the few surviving villagers who had escaped the guards initial search had located him, still curled up in his father's oversized shirt in the storage room under the shop.

Ryder shook his head to dispel the sad memories. He grinned at Cayden. "I would like nothing better than to cause some havoc at their camp. Drink up and let's get out of here before any of them come inside."

They downed their beers and left through the back door of the inn, taking the hallway leading out of the rear of the common room.

Cayden and Ryder headed for the stables at the back of the inn. They opened the stable door and trotted through the dim interior of the barn. They exited via the wooden double doors at the rear onto a paddock which edged a rough lane leading back to the forest road. They followed the lane until they found the deer trail skirting the edge of the forest. Walking for about half a mile, they crested a hill and suddenly they spied the legion's camp.

They ducked into the trees so they wouldn't be spotted and slipped through the underbrush of silver leaf dogwood, keeping well-hidden in the leafy ground cover. Dropping to their knees and eventually their bellies, they crawled to the edge of the forest and stared.

The camp appeared to set out in squares. Each unit contained a series of ten tents, which surrounded an area in the middle where horses were hobbled.

Cook fires were set up every four squares, and men lined up to receive their evening meals served from a large kettle hung from a collapsible roasting rack. In the center of the camp was a larger tent, which was topped with the queen's flag announcing the command tent. On the forest side of the camp, a row of pits had been dug into the ground. *The latrines*, Cayden thought from the smell emanating from the area.

"There must be three hundred or more men in that camp," Cayden whispered to Ryder, turning his head. Ryder nodded in agreement.

"They don't appear much older than us. Do you think they are all new recruits? I mean, would you settle in all comfy like that if you had been snatched away from your family recently?"

Ryder growled low in his throat. "I would never settle in. Try to recruit me and I would fight them with every fibre of my being. I would never stay." He lowered his eyes. "They would end up killing me before I ever gave in. They are pigs!" He spat in the dirt in front of him to emphasize his words.

Cayden nodded his agreement. The very thought of being forced into the legion appalled him.

"I will never serve the queen. I will die first, by the gods, I swear it!" Ryder said his fists clenched so tightly his knuckles whitened under his skin.

"So...where do you think we should strike? I like our chances with the unit over there by the latrines," said Cayden, attempting to lighten the mood. "They are trying to stay as far away from their post as possible probably because of the smell." Cayden sniffed the air and pointed at the bored-looking soldiers stationed to their left at the base of the hill.

Ryder studied the latrines and then his eyes wandered over the hillside, scanning the perimeter of the camp. "Do you see any sentries? Shouldn't there be some patrolling the area here too?"

"No...wait, yes, on the far side, inside the tree line." Cayden pointed across the field to a man who was standing in the shadow of a cottonwood tree, bow in hand and arrow nocked but not drawn. "Can you see any more around?"

"No. Nervous bunch, aren't they?" Ryder said. "Why post sentries in the daylight? Who is going to sneak up on them?"

"People like us, Ryder!" Cayden grinned. Ryder grinned back.

Suddenly, they heard a sound like metal sliding over metal above them, the sound of swords being drawn.

Rolling over, they froze in horror. Cayden sucked in his breath, and Ryder swore under his. Three men stood behind them, swords drawn and pointing at their throats. All three were Queen's Guard scouts.

"I think we found the other scouts, Ryder."

Thunder rumbled overhead.

Chapter 6

ROUGH HANDS GRABBED CAYDEN AND RYDER by their arms and pulled them to their feet. "Well what do we have here? It looks to me like we got us a couple of volunteers." His two companions laughed. "So nice when we don't have to go searching for them. It lets us get back to our gaming that much faster!"

"We are not here to volunteer," Cayden said quickly. "We wanted to see what the camp looked like, that's all." Ryder nodded his head in agreement, keeping his gaze on his boots. He strained to control his temper. Panic bubbled in the pit of his stomach. He felt like a lit firecracker fuse. Ryder tensed against the two men holding him.

"I'm afraid that qualifies as volunteering, lad. Now get moving." Rough hands shoved them in the direction of the camp. That was all it took. At the soldier's touch, Ryder snapped. With a bellow, he swung at the man holding him, his ham-like fist connecting with the man's right ear, knocking the soldier to his knees. Ryder kicked out with his right leg, sweeping the soldier's legs out from under him. He fell into the second scout who was bowled over. The scout's head hit a rock and he didn't move.

Cayden swung around and grappled with the scout holding him, right hand grabbing his thick-whiskered throat and his left hand wrapped around the weapon-wielding wrist forcing his flailing sword above his head. Cayden squeezed with all his might as the scout struggled. The man's eyes bulged. His grip on his sword weakened and it dropped to the ground. Cayden continued to squeeze, until the man's eyes rolled back in his head. Cayden let the man drop. He did not want to kill him; he only wanted to incapacitate him.

Turning, he saw Ryder's original attacker rising to his feet again. Cayden picked up the sword on the ground. He smashed the hilt of the sword down on the head of the strangled scout who was stirring and he crumpled back to the ground.

The last soldier advanced on Cayden, arms outstretched, wary of the blade in Cayden's hand. Cayden shifted his weight from one foot to the other, nervously watching the scout. He had no intention of using the sword. *What possessed me to pick it up?* Cayden wondered as he adjusted his stance, as a malicious grin spread across the face of the scout.

"Drop the sword, little boy," sneered the scout. "You will accidently cut off your own fingers, and then how will you fight? I promise you, if you continue this futile resistance, I will make sure you pay." He looked around at his companions. "In fact, I think you are already in deep trouble. You do know the penalty for attacking a member of the Queen's Guard? No?" His eyes taunted Cayden, noting the trembling in his arms. "Let me inform you. First offense is five years in prison in Cathair. I hear the rats are better fed than the prisoners."

While the scout's attention was focused on Cayden, Ryder scooped up a fallen scout's sword. A bright red flush covered his neck and cheeks, the combination of fear and adrenaline causing a roaring in his ears. His eyes were wild, so wide open that the whites dominated and his nostrils flared as he sucked in huge amounts of air. Yelling, he launched himself at the guard, swinging wildly at him. The blade was heavy in his hand and he tripped over a body as he swung, nearly falling on the blade himself as he tumbled to his knees on the rocky ground. The guard laughed and ignored Ryder.

"Sit down, boy," the scout said to Cayden, "while I dispatch this one. He seems eager to battle. I will deal with you in a moment."

Still on one knee, Ryder watched the scout approach through a mist of anger. Panic seized him and with a bellowing roar, Ryder hoisted the heavy sword with both hands and swung it in an arc curving upward meant for the sword hand of the soldier. However, at the last minute, the soldier turned, and the upward swing of the blade instead found the meaty throat of the guard, slicing the man's jugular. Ryder felt the momentary resistance as the sword caught in the flesh of the man's throat, and then bright red blood sprayed out from the gash, pumped at an alarming rate by a heart that did not know it was doomed. The scout's head flopped to one side and he tumbled to the ground.

Cayden stood stock still, watching as the man's blood pulsed out onto the soil, darkening the stones as it spread out in a pool.

Ryder's shocked eyes looked at the sword in his hand, slick with blood.

Cayden grabbed Ryder by the front of his shirt and pulled him. "Come on! We have to get out of here! Quickly!" he yelled. Turning, he ran back into the woods, as though the hounds of hell were on their trail. Ryder followed in equal haste, the swords in their hands forgotten in their panic to flee the scene of their skirmish.

They ran for roughly a mile, eventually joining up with the stream that had made for an ideal campground for the legion. Keeping to the water-slicked rocks along the edge, they headed up river toward Cayden's farm. Lightning flashed and fresh rumbles of thunder were accompanied by the skies opening up. A heavy downpour followed them, soaking them from above, while the river took care of the rest. They left the stream about two miles past the Tiernan farm, dripping from head to toe and cut across the pastures Cayden knew so well. Cayden led Ryder to the cliffs by the sea and to a cave he had discovered long ago, a secret place known only to him and Avery, and now Ryder.

The cave faced the ocean and was hidden to any who did not appreciate heights. A rocky goat path was the only access and Cayden led Ryder along the outcroppings, showing him the handholds and footholds that were true in the rocky slide. The cave opening was a tall and narrow slit in the cliff face. When they entered, the bats that made this cave their home screeched and swooped around before settling back down to perch upside down from the cave ceiling.

"The bats are great sentries," Cayden said, as he dropped to his knees in the egg-shaped room. The tall slit allowed enough light to see their surroundings in a twilight grey. Ryder collapsed down beside him on the cool rocks, gasping for air, swords clanking as they dropped them. Cayden groaned and rolled onto his back, staring at the roof of the cave. Ryder hung his head; his eyes squeezed shut, body still quivering with nerves and fright. *I killed a man*, Ryder thought to himself, shuddering with the memory.

Cayden reached over, grabbed Ryder's shoulder and shook him. "Are you OK, Ryder?"

Ryder swallowed hard and opened his eyes. "I didn't mean to kill him. I panicked, Cayden, and the sword was in my hands and I swung it. I didn't mean to kill him, only wound him. Good lord, what have I done?"

He squeezed his eyes shut again and his big hands clutched at his head. "I was so scared! I was afraid to be taken," he shuddered. "I was five years old again and trapped in that basement, helpless and terrified. I snapped." His eyes opened again, regret shadowing in their blue depths.

"We can't go back to the village. That much is obvious. They will be searching everywhere for us," said Cayden. "I think they will round up everyone and will try to force them to identify who is missing. Ryder, I am scared of what will happen if the villagers resist."

Ryder straightened up. "Then maybe we should go back to the village? If someone is missing and they cover for us, then the soldiers will burn the town again like before."

Cayden plucked at a hole in his sleeve, thinking. "If we go back, they may find out it was us and capture us. Killing a Queen's Guard is punishable by death. They could kill us instantly or, worse yet, force us into their army. If we return, Ryder, we will be giving them what they want. We can't go back there now. It would be suicide."

Ryder began knocking his head against the rock, groaning. "What can we do? We have to do something. Gods, what a mess!" They lapsed into an uneasy silence, thinking.

Suddenly, Cayden sat up and pulled Ryder up beside him.

"What if we were to volunteer now? No, hear me out," he said holding up his hands as Ryder opened his mouth to protest. "What if we return to the village before they discover the guard's death? Maybe it would throw them off the scent. They can't know it was you, Ryder, who killed that soldier."

"But how would that protect the town?"

"If everyone was accounted for at the beginning, then they might conclude the person they hunted was a soldier in their midst already or it was an outsider to the village who had slipped away. The town might be spared either way."

Ryder idly picked up a stone from the floor as he thought over Cayden's words. "But if they do think the murderer is in the village, why would they let everyone go?"

"Because their mission here is to recruit soldiers, not to avenge a soldier whose death may be the result of one of their own. They would have to look at all the possibilities and, who knows, maybe those scouts have some enemies. Maybe someone owes them some money. The one did mention playing cards; perhaps they cheated someone in a past village, and that person confronted them. They can't know exactly what happened." Even to his ears, the argument sounded weak.

Cayden sat for a moment, plucking at the tear in his shirt sleeve, thinking things over. "Only one of us need volunteer and I think it should be me," he whispered and then shook his head when Ryder protested. "Listen, if I volunteer I can finally see some of the world, you know go on one of those grand adventures we always talked about." He grinned at Ryder, brightening at the thought. "I have always wanted to visit Cathair." He gaze lifted towards the bats in the cave, his mind imagining the trek to capital city. He felt an irresistible draw to the king's city, which now housed the queen. "You know I have always talked of going there. But you, if you get sucked into that legion, you will never realize your dream of becoming a knight. You will never get away. They don't recruit blacksmiths by the queen's decree, so you are in the clear, even if they did discover you killed the guard. But that doesn't mean they won't take one that volunteers, and that service will be for life."

"No, I would be soon dead if I was forced into that legion." Ryder snorted in disgust. "Cayden, there is no king, so how can I be a knight anyways? It was only a childish dream."

"It won't always be this way, Ryder. You will see. Someone will overthrow the queen." Cayden sighed. "So, it is decided. I will volunteer for the legion. With their quota fulfilled, they will leave town. And you, you must go back to the blacksmith shop. You are safe there. You are too valuable a resource for the queen's legions."

Ryder grabbed Cayden's sleeve. "Cayden, don't do this! We will think of another way."

"We don't have the time to sit here and plan, Ryder. With every minute that passes, we endanger the town. It's the only solution I can think of. We have to give them a reason to leave, to look no further. If you can think of another plan, some other way to save the town, I'm listening." Cayden looked hopefully at Ryder, and then as Ryder remained silent, the hope faded and his expression became somber.

Ryder's sad eyes locked onto Cayden's resolved ones. He shook his head. "I never meant for this to happen."

"I know," said Cayden softly. "Slip into the village by the back way and go home. Climb in a window so no one sees you returning. I will grab some clothes and supplies from the farm and make it appear that I was on my way to volunteer."

Cayden got to his feet, brushing off his clothes.

Ryder rose to his feet and took his friend in a long fierce bear hug. Tears sparkled in his baby blue eyes. "You make sure you take care of yourself in there. Learn all you can. It will keep you alive. Try to get away in time. I will find you some day. You can count on it." He grabbed Cayden a second time, crushing him, and then he exited the cave.

Chapter 7

QUEEN ALCINA TURNED THE CORNER of the corridor and walked briskly toward an alcove filled with bright sunlight, the stained-glass windows casting a distorted wave of colour across the tiled floor.

She pushed open a painted oak door that led to a little-used chamber, barely as big as a broom cupboard, used to store old carpets and tufting materials for repairs. She bypassed the clutter and passed through a curved opening in the back wall, which opened into a dark circular room with no windows and no doors.

"Great Mistress?" she whispered, peering around anxiously at the creeping shadows that lurked the corners of her vision.

Suddenly, the room filled with a heavy, oppressive presence. The little light remaining in the room fled and the darkness became complete. Alcina dropped to her knees, trembling as the presence filled the room, shutting out all other sounds.

"Alcina, what do you have to report?"

"Great One, we have picked up a trail that may lead us to whom we seek. We have heard rumours of a presence in the north country by the sea that could be promising."

The shadows trembled. "Rumours do not produce the prophesied heir. I feel that your motivation is not strong enough in this matter. Perhaps a demonstration is in order?"

"No!" gasped Alcina. "No, Great Mistress! I desire to find this usurper to my throne! I will not stand to have our plans…I mean, your plans…derailed at this time! I long to serve beside you…I mean beneath you," she hastily amended at the growl of the Goddess, "for all eternity!"

She panted, trying to slow her racing heart, fear prickling along the nerve endings of her hair, which tried to stand on end in response.

"See that you do not forget who the goddess is here, Alcina. I will grant immortality to those who serve me well. As for those who do not, they will also live forever. But I do not believe that they will find it a pleasant experience." She chuckled and the sound was as if she dragged her fingernails down a chalkboard. The sound shrieked through Alcina's soul, deafening her to all but her own fear.

"I will not fail you, Mistress!"

"See that you do not," the goddess replied as she faded from the room.

***

Cayden eased himself out of the cave and stood facing the sea. He breathed in deeply, eyes closed, tongue tasting the salty tang in the air. He exhaled, seeking calm and courage in the shushing of the waves over the rocks below. He reached out with his senses and found the shadows of those animals now bound to him by his flutes and felt at peace with his decision.

Opening his eyes, Cayden climbed back to the ridge, then examined the forest ahead, as he crossed the clearing. He saw the crown of the ancient oak towering above the rest of its prodigy on the forest floor. He trotted toward the matriarch to retrieve a flute or two to keep him company during his travels, wherever the legion took him.

Reaching the base of the tree, he knelt down and scooped away the leaves and branches hiding the entrance. Reaching inside, he retrieved the brown bag and untied the drawstrings.

He took out the longer, thicker flute, the base of which he had carved with a symbol vaguely reminding him of a paw print. The other one he selected was narrow and thin, delicate like the bones in the wing of a bird. The song of this flute was the cry of an eagle on the hunt.

He left the remaining flutes in the bag and secured it back under the roots, carefully covering the opening with more leaves and sticks.

His feet retraced the familiar, well-worn path home that he had trod most of his life. As he approached the farm's boundary, the sheep in the closed pasture bleated to him in greeting.

He entered the squat cabin, took a leather satchel from a post by the door, and then hurried into his room. He grabbed a coil of string used for snaring and a hook with line used for fishing, shoving both into a pocket of his oiled leather duster. In the other pocket, he put a short-bladed knife and sheath and a piece of flint and striker stone. Into the bottom of his satchel, he put the two flutes he had retrieved and the one he had carved that day, wrapping them with his woolen socks.

Next to go in were two wool sweaters, two lightweight shirts with leather lacings, and a spare pair of pants. A bar of soap and some shaving supplies followed the clothing. He took one last look around, before throwing his duster on over his clothes.

As he turned towards the door, his eyes fell on the blue agate stone his sister had given him. She had sworn she could always find him if he kept it on his person. He had laughed off her claims as childish fantasies, but in light of his own abilities, he decided to take it with him. Besides, it would help remind him of home and why he was choosing to join the legion in the first place. He tucked the stone into a hidden inner pocket of his shirt, close to his heart.

The next stop was the kitchen, where he grabbed some dried beans, dried mutton, a small cooking pot, and a leather waterskin. These were also placed in his satchel.

He snatched up the quill and ink jar, lying on the table, unstoppered the jar, then retrieved a piece of parchment and a quill and quickly scrawled a note. Dipping the tip in the ink, he wrote:

"Father, I know this decision of mine will seem sudden to you, but you have always known of my desire to see the world and especially Cathair and joining the legion seems the perfect opportunity to do so. Know that I choose this of my own free will and do not follow me. Take care of Avery. Give her my love. I will send word when I am able." All of the above was a lie, of course.

Cayden knew his father would see through the ruse, but he was afraid to leave a more personal and incriminating note. He signed his name and placed the note under the kettle sitting on the counter.

Picking up his bow and quiver, he committed this last view of his childhood home to memory.

Closing the door behind him, Cayden left the cabin.

Chapter 8

"What is the price of freedom? What is the cost of war? As the storm crashes against the mountain so shall be the salvation of the world."

—EXCERPT FROM THE *TOME OF SALVATION*

CAYDEN STEPPED ONTO THE DUSTY ROAD at the outer edge of the last farm, leading his horse. An eerie quiet hung over the town as he entered in sharp contrast to the Beltane bustle present a few hours earlier. The reason became evident as he rounded the corner of the building leading to the village square.

The buildings making up the village had been emptied and everyone herded to the village square. A ring of soldiers, swords drawn, surrounded the men, women, and children huddled together with their heads bowed. Cayden spied Ryder in the group, head bent in a submissive posture. Ryder avoided his eyes, although Cayden could feel his gaze.

Cayden stopped walking. His gaze swung to the tall man he had seen earlier on horseback, who was gripping the front of Cayden's father's shirt. Blood trickled from his split lip and he spat to the side.

"I told you. I have not seen my son since noon, my lord," Cayden's father said quietly.

"He is the only person not accounted for in this hellhole of a village. I will know where he is or this town will rue the day he was born. Now tell the truth!"

The two men holding Cayden's father's arms tightened their grip in anticipation of another blow from the lord.

"I am here!" Cayden cried out. He strode toward the small group of soldiers.

At his words, heads swung in his direction, and he felt his father's sorrowful face following his path, full of disappointment. A contingent of soldiers detached themselves and with weapons drawn, surrounded Cayden, as he walked up to his father.

The high lord grabbed Cayden by his coat front. "Where have you been hiding, boy?" he snarled.

"I haven't been hiding anywhere. I was at home gathering some things together to volunteer for the queen's service."

"No one volunteers for the queen's service from these parts," he snarled into Cayden's face. "Volunteer service is for ten years. Conscription is for an additional five years, and a liar's service? That is for life, as we make sure they do not make it through the fifteen years." The soldiers surrounding Cayden barked a laugh, eyeing the skinny frame of the new recruit. "Now tell me again. Why would a farm boy like you volunteer?"

Cayden's father, Gaius, blinked in confusion. Pride shone from his eyes, shadowed with worry.

I'm sorry, Father. Cayden apologized with a mental grimace for the lie, as he opened his mouth to respond. "I have hated the farm my entire life. Who wants to chase sheep for the rest of their days?" Cayden announced loudly. "I have yearned to travel and see the world. What better way than in the Queen's Guard?"

At that moment, a rider from the legion camp galloped into the village, dirt flying beneath his horse's hooves. Hauling his sweaty mount to a halt, he saluted. "My lord! One of the scouts has been murdered, my lord. His throat was cut on patrol. The other two scouts say two men jumped them in the woods and fled after they were confronted."

"They have tracked these men back to their camp?"

"No, my lord. They said they followed their trail to the river where they lost them."

The high lord grimaced and waved the guard away. "Likely they were thieves attempting to rob the camp, scavengers from this sorry, godforsaken backwater." He returned his focus to Cayden and hatred of his duty transferred to the fresh recruit in front of him. "Since you are so eager to join our ranks, you will return with this rider to the recruitment tents. Guardsman, escort our fine new volunteer back to camp."

Saluting, the mounted guardsman prodded Cayden with his booted foot. "Get moving, recruit," he said, pointing in the direction of the camp.

Cayden's father made to grab him, but the lord promptly struck him across the face, knocking him to the ground again.

Cayden's heart lurched. "Please, Father, accept my decision. I will write when I have time." Cayden mounted up and joined the soldiers. He did not look back.

***

Avery watched from the midst of the huddled people in the middle of the square. Mothers clutched their children to their skirts and the men's eyes darted around, anxiously watching the sharp swords surrounding them.

Avery's heart sank as she watched her brother walk up to her father. She could not hear his words, but she saw her father's expression. She knew. It was as she had foreseen.

Her brother glowed with a soft blue aura that never left him. The light pulsed with his feelings. She sensed a riot of emotions although outwardly his face was calm. He was fury mixed with fear, but overriding it all was concern for their father.

The elder lord struck her father again and Cayden's aura pulsed angrily even though his face remained expressionless. *He is hiding his true intentions,* she thought to herself. *Why? And why is he carrying his satchel as though he planned…No! He is planning to join them?*

She stifled a cry as he rode away in front of the mounted guardsman. Cayden picked her out of the crowd and grinned at her. She felt waves of reassurance coming from him.

He has my stone, she realized suddenly.

"Release them!" the lord snapped to the guards who still surrounded the villagers. "They are of no further use to us. Report back to camp."

The men sheathed their swords and swung into saddles. Forming up, they clattered back down the street, following Cayden and the lone guardsman.

The lord addressed Avery's father. The men holding Gaius let go of him and he collapsed to the dirt of the street. With a final kick to the ribs, they left him lying curled in a ball and, laughing, mounted their waiting horses and rode away.

Avery ran over to her father and knelt down beside him, grasping his shoulder and rolling him over onto his back.

"Are you OK? What did they want with Cayden, Father?" Avery said, running her hands over his ribs checking for broken bones.

"They were searching for new conscriptions and Cayden was missing. I tried to hold them off, but then Cayden walks right up to them and volunteers! What in the world was he thinking? He should have hid until they left."

Avery glanced in the direction of the road that had swallowed Cayden's form. "I don't think they would have left, Father. I think they were determined to take away one person from this village. Cayden is up to something. I know it."

Gaius sat up, wincing at the pain in his side. Avery helped him to his feet. Gaius did not understand the connection between the twins, but he knew it was real. He had observed it from their first breaths. His wife used to say it was like they drew the same breath. And yet, they were very different. If Avery said Cayden was up to something, he was.

Turning, she helped him back to the inn and onto a chair by a table inside the door. Ryder Briarman walked in right behind them and paused by their table. His face was stiff, lips compressed into a straight line.

"I need to speak to you both. Not here not where we can be overheard. Join me in the corner booth by the fireplace?"

They nodded, claiming the table in the corner, sliding onto the bench side by side. Ryder strode to the bar and ordered three mugs of ale. Collecting them from the barmaid, he carried them to the booth and placed a mug of beer before each of them. Gaius accepted gratefully, taking a tender sip. He dabbed at his split lip with a handkerchief from his pocket. Ryder slid onto the bench across from them, eyes downcast.

Avery starred impatiently, mug untouched, and waited for Ryder to speak. Reluctantly, he met her eyes.

"You know what is going on with Cayden," she stated. "You know what this is all about. Cayden would never volunteer for the legion. He hates violence and everything to do with it. He is afraid of violence. What's going on, Ryder?"

Ryder opened his mouth and, voice soft, told them what had happened.

Gaius frowned and Avery gasped, flinging hands over her mouth to stifle the sound. Ryder hung his head and his voice quivered when he reached the part where he admitted to killing the guard. Gaius bolted to his feet jostling the table in his haste. Avery pulled him back down with a quick glance around the inn. Thankfully the room was empty as the villagers had gone home with their families.

"It was the only solution we could come up with, at the time." Ryder's shoulders drooped. "I didn't want him to do this, but he insisted. He did not want a repeat of what happened to my village all those years ago."

Ryder hugged his body, his beefy arms bulging with the effort to hold in his pain. His fists clenched, the veins in his arms bulging with tension. *My best friend is gone. When will I ever see him again?*

Avery reached across the table, unfolded the fingers, and took his big rough hand in hers in comfort.

Gaius's face was pale and etched with sad lines. He took a deep breath.

"We know you did not want him to go alone." Frowning, he voiced his thought aloud. "Do you think the other two guards will recognize Cayden?"

Ryder's heart jumped in his chest with fear. He groaned, guilt wriggling in his chest as though the snakes of Cayden's prank resided there. "Oh lords! What will they do to him if they realize he was with me?"

"We will have to trust Cayden to this," Gaius said. "He is a smart lad. He will figure out a way to survive in the legion. One thing is certain. We must play along with his ruse or we will draw attention to the timing of his choice."

Worry etched all their faces as they contemplated the reality of all that had transpired.

"Did they take any other boys?"

Gaius shook his head. "Not from this village. I heard they took two boys from Maiden's Head a week back, but I know of no others."

Gaius stood, drawing Avery up with him. "It's time to get back to the farm, if we are to arrive before the sun sets. Thank you for telling us this." He gripped Ryder's shoulder for a moment and then they were gone.

Ryder watched them both leave the inn. He had never felt so alone in his life. Not since those early days so long ago. Cayden was gone and Ryder had no idea when he would ever see him again. Ryder put his head down on his arms. His great shoulders shook with pent-up grief.

Chapter 9

THE PEOPLE OF THE VILLAGE of Lower Cathair watched from windows and doors as the formation of the Queen's Guard marched past the town in orderly rows, their pikes and halberds stowed on backs bristling like porcupines. Most of the watchers were grey-haired men, backs curving with age, weary-eyed from their toils of the day in the hot spring sun.

The soldiers paid little attention to the villagers as they marched past. This town had been cleared of young men long ago, as its proximity to the castle gate assured men of conscription age had been identified and secured for the throne.

Dust stirred in the wake of the stomping boots and drifted in a cloud behind the thousand or so troops, as they disappeared over the rise of the hill.

Denzik frowned and lowered the pipe from his mouth, watching the retreating backs of the soldiers.

He was a good Kingsman, when such things had been allowed, and he still considered himself such. No kingdom should be ruled by a queen and especially not one acquiring power in the manner of the current one.

He had not reached sixty years of age without having seen a thing or two in his time. Rumours or no, the power of the land was held by the queen, and it seemed might made right…for now at least.

Glancing down, he noticed his pipe had gone cold. He reached inside his pocket, took out his tobacco pouch, and pinched enough to fill his pipe bowl between his forefinger and his thumb. He used his thumb to compact it in place and then leaning over, took a small stick and lit it in the fireplace by his side. He brought the glowing end to the bowl of his pipe and puffed it into flame. Smoke curled up to form a haze around his head.

He opened the front door and stepped out onto his porch. By the central well stood the village baker, Fabian Tavish, and beside him was Nelson McDermid, the owner of The Kings Steed, the village pub and inn. Denzik stepped off his porch and walked over to join the two men.

Fabian was short and as round as the sticky honey buns that had made him famous across the valley. Many rumoured he sampled every batch he made to be assured they were the finest. Denzik mused that it might even be true; however, it was best not to judge the baker by his girth as he had been one of the best captains ever to ride in the King's Cavalry, before their abrupt dismissal.

Nelson was equally as short but skinny and leathery as though the food served at his inn was not fit to eat. That did not stop the locals from flocking to the inn before heading home in the evenings to gossip and share news of the day over a cold pint. Nelson ran his inn with a strict hand. The pub and inn were scrupulously clean, the food served piping hot, and the ale chilled in the stream behind the inn where Nelson had hollowed out an underground cellar and plumbed in water to act as a cooling system. The underground room also served as a cold cellar where he refrigerated his food supplies. It was the envy of the town. Sometimes he even managed to make iced creams, a delicacy reminding Denzik of sweetened butter.

Nelson ran his inn with a military flair, having learned his skills in the army camp kitchens. In the King's Army, he had been the head of supply and his contacts across the realm were secondary only to the king's scouts and better than the king's own spy system.

Denzik frowned at the memory. Had the king's spies not betrayed him, then the king would still live. *But*, he thought to himself, *who spies on the spies?*

Reaching the pair, he raised his hand in greeting. "Enjoying the parade?"

Nelson spat in the dirt at his feet and then realizing what he had done looked around surreptitiously.

"Dirty grovelling worms," he growled. "All dressed up pretty, but not a one knows a damn thing about soldiering. Young whelps. Should still be on their mother's apron strings, I say."

Fabian gazed off in the direction where the soldiers had disappeared. "I doubt they had any choice. Likely they were conscripted into the service, their heads stuffed with stories of the glory of serving the queen in some divine task or another. She'd have patted them on their collective heads and then shooed them away to root out the 'heretics of the realm.'" Fabian snorted his disgust.

Nelson grunted and spat again in the dirt. "They will be dead inside of two weeks with arrows of Primordials stuck in their chests, if they don't starve to death first. Their families will never know what happened to them. Bloody mess the queen is making of things."

Nelson checked to see if anyone was listening then lowered his voice. "The king would never have done such a thing. He was working to unite all peoples, not slaughter them. I suspect that's why he was assassinated. Queen Alcina is my first suspect. Her hands are dirty in this."

"Shush, you old fool!" Denzik hushed. "We do not know who listens in this village. We were told to wait, to watch, and to prepare. You know our mandate. We must go about our lives, knowing someday *he* will come. In the meantime, we must play our roles well. The information we gather daily is vital."

Fabian leaned in and muttered in a barely audible whisper, "When do we meet next?"

"I will let you know before time. It is the safest way to be certain we are not surprised or tracked," murmured Denzik quietly.

"Agreed, I had better get back to the inn," Nelson whispered.

In a louder voice, he announced, "Tabitha is likely overcooking that glorious side of mutton again. Thinks none of us have teeth, she does." Grumbling under his breath, he walked off to the inn.

Fabian twitched into action. "I had better get back to baking. These foot soldiers clean me out every time they pass," he grumbled, "and the set before last didn't even pay me. Told me I was lucky and I could keep the rest of my fingers to keep baking with." He held up his right hand with the missing index finger and waved it in farewell. He subconsciously rubbed at the missing digit's phantom pain as he walked away.

Denzik walked back to his own dwelling. Dusk was falling now, and lights flickered in the windows of the various dwellings as lamps were lit.

Entering his own home, he trimmed the wick on the lantern by the door and, using the same stick he had used to light his pipe, lit the lamp, waving it to extinguish the flaming tip and placed the stick back on the mantle.

Denzik carried the lamp into the small kitchen area of his cabin and pulled out bread, cheese, and some leftover ham from his cold storage. He sliced off two slabs of bread, a hunk of cheese, and a piece of ham. Wrapping them back up, he placed them back in the cold storage.

Cold storage...he snorted at the thought. The only way it stayed cold was to either leave the door open to the cabin or to put cold water in a pitcher in the cupboard. He had put a small hole in the back of the cabinet to allow cold air to seep into the chamber and cool the contents, and for three seasons of the year it worked fairly well.

Sitting down in his overstuffed chair, Denzik mechanically ate his dinner, giving no thought to the food. He mulled over the last seventeen years in his mind. All of the men in this village were misfits. The majority were ex-Kingsmen who had been ousted from the castle on threat of death. He remembered it still, the memory slap as sharp as the day it happened.

The coup had been silent, really. They were on their regular assignments within the castle when Cyrus, the Lord General of the Kingsmen, had called them all to attendance in the main yard. He stood on the balcony of the royal apartments and addressed the assembled men.

There, he had announced the king was dead, as were Prince Alexander and his consort, Gwendolyn. No cause of death had been announced, and the future queen, from her self-imposed isolation, had commanded Lord Cyrus to gather all the Kingsmen to hear her decision. The Kingsmen were to be disbanded across the realm. The official version was that as the perpetrator was still at large she feared being surrounded by potential assassins. That so great a tragedy could occur within the castle grounds and without an alarm being raised was a shame on all the Kingsmen and she had refused to place her trust in any of them.

Lord Cyrus's voice had boomed from the wall top, reverberating off the walls across the parade ground. "Effective immediately, I will be taking over command of the newly formed Queen's Guard for the queen-elect. You are hereby ordered to pack the few belongings in your possession and collect your final pay at the gate as you are leaving the castle grounds, which you will do immediately." On the last word, doors on lower level opened out marched an army of new soldiers, all dressed in the queen's colours.

An outraged cry had arisen from the men in the courtyard. The strange men in new Queen's Guard uniforms fanned out and surrounded the Kingsmen. Pikes were lowered and swords drawn. Swords were drawn amongst the Kingsmen too, the blades making a ringing sound of steel on steel as they were drawn from their sheaths.

Lord Cyrus had spoken in a loud voice over the grumbling of the Kingsmen. "You will be escorted in groups of ten to your barracks and then to the gate. This is the only warning you will receive. If you resist in any fashion, the new Guard have been advised to cut you down where you stand. You are to be removed from the castle grounds and released to go wherever you wish. You are never to return to the castle. You may not come within a two-mile radius of Castle Cathair or the village of Upper Cathair. If you do, you will die. This is the royal decree and so it is law."

Turning, he left the balcony and re-entered the royal chambers.

The Kingsmen had found themselves outside the castle gates within two hours. A contingent of Queen's Guards ten deep and the width of the main avenue to the gates had formed up as the last Kingsman exited under escort. The gates swung shut behind them and were sealed.

The men headed up the road, two hundred of them in total. Most carried on up the road and settled in villages along the way and were absorbed into the bigger towns away from the capital.

About twenty of them, Denzik, Fabian, and Nelson in the group, settled in the first hamlet outside the radius, a fly-speck village called Lower Cathair. They virtually doubled the size of the town that night, but the choice of location was not random. As longstanding members of the Kingsmen, they had explored every nook and cranny of Castle Cathair during those twenty-five-odd years of service. They had gone places no one knew existed.

One thing was always consistent about being a Kingsman. On those long cold winter's nights guarding the outer walls, there was nothing more welcome than a nice shot of brandy in your flask. *Of course,* Denzik thought, *only those foolish enough to volunteer for that duty had any right to know the secret.* He smiled to himself in memory.

The small room Denzik had discovered when he was twenty-seven had actually been shown to him on his promotion to captain of the guard by the former captain, Jonathan O'Reilly. He, in turn, had learned it of it from another retiring Kingsman. He warned young Denzik to not reveal the presence of the sealed room to anyone else. It was a sacred trust, and it had to be kept a close secret.

The hidden room was in a false wall off the exercise courtyard for the prisoner cells. Denzik suspected it was originally used to hide high-profile prisoners or political enemies of the crown. During his years in the castle, it had never been used by the royal family, and he believed they had forgotten about it. The only memory of this room remained with the captain of the Kingsman guards, who retained this knowledge as a trusted servant keeps their masters secrets. This secret had been passed down from captain to captain, since there the beginning of the Kingsmen.

Of course, during his time in the Kingsman guard, they had used this room to hide the barrels of brandy they smuggled into the castle for the men of the wall. It had a secret door cleverly concealed in the stone wall at the rear, which led to a tunnel system under the castle.

Denzik had never had an opportunity to fully explore all the tunnels, although he suspected they were extensive. Likely the system had been designed as an escape route for the royal family should the castle ever fall under siege or if the walls be breached. The royal family had to have been aware of some of the tunnels. He did not believe the queen or her counsellors knew of the ones he had used, however. The tunnels they had used had led to the inner city, outside the castle proper but still inside the city walls.

Fabian had suggested the plan as they were marching away from the castle that fateful evening seventeen years ago. They had started planning the very next day, after scabbing together some temporary lodgings. Over the next few months, they purchased a collection of abandoned buildings and lands from the absentee land owners with the dismal balance of their dismissal pay, buildings strategically located. They wasted no time launching the tunnelling underground, aiming to connect with the smuggling tunnel, and it had been their life's work ever since. If they found the tunnels he had used to store those barrels in, all those years ago, it would give them secret access to the castle…and to the queen. The entrance was within the two-mile boundary set by the queen. It was pretty much under her bedroom window.

They were close now.

Finishing his meal, he brought his empty plate to his small kitchen. Sitting back down, he put his feet up and pulled a book entitled *A History of the Royal Family of Cathair* from the table beside him, opening it to his bookmarked spot.

The real work of this day would begin in another couple hours when the main residents of this hamlet were safely tucked into their beds, oblivious to the work being performed under the inn by the river. Denzik settled down to read.

Chapter 10

ZIONA TIED THE LEATHER THONGS of her pack closed. Hefting it onto her shoulder, she took one last look around the cave. All evidence of anyone having camped in the hollow had been eliminated. The fire ashes had been swept up and buried outside.

Sharisha's horse stamped its hoof. Sharisha, already mounted, headed off into the trees, selecting a deer trail leading in the direction of the village. Ziona secured her pack to the back of the saddle and then clambered aboard her roan mare and followed.

As they drew parallel to the farm, Sharisha guided her grey gelding to a path emptying out beside the main gate to the farm. Ziona felt urgency about their task, like an itch behind her shoulder blade she could not scratch. Something felt wrong this morning, as though her quarry were dissolving like a mist before the morning sun. She followed Sharisha, yet her instincts told her she would not find the boy when they arrived.

A shaft of sunlight pierced the yard as they rode through the gates. A man, hearing the chickens clucking in the yard, came out of the house, a walking stave in hand. There was no hesitancy in his step; the stick was obviously not a cane.

Eyeing the two women, he stepped off the porch and approached them.

"Good morning, ladies! What brings you to my place so early this morning?"

Sharisha spoke first. "We have come to speak to your children, kind sir."

"And what business could two strangers possibly have with my children?"

"We believe they are two people we have been seeking for a very long time. You see, we are Primordial kind." Sharisha tucked back the braided coils on her head to reveal the tips of her ears.

Gaius stared at her for a moment. There was no surprise in his expression. With a resigned shrug to his shoulders, he motioned for them to dismount. He took the reins from each mount and tied them to the hitching post at the side of the house.

"This is not a conversation to have out in the open." He gestured toward the stairs to the house. He left the front door open in invitation to enter as he passed through the doorway.

The interior of the cabin was cozy and comfortable. Several overstuffed chairs were set to take advantage of the light coming in from the windows on either side of the rectangular room for reading. They flanked a broad fireplace serving as the main cooking arena, a braided rug warming the floor.

Gaius waved them toward the fireplace. "Tea?"

Nodding their acceptance, Sharisha and Ziona settled into the chairs.

"Avery!" he called. "Would you come here please? We have company."

Avery entered the room a few minutes later, her eyes settling immediately on their guests. They widened as she took in their fair features.

"Please make some tea for our guests. Now, ladies, if you would be so kind as to advise us as to why you are here?"

Avery filled a kettle with water at the small sink in the kitchen, pumping the pump handle to draw the water. She hung the kettle on the cast iron hook suspended above the hot coals left from their morning breakfast in the open-hearth fireplace.

"We are here because of an ancient sacred text of our people called *The Divination of the Divine*. Our Elder Scrolls speak of the birth of two individuals who will have the ability to intercede in the events of the future, who will be the key to preventing the destruction of this world," Sharisha explained. "We do not understand how or why they are important, but certain key events have been foreshadowed and have brought us to this time and place."

Avery hung on every word. Pulling the tin of loose tea from the shelf above the fireplace, she opened it and filled the tea ball with fragrant crushed herbs. She then gathered four mugs and poured tea, passing a steaming cup to each of their guests and then one to her father. Avery settled back on the rough carpet, sitting cross-legged, cradling the warm cup in her hands.

"Where is your son?" Ziona glanced around the room once more.

"He is gone."

"Gone? What do you mean, he's gone?" Ziona said sharply.

"He volunteered for the legion last night."

"What?" Ziona shot to her feet, tea sloshing over the sides of her cup.

"He had no choice. The legion had dragged the entire town out of their homes and shops and was systematically sorting through the assembled people for young men of recruitment age. Although I must say, Cayden came to town prepared. He intended to volunteer."

"Why would he volunteer for such service?"

"I believe he was in some kind of trouble." Gaius was intentionally vague. He was unsure how much of Ryder's confession he should share with these strangers. "You have still not explained why you are interested in my children," he said, his eyes now sharp on their faces.

Instead of answering his question, Sharisha turned to Avery and commanded, "Look at me, child." Avery obeyed, startled by the request. "What is the first memory you can remember? No matter how vague, how shadowed it may seem. What is the first thought you can remember since your birth? Relax your mind and think."

Avery frowned and thought. What was her earliest thought? What was her first memory? She closed her eyes and relaxed her mind. The familiar sensation of being able to smell the mood of things around her filled her. She smelled anxiety on her father and excitement and curiosity from the two Primordial ladies in front of her.

Avery relaxed her mind even further, her breathing slowing, her senses expanding. Lighter than a breeze, softer than a feather, she floated out the door and into the meadow beside the barn. She sensed the industriousness of the ants crawling over the decaying apples fallen from the tree and the serious concentration of the spider spinning a new ground web in the tall grasses near the ant hole.

"Concentrate, child," Sharisha whispered, "and think back to the beginning."

Avery let her mind wander down the familiar path of her childhood memories, moving backward in her mind. Her earliest memory...she sorted sensations and emotions overlaid with thoughts and conversations...and suddenly she had it.

"I remember a storm-filled night," she murmured. "I remember flying. I remember a candle in a window. I remember holding my brother's hand. I remember joy and pain...but joy and pain twice." Avery's eyes shot open. Shock rippled through her and she grabbed her father's hands. "I remember us being born, but I remember it twice! How is that possible?"

Sharisha and Ziona stared at each other, surprise written on their faces also.

Gaius walked over to the fireplace and leaned an arm on the mantle, staring into the amber coals, lost in thought. "Let me tell you the story of their birth," he said in a voice barely above a whisper.

***

Thunder rumbled high above the sheer rocky cliffs of the cove. Lightning flashed in the leaden skies above and the waves of the sea below churned in concert, sending plumes of water into the air then splashing back to the stormy sea.

A tiny light flickered in the window of a small wooden cabin facing the sea, the window open to tempt a cooling breeze. The candle sputtered but then settled back to burning clear and bright.

Gaius swiped a nervous hand across his sweaty brow and glanced out the window. Lightning flashed again and a sonorous boom sounded.

At exactly the same moment, seemingly in concert, his wife Melle screamed in the next room and low murmurs reached his ears, soothing sounds of the woman assisting her. He heard his wife's agonizing wail once more and then...the sound of a baby crying.

He ran to the bedroom and opened up the door. Inside he saw not one, but two babies, lying at the foot of the bed. The last one was being gently wiped down by the midwife and wrapped in a clean blanket. She picked up the two babes, placed them in his wife's arms and stepped back.

He walked quietly over to his wife's side. Two bright-eyed children stared back at him. He saw intelligence sparkling in their eyes, and something more, something he couldn't define.

Gaius gazed down into his wife's beaming face. Her hair was in sweat-soaked tangles and her eyes were tired but gleaming with pride. "Two babes, Gaius, a boy and a girl, and both as healthy as can be!"

As he gazed down at his children, lightning flashed again.

With their faces highlighted in the sudden glare, he noticed a birthmark in the shape of an oak leaf on each of their right cheeks. The lightning faded and with it the birthmark. He bent to take a closer look. There was nothing to see.

***

Gaius sat with elbows on knees, hands clasped, and head bowed. Silence followed his words.

Avery remembered it as clearly as if it had just happened. But she also remembered more. There had been another woman and man, another room, a room of stone. Her senses told her that woman was also her mother. She shook her head in confusion. How could it be? Yet she knew it for the truth...she *felt* the truth of it.

Sharisha and Ziona exchanged glances. They did not understand it either, but one thing was evident. Gaius had spoken of a birthmark which had faded away after a glance. Could this be another of the signs they sought?

There could be no doubt these two children were the ones they had travelled to locate.

And now one was being carried away into the mouth of the beast.

Ziona stood up abruptly. "I must go," she stated. "The legion already has too great of a lead on me."

Sharisha stood also. "How do you plan to approach him?"

"I will attach myself to their travelling supply train. It is the simplest answer. I shall present myself as a merchant seamstress who can sew uniforms for the new recruits. It should allow me access to most of the camp. I will be able to follow them the entire time."

Sharisha nodded her acceptance of the plan.

Ziona stood and bowed to Gaius and Avery. Avery blushed in surprise. "Until we meet again, Mistress Avery. Sir. " Ziona left the cabin, closing the door quietly behind her.

Sharisha directed her words at Avery. "You must come with me back to my homeland. Only there can I protect you."

"Protect me from what? What is it we are supposed to be in danger from? I don't understand any of this. Who are you anyways? And what is she"—Avery pointed at the recently closed door—"going to do with Cayden?" Avery took the seat vacated by Ziona and waited, arms folded across her chest defiantly.

Gaius looked up from the contemplation of his hands. He appeared years older suddenly.

"There were always little things with them both, right from the beginning. Avery, on her second birthday toddled over to her mother's side where she was hanging laundry on the line, jabbering away that Cayden was about to get hurt. She saw Cayden playing with a rattlesnake which had crawled out from under the rock pile to sun. The odd thing was, it seemed as if the rattler and Cayden were having a conversation. There was no aggressive behaviour in the snake. She shooed it away and it left. Cayden later said the snake was watching over them. He babbled on about his guardian snake for days afterward. We thought it was childish talk at the time..." His voice faded off in thought.

"And then there was the time Avery warned me of the thieves who intended to rob us as we came back from town one evening. A couple of bandits, a man and a woman dressed as common folk, were at the side of the road, pretending to fix the wheel of their wagon. The wagon was blocking a good section of the road, enough to cause us to stop or go around. Avery was about four and she was sitting in front of me in the saddle. She said to me very clearly, 'Papa, those people want to hurt us. Their wagon is not broken.' I watched the pair as they waved at us to assist them. It was then that I spied the third person, hiding under the canvas in the wagon with bow drawn and arrow knocked. I heeled my mare and we leapt into the woods at the side of the road. The arrow lodged itself into the tree beside my head as we gained the cover of the woods. How she knew, I never figured out, but she was right and she saved both of our lives that day. The thieves were gone by the time I was able to return with help."

Avery remembered the incident too. "There were four people, Papa. Another man was hidden on the other side of the wagon. They were slavers. They were after children to kidnap and sell. At least that was what I felt from them."

Both Gaius and Sharisha stared at her.

Avery gazed back at them and shrugged, plucking at a pull in her sweater.

Gaius rose abruptly, decision made, placing his cup on the table beside the chair.

"I need to make arrangements for the farm." Gaius rose from his chair. "We will leave in the morning."

Sharisha nodded in acceptance.

Avery stared at him, dumbfounded.

Gaius picked up his hat from the peg by the door and left the cabin.

Chapter 11

CAYDEN RODE BEHIND THE SCOUT. The riders formed up and followed them out of town, soon overtaking them, kicking up a cloud of dust as they passed. Cayden coughed and covered his nose with his sleeve until the dust settled. The scout ahead of him was keeping his mount to a brisk walk.

Cayden longed to enter the dense trees. It would be so easy to slip away into them and forget about this hair-brained scheme, but he knew others would suffer if he did so. So he kept his eyes on the horse in front of him and followed placidly.

They crested the hill and the camp spread out like lava on the slopes of the valley below. There were a few merchant wagons set up along the roadside, their canvas sides rolled up to display their merchandise for sale. They cried out in loud voices at the mounted men riding toward the camp, hawking wares from needles and tobacco to knives, flint, and candy. The riders did not slow until they had entered the perimeter of the camp.

Cayden slowed his mount in order to take in the goods on display. There was little that would be useful to a soldier on the march. A broad rim hat of dyed calf's leather in a dark green shade caught his eye. It would be very useful for keeping the sun out of his eyes. Perhaps, when he earned some pay in the service of the queen, he would return to buy it.

"Magnus, I have a new recruit for you," called the scout to a beefy man standing inside the main entrance of the boundary containing the camp. Magnus walked over to where Cayden had dismounted. He walked around Cayden, sizing him up. He paused in front of him, turned his head and spat at the ground. A stream of foul brown liquid jetted from his mouth. He rolled the chew of tobacco over to the other side of his mouth, tucking it in his cheek and then leered at Cayden, showing yellowed teeth.

"Scrawny thing, but we will soon toughen him up. Ranolph!" he bellowed to another man standing over his shoulder. "Get over here and take the new recruit to the supply tent. Find him a uniform to wear that doesn't fall down around his knees. Bunk him in with the recruits from the last village."

"Aye, sir!" said Ranolph with a quick salute. "Follow me."

Cayden followed Ranolph to the eastern side of the camp, wending his way between tent pegs and cooking fires. The men in the camp seemed a well fed but surly lot. There was no laughter, no music, and no camaraderie. The men sharpened their swords, polished boots, or tended their cook fires but all with an air of workers sharing the same drudgery. Boredom seeped from every pore. Suspicious eyes followed Cayden's journey through the camp. The men sported various injuries and somehow Cayden did not think they were all a result of battle. Many a man was wrapped in bandages, while others used roughly carved crutches to hobble about the camp. *If these are not battle wounds, they can only be training or brawl related,* Cayden thought. He shivered. He thought all it would take was one spark and the camp would erupt like a firework dropped in a campfire.

Cayden was relieved when they reached the supply tent without incident. Drawing the flap aside, he entered the dim interior. A man was seated behind a makeshift desk, making notations in what appeared to be a supply catalog.

He squinted at the newcomers through spectacles perched on the end of his nose. The reading glasses slipped a little as he harrumphed, "New recruit?" He eyed Cayden up and down and then rose and walked over to a trunk. Opening the lid, he pulled out a tan shirt, a pair of dark brown pants, and a belt. He closed the lid of the trunk and then opened an identical one sitting beside it. He pulled out a brown cap and a leather jerkin from its depths. He glanced at Cayden's feet and then reached into the portable cupboard behind him and produced a worn pair of work leather boots. He handed the bundle of clothing to Cayden and jotted the transaction into his ledger, dismissing them with a vague nod of the head.

Cayden followed Ranolph out of the supply tent and then a short distance away to a long horse picket. Ranolph indicated that he tie his horse to the end of the line.

They then approached a low tent off to one side, much larger than the ones surrounding it. Ducking inside this tent, Cayden saw two rows of sleeping mats laid out, ten in total. Each mat had a blanket. All the mats were currently occupied with the exception of one right at the entrance flap, the coldest and noisiest spot in the tent.

"This is where you will sleep. Roll call is at six o'clock every morning. Change into your uniform and come outside. I will take you to your new mates."

He changed quickly and then followed Ranolph out into the camp again. They passed the latrines he had spotted from their earlier spy trip and ended up at the edge of the camp where a practice battle range had been set up.

At the far end of the field they entered the practice range. A group of men about Cayden's age shot arrows at straw targets. Closer in, men worked with practice swords under the careful eye of a trainer. Closer still, Cayden picked out men working with pikes and halberds, dodging the wrapped blades.

Ranolph handed Cayden over to the training sergeant, a balding man with arms and legs like an elephant. His shirt strained across his chest. "Well, well, boys! Look here. We got ourselves a rabbit."

The others stopped their practice and sauntered over, raw aggression evident in their stiff gait.

The sergeant bared his teeth in a predatory smile. "Rabbits run, boy. I suggest you get going."

With a holler the entire practice yard raised weapons and ran at Cayden. Cayden yelped and grabbed a wooden staff from a nearby barrel. He fled out of the yard, only to find his path blocked by more soldiers.

Cayden shot off to the right, toward the practice dummies, the men behind him yelling and catcalling, waving their various weapons at him. He ducked behind a practice dummy, which shuddered as a sword was thrust through it, the tip of the blunt wooden blade stopping a bare inch from Cayden's belly.

He leapt back in shock, but not in time to avoid a blow from a wooden practice mace to his head. His ears rang and the world spun. Staggering away, he launched himself into motion again, this time running toward some wooden boxes arranged in another corner of the yard.

Reaching the boxes, he jumped on top of them and brought his staff around in front of him. With a wild swing, he pushed the five men in front of him back. Two more closed in from the right side, one with a wicked looking blunt steel-tipped spear. The man jabbed the spear at Cayden, catching him on his thigh and ripping a gash in his pant leg, quickly soaking it in blood.

Cayden yelped and swung the staff clumsily once again. A man on his right stabbed at him with a short sword, catching him on the left knee. Cayden hopped back in pain and failed to see the man right in front of him who lifted his own staff and jabbed Cayden in the stomach. Cayden doubled over in pain, gasping for air. A fourth man stepped up to him and with the blunt end of his sword, struck Cayden on the head. Everything went black and Cayden toppled from the crates to land face down in the dirt.

Cayden came to, eyes creeping open to see a pair of polished black boots in front of his nose. He groaned, the light making his head pound. He pushed himself to a sitting position. Sergeant Perez stood in front of him, his icy smile freezing him in place. Cayden reached back and found a large lump on the back of his head. The sergeant sniggered.

"Every morning you will report to this yard. You will be taught defensive skills during the course of the day. Every evening at quitting time, you will become the rabbit. You must not only survive in this arena for ten minutes. You must also take out a minimum of two of your opponents. If you fail, you will repeat the process the next day…and the next day until you learn to defend yourself. Only then will you be taught offensive skills."

Cayden counted the other men. They stood smirking. There was no compassion on any of their faces. He knew he would receive no mercy from this group.

"The day is done. Dismissed!"

The assembled men stored their weapons and walked away.

Cayden got woozily to his feet. His knee was bleeding and blood trickled down into his boot. He limped after the men. He needed to be stitched if there was any kind of healer in the camp.

Ranolph met him as he came out and with a curt nod indicated that Cayden was to follow him again. Cayden limped behind him to a large central tent with a flag hanging limply from a pole by the entrance. The flag fluttered and Cayden caught a glimpse of various leaf shapes imprinted on the flag. This was the healer's tent. He gestured for Cayden to enter the tent. "I will leave you here."

Cayden opened the flap and entered. A middle-aged woman was standing at a scrubbed table, mashing the contents of a stone bowl with a pestle. She added a little water and continued mashing. "Have a seat in that chair by the lamp."

Cayden did as instructed, groaning softly as he eased himself into the chair.

Grumbling to herself, she added a few more drops of water and then turned to face Cayden.

"Always the same time every day, always the same ones." She stopped in surprise. "You're new. When did you arrive?"

"About an hour ago," Cayden said. "About an hour too soon I think."

She laughed, kind eyes twinkling. A slow smile twitched on Cayden's face.

"I'm quite the mess." Cayden sheepishly gestured to his thigh and knee.

She walked over to him, setting the bowl down on the small table holding the lamp. She knelt beside him and inspected his wounds. She stood up and drew his shirt off over his head, examining the bruise on his stomach and probing with tender hands. She then examined his head, Cayden wincing at the slight pressure she applied while searching the wound. She pulled open one eye and then the other.

"My name is Laurista. It appears you will survive, although I would recommend you strive to not take any more beatings like this. The head is a very fragile thing and a man can die from too much head trauma."

Cayden shook his head ruefully, causing the world to spin. "My name is Cayden. And it was not my idea. They tossed me in there with no warning."

"Yes, that is how it is done, and I get stuck with trying to patch everyone back together. It's brutal, yet oddly effective, I think, when it comes to skills training. I am not much of a fan of the attitudes spawned by it, however. You need to watch yourself in this camp. None will call you friend."

"Why would they have a grudge against me? I just arrived," he growled defensively.

"They view all from this area as outsiders. Your villages are so far removed from the capital and your people from the main fighting for so long, that they see you as cowards, cheats who have somehow ducked their duty to the queen. They think it is their right to teach you a lesson. They think you believe yourselves to be better than them, above them. They hope to prove otherwise, I am afraid. You can expect no mercy."

Laurista reached down and scooped up some of the poultice she had been mixing. She gently spread the greenish mixture on both cuts and then applied a wrapping around each location. The mixture stung as it entered the wound and then faded, taking the pain with it. Cayden was caught by surprise. "Hey, that works really well!" He gingerly moved his limbs. "Thank you."

Laurista's lips ghosted a smile at him. She reached into a travel cupboard set on the table, withdrawing a bottle of purple liquid. She added a few drops of the liquid with some water and returned to him.

"Drink this. It will help with the dizziness."

Cayden drank the liquid, which tasted like berries. His vision steadied.

"I'm finished with you. You should go get something to eat and rest. It is a narrow window when they serve meals." She collected up her bowl and vial and set them back down on the table.

"Thank you again. I really appreciate it and the advice. I will take it to heart and head." He grimaced. "Until next time?" Grinning, he stood and waved a friendly goodbye and sauntered out the tent.

Laurista watched him go, a tiny frown creasing her forehead. There was something different about that boy, something very different indeed.

Chapter 12

AVERY FOLLOWED HER FATHER and the Primordial woman through the twisting path created by the stream bed. Their horses gingerly picked their way amongst the loose stones at the side of the stream.

Reaching a fainter path created by some animal, they ascended into to the wooded mountainside, the foothills of the Highland Needle range. Far above, Avery saw a cleft in the rocks, a natural divide backlit from the far side by a sun that had not yet reached the zenith of the mountain.

The animal trail meandered back and forth on the climb, finding the best purchase for an animal with hooves. The morning dew clung to the branches and leaves of the underbrush and soon soaked through their clothing. Avery drew her cloak tighter as she shivered.

They had been travelling for several days now, always during the early morning hours when the dew was fresh. Sharisha had said little more about their purpose in going to the Primordial lands and Avery's father had been equally withdrawn and tight-lipped, as though he didn't want to know what would be revealed there.

Avery sensed the worry and anger he held tightly. Ever since her mother died when she and Cayden were little, their father had protected them with an almost religious fervour, allowing nothing to come too near them, human or animal.

The day her mother had died, she had gone alone to collect blueberries from the scrubby plants that loved to nestle amongst the rocky hillsides. She did not return. The next day, her father had found the body. Her mother had been attacked, torn to shreds by some animal or animals they had never seen or been able to find, although her father and some of the other villagers had attempted to hunt it down. Avery had been five years old.

From that point on, he refused to speak of it to them, but her father had changed that day. Something other than her mother's death had scared him; Avery sensed it. She shook her head. Why was she revisiting that memory this morning of all mornings? Perhaps it was the rocky terrain recalling the time to her. Suddenly she realized her father was thinking these thoughts also and as she dwelled on that idea, his thoughts nearly congealed into a solid form right in front of her.

"Papa, are you thinking about the day Mother died?"

Her father gave a surprised start in his saddle, his head whipping around.

"How did you know that?" he challenged.

Sharisha's dark eyes settled on Avery's green ones.

"I...don't know...," Avery puzzled. "I saw a mental image of what you were thinking."

Sharisha watched the exchange, her cool gaze hinting at hidden knowledge. She twisted back around in her saddle. "Come. The pass is just ahead. We can easily reach it by noon. We will break for food there."

***

Cayden unconsciously shoved his blankets off to his knees. He rolled onto his side and settled back to an uneasy sleep filled with dreams. Thunder rolled, lightning flashed.

An eagle soared in the midst of the storm, carrying a blanket woven of curly goat hair in its beak. The eagle dived through the tempest, alighting on the stone sill of a window set in a cottage wall. The ghostly bird hopped down into the room and onto the shadowed arm of the tall thin man who greeted the eagle like an old friend. He carried the shadow eagle over to where a woman in the throes of giving birth writhed in a bed, clearly in pain. The bird lowered the shimmering blanket to the floor.

The shadowed old man murmured a spell that enveloped the body of the woman. A midwife knelt at the foot of the bed, giving no indication she saw the man or the eagle.

She eased the children from the woman's body and one by one, placed them on a soft blanket folded multiple times and placed on the floor in front of the eagle she could not see. The midwife dipped a cloth into the bucket of warm water and began to bathe the twins. She wrapped the infants in soft blankets and then left them while she ministered to the mother.

Cocking its head to one side, the eagle gazed at the children.

The wisp of a man then began to utter a rhythmic prayer, pulling a vial of liquid from his robes. He dipped his finger in the vial and traced the outline of a leaf on the cheek of each child with a stroke of his finger. The outline flared blue and faded, as the chant continued.

The eagle screeched and hopped closer to the children. It swayed to the rhythm of the chant, bobbling its head and flapping its wings.

Suddenly, the man clapped his hands and the thunder crashed, shaking the cottage, its sound echoing off the polished logs. Blue lightning flickered into the room and touched each of the inhabitants, including the eagle, bathing the room in an effervescent glow.

When the lighting faded, the eagle flew back to the window, blanket in its beak and hurled itself into the storm. Lightning flashed once again, striking the eagle. The blanket vanished. The eagle plummeted into the waves below.

Cayden rolled over once more. His breathing steadied as the storm overhead departed. He did not remember the dream in the morning.

Chapter 13

CAYDEN WOKE TO THE SOUND of movement in the tent. The other men were already dressed, stuffing their belongings into packs and rolling up their sleeping pallets and blankets. Cayden scrambled up and dressed quickly.

"Are we breaking camp?" he spoke aloud to no one in particular.

"No, we are going on a picnic," a pockmarked face sneered. *Powell is his name,* Cayden thought. Laughter filled the tent.

The flap opened and in stomped Sergeant Perez. The men in the tent snapped to attention. Cayden went rigid.

"You have two minutes to report to the central practice grounds. Last man to report in will be taking the place of one of the pack mules that has come up lame." Sneering at Cayden, who was standing with one sock on and the other still in hand, he left the tent.

The tent emptied faster than a stirred hornet's nest. Cayden tugged on his boots. Gathering up his gear, he left the tent for the horse lines. There, he found his mare mixed in with the army's horses. As he went to fetch his saddle and gear from the storage tent, a soldier stepped up to him.

"You cannot take that horse, son. It is now the property of the legion. Don't you have a squad you have been assigned to?"

"Yes, sir."

"Then I suggest you form up with them."

Frowning, Cayden trotted back to the practice grounds. He was the last one to arrive, much to the glee of his bunk mates and the sergeant.

"Will you look at this? The rabbit has volunteered to replace the mule," scoffed Perez. "Get over here so we can get you harnessed."

Cayden walked toward the wood-sided wagon piled high with gear. Attached to the front yoke, where normally a pair of mules would have stood, was a freckle-faced lad Cayden's age. He was one of the men sharing Cayden's tent. He stared at his feet, face red as his hair.

Perez grabbed Cayden's arm and shoved him in beside the other young man. Rough leather straps were wound around his shoulders and across his chest and buckled behind him. Attached to either side of the harness was a set of reins which were looped around a piece of wood on the front of the wagon.

Sergeant Perez bellowed for the men to form marching units. He clambered up the side, rocking the wagon with his weight then settled onto the rough seat. One beefy hand took up the reins and the second picked up the horsewhip.

With an exaggerated flick of the reins, he shouted a command to leave. The whip whistled through the air and snapped the tip of Cayden's ear. Cayden cried out, clasping a hand over the reddening curve, protecting it from further harm. Cayden swore loudly and pulled on the straps. The other lad did the same as they strained to get the wagon into motion. The whip flicked out again and this time the lad beside Cayden yelped and jumped. The whip had caught him on the side of the forehead, leaving a swelling welt.

Cayden's anger flamed and his face reddened. The rest of the camp was in various stages of preparation to leave. It appeared they were the first group to actually do so.

As they strained to start the wagon rolling, random soldiers lifted bowls of steaming food to them in a mock salute. Cayden's stomach rumbled loudly. Others laughed and pointed. Perez smirked and flicked the whip again. Cayden's shoulder stung. Cayden kept his gaze fixed ahead on the path straining against the straps to climb out of the meadow and into the trees. Sweat broke out on his brow and his blood thundered in his ears. He felt a surge rise up his neck and into his face but not from exertion. Fury hummed along his veins, adrenaline pumping.

"My name is Cayden. What's yours?" he said to the lanky lad yoked beside him, trying to distract himself from his anger.

"Darius," the lad answered hoarsely.

"How did you end up here beside me?"

"I didn't get the sergeant's boots polished in time."

"You polish his boots? Why in the world would you do that?"

"Well, because otherwise I will end up as the rabbit." A brief grin flashed across his face.

"Oh," said Cayden, nonplussed. "I guess that's a good reason. It is my honoured position right now, at least until someone new comes to camp."

"I doubt it will make a difference even then." Darius glanced back over at Cayden, adjusting his grip on the leather straps on his chest for better leverage. Cayden thought he saw pity in his grey eyes.

Frowning, Cayden gazed sightlessly down the road they travelled.

"Why should I be singled out? I just got to camp. I haven't even had a chance to prove myself."

"It doesn't matter what you do, Cayden. You are from the cliffs. You are automatically classed as an outsider. You will never be allowed to advance. You will never be given rank. You will be pushed and punished until you break." Darius shrugged uncomfortably at his own words.

"Then why accept my offer to serve? That makes no sense."

"No one from your area ever volunteers for service in the legion." Darius tilted his head at Cayden quizzically. "Why did you? There is no way it's because you love the legion. No one would believe it even if you swore on the queen's crown."

"No, it was not for love of the queen." Cayden thought quickly. "I want to see the world outside of the cliffs because, as you said, no one ever comes away from the cliffs to see the world. I thought this would be a good way to do it. Food, a place to sleep, you know, some wages to go with it along the way?"

"And the occasional skirmish where you get to stick your sword in someone. Yeah, I know." Darius was grinning openly now.

Cayden shrugged again, the movement restricted by the leather harness. He was not thrilled by the idea of sticking his sword in anyone. He felt a sick squirm in his stomach at the thought.

"Why did you join?"

"Well, I am from the plains at the base of the Highland Needle, you see. It is grasslands mostly and not a tree to be seen. It's always dry, even desert-like in some areas. My folks, they have nine kids. I am the eldest. Last year was a hard year. The crops never sprouted as the spring rains didn't come until it was too late. My pa scraped together a grub stake and gave me my clothes, a good hunting knife, and a skin of water and told me it was time to make my own way in the world. I left that very night and haven't seen them since."

Darius paused, thinking. "Then about six months back, near starvation and thinking I would need to steal food from the farms I passed, I bumped into the legion. Well, in actual fact, I passed out in the middle of the roadway and they nearly ran me over. When I came to, I was in the healer's tent and being shoved into a uniform as soon as I could stand. Guess I got recruited while I was passed out. It's not such a bad life. I get regular meals and my clothes are taken care of. I get to train on weapons, which is fun…as long as I don't get stuck by anything. I haven't seen any real fighting yet." He paused, his forehead wrinkling, concerned at that thought, but continued his story. "Not sure how that will go, to tell the truth. I was a farm boy. I don't know anything about fighting, only about vegetables."

He lapsed into silence. Cayden felt sorry for him. Although he wasn't much older, he felt ancient in comparison. He grinned over at Darius. "I could use a friend and who better than the guy being forced to help me drag his sorry carcass all the way to the next camp?" He jerked his head back at the sergeant lounging in his wagon seat.

Not surprisingly, Perez guessed at the conversation. The cruel whip flicked out again and this time it cut Cayden's cheek below the eye, his head still turned in Darius's direction. Cayden's hand jerked to his cheek, pulling it away to show a bloody smear.

Darius snapped his head back straight and focused on pulling the cart.

Cayden glared back over his shoulder, his hatred naked on his face. Perez grinned evilly as he pulled out his short knife and proceeded to scrape dirt out from under his fingernails.

Cayden whispered fiercely, "We will come out of this fine, Darius. You'll see. Don't let them get to you. If I won't break, you are not allowed to either. We are a team, you and me. OK?"

"OK," whispered Darius.

They lapsed into silence, each alone with his thoughts. Dust puffed under their feet as they walked.

Chapter 14

THE AIR AT THE TOP OF THE PASS was cool and thin. Avery took a deep breath and still wanted more. The horses didn't seem bothered by the thin air, but the short exercise of gathering firewood from the scrub brush around their campsite had her wheezing like the bellows at Ryder's forges.

Sharisha put a kettle over the fire to brew a pot of tea. From his saddlebag, Gaius retrieved some dried mutton and some flatbread. Avery retrieved some dried berries from her saddlebags, which with the addition of water plumped back up in a few minutes.

Sharisha walked away into the trees and collected some bright green fiddleheads and a full bowl of wild mushrooms, which she then added to a pot with the dried mutton and water and set it to simmer on the coals.

Avery lowered herself to sit on a blanket on the ground near the fire. She was quiet, thinking about the last conversation.

Sharisha had brought her horse up alongside of hers, matching her pace.

"What you do is a very rare gift, my child."

"What is it I do?"

"You have the ability to sense the feelings of others. You can also sense their truths, their honesty, or their lies. You can tell if they believe what they are saying or whether they lie to themselves and to others. This can be a two-edged sword. The fanatical do what they do, convinced what they believe is the truth, even if it is the most diabolical of actions. The radical will kill in the name of the lesser gods to please them and the same men will spare wicked lives to avoid the attention of the Great Goddess of the Dark. Knowing what they believe is not necessarily knowing truth and acting on what you believe to be their intent can cause grief beyond measure. This is in part why we are bringing you to Faylea, our capital city. We have elders there who are able to help train you in your abilities and give you guidance. The head of our order, the Spirit High Priestess resides there, and of course the Shining Temple is at the very heart of Faylea. Faylea is the home of the Spirit Clans."

Gaius rode up on Avery's other side and focused on Sharisha. "Why does she have them, these special abilities you mention? Where did they come from? Is it something genetic?"

Sharisha gazed solemnly at him. "I cannot say. I do not have that knowledge. The elders will know. They will be able to say for certain. I am merely a Seeker sent to search for those who may be spoken of in our prophecies. We are trained from birth and made to memorize the Elder Scrolls so that we may perform this sacred duty."

Avery checked the stew. She took the pot off the coals and ladled the bubbling contents into wooden bowls. She handed them around, not meeting either set of eyes. She blew gently on her stew and then took a mouthful.

As she chewed her food, her thoughts strayed to Cayden. Unconsciously, she touched the stone on the chain around her neck. It warmed to her touch and pulsed in her hand. He was alive, if not happy.

She sensed he was spitting mad at the moment. Not unexpected, considering what he had chosen to do. He would have a rough road ahead of him. But there was no reason why he shouldn't come out of it fine. She hoped.

Meal finished, they doused the fire and packed up their belongings, setting the horses off on a slow walk as the descent was as steep as the upward climb had been.

The thin scrub brush gave way to taller and taller trees. The heat of the day was undiluted on this side of the pass and the day warmed quickly. As they descended, the air grew thick with humidity due to the lower altitude on this side of the mountain range. Flowers appeared, dotting the hillside in pockets. Avery sniffed appreciatively and then pulled back on the reins abruptly.

That flower...it was the one she had smelled in her mind when she fell from Sunny's back. Avery leapt from her saddle and ran toward the now familiar scent. In the crevice of a rock a fragile orchid bloomed, its white flesh striped with thin veins of pink and blue. The flower bobbed on a bright green bulbous stem that continuously fed it rare nutrients to keep it blooming year around.

Avery dropped to her knees and gently cradled the flower in her hand. She *knew* this flower. How was that possible? She had never seen it before.

Sharisha watched from her mount, as Avery examined the flower. "It is called Heavensmist. The plant is known to have healing powers beyond the extraordinary. It is never to be moved. If you dig it up, it will die. This is the only place it grows naturally, here at the height of the pass. The plant is protected by our people. We harvest its seeds and grow a lesser, cultivated variety of it on our farms. The pure natural stock is sacred, however. It will cure you if you ingest it, if you are an inch from death, but at the cost of its own life. All of its offspring plants die too. We do not understand why."

Avery gently stroked the fragile petals. They quivered in response to her touch, the flower turning toward her hand. Sensation shivered through it, like a cymbal vibration. She felt life and spirit rush into her. She breathed deeply and felt completely rejuvenated.

"Come," Sharisha commanded. "We should reach the first Spirit clan village by nightfall."

Chapter 15

ZIONA CAUGHT UP TO THE LEGION when the sun was still about two hours in the sky. She was riding her mare named Seeker, after her task that had brought her to this area of the word, and leading a pack mule she had not yet named. Judging by the way it resisted doing any work, she was thinking Troll might be a good one.

When she caught up to the legion, she found them settling into a clearing bordered by cliffs on one side and a small tributary of the larger river on the left. The flats were usually flooded during the spring rains, but at this time, they were dry.

She joined the rest of the camp followers, riding up to a round woman sitting on the bench of a wagon loaded with goods.

"Good day, mistress," Ziona said politely. "Where might I find the supply clerk of the legion?"

The woman's eyes peered out at her from a dusty bonnet. "Quartermaster Higgs is the short, balding man other there." She pointed to the left side of the camp where it appeared a large tent was being erected. She eyed Ziona's packs with interest.

"Thank you, mistress." Ziona rode toward the edge of the camp.

A pair of soldiers stepped into her path before she was able to cross half the distance to the tent. "What is the nature of your business?" the larger of the two demanded.

"I have come to see the quartermaster, good sirs. I wish to offer my services to the camp as a seamstress of renown. I have experience creating army garments for the lowest recruit to the highest ranked officer. I assure you my prices are very reasonable."

"Very well, report directly to the quartermaster. He will tell you where you are permitted to set up camp."

Ziona nudged her mare forward and rode the short distance to the quartermaster's tent. She dismounted and then pulled a bundle of samples from her side pack. As she entered the tent, she observed a flurry of motion, as supplies were unloaded and stacked onto makeshift shelving. It appeared they intended to stay for a few days.

She approached the man who appeared to be in charge. "Good sir? May I speak with you a moment."

The hulking quartermaster, annoyed with the interruption, barked, "What do you want?"

"The good men at the entrance told me to come see you. Where should I set up my seamstress's tent?" She held out the samples for his inspection. "They are of the finest quality, I assure you."

He glanced at them and waved her away. "You can leave those here and set up your tent with the other merchants. I will come find you."

"Thank you, good sir." She left the tent.

On her way out of the camp, she spied activity on the back side, where a practice yard appeared to have been set up. A group of men were chasing a lad about Avery's age. He dashed here and there, trying to avoid their weapons. He glowed blue the entire time.

Smiling to herself, she searched for a place to set up camp.

***

Cayden dodged to the left, rounding a tree which saved his head from being split open by the wooden mace swung into it. He had not been issued any weapons, not having earned the right by keeping his feet for ten minutes. He was at eight and a half minutes now by his reckoning. However, Sergeant Perez seemed to have a longer accounting of time.

Cayden had dropped one of the trainees, having kicked him as he swung his weapon, a staff, leaving is belly exposed. He had gained a weapon at last out of the exchange, but it was impossible to swing it in the trees where he had fled, the men chasing after him.

His eyes searched frantically for a spot from which to defend himself with his commandeered weapon. He spied an outcropping of rock too steep to climb. It would protect his back, however. He sprinted toward it, arriving just in time to spin into a defensive position.

He couldn't only defend. He had to attack. He had been the rabbit for two weeks now. The daily beatings were wearing him down. He was a mass of bruises and cuts even Laurista's administrations couldn't eliminate. Seven men were left and they formed up around him. Two were short, three were tall, and the other two were of medium height.

Cayden took a deep breath and calmed himself. He thought about the eagle he had called when carving its flute back home. Thinking of the eagle gave him an idea. He reached out with his senses and found an eagle nearby in the forest. He nudged it with his subconscious mind and the eagle responded, winging toward the camp.

The tall man on the left swung at Cayden with his sword. Cayden easily deflected it with the long staff. A man on his right dashed in with another sword, which was easily pushed aside. Suddenly, they rushed him at once, attempting to overwhelm him by sheer numbers. Cayden lay about with the staff, panic lending him speed if not accuracy. He knocked one on the head, dropping him to the ground, out cold. On his return swing, he took two more out at the knees. They fell on top of one another. A sword caught him, slashing a long cut down his upper arm. Thankfully the practice swords were left somewhat dull; however, they could still break bones and blood welled from the wound, dripping down to his hand and making the already slick staff, slippery in his grip. Cayden butted his attacker in the stomach while his sword completed its arc past his arm and he doubled over in pain, retching. He did not get back up. The remaining men backed off and reorganized. The two he had tripped got back to their feet. They moved a little more warily now, attempting to flank him.

Cayden breathed heavily, sweat pouring from his pores and mixing with the blood of his cut, causing it to sting and burn. Suddenly, he heard a screech from the sky. A lone eagle circled above him and then dived toward Cayden. The men glanced up at the sky, alarmed by the plummeting eagle.

Cayden swung his staff, clipping the nearest man on his ear. He fell to the ground, out cold. Cayden pulled back on his staff and rammed the butt end into the stomach of the man standing opposite. He clutched his stomach and spilled its contents, dropping to his knees.

Cayden then swung at the third man who raised his sword arm in defence. Cayden rapped his wrist, causing it to go numb and drop the sword. Cayden then tapped the man in the head and he dropped.

The eagle clawed at the remaining two men, wings flapping, talons raking their backs and arms. Sergeant Perez, watching from the sidelines, cursed and called for archers. Cayden cried out to the eagle to flee. The eagle lifted back into the sky and vanished into the trees. Cayden lowered his staff. The remaining two men were no longer interested in fighting. Blood dripped from the shredded skin on their backs. Cayden breathed in heavily, trying to catch his breath. He had won for a change.

Sergeant Perez marched over to where the men lay groaning on the ground. He glanced at them and then frowned at Cayden. Cayden thought he saw a glimmer of respect in his eyes. Respect, yes, but hatred was reflected there too.

"So the rabbit has teeth at last. It's about bloody time. Lucky for you the eagle took a liking to their arms. You lot, up on your feet and off to the healer's tent. Since you helped cause this mess, you can help get them there, Cayden. Dismissed!"

Chapter 16

NELSON SQUEEZED HIS SKINNY FRAME into the gap, holding his lantern aloft as he shuffled sideways through the break in the stone wall. Hands took the lantern from him and then grasped his arm to give him a tug. He popped out of the crevice like a cork from a bottle, overbalancing on the landing.

He brushed his shirt and pants down and then examined his surroundings. He found himself in a rough, naturally formed cavern about the size of the stables of his inn. The ceiling was covered in stalactites at one end, close to a narrow stream of water that trickled through the rear of the cave. Matching stalagmites formed on the floor, giving the appearance of a tooth-filled jaw about to snap shut.

This limestone cave was promising. Of all the stones they had tunnelled through to date, this was the first that matched the stone construction inside the castle. The castle foundations were built on limestone, but the upper structure was of quarried granite from the mountain ranges to the northeast. Finding a limestone deposit was like finding gold. They were not far from their goal.

"Hector, how far does this cave extend? Have you had a chance to explore deeper yet?"

Hector rubbed his dark chin in thought, rough hand rasping across the stubble. "Yes, sir. However, we ran low on lantern fuel and had to turn back. If we follow the stream, it runs in a southeast direction that should bring us inside the castle walls. The stream is flowing away from the castle, which means there must be a water source up ahead. I suspect a spring of some sort."

Nelson nodded. The spring could be the one that fed the wells inside the castle.

"OK, let's work on widening this cleft. It needs to be wide enough for men and supplies to pass." Hector nodded his head in acknowledgement of the instructions. "I think this is a good place to set up a base camp. The cavern is wide enough to hold twenty men plus supplies. I'll head back and let Denzik know of our find. Erik, Hector, come with me and put together an exploration crew."

They squeezed back out through the crack and into the main tunnel. Men were busy clearing the debris from the latest tunnelling efforts. They were using pickaxes and water combined with fungus to soften the limestone wall. One of the men had discovered the pasty mixture easily dissolved the white powdery veins in the limestone rock, making it easier to knock out larger pieces of stone. The pickaxes clanked against the stone surface as they chipped away at the walls.

They exited the caves into the cellar of his basement. Nelson climbed back up into the inn and set off across the village square to Denzik's home. He found him out back tending to the vegetables in his meager garden. Denzik was bent over his hoe, chopping at the weeds attempting to take over the bed. Sweat glistened, streaking the dust coating his shirtless back as he hoed. Nelson stepped up to the side of a row of string beans, and peering over the laced stakes, he whispered, "The men have made a discovery. You need to come have a look at this."

Denzik straightened from his work, swiping his arm across his forehead and leaving a dirty smear. He nodded. He worried about what ears were about during the daylight hours. "I will share a pint with you as soon as I am finished here. I accept your invitation gratefully. There is nothing like cold ale after slaving away in the hot sun," he announced in a loud voice.

He nodded and Nelson headed off for the bakery.

Opening the door set the chimes to tinkling. His senses were overwhelmed by the sweet spicy scent of apple dumplings. He spied Fabian with his head emerging from a wall oven, a steaming tray of the sugary treats in his hands. At the sound of the bell, he spotted Nelson.

"Some great things are cooking in my kitchen too. Care to stop by for a bite after work?" It was his code to Fabian.

Fabian lips twitched. "I would be delighted to stop in. It beats going home for a lonely dinner. Around the usual time?"

"Certainly, I will save a table for you. In the meantime, I need fifty of your crusty dinner rolls for this evening."

Fabian rounded up the requested rolls and placed them in a paper sack for Fabian. "Cash or on account?" he enquired as he placed them on the counter.

"On account, if you please. See you at dinner." Picking up the bag of buns, Nelson walked out of the bakery and back down the dusty street to his inn.

The inn was a two-story wooden structure, framed by a verandah running the length of the front exposure. Rocking chairs were placed randomly along the front and were frequently used by guests to relax after their evening meal, lit pipe in one hand and a brandy glass in the other. The porch afforded a clear view of the highway, which did not disappoint for entertainment, day or night. A constant stream of traffic moved back and forth from the castle.

When Nelson had taken it over, the entire building had had a definite lean to the right. The wooden shutters were missing slats and the door creaked on hinges nearly seized up. The inside had been infested with mice and rats. Nelson walked up onto the porch and bent down to scratch his favourite cat, Sally, under her chin. She purred and wound around his legs, tail held rigidly in the air. He had found her, drowning in the rain barrel she had fallen into while attempting to get a drink. Scrawny and near dead, he had taken the kitten in. She had rewarded him by becoming a prime mouser, earning her keep every day. In fact, she was the best mouser he had ever had.

Entering the inn, Nelson waved to the assembled patrons who called out greetings. He stepped up behind the bar and put a note in the store's ledger about the bun purchase and then delivered them to the kitchen.

Inside he found his head cook, Tabitha, spoon in hand, tasting the broth from her soup pot. With a satisfied smacking of her lips, she gave the pot another stir and placed the lid back on it with a clatter. He handed off the rolls to her.

"There will be a few extra for dinner tonight. I hope you have made enough to feed everyone." She squinted at him and seeing his expression, nodded.

"I always cook for the regular crowd plus ten percent in case we have unexpected company like those soldiers that came through. Why don't you check the pantry and see for yourself? I will not be accused of slacking in my duties. Now let me get back to my work," she said primly. Scowling, she focused her attention on the large bowl of potatoes waiting to be peeled.

Nelson snorted a laugh then wandered off to the pantry. She really was the best cook he had ever had…along with being the main food supplier for their underground endeavors. It amazed him how she stretched the inn's budget to keep the underground crews fed. *I really must give her a raise some time,* he thought.

The pantry was located in a separate room from the kitchen. This was also where the trap door to his cellar was located. Usually, it was covered with a woven mat and a vat of potatoes sat on it to disguise its presence. The mat was attached to the door so it would settle back into place when someone pulled the hatch closed after lowering themselves into the cellar, effectively disguising the entrance on entering or exiting.

Hector and Erik were waiting for him when he entered the room.

"The men are assembled and the supplies are down in the tunnel. The crews are about halfway through the cleft. I would say it will be about another hour or two before they have it fully opened," Erik said.

"Good work. Head into the common room and get yourselves something to eat. It might be a long night."

The pair left as instructed. Nelson approached the left wall of the storage chamber. He stored his extra lamps next to a large barrel of lamp oil he kept for just this kind of occasion. He pulled out twenty lamps and began filling their bellies, trimming the wicks as he did so. Task completed, he placed them on a shelf near the entrance to the basement.

Next, he pulled a blanket off of a storage chest. Fishing his key ring out of his pocket, he searched for the brass key that matched the lock. He turned the key in the lock and it opened with a metallic click. Stored inside was a stash of weapons, swords and halberds, spears, and shields. He hesitated and then took out five of the swords and placed them beside the trunk. He locked it back up and replaced the blanket, concealing the trunk from curious eyes. Wrapping the swords in spare linen from the cupboard, he placed the bundle behind the lanterns and left the room.

Chapter 17

CAYDEN STRETCHED AND RELAXED HIS SORE MUSCLES as he lay on his pallet, idly rolling the stone his sister had given him between his fingers. The stone felt curiously warm, like it had been sitting in the sun of the south-facing garden of their cabin all day.

The tent flap opened and half of his tent mates clambered in, returning from dinner and flopping on their respective mats.

Darius dropped onto the pallet next to Cayden's, groaning in contentment. He rubbed his distended belly. "I don't know whether the eats were better than normal tonight or if I was extra hungry."

Pieter, the lad next to Darius, snorted and with a laugh flopped down on his own space. "If it wasn't for Cayden whooping us out in the practice yard, we wouldn't have been allowed those extra helpings. So kind of Laurista to send that note with us saying we required 'extra helpings' to assist with her healing…and so kind of the cook to oblige."

"Well, I for one do not plan to have Cayden 'whoop us' again anytime soon. He got lucky. That's all there was to it," said a third tent mate, James.

"How so? I was out cold from the beginning." Darius gazed intently at Cayden, his stare so intense that Cayden looked away.

"You missed the eagle attack," said James. "I've never seen such a thing before. That eagle dived from a clear blue sky and went straight for those of us who were attacking Cayden. Cayden didn't get a scratch from the bird. It was like it was protecting him." James stared at Cayden.

The others' eyes fell on Cayden too, watching his reaction. Cayden sat up, tucking the stone in his pocket. He stared back at the others, trying to think of what to say. A slow flush crawled up his neck. His ears heated.

"I can't explain what happened. I was as shocked as any of you when the eagle appeared." He dropped his eyes. This was stretching the truth, he knew, which only made the flush rise higher. "I'm not sad for its help, though."

Darius's toothy grin broadened, seeing his friend's embarrassment. "You beat us fair and square, Cayden. We all know it. We were curious about the bird, that's all. It did seem like it was protecting you or something. I know Perez was livid after you left. He felt you had cheated somehow. We can't see how that's possible, though."

The rest of the tent residents filed in at that moment, interrupting their conversation.

"Oh, before I forget," said Darius. "Perez says that you are to report to the supply tent first thing in the morning. You are to be fitted for a private's uniform like ours." Darius leaned over and whispered softly, "If you ever need someone to talk to, I am here for you."

"Thanks. I think I will sleep now." Cayden pulled his blankets up to his chin, rolled on his side. Before the lamps were dimmed, he was fast asleep.

***

The morning dawned cloudy and grey. A damp mist hung in the air, which soaked through Cayden's shirt long before he reached the supply tent. He wished he had pulled out his cloak, although it was really too warm for such a heavy garment.

He knocked on the wooden plate at the door of the supply tent, announcing his arrival. "Come!" Drawing aside the flap, he entered the tent he had visited on his first day. The supply clerk was seated at his makeshift table, scribbling in a ledger. He glanced at Cayden as he entered. "Name?"

"Cayden Tiernan, sir."

"Ah yes…seems you have completed your basic training. You are to report to the seamstress's tent which can be found in the merchant's camp outside our camp perimeter. You are to have three uniforms made." He tossed a coin purse at him. "Inside are your wages for the last two weeks. You are to pay her from your own pay, understand?"

"Yes, sir!"

"Then go. After meeting with her, you are to report back to your unit."

"Yes, sir. Thank you, sir!" Cayden saluted and left the tent.

Cayden stopped by the mess tent and grabbed a couple bread rolls and some cheese. He pocketed these and then headed for the perimeter of the camp. Dawn was breaking the horizon, flooding the sky with purple and pink. He had about an hour to run his errand before he was due back at camp. Quickening his steps, he jogged to the perimeter. Nodding to the guards, he passed through and out into the merchant's camp.

His spirits lifted as he left the military camp behind. He was free again for a short period. He breathed in deeply, smelling the earthy smells of springtime, his heart light. He gazed around at the landscape as he walked and munched on his cheese and bread, taking in the canopy of the great trees. A golden shaft of morning sun struck the leaves, the brilliant spotlight exploding his senses with the vibrant greens of new growth. Birds warbled and cooed, welcoming the day. It was a glorious morning and Cayden was happy to be alive in it.

Other than the few stolen moments alone with his flutes, he had not been able to escape his voluntary imprisonment. He wondered idly how Ryder was doing. He felt a pang of homesickness. The spring lambs would be coming soon. How would his father manage everything without him?

Cayden entered the merchants' camp and dropped to a walk, strolling along the makeshift road between the wagons. A man backing out of a covered wagon nearly bowled Cayden over. Cayden stepped out of the way just in time and then asked where to find the seamstress's tent. The man gestured down an aisle to the right.

At the end of the grass path, Cayden found a tent of bright green erected between two large maples. Smoke curled out of the center vent of the tent. He stepped up to the flap and knocked on the wooden shingle hung by the flap. "Mistress, would you be awake?"

A head popped out of the tent. Cayden found himself staring into the most beautiful eyes he had ever seen. Emerald green, almond-shaped eyes gazed at him from a heart-shaped face framed by curly wisps of hair. Cayden's heart stopped. Fumbling for speech, the words tumbled from his lips. "Sorry to disturb you. I need you to help me find my pants…No, to get some pants. I mean I have pants, but I need new pants. These are no good…" He stumbled to a halt, blushing, as he saw a grin split her face. Laughter sparkled in her eyes. Groaning, he took a deep breath to calm himself. "I sound like an idiot."

"Not at all," she laughed. Her laughter sounded like chimes dancing in a breeze. "I assume you are here for a uniform?"

"Yes." Cayden sheepishly tugged at his collar.

"Come inside then. What is your name?"

"Cayden Tiernan. I am a new private and I was told you made uniforms."

He followed her into the tent, noting the neatly arranged seamstress supplies. Bolts of cloths were stacked in piles along one wall. A table set with spools of threads in various colours, jars of buttons and zippers, scissors, measuring tapes, and other supplies Cayden didn't recognize lined the opposite wall.

At the back of the tent sat a small narrow cot and a banded flat-topped chest with an oil lamp set on top of it. A small fireplace was centered in the tent, a wisp of smoke curling out the hole from the banked coals.

"Please, sit." Ziona motioned to the chair set by the table of notions. "Tea? I made a pot a few minutes ago."

"Yes, thank you." Cayden gratefully sank into the chair indicated, wincing slightly. She poured tea into two ceramic cups and handing one to him and then perched on her table, one leg dangling over the side.

She studied him with interest. "I have been waiting for you to come see me. My name is Ziona Aspenwood." She studied him, taking dainty sips of her tea.

Cayden's studied her with curiosity. "You have? Why?" He met her frank gaze and, blushing again, dropped his eyes.

"So shy…," she murmured. "Do you know who you are?" The blue aura pulsed around him, rising and falling as his emotions swung between curiosity and surprise.

Cayden's eyes shot back to her. "What do you mean? I told you who I am."

"I see…well." Her eyes travelled up and down him. "I wish you could see what I see…It is all good. Believe me." Her appreciative eyes roved over him, taking in his lean torso, blond curly hair, and vivid green eyes. Cayden blushed again under the scrutiny, his heart galloping and a chill of excitement shivered down his back.

"We have been destined to meet. I am here not merely as a merchant seamstress. I am what they call a Seeker. My people have sent me to be of assistance to you. Of course, I had to find you first."

Cayden locked his eyes on hers. "You have been following me?" He frowned. "It was you! That day in the high pasture…I thought I saw something in the trees. Was that you?" He watched her eyes, gauging her reaction to his words.

It was Ziona's turn to be surprised. "I didn't think you had seen me." Her eyebrows rose in disbelief. "Human eyesight should not have been able to spot me at such a distance."

"I didn't see you, not exactly. It was more like I sensed where you were."

Ziona nodded her head, satisfied.

"Who sent you? What is a Seeker?" Taking another sip of his tea he tried to calm his racing heart. He was aware of her in a way he had never been before with any other woman. He inhaled her woodsy scent without thinking and then blushed again.

On impulse, Ziona reached up and unwound her braid from around her head, revealing her ears.

Cayden gasped, "You're Primordial! " His eyes searched quickly for spying eyes. "You shouldn't be here! It's extremely dangerous! They would hang you on sight, Ziona, if they ever found out what you are! You must go quickly!"

Ziona shook her head. She rewound her hair to hide her ears. "I am here for you. You are my destiny, Cayden. I set out with one other, Sharisha, seventeen years ago to find the prophesied children. We did not know where to go or even what they would look like. We only knew to watch for the signs. We have been searching for you and your sister for seventeen years. We are your guardians. And we are your friends."

Cayden clutched at his tea, trying to warm his suddenly chilled fingers. He shook his head, trying to clear it. "Wait...seventeen years? How old are you?" She appeared to be no more than a couple years older than him.

She again laughed. "We are a very long-lived race, but by Primordial reckoning, I would be of a similar age to you."

"Is this a safe place," Cayden asked, "to have this kind of conversation?"

"I have placed wards in the soil around the tent to prevent eavesdropping. It is part of my earth magic."

"You have done what?"

"A ward is an invisible barrier. In this case, it keeps sound from travelling in or out from the boundary it surrounds. It is centered on me."

"Oh. So why are you so interested in me? Frankly, I think you have it all wrong. I have never even seen a Primordial prior to this. I have barely been out of my village, except to go to the market in the next village over. What does my sister have to do with any of this?"

"Cayden, look at me." Cayden met her gaze with defiance and a trace of fear visible in his green depths. "You have special abilities, don't you?" His eyes widened, as fear leapt within him. "When I really look at you, I see a blue aura surrounding you. It pulses like waves lapping at a shoreline. We see it around your sister too."

Cayden's eyes locked on hers, searched hers, seeking her sincerity, examining her heart. Ziona shivered under the intense scrutiny. Here was someone she could not lie to. His eyes commanded truth.

"We believe you have abilities you are hiding, or perhaps are not aware of yet. The queen, if she were to capture you, would order your execution on the spot. She has searched her entire reign to find you and your sister for she is aware of our prophecies, even if she does not believe in them.

"She sends soldiers into our lands, in an attempt to wipe out our peoples so no one will be able to aid you. She makes war on our villages, and we have had to abandon our homes, retreating to a sanctuary she does not know of. Even now, a new assault has been ordered and her soldiers march for the three passes into the Primordial lands across the Great Spine. She does all of this to try and find you and Avery…and here you sit right under her nose. Your sister is on her way to the sanctuary as we speak." Cayden tried to absorb Ziona's words. He tried to deny what she said, but the words rang true in his head.

"Avery glows too," he murmured absently.

Ziona paused. "You can see her glow?"

"Yes. I have always been able to see her glow. Why do others not see it?"

Ziona nodded. "It is because they are not of the blood."

"What blood?" Cayden asked, pinning her with his bright eyes again.

"Primordial blood Cayden, Royal Primordial blood." She waited for the explosion. She didn't have to wait for long.

Cayden stood up abruptly. "There is no way I am Primordial! I know who my mother and father are and they are not Primordial! What kind of foolishness is this?"

"The prophecies foretell of a prince and princess who would be born to humans but are of the blood. We do not understand how this is possible either. The prophecies do not explain it. Finding you both with this sign makes it ironclad. There can be no doubt as to who you two are."

Cayden sank back into his chair shaking his head in disbelief. *It isn't possible…is it? It's outlandish and absurd!* He was not of royal birth; he wasn't even important in his village. He was a farmer playing soldier.

Your flutes are an unusual talent, his conscience whispered; *a very dangerous talent.* If news of that particular talent were to reach the wrong ears, it would put a price on his head. He knew he would be hunted day and night. He frowned. Maybe the hunting had already started?

He lifted his head to meet her eyes, hands clasped in front, arms resting on his thighs. "You wanted to know about my abilities. Would you know if they are related to this theory of yours?"

"What kind of abilities?" Ziona cocked her head to one side, studying him.

"It must be kept an absolute secret. No one must ever know about it. It would be very dangerous news to share, especially in our present company. I like to carve. Flutes are my specialty. But when I play them animals gather."

He watched her closely, gauging her reaction to his words.

Ziona frowned. "I have never heard of any Shamanic prophecies associated with you. Are these animals real?"

"Of course they are real. They seem to be called by the music of my flutes."

"I have no idea." She hopped off the table and walked over to him. "We need to get you measured for those uniforms. Stand, please?"

Cayden stood up and at her prompting, held his arms out parallel to the floor. Ziona picked up a tape measure and measured the under arm measurement, armpit to wrist. She then jotted this measure in a book at her side. Next she measured his bicep circumference, wrist, neck, and waist. She then measured from the lowest neck bone down his back to his waist and then from his waist to the floor.

"It will take me about a week to make these up. I would like you to come back for a fitting every day at dinnertime. Do not worry about getting dinner in the camp. You can share my dinner and we can talk further then in private."

Cayden nodded. "Would you sew some hidden pockets in my uniform? I'd like a place to store my flutes on my person."

"I will put a pocket right here," she tapped his chest, over his heart, "and in the pant right here." She said, pointing at his thigh.

"I should be getting back to camp." He glanced back at her. "I am not sure I believe anything you have told me. But I do know one thing, I am no hero. I couldn't kill an animal, let alone a person. I have no stomach for it."

"What do you intend to do when a battle comes? You're a soldier in the legion. How can you avoid hurting anyone in battle?"

"I don't intend to be here long. I never did. I volunteered for reasons I would rather keep private, but it wasn't because I wanted to serve."

Ziona fingered her list of measurements, thinking. "Then perhaps we should make plans to break from the legion. It would be easiest to slip away when the legion is on the move," she mused. "Let me think on it. We will talk tomorrow when you return for your fitting. I will have one set ready by then."

Chapter 18

CAYDEN FINISHED SKINNING THE BARK off the willow branch. The supple wood was easy to strip, the bark falling away in curls. He was seated on a rotting log at the edge of a meadow. Two deer grazed knee-deep in the pasture in front of him, their heads popping up from the lush grasses every once in a while to check on his position. Free time was a rare commodity but when the opportunity presented itself, he could not resist the lure of the woods and his hands itched to carve. Carving soothed his wounded spirit and took his mind off the residual aches and pains of training.

As he carved, the bark-less wood revealed veins of yellow, green and—of all colours—pink. He spit on the wood and rubbed it in. The colours glowed. Fascinated, he trimmed the length to six and a half inches and then began to hollow out the middle. The pliable wood bent under his ministrations, soft as butter in his hands. He flared the end of the pipe into more of a bell shape. He hollowed out several petite finger holes along the shaft.

Putting down his tools, he inspected his work. The flute seemed feminine to him somehow, as though he was carving a little girl's doll. He fancied the bell-shaped bottom looked like the billowing form of a child's skirt as she twirled. His fingers followed the coloured lines of the wood. At the base, he carved small wing-like symbols and the oak symbol.

He then took out a soft cloth and picking up a small pot with some beeswax he had secured from the cook, rubbed the soft wax into the surface of the flute. The colours glowed like a rainbow. His heart swelled with pride and a grin spread across his face.

Satisfaction oozed from every pore. He closed up the pot and put it and the cloth back in his pocket.

Closing his eyes, he put pipe to lips and gently blew. A tinkling sound like a child's laughter sprang from the flute and danced across the air. The deer raised their heads in unison, ears twitching in interest.

This time, no animal came to him. When he opened his eyes, a child was standing in front of him in a shimmering turquoise tunic. She smiled at him impishly, foot tapping to the music. Cayden spilled backward off the log in surprise, yelping as he hit the ground. Pain flared in his overtaxed body. He scrambled around on all fours to see if she was still there.

She waggled her fingers at him, mystery and mischief in her eyes.

Cayden, his mouth dry, croaked, "Who are you? How did you get here?"

"I am called Aossi and I live here. How did you get here?"

Cayden slowly sat back on the ground, afraid she would run away. He ignored the question.

"Why are you here?"

"You called me, didn't you?" She touched a hand to his flute.

"I called you? How can that be? My flutes have only attracted animals before." The words were out of his mouth before he realized he had spoken them aloud.

"Do you imagine only animals are attracted to your songs?" She tilted her head to one side, studying him. "Why play if not to have others enjoy it?"

Cayden shook his head, bemused. "Of course, I play for others to enjoy." He felt a twinge of guilt at the lie. He had never played his flutes for anyone. She winked at him, knowing it to be a lie. Cayden flushed in embarrassment.

"Let me tell you something, Cayden of the Cliffs. Music is a life force, a common well of unity that all may freely drink from. Music is a magic that can bind the worlds together. The soul of music is the very breath of life. All creation is bound together through this, yes?" She studied him further. "I think you know this already." Her mouth curved into an ear-splitting smile that lit up her face. "So why are you surprised that I came to hear you play?"

"But…what are you?" Cayden asked, bemused.

Aossi grinned and ignored his question. "That is a conversation for another day. For now, I must go, but know that I am only ever a song away." With a spin and a twirl of turquoise, she vanished right before his eyes.

Cayden gasped and slipped as he spun around, trying to see where she had gone. The deer lowered their heads and went back to munching on the grass. Cayden carefully placed the flute in the lined inner pocket Ziona had sewn for him.

He sat back down on the log, hands clasped and arms resting on his knees. Who was she and how did she vanish into thin air? He never had a person show up before. *Wait*. Was she a person? How had she known his name?

A harsh cry pierced the silence of the woods, and glancing up, he spied eagles soaring in lazy circles above his head. There were four of them, uncharacteristically grouped and circling in slow patterns above him.

He walked back over to the willow tree where he had found the branch. It was a huge tree, like the old oak tree back home, its crown high in the sky and its sprawling branches swooning back to the ground, its roots dug deeply into the bank of the river. It was ancient.

Suddenly, the deer's heads shot up and they froze. The eagles screeched, as one of their members plummeted from the sky. The eagle crashed to earth a short distance from where Cayden sat. The deer bounded away into the safety of the woods.

Cayden ran over to where the eagle was lying. It lay on its back, flapping its wings feebly. An arrow had pierced its body. Cayden knelt beside the dying bird. The eagle locked eyes on him and stopped flapping. Cayden *felt* its thoughts. It seemed at peace and glad of his presence. He placed his hand on the bird's breast, thinking to comfort it.

A jolt of searing pain ran up Cayden's arm like an electric shock. The bird arched its back and flopped back down, no longer breathing. At the same moment, Cayden saw a bluish mist rise from the bird. The mist gathered into a semi-transparent form of a bird with a wingspan as tall as a man. Its feathers were layered in blues and reds and purples. Its head was bald except for a small curl of feather on its crest. Cayden thought it resembled his mental picture of thunderbirds in the tales he had been told as a child.

The apparition steadied and Cayden felt thoughts being pushed into his head. The foreign intrusion made his head explode with pain. "Are you Mac Mak? The thunderbird of the stories?" He clutched at his head, trying to still the pain of the foreign communication.

"*Mick-mak.* My name is Mik'maq. In the old tongue, it means Allied Brothers. Thank you for aiding in my rebirth, young Cayden." Cayden didn't reply. His mind was foggy and slow with the pain in his arm and mind. "You and I are now brothers. You may call on me at any time and I will answer that call."

The thunderbird launched itself into the air, soaring over the clearing, and disappeared into the distance. The remaining eagles followed it. Cayden eyes followed the eagles' flight and abruptly he found himself seeing through the thunderbird's eyes. His focus narrowed and sharpened as he flew over the land. His stomach lurched as it dived steeply toward the ground. Cayden cried out in alarm, squeezing his eyes shut and throwing out his hands to stop his fall, landing on his hands and knees on the dirt. The thunderbird chuckled in his mind and then broke contact.

Cayden gulped and opened his eyes. He was still in the meadow on his hands and knees. He stood up, legs quivering and as he did so. Two men walked into view about twenty feet away from him. They both carried bows. Spotting Cayden, they walked over.

"You found the eagle! We weren't sure whether we had hit it or not!" The younger man picked up the eagle by its feet. "These feathers should be worth something in trade with the merchants. I guess it wasn't a complete waste of a hunting trip." They walked away, not waiting for a reply.

Cayden shivered. He felt chilled, as though he was catching a cold. His awareness of the eagles did not diminish. He felt stronger in aspects, his eyesight was sharper, his focus clearer, yet he shivered. *What is happening to me?*

Rubbing his arms, he headed back to camp. He couldn't help glancing at the sky.

Chapter 19

THE FOLLOWING DAYS SETTLED into a pattern for Cayden. Roll call at dawn, breakfast, sword training, archery training, pike drills, a break for lunch, and then hand to hand combat, flail and shields, and finally ending with halberds. Dinner would follow and then roll call before settling down for the night. He slipped off to Ziona's for his "fittings," sharing dinner with her on those evenings. He found her to be a smart and engaging companion, quick of wit and with a cheery disposition. He enjoyed her company immensely.

Cayden discovered he also enjoyed learning the forms of the sword and the pike drills. The flail drills usually left him heavily bruised as he was not as tall or as strong as the others in his training group. Some of those men reminded him of gorillas because their arms were so long. Cayden swore they would drag on the ground if they relaxed them enough. Cayden, however, was quick and light on his feet, perfectly suited to sword play. His skills improved rapidly.

Sergeant Perez never failed to set Cayden up to receive the worst positions with the worst equipment he could find. Sergeant Perez loathed Cayden. His narrowed eyes followed him everywhere, his hatred nakedly displayed on his face. Cayden found himself watching his back. Sergeant Perez had gathered a set of sycophants, who shadowed him like he was a lord.

Two weeks into this new routine, Sergeant Perez arrived at the training grounds with some older men of higher rank.

Sergeant Perez's evil grin split his fleshy lips, displaying yellowed teeth, and a satisfied expression spread across his face. *He looks triumphant.* Cayden broke out in a sweat, shivering in the breeze tugging his shirt. Someone had just walked across his grave.

"Line up, you lazy scum! Inspection!" Perez roared. They took their positions and snapped to attention.

The tall thin officer had a hooked nose that he stabbed into each of the men's faces, inspecting them with an intensity that frightened Cayden. Perez followed in his wake, re-inspecting the line of nervous men, as though attempting to read the secrets they hid. Perez, arms clasped behind his back, watched the reaction of the officer as he walked the line, intently examining each face. He paused when he reached Cayden, his narrow eyes searching his face.

"Bring the two guards who were with Sandez on guard duty that day." Perez's grin widened maliciously.

Two men jogged up to the group, dressed in scout's camouflage and saluted before Perez. Cayden had not seen them in the camp since their arrival. "Sir!" they snapped to the two officers.

"Do either of you recognize any of the men in this line up?"

The two scouts slowly walked past the line of men at attention and one paused directly in front of Cayden. His eyes roved over Cayden's features, studying him intently. Straightening, he turned to Sergeant Perez and said, "Yes! This man was with the heavier set man, who fought like a cornered badger. I do not know if he killed Sandez though."

It was enough for Perez, however.

"Cayden Tiernan, you are under arrest for murder!" He motioned to a couple of his cronies standing a little ways back. "Bind his hands and take him to the prisoner tents."

Cayden's tent mates roared their disapproval as he was roughly dragged out of line and his arms yanked behind him and tied securely with a length of rope.

"Back in line, you scum, unless you want to join him?"

Darius caught his eye, shock and sadness painted on his face. Cayden shook his head slightly, warning him to not get involved.

Cayden recognized the soldier who had identified him now. He was one of the three who had surprised him and Ryder that miserable day. The nameless soldier grinned as evilly as Perez did. "You thought to escape our justice by hiding in our midst? You will live to regret that day, boy. You will regret it very much, I think," he said softly. The threat in his voice made Cayden's mouth go dry. He did not answer.

The guard-turned-scout punched him hard in the stomach. Cayden doubled over, vomiting on the grass. He only kept his feet because his arms were being held by the two soldiers who had bound him. The soldier lifted his head and punched him in the face. Cayden's head snapped back and he felt his nose break. Blood spurted and ran down his face, dripping off his chin.

Rough hands jerked on his arms, hauling him away. A canvas sack was pulled over his head. He stumbled in his captor's grip, the uneven ground tripping his feet. His eyes watered with the pain of his broken nose. Twice more he was randomly punched in the stomach, eliciting a groan. Once they let him fall to the ground and then proceeded to kick him with sharp-toed boots. Cayden thought he heard Perez chuckle. Cayden felt a rib crack. Groaning, he could do nothing to stop the beating. He couldn't even protect himself with his hands tied behind his back.

Suddenly, it stopped and Cayden was hauled to his feet again. He collapsed as the world tilted around him. They dragged him the rest of the way and with a last shove, threw him into what felt like a cart. The bag was ripped from his head as he fell, still bound. A metal-sounding door clanged shut and there was a sound of a key being turned in a lock. Waves of nausea washed over Cayden as the world spun and he vomited. Everything receded from Cayden in a rush and he slumped, unconscious to the wooden floor.

Chapter 20

WHEN HE CAME TO, it was fully dark. He tried to move, only to find his hands were still tied. He felt around in his mouth with his tongue. All of his teeth seemed to be intact. He spit the blood out. The simple act of lifting his head caused searing pain in his ribs. He groaned out loud. He had definitely broken a rib or two. He moved his legs, moaning with the effort. *Nothing broken there*, he thought, panting with the exertion.

He peered around cautiously. He appeared to be in a metal cage of some sort outside of the camp. He thought it was one of the cages used by one of the butchers who supplied the camp with meat to haul livestock. Why was he outside the camp? This was not the prisoner tents. What was Perez playing at?

Cayden did not spot a sentry, which didn't mean there wasn't one. He tested his bonds, wriggling his fingers and trying to loosen the ropes. He felt around for the tied ends. His eyes searched the cage, looking for a nail or a sharp metal edge to fray the ropes on. There was nothing in his immediate line of sight. He tried to shift his position, but the flash of pain in his ribs made him suck in a deep breath and groan aloud.

"Cayden…Cayden, are you awake?" Darius's shadowed face appeared over the edge of the cage floor. "I came as soon as I could sneak past the patrol," Darius whispered.

"I am awake," Cayden whispered back.

"I went to the prisoner tents to see you, but they said you were not brought to them. Rather than hang around and ask questions that would raise suspicion, I left. On the way back to our tent, I saw one of Perez's cronies slip off in this direction. I decided to follow him and he led me straight to here. He was replacing another guard. Don't worry. He is out cold."

"That's great," Cayden croaked. He could barely speak; he was so thirsty. "He wouldn't happen to have had the key on him for this buggy?"

Darius grinned, holding up a round key ring. "Let's find out, shall we?" Darius reached for the lock on the back of the cage. Cayden lost sight of him, but he heard the key scraping in the lock.

It clicked open and Darius hopped in beside him. He produced a knife and quickly cut the ropes binding Cayden. Darius helped him to sit up. Cayden groaned and clutched his stomach. "You shouldn't have helped me. They will have no compunction about killing you for helping me."

"Never mind about that right now. Where should we go? You can't travel far in your current condition."

"Take me to Ziona's tent. She will know what to do."

Placing Cayden's arm over his shoulders, Darius helped Cayden get to his feet. Cayden bit down hard on his lip to keep from crying out. The cage spun crazily in his vision and he nearly fainted. Deep breaths were agony due to the broken ribs.

"Come on, Cayden, we have to get out of here. If you pass out, I will have to carry you."

Darius helped Cayden to the door and then gently lowered him to sit on the edge of the opening. Hopping down, he put Cayden's arm around his shoulders again and pulled him into a quick walk. Cayden stumbled and passed out twice during the short journey, ending in front of Ziona's tent. Ziona took his other side and helped bring him in, lowering him onto her cot. Cayden did not remember actually hitting the cot. Everything went black.

When he came to again, darkness was fading into dawn. Darius slumped in the chair, snoring softly. He appeared uncomfortable but slept on.

Ziona bent over Cayden, slightly out of focus. She pried one eye open and flashed the light from a tinder stick in front of his eyes. She then did the same to the other. Satisfied, she raised his shirt and examined the poultice she had placed on his ribs. She lifted the edge of the cloth and then placed it back down again.

"How are you feeling?" Her green eyes loomed large in his sight.

Cayden thought that her eyes were the eyes of an angel. His lips to curved in response or at least they tried to. His lip was too swollen to form the proper shape. Raising his hand to his face, he winced as he touched his nose. It felt like badly mashed potatoes to him, all lumpy and squishy.

"I have had better nights." He grinned crookedly. "Why did you let Darius stay? He should have snuck back into camp. Now everyone will know he is with me. He will be a wanted man too."

"He refused to leave. He said you two were a team and he had pledged himself to you a few weeks ago?" She raised her eyebrows in enquiry.

"Oh…that…well I didn't mean it literally. I didn't mean for him to follow me into trouble."

"That's what friends do, Cayden."

Ziona reached over for a pitcher of water and poured a glass for Cayden. She held up his head and helped tip the liquid into his mouth. He swallowed gratefully, washing the tinny taste of blood from his mouth.

Replacing the glass on the chest, Ziona sat down on the edge of the cot. "So, are you going to tell me what this is all about? Somehow I think I am going to learn why you decided to join the legion in the first place."

Cayden nodded and quickly told her about the incident with Ryder. Toward the end of the telling, he noticed Darius had woken and was listening intently also.

"So you didn't actually kill that soldier? Ryder did?" Darius asked.

"Yes. I had to hide him and protect the village."

"Then you are innocent," said Darius.

"Or guilty by association," said Ziona.

"None of this explains why they put me in a cage outside of the camp." Cayden eyes flicked from one set to the other. "If this was about that night, I should be standing trial for the legion. But they didn't even report they had found me. Something else is going on."

"I quite agree," said Ziona. "However, short of capturing and interrogating Perez and the mysterious second soldier, we cannot know what their motives are. What is certain is that there are parties interested in you, Cayden, outside of the legion itself."

Darius stared at Cayden, puzzled. Cayden felt equally mystified.

"I have done some healing to your ribs overnight. There were two cracked on the left side, but I think you will find they have mended now. Try to sit up, slowly now."

They helped Cayden sit up. The pain was still present, but it was a shadow of what it had been before.

"How were you able to heal my ribs so quickly?"

"I will explain another time," Ziona said with a glance at Darius. "Now, what do we do with you, young man?" She turned to face Darius fully, arms crossed over her chest.

"I'm not going anywhere without Cayden. I swore to help him and that is exactly what I intend to do." Darius scrubbed the toe of his boot on the soft ground. "That is, if you will allow me to stay, mistress. I go where Cayden goes."

"Well I think it is time we packed up and got away from this arena. It will be too difficult for you to be outside, Cayden. Too many people know you. You have approximately an hour and a half until dawn and an hour before roll call." Darius nodded. "I need you to slip back into camp and gather your and Cayden's satchels. Take only your satchels. Anything else will slow you down. Meet me back here in forty-five minutes. Be warned. If you are discovered, we will not be rescuing you nor will we wait for you."

"I understand, mistress." Darius left the tent.

"Now, we gather what we need. I have supplies stashed in other locations. There is nothing in this tent that I cannot carry in my satchel and leaving the tent up will give the appearance I am gone for the day and will return. I will leave word with a neighbouring tent that I have gone to the last village we passed to purchase some supplies. You will go into the woods out the back of my tent." She reached for a knife sitting on the cutting table and quickly slit the tent back at a seam. "Head out into the woods. I want you to make a wide circle around the camp and then join back up with the road about three miles west of here. You will find an ancient Primordial pine in the meadow off to the side of the road. Behind the great pine is a cave. I will meet you there in a day or two. There are supplies in the cave. You will stay there until I can meet up with you, all right? I want to be sure no one connects my disappearance with yours." *And I want to find out who is interested in you enough to try to kidnap you out of the middle of the legion,* she thought to herself.

Handing him a flask of water and slipping some bread and cheese into his pockets, she gestured towards the slit canvas. "I have put more medicine in the flask of water. It will heal you as you travel. Now go. I will send Darius after you as soon as he arrives, but you must go."

Cayden stood up slowly. His concern for her reflected in his green eyes. "Stay safe, OK?" He bent down and hugged her fiercely and then slipped out the back of the tent, disappearing into the trees.

Chapter 21

ZIONA GATHERED HER SATCHEL and flipped back the flap. In went the potions she had made for the journey, bandages, her Primordial clothing, and several human changes of clothes. She carefully packed anything that would reveal her true ethnic roots. She must remain anonymous. She gathered thread and a large stitching awl to repair the tent seam after Darius arrived. She burned the leftover dressings from tending to Cayden's wounds in the fire pit in the middle of her tent. The flames sparked and eagerly consumed the offering.

Her thoughts drifted back to Cayden. Who was after him? Did they know who and what he was? She shivered at the thought. She had suspicions as to who might be behind the kidnapping, for that was what it had been in reality. He had been kidnapped in broad daylight with over twenty witnesses. It was a boldly brilliant move by a dangerous adversary. She would have to stick as close as bark on a tree to him from now on.

She doused the fire with the last of the water from her basin and then pulled out several unfinished garments and laid them out on the table. She placed scissors and a spool of thread next to them, putting them down carelessly as though she had stopped in the middle of working on them. She partially straightened the blankets on the cot, mussing them enough to appear to have been slept in. With a last glance around, she buckled her travel bag and waited.

Five minutes later, Darius's head popped into the tent, followed by his body. He was not alone. Five of Cayden's tent mates filed into the tent behind him.

Darius carried his and Cayden's satchels. The other five men were likewise attired, carrying packs on their backs.

"What is the meaning of this?" Ziona snapped at him, frowning with displeasure.

"When I got back, these guys were awake and whispering in the tent. They had also gone to check on Cayden and had received the same response. They were trying to decide where to go searching when I arrived. I couldn't think of anything else to do but bring them along, seeing as they knew I had been out all night searching for Cayden."

"Mistress," piped up James, "Cayden is a good lad. He didn't deserve how they treated him. Something is wrong with Sergeant Perez. He didn't report back for roll call last night. It's like he disappeared right after he arrested Cayden." He shrugged at his companions. "Well, we figured there was something rotten in the camp and it was time we decided where our loyalties lie. We want to help Cayden escape." The others nodded their heads in agreement.

"All right, I don't have time for this. Darius, you are to take your companions and follow Cayden." She quickly went over the instructions she had given Cayden. "You are to hold at the cave and stay out of sight! Do not leave the cave until I arrive. Is that clear?" Heads bobbed in understanding. "Now go, it will soon be light. Be as silent as a hawk on the wing." She held back the cut canvas, and Darius led the way out the back of the tent. They were soon swallowed by the forest.

As soon as the last man exited, Ziona stitched up the slice in the canvas. It took about ten minutes to repair the damage, but in the end, it was completely invisible to the eye.

With a last inspection, Ziona picked up her travel bag and slung it on her shoulder. She went to her horse and saddled the mare quickly. Next, she threw a halter on the mule and led both animals away from her tent.

She stopped at the next tent and called out to the occupant. "Mandy, would you watch my tent for a few hours? I need to go back to Tintern to pick up some more supplies."

"No problem, Ziona. I will take care of things here till you get back."

"Thanks! I should be back before dark, but I may also stay over in the town. I fancy a hot meal and a bath."

"Not to worry!" Mandy hollered through the tent wall.

Ziona mounted her horse and with a gentle pat on her neck, urged her into a slow walk, the mule following with a plod.

She took the road leading away from the camp. It disappeared from view as the sun split the horizon. She was unsure if anyone was watching her, so for that reason alone, she decided she must make the journey all the way to Tintern. Her plan was to purchase some supplies, book a room at the inn, and then quietly leave again after dark and travel by night back to Cayden. If her suspicions were correct as to who had attempted to kidnap him, then perhaps she was being watched also. She kept her pace leisurely, as though she didn't have a care in the world.

She reached the village about noon and dismounted at the inn, a shabby establishment called The King's Ransom. *The cost lived up to its name,* she thought, as she laid out the coin for her night's stay. The innkeeper, a portly man with a balding pate, provided her a main floor room by the rear door as requested so "she would have the quietest room in the inn away from the rowdy late night crowd." She picked up her key and nodded her thanks.

She gathered her horse and mule and led them around the back to the stables. She handed them off to the stable boy and requested they each get an extra measure of grain each and a good rubdown. She flipped him a coin for his consideration and he grinned back in thanks.

She paused in thought. "Oh and when you are done grooming my mare, please saddle her again? I may decide to go for a gentle ride later this afternoon. Leave her in her stall, saddled." He nodded and led the animals away.

Ziona carried her travel bag to her room. Opening the door, she found a modest room, outfitted with a simple bed, a lumpy mattress, a wash stand with a chipped bowl and mismatched pitcher. On the wall hung a scratched silver mirror and a ladder back chair placed under the window completed the furnishings.

She closed the door and locked it. She was weary and needed rest. She had not dared to sleep after Cayden had arrived injured so severely. Besides, he had been in her bed. She stretched out on the lumpy mattress, fully clothed, and closed her eyes. It felt like heaven. In less than a minute, she was fast asleep.

Chapter 22

SERGEANT PEREZ CRINGED as the deeply hooded figure paused in front of him. It was a full foot taller and Perez imagined cold slimy hands were hidden by the long full sleeves. Death stalked him and played with him.

"You let him escape," the voice hissed, not quite human sounding. "You had him tied and locked in a metal cage and he still escaped."

"No, my lord!" Perez trembled, afraid to gaze too deeply into the hood. "The boy was aided by friends. Our guard was knocked out. We do not know how they found out where he was being held. Please, my lord, I can find him." Eager to please, he implored the Charun, tenting his fingers in supplication.

"You failed," hissed the faceless voice, "and I have no use for defective tools." It reached out with scaly hands and grabbed Perez by the throat. Perez eyes bulged as his air was cut off. The spectral figure squeezed and bones snapped. Perez dropped to the dirt below like a practice dummy with its ties cut.

The figure seemed to float as it rotated. Three other eerie figures, similarly garbed, stood silently waiting. "Eliminate the humans. Leave none alive."

Heads bowed in acceptance of the order. They ghosted from the room, black phantoms of death descending on an unsuspecting foe.

***

Cayden wearily sank down onto a fallen tree blocking his path. He had been walking for several hours now. Dawn had arrived but the rising sun was not able to penetrate the dense vegetation surrounding him. He had stayed deep in the woods, using the fading darkness as a compass to keep him going west.

He pulled the flask of water from his pocket and took a swig. It was cool and minty tasting. His ribs ached still, but the pain was bearable. He shook his head, amazed. How had Ziona been able to heal him so quickly? His insides warmed as the liquid reached his stomach and he felt strength returning to his muscles. He took a deep breath. The pain in his ribs receded to a whisper. His nose had also returned to a normal shape and size.

A twig snapped. Cayden's head shot up, examining the forest to the west. He froze, his ears straining to catch any out-of-place sound. The brush quivered and parted, revealing a silver-haired wolf. The wolf sniffed the air then limped toward him. An arrow was jutting from her body. She sat down beside Cayden and looked at him, pain shadowing her eyes. The arrow had entered the right shoulder near the neck. The arrowhead and gone clean through and was sticking out from the underside of the shoulder blade.

Cayden, without giving it any thought to his actions, knelt beside the wolf. Blood stained her silvery coat. The wolf fixed her ice blue eyes on him and whined. Cayden reached for his water bottle and poured a small amount of the water into the lid of the flask. He offered it to the wolf, who slurped it up gratefully. The pain receded from her eyes.

"I can't take the arrow out here. Can you come with me to a safe place?" The wolf cocked its head, listening. Cayden felt her acceptance. She licked his hand and then grabbed his pant leg and started pulling on it. She walked a little ways away and then came back and pulled on his pant leg again. "You want me to follow you?" She sat down and waited, licking at her wound.

Cayden replaced the flask and stood up. "OK. Lead the way."

The wolf headed back into the trees in a westerly direction. They had pushed through the brush for a time when they came to a small clearing. A pungent odour assaulted his nose. It wrinkled in response. A wolf pack of about fifteen animals lay bleeding in the field. Flies buzzed and rose from the carcasses as Cayden walked through the slaughter field, examining the scene. The wolves had all been shot by arrows. Hoof prints mixed in with the blood had churned up a reddish mud. The attackers had been on horseback. Why would anyone attack a wolf pack? It made no sense.

The silvery wolf yipped to gain Cayden's attention. He walked over to her, where she pawed at a jet black wolf lying on its side, three black-shafted, black-tipped arrows piercing its body. This one was male. The one blue eye seemed to plead with Cayden. The wolf was still alive.

Hesitant, Cayden placed a hand gently on his head. A jolt of liquid fire shot up his arm and a conscience pressed hard on his brain. Cayden cried out as the wolf's essence was transferred to him. Cayden fell on his side, twitching, his limbs jerking uncontrollably. Slowly, the tremors left his body. The wolf took one last breath, trembled, and was still.

From the body of the wolf rose a form of a wolf but larger, three times the size of the wolf dead on the ground. The form solidified and unfolded as though in slow motion to stand on its hind legs. Hairy arms rippled with cords of muscles that flowed across to join an equally muscled chest matted with hair. The face of the dead wolf gazed at Cayden with long wicked teeth curling from its snout. It snorted and Cayden cringed back in fright. "Do not be afraid. You have given me the chance to live again. I have given you my mortal energy and spirit and you have given me my mythical form."

Cayden gazed back at the creature in shock. "What are you?" he croaked.

"I am a werewolf. We are often thought of as evil, just as the wolf is misunderstood. I and my kind will serve you. You need only to call." The werewolf glanced around at the killing field and a ferocious light blazed to life in his eyes. "Look closely at this scene for you can learn much about what hunts you. We were slaughtered to keep from bringing you warning." He gazed at the silvery wolf beside Cayden. "Take care of Sheba for she was my she-alpha."

With a final glance around, the werewolf bounded off and was soon swallowed in the trees. Cayden sensed his passing but still retained a connection to the werewolf and could sense his presence in his mind.

Cayden collected several of the arrows lying around, wrapping them in leaves and then tucked them in his pocket, careful to not touch the blackened tips. As he headed west again, he noticed a dead wolf with a piece of cloth clamped in its jaws. He pried the cloth loose and placed it in his pocket with the arrows.

He stroked Sheba's soft head. "Are you ready to go, girl?" She raised her head and then lowered it, nudging the dead black wolf, urging him to rise. When he did not move, she raised her muzzle to the sky and howled a long, sad call. The sound was so mournful Cayden's chest constricted. There was no answering call. Tears sparked in his eyes. She trotted off toward the west. Cayden followed.

***

Ryder gagged as vomit welled up into his throat, burning with the intensity of his disgust. He swallowed, the acidic lump burning a path back down into his queasy stomach. The tinny, maggoty smells of blood and body fluids clogged his nose and added a sauce to the bile attempting to escape his body.

The carnage was beyond his experience. His gaze took in a decapitated head sitting on top of a tent pole, blood staining the wooden shaft and pooling on the ground below. The tent was whole and untouched; however, the canvas surface was sprayed with pieces of entrails and bits of bone. The part of his brain protecting his mind from shock logically attempted to compute the amount of human residue needed to constitute an entire body. Whether a part or whole body, it was clear it had exploded on the side of the tent.

Gingerly, Ryder stepped around a corpse lying at his feet, careful not to step on the flayed remains.

This scene was repeated throughout the camp with little variation. The attack appeared to have been designed to create the maximum amount of carnage. Ryder could only think of one reason to do so: to elicit stark terror from any who viewed the scene. *It's working!* His limbs trembled as he fought them for control. Behind him, he heard noisy retching from his companions.

He forced himself to turn in a complete circle to survey the scene. Cayden could be in here somewhere, still alive. They had to search.

"Break into groups of two and search for survivors." He did not need to mention which survivor they were to search for.

The group of twenty men split into teams and fanned out through what remained of the legion. Ryder was joined by the baker's son, Joshua, who had begged to come with him when he had left home. Ryder had initially refused to take him along as he was only fifteen, but in the end Joshua had followed them out of town and continued to follow despite Ryder's repeated urgings for Joshua to go home.

Everyone with Ryder was a volunteer from the village. Rumours of Ryder's plan to help Cayden escape the legion had been whispered through town and one by one they had begged to come with him. Ryder now wished he had set out alone. This was not what he had expected to find. It seemed they had walked into the middle of a war...but what war? He had not heard any rumours the entire trip while following the path of the legion.

Joshua, swallowing heavily and wiping his mouth on the sleeve of his jacket, picked up a broken spear and prodded at the bodies they passed to see if any stirred. Flies buzzed around the carcasses, billowing up and resettling on the bodies after they passed. Vultures huddled in groups at one edge of the camp, squawking and fighting over a body. They had had to chase them off at first, but the vultures were overcoming their fear of the boys quickly.

Nothing moved except for the vultures and the flies. Nothing stirred.

The strange thing was Ryder did not see any enemy soldiers amongst the dead. *Surely they had killed some of the attacking force. Had the attackers carried off their dead then to hide their identities? If so, why was there no trail away from the camp?* They had scouted the perimeter to be sure there was no ambush waiting for them. There was no sign of a retreating army. Not even of fleeing soldiers.

Nothing about the scene before him made sense. He shivered, fear making his heart thunder in his head. He wanted to be away from this place. He wanted to run. But he searched on.

Joshua flipped over a tumbled water cart and jumped back in surprise. Huddled beneath the overturned wagon covered in mud and blood was a lad about Joshua's age. His eyes were wild in his ashen face. He was not wearing a uniform. The lad raised terrified eyes to Joshua and then cried out in relief, the flood of tears streaking his face.

Hearing the sound, Ryder strode over to the survivor. A witness had been found.

Ryder squatted down and gently gripped the lad's shoulders. "It's OK. We are here to help you. My name is Ryder. Who are you?"

The lad gulped and whispered, "Michale, sir."

"What has happened here, Michale? Who did this?" Joshua knelt beside Ryder, blocking the scene from Michale's eyes.

Fixing his gaze on Ryder, Michale whispered, "Black phantoms."

This was incomprehensible to Ryder. *What is this black phantom? A kind of ghost? Or an evil spirit?*

"Do you know Cayden Tiernan? Did you see him? Is he here in the camp still?"

"He was here, sir, but he left two days ago. Or maybe he was arrested. I saw some men taking him away. He was not here when the camp was attacked."

Ryder blew out the breath he hadn't realized he was holding. They did not need to linger on the dead, only confirm there were no other survivors.

He helped pull Michale to his feet and led him back to their horses on the west side of the camp. Michale kept his face averted from the scene surrounding him and allowed Ryder to blindly lead him out of the camp.

Reaching the horses, Ryder sat Michale on the ground. "Stay with him, Joshua. Get him something to eat from our packs and some water. I will be back shortly."

Relief flooded over Ryder as he went back into the camp turned graveyard, his steps a little lighter for the news. Cayden was not here when this happened. They would continue to search for him. He would find him.

His men were gathered on the eastern edge of the camp. When Ryder reached them, they confirmed they had found no other survivors.

"Gather up as many useful weapons as you can find. We will load them on the spare mule. Whoever did this may still be around and I, personally, would like to be armed if they return. In fact, I would rather not be here at all." The weapons would not help them repel such a foe, based on what had happened here. *Would any weapon be effective?*

"Also, gather any of the horses that are still nearby. We may need a change of mount along the way." Curiously, no horses had been harmed and they grazed in groups at the edge of the camp.

Twenty men had arrived at the camp that morning. Twenty-one left the camp heading along the western road in search of Cayden. The vultures resettled to feast as they rode away.

Chapter 23

CAYDEN REACHED THE CAVE just before dark. It was cleverly hidden. The entrance was a slit in the stone outcropping, the angle left the opening in perpetual shadow. One could walk within ten feet of the opening and not see it unless one knew to look for it.

Entering the cave, he found a large cavern hollowed back into the hillside. The cave was stocked with supplies. A racking system had been installed along one wall that contained thrush sleeping mats, blankets stacked in neat piles, lanterns and lantern fuel, and cooking utensils and pots on the top shelf.

The bottom shelf contained sacks of dried beans, corn and peas, ground flour, bottles of oil, bags of dried berries, fruits, and nuts. Dried meats rounded out the basic supplies. A small spring bubbled at the back of the cave.

Selecting a lantern already half full of oil, Cayden carried it over to the mud brick cooking oven already stacked with kindling. He gathered the flint and steel from the shelf and, kneeling, rained sparks into the fluffy starter. It leapt to life and caught the dried sticks above. Cayden added a couple of smaller pieces of wood from the stacked wood pile at the back to the fire. Soon a cheery blaze was burning in the hearth. He fetched a pot and a kettle and filled both at the spring then set them atop the cooking hearth.

Sheba watched all this from a position she had taken up at the cave entrance. Cayden knew she was guarding his back while he worked. He felt her presence in his mind and the other wolves distantly. None remained of Sheba's pack.

The water in the pot bubbled. Cayden added some dried salt pork, dried beans, and some dried onions. He gave the mixture a quick stir and the fetched the tin of tea from the shelf, sprinkling a hand full of leaves into the kettle.

He then joined Sheba at the mouth of the cave, satchel in hand. He sat down beside her, pulled out his flask with the healing water, a sharp knife, and some bandaging material. He stroked her fur. She rested her chin on his thigh.

"I need to take that arrow out now, girl." She lifted her eyes in response to his voice, trust in her eyes. "I will snap the shaft off as close to the entry point as I can. I need to pull on the arrow to get the rest out of you. OK?" He did not know if she understood his words or if it was the tone of his voice.

Gritting his teeth, he set to cutting the shaft of the arrow. Sheba growled and squirmed as the bolt shifted in her skin. The shaft broke off with a snap. "I am going to pull on the arrowhead here now. OK?" She panted, seeming to understand. Cayden gripped the arrowhead and quickly pulled. Sheba yelped and whimpered. The arrow pulled free. Fresh blood poured from the wound. Cayden quickly soaked two bandages in the water and pressed them to the wounds and held them. Sheba shuddered and lowered her head to her paws, panting. Slowly she relaxed as the water's soothing healing took effect. Cayden wrapped the cloths in place with more bandaging and tied them off. He then fetched a bowl from the shelf and poured the last of the water into it and placed it in front of Sheba. She thirstily drank it down.

Suddenly, Sheba's head came up and she growled a low growl. She stood up, hackles rising along her back. Cayden got to his feet and peered out of the cleft. Men were approaching on foot. The lead man paused and knelt examining Cayden's trail, and then their heads swivelled toward the cave.

"Do not move!" Cayden commanded, as he grabbed Sheba's scruff. He wished he had a weapon. Sheba would have to do. She growled low in her throat and shifted in front of Cayden, sensing his alarm.

"Cayden, it's me, Darius." Darius stepped forward, hands displayed for Cayden. He jerked his head towards his companions. "They wanted to come help you. They were waiting for me when I returned to the tent."

"It's OK, Sheba. They are friends." She continued to growl protectively and then licked his hand. He scratched her behind the ear.

They approached the cave and came to an abrupt halt as the wolf growled warningly at them from the shadowed entrance. Darius stopped in surprise. "What are you doing with a wolf?" Darius handed Cayden his satchel that he had retrieved from their shared tent. Sheba's lips curled back in warning at the movement. Darius snatched his hand away and backed up.

Cayden patted Sheba comfortingly. "We found we needed each other and joined forces. Never hurts to have an extra pair of eyes, especially ones as sharp as hers."

"Yes…but a wolf?" The others crowded in around Darius, leery of approaching Cayden while Sheba still rumbled warning.

Cayden shrugged. "Come on in. I have a stew cooking. With a few more beans, there should be enough for everyone." Sheba followed him back to the fire as the men filtered in and took up positions along the one wall. Her eyes followed them, marking their movements. She took up her position at the door again and lay down, clearly guarding the entrance once more.

The smell of the cooking stew drew the men like butterflies to nectar and they crowded around the pot, sniffing appreciatively. Cayden tossed in some more beans and some additional dried pork and let the stew cook while he sorted through the contents of his satchel. He felt around the base and found that all his essentials were there. He could feel his flutes in the bottom of his satchel, untouched.

Cayden gave the pot a final stir and then ladled stew into the wooden bowls. Famished, they set to eating, gobbling down the food without speaking.

After pouring a cup of tea for himself, Cayden brought a bowl with pork scraps to Sheba. He then settled with his back against the wall between the newcomers and Sheba. She thumped her tail and ate the offering hungrily.

"So tell me, Darius, how did you all come to be here?" Cayden's gaze took in all five men. *How well do I really know them?*

"We insisted on coming, Cayden." Pieter poured himself a cup of tea also. "We all felt bad about what went down back at camp. Sergeant Perez was completely out of line. When we couldn't find you or Darius later on, we knew something bad was going on. He acted strangely toward you from the first day. We all saw it."

Darius took up the story. "So they followed me back to where Ziona was waiting. Sergeant Perez never showed up for roll call, not the evening or the morning one. Ziona sent us on this way to catch up with you."

"Cayden, what's going on? Why did they accuse you of murdering a soldier?" Pieter asked. "The man with Sergeant Perez, he's not a regular soldier of the legion. He arrived a couple days before you did." The other men nodded in agreement.

"We were told he was sent by the queen. He roamed around the camp, checking out the younger recruits. We never saw him do much of anything else," said James. "I think he is some kind of military police or the queen's personal guard. He asked a lot of questions about everyone's background, where they were from, that kind of thing. Strange man, we all thought. It was like he was hunting someone though. We dubbed him 'the Inquisitor' as a nickname." He peered curiously at Cayden.

Cayden stared into his cup of tea. He had no idea who the officer was. He had not worn any insignia. If he had arrived just before Cayden volunteered, that would mean he was the lord that rode into town with the legion on the first day. Obviously, he was not searching for a murderer as that event occurred later. Cayden remembered the hatred in his eyes when he had glimpsed him outside of the inn.

He looked around at the silently waiting men. How much should he tell them? They deserved some of the truth. They had irrevocably bound their lives to his in deciding to follow after him. Foolish as it was, they had shown themselves to be friends and he decided they should not be left totally in the dark. He raised his head to find their faces staring at him.

"I did not kill anyone. My friend did." Leaving names out of the story, he told them what had happened that day. It seemed so long ago. Heads nodded as the story progressed. When Cayden finished speaking, silence descended on the cave. Cayden got up, retrieved another lamp from the shelf, and lit the wick.

"So this Inquisitor, what is his reason for being here? We assumed he was sent by the queen too," Darius said.

Cayden shrugged. He had no answer for them.

"You sure know how to make friends, Cayden," Pieter laughed. "I mean, we walk up and say hello while you cliff folk stick 'em with steel. Mind you, he probably deserved it, that one. Dangerous enemies to have though, I think."

"Now you know why you shouldn't be following me," Cayden urged. "I will be hunted, now they know I am out here. There are sure to be soldiers following me. If I were you, I'd sneak away and go back home. Best not to be found anywhere near me."

The others laughed.

"We are no longer farm boys, Cayden, any more than you are," Pieter said. "I fancy seeing a bit of the world, so I will stick around, if it's all the same." Heads bobbed in agreement.

Cayden shook his head, frustrated with their foolishness.

"I think I will turn in." Cayden tried to suppress the yawn in his voice. "I really didn't get much sleep last night." He grabbed a blanket and a mat from the rack and unrolled them near Sheba. Opening his satchel, he extracted his short knife and placed it within reach of his hand. He crawled under the blanket and Sheba nestled in beside him. They were asleep before the rest had finished their teas.

Cayden woke with a start about five hours later. Sheba's head came up at the same time. Someone approached the cave with a soft-booted walk. Strangely, Sheba did not growl. Cayden placed his hand on the knife. The moon silhouetted a figure, standing in the entrance of the cave. Ziona entered and spied Cayden. Sheba huffed and then put her head back down on her paws. Ziona placed her bag on the floor and, gathering a mat and blanket, stretched out near them with relief. She closed her eyes and fell promptly to sleep.

Chapter 24

DAWN LIGHT FILTERED into the opening of the cave, announcing a new day. Cayden sat up, rubbing his eyes. He stretched his ribs and found only a very slight tenderness remained. His ribs were fully healed, marvelling again at the potion Ziona had concocted for him.

He glanced over to see her eyes open and staring at him. She put a finger to her lips and then motioned for him to follow her outside. Sheba rose and followed, her limp much improved this morning. Cayden followed Ziona to the edge of the trees away from the cave, so as to not disturb the sleeping occupants. Cayden stopped in front of her, gathering her beautiful green eyes to his, and promptly became lost in them. He shook his head to dispel the spell.

"Thank you for helping me yesterday. What was in that water? It worked miracles."

Ziona stroked his face. "I will show you how to prepare it. It is a simple preparation but requires very rare ingredients. Sufficed to say, I made enough to keep us for a time if used sparingly. Your legion mates found you," she said, waving in the direction of the cave. "They made good time."

"Yes, they arrived late yesterday afternoon. Where have you been?"

"I had to make sure my back trail was clear before coming on to you. Rest assured no one has followed you to this site, other than those whom I have sent." She glanced down at Sheba. "Is she from the pack of dead wolves I found back in the woods?"

"Yes. I don't know who did this, but I did keep some arrows and a piece of a cloak one of the wolves had torn off in the fighting. Do you want me to get them?"

"Yes, let's take a look at them."

Cayden walked back to the cave and retrieved his satchel into which he had tucked the strange arrows. He extracted them and turned them over in his hands, examining the black fletching and shortened shafts. He handed them carefully to Ziona along with the torn piece of black cloth. Sheba whined and trotted off into the woods. Cayden didn't blame her; the memories were sad ones for him also.

Ziona examined the arrows. She frowned and then took the cloth from him. The fabric was light as gossamer silk yet resisted tearing or fraying. It must have taken the wolf a lot of strength to pull it free. Ziona's thoughts returned to a large male wolf she had spied in the forest, lying dead on ground. If the same wolf that tore this piece of cloth free, the three arrows in its body was a testament to his determination to not let go.

Ziona's brows drew down in a scowl. "Walk with me, Cayden." She strode away, stiff-backed from the cave. Reaching the woods, she ducked behind the large willow and spun to him. "Do you have any idea who hunts you?" she demanded.

Cayden frowned and shook his head. "No, there were none present when Sheba took me there. She led me to the site. I think she was the only one to survive. She had an arrow through her shoulder when she found me. Why do you assume they were hunting me?"

"You had better thank your lucky stars they were not around. They were hunting *you*. Of that there can be no question."

Cayden's eyes widened, meeting her earnest ones.

"What hunts you is called the Charun. They are the dead spirits of our land, Primordials who have been slain in battle and their souls received by the Goddess of the Dead, Helga. For them to walk the land again, they must be summoned by a Dark Primordial High Priest or Priestess. I did not believe that the legend had survived till this time, let alone the knowledge of how to animate them." She walked away and paced five stiff steps and then five stiff steps back, stopping in front of him.

She grasped his arms reading the fear in his green eyes. "The Seekers were taught about Charun by the Mother Priestess as part of our training. This knowledge is only passed to a few chosen ones. The knowledge of how to raise the Charun from the dead is kept strictly with the High Priestess, of course. The implications of them being here is worrisome."

Cayden struggled to get his lips to move. They had frozen in a perfect *O* shape of horror at her words. Charun! *But the Charun are a myth! Minions of the underworld; legendary creatures used by village parents to frighten disobedient children.* In all the old stories, they were described as loathsome creatures, terrifying to behold and now walking the earth...*hunting him.* Wait! Hunting him?

"Charun are, of course, already dead. It is very difficult, therefore; to kill one...or de-animate one would be a better description. One cannot kill what is already dead." She looked back when she realized he hadn't moved. He was frozen to the spot, horror freezing his limbs as though encased in ice.

Ziona took his hands in hers. She touched him this time, not to measure for clothes, not to heal, but to provide comfort and solace. She tugged on his hands pulling him close and wrapped her arms around him, drawing him into her embrace.

Cayden found it hard to unbend, to relax. He was shocked to his very core. Confusion had his thoughts running in all directions. Should he flee? Should he hide? Should he fight? But how? Where? Why? Above all, the question *why* was stuck in his mind. Why was this happening to him? Answers...he needed answers. Someone must know why!

He shuddered in her arms. Ziona soothed his back with a gentle hand. He met her eyes at last and asked the simple question, burning within him.

"Why, Ziona?"

"I don't have all the answers, Cayden. I know you are special and they seem to know it too. How knowledge of you reached their masters, I do not know either. I am glad I found you in time. And know this for a fact. I will protect your life before my own. From here on out, we will not be separated." She released him and checked the cave entrance again. All was still; the men slept on. "You are collecting quite a following. Something about you calls to the men around you. They sense something special about you, I think, greatness yet to fully flower. They are unconsciously answering that call. You will have to lead them."

Cayden snorted. "Lead them? Lead them where? If I am being chased by Charun, then I should tell them all to leave me and flee! It would be stupid of them to follow me, maybe even fatal!"

"You need them, Cayden. You cannot do this alone. They follow you out of choice. No man should take that choice away from them. You can explain the risk, but in the end the choice remains theirs."

"What is it I am supposed to do, Ziona? I don't understand what is happening. I don't know where to go."

Ziona gazed at him a long while. "I think you do know what to do. Where does your heart say to go? What are your instincts? Close your eyes and clear your mind. What feels right?"

Cayden closed his eyes. He slowed his breathing, stilling his racing heart. Ziona placed her fingertips at his temple and massaged in a slow circle. Peace flowed into him.

Where do I need to go? He let his mind float and suddenly there bloomed into his mind a castle wall surrounding tall towers of stone soaring above the ramparts. A flag snapped in the breeze…the flag of the queen.

His eyes jerked open. Ziona's were inches from his. He felt her sweet breath on his cheek. He stepped back, breaking contact. "I saw a castle. The queen's flag was flying there."

She frowned. "You are being drawn to the castle of she who is likely behind all of this?" Ziona shook her head in puzzlement. "What could possibly lie that way but death?" She hugged her arms around her middle as she paced. "Sharisha warned me not to interfere with your choices, but this hardly seems wise." She stopped in front of him, studying him again. "All right, we do it your way. We travel for the capital city of Cathair. It's time we roused the men. We need to keep moving." She headed back to the cave, Cayden following in her wake.

Sheba returned from her hunt with a rabbit clutched in her jaws. She trotted up beside Cayden and then growled a warning once again. Her eyes were fixed down the road to the east. Cayden squinted and saw a faint dust cloud rising to announce the presence of riders, multiple riders by the amount of dust in the air. He called out to Ziona and pointed in the direction of the cloud. By unspoken mutual agreement, they slid back into the trees to watch the oncoming riders.

The dust storm resolved into about fifty horses, only half of which were actually being ridden. Each rider led an empty-saddled mount. They were not soldiers. There were no wagons, which ruled out a merchant train.

The lead rider came into view and with a yelp, Cayden leapt from the trees and bolted out into the field and started waving his arms like a windmill. Sheba bounded after him and took up a defensive position in front of him. Ziona hissed and quickly followed, pulling a set of sharp knives from her sleeves and brandishing them.

Cayden stopped in surprise and then grinned. "It's my best friend, Ryder!" He swung back to the road and hollered, "Ryder, you big lump, I'm over here!" He wasn't sure if it was his hollering or if it was the flapping arms, but Ryder slowed and turned his mount toward him.

Suddenly, Ryder put boot to ribs and his horse bolted toward Cayden. Just as suddenly, the horse shied and Ryder nearly went straight over his horse's neck. His mount had spotted Sheba, who had grown to twice her normal size, fur distended from her body.

Ryder leapt down from his mount and continued on foot. Cayden patted Sheba and told her it was all right. She slowly relaxed but continued to growl softly. Ryder glanced at the wolf and stopped. "Is that you, Cayden?"

Cayden covered the distance between them and grabbed Ryder in a bear hug in response. Ryder crushed him back and then they were both talking at once. The men riding with Ryder halted on the road, watching the reunion.

Ziona walked up, tucking the knives back up her sleeves as she approached.

Behind her, the cave suddenly erupted with men, all brandishing weapons and running towards Cayden and Ziona.

Cayden held up his hand in a halting gesture with a quick glance over his shoulder. "These are friends. Please lower your weapons." Swords slowly dropped.

"Now that is what I call a welcoming party." Ryder grinned, surveying the partially clothed men. "There are strange things happening in the world." The grin slid from Ryder's face as he turned back to Cayden.

Cayden saw sadness touched with fear replace the joy of a few moments ago in Ryder's eyes. "We need to talk, Cayden." He looked at Ziona and raised an eyebrow in query.

Cayden reached back and took Ziona's hand, drawing her forward. "Ryder, this is Ziona. She has been a great help to me. Let's get your men settled and the horses picketed, and then we can talk."

Ryder motioned for the riders to approach and they filed in with their mounts.

"Why do you have all the extra horses?" Cayden was curious at the string of horse flesh being pulled along with the riders.

"I will explain in a minute."

They hobbled and picketed the horses, allowing them to graze. They remained saddled, however. Cayden noted the precaution.

"Please make these men comfortable and scrounge up a meal for them," Cayden instructed his companions. Ryder's men followed them back into the cave.

"Why are you here, Ryder?"

Ryder withdrew his waterskin from his saddlebag and leaned against a tree trunk. He uncorked it and took a long drink to quench his thirst and then described everything that had transpired up to their arrival a few minutes ago.

Ziona and Cayden took turns describing their flight from the legion's camp.

"We were so afraid you were lying dead in that horrible place." Ryder grimaced as the unwanted images passed before his eyes.

"One thing is certain." Ziona pinned Cayden with a look. "That camp was attacked because of you. You must take my warning seriously, Cayden. Men are dying for it."

Cayden raked his hands through his hair. He nodded. He looked to the south in the direction of Cathair. Something tugged at him, urging him to go in that direction.

That quickly, Cayden's band became thirty. There would be no more hiding their travels. From here on out, they would be riding in the open and much easier to spot.

Chapter 25

AVERY CROUCHED IN THE BUSHES between her father and Sharisha. The scene before them was eerily silent. A door swung back and forth in the breeze, creaking on rusting hinges. A lone chicken strutted across the empty street and disappeared into a flower bed to the right of the loose door. Nothing disturbed its passage.

The town seemed deserted. No smoke rose from the hearth chimneys. No children played in the warm sunshine. No laundry was strung from the drying lines in the backyards.

Sharisha stood up suddenly and strode forward into the village. Gaius and Avery followed, but at a much slower pace. Avery felt a great sadness about the town and a deep-rooted terror. Sharisha entered the dwelling with the creaking door. Inside was a comfortable living room. The chairs were covered with bright quilted pillow seats, the floors adorned with woven mats. Matching curtains fluttered in the windows.

The table in the kitchen was set with four bowls. A roast sat in the middle of the table, carving knife and fork resting on the side of the platter. Several slices had been carved from the roast and lay ready for serving. A bowl of potatoes and a bowl of peas were also on the table. The fly-covered food had spoiled as had the meat. There was no one home. The house sat empty.

Avery touched the tabletop and a flash of pure emotion assailed her. She gasped. For a second, she saw the family seated before her at the table. The woman wrestled two young children into their chairs. Her husband stood carving the meat. Suddenly, they both glanced toward the doorway. Horror sprang into their eyes and their mouths opened to scream. There was a sudden bright flash and everyone vanished.

Avery stumbled back from the table as the vision faded. Tears sprang to her eyes and she gasped, hands over her mouth. She collapsed to the floor. Sharisha bent down and eased her to a sitting position.

"What was it, Avery? What did you see?"

Avery described the vision, blinking away tears that misted her vision. Gaius frowned at the table.

"Was that an actual vision? Or was it my imagination?"

Sharisha helped her to her feet. "Oh, I think it was a true vision. As to what could cause people to vanish, I know of only one possibility." Sharisha strode out the door and continued to search the other dwellings. All were empty of inhabitants.

In the barn, they found a hay fork dropped beside a loose bale of hay. The stall door beside it was broken. The horse had kicked it down to get to the food. They searched the barn. None of the animal fodder had spoiled. Only the human and Primordial food was going bad. They found the horse out the back of the barn, happily munching on the flowers planted along the side of the inn next door.

"We need to leave this place," Sharisha said. They hurried back to their horses, which they had tied off in the woods. Mounting up, they skirted the village and continued on down the road.

The next three villages they reached were similarly abandoned, their inhabitants seeming to have disappeared midway through activities. The farms they found in between villages were also empty of human life.

They set up camp for the evening in the yard of one such farm, where they turned out the horses to graze. No one wished to sleep inside, even though it was obvious no one was returning to the houses. Settling down around their campfire, Avery turned to Sharisha. "Tell me what is going on. Where is everyone?"

Worry drew Sharisha's brows together. "These are villages of the spirit clans. The Primordial of this area have been taken by the Paimon. The Paimon is the king of the underworld who manages the armies of the dead for both the Mother Goddess and the Great Goddess of the Dark. Humans would know the armies of the Mother

Goddess as angels, the armies of the Dark as demons. It would appear the Paimon is recruiting for both armies."

Avery and Gaius gasped in unison.

"I think it is safe to say war is imminent, if not already occurring. Recruitment in this fashion is usually a result of unrest in the underworld." She addressed Avery. "The prophecies speak of a saviour to be born who will heal the land and its peoples and will lead the armies of righteousness against the forces of the Dark One, and who will unite all peoples in the final days." She looked away. "It seems those days are upon us now. It is time to rest. We will reach my people with one more day's hard ride."

Avery crawled under her blankets, her thoughts full of what she had seen. She eventually dropped into a troubled sleep, a sleep where she dreamed of Cayden in a cage and a ghostly hooded figure standing over him with a bloody knife. She cried out a warning, then rolled over and drifted back to sleep.

Chapter 26

CAYDEN AND RYDER assembled the men. They were a ragtag bunch in farmer's woolens and former legion uniforms. Joshua scratched at his arm where the itchy wool rubbed against his sweaty skin.

Silence fell as Cayden stepped forward to address them, Ryder at his side. Sheba took up a position on the other side of Cayden.

"We wish to speak to you about your presence here." Cayden glanced at Ryder, who nodded encouragingly. "I want you to know that I truly appreciate your care and concern in coming to rescue me." He gripped Darius on the shoulder. "Without your help, I would still be captured and possibly dead by now." Darius smiled, accepting the nod in his direction. "I must make you all understand the danger you are placing yourselves in by staying with me. Something is hunting me. I do not understand what or why. But understand this. Everything you have seen since leaving your homes is related to these enemies. They will not quit pursuing me. If you stay with me, there is every chance you will die doing so."

His gaze touched each of them briefly. "I cannot ask you to stay. There is no shame in going home after what you have seen these past few days. However, if you are willing, we would be glad to have your help and assistance. We will be travelling to the capital city of Cathair."

Ryder stepped in at this point. "If you choose to stay, the men who followed Cayden out of the legion will be training you all in battle and weapons techniques beginning today. You need to learn fighting skills if we are to survive. You have seen what we face. The legion was killed to a last man…except for those who had left earlier."

"What killed the men in the camp?" asked a pale-faced Joshua.

Ziona took over and painted a gruesome picture of the Charun for the men. Faces paled and many men swallowed, panic striking their hearts. Ziona then reached up and uncoiled her hair, revealing her Primordial features. The assembled men gasped in surprise. Murmuring arose from the crowd.

"Know this!" Ziona's voice rang out. "Cayden is not alone. He has the support of the Primordial people in this quest given to him. He does not fight alone! Do you stand with him?" She surveyed the men. "There can be no doubt in your decision. The world is changing and he is central to it. Choose now, but choose carefully for you will not be asked again. Stay and help; fight and die if necessary. Or leave. There is no shame in doing so. But you must choose now. If you leave later, it will be viewed as treason. There is no turning back."

The youths from Cayden's village shuffled their feet and as a man, looked to Ryder. Ryder nodded to them, feet spread wide and beefy arms crossed across his chest.

Michale stepped forward. "I think I speak for all the men here," he trembled, his voice breaking, "when I say we will stay. What hope is there for the souls of the living if things like the Charun are allowed to roam the world? We are all doomed if we do not take action. Stay or go home, but at least we know what is out there now. The people in the villages and farms across this land have no idea." He met Ziona's eyes and his hardened with determination. "If the Primordial people are willing to back Cayden, then I stand with Cayden." He stepped forward and knelt in front of Cayden, head bowed. "I pledge my life, body, and soul to you, Cayden Tiernan. I am your sword."

All of the men followed suit, going to one knee where they stood and repeated the pledge.

Cayden's jaw dropped open in surprise. Ziona nudged his arm. His jaw snapped shut.

Cayden cleared his throat. "Rise, men," he squeaked. They rose as one, flashing grins at each other. *It's like they think this is a grand adventure.* Cayden struggled to keep the grimace off his face. He felt completely foolish commanding them to rise, like some lord.

Cayden grabbed Ryder by the sleeve, hauling him around so their backs were to the men, their faces hidden. "We need to get going. We can't stay here. Can you organize them? Darius is a good man and well trained. He would make an excellent second-in-command for you."

"I will take care of it."

"Darius, step forward," Ryder commanded, turning back to the crowd. Darius took two strides forward and snapped a sharp salute. Ryder pulled his sword and in the fashion he imagined the knights of old would have performed this ritual, he commanded Darius to kneel. Darius sank to his knees and bowed his head. "Darius, you are hereby raised to the rank of captain and you are now my second-in-command." He lightly touched the blade to each shoulder then raised it straight, before dropping his arm to his side. His eyes took in all his men. "You will take orders from Captain Darius as you do me. Rise, captain."

"Your first task as captain is to get every man to a horse and to distribute the weapons we brought. Your men must be armed. Your second task is to arrange the men into fighting units. Choose a capable man to be in charge of supplies and have him gather men to secure provisions from the cave to be packed on the spare horses. We break camp in an hour. Dismissed!"

The men followed Darius back toward the cave and hobbled horses to begin preparations to leave.

Ziona moved closer to Cayden and Ryder. "We need maps. I will ride ahead and gather some maps in the next village. A lone woman will not be suspicious. Stay away from the main roads where ever possible. Try to keep the men on a parallel course to the road and use scouts to keep track of your relationship to the road. I will join back up with the band by sunset." She glanced at the sky. "The Charun prefer to move about in the darkness for they are creatures of shadow. Evening will be a dangerous time. Travel during the day should be relatively safe, provided there are no other forces out there hunting you, Cayden."

She retrieved her pack and sleeping roll and some basic supplies from the cave, gathered her horse and mule and with a quick hug for Cayden, mounted and rode off to the west.

Chapter 27

LAURISTA STUMBLED OUT OF THE BUSH, the gash on her head bleeding through the cloth she had hastily tied around her forehead. She limped slowly over toward the trembling horse. It was clearly terrified of her, nostrils flaring and eyes rolling back. It bared its teeth in warning.

She murmured soft words to it and held out the apple once again. She knew she would not survive unless she could ride for help. She stumbled and fell to the ground. The horse snorted and backed up further.

Her world spun. *Light-headed from blood loss,* her mushy brain told her. She reached up and applied pressure once again to her head wound. The world swam and she fainted.

A velvety soft muzzle nuzzling her hand roused her once more. The apple was gone. The horse snorted gently and took a step closer, searching her body for more apples. Laurista opened her eyes and stared it in the face. Slowly, she reached up her hand and patted its muzzle. Her hand closed on the bridle and she pulled herself up as the horse stepped back, pulling her to her feet.

She made a shushing noise, moving slowly to calm it. It stood still, permitting her touch. The gelding was still saddled. It had been one of the scouts' mounts. She gathered the reins and pulled herself into the saddle.

She pointed it west and nudged it into a walk, hanging on its neck to keep from sliding back to the ground.

***

Ziona paused, hearing the sound of movement in the bush. She faded back into the trees, watching the approach of some animal. Her horse whinnied in greeting. A grey gelding stepped out of the bush, carrying a rider slumped over in the saddle. Ziona urged her mount forward and approached the unconscious person. She dismounted and cautiously approached the woman whose blue dress was covered in blood, the once white sleeves stiffened in gore. The woman slid sideways out of the saddle, as her mount came to a halt. Ziona caught her and lowered her gently to the ground. She tied the horse with her own and retrieved her medicine bag, her precious potion, her skin of water, and soft rags.

Kneeling by the woman, Ziona forced some of their precious potion between her chapped lips. The woman swallowed it automatically, but her eyes remained closed. Ziona unstopped her water bottle and then unwound the hastily applied bandage around the lady's head. A large gash pulsed with blood, beginning to trickle down her forehead and into her matted hairline, remoistening the blood already soaking it.

Ziona washed the gash and then pulled a needle and thread from her pocket and stitched the large wound. It took forty stitches to close the gap. She examined her skull and was relieved to find no fracture. She knew that did not mean there was not some swelling under the skull.

She washed off the remaining blood and affixed a smaller bandage in place over the cut. She poured a little more potion down the woman's throat, which she swallowed again.

Next, she examined the rest of the woman. There were no other severe injuries. There was a slice in her sleeve, revealing a superficial cut on the arm that had long since stopped bleeding. Ziona cleaned that wound too.

Ziona leaned back to examine the woman. Obviously, the gore on her dress was not her own. She stripped the woman down to her smallclothes and then redressed her with a soft robe from her own pack.

As she finished her ministrations, the woman stirred. Her hazel eyes fluttered open and focused on Ziona's face.

"You are the seamstress from the merchant's camp," she croaked. She reached up and touched her forehead. Her eyes flew open. "You have stitched it already?" She struggled to sit up and Ziona assisted her. The woman trembled weakly. However, she felt herself strengthening dramatically. She peered closer at Ziona. "You are not what you seem, are you?"

"I am a friend. Now that I know where you came from, I understand the gore all over you. Come, we need to keep moving, those who attacked the camp are still nearby."

She helped her back onto her horse, repacked her supplies into her saddlebags, and mounted up beside the woman. "My name is Ziona."

"My name is Laurista. Your name is Primordial?"

"Yes. Let's go."

Laurista followed Ziona's retreating horse, eyes thoughtful.

They reached the village of Stonytrail about two hours later. Laurista donned Ziona's cloak to disguise her lack of proper clothing. They had stopped to bathe in a secluded bend of the river. Laurista joyfully sluiced away the gore and the stink of death from her skin and hair. They had not spoken much during the ride, Laurista too exhausted to do more than concentrate on keeping her balance in the saddle, Ziona deep in thought and planning.

They skirted the village and set up a meager camp on the western edge of the village in a small dense grove of cottonwoods. Approaching the town, they entered a dressmaker's shop and purchased two changes of clothing for Laurista. Ziona handed over the coins and nodded to Laurista's hastily whispered thanks.

"Is there a mapmaker in town?" Ziona asked the merchant.

"No mapmaker, but the village mayor keeps a stock of such items. He is the fifth house down on the riverside."

They made their way to the indicated dwelling and knocked on the red-painted door. A maid opened it and ushered them into a small waiting alcove. She returned a few minutes later with the mayor, a tall dark-haired man sporting a handlebar mustache that he twisted between his fingers as he listened to their request.

"I may have a map I can spare, but it was done for a mining survey, so it does not show the roads so much as the areas where caves are located. Would that suffice?"

"Yes, that would be fine, good sir." The mayor fetched the map and spread it out on a table before them. Ziona inspected it and then rolled it up tightly, slipping it into its protective sleeve. She handed over several coins in payment and thanked the mayor.

"Be careful in your travels, ladies. There are strange men and creatures afoot," he called to their retreating backs, closing the doors behind them.

Chapter 28

NELSON SET TWO STEAMING PLATES OF FOOD on the table, one in front of Denzik and the other in front of Fabian. Fabian rubbed his hands together, smacking his lips in anticipation. Thick cuts of pork adorned his plate, dripping in rich gravy. Roasted potatoes and freshly snapped peas were piled high in accompaniment. Nelson carried three beer steins over to the table, set them before the men, and then slid in beside Denzik at the booth.

Forks and knives scraped and glasses clinked while they cleaned their plates. Nelson sipped his beer, watching the room. No one seemed to be paying any attention to them. His serving staff drifted between tables and a happy hum hung in the air as the patrons ate and conversed.

Nelson took another sip and then set down his mug. "We discovered a promising cave this morning. It had too narrow of an opening to get through, so I set the men to enlarging it. It is now ready. Supplies have been brought down into the cavern and a crew of eight men are waiting for us," he murmured in a voice low enough to not carry past their table.

"As we get closer to our target, we will have to be careful about when we are excavating. Sound travels far in tunnels and we do not want to alert anyone on the inside to our presence," Denzik said. "The patrols are at their thinnest in the early morning hours and we should tackle the heavy excavation work then."

"It's also time we attempted to sneak someone into the castle grounds to spy out the guards' schedules. For the final wall breach, we may need an external distraction to take the guards away from the breach point," said Nelson.

"I agree," said Fabian. "And I think I know of just the person. The queen has a soft spot for my sticky buns. I believe we should send along my apprentice, Anthony, on the next delivery. He will be able to get right inside the castle and into the kitchens themselves."

Fabian dunked one of his rolls into the leftover gravy on his plate, smeared it around, and then popped the bite into his mouth. He chewed in satisfaction. "Excellent meal, as usual," he said in a louder voice to Nelson. "Please pass on my compliments to your splendid cook." He picked up his mug and drank deeply.

Nelson spoke up too. "Why don't you come back and compliment her yourself? She'd rather hear it from you than from me, I expect."

"Certainly, lead the way, good man!" They rose and followed Nelson through the back hallway to the kitchen. Warm fragrant air assailed them as the door opened, revealing a bustling room full of servers. Tabitha stood, waving her spoon toward a young girl, who was lifting a tray loaded with plates. "There's a good girl. Balance it on your shoulder and use the front hand to guide it. That's it. Now off with you!" They stepped back out of the way to give the girl a clear passage out the door. It swung shut behind her as she left.

Tabitha frowned at the intrusion and marched over to them. "You had better be bringing more supplies! I have been waiting for them for over a day now." She lowered her voice and nodded toward the small door at the back of the kitchen. "They are waiting for you out back."

"Thank you, kind mistress, for the delicious dinner. I would be honoured to unload the supplies for you. Carry on, my good woman!" Fabian smacked his middle in appreciation and headed off toward the rear door. Denzik followed with Nelson bringing up the rear. As they exited the kitchen, they found Erik standing in the back corridor.

"All is arranged, sir. The men are waiting for you below." He stood to the side to allow them to pass. They quickly entered the supply room and crawled down the ladder into the hidden cellar below. Erik pulled the trapdoor closed behind him.

Grabbing a lantern each, they trekked into the limestone cavern. The walk took about thirty minutes, during which Denzik admired their handiwork of the intervening seventeen years.

A great amount of time and effort and secrecy had gone into this project; but perhaps this evening would be the night they saw the fruit of their efforts. The tunnel was tall enough for them to walk fully upright and three abreast. Every hundred yards or so a side shaft had been cut, rising back to the surface for ventilation. Occasionally, during their excavations, they stumbled on another naturally formed cave and these were back-filled with the debris and stones chipped away during their tunnelling efforts.

Of course, the truly remarkable discoveries had come when they had uncovered the black rock in one of the side shafts. The men swore the stuff would burn better and longer than wood. It seemed strange to Denzik that a rock would burn, but the men assured him it was so. They gathered the flammable rock and separated it to be stored in an empty building in town. Perhaps they could sell some of it.

The end of the tunnel lightened and sloped slightly under Denzik's feet. Lanterns had been hung from pegs driven into the walls every twenty feet along the passage. The light resolved into a widened passage, where two men stood guard at the entrance they had widened.

Denzik stepped past the men and into the cavern. He stopped dead in amazement. The cavern, now lit by the twenty lanterns Nelson had prepared earlier, shone with an eerie beauty. The strangeness of the cave made Nelson feel as though he had stepped into another world. Perhaps he had.

He moved forward toward the men gathered in the center of the cavern. They all carried packs with shovels, picks, and gear to camp if necessary. Each carried a lantern and a walking stick to prod ahead and check their footing as they walked. No one wanted to step into a crevice or onto a fragile ledge that gave way underfoot.

They picked up the three spare packs waiting for them and slung them onto their backs.

"Lead the way, gentlemen," Denzik called to the men. One by one, they filed off down the cave, following the water source into the darkness. The cave narrowed and they followed the stream, the rocks slick and coated with an oily film. Nelson's booted foot slipped and splashed into the streambed. The footing was treacherous as they traversed the slimy, stony floor.

Half an hour later, the stream disappeared into a thin crevice in the wall and the tunnel they were following abruptly ended.

"Raise your lanterns and see if you can find any other openings in the rock face," Denzik called out.

They raised their lanterns, scanning the walls on either side of them.

Nelson raised his arm and pointed. Above the rocky face in front of them, about ten feet in the air, was a door-sized opening, obscured by deep shadows. Everyone raised their lamps, adding more light to flood the surface of the rock face.

There was an actual door in the opening. A thick iron-bound wooden door…a door that appeared very much like the doors found throughout the castle dungeons. They murmured to each other and searched to see if there were any other such openings. There was no ladder to the door and the face of the rock was smooth and unbroken. There was no door handle. It appeared it was meant to be opened on one side only.

Denzik scratched his day-old grey beard, eyes narrowed in thought.

"Have the men spread out. I want them to search this area. The door must have a purpose and I would prefer knowing what it is before we attempt to open it."

They scattered through the cave, searching for a clue to explain the door's presence.

One of the men wandered back into a shadowed corner and suddenly called out in alarm. They rushed over and found him staring down at a skeleton of a man in a Kingsmen uniform. The flesh had shrunk and shrivelled, covering the skull like a papier mâché mask. He lay on his back, head leaning against the rock, and clutched in his curled hand was a rotting leather bag.

Denzik reached down and picked up the bag, which crumbled to dust as he took it. Inside were twenty pieces of silver.

Denzik studied the door again. *This must be the Traitor's Gate,* he thought. At least he knew where they were now.

Denzik searched the body, but no clues were found as to his identity.

The others spread out and found five more bodies scattered in the area. They all appeared to have died around the same time. On the last one, Denzik found an insignia made of bronze, a captain of the King's Guard. He knelt down and examined the skeleton.

"There you are, Captain O'Reilly. I always wondered why you never came back to visit after your retirement. You never had a chance, did you?" he said softly. Denzik gazed around at the other men. He knew who they were now. The rest of O'Reilly's squad, the one he had taken over for all those years ago.

"I kept your secret safe all these years. Rest in peace, my friend."

He stood up. He had missed Nelson and Fabian's approach. He gestured to the bones at his feet. "Captain O'Reilly." Nelson and Fabian nodded in understanding.

He raised his voice to encompass all the men. "This is the Traitor's Gate. I do not believe it has been used in decades. It may be unguarded. If so, it's good news for us. If not, we must be prepared for battle.

"We have found a path to the one door no one wants to be put out of." He ran his hand over the rough stubble on his chin, considering the wall. "We need to build a staircase to access that door and outfit it with a handle on this side."

Denzik reached down pulled out a silver coin from Captain O'Reilly's bag. Heads, they pushed on tonight; tails, they went back to prepare. He flipped the coin and it sparkled in the wavering light of the lanterns. He caught it and slapped against the back of his left hand. Tails.

"We are going back to our staging area. Be sure to leave no clues to our presence here. We will not even post a guard, until such time as we begin construction."

One of the crew began to take measurements of the area, preparing a checklist of materials needed at the staging site.

Denzik's gaze lingered on Captain O'Reilly's bones. "You will have a proper burial, my friend. We will be back for you."

He headed back up the passage, the men trailing in his wake.

Chapter 29

THE DENSE FORESTS GAVE WAY to rolling hills dotted with trees. The River Erinn broadened and slowed, its banks flattening. Fishing along its banks had been excellent and most of Cayden's evenings had been spent catching, cleaning, and roasting speckled trout over open cook fires. Fresh game and fish would help extend their supplies and so Cayden led the hunting party that morning. In truth, Cayden was leery about hunting animals for meat. His experiences with his flutes left him confused about the animals. He knew his men needed to eat meat to survive, yet the idea of killing an animal sickened him.

Peering around a large tree, he spied a group of five deer grazing at the edge of the bush line across the meadow. He waved his men forward and into bow range. They knelt and drew on their bows. Four arrows zipped away and two of the deer dropped. The other three bounded away into the forest cover.

Cayden's men whooped and ran forward to check on their kill. Cayden followed. The two deer had died instantly. His men pulled out hunting knives to skin them, keeping the deerskin, quartering the meat and leaving the bones and viscera behind for the scavengers to clean up. They hauled the heavy load back to camp on a makeshift sled they had brought along for that purpose.

A round-bellied man named Tucker from the village of Maiden's Head had been appointed the head cook of the camp. He met them and he took control of the deer when it arrived back at camp. He had been an apprentice to the butcher there and would see to its preservation and storage.

Cayden strode over to where Ryder was watching Darius run the balance of the men through training drills. Cayden joined Ryder and leaned against the broad tree trunk, eyes following the men's practice.

"Ryder, what are we doing out here? I don't understand why we are here."

Ryder watched the men training and did not reply.

"Surely this was all chance? We've had a run of bad luck, right? We are simple farmers. We are not soldiers. Why are we out here?"

Ryder shrugged his broad shoulders. "Do you think the fates leave everything to chance? Even fate has design. A tree toppled by the wind may think why me? Why now? But in the end, it still feeds the forest floor."

Cayden grinned. "When did you become a philosopher?"

Ryder shrugged again. "Probably about the time I let my best friend be dragged off by the enemy to save me from my fate. There is more to this than we realize, Cayden. Can't you see it? The world is changing and somehow you are central to it." He clapped Cayden on his shoulder. "We will face it together. I promise you that."

At that moment, Ziona entered the camp, accompanied by another woman, whom Cayden recognized instantly. He ran over to where they sat their horses.

"Laurista, you are safe!" Cayden reached up a hand to help Laurista dismount and then gently hugged her. She hugged him back.

"I am happy to see you are safe too, young Cayden!" She looked him up and down. Ziona raised her eyebrow in question at this greeting.

"Where ever did you find her, Ziona? Laurista is one of the best healers I have ever seen." Noting Ziona's expression, he added, "Next to you, of course." Cayden turned to hug Ziona next, but she held up her hand to stop him. Cayden blushed.

"We must keep moving, Cayden. This camp is too exposed. It attracts attention. How long have you been camped in this area?"

"We have kept moving." He frowned at her. "We haven't stayed long at any one spot."

"Your trail was as clear as if you had left me bread crumbs. If I can find you this easily, the enemies' spies certainly know where you are. We must move on quickly."

Ryder whistled for Darius, who came running over saluting.

"Advise the men we are breaking camp. We leave within the hour."

"Yes, sir!" Darius trotted back to the men he had been training. After an exchange of words, they dispersed through the tents, to break down the camp.

"I am sticking to you so closely you will think I am a tick on your back, Cayden," said Ziona. "I will not have you out of my sight again." Ziona raised her pointed eyebrows in challenge.

Cayden glanced at her in surprise. "What has happened, Ziona? You are wound up tighter than those sewing spools of yours."

She sighed, rubbing her arms. "I don't know, Cayden. Something isn't right. I feel like we are standing in quicksand and sinking, yet we can't see the bog."

She slapped at her neck as a bug bit her. She pulled away her hand, observing the squashed insect. "Spies can take many forms..." Her voice trailed off as she gazed at her hand, frowning.

Ziona's gaze took in the camp, watching the men. They worked with concentration, packing up tents and belongings and storing them on their horses, which stood saddled at the ready. Occasionally, one of the men would slap at their arms or neck as Ziona had done.

"I want you to put your cloak on and draw up your hood tight. Pass the same instructions to all the men. Despite it being a warm day, we need to not be instantly recognizable," Ziona said as she climbed back into her saddle, pulling up her hood and drawing it tight around her face.

Cayden pulled his cloak from his satchel and did as instructed. He quickly collapsed his tent and bound it to his saddle at the rear. Mounting his white mare, he rode over to Ziona.

They led the way out of the camp, taking a path that led away from the river and into some stands of scrub brush to the south. The river continued on to the west and soon was lost from view.

Over Cayden's shoulder the band strung out behind him, following his meandering path to the south. The land flattened into grasslands with an occasional tree or outcropping of rock to break up the flatness. Cayden shaded his eyes and squinted. The horizon stretched for miles in every direction. There was no way an enemy could sneak up on them. Yet, his nerves itched, along with his neck where a black fly had bitten him too. The sun was directly overhead when they stopped for a quick bite to eat and to rest the horses. Everyone sat on the ground by their mounts, eating some dried meat and washing it down with tepid water from their flasks.

As Cayden ate, he stared around at the unbroken flat expanse of sky in front of him. His gut pulled him south. It was getting stronger. He had absolutely no idea what it was, but still it called to him, tickling his mind. He pondered what was out there that could attract him so, eyes slightly out of focus as he searched inside himself. He was so self-absorbed that he didn't realize at first that the hazy black specks on the horizon were becoming larger.

Suddenly, Darius jumped up and yelled, "Riders!" Cayden jumped to his feet along with the rest of the men and quickly mounted. The specks grew and separated into what appeared to be a group of riders on the ground and some type of bird in the air following the riders.

Ziona hissed and heeled her mount. "By the gods! *Mount up! Now!*" she screamed at the men. "We must flee! It's the Charun! *Go now!* Scatter. Do not stay together!" The men, including Cayden, leapt into their saddles. Ziona reared her horse in urgency, causing the other horses to snort and begin to run in all directions.

Ziona grabbed Cayden's bridle and pulled his mount after hers, heading in a direction leading away from the main body of men. She bent over her horse's neck, urging it to greater and greater speed, murmuring to it in Primordial. The horse's ears were laid back as it ran, eyes wild. Cayden's mare kept her nose in the stallion's flank as if an invisible cord bound them together.

They ran into a gulley with a small stream trickling through its base. The lower terrain partially hid their silhouettes and allowed them to disappear in the grasses. They followed the gulley to an outcropping of rock jutting up from the flatlands. Ziona pulled her mount to a halt and dropped down to the ground. She handed the reins to Cayden and then climbed carefully to the top of the stone pile to check for pursuit. Cayden slithered up beside her to gaze down at the plain.

The Charun had reached the spot of their recently vacated campsite. There were three of them in total. They sat on black horses, examining the spot where Cayden's men had been. Overhead, half a dozen large black birds circled. Their heads were featherless, their large wings spiked with clawed tips. Vultures. Were they the same ones Ryder had seen in the legion camp?

A fourth black rider galloped up to the group, carrying a struggling person in its grip. Cayden felt alarm spike through his body. The man was dropped to the ground and as he tried to run away the creature grabbed him by the hair from horseback and held him still. A second rider dropped to the ground and floated up to the prisoner.

Cayden saw the prisoner shake his head in response to a question being asked. The Charun reached out with a clawed hand and hooked a digit into the prisoner's chest, causing him to scream. The first Charun hauled him back upright by his scalp, blood oozing down the man's chest.

Cayden felt his stomach roil, sickened by the scene. He recognized who the prisoner was. It was James. Ziona gripped his arm in warning. "Stay still," she hissed.

The second Charun hauled out a knife and sliced off the scalp of the prisoner while he screamed and screamed. Abruptly James fell to the ground as the scalp came free. Blood sprayed fountaining through the air.

Floating back to their beasts, the Charun mounted up and headed north. As they drifted away, the vultures fell from the sky, obscuring James's body from view.

Chapter 30

CAYDEN ROLLED OVER ONTO HIS BACK, eyes squeezed shut, trying to wipe out the scene behind him. It did not, unfortunately, stop sound from reaching his ears. The vultures screeched and fought over James's remains.

Cayden thought he was going to be sick, right there, right then. His stomach heaved and he broke into a sweat, trying to keep from throwing up. He failed. Rolling onto his side, he spewed his stomach's contents over the rocks at his side. Swiping the back of his hand across his lips, he panted, chest and belly heaving.

He sensed rather than heard movement at the base of the rocks. Sheba sat, staring up at them both and whined. He had almost forgotten about her in their recent flight.

Ziona edged back from the lip of the rock face and sat beside Cayden. Sheba crawled up onto the rock and rested her chin in Cayden's lap. He petted her soft head, drawing comfort from her presence.

"I can't rejoin them, can I, Ziona? I put them all in danger whenever I am near them."

Ziona nodded. "We cannot go back to them. The Charun are tracking us with black flies. Black flies can always find people, as they feed on blood. They are attracted to death and all life is slowly dying. They know what they hunt. If we leave, they will follow us. The others will be safer if we are not with them. They have no interest in them other than to find you."

Ziona crawled back up and checked the horizon. Nothing moved, except for the vultures. The others would not return as long as they were present.

"We need to go. I think James bought us some time, sending them off in the wrong direction. We need to use the time he bought us with his life," said Cayden.

"We will ride hard. We should be able to reach Cathair within two days if we do. We stop for short periods only and take shifts standing guard while the other sleeps."

They slid back down to their horses. Cayden took a swig of his water to rinse his mouth, spitting it out on the ground. He patted Sheba on the head and whispered, "Keep up, girl, and keep your eyes open, OK?" She licked his hand and tilted her head, listening. She trotted off ahead of them, seeming to lead the way.

They rode hard and by nightfall the area of the attack was far behind them. They did not see any sign of the band or any sign of their pursuers. The flies also disappeared. That evening they ate a cold dinner, not wishing to alert anyone to their presence. They hobbled their horses and allowed them to graze close to their camp, but they remained saddled. They slept under the open stars under a blanket, fully clothed.

Sheba sat with Cayden and watched with him while Ziona slept. All was still. She gnawed on the thigh bone of the rabbit she had caught for her dinner. Cayden pulled out his flutes and rolled them in his hands. He pondered their use, beyond calling the creatures to him. Was it possible they could help him in some other way?

He sensed Sheba's presence separately from the other wolves around them. He thought about his flutes tucked back under the grandfather oak tree back home. He wished he had brought them all along now.

If Ziona played the flute, would the animals come to her? He had never considered what would happen if others played them. He would have to have Ziona try it when she awoke.

Worried about what had happened to the others, Cayden unconsciously ground his teeth. *Surely they had escaped. There were only four of those creatures. The band would be OK. They had to be.* Cayden's frustration mounted as his ever-present worry about his friends came back full force. Was there anything to be done differently to protect them? They were dying because of him and he didn't understand why. He needed answers and he needed them now. His eyes were drawn south again toward that persistent nagging tug at his soul. Answers were waiting for him in Cathair and he was anxious to get there.

He glanced at the sky and saw the moon was about three quarters gone. Dawn would be arriving in about three hours. He got up and shook Ziona awake, changing places. Crawling under the covers, he fell into a restless sleep in which werewolves stood guard while demons played his flutes and the dead clapped along.

***

Ryder huddled with the band members, midstream of the river. Their horses quivered with fear and exhaustion. The flies did not seem to like the water and refused to follow them into the streambed, a lucky break for them. Ryder took a quick head count. Everyone was accounted for except for Cayden, Ziona, and James.

Ryder prayed they were safe. "All right, here is what we are going to do. We will ride downstream toward Cathair for a couple of miles in this river. When we find a good location, we will exit the stream on the opposite side of where the Charun are located. Their flying spies should not be able to find us at least until the Charun cross over. Hopefully, they never do."

In their mad flight, they had headed north for a mile or so and then cut back to the river. The last few stragglers of the band had finally caught up to them. This had been the fallback plan Darius had discussed with the band in case they were separated. He had not shared this with Cayden or Ryder in the hope that if disaster struck they would leave on their own as the band led any danger away from Cayden. Ryder thought this plan rather brilliant of Darius. He would need to promote the man earlier than he thought.

"Let's head out!"

They splashed down stream for a few miles and eventually came to a sandbar extending out from the right-hand shoreline. The horses scrambled up out of the river happy to regain the solid ground of the riverbank, spreading out onto the grassland on the west side of the river.

Glancing at the sky, Ryder judged they had roughly three hours of daylight left to them. Their sidetrack had taken them another two hours off the path. Assuming Cayden, Ziona, and James headed due south they now had a five-hour lead on the band. Ryder's gut told him Cayden would push hard to reach Cathair now. He would not attempt to rejoin them.

Laurista rode up to Ryder and placed a hand on his arm. "The men are tired, my lord. They need to rest, as do the horses. To push on now would not be wise. There are injuries amongst the men I need to attend to."

He glanced down at her. "I am not a lord, Laurista. My name is Ryder."

She looked askance at him. "Of course, my lord."

He frowned, not understanding what she meant.

"Darius, have the men make camp, but they must be prepared to ride at a moment's notice. No cook fires, understand?"

"It will be as you command, sir." Ryder returned the salute from his captain and then followed Laurista back to her tent that was now acting as a field hospital. A small service tent had been set up to receive the wounded. Most injuries were not serious, cuts and scrapes and one arm broken when the man had tried to outrun the Charun. His horse had stumbled, throwing him, but he had managed to remount and escape. All in all, they had survived this first test and come through the other side relatively unscathed.

Ryder was sure it would have been worse if they hadn't discovered the flies' weakness. He was also sure they had been tracking them and would return to the hunt once the Charun discovered their prey had escaped once again. There was no doubt in Ryder's mind they were after Cayden, which meant he was in danger every second of every day.

Ryder strode over to Darius. "Captain Darius, I need you to select four men with demonstrated skills to perform as scouts."

Darius surveyed the men. "Gregory, Samuel, Phillip, and Macon, with me." The four soldiers walked up to him and Ryder. "These four have excellent horsemanship. Gregory and Samuel have served as trackers and scouts in the legion already. Phillip is from my village and can track a squirrel up a tree to its den. Macon can smell a rat even if it has been pickled and stuffed in a jar."

"Excellent." Ryder examined the four men. All were of a wiry build and short. "We need to know what we are riding into and who may be trailing us. Your job will be to continuously scout for enemies. I want one man out front as we advance and one checking our back trail as we march. The other two are your relief. You will scout day and night in six-hour shifts. I will leave you to arrange your scheduling, but it begins immediately. I do not want to be surprised ever again."

Ryder strode away, leaving the men to carry out his orders.

Chapter 31

THE WIZARD STIRRED ON HIS FILTHY PALLET on the floor. The cave-like cell was dank and damp, having been formed out of a natural occlusion in the limestone rock. In the corner stalactites and stalagmites, created by a steady drip of water, formed a jagged toothy cavity perfect for hiding small treasures he wished to keep out of sight of his hosts. He thought they were actually quite a bit longer than when he had taken up residence in the cave seventeen years ago.

The only reason he knew it had been seventeen years was because of the rough calendar he had gouged into the soft rock with a piece of calcite. That stone made a perfect chalk and it was plentiful in the cave. The difficult part was getting enough light to see to be able to write anything by. The few stubs of candles left behind by the guards soon sputtered and died, giving barely enough light to eat and perform his toilet once a day.

The door rattled and his usual jailer, Wendell, poked his head in.

"When are you going to die?" he puffed, dragging in a bucket and a plate with gruel. "You make me work so hard, hauling this slop up and down the stairs all the time."

"I am indeed sorry to inconvenience you, my good man. As luxurious as my accommodation is, I would hate to leave it empty. Now tell me, where would you ever find such an excellent tenant? Why, you would be retired and bouncing your grandkids on your knee before you could find a suitable replacement."

Wendell snorted and plopped down the bucket with an audible splash.

He set the lantern on a peg by the door, illuminating the cell for a short time. The old man sat on his pallet as always, long white hair flowing over his shoulders and onto his chest. It curled at the ends, reminding Wendell of a horse mane.

"Well, at least I don't have to shave you anymore, not that they ever checked on it. I need that shave more than you do. The lice are your buddies now, right? Bed bugs keep you company at night." He chuckled at his own dark humour.

"Alas, they certainly do," the wizard agreed pleasantly.

"Well here are your candle stubs." Wendell lit one and placed it on the ground. "I have a special treat for you tonight. Don't go expecting it every day, mind you. I had to sneak this in for you." He frowned at the wizard, suddenly unsure if this was a good idea after all. Shrugging, he tossed a package to the wizard. The small bag was made of old leather and tied with a drawstring.

"There is an extra candle strapped to the base of the water bucket. Enjoy your few extra minutes of light."

Wendell backed out of the cell with the full slop bucket and took up the lantern from the peg on his way out. The light dimmed and the key squawked in the lock. The sound of boots on stone faded with the light.

Mordecai Ben-Moses was a practical wizard. When materials presented themselves, there was no reason to flaunt one's powers. He retrieved the candle from under the bucket and set it aside so the wick would not be wetted by his ablutions.

He picked up the bag and tugged on the drawstring, dumping its contents onto his filthy robes. Out tumbled a multifaceted crystal, its cut surfaces sending rainbows of light flashing around the cell from the candle's flickering flame.

Mordecai grinned. Finally, his hard work was paying off. It had taken seventeen years of chit-chat and conversation to win the reticent Wendell over to his side. Now Mordecai had his focus stone back in his possession. The time was close; he knew it.

Mordecai felt him coming. *The bond was working. Gwen would be pleased that their plans of so long ago were coming to fruition.* His grin widened and then he set about bathing and eating his meal just as the liquefied stub of candle sputtered out.

He snapped his fingers and a flame danced to light on his fingertips. He checked another day off his chalk calendar and then lay back down to sleep. He snapped his fingers and the light extinguished. Closing his eyes, he reached out to the boy in his dreams, calling him to his destiny.

***

Cayden's band settled in a copse of trees nestled in a valley about half a mile off the main road. An animal trail had led back to the spot and, as Cayden had suspected, a small spring bubbled from the rocks near the trees.

A light rain continued to fall so they took luxury in putting up both tents, stretching a canopy between the two to keep their small fire dry and give them a spot to sit together.

Cayden scoured the underbrush to find kindling and dry wood for their fire. He located a very old birch tree, the white bark peeling in long curls. Perfect kindling lay at its base and he collected that along with some more substantial branches. One in particular was of great interest.

Arriving back at their campsite, he started a fire, while Ziona pulled food from their packs. She suspended a pot and a kettle from the arm of a tripod and added dried meat, beans, and water to the one and tea leaves to the other.

Cayden grabbed his satchel and lowered himself to the ground under the canopy, pulling out his carving tools.

Sheba trotted in from the scrub line, another rabbit clenched in her jaws. She settled on her belly beside Cayden and tore into her meal.

Ziona sat down beside him, watching. "Do you mind if I look at your flutes?"

Cayden reached into the bottom of his satchel and pulled out the three flutes he had stored there.

"These two, I carved back home and this one I made while I was in the legion camp." He hesitated before handing them over.

Ziona examined them, her slender fingers tracing the designs he had carved into them.

"Do you know what these symbols are?" Her nimble fingers followed the serpentine marks on the snake flute.

"They are designs, I imagine...aren't they? I carved whatever inspiration came to me at the time."

"I don't think so, Cayden. They look like runes to me."

Cayden paused halfway through reaching into his satchel again, eyes flashing to hers.

"Runes? I know nothing of runes. That is not possible."

"Nevertheless, it is what they appear to be." She smiled at him. "If you have discovered a talent for the ancient rune language, you are unique, Cayden. The knowledge of runes vanished over a thousand years ago. What do you want to do with them?" She held them up for his inspection. "Shall I play them for you? Or do you want to play them?"

Cayden studied her. Then he took back the ones he had carved at home, leaving the rainbow-barked one he had carved that day in the meadow in her hands.

"Play this one. I know what happens when I play it. You try it. Play any song that comes to mind."

Ziona put the flute to her lips and played. *The flute sounded...well, like a flute*, Cayden thought. The music was pleasant, the song pleasing. She played on for a few minutes. Then, she lowered the flute, eyebrows raised in enquiry.

Cayden shook his head. "Nothing happened, Ziona." He took back the flute, examining it. It was still the same as when he had played it. "It played nicely, but the song...the sound was different than when I play it."

Ziona did not seem surprised. "I think, Cayden, it is because this flute is bound to you. To anyone else, it will be a pretty flute. Only you have the ability to make it come alive. Come, you play it for me. Maybe I can see the effects, even if I can't make them happen."

Cayden put his lips to the flute and played. Instantly, the tone changed and laughter bounced out of the flute. The song giggled with light notes and a breeze gusted, swirling the leaves on the ground. This time when the child appeared in response to his playing, she was dressed in vivid green gossamer skirts and a halo of flowers nestled in her curls. She spun in a circle, dancing a jig to the music Cayden played.

Sheba raised her head and watched attentively. She did not growl or show any aggression at all. She seemed to accept the girl as normal. She went back to chewing on her rabbit.

Cayden lowered his flute and grinned at the familiar figure that appeared.

"'Tis a much better song than the last time, Cayden of the Cliffs," she said in a lilting accent.

Ziona, however, gasped and fell to her knees face down in the dirt in front of the child. "I am honoured and humbled by your presence, Great Aossi!" She pressed her forehead to the ground. Cayden was stunned. Aossi winked merrily at him again and skipped over to Ziona. She placed her hand on her hair and murmured something to Ziona in the Primordial tongue. Cayden thought it might be a blessing of sorts. He gazed at the scene in amazement. Tough, commanding Ziona on her knees to a child, albeit a magical one. Ziona rose from her subservient position and backed up beside Cayden. Her face was alive with joy.

"Tell us why you have come, ancient one?" Cayden's eyes jerked back to Ziona's at her words.

"Cayden has summoned us from our retreat." She twirled, her prismatic skirts swirling on feet floating above the ground. "Even we could not resist the spell of his music."

She danced over and placed a hand on the curve of Cayden's cheek. "He is so very special, even if he does not yet understand how. We know and we come as called." She grinned again and a finger tapped his cheek. He instantly felt a rush of joy swell in his chest. She soothed his worries and peace stole over him. She gazed into his eyes and they grew serious, a strange expression for her nature.

"Cayden, you are the one all creation has been waiting for. That we have been waiting for. Hidden within you is the ability to save this world, poised on the brink of destruction. You and your sister have great gifts, which you are only beginning to understand. You are prophesied to do great things. Many have sacrificed their lives to give the world this chance. We bow to you and are in your service." She knelt before him, head bowed. Ziona knelt beside Aossi also.

Cayden backed up in shock.

"Stop that! I don't understand any of this!" he croaked. "Would someone please tell me what is going on? Everyone seems to know far more than me." Frustration made his voice sharpen. "I need answers and I need them now!"

Aossi stood up and smiled at him. "That is the response I was waiting for. Take command, Cayden. Do not be afraid to lead. A king must be able to stand tall and with assurance. He must be able to make decisions sometimes with little or no knowledge. This is your destiny. The city you march toward is your home, Cayden. It is your heritage and your promise. The present queen is a usurper and must be deposed. There is one there, who is calling to you from within the city walls. It is so, yes?"

Cayden's eyes met hers and he nodded.

"Find him. He is a wizard of great power. He has been imprisoned there since your birth. He has been waiting for you. He has the answers you seek. You must free him and take back control of your capital."

"I am no king." Cayden rejected the charge automatically.

"You do not know who and what you are." Aossi studied him. "Find the wizard. He will help you to understand."

To Ziona, she said, "You are his guide, yes?" Ziona nodded reverently, bowing her head once again. "You must stay with him every minute of every day. There are many seeking him on behalf of the queen. She has entire legions of soldiers searching for him. She may even know you are coming. But they are not the only ones. There are deeper, darker stirrings."

Ziona nodded again. She straightened her posture, grim determination etching her face.

Aossi's smile dimpled her cheek, once again becoming the impish little girl.

"All you ever need to do, Cayden, is call for us. Protect that flute. Know that it works only for you. If you should ever lose it, you may also find us here." She poked his chest where his heart beat. "And here." She tapped his temple. "We will be watching over you too." With a swirl of green skirts that felt like a breath of warm spring air, Aossi vanished.

Ziona sank back to the ground, her eyes clouded over in thought.

Cayden placed the flute back in his satchel and then went over to the pot of stew bubbling and gave it a stir, his thoughts full of the conversation. At least now he knew who was calling him in Cathair. *But take the city?* He snorted to himself. How in heaven and earth would he accomplish such a task? It seemed ridiculous to contemplate. He laughed out loud. *I am no king. What a ridiculous concept.* He opened his mouth to say those exact words, but the look on Ziona's face stopped him.

She stared at him in fascination, and she was bowing before him once again. Cayden blushed deeply and reached down and pulled her to her feet. "Stop that. You are totally embarrassing me, Ziona! Get a grip on yourself, would you? She was just a little fairy person. What does she know about the future or about who I am?"

Ziona shook her head, marvelling at his innocence.

She sat down, drawing him down beside her. "Your Majesty." Cayden went to interrupt, but she plowed right over top of him. "You did not tell me you had summoned the Aossi."

Cayden frowned at her. "What is so important about them? They look like fairies to me."

"They are related to fairies, yes. But they are much, much more than mere fairies. They are of the Mother Goddess herself. They are the guardians of the spirits of nature; the chief stewards who protect the world and keep it in spiritual balance. It is said that they are immortal and exist on a plane between the mortal and immortal worlds. And..."—she raised a finger in emphasis—"they have not been seen in a millennium."

Cayden's mouth snapped shut. "So...they are...what? Angels? What do they do?"

"They maintain the status quo between good and evil, Cayden. Think of it this way. When the autumn comes and the leaves fall, what happens to them? They become part of the forest floor and in the spring the worms grind them into fertilizer to feed the tree, which in turn feeds the leaves of the new season. Death begets life and life falls to death. Harmony and balance are maintained in the circle of life that the Mother Goddess created. For good to exist, so must evil, for one cannot exist without the other. They are the balance."

"But why have they appeared to me?"

"You are significant to their plans or to their existence or both. You are somehow tied to them and them to you. They aid you because they must, because it is part of what was and what will be."

Cayden stood and went back to the pot. The stew was done. He ladled their dinner into two bowls and brought one to Ziona.

Ziona observed his stiff and jerky motions, frustration displayed in his every movement. "I know this is hard for you, Cayden, but you will find your answers in time. I am here to help you. At least we know one thing for certain."

"What do we know?"

"We know you were right to head to Cathair. And we now know why. Who is this wizard?" she mused.

"I have no idea. I have never met a wizard before." Cayden shrugged. "Can I ask you a favour?"

"Certainly, what is it?"

"Please do not call me 'Your Majesty' ever again."

Ziona shook her head, amused. "I cannot promise that, Cayden. However, I do believe it unwise to flaunt such knowledge to the common listener. Your secret is safe with me…for the time being at least." She regarded him once again. "I would never have believed starting out that this journey would bring me to this place and time. The Mother Goddess works in mysterious ways."

Cayden frowned, clearly not amused. They cleared up the dishes, working side by side, and then settled back with their tea. Curling his hands around the warm cup, he gazed into its murky depths. "I wonder why you couldn't summon the Aossi." He took a sip in contemplation.

"A good question. I believe those flutes are attuned to you and they will only respond to your touch in any magical fashion. Should anyone else pick them up, they will simply be what they seem, wooden flutes. I think it must have something to do with the runes. There is a magic in runes that is unique. The symbols have meaning beyond the actual shapes they form."

Cayden took another sip. "Maybe this wizard will know. Do you have any idea how to find him?"

"Well, if he is a prisoner, he is likely held in one of the prison cells, right?"

"That would make sense, yes. So do you have any ideas on how to go about breaking a wizard out of a prison cell? Why can't he break himself out?"

"I can think of many reasons why he might still be in that cell, Cayden, but none of them really help us. I think we need to enter the city and see what it is like before we try to form a plan to get him out. I know nothing about the palace and I assume you are equally in the dark about it?"

He nodded.

"Well then, we should get some rest, Your Majesty." She giggled and headed off to her tent. She glanced back over her shoulder and spied his look of consternation. Laughing, she let the tent flaps close behind her.

Chapter 32

NELSON AND FABIAN PAUSED, pulling Denzik to the side. They let the men pull ahead, so they were the last to leave the Traitor's Gate.

"This is the wrong opening," Nelson whispered.

Fabian nodded. "Yes, I think so too. A lucky discovery, but we were led to believe that the path to the proper insertion point would be more to the east."

"Then we must have walked right past it. Let's keep our eyes sharp on the way back." Denzik took the lead.

They headed off down the stream side path, keeping their eyes peeled for an opening in the rocky cavern face. The cave widened and narrowed in several places. About one hundred yards from the Traitor's Gate, Fabian pointed out a shadowed area partially concealed behind a stalagmite formation. From the other direction, the opening had been completely covered.

They scrambled up over the short rise of floor to the opening. It appeared to be high enough to allow a slightly stooped tall man to enter. Denzik and his companions, not being tall men, were able to stand straight, their hair brushing the stone above. Denzik shoved his lantern hand into the opening and a narrow passage opened up before them. It was not a natural formation. Small sharp grooves marked the surface of the tunnel.

"This may be it. Nelson, go inform our men that we are staying behind for a little while longer. We need to see where this path goes."

Nelson trotted off to do as bidden and returned a few minutes later, carrying an extra couple of lanterns.

Denzik led the way into the tunnel, which twisted around, its path seeming to follow the softer sections of the rock. After about ten minutes, during which they became completely disoriented, the path emptied onto a flat expanse of rock glowing with an eerie light. Some sort of fluorescent substance lined the cave, giving it a greenish glow. They spread out, approaching the wall in front of them. It was also plain but obviously made of limestone, and this time there was no question that it was man made. Large smoothed blocks of seamless limestone were stacked precisely, the stone quarried to the slightest of tolerances.

Denzik stepped up to the wall, searching its surface by lantern light. He ran his fingers across the surface, looking for anything to indicate they were at the right spot. The others searched alongside him. He moved down the wall, right into the corner where the massive foundation disappeared back into the natural rock. His fingers paused over an indentation about chest height shaped like a sword.

"Here, this might be it. Give me some more light." Nelson and Fabian raised lanterns, flooding the area with a flickering bright light.

Denzik rubbed the surface, scratching away years of dust and dirt to reveal the symbol. He backed up, eyes scanning the wall. "This must be it." He scratched at his beard in thought. "I have no idea what is on the other side."

"Why don't we tap on the wall and see if we get a response? After all, these are likely to be the deepest cells of the castle, correct? They must be prisoner cells."

"All right. I guess there is no way our tapping would alert any guards. Their stations are on the next level up." He gazed up the wall to where it disappeared into the cavern's ceiling.

"Here is a rock." Nelson pushed a stone into each of their hands.

"Let's tap the call to arms from the King's Guard. The current guard would not recognize it," Fabian suggested.

"An excellent idea." Denzik clapped Fabian on the shoulder appreciatively. It seemed fitting to attack the walls with sounds that had been banished from them.

They tapped out the bugle call, the rhythm coming naturally to them as though no time had passed. They paused at the end, waiting to see if there was any response.

Silence filled the cave...and then they heard a faint echo of their tapping. It was the same call, but coming from the other side of the rock. Someone was tapping in response.

Denzik switched over to the proper tapping code of the sentries and tapped on the wall, "Who are you?"

The reply, when it came, shocked them. "Mordecai Ben-Moses, First Wizard of the Fell. I have been waiting for you."

Chapter 33

THEY BROKE CAMP TO A FINE DRIZZLE that soaked the tents and ground. Ryder settled his cloak around his broad shoulders and drew up his deep hood to fend off the persistent moisture. The evening had passed peacefully. He tightened the girth on his horse, checking its catch. He tied his pack in place behind his saddle and mounted up.

The men were ready to go. *They have become quite good at this. Slowly, we are being transformed from a bunch of farmers into a real soldiering unit,* Ryder thought.

The once-boys-now-men laughed and joked as they went about their tasks, clearly happy to be in the band.

Last night around the campfire, they had finally chosen a name for themselves. They argued that all excellent fighting forces had a name. They approached Ryder for his permission to raise a banner in their chosen name. And so the Band of the Rebels' Land was formed. Darius led the name choice. Ryder had tried to talk him out of it initially.

"I don't know if it's such a good idea, Darius," Ryder said, the presence of the men standing behind him softening his words. "By choosing that name, you are announcing to the entire world that you are set against the queen and in open rebellion against her rule and her authority. You are painting bull's eyes on their backs."

"Exactly! Don't you see? By loudly proclaiming our allegiance to our homeland, we will attract like-minded men who are not organized but who wish to stand in revolt. We are not the only ones out here, Ryder."

Ryder scanned the eager faces around him and crossed his arms over his chest, pondering their choice. Yes, they would attract attention, but enough of the right kind to offset the expected whiplash when the queen learned of their presence and declared purpose? What if she sent her own forces against them? Experienced battle-trained troops!

"Then in the morning, we ride. We ride hard. For in announcing our intentions, we sacrifice the luxury of remaining hidden."

Laurista worked long into the night to fashion a banner. They located some royal blue cloth onto which they had sewn a circle embroidered with a bright golden eagle clutching a branch in its talons. The banner was hoisted into the air on a stout wooden pole they had foraged for in the woods. After arguing over who would have the first honour, Darius took it and rode up beside Ryder. The rest of the band formed up behind them to begin the long journey south, allegiance proudly displayed for all to see. They broke into song, singing a battle hymn of their own making:

> "Hoist the flag and proudly fly
> Our pride soars into the sky
> War will find us come what may
> Bring it on, we proudly say
> We march no matter what the cost
> In remembrance of what was lost
> Our proud king stolen away
> Will rise again on that day
> Hoist the flag and proudly sing
> Freedom comes on eagle's wings!"

Ryder hummed along as the drizzle dripped off his coat.

They followed the River Erinn for most of the day. Toward dusk, they came upon the outskirts of a small village set back from the river. A long stone arch bridged the river from shore to shore, wide enough to accommodate two wagons passing at mid-span.

The village was surrounded by farms, bordered with neatly trimmed hedge rows and low fieldstone walls. A dirt road opened up between the farms and led directly to the central village square. A sign announced the village as Erinnshire.

They rode into the village and stopped at the fountain in the center of the square. The new banner snapped in the wind announcing the band's arrival. Ryder gazed around and then dismounted. The villagers went about their business taking no particular interest in the newcomers.

Ryder spied the village inn on the south side of the square. It was a two-story structure, covered with mud plaster and peeling white paint. Wooden shutters painted a bright blue provided a splash of colour on the otherwise plain façade of the building. A sign hanging over the front entrance announced the name of the inn as The Frosty Mug. A tall glass of ale with a bead of moisture slipping down the side decorated the sign. The men eyed the sign and licked their lips in anticipation.

"Stay here," Ryder commanded, "while I seek out the mayor and ask him for a suitable location to set up camp. If he is agreeable to having the entire band in town, we will come back and fetch everyone."

Ryder was joined by Darius and Laurista as he entered the inn's dim interior.

A woman with a mass of curls piled high on her head straightened from wiping a table and inspected the newcomers. She wore a yellow ankle-length skirt and matching shirt, accented by a crocheted tan vest. Her friendly eyes greeted them.

"How may I help you, gentlemen and lady?"

"We have come with about thirty men and are planning to have them camp at the edge of town. Would the mayor be available to speak to us? We wish to ask where it would be the least intrusive to settle down for the night."

"I am the mayor. I am also the proprietress of this inn. My name is Simona."

"Pleased to make your acquaintance, madam. I am Ryder." He motioned to his companions and made introductions.

"I believe Old Man Jacoby has a field lying fallow this year. He may be willing to allow you to set up camp there for a small fee." She gave directions to the farm on the south side of town. "Will your men be coming into town later? I ask so I can let the cooks know of a larger crowd than usual." She glanced around her common room, which was presently about a quarter full.

"Yes, I believe they would be happy to avail themselves of your fine inn."

"Until then," she curtsied lightly, "gentlemen and lady." She marched off to the kitchens.

They left the inn and were surprised to find a small crowd had gathered around the band in the short time they were inside. Most were young men, but some were old gents, all speaking with the band and asking questions. As Ryder strode up, he heard one of the band say in a loud voice, "Yes, we have been travelling with a young prince. You would believe it too if you saw him. We got separated, but he is of princely seed. You know it to look at him. We are going to recover his throne for him. You'll see." Murmurs greeted these words as the crowd repeated the conversation to others too far away to hear.

Ryder mounted his horse again and motioned for the men to follow him. He glanced at Darius, who shrugged as if to say *don't look at me.* "They came to that conclusion all on their own."

A short ride brought them to the farm and an even shorter negotiation had them setting up camp in an empty hayfield with access to the farmer's well for watering their horses. The rain had let up and a watery sun poked through on the western horizon.

Darius set a few men to guarding the camp while the rest of the men found wash buckets and clean clothes. Then they walked back into town in threes and fours, hot food and cold ale on their minds.

Ryder, Darius, and Laurista strolled back to town also, drawn to the comforts of the village and also keen to hear some of the local gossip. Ryder knew their presence was being noted and he felt this would be the first true test of the band's acceptance or rejection by those they hoped to recruit in time.

They entered the inn and the band quickly filled the available tables, mixing in with the local men and beginning conversations. Ryder, Darius, and Laurista settled in at a table close to the door, so as to watch the people who entered.

A serving girl stopped at their table to place a basket of hot bread on the table. A barmaid stopped by next and took their drink order, retrieving three mugs of mulled wine for their table. Ryder spied the innkeeper who doubled as the town mayor and waved her over to their table.

"Simona, I was wondering if you would point out the local merchants. I find I am in need of a good tailor."

Simona peered around and then pointed to a pinched-faced, balding man sitting at a small table by the window. "He travels between villages and into the capital once a month to purchase supplies."

"That's great. Thank you." Ryder stood up and walked over to the man. He was absorbed in his plate of thinly sliced lamb and potatoes as Ryder paused by his table.

"Good evening. May I join you?"

The man shrugged and gestured to the chair opposite him. Ryder sat.

"My name is Ryder. I need to have some sashes made for me and my men. I am trying to locate someone who sews."

The man studied him. He did not give his name. "What kind of sashes?"

"They would be made to sit at the hip, solid colour with braiding along the edges, and a little embroidery on the front."

"The queen has forbidden the creation of any garment for armed men who have not received her seal sanctioning its making in advance." He squinted at Ryder, taking in his sword at his hip. "What you ask me to do might be viewed as treason."

Ryder frowned at the man. "I apologize. We are not from the area and we were unaware this law. Please forgive my impertinent request." Ryder stood, bowed stiffly to the man and withdrew back to his table.

He relayed the conversation to Darius and Laurista. She also frowned at the information. "If that is the case, there is a ban on selling materials that might be made into uniforms as well. It may be that this cloth is as strictly controlled as the sale of weapons. You might commission one sword, but you are sure to attract attention if you commissioned for, say, two hundred of them."

"Fortunately, we have a good number of those already courtesy of the legion. We will need to find a way to buy the proper cloth. Perhaps we can purchase some in several different villages, not enough in any one village to raise suspicions?"

"Why this sudden interest in uniforms?" asked Laurista.

"It occurred to me that in a battle, unless it is with the queen's forces, we would not be able to tell friend from foe. We need some way of identifying ourselves to one another, especially if our numbers grow."

"Good point." Darius picked up his fork, his stomach growling as the spicy meal arrived. They had taken no more than three bites when a large thud occurred, instantly followed by a flash of bright light and a shuddering crash. The windows of the inn blew in, glass shattering and spinning through the air. Screams of pain filled the room as those closest to the windows were impaled with the airborne shards.

Ryder leapt to his feet and drew his sword. The other band members, who had not been cut by the flying glass, also drew theirs. The windows filled with a howling rush of sound and then all went still.

Ryder ran out the door, followed by Darius and Laurista, who had a small sharp dagger in her hand.

The village square was strewn with debris. Trees had been snapped in two. The central fountain had been toppled, the basin cracked and water was flowing out onto the ground. Several people were getting slowly to their feet, while others did not move. In the center of the square, where their band had originally stopped, was a large blackened crater. Smoke curled from the edges of the depression and a flickering flame rose from the center.

Ryder strode up to the edge of the hole and looked down. A large glowing rock sat in the center of the depression, pulsing with the dull red of a horseshoe freshly out of the forge. The roughly shaped metal ball was about the size of a church bell. Ryder examined the hole, trying to gauge the direction the iron ball had come from. To launch a ball that large, it would take something larger than any catapult siege engine he had ever heard of. It would not have that long of a range, however. Puzzled, he found nothing in the area to suggest where the iron ball had come from.

Ryder bent to a nearby man and felt for a pulse. When none could be found, he moved on to a young child who was partially buried under the body of his mother. The woman's body was twisted in a grotesque form only possible if her back was broken. The child was stirring and crying, unable to push his mother's body off of him. Ryder rolled the woman over and picked up the child, ducking his head against his shoulder to shield his view of his mother's broken, bleeding body.

He sprinted toward the inn with the child clutched to his chest, meeting Laurista halfway. He pushed the boy into her arms without speaking. The child wailed for his mother. Laurista ran back toward the inn, the child's cries mingling with the moans of the injured.

Ryder saw the men of the band spread out, searching the carnage for survivors. Other people from the town were gathering on the square. Ryder followed Laurista back into the inn, where he found the mayor directing the serving girls to push the wooden tables off to the sides of the rooms, creating a triage area in the middle of the empty floor.

The cook appeared from the kitchen area with a virtual army of young men hauling buckets of water and what appeared to be the entire stock of towels and linens. They placed them on the tables at the side of the room.

Ryder walked over to the window where the glass had blown in. The merchant he'd been speaking to a few moments ago was slumped over his table, a chunk of glass from the window imbedded in his temple. Ryder turned him over. He was clearly dead. Ryder hoisted him onto his shoulder and his torso flopped over his back. He carried the dead man outside to the fountain area and laid him beside the other ten people who had been deposited there by the band in a makeshift morgue beside the fountain. As Ryder knelt to lay the man down, an object rolled out of the man's waistcoat pocket and dropped to the ground.

Ryder bent down and picked it up. It was a curiously shaped coin, octagonal in shape, and made of a strange silvery metal that seemed hot to the touch. On one side was a picture of the sun and on the other side what resembled a bear. Ryder pocketed the coin, not because it was valuable but because it seemed out of place. He quickly searched the man for identification but found nothing to tell him who the man had been.

Ryder straightened and walked back to the remains of the fountain. Something strange was happening and he itched to know what it was. He sent prayerful thoughts in the direction he hoped Cayden was riding.

Ride, Cayden, ride! I am not sure how long we can hold them from your back, whoever they are.

Chapter 34

THE FURTHER SOUTH CAYDEN AND ZIONA RODE, the more populated the area became. Grasslands gave way to rolling hills dotted with willowy branched trees that bent back to the earth. A fuzzy grey seemed to coat them. On closer inspection, Cayden realized moss was hanging from the branches, swaying in the breeze. Colourful birds flashed through the treetops, calling to each other as they passed.

As heat grew so did the humidity. The soil churned into ruddy clay that clung to their boots and to the hooves of the horses. Even though it was spring, the muggy air felt like midsummer at home.

They came to fields cultivated with a twiggy plant set in straight rows. They marched off in parallel green rows over the rise of the hill. Cayden examined them as he rode past. He had no idea what they were and his puzzlement must have shown because Ziona spoke up. "Those are cotton plants. They are native to this area, and it appears the local farmers are cultivating them rather than gathering and harvesting from the wild."

"If they are growing cotton in this quantity, then they must have a place to sell it. Who do you think is able to buy all this?"

"Likely local merchants buy it and ship it to the weavers on the southern coast. There is a large guild of wool and cotton weavers on the coast, and the most famous looms for these fabrics are to be found in the town of Seaside."

As they crested the hill, they came upon a small village. A weathered wooden sign hanging from a post announced the hamlet of Cottonham. The tidy fields were cultivated right up to the low stone wall. Past the wall, buildings sprung up and an assortment of people wandered about inside the town going about their daily routines.

"Should we go into the town?" Cayden enquired of Ziona.

She frowned, thinking. "It should be safe enough, but I think we should pose as a married couple. That way we can stay together without suspicion."

"We should be able to blend in fine, two simple travellers passing through."

Sheba shadowed them from the woods. She never entered the villages. She did not like large groups of humans. Ziona nudged her horse, encouraging a slow walk. They rode side by side and were soon entering the town.

Cayden sat tall, back straight and alert in his saddle. Ziona observed him from the corner of her eye. He sat like a monarch, even though he was simply dressed in his woolen cloak, tan pants, and boots. He did not realize his bearing screamed royalty. She saw his chin firm as his eyes surveyed the scene before him. A woman paused in the midst of pinning a blouse to a clothesline to watch him pass. Ziona hid her smile. *It was not every day you saw a king being molded and formed right before your eyes,* she mused.

Several men, gathered around what looked to be the local smithy's shop, watched them pass. They slowly followed after them, drawn to Cayden.

Cayden, completely oblivious to the attention he was attracting, dismounted in front of the inn, looping the reins over the railing. Ziona mirrored his actions and then stepped up onto the boardwalk beside him.

Cayden glanced down at her, wondering at his luck to have her beside him. He offered her his arm and she lightly placed her left hand on it. Together, they entered the tavern beneath a weathered sign announcing it to be the Cotton Gin Inn.

Inside the brightly lit interior, large quilts of cotton were proudly displayed on the walls and ruffled curtains of a similar fabric draped the windows. A round woman with grey hair secured in a tight bun on the top of her head greeted them as they entered. She took one look at the pair of them and dropped a deep curtsey.

"How may I be of service to my lord and lady?"

"We require lodgings and a hot meal served to our room. We would also ask the horses be given an extra measure of grain this evening."

"It shall be as you ask, my lord. Will your manservant be bringing your things?"

"We are travelling light. We will bring our own things up."

"Certainly, please follow me." She headed up the stairs to the right of the door. She led them to a room at the far end of the hall and around a corner. It was obviously the only room in this section, situated over storage rooms below.

She opened the door with a large iron key and then stepped back to allow them to view the room. A small suite was revealed, a large four-poster bed centered in the room with tall curtained windows flanking it. A tall boy dresser in a rich oak adorned one wall, while the opposite side held a petite ladies table with a wash bowl and pitcher. Fresh flowers sweetened the air with their perfume. "Our quietest and most private suite," she announced as they stepped across the threshold.

Ziona perused the room and dismissed the woman with "These rooms are suitable. Thank you." The plump proprietress curtsied roughly and then pulled the door closed behind her.

Cayden groaned and closed his eyes. "There is only one bed." The beginnings of a flush violently rose through the collar of his shirt. Ziona grinned at him, clearly enjoying his discomfort.

"Well, I suppose we do not have to worry about being cold tonight." She laughed as the colour climbed up into his cheeks. "Come, let us retrieve our gear and get a bite to eat."

They descended the stairs together to find a crowd gathered at the base of them. The villagers, including the women and men Ziona had noticed earlier, quieted as they spied Cayden and Ziona at the top of the stairs. Cayden instinctively placed his hand on his sword, eyes measuring the men and women in front of him. No weapons were visible, but it did not mean they were friendly.

They, in turn, doffed hats and made bows to him as he drew eye level with them.

"My lord," a man spoke up, drawing Cayden's attention. The man stared at Cayden with one wild eye that wandered when he tried to focus. A long scar ran from the corner of the wandering eye and disappeared into his rapidly receding hairline. "We could not help but notice your arrival. May we ask your name, sir?"

"My name is Cayden Tiernan." Cayden gazed at the men. There were a good twenty of them and about half as many women assembled. The innkeeper peeked from the door of the kitchen, listening with all her might. Cayden found it odd she would feel the need to sneak inside her own inn.

"And where are you from, my lord?" This came from a redheaded man not much older than Cayden.

"I am from the village of Sanctuary-by-the-Sea. Do you know it?" Cayden glanced around. The men shook their heads at the name. "Why do you ask?"

A middle-aged woman spoke up for the first time. Her blond hair liberally sprinkled with grey fell straight to her waist and her blue eyes were framed by thick eyelashes. She spread her skirts in a deep curtsey. "I'm Catriona, my lord." Peeking at him from under her lashes, she said, "You look like the king." Her voice trembled. "You are the spitting image of the king, may he rest in peace." She made a symbol with her fingers as she breathed a blessing, the crook of her fingers like an eagle's beak.

Ziona glanced sharply at the woman. "How would you know what the king looked like? He has been dead for over seventeen years. Where did you learn that sign? "

The woman cowered back as Ziona's gaze pinned her.

"Please, my lady. I worked as a maid in the castle when I was young. I was a maidservant to the royal family. Although I did not personally attend the king and queen, I had opportunity to see them in the halls. I was a servant to the prince and princess consort. Please, my lord, you have the same colouring and bearing as the king except for the eyes. They are different." The men around her nodded their heads in agreement. "These men, they also served in the castle. They served with the Kingsmen. All except Jakob; he was born here in the village. We beg you to tell us who you really are."

Cayden and Ziona gazed around at them all, stunned.

He had not expected to find people who would seem to recognize him, maybe even be able to identify him. These people appeared friendly, but what of his enemies? Would they be able to recognize him as well? *What am I saying? I am no king. This is foolishness!*

Ziona took control of the crowd by shouldering her way through them, dragging Cayden behind her by his sleeve. Gaining the open air outside the inn, they found an even larger group of people assembled. It appeared half the town was gathered; a good hundred people had congregated out front of the inn in less than ten minutes. Cayden and Ziona's horses had been swallowed up by the crowd but appeared untouched.

Cayden stopped cold, frozen in shock.

The crowd bowed and curtsied as he stepped onto the boardwalk outside the inn. The front row of men melted before him.

"My lord. My prince." A gnarled man in a worn and patched Kingsman uniform rose from the dirt and, with head lowered, spoke. "I pledge my life to your service. We have waited, watched, and prepared for this day as we were instructed to do." He bowed at the waist, his sword extended, grip toward Cayden. "My sword is yours. My life is yours to do with as you please."

The rest of the crowd kneeled behind the first row and repeated the pledge, man and woman alike.

Cayden found his tongue at last. "Stop!" he said, aghast. "What do you think you are doing? You have no idea who I am or where we are going."

Ziona placed a hand on his arm again and stopped his automatic rejection. She leaned over and whispered in his ear. "You are prophesied to save these people. Do you not think it is possible they have prophesies that speak of this day? Hear them out and ask them for their faith and knowledge."

Cayden gazed into her calm emerald eyes and his panic stilled.

He raised his hands to the crowd, who now stood in front of him and behind him, the group from the inn peering out the door.

He felt a feather-like touch along his cheek and heard a thunk. His mind had barely registered the fact that an arrow had imbedded itself in the door frame by his head, when a second arrow pierced his shoulder tossing him backward onto the boardwalk.

Ziona cried out and flung her body over his, shielding him from any more arrows. The first row of the sworn men scrambled upright and formed a human barricade around him, allowing no one access. One man pointed at the rooftop of the building across the street, where a man was seen running off toward the back of the building. Several men took off in pursuit.

Cayden groaned, blood gushing from his right shoulder and soaking his cloak and shirt. Ziona eased back off of him and glared at the men assembled around her. A sharp wicked knife with an obsidian handle gleamed in her hand.

"Be true to your oaths, gentlemen, or be prepared to pay this day with your life," she growled at them all. She flashed the knife and the men backed away slightly. The man with the wandering eye spoke up. He had pushed his way outside to help form part of the men protecting Cayden after he was hit.

"We have been sworn to defend the royal family since we were children. We will defend his life with our own. This we have always done and now that we have found him, this we will do with our last breath."

Ziona locked her eyes on his, dragging the truth from him. Seeing the honesty there, she nodded. "What is your name?"

"Tobias, my lady."

"Help me get Cayden back inside to our room."

Tobias gestured to another man beside him and together they lifted Cayden. He groaned in pain and his eyes rolled, sweat beading on his brow. They carried him back up the stairs as smoothly as possible and gently lowered his unconscious form onto the bed.

"Do you have a healer in this town?"

"We have a midwife, but she is used to setting bones. Perhaps she can be of assistance."

"Fetch her." The second man left.

"Tobias, I want a guard placed on this room, twenty-four hours a day. Do you understand me?" Tobias nodded. "Also, I want you to find the innkeeper and bring her to me. She is involved in this assassination attempt in some way."

"Yes, my lady, it shall be done. I will send up two men I trust to begin guarding the door immediately. I will also see to your horses, my lady." With that, he bowed and left the room, closing the door behind him.

Chapter 35

NELSON PEERED AT THE GLOWING GREEN WALL. Surely it was easier to build a ramp or a staircase to the suspended door than it was to assail the foundation wall of a tower that soared eight stories above the four stories buried deep underground, the fourth of which he was reduced to staring at as he attempted to form a plan to get through it. "Fabian has the easier of the two assignments," grumbled Nelson.

Nelson could try tunnelling deeper, but he suspected the foundation sat on bedrock. He could try blowing it up, but the resultant explosion would alert everyone inside the castle to his activities and most likely bring the upper four stories of natural caverns down on his head, and be insufficient to breach the wall in the end. There was insufficient water available to wear away the stone like he had done with his cold storage back at the inn in the village.

He ran his hand over his chin, scratching the day's growth of stubble. Absently, he reached for his cup of cold water sitting on a narrow stone ledge where he had placed it an hour ago.

The lad at his elbow spoke up. "Did you require anything more, sir?"

"Yes. I need a way to get through this section of wall, but I am stumped as to how to do it."

The lad peered at the limestone block in front of them. It was a faint pink colour and marbled with white veins. "We could use the same fungal paste we were using earlier, sir, if you are interested. You know it, the paste we used to widen the passageway. It worked quite quickly." He waved his hand in the general direction of the limestone block. "The mortar is made of the same substance as the veins of this block. We should be able to dissolve the white material completely."

Nelson smacked his head. Of course, how could he have forgotten? *Stupid old age is creeping up on me.* He frowned at the rock. "How long will it take?"

The lad paused, thinking. "Two days to make enough paste, I think…and maybe a week to dissolve the veins?"

Nelson clapped him on his shoulder. "Get it done in four days, and I have free ale for the night for you and your crew at the inn."

The lad whooped and ran from the cavern to gather his team.

***

Fabian sat back and munched on one of his sticky buns that he had brought along as an incentive to his crew. The icing oozed onto his fingers and he licked them, eyeing the proceedings.

The first stage was constructed, a wooden platform levelling out the bottom of the construct. Risers were being erected on the first stage and fastened in place. In all, they needed to rise about three stories to parallel the door of the Traitor's Gate.

Construction was going slower than he had hoped for. He had a shiny silver piece at risk, should his crew fail to gain entrance before Nelson's. He knew the old innkeeper was as stingy as a washwoman during a drought. He had to be in well ahead of time or kiss his coin goodbye.

Denzik strolled out of the mouth of the passage and paused beside him, watching the workers. He reached into the basket and picked up a sticky bun and bit deeply into its cinnamon center.

"I heard frum sum of the earz today," he mumbled around the delicious mouthful. He swallowed and continued, "There are rumours of a young man moving in this direction who is gathering quite the following." He popped in the last mouthful and chewed slowly. "Some say he has the look of our former king, although how that would be possible, I have no idea."

Fabian tore his gaze from his contemplation of the stairs and raised his eyebrows. "Is it possible, do you think? Is this the one?"

"Yes…yes I think so," Denzik said slowly. "So many things have been happening lately, fortuitous events. It's as if the fates or the Mother Goddess herself is taking an active hand. The ears are very active. Rumours are flooding into the system. Some speak of spirits on the move, haunting armies and laying waste to any that stand in their paths. Others speak of Nature herself rising up, wolves roaming, birds gathering, as though being called to battle. There are even rumours of Primordial warriors past our borders. Something is happening. We need to be ready."

Fabian nodded, thoughtful. "Have you alerted our branches to gather their men and prepare?"

"Yes, I did, as soon as we discovered the wizard. They are on high alert and sharing the watch, ready to respond. One village north of us has already gone silent. It is the area where the lad was rumoured to have been last seen. I can only hope it is positive news of them on the march."

"Time is short then."

Denzik nodded.

"Well we need a couple more days here, four at the most."

Denzik nodded again and then left to relay the news to Nelson.

Time is indeed short, Denzik thought. If this was the moment they had waited and prepared for all these years, they were actually out of time.

Chapter 36

CAYDEN WOKE TO A SOFT TONGUE lapping at his face. He opened his eyes to focus on two large ice blue eyes staring at him. Sheba was stretched out along the left side of his body on the bed. He attempted to sit up but immediately sank back in a groan, realizing for the first time that his right shoulder was swathed in bandages.

"She has not left your side. As soon as you were struck, she bounded out of the woods. I had to convince the men that she was your guardian also. She was frantic to get to you, so frantic that she has ignored her fear of men." Ziona sat in a chair to the right side of the bed observing Cayden. "She snapped at the hand of anyone who got too close. Remarkable restraint for a wild animal, I'd say." Ziona ruffled Sheba's fur.

They have worked out an understanding, Cayden thought.

"What day is it?" Sunlight streamed through the eastern-facing window.

"It's early the next morning. I thought it best to keep you sedated while we took the arrow out and healed your wound. It was deep and hit the bone. We had to remove some bone fragments that splintered, so you will be sore while it heals. I can speed up the process, but it still uses your body strength to heal, so the best thing is rest."

Cayden moved his right arm in a circle, rotating it carefully, testing its limitations.

"Did you catch the archer? Did you find the one who shot me?"

Ziona shook her head. "No. He seems to have had his escape route planned in advance. The innkeeper has disappeared also."

"What of all the people in the square? Are they all right?"

Ziona smiled. "I think I will let them tell you. It is very interesting what they have to say." She stood up and tucked his blankets in more closely to him. "I will go get you some food. Tobias is standing watch at your door. He has refused to rest until he saw you were fine with his own eyes. I will send him in to chat. He can be trusted."

She walked across the room to the door. Sheba's head swivelled to watch her go, eyes intent on the door and what lay beyond. She sniffed the air. Cayden stroked her fur and sensed her contentment at his touch.

Ziona was replaced by Tobias, who entered, closing the door behind him and then snapped to attention. "My lord, you wished to speak to me, sir?"

Cayden watched the man's lazy eye twitch in its socket. The scar was more pronounced this morning, possibly due to his tiredness at standing guard all night.

"How did you receive that scar?"

"I was in the Kingsmen Cavalry, my lord. I served during the Daimonic wars. During the Primordial uprising of Daimon Ford, I was speared by a Primordial soldier who had gotten inside the perimeter guard of the High Prince."

The door opened and another man walked in behind Tobias, the second man who had stood guard through the night. "My name is Stephanos, my lord. What he doesn't tell you is that he took down six other Primordial soldiers while having three arrows stuck in his body, saving the life of the High Prince."

Tobias shrugged. "I refused to allow them to hurt the prince." He bowed his head to Cayden. "But I have failed you, my lord, and I will accept any punishment you see fit. I should have seen the assassin on the top of the building." Tobias knelt by Cayden's bedside on one knee, hands clasped on his knee and head lowered. He looked like a condemned man waiting for the headman's axe.

Cayden struggled to sit up, gasped with the pain and sunk back. Sheba emitted a low growl but did not move.

"Don't be a fool," Cayden gasped, wheezing. *One of those bones the arrow struck must be related to my ribs,* he thought. "We had only arrived. There was no way to anticipate that attack. It must have been totally impromptu." Cayden frowned. "Rise, would you? You are embarrassing me. Besides, I can't see you on the floor."

Tobias scrambled to his feet, his face flaming. "I apologize again, my lord. I didn't mean to embarrass you."

Stephanos chuckled. "My lord, our friend Tobias here is a very literal person. I suggest you speak true every time and hold thoughts you may not wish taken to heart for he will see every word spoken as a command."

Cayden puzzled over what he was expected to do with the two men.

They were dressed similarly in tan pants made from a homespun cloth. Leather vests topped laced shirts with loose sleeves. Both men wore broadswords strapped to their backs. Stephanos's dark beard hid a pointed chin.

"I have the impression you were somehow waiting for me to come, although I cannot figure out any reason for a large contingent of king's soldiers to be holed up in this town."

"That is easily explained, my lord. We have been living our lives in this town since we were dismissed from the king's service seventeen years ago. The queen dismissed all those loyal to the king. We have raised families here." Stephanos fiddled with his bearded chin, nervously.

Tobias grimaced and spat on the floor and then realizing what he had done, shifted uncomfortably. "Sorry, my lord," he murmured. "The queen did not dismiss us. She rode us out of town on threat of death. What she did not realize is that our oaths are for life. She should have killed us." He made to spit again, but then thinking better of it he swallowed back his spittle.

"She did reconsider after the fact. We had to disband in order to not be hunted down like rabid animals. We dispersed," continued Stephanos, "settling in small villages and towns across the land, blending in with the locals, never together in numbers so large as to be noticed. But we did not disband. We have continued to work against the queen and have undermined her reign since the beginning. We have worked to sabotage her supply lines to make her forces ill. We have stolen horses, interrupted couriers, whatever came to mind to create mayhem for her legions. Many of these events she has blamed on the Primordials. All the while, we remained hidden and waited for the return of the prophesied king." He bowed to Cayden once again.

Cayden looked from one to the other and finally spoke what he dreaded saying, "And you think I am this king?"

Tobias caught his eye and grinned. "Of that, my lord, there is no doubt. You will see when we get closer to the capital. There are statues, my lord, in the central square that could have been molded from your form."

Cayden shook his head, dizzy as the implications washed over him. He could not move freely. He would be immediately recognized wherever he went. A part of him wanted to jump to his feet and flee, run as far and fast as he could as fate squeezed him to this path. He saw a great cage looming overhead, one he would never be able to escape, responsibility such as he had never wanted or known.

"My lord," Stephanos spoke this time. "We have heard it is prophesied you will free your people from the queen's grasp. We have waited these long years, working and preparing for this day. We have raised families and have sons and daughters pledged to your service. We are yours, as we pledged yesterday."

Cayden saw Stephanos was completely earnest in his words. Curious, he asked, "How many Kingsmen are we speaking of, Stephanos?"

"We are only one of many groups, my lord. The head of our organization is a man who is near the capital. We do not know his name, as we have only ever known those in our closest units to protect the others should some of us be captured. But at last count, your men totalled around twenty thousand troops, my lord."

Cayden sat bolt upright despite the pain. "*Twenty thousand?*" he exclaimed.

"Yes, my lord. They are scattered and would take time to assemble, but they exist, my lord."

"Oh sweet Mother of Earth," Cayden swore. What was he to do with so many people looking to him...to do what? He didn't even know what he was to do. He sank back to his pillows with a loud, extended groan. It was only partially due to the pain of his injuries, but the two soldiers believed he was tiring and backed out the door with low bows.

"We will leave you to rest, my lord. Have no fear; we are standing guard while you sleep." They withdrew with many more bows and closed the door behind them with a click.

Cayden flung his arms over his eyes, trying to hide from the cage closing on him, but there was nowhere to go.

Chapter 37

RYDER LED HIS MEN AWAY FROM THE TOWN two days after the attack. His men insisted on helping to bury the dead and making a start on repairing the damage to the inn and other buildings in the village. They could not stay for long, however, and after a couple days, they mounted up. As they rode away, Ryder found his ranks had swelled from their original thirty to nearly one hundred.

A sizeable portion of the villagers revealed themselves to be Kingsmen who had settled in the town around the time of Cayden's and Ryder's birth. The men had approached Darius and expressed their desire to assist with the young lord's adventure, as Darius had put it. Ryder suspected the men knew more than they were letting on.

For one, they had assembled on the morning of departure, fully outfitted and ready for a long campaign. Each man had brought his own mount, pack, supplies, and weapons. Each man had also donned his former King's Guard uniform. Some strained around girths that had realigned themselves south over the intervening seventeen years. However, all the men wore them proudly.

They rode into the camp and sat their mounts, waiting and expectant.

Darius had approached the lead man or who Ryder assumed was their leader. After a quick conversation, Darius had walked over to where Ryder had been saddling his mount.

"They want to join us."

Ryder had inspected the men. *It would be stupid to refuse such a well-trained group of soldiers who were not mercenaries, even if they were old enough to be his father. Their skills would be invaluable.*

"Let's make use of them. See that our men are mixed into their units. With their obvious military training, they should be able to teach cavalry charges and the like. They are to report to you as their superior. Select the men who are capable leaders and bring them to me. We will assign them rank."

Darius had done as instructed and now the reformed band had an orderly march, the men set in fighting units.

Ryder rode, flanked on one side by the chosen bannermen of the day and by Darius on his other side. He twisted in his saddle, gazing back at the band of men following him. They had not seen any fighting yet, but he knew deep down it was coming. There was no way for them to reach the capital city without bumping into the queen's legions. And then there were those Charun following them. He felt as though he was being squeezed through a cattle chute toward a dark and dangerous future.

His scouts patrolled ahead and behind the large body of men, now making its way south. Every few minutes, a rider would approach the band, sometimes in groups of twos and threes. More often than not, they also wore the King's Guard uniform. It seemed word was spreading of Ryder's band and the young prince they followed.

They kept moving, stopping for brief periods to sleep but for no longer than six hours at a time. They passed by smaller villages and towns, but they did not pause. Ryder sent teams of men into the towns to purchase supplies as they went. The gold they had brought from Ziona's cave gave them the funds they needed, however as their ranks grew, Ryder became more and more concerned about conserving their funds.

By the time they were two days distant from Devonshire, their numbers had doubled again, as more and more former King's Guard joined their ranks.

The annoying itch that had begun between Ryder's shoulder blades as they fled from the Charun grew worse, the closer they came to the capital city of Cathair.

On the third day, they reached the town of Pert Soaidh, which in the ancient tongue translated into "The Wooded Place of Heroes." Ryder gazed around in open interest as they approached the fringes of the town. It appeared to have been swallowed by a dense forest. There was only one road, split by the town, so that the one on which they travelled lead in from the north and formed again on the far side, departing to the south.

The town boasted the first true fortifications Ryder had seen. The wooden palisade surrounding the town was located on top of a steep-sided earthen mound that rose from a water-filled moat. A wooden drawbridge flanked by guard towers with archery slits adorned both entrance and exit. The middle of the town was split by a river flowing on its east-west axis.

This town would be able to withstand a siege, Ryder noted, as he rode through the gates and into the town proper. His men followed, arranged in precise units, trotted along behind him. No one challenged their entry.

The town was the largest they had seen so far. Wooden houses and shops lined the walls and dirt road, which curved to the right and followed the basic line of the palisade. Streets intersected the curving road like spokes of a wheel within a wheel. The spokes did not run straight to the center of the town but rather they were offset on the next wheel.

There was no straight line to the center of the town, which Ryder identified by a flag flying on top of the tallest structure. The ring roads of the wagon wheel offered the most direct approach. Ryder felt dizzy and confined within the curving streets.

The cobblestone was busy but not overly full, considering it was midday. Tall palisades cast deep shadows on the street below, creating a semi-permanent twilight. Shadows blurred the outlines of the buildings they passed. Ryder thought the design was brilliant; an invading force would be fighting in twilight conditions even in the full light of day, while the residents eyes were accustom to the gloom.

Indeed, as they rode past, they belatedly noticed the armed men watching them from the shadowed alleys between buildings. The itch between Ryder's shoulder blades grew.

As they rounded the curve on the far end of town, their way was blocked by row on row of armoured soldiers, pikes lowered to the oncoming horsemen. Archers stepped to the edge of the two-story buildings above, surrounding them, aiming down on their position. The shadowy figures from the alleys stepped forward. The rear of their procession closed with an equal number of pikes.

Ryder's men drew their swords, steel ringing as they slid them out of scabbards.

Ryder raised his arm signalling a halt and to hold position.

Ryder did not want to trigger a confrontation in the middle of the town. He nudged his horse in the ribs making it walk forward toward the waiting pikes.

"Who here speaks for you men?" He spoke loudly to the men gazing around. "I would speak to your captain."

The men remained in position, pikes lowered. Someone coughed in the group. A voice called from the side and a tall balding man, dressed in a red and blue tunic stepped forward. His blue pants were tucked into tall boots that clicked on the cobblestones as he walked forward. A large feather bobbed on the ornate hat he wore. He did not carry any weapons visible to Ryder.

"I do be the magistrate of this fair town," he announced in a bored voice, "and I do be afraid you intend to pass through without paying the customary levy for the use of our fine streets."

Ryder dismounted and approached the man on foot. "I apologize on behalf of myself and my men for the intrusion. We were unaware a toll had been set for the use of this road. If you could advise the appropriate fee, we will pay it and be on our way."

The magistrate looked Ryder up and down, taking in his dusty country garb. The corners of his mouth turned down in disgust. He ignored Ryder and addressed the eldest of the captains leading the team behind Ryder. "You, good sir, look to be a man of means, please instruct your servant here to remain silent in the presence of a lord."

The King's Guard, a man by the name of Lazaro, rode up beside Ryder. He removed his hat and bowed from the saddle. "You are mistaken, my lord. Sir Ryder is the lord of this band and it is to him you will answer."

The magistrate's eyes widened and his gaze swung back to Ryder. He bowed a short bow that was nearly an insult, for one of equal rank. "My apologies, my lord, I did not realize." He stepped back and gazed around at the tense soldiers on both sides. "Please, allow me to make up for my error. Let us talk over refreshments." He waved his hand and the pikes lowered. The archers eased back on their bows and relaxed.

Ryder nodded to Lazaro, who selected an honour guard for Ryder. Darius accompanied Lazaro and two other men. Laurista rounded out the group.

"Your men are to continue through town and may make use of the wagon staging grounds outside the palisade wall to the south. They will wait for you there."

The pike men separated and formed a gauntlet of steel down which The Band of the Rebel's Land continued to march.

Ryder followed the magistrate who was walking with his own contingent of guards toward a full log building set against an inner palisade wall. It was a two-story structure, the windows fitted with metal bars on the main floor. Stone steps rose to a set of carved double doors, which were opened at their approach by two ceremonial guards, dressed as flamboyantly as the magistrate.

The interior was lit by lamps hung from ornate metal arms, which were attached to the walls at even intervals. Long raised benches lined the back wall and a plain door was visible behind them. Smaller tables and chairs were scattered throughout the balance of the room with doors leading to other rooms on the side. Books lined the walls, their shelves reaching close to ceiling height. Between the doors, hung on the wall was an assortment of portraits of Queen Alcina. Ryder stared at the portraits as they passed.

"You admire my portraits of the queen? She graced me with her presence when she first came to the throne and privileged me with the opportunity to paint Her Grace. She was pleased to find that, as Pert is strategically placed on the road to the capital, her inhabitants are loyal to the throne." His lips curved into a smile that did not reach his eyes.

We have wandered into the mouth of the lion, thought Ryder. *Somehow I do not believe he intends for us to pass through his town.*

The magistrate led them through the end side door and into a room comfortably arranged with overstuffed couches that flanked a cold stone fireplace. Tall windows let in a gloomy light that passed for daylight in the shadow of the palisade wall.

"Please, gentlemen, lady, have a seat. I will call for refreshments."

The magistrate pulled on a silk cord and Ryder heard a bell ring in another room.

A maid dressed in blue livery entered and curtsied. "Please bring tea and scones for our guests, Sharona." She curtsied again and left the room.

"Let me introduce myself. My name is Samuel de Champagne and I am the magistrate and high official of this town." He gestured around at his surroundings. "This building is the courthouse and also houses the trade and taxation departments. Handy if someone do be trying to skip their duties. If they cannot pay their taxes, it do be but a short walk to their cell." He chuckled at the assembled men, who had not yet seated themselves.

"Please, please sit. We have things to discuss." He seated himself in a plush armchair. His guard took up position behind his back, watching the room and its occupants.

Ryder sat in a stiff-backed chair that allowed him free movement. The itch between his shoulders had not left with the disappearance of the town's soldiers. Laurista seated herself in a couch to his left and his escort arranged themselves similarly behind Ryder.

The maid re-entered and placed a tray with cups, teapot, and a plate of scones on a low table by the fireplace. She filled a cup of tea from the teapot and brought it over to Samuel, who took a sip of the brew. She did not serve the others.

"Come, help yourselves to tea." No one moved.

Ryder spoke for the first time. "We do not plan to linger in your town, my Lord Champagne. We intended to pass through on our way south. If you would advise the amount of the tariff, we will be on our way."

He sipped at his tea, considering eyes flicking over the audience in front of him. He set his cup down on the carved table beside his chair.

"Well, first I need to know the purpose of your journey. There are many different levies, depending on the purpose of passing through. For instance, if you are a merchant, moving wool to the looms of the coast, the appropriate levy may be a percentage of what trade you take away from the local wool farmers. If you are a trader in rare metals and coin, perhaps the appropriate levy is a donation to the fund of the poor as you are leaving nothing of value behind for my people.

"The law do be very broad in these areas, you see...and flexible to meet the need." He waved his hand at the books on the other side of the wall. "Our lawmakers have been very meticulous at recording every passerby and the levy imposed in order to keep the assessments fair. However, we have never had an army decide to ride through. They do normally take a route to bypass our fair town." He once again scrutinized the group. "Yes, indeed, you will make for a very interesting test case, I believe." He picked up his tea again, sipping it.

Ryder frowned at the floor, thinking. The magistrate demanded a levy yet he could not advise what was appropriate. Surely they were not the only travellers to pass through the town? Not all could be merchants. So how did they assess the levy against a single traveller or a family? Ryder shifted in his chair, wishing momentarily that he had chosen a softer one.

"We have nothing to trade. We are purchasing supplies as we travel. What would you have us give you?"

"Well you have hit the hammer right on the head, haven't you? You do be passing through and do be taking the supplies of the local farmers. You may even pay for them. If it had not been so, I am sure I would have heard of your band long before now.

"However, merely paying the farmer does not compensate this town for the use of the roads we maintain, so you can reach the farmer in the first place. It does not pay for the protection we give the farmer from bandits...or even rogue armies," he said with a languid smile that did not reach his eyes.

Laurista abruptly stood up and walked over to the cooling tea tray, pouring herself a cup of tea. She met Ryder's eyes and blinked as she took a sip. The magistrate's smile widened. She put it down and then brought Ryder a cup and returned to fetch hers.

She sat and sipped at her tea with Ryder doing likewise.

The magistrate froze, watching them intently. *So the tea was poisoned*, Laurista guessed. They continued to sip. Nothing happened.

The magistrate's eyes widened in shock as the poison appeared to have no effect.

"My Lord Champagne, poisoned tea is a very old ruse. Surely your healers have developed a counteragent to this particular kind?" She continued to sip her tea, as Ryder did his. "Obviously, your cup is not poisoned. Ours, I suspect, most definitely are."

"Perhaps"—Ryder pinned the magistrate with his hot glare—"we have found our levy."

The magistrate assessed him with roving eyes. "I do believe we have, my boy...I do believe, indeed."

Chapter 38

"HERE, PUT THE PRY BAR IN THIS WAY." Nelson flipped the bar over and wedged it back into the side slot of the limestone block closer to the top. A gap had appeared where the paste had done its job. "Now, give it a good heave and keep working it in the crack, back and forth. Then, alternate with the other side of the rock like this." Nelson handed the pry bar back to the Kingsman and stepped back out of the way.

They worked the pry bars, scraping aside mortar and wedging the steel under the lip of rock, shifting it by the tiniest of increments. The men had to take turns, working the block side by side, rocking it back and forth until a good three inches had been moved out from the face of the wall.

Suddenly, a tapping reply issued from the rock. Nelson flapped his arms, hushing the men. "Tap, tap…Tap, tap, tap…" went the message, repeating itself. Nelson listened intently. "Back…stand…back…," he murmured, sounding the code out. *Stand back?*

A great crash filled the cavern as the block popped out of the hole like the plug out of a dam. The one-hundred-pound rock fell to the floor and tumbled a couple of times before coming to rest. The men leapt back to preserve their toes as it rumbled past, churning centuries old dust into the air.

Nelson waved his hand in front of his face, coughing, and squinted at the now sizeable hole. A man stared back at him, white hair and beard streaming past his shoulders.

Nelson moved closer to the hole. "Mordecai Ben-Moses, I presume?"

"Alas it is I, or that was what I was called when I was locked away in here seventeen years ago."

"How did you do that?" Nelson said, peering at the old man as the dust from the collapse settled to the floor. He waved a hand to clear the lingering haze.

"Oh, a bit of this and a bit of that...some hocus pocus and there you have it." He grinned at the bewildered expression on Nelson's face. "Come, come surely the world has not forgotten about magic?" He *tsked* and shook his head sadly. "Magic surrounds us. All it needs is a disciplined mind, some focused intent and the will to see the thing through. This"—he held up his crystal—"also comes in useful."

Nelson's eyes squinted, more confused, not less.

Mordecai sighed. "I presume they did not announce my untimely death or any such thing in my absence? I would not relish having to explain how I am still alive when everyone who loved me has forgotten me and those who hated me are alive to hate me still."

Nelson chuckled. "No, they did not announce your death, although I think most have forgotten you existed. They never announced your capture. You were never spoken of again. Most thought you had died, so I suppose it is the same thing."

Mordecai chuckled softly. "Certainly, I can make use of being dead. Few souls have the opportunity to walk the land again in the same bodies that dressed them originally. I must admit, though, this cell has become quite wearisome in the intervening years. It is time I took up new residence elsewhere...but not quite yet. I am expecting a very important visitor shortly."

Nelson frowned. "They allow you company?"

"Certainly not—I don't exist, remember? No, this company will be dropped into my lap, quite literally, I believe." One eye stared through the crack. "Keep enlarging this hole for I foresee a time in the near future when it will come in quite useful. But you must replace all the stones at the end of the day. I will disguise the work from my side."

Nelson nodded. "I will bring Denzik to see you tomorrow. He's the brains of this outfit."

"Now, would you pass me one of those wonderful sticky buns I have smelled for the last hour? It's been so long." Mordecai sniffed the air in appreciation.

"I will never hear the end of it from Fabian," Nelson grumbled, passing the bag of sticky buns through to the grizzled old wizard.

* * *

Fabian grunted. The steps were finally in place and the door facing him at eye level. He ran his hand down the stubble on his unshaven chin and grunted again. He still had no idea how to open it. The thick oak door's hinges were covered in thick rust, proof positive of inactivity. He doubted if they had been opened since Captain O'Reilly and his men had taken up residence in the chamber. Fabian scratched his head, examining the problem.

Nelson must be close to getting through the block wall. Who would have thought he could chisel through a castle wall faster than I could assemble a staircase?

The lead carpenter squeezed past him, picking up his tools and dropping them into a tool belt strapped around his waist. Fabian grabbed his arm, halting him. "Tell me, how would you break open that door if it was up to you?"

The carpenter paused, glancing at the door. "You want to get into the next room?"

"Yes, I do."

"Well, why don't you have someone open it from the other side?"

"I don't know if anyone is on the other side."

"So, why don't you get someone to go and open it for you?"

Fabian stared at him. The idea wasn't as dumb as it sounded at first. "You do know who is on the other side?"

"Well, as this would be the prison section, I would assume some of the Queen's Guard."

"That is correct. Why would they help us?"

"They wouldn't...but one of the serving staff might. They feed the prisoners on a regular basis, right? So they have access to the prisoner cells." He headed down the stairs and back to the crew who were waiting below.

Fabian gazed after the man and then at the door again and laughed silently. It was time to arrange for a delivery of sweet buns to the castle. Nothing opens doors like the smell of food, and those sweet buns were a cinnamon-crusted golden key to the castle and to the corridors beyond.

Chapter 39

LAURISTA LEANED IN TOWARD RYDER as they walked down the steps of the government house. "Well played, my lord," she whispered, eyes darting around at the guards on either side of the double doors.

"So the tea was poisoned?"

"No, the cup was. The maid poured tea in his cup only to make sure he got the clean cup. I quickly rinsed your cup with the tea I poured, and then I combined it into mine while his attention was on you. I emptied the poison into my cup."

Ryder's head swung in her direction, alarm in his expression. "How are you still standing then?"

"I didn't drink any of the tea. I only pretended to. The tea never touched my lips."

The corner of Ryder's eyes crinkled in laughter. "Where did you learn to be so devious?"

She stepped along, raising her skirts to avoid the puddles left over from a passing shower. "I was the king's taster in my younger years."

Ryder's eyes widened, in response to her words. "You were in the royal court? Why did you leave?"

"I was reassigned to some country lord who was in charge of the legions in the outer territories. When he died during a siege, I ended up assisting the healer to the legion. Funny enough, everyone in the royal court was dead within a year of my dismissal from my post...with the exception of the queen, of course. I suspect they all died of poisoning, although it is considered treason to voice that opinion."

"Well, I am certainly happy to have found you. Do you really know the antidote to that poison?"

"Yes, I recognized the herb being used. I can make an antidote for it." She laughed. "The magistrate may not be pleased with its side effects, however, as unfortunately you find yourself with wicked cramps that require an inordinate amount of time spent in the privy."

Ryder laughed in response. He intended to be far away before the magistrate found the need to use that particular remedy.

***

Ryder and the band left the fortified town the following morning. Once the levy had been arranged and paid for, they were invited to trade openly with the townsfolk, who were happy to entice the soldiers with wares gathered from the four corners of the queendom. The men were allowed to return to the town in groups no larger than ten. They were required to sign in and out before the next group entered.

Despite the restrictions, the townsfolk were eager for news from the outside word. It seemed merchant caravans avoided the town due to the taxes levied. A vigorous smuggling trade was the result with an active underground component.

Ryder chose what was purported to be the best inn in the town, the Flaming Phoenix. They took a quiet booth in a corner away from the crowd of locals who appeared to be flocking into the inn for an evening of entertainment.

Ryder sipped on the house specialty, a spiced rum punch served in a mug decorated with a hand-painted phoenix. Ryder thought they looked like flamingoes with attitude. Laurista sat beside him, as did Darius and Lazaro who had insisted on accompanying them.

The inn's entertainment for the evening was provided by a man playing a dulcimer while a middle-aged woman sang. The townsfolk formed squares and began to perform a dance unfamiliar to Ryder. He watched while sipping his drink. People clapped along in time to the music.

A short muscular man took a winding path through the crowd to Ryder's table. He swept the hat from his head and then bowed to Ryder and said quietly, "My lord, I would speak with you, if it pleases you?"

Ryder nodded and motioned to the seat across from him.

"My lord, I have been told to enquire about your purpose in passing through our town?"

"We seek to catch up to some companions we were separated from."

The man nodded. "We have been commissioned to pass a message to the man who hails from the cliffs. Is this the man you seek?"

Ryder observed the man, trying to get his measure.

"Perhaps."

The man lowered his voice to prevent being overheard.

"Would you be headed for the capital?"

"It's possible."

"I have a contact in a village outside of the capital in a town called Lower Cathair. I have been instructed to advise the leader of the band from the cliffs when he passes through to find a man named Denzik."

The man glanced around again quickly, checking the crowd. The noise of the dancers drowned their voices and made listening in by normal means impossible.

"I am also to give you this." He slid a leather pouch across the table. "Do not open it here. Open it in private."

Ryder picked up the bag and tucked it into an inner pocket of his cloak.

"Please pass this message to Denzik when you see him. Tell him we stand ready to serve. The watchtowers are manned."

Ryder nodded.

The man stood up and without a backward glance walked away.

Laurista leaned her arms on the table to watch the man depart.

"Kingsman, do you think? Or a spy for the queen?"

"Could be both. What do we know of the politics in this area? It's time we moved on though. It's dangerous to stay in one spot for too long. Let's head back to camp."

Chapter 40

THE PEOPLE ASSEMBLED BEFORE CAYDEN were the ragtag remnants who had managed to flee before the legions descended on the outlying villages of Cathair. They had joined the Kingsmen's flight as they left the capital, blending into their ranks and fading into other villages, establishing new lives in order to protect their sons from the conscription teams. The light of rebellion shone in their eyes. Men and women alike were armed, the men donning pants and armour they had obviously created for themselves. Hand-tooled leather fashioned to fit each individual was proudly worn complete with leg chaps and arm guards.

The women had shorn their hair into a pageboy style that somewhat disguised their gender. They had fashioned linen amour that molded to their feminine forms, layers on layers of tightly woven linen, bound together and as thick as Cayden's thumb. Each woman's armour was specially made for her body and dyed vibrant hues of red, green, yellow, and blue. The amour made them look as intimidating as female dragons guarding their nest of younglings. To Cayden's eyes, they appeared every bit as fierce as the men.

Cayden nudged his horse into a slow walk. The sun had cleared the treetops. It promised to be a hot day.

Tobias advised they would reach the castle with two days of steady travel. He had sent runners ahead to scout the way and locate a promising area to camp their large band.

The wind rustled the treetops and played with the edge of his cloak. One of the women of the village had produced a fine silk cape made of a deep purple with golden crowns embroidered on the hem.

The crest of the king was embroidered over the right breast. It had been part of the ceremonial uniform of the King's Guard and the men had insisted Cayden wear it in their honour. Cayden had refused the gift, of course, but with Ziona's frown and the men's disappointment clearly etched on their faces, he had succumbed and now it was fastened around his throat with a fine golden clasp shaped like an eagle.

"I feel like a circus monkey," he said, tugging at the clasp.

"You are the image of the king. Yes, you are or soon will be." Ziona laughed as he grimaced.

His frustrated posture made her smile widen and she leaned over to straighten his collar. "Smile, the people are watching. You cannot let them see your insecurity or uncertainty. You must always display confidence and courage. They draw strength from you."

"Let's get this circus on the road," he said with a wobbly twist of his lips. He booted his mare to a trot, his guard spreading out around his mount.

They kept a steady pace throughout the day, catching up to the scouts about an hour before dark. The spot they had chosen for the camp was bordered by a stream on the west and the east was boarded by the road, which had been strangely empty all day. They settled in a meadow knee high in grass. The men and ladies quickly dismounted, hobbling their horses and giving them quick rubdowns before saddling them again. They set up a quick camp without tents, prepared to move quickly as they entered the area patrolled by the queen's guards. Small fires were lit, and as soon as the meal was prepared, they were doused and buried.

Cayden settled down in his blankets and gazed up at the stars glimmering above. He sensed the wolves nearby. Sheba was off meeting with the packs around their camp. He felt she was setting up her own guard, unbeknownst to the group surrounding him.

Ziona leaned over and checked his shoulder again. The arrow wound was a faint pucker now, the skin pink and healthy.

"Rest well, Your Majesty," she grinned and with a quick curtsey, dropped down, and buried herself in her blankets, giggling at his reaction.

Cayden grimaced and then a grin tugged at the side of his mouth. He chuckled as he relaxed, stretching an arm behind his head for a pillow. He drifted off to sleep, secure in the fact Sheba was watching out for him.

He jerked awake what seemed a short time later, to Sheba's howls combining with the howls of a dozen other wolves. He leapt to his feet, grabbing his sword as the urgency of her cries pierced his mind.

"To arms," he shouted before he even cleared his blankets.

Shadows flitted at the edge of his vision, as Ziona shot to her feet at his call. Cayden continued to holler and the camp erupted, the shadowy forms coalescing into soldiers brandishing swords and cudgels. Battle erupted around Cayden, who found himself in hand-to-hand combat for the first time since his arrest and attempted abduction from the legion. He scrambled to right himself then deflected a blow aimed at his head, the sword skidding along his blade and bouncing off his guard at the last second.

He shouldered the soldier, throwing him off balance and Ziona stabbed the fallen man. She backed up to Cayden and as a unit they battled the oncoming soldiers. Cayden's downward stroke sliced the wrist of the next soldier, as he attempted to stab Cayden in the thigh. Ziona's swing took the soldier in the throat and the man fell, blood spurting from his opened neck.

Cayden felt sickened. He did not want to kill. *I could not kill…not even to save myself.*

Ziona felt no such compunction. She fought like a cornered badger; her every intent to kill. Ziona shoved Cayden behind her, shouting, "Cayden! Do not worry about attacking to kill. Just wound. I will finish them."

The enemy soldiers surrounding them hesitated when the pair began fighting as a cohesive whole. Suddenly, all four soldiers attacked at once. Cayden's mind flashed back to his days as the rabbit and he sought a low center, his back guarded by the rock that was Ziona. Cayden dodged the first sword and ducked under the cudgel swung at his head. His sword arced, slicing through two sets of kneecaps, causing the two soldiers to stumble.

Ziona's sword decapitated the closest soldier, his head bouncing across the trampled grass, the soil darkening with his blood, even as she stabbed the second facing her in the shoulder causing him to curse and stumble away from her. He was lost from Cayden's view.

Cayden saw the two soldiers facing him pause, drawing back to reassess their opponents. Then they rushed him together and he sought to keep them at arm's length. He felt Ziona jerk behind him and heard the lone soldier facing her grunt.

The sounds of battle were suddenly muted under the howl of wolves. From the corner of his eye he saw multiple sets of glowing eyes, a second before the wolves attacked.

The air around them exploded as the snarling pack of wolves fell on the enemy soldiers. They fell back, attempting to guard their throats from the razor sharp fangs and curled claws. Men fell, hamstrung and ravaged by the savage attack.

Cayden stopped fighting, mesmerized. He could understand the communication between the pack members. He could *hear* what they were thinking. He knew where the wolves would attack next. His focus switched to an unfortunate soldier, who had been attempting to flank Cayden and Ziona, by taking advantage of the confusion caused by the wolves' arrival. The soldier realized his mistake a moment too late and with an agonized cry, disappeared beneath three large wolves.

The rest of the camp fought on, but the attacking forces were disorganized now, the wolves putting a panic into the defeated troops. Within a few minutes, all fell still, the few remaining legionaries retreating and disappearing into the trees on the opposite side of the road.

The wolves disappeared, silently sliding back into the shadows. Sheba padded up to Cayden and sat down at his side. She cocked her head to one side, panting at him. Cayden knew she was asking for confirmation she had done well. Cayden knelt beside her and hugged her. He cupped her wolf face between his palms. "You did great, Sheba. Well done!" Her tongue flopped out to the side for a second, and then she licked his hand. She trotted back into the woods, seeking her kin.

Cayden stood up and turned to speak to Ziona. It was only then he saw her swaying on her feet. Scarlet blood soaked the left side of her tunic. Cayden grabbed her as a surprised "Oh!" popped out and she collapsed in a heap.

Chapter 41

"ZIONA, YOU'RE HURT!" Frantically, Cayden pulled open her tunic to see a deep cut had opened up a belly wound, her intestines clearly showing through the open flap of skin. Cayden gasped and clasped his hand over the wound, attempting to keep her together.

Ziona's eyes glazed in pain. As she stared at Cayden, his silhouette glowed as blue and clean and clear as a summer sky. His silhouette shimmered and blurred as she struggled to focus on him. She knew it was blood loss, but in another part of her she saw his soul pulsing with life and comfort. She knew she was gazing at a god.

She smiled at him. "I am not afraid, Cayden. I see you clearly for the first time. I am yours; my soul is yours to do with as you please. I do not fear death when you are near." Her eyes drifted closed.

Cayden's heart burst within him. He shuddered and yelled, "Ziona, don't you give up on me. You cannot die! I need you. Please!" He shook her shoulder, begging. "Please, Ziona, stay with me!" Ziona did not respond. As he gazed at her, he saw a mist begin to rise from her body.

He pulled her body tightly to him, sheltering her in his strong arms. Hot tears slid down his cheeks as he gazed at her bloodied form. They dripped unchecked from the end of his nose and splashed onto her smooth alabaster cheek, sliding to join the dusting of black-tipped lashes feathered under her eyes. His soul was as parched as the desert, soaking up her life essence. Love, pure sweet love, slipped past his barriers, breaking free, gathering into a tempest that beat inside of him, an avalanche of feelings long resisted and buried deep. *Ziona, my heart, you cannot die! I will be lost without you! You are the completion of my soul. Please do not leave me. Please, I beg you! I beg you!*

Cayden shook, his body quaking, refusing to accept what he was seeing. He threw back his head and howled, his soul screaming in pain. He expanded his will and called frantically to the spirit of the Aossi, his tears and his voice recreating the song of the flute, but this time it played from his inner being. His lips formed words into a chant he did not know the source of. Nonsense tumbled from his lips as he prayed.

He opened his eyes and saw time had frozen around him. The men who had reacted to his scream had slowed, as though they were walking through air thickened by molasses. Surprise slowly spread across their faces as they moved with the tiniest of increments. He focused on Ziona and saw the mist had slowed also.

Aossi walked up to Cayden and placed a hand on his shoulder, sharing his view of the still woman.

"It is not so easy to watch them die, is it, young one? Yet they pass their spirit to you without a thought. They trust you to care for them both before and after death. It is what being a god is about."

Cayden eyes filled with tears, his chest constricted in anguish so tight he struggled to draw breath. He could not focus on her words.

"She cannot die. I need her, Aossi! She is my guide. I am lost without her."

"Yes, she is your guide. You chose her long ago and you chose well." She tilted her head observing the woman and then looked back at Cayden. "I can do nothing for her soul. That is her gift to you. I can return her body, heal her wounds, as she is not completely gone from this world as of yet. But only you can return her soul to her."

Cayden looked away from Aossi, wiping tears from his face. "I do not know how."

Aossi grinned impishly and tapped Cayden's nose with her finger. "I think you do, young one. You stilled time so you would have the time to save her. You also know how to return it. It is a similar thing to return her soul to her body. But be warned, the power of a god is not without repercussions. She will live in a half world from this moment on. Half of her soul is bound to you in truth as she had begun the process of the transfer. Return it to her now and you are also bound to her. You will feel her near or far, forever more." She fondly lifted his chin, meeting his eyes. "You already share such a bond, do you not…with your sister?"

Cayden considered her words, frowning. It was true. He could always tell where Avery was. He nodded his agreement with her words.

"Let us begin then." Aossi knelt down and replaced Cayden's blood-soaked hands with her own. She traced the line of the sword slash, humming a tune that brought a mental image of butterflies in a garden, lush with flowers, their wings sighing on the breeze. The skin knitted together. The mist remained frozen in time.

Cayden closed his eyes and concentrated on Ziona, seeking her essence in the air, gathering the pearls of her personality and tiny shards of her sensitivity, the wisps of her soul, and pulled them into a tight ball of bright being. Some of his own soul blended with the compact point of light, surrounding it and containing Ziona's spirit. He then pushed with his own soul, taking the point of life and forcing it back into the body lying on the ground. He didn't understand what he was doing, working with raw instinct as he searched for a spark to attach the light to. His soul touched her mind and prodded it to accept the blended essence.

Aossi drifted down and gently pumped Ziona's chest, forcing her heart to move and circulate its blood again. Cayden bent over and placed his lips on Ziona's and breathed a long soulful breath into her lungs. Her body jerked as his breath inflated her lungs and the heart took over pumping her blood.

Aossi grinned and pinched his cheek, laughing at the blush that grew there.

"Remember what I said, young one. " She winked at him one last time and disappeared.

The time bubble dropped and real time returned.

Ziona's eyes shot open and she gasped at the gentle pressure of Cayden's lips meeting hers.

The soldiers of the camp ran over form a solid barrier around them.

Cayden cupped Ziona's cheek and gazed into her eyes. "I nearly lost you."

Ziona cupped his cheek in response, holding him to her with the touch, her eyes searching his. "I am with you always to the end of days."

Cayden's eyes crinkled at the corners with joy. Vibrant green eyes locked onto hummingbird green and the bond flared between them.

Can you hear my thoughts? Cayden sent his thoughts to her with his mind.

Ziona's eyes widened in surprise and she sent back: *Yes, is that really you? I can hear your thoughts in my head!*

Yes, it's me, but I have no idea how I am doing it. Aossi said we would have a bond from this moment on, something about how we saved your life.

Aossi was here? She swivelled her head, her eyes searching for Aossi's form.

Cayden cleared his throat and resumed normal speech. "Can you sit up yet, Ziona?"

She stared down at her torso, observing the tattered clothing and the large pool of blood all around her. She ran her hand over the mended skin in wonder.

"I should be dead," she whispered.

Cayden helped her to a sitting position as Tobias arrived.

"My lord! My apologies, my lord! We were blocked by a large group of soldiers. We fought our way through them just now. They were intentionally delaying us." Tobias gasped as his gaze switched to Ziona for the first time. "My lady, you have been wounded!" He spun on his feet and bellowed, "Medic, get over here now!"

Cayden caught his arm. "It's OK, Tobias. I have tended to Ziona. She is fine now. She will need rest, but I am sure there are other more critically wounded."

Tobias took a closer look at Ziona. His hand trembled over the healed skin where her belly wound had been. He instantly dropped to his knees, bowing his head to the earth. "My lord, forgive me for my lack of faith. You are as great as we have been told. Praise to the king, the Protector of Souls! Praised be the Spirit Shield, true heir of Cathair!"

The soldiers around Cayden and Ziona instantly followed suit, picking up the chant and kneeling where they stood.

Cayden scrambled to his feet and held up his hands to quiet the men.

"Please, we have no time. Tend to your brothers and sisters in arms."

They rose and resumed their duties. As they did so, Cayden heard the whispering tale take flight amongst the troops.

In no time at all, word spread to every soldier and cook in the company or at least their version of it. The story would grow and evolve with the retelling, as all great tales do, but for those lucky few who were present for the event, there was no doubt in their minds they had witnessed the birth of a legend.

Chapter 42

THE CITY GATES WERE FLUNG WIDE OPEN under the brilliant sky. The curved gate was broad enough for three carts to travel side by side with ease. They dwarfed the farmers' and merchants' wagons moving in and out in a steady stream. Dust stirred in the air, brought in on the hooves of horses and wheels of the wagons, despite the smooth paving stones lining the road.

The dust is lesser here than on the open road beyond the two-mile marker, Fabian thought, *but still the buns are sticky and any dirt is unacceptable.* He glanced back into his covered wagon where sat three of his apprentices. They maintained a tight grip on the stacked trays of buns, adjusting the cloth covers to prevent the dusty air from settling on them. The heat of the day brought out the smells of cinnamon and the caramelized sugar glaze that was the hallmark of his recipe. Others had tried to emulate it but had failed. His were simply the best.

He drew up at the checkpoint and nodded to the officer who approached his wagon.

"Destination?" he yawned around the words in a bored voice.

"Castle cook's kitchen. I have a delivery of sticky buns."

The officer sniffed the air and then, in a voice filled with longing, groaned. "I have always wanted to try one of those."

"We don't often make the market these days. They are sold out long before I can get them here."

Fabian studied the officer for a moment and then snapped his fingers, as if a thought had just occurred to him. "Say, maybe we can make a deal. I need a guard till we reach the kitchens. Oh, not a real guard, someone to keep the crowds away from the wagon so these arrive fresh and hot, the way Her Majesty likes them. Spare a lad, say that one over there…to give us a hand?"

The officer motioned to the young recruit who was lounging against the wall, appearing as bored as his superior.

"Anthony!" he called.

The recruit marched over and snapped to attention. "Yes, sir!"

"Escort this wagon to the castle kitchens. They are not to be disturbed. Understood? Keep the crowds away. This is a delivery for the queen."

"Yes, sir!" Anthony took up position beside the horse team's head.

"Thank you, Captain, and please enjoy this with our compliments." He handed down a huge sticky bun oozing with caramelized sugar resting on a paper napkin.

The officer grinned and waved Fabian on. Fabian clucked to the horses and they clopped forward with a jingle of the harness.

Anthony temporarily slowed his gate, allowing Fabian to pull up beside him. Keeping his eyes forward, Fabian muttered in a low voice, "Good to see you again, Anthony. Is all prepared?"

"Yes, I have people in place within the castle with access to the dungeons. They are ready to act when we are."

"Excellent. Now let's see if we can get there safely without getting mugged for our load of sticky buns."

The cart horse plodded along, the way through the streets a familiar route for the old mare. As they approached the castle, she automatically turned down a side alley, cast in deep shadow from the wall of the castle on one side and a two-story building on the other. The alley narrowed to a width that barely allowed the cart through without scraping the sides. After three hundred paces, it opened into a small square. The castle wall was set with solid wooden doors, their heavy iron hinges recessed into the native limestone.

The square was a dead end. Directly ahead was the entrance to a set of stables. Two guards stood at the entrance. The horses of visiting lords and ladies were typically housed within these stables. The royal stables backed up to them through a common door in the castle wall that was never opened unless for an emergency and then only with the proper password.

Fabian halted at the gate and Anthony stepped forward to introduce the arrival to the guards posted at the kitchen receiving gate. He was greeted jovially and with much back slapping. Fabian overheard the words "...sticky buns?" and "...would be worth the lecture for a taste..."

The guards signaled to the watchman high on the wall and the gates rolled back on wheels set to assist the movement of their ponderous weight. The sunny inner courtyard slowly revealed women and men dressed in service livery, some carrying baskets balanced on their shoulders and others carrying pails or pulling small carts loaded with supplies. To the right, teams of horses and wagons were lined up, their owners waving their hands, instructing the servants on the delivery of their goods.

Fabian pulled up beside the last delivery and hopped down from his wagon. Anthony waited for Fabian at the back of the wagon and then whispered, "I can't remain here for long, but I can see you safely inside and to our contact." In a louder voice he said, "This way, please."

Fabian's assistants jumped down from the wagon bed and pulled out the sticky bun trays. They each carried two trays and left Fabian to pick up the last two and follow them.

The procession was keenly watched, as hungry workers caught a whiff of the delectable treats that drifted in their direction. Fabian glanced around and thought his plan for an escort was wise regardless of his other plans. He shook his head, bemused at the attention his wares were gleaning.

They reached the kitchen delivery doors without incident and crossed into the comparatively cooler interior. It took a moment for their eyes to adjust after the brilliant sunlight of the courtyard. They blinked, hastening the adjustment of their eyes to the dimmer setting. The main kitchen was a large three-sided stone room, the fourth set with large windows facing the courtyard. Long wooden shutters were thrown open to allow the heat to escape and to tease a breeze into the warm interior.

Three wooden tables ran parallel to the length of the room, stacked with plates and bowls and food in various stages of completion.

Large-bricked wall ovens flanked the end wall and in each open hearth, spits of meat sizzled as they were rotated, the metal spit attached to a wheel which was in turn was connected to a larger wheel set with handles. The spit boy cranked the wheel slowly, as he had been taught, wiping his sweaty forehead on a towel draped over his shoulder on one side. Fabian observed him crank the wheel five times, which set up the spring and the spit turned as it slowly unwound. The boy then moved to the next and then the next and by the time he finished the entire row, the first oven was ready to be wound again.

"Now isn't that efficient," said Fabian, gesturing to the lad.

"Sir, if you will follow me." Anthony marched away down a side corridor out of the main kitchen.

They followed Anthony down the corridor, the heat fading somewhat as they walked. At the end of the hallway, they entered a stone passageway that led to a set of circular stairs disappearing into the gloom. A hole in the wall displayed a wooden platform and a set of ropes alongside it. *A dumb waiter*, Fabian guessed.

They walked carefully down the curving staircase, eventually reaching the dim recesses below. A hallway led back underneath the main kitchen. A wooden door blocked the end of the dark hallway, which was lit by a couple of torches.

"This is the refrigeration room," Anthony explained. "You may store your baked goods here." He pulled on the door, swinging it open. Inside were wooden shelves lined with supplies; bags of potatoes and carrots, heads of cabbage, onions, and apples in bushel baskets rested on the floor.

Fabian found a spot on the far wall cleared for their trays. They placed them carefully on the rack.

"The queen requests that you stay and enjoy the hospitality of the castle." Anthony bowed to Fabian. "Your apprentices may join in with the other serving staff and enjoy the evening."

Fabian nodded to the staff, dismissing them. They grinned and trotted quickly out of the cold room, happy for an early beginning to a day in the capital. They quickly disappeared back up the winding stairs.

Once they were alone, Anthony dropped all formality.

"Come, we only have a couple hours before you will be expected to be in Her Majesty's presence. She has wanted to meet the creator of her favourite sweet for ages."

They pulled closed the cold storage door, and then Anthony led Fabian off down a side passage leading back toward the east end of the castle. He lifted a lantern from a wall stand and lit it, carrying it along in front of him. After about three hundred feet, they arrived at another set of stairs, carved directly out of the limestone which made up the base of the castle. They wound down the worn steps which opened out onto a railed stone landing. Fabian stepped up to the railing and gazed over the edge. Wooden doors with iron grills were set into either end.

Below a set of guards were seated with their booted feet up on a trestle table. Their swords were resting on the table beside their boots, reflecting the light of the lantern hung on a peg above their heads. Both guards held cards in their hands, intently studying the faces on each one. One guard leaned forward and tossed a card on the stack in the center on the table.

"Sire of hearts," he said. The other guard grunted.

"Squire of diamonds," he huffed, throwing his card on the pile.

"You know, they had better arrive soon. Our shift is almost over," said the first guard. The second grunted once more.

"Sire, consort, and bastard of diamonds. I win." The second tossed his remaining cards on the table.

The first growled and peered over his feet at the display, suspicious.

"You always pull that set. How is it you always get those cards?" The second guard shrugged, grinning.

Anthony harrumphed loudly from the landing.

Both guards shot to their feet, peering up at the balcony above. Spying Anthony, they relaxed.

"About time you got here! What took you so long?"

"There was a near riot in the courtyard for this guy's sticky buns. He attracts more flies than...well you know, that's not important now." Anthony opened the door on the left and headed down the stairs approaching the guards, Fabian trailing in his wake.

"When will the meal guard be around?"

"Soon. Wendell usually arrives about a quarter to the hour which should be any time now."

"You are sure he is on board?"

"Yeah, he has been doing this duty for twenty years. Sour to it, he is, always passed over for a promotion. He is keen to earn some gold though…and to get away from carrying chamber pots." He chuckled, while reaching for a lantern.

"This is Fabian, the one I told you about," he said, waving vaguely in his direction. "Come on. Let's find Wendell so we can get these cells open."

The second guard stood and produced a rusty keychain on which dangled around twenty long metal-toothed keys. It rattled as he searched for the correct key, and then he inserted it into the lock. With a creak of rusting hinges, the door opened to a gloomy interior hallway.

The wavering light fell immediately on a ruddy face, lips parted to reveal a swollen tongue. Glassy eyes bulged as the corpse's hands clutched the rope around his neck. The rope led up and over a crossbeam inside the doorway. His feet dangled as the body swayed mere inches from the floor.

Chapter 43

RYDER CHEWED HIS LOWER LIP AND THOUGHT. He chewed it some more and stewed over his choices. How does one hide five hundred plus soldiers from the eyes of the queen of the land as one descends on her city? His thoughts ran round and round in his head, but no answer presented itself.

The swelling band pushed their way slowly through a rough terrain consisting of scrub brush and rocky abandoned farmers' fields, keeping away from the main roads.

The recent rains had left flooded pockets of mud, their path clearly visible to any who wished to follow. He hoped no one was interested in them. He snorted in response to the absurdity of his own thoughts, as more people drifted into his ranks on a daily basis. He feared the news of their movements was far outstripping their progress.

Darius rode at his one shoulder, Laurista at his other. Both examined the shoreline ahead as they approached the banks of the river once more. They needed to find a good place to ford the river before they reached the capital proper.

One of the scouts appeared out of a stand of trees about two hundred yards ahead of their location. Ryder saw it was the young lad Michale they had rescued from the legion camp. Ryder hadn't realized Darius had recruited him into the scouting ranks.

The lad rode up and joined Darius to give his report.

"My lord, there is a good fording point not far from our location. The river widens and there are sandy shoals for about half of the river."

Ryder acknowledged the report with a nod. "Darius, alert the men and women and let the wagon drivers know we are going to attempt a fording of the river. They may need to lighten their loads."

"Yes, sir." He saluted and rode off to give the orders. Michale claimed a position out front, leading the way.

Laurista watched the young man ride away. "He is adjusting well to his new duties. I had feared for his sanity when he was first brought to me. He was barely coherent. He is still a boy, only now entering his manly years."

"Yes, but war and violence will make a man of a boy before he realizes what has happened. One cannot witness what he did and not have his innocence stripped from him." Ryder followed the lad's progress with his eyes. He reached into his pocket and fingered the pouch he had received from the mysterious man in Pert Soaidh. It contained a coin to match the one he had recovered in Cottonham and a brooch with the insignia of the Royal House of Cathair, a golden shield wreathed in blue spirits.

Laurista regarded Ryder. "Yes, it changes a boy into a man, doesn't it?" She lifted an eyebrow knowingly at him.

Ryder shifted in his saddle and chose to ignore her.

The Band of the Rebel's Land had swollen to over five hundred men. Ryder felt the weight of responsibility keenly. He had dreamed of becoming a knight, not the general of an army. He knew nothing of battle strategy or of fighting. Cayden had at least received some training. Ryder had none.

Yet Cayden was relying on him to help and he would do exactly that. *Cayden was changing too,* Ryder mused; they all were.

He had instructed Darius to search amongst the new volunteers for those men (and women) with battle experience. He had then seen them organized them into a rough command structure. He prayed it would be enough for he also realized they would be put to a true test one day soon. Every day they moved closer to the capital, and it pulled them closer to a confrontation with the Cathair garrison. He had no intention of riding up to the city gates alone. It would be suicide.

By the scouting reports, it appeared they would reach the outskirts of the town in about two days.

"Laurista, I plan to leave the band at our campsite this evening and go on ahead. I want to scout out this Denzik fellow and see what he has to say. I would like you to accompany me."

She nodded. "Yes, and we should take a couple of the old Kingsmen along. They may recognize this fellow."

They arrived at the shoreline of the river, the banks gently sloping toward the water's edge. The river slowed and almost stilled as it widened, and lily pads adorned with fuchsia blooms dotted the marshes formed by the sluggish flow. Frogs made plopping sounds as they launched themselves into the water and out of the path of the horse hooves. The trail led directly out onto a sandbar and disappeared off the end.

One of the scouts waved from the opposite shoreline where the trail picked up again after exiting the river. Ryder gazed up and down the river. It felt strange to be exposed after attempting to hide from enemies' eyes for so many miles. Shrugging his shoulders, he touched heel to flank and urged his mount into the waters. Laurista followed.

About halfway across, the sandbar ended and a rocky stream bed was exposed, the water tumbling over the slippery surface. The horses picked their way slowly across the river bottom and reached the other side without incident.

Darius crossed behind them with two other band members to join the scouts. Both men who had come with Darius were Kingsmen. Darius trotted up to Ryder as his horse climbed the bank, water streaming from her legs.

"Are you going on ahead, sir?"

"Yes, that was my intention."

"We would like to accompany you, if we may. You should not go off alone. There are those who would love to know who leads the band, I think. I fear for your safety."

Ryder frowned at the words. He did not like the idea of having a guard, in truth. He understood having an honour guard to create an image of power, but only in special circumstances.

"I think they are right, my lord," said Laurista.

"Very well, but you are *not* my guard, understand? We leave as soon as the band has safely crossed."

The band set up on the riverside for the evening, their tents sprawling in a semicircle from the banks of the river. The smell of roasting fish permeated the air.

Two hours later found the seven of them riding away from the camp. The scouts led the way, taking a direct route through the trees ending at the Cathair Road. An hour of such travel dumped them onto a rough stone and dirt roadway. They headed south, passing occasional wagons and the lone rider, but traffic was sparse, most having reached their destination before the sun stretched on the horizon.

Near dusk, they came upon a wagon train pulled off the road and under a grove of trees for the evening. Ryder motioned the others to stay back and dismounted, approaching the campsite on foot. A man and a woman tended a cooking fire and started at his sudden appearance.

"Good evening, kind sir and miss. What news from the road?"

"Good evening to you also. As we are travelling the same direction, how could you have not heard the news?"

"My companions and I have been travelling cross-country and only just arrived at the main road. We are curious as to the news in these parts."

The man and woman gazed back to Ryder's companions. "Would you like to join our camp this evening? We have some provisions to share."

"That is very kind of you. Perhaps we can share conversation and a meal, but we will be travelling further this evening."

Ryder tied his mount's reins to a low branch, allowing some slack for grazing then motioned the others to approach.

"My name is Mark and this is my wife, Joy. We are wool-dye merchants, bringing dyes to the mills on the coast." He motioned toward his wagons, their contents shrouded under large tan canvas tarps.

"I'm Ryder, and this is Laurista." He made introductions of the other men. "We are travelling to Cathair to meet up with a friend, who preceded us to town. We have heard talk of legions on the move and were wondering if there is unrest on the road ahead? Have you heard any news?"

Joy stirred their bubbling pot of stew and then moved over to make room for Laurista to sit beside her on the ground. Laurista smiled her thanks then settled in to listen to the men speak.

"There have been rumours of a great battle between a legion division and some rogue men. Some of the rumours say they are

Kingsmen although everyone knows they have been gone for near twenty years. Others say they are rogue bands from the north, come south to challenge Her Majesty's conscription laws. One such rumour, I credit more than the others. A wounded soldier stopped us by the roadside early in the morning today to beg water and a change of clothes. He was bloodied from head to toe and spoke of wolves attacking them in the midst of a battle." Mark frowned at the spoon in his hand. "One thing was certain. By the rips in his clothing and the scratches and gouges on his limbs, he did appear to have battled wolves. He spoke of an encampment of men who were being led by a dangerous young lord sought by the queen for treason. They had been sent to secure the peace, but then the wolves attacked and they fled."

Ryder sat up straight at the mention of the wolves. *Cayden,* he thought.

"Did this man speak of where this battle had occurred?"

"It was not far from here…a few miles ahead as the road goes."

"So this soldier was returning to his legion?"

"No, he was heading to the capital to gather reinforcements, I believe," said Mark. His wife nodded in agreement. "We had been considering turning around because of this news. War is never good for commerce, you know, unless you are a camp follower. Perhaps you would be so kind as to accompany us for as long as you can? An armed guard is not a bad thing in these troubling times and we can see by your posture and by the weapons on your mounts that you and your men are not unaccustomed to danger. There is greater safety in numbers."

Darius and Laurista exchanged glances. Ryder spoke in response to her affirmative nod. "We would be happy to have you journey with us. We are headed for a small village on the outskirts of the capital. Our friend's name is Denzik, perhaps you know him?"

"I can't say I do. However, there is a small village called Lower Cathair with a marvelous inn and the best bakery in the realm. We stay there often. Perhaps we can find your friend there if we ask around."

"How much further is this village?" Ryder scanned the horizon, judging the amount of daylight left.

"It is about a three-hour ride from here."

"I would prefer to continue on this evening then, if you are not too weary from your travels."

"It would be nice to sleep in a bed this evening, if one would be available," Mark said.

"And have a proper bath," piped up Joy.

"It is settled then. We leave as soon as we finish eating."

Chapter 44

THE CAMP AROUND CAYDEN STIRRED like a kicked anthill. Some men swarmed over the wounded, while others picked up their fallen comrades and carried them to the perimeter of the camp to prepare them for burial. The few dead wolves were also picked up and carried to the edge of the camp.

Ziona rested in her tent, having fallen asleep after sipping some of her potion. She had insisted the rest she had prepared be shared with the wounded men and it was being passed around from soldier to wounded soldier.

The decision had been made to not move the camp that night. Their presence was obviously known as was their destination.

The few soldiers who had escaped were no longer a threat. Whether they returned to their base camp or travelled directly to the capital to give warning and an account of the battle to their superiors, either meant they were no longer a direct threat.

Another attack was slim, yet they doubled the patrols, just in case.

Tobias became Cayden's self-appointed bodyguard by refusing to leave his side. He stood a short distance away from Cayden, legs spread, feet firmly planted, arms folded across his chest. His scar stood out lividly against his pale skin and his lazy eye jerked from the glare he shared with all who approached Cayden. *The effect was quite frightening,* Cayden thought, as he rested against a log outside of Ziona's tent.

Cayden picked up the branch he had found and turned it over in his hands, inspecting it, but for once carving held no interest for him. The peace he normally found in the familiar activity eluded him. *The events of the last few hours have unnerved me,* he admitted reluctantly to himself. He felt Ziona's presence behind him. He could almost see her dreams as she slept. Flashes of images crossed his mind when he focused on her, a wooded glade with tall ferns swaying and a door set in the trunk of a tree.

He shook his head to clear his thoughts and focused on Avery instead. It had been ages since he had thought about his sister. He felt worry and concern in the air and a spikey wave of fear assailed his senses. She was in trouble and he felt it as intensely as if he was standing beside her.

Avery? He called to her mentally, trying the same method of communication he had done with Ziona. Surprise and caution flooded back at him.

Cayden, is that you?

Yes. Are you all right? I sense fear in you.

After you left, Father and I left with a Primordial woman named Sharisha to go to the land of the Primordials. Right now, we are in the pass to the Primordial lands. There is a huge army camped at the foot of the pass, thousands of legionnaires. The Primordials are also massed in the mountains, and I fear that there will be an invasion soon. I will contact you later.

Stay safe! he whispered back with his mind, out of habit, and the connection broke. He sucked in a deep breath. The fear he felt through the bond was incredible. It made him itch. He felt an urge to leap to his feet and draw his sword, yet there was no enemy in range. Instead, he began pacing, back and forth in front of his tent. Five steps. Stop. Pivot. Five more steps. Stop. Pivot. Tobias kept pace with him, and sensing Cayden's distress, dropped his arms to his side, one hand resting on his sword hilt.

Cayden stopped pacing and stopped to stare in the exact direction of Cathair. That tugging was back, but stronger and more intense. He felt...well, it felt like a massive mind was pulling at his, calling to him. It was impossible to focus on any one thought; although he sensed a vast intelligence behind it.

He must get to Cathair. Further delay was pointless. *Whatever is pulling at me will not leave me alone, and delay would not assist Avery. I must continue on the path laid out for me and confront it.* It was time.

***

Mordecai sat in the semi-darkness, eyes partially closed. A flame danced on the upturned palm of his hand. He focused on the flame and observed the quality of the light, the prisms of colour in the flickering flame. The heat source pulsed, a heartbeat of light. Into the flame he poured his conscious thoughts and the flame expanded them, lightened them, causing them to drift to the roof of the cavern cell, up through the floors above and into the open air.

His will continued to expand, ever wider and wider, seeking the destination created in his mind. His thoughts searched, shifting on the winds, sliding here and there over man and beast, to finally settle on a young man asleep in his tent.

"Cayden," he whispered. "Cayden, you must come to me. Do not delay." Cayden rolled over in his sleep, mumbling. "You must hurry. Time is short. Seek out Denzik. He can be found in Lower Cathair."

"Lower Cathair," Cayden mumbled to himself, still asleep.

"I will be waiting for you here."

"Lower Cathair...Denzik..." Cayden snorted and then rolled onto his back and snored as his mouth dropped open.

***

The guards drew their swords and quickly checked the shadowed chamber. Anthony stepped up to the body and examined the middle-aged man. There was no wound visible on the body.

Anthony lifted the man as Fabian untied the rope from the lantern bracket, allowing the body to be lowered to the floor.

"Who is he?" Fabian asked the guards as they approached, having determined there was no one present in the hallway.

"This is Wendell. He is the meal and chamber steward that we bribed, the one we were supposed to meet. He must have come down early?"

The taller of the two guards shrugged as they exchanged glances. "We did not let him in though, so how did he get here?"

"If he was here to work, then where are the chamber pots he should be removing? Perhaps he had not reached his destination? In which case, where are the meals he was to deliver?" Fabian walked around the man, examining the body.

The guards noted the lack of any work-related objects. They frowned in unison, clearly perplexed.

"When did you two come on shift?" Anthony asked.

"We have been on since early this morning, our normal eight-hour shift, seven in the morning till three in the afternoon," said the shorter of the two.

"And you let no one into these access halls?" asked Fabian.

"No one has come down to the dungeons in the past eight hours. We have the keys right here for this door." He shook the key ring and the keys rattled. "The only other set is with the queen, but we would know if the queen came to inspect the prisoners."

Fabian frowned at the men. "You realize you are incriminating yourselves?"

The two guards frowned, consternation playing across their faces. "We patrol these halls every two hours," said the shorter one.

Fabian touched the dead man's body. He was cold, but rigor mortis had not set in yet. "His death occurred within the last two hours. It's odd, though; his body shows no sign of other injuries, no indication of a struggle. I believe he knew his killer."

Anthony walked around the body and nodded in agreement. "We need to check the prisoner cells and make sure he was the only victim."

The four of them spread out to search. The hallway was intersected in quick order by narrower halls, lined with cells, four on either side of their main hall.

The two guards took the first set of intersecting hallways and Fabian and Anthony continued on. The lantern light flickered in the cool ventilation breeze, a constant feature of the clammy dungeon. The two guards' shadows overtook them as they checked the cells at the next intersection to check the next section. Most cells were empty, and in the few occupied the prisoners were unhurt.

Eventually, Fabian and Anthony came to the hallway level with the Traitor's Gate doorway. This intersection had only one branch to the left with a spiral set of stairs winding deeper into the earth. With a nod, Anthony took the hallway toward the suspected location of the Traitor's Gate, drawing his sword as he left, lantern light bobbling in his wake.

Fabian held his lantern high to light the treacherous stairway. At the base of the spiral, he nearly tripped over a tray of congealed food and an abandoned chamber pot which had been hastily put down. The contents coated the stone floor.

Fabian stepped around the mess, wrinkling his nose, and then continued down the rough-cut passage. This deep in the dungeon, the corridor was roughly hewn as though it had been hastily chiseled as an afterthought. Only two cells were found this deep down in the passage and were reserved for the most heinous of prisoners. Fabian walked up to the left-hand cell and raised his lantern, light flooding the chamber. A white-haired elderly man blinked at him in the sudden light.

"I am relieved to find you well, Mordecai," said Fabian.

"Was there ever a doubt?" Mordecai rose to his feet and walked over to the door. "I fear my dear friend Wendell has not been so lucky. I heard a commotion at the end of the hallway as he left my chamber and a short while later I heard voices echoing down to my cell. They shone a light on me and then left. I am sure I recognized the voice. It has been many years and not nearly long enough since I heard it last."

"The guards' keys are accounted for, so unless someone copied them, there is only one other possibility," said Fabian.

"No doubt the keys have been copied, but I have not seen any recent use of them. No, I believe this was a random inspection by the queen, checking on her prize prisoner. Wendell is dead, I take it?"

Fabian unlocked the cell door. "Yes, he was found hanged inside the cell access chamber."

"Made to appear as a suicide?" Mordecai asked.

"Yes, I think that was the idea," said Fabian.

"Poor fellow, he was a good chap in the end. I am truly sorry he was on duty tonight. Queen Alcina felt the need on this particular evening to check on me. Unfortunately, Wendell spied her leaving my cell. I believe she did not want any witnesses to her interest in me. Would you see to it his widow receives this?" The wizard reached up into his sleeve and pulled out a leather purse, bulging with coins.

"How in the world did you manage to acquire all that in a prison cell?" Anthony's eyes widened, in surprise.

"The guards get as lonely as the prisoners do. What harm can come of relieving a poor prisoner of his coin?" Mordecai chuckled. "Fortunately, I am rather fond of cards and possess a keen eye, so I am rather lucky as a result."

"Aren't you leaving with us?" Fabian frowned at the wizard.

"No…no, not quite yet, I think. I believe it would give the game away and it appears Her Majesty is growing nervous and suspicious, hence her visit to me this afternoon. There is a secret passage from the royal suites to the prisoner cells. Did you know that?"

Fabian shook his head, bemused.

"She often visited me in the early years after my capture," mused Mordecai. "She thought she could torture a first wizard and have him tell his secrets. I am happy to report she was wrong." A smile lit his wrinkled cheeks. "Soon I shall leave these cells behind, but not quite yet. You, however, must be prepared. Gather the Kingsmen where ever you can find them. The time to reclaim the kingdom approaches. Let those loyal to the true House of Cathair know. Let the people of the Spirit Shield know their king has returned."

Fabian nodded in understanding. "Diversions have been set up within the castle, as we planned. Our people are in place." Fabian chuckled. "Nelson owes me some coins as I finished first." Fabian turned the key in the lock to Mordecai's cell and retraced his steps up the hallway to the stairs.

The voice of the wizard drifted up the passageway to Fabian. "Nelson asked me to pass on a message. He says dinner is on him when you get back and bring your coin purse. He arrived at the wall here about three hours ago."

Chapter 45

THE BALANCE OF THE JOURNEY to the outlying village of the capital was unremarkable. Few people travelled at night and the road was in use only by merchant trains running tight schedules of perishable goods.

Ryder peered at the indistinct forms as they approached and resolved into horse teams and wagons. Drivers raised a hand in greeting but did not slow as they passed.

They reached Lower Cathair as the moon broke the horizon. The area was suddenly bathed in a cool white glow, revealing low rugged fieldstone buildings with thatched roofs. A lower stone wall followed the road, guiding traffic to the main crossroad. Most traffic passed right by the village, focused on reaching the capital.

The windows of the houses were dark as they passed, the hour being late. The village slumbered. It wasn't until they left the road and entered into the village proper that they spied the inn tucked back against the river. Light spilled from the windows of the main floor illuminating the wooden front verandah.

They pulled up at the inn's entrance. Strains of music drifted out the door as a man and woman exited the tavern and walked off down the street, arm in arm.

Ryder and Laurista dismounted, leaving Darius to take the horses around to the inn's stable located at the side of the building. Mark followed Darius with his team and Joy accompanied them inside. The interior of the inn was warmed by two large stone fireplaces set at either end, crackling with a merry fire of dried logs. The locals were listening to a woman singing and playing a guitar situated on a raised platform to the right of the fireplace.

Joy placed a hand on Ryder's arm and pointed to a man standing behind the bar to the right of them. Ryder followed her to the barkeep and they each took a stool at the bar. A short wiry man stood polishing glasses in front of the bottles lined up under the etched mirror. He called a welcome over his shoulder without pausing from his work. "What can I get you all?"

"Mulled wine for me," said Ryder, peering at his companions and at a nod from Laurista and Joy: "and also for the ladies. We are also looking for information."

"Three mulled wines. An easy order to fill," he said as he pulled three mugs from under the bar and took up a pitcher of wine from the back counter, pouring as he spoke. "But as to information, well, that usually depends on who is asking and why?" His gaze finally rested on them, measuring.

Joy spoke up first. "We are looking for a gentleman named Denzik. We have business with him. It's important." Ryder looked at her, a quizzical look in his eyes.

The barkeep squinted at her and then looked at Ryder. "Your accent isn't from these parts. If I were to hazard a guess, I would say you hail from a village on the coast. Tell me why you are so far from home at such a young age?"

Laurista and Ryder exchanged glances then he shrugged. "We are looking for a friend of ours who was headed this way when we became separated. We have reason to believe he may seek this man named Denzik and wished to know if he has arrived yet."

"We also require rooms for the night," Joy said.

"A hot bath too," Laurista added.

"Now that is something I can arrange," said the barkeep. "A meal comes with the room, so why don't you eat and relax while we prepare your lodgings. I will see what I can do about your other request in the meantime." He flagged down a serving girl, who went off to the kitchens and returned with three steaming plates of roast chicken and potatoes. The barkeep wandered off into the back of the inn as they set about their meals. Darius and Mark soon joined them and two more plates arrived in short order.

***

Nelson let the door swing shut behind him and spoke to the head cook, Tabitha. "Keep that group at the bar busy. I have to go speak to Denzik. They asked for him specifically." He grabbed his coat from a hook by the back door to the kitchen and let himself out into the rear yard of his inn. He quickly found his way to a small gate set in the stone wall and briskly strode down the dirt path leading to the river.

Five minutes of energized walking brought him to Denzik's door. The lights were out. He knocked on his door and waited, fidgeting. His heart was thumping in his chest as though he had jogged the short distance.

A light flared in the window and then the door opened a crack and a sleepy-eyed Denzik peered out. Seeing Nelson standing there, he opened the door further to allow him to enter.

"What's up?" He walked back into his living room and sank down in his favourite chair.

"A group of out-of-towners are asking for you by name at the inn. They have accents from the coast...the northwest coast."

Denzik's posture straightened and Nelson imagined great mental gears whirling in his head. "What did they want?"

"They say they are searching for a friend who they were separated from and they thought he would come looking for you."

Denzik frowned. "I do not know anyone from that area of the province." He reached into his upper pocket and pulled out his pipe. With his left hand, he searched his other pocket for his pouch of tobacco. He pulled it out and packed the fragrant leaves into his pipe. The routineness of the action calmed his nerves and cleared his head.

"I doubt he is the one we seek. But he may have a connection to him. We need to speak to him privately, away from the villagers. The inn is no good. Go back, and after they are seen to their rooms, bring him along with you to my house here so we can talk privately. If it's nothing, I can spend a quiet hour or so sharing tea with a stranger from the coast."

Nelson nodded in agreement and left Denzik still packing his pipe and studying the patterns on the rug under his feet without seeing either of them.

***

Darius's room was at the far back of the inn, tucked under the roof line. The ceiling slanted to meet the walls about a third of the way down. His bed was pushed up against the wall, which suited him fine as who stood up on a bed anyways? He peered out his window which overlooked the back garden of the inn. Two shadows appeared in the garden below, hurrying toward the gate. One of those shadows resolved into Ryder, accompanied by the innkeeper.

He waited until they had disappeared from view, and then he donned his coat and picked up his saddlebags which sat on the floor beside him, still packed. He swung the pack over his shoulder and exited his room, quickly descending the back staircase and out to the stable where his horse was waiting in its stall, still saddled.

He flipped the groom a coin as he rode out of the stable and off into the night.

***

Denzik's kettle was boiling by the time Nelson arrived back at his doorstep with a stocky solid lad in tow. Tall of stature, the youth moved with a grace that spoke of confidence and grounding. *Now this is a good, solid soldier,* Denzik thought, as though measuring him up for a post in the Kingsmen ranks.

"Please, enter." He stepped aside for the lad, Nelson on his heels. He motioned to the chairs in the living room. "Tea?"

"Yes, thank you," said the stranger politely.

"I will take a cup too," said Nelson, leading the way into the living room.

Ryder inspected comfortable but sparse furnishings, noting the fine sword displayed over the fireplace mantle. It appeared to be sharp, and well used. Not a display piece at all. He frowned at it, studying it closely. *What was that marking on the hilt?*

"You are examining my sword very closely, lad. Do you know about swords?" Denzik set a cup of tea down in front of his two guests.

"I am an apprentice blacksmith. I have had the opportunity to work with steel such as this on occasion"—Ryder's head swung back to Denzik—"but never so fine a blade as that, sir. Where did you get it?"

"It's mine." Denzik lowered himself into his favourite chair and took a sip from his cup. "I am a retired Kingsman. It was my blade while in service to the king. I keep it polished and sharpened, but obviously it hasn't seen much action in the last twenty years. Still, old habits die hard. Tell me, why are you looking for me?" He studied Ryder over the rim of his steaming cup and noted the clear gaze he received in return. *This is an honest lad,* he thought.

Ryder took a sip of his tea. "I left Sanctuary-by-the-Sea roughly three weeks ago to catch up with a friend, who had been pressed into the queen's legions. By the time I caught up..." As Ryder recounted the tale of his travels, the words spilled from his lips in a torrent. He spoke of Cayden and their parting, and the men who followed him; the attack by the Charun, their separation, and his search since then to locate Cayden. He did not speak of Cayden's strange abilities but focused on the Kingsmen who had joined his ranks and his concern to reach Cayden before anything else happened to him. As he wound down his discourse, a stunned silence filled the room.

Denzik and Nelson exchanged glances and Nelson nodded.

"Son, we have been waiting for you and young Cayden for seventeen years."

***

It was predawn when Darius located them. As he suspected, their camp was located in the woods off of the main road. It seemed Cayden had acquired a bunch of soldiers, same as Ryder, but this bunch seemed less military and more like families. Darius marched up to the ring of guards and identified himself. He was escorted to Cayden immediately, who exited his tent and gave him a hug in welcome.

"I am so glad I found you! Have you been hiding here the whole time?" asked Darius.

"Nah, been trying to make our way south without running into the Charun. We ran into some legionaries recently. I am beginning to worry that our presence is known to the queen."

"Well, Ryder wants to talk to you. He's in the village ahead. Come with me for a quick ride?"

Cayden observed the quiet camp. Most of the men were bedded down. Ziona slept peacefully; he felt her nestled in his head. Tobias had finally gone to bed but set two guards for Cayden while he rested, as though it took two to replace him.

"OK, but I will need two escorts or there will be hell to pay when I get back."

Darius grinned. "OK. Grab your horses and personal guard, and follow me."

A short time later, Cayden and the two guards rode up to Darius, where he sat astride his horse. At Cayden's nod, they headed off into the woods, Darius taking the lead. The moon had fully risen now, and visibility was good for the horses. After about an hour of winding through the woods, they came to an opening in the forest wall and rode into a small meadow with knee-high grass. They rode out of the trees side by side and as they did so, the shadows of the forest elongated after them and resolved themselves into three tall, eerily still Charun. Three more glided out in front of them, encircling their small group. Cayden yelled and attempted to boot his horse into action, but the animal snorted and reared in fright at the sight of the Charun. His two guards, on either side, drew swords and booted their mounts, charging the Charun ahead of them. The Charun let them come.

The guards had almost reached the Charun when black arrows from the edge of the forest struck both rushing guards in the back, and they toppled off their mounts to the ground. Their horses bolted past the Charun and disappeared into the trees.

Cayden's eyes widened as he caught sight of Darius lowering his bow. A fourth black tipped arrow was notched in his bow and swung Cayden's direction. He sat calmly in his saddle, slightly behind Cayden, who had finally brought his mount under control.

"There is no sense fighting them, Cayden. You cannot win."

Cayden, seeing Darius's total lack of concern over the presence of so many Charun, felt his fear ratchet higher. "You brought them," he whispered, shocked. "You betrayed me! Why?"

Darius's lips twisted in a cold smile. "You didn't listen to what I said when we first met, did you? I joined the legion when they found me, but it was more than that. They needed a spy, someone to infiltrate the locals where ever we went with the sole purpose of finding you. The queen's bounty on your head has made me rich and I will live easy the rest of my days. I will finally be able to go home and help my family.

"Unfortunately for Sergeant Perez, he became rather greedy. He did not want to share the prize money for turning you in. So I had to steal you away from him…and what better way than by befriending and freeing you? Now I have tracked you all the way to the castle and will deliver you straight into the queen's waiting arms. I have you trussed tighter than a festive turkey. So much simpler to make sure I was the one who benefited in the end. Poor Perez. I doubt the Charun were very kind to him."

He turned his back on Cayden. "He is yours now," Darius said to the Charun. "Be sure to not harm him in any way. Take him to the queen whole and undamaged."

He spurred his mount and trotted back off into the trees. The Charun closed in on Cayden and claw-like hands reached for him. His horse snorted and shied away from the Charun. Refusing to wait to be captured, Cayden booted his horse in the ribs and it shot forward, galloping toward the oncoming Charun.

The Charun pulled out long hook poles and swung the loops forward, dropping two of them over Cayden's body even as he ducked to avoid them. The loops tugged tight, binding his arms to his side and yanking him out of the saddle to hang by the loops in midair. A third Charun, red eyes glowing from under its hood, glided forward and pressed an oily cloth to his face even as he struggled in their grip. The fumes stung Cayden's eyes and lungs, even as his senses faded into nothingness.

***

Ziona sat bolt upright on her cot. Terror spiked through her like a living thing, rioting her into motion. Sweat popped out in beads on her skin and she shivered as fear rolled over her waves through her connection to Cayden. She jumped to her feet and took three steps before exhaustion hit her like a club. She stumbled and grabbed on to the central tent pole to keep from collapsing to the ground. The room spun and she fought to keep her eyes open. "Help!" she cried out weakly. "Help!" she cried again, a little louder. She let go of the post and stumbled to the tent entrance, falling to her hands and knees and spilling out of the flap. She shivered again, dressed in nothing but her thin shift. The world spun and she slumped to the ground, helpless to stop herself from doing so.

Hands reached down and helped her to her feet, where she swayed in their grip, fighting to keep her eyes open. Bleary eyes attempted to focus on Tobias and another soldier, their grip on her arms the only thing keeping her on her feet.

"Let me help you to a seat, my lady," Tobias said.

Ziona shook her head and slurred drunkenly, "Its Cayden...He..." She swallowed past the dry lump in her throat. "He's in trouble...some kind of trouble...," she slurred. Ziona shook her head to try to clear it, but it only made things worse. "He's been drugged, I think." Her eyes drifted closed and she sagged in their arms.

Tobias bolted into Cayden's tent and found no sign of him. His fear mounting, he yelled for his men, who came running from all directions of the camp. "Search the camp and find him and his horse," he snapped to the guards stationed around him. "I want to know who is missing from this camp.

"Roll call *now!*" Tobias bellowed to the men standing around him. A bugle was brought forth and blared. Men tumbled from their tents to answer the summons.

Tobias lowered Ziona to the ground and grabbed one of the Kingsmen as he passed. "Take her back inside her tent and stay with her at all times. If she comes to again, I want to know immediately!" The soldier saluted and picked up the unconscious woman and carried her back to her tent.

Far away across the realm, Avery stumbled in her tent and fell to the ground, her voice slurring unintelligibly before she succumbed to the drugging fumes.

Chapter 46

THE SUN WAS PEEKING OVER THE HORIZON when Ryder, Laurista, Denzik, Nelson, and Fabian rode out of the village. They had waited as long as they could for Darius. If he had wandered off in the middle of the night without leave, he would be court-marshalled. They had been warned. It bothered Ryder, but he could find no answer for the strange behaviour. Nelson reported Darius's bed had not been slept in and the serving staff advised he had not been in the common room that evening.

Perhaps he had ridden on into the capital to find a greater selection of entertainments. Ryder tried to put it out of his mind. He had more important things to think about, but the absence weighed on his mind, making him uneasy.

The revelations of the previous evening still spun in his head. He had stumbled on, or been guided to, an underground movement of people with imbedded ties and loyalties to the former king. *He rode beside a knight...a real knight of the realm.* Ryder shook his head in wonderment, bemused by his thoughts, pushing down the giddy glee he felt.

They had explained their years of preparations and had given Ryder a quick tour of the beginning of the tunnel system to the capital. They had also been already aware of his and Cayden's bands—armies, they called them. Ryder thought it was going too far. His band of men and women were untested in battle and more of a rabble than a trained force. However, the drills were working and he did see improvement in them.

Denzik, Fabian, and Nelson were excited to meet up with Cayden and happy to lend their assistance in locating the other band through their eyes-and-ears network. Now that they knew what to look for, they were confident that someone would get back to them within a day as to the location of Cayden's camp. It was funny to think that Cayden had gathered a force of men and women in much the same way as he had.

They reached the camp about noon. As they rode in, Ryder looked around for Darius's cheery face. He could not locate him in the sea of faces saluting as they rode past. Cheers rose around him as he reined in at the command tent set up in the middle of the band.

Young boyish-faced Joshua, a familiar face from back home, came running forward to hold his and Denzik's bridles while they dismounted. Two other men stepped forward, and then they led the horses away to be cared for.

Denzik examined Ryder with interest as did Fabian and Nelson. The camp was filled with the sounds and smells of men and women sharpening blades, fletching arrows, and cooking meals over cook fires with the happy chatter of people who had found contentment in a common purpose.

Denzik nodded approvingly. "You run a fine camp here, Ryder. Yes, very fine indeed. I would like to do a walk about to inspect the camp." Ryder nodded and led the way out into the main body of his band.

The first section of tents housed a group of ladies who had joined them from the last village. Hair cut in the male fashion and dressed in tan pants and leather vests, it took Denzik and the rest a moment to realize they were women. When they did, they stopped dead. The women sat around their campfire, sharpening stones rasping along the blades of their swords. It was obvious they were well practiced at the skill. The closest woman tested the edge against her thumb and grunted in satisfaction as a small cut appeared across it.

Nelson approached the woman and paused beside her. "That's a fine edge you have put on your blade. Do you know how to use it?" The woman glared at him and then stood. She towered over him by a good eight inches. Nelson squinted up at her and the corner of his mouth twitched, holding back a grin.

She eyed him up and down. "I would not worry about my skills, little man, but more so about your reach." Ryder shook his head, making a mental note to speak to them about tact.

Nelson's grin burst on to his face. "What is your name?" he asked, laughing in earnest.

"My name is Candice, daughter of Sophia and Armando, knight of the realm, fallen in battle, may the gods bless them." She stood tall and menacing, evidently attempting to decide whether he was truly threatening, or just plain dumb.

Fabian walked up, chuckling. "Last time we saw you, Candice, you were but a babe in arms, but there is no mistaking your mother's good looks." Her eyes flickered over them all then settled on Denzik.

"I'm sorry, but you have me at a disadvantage. Should I know you?"

"No, my dear, we served alongside your father, and we are pleased to see you doing so well. Welcome to the fight."

Candice nodded with pride, winked at Ryder, and sat back down to resume her work.

Fabian wolf-whistled softly under his breath and strode away.

"You always did have a soft spot for Sophia. You never could keep your eyes off her legs," said Nelson.

Fabian's whistling stopped abruptly, like a cork plugging a bottle, and he quickly glanced over his shoulder to see if Candice had overheard. Denzik laughed out loud. Ryder found himself chuckling too.

They toured the laundry areas, the latrines, the kitchen, the small portable smithies, the supply tents, and the makeshift stables. Completing the circuit, Denzik ducked his head and entered the command tent. Spying a frosted pitcher and some glasses, he poured a drink and took a seat at a table consisting of three wooden boxes set close together in the middle of the room. Ryder joined him with his own glass.

"I am glad to be able to turn this venture over to your more experienced hands. Cayden asked me to help him, but I am sure he'd prefer to have someone in charge who knew what they were doing." He sat down and took a long drink of the cool lemonade.

Denzik studied him as did the other two. Ryder lowered his glass and his eyes travelled between the three men. "What?"

"We have no intention of taking over your camp or your men," Denzik said. "They are gathered together and are loyal to you. You and you alone are their leader. They would not do half as well under another's command."

Ryder frowned. "They are here because they wanted to help in recapturing the castle to oust the queen. It has nothing to do with me."

Nelson spoke this time. "I doubt that's true, lad, but you are the one who showed them the way and that makes you their leader. They trust you."

"But I know nothing of wars or battles. Sure, I once dreamed of becoming a knight, but it was a childish dream. I cannot captain these men, not in a real battle," Ryder protested.

"A true captain points the way. He doesn't do the majority of the battling. Fighting is what his troops do. And a wise general places many capable captains under his command. Do you have a title? What do the men call you?" said Fabian.

"I...well actually they call me 'sir' or 'lord.' Only those in command have titles and they are all captains."

"Then by your own command structure, you have assigned yourself the role of Captain General of the Band. Congratulations on your promotion, General." Denzik clapped him on the shoulder, grinning. Ryder groaned as the three men laughed at his stunned expression.

"Now, let us make plans for moving this army forward. By the time we are finished here, our scout should be back with the other band's location."

Chapter 47

CAYDEN WOKE SLOWLY, his mind fuzzy and his tongue dry as though coated in chalk. He tried to swallow, but his tongue stuck to his cheek with the gummy glue of his saliva. He dozed, the effort of lifting his head an impossible task. He dreamed he was surrounded by people, arms reaching out to him, begging him to hold them, yet he was only one man. How could he hold and comfort them all at once?

He jerked at a loud noise and began the climb toward consciousness, but then the sound went away and he succumbed to the darkness again.

"When is he going to wake?"

"You wanted us to keep him drugged. We have done exactly what you told us to do."

"We don't even know if he is the one we seek. I will not carry word of this man to Her Majesty without knowing for certain. You will discontinue the drugging and let him wake. The minute he does awaken, you will summon me and only me in person and with the utmost secrecy. Understood?"

"Yes, my lord. It will be as you command."

Cayden drifted in semi-consciousness. *Were those real people, real voices? Or were they more muddled dreams?* He wasn't sure. He thought he heard a key rattle in a metal lock, but maybe that was his imagination too. He had had so many dreams he couldn't begin to sort reality from fiction.

Yesterday—at least he thought it was yesterday—he had dreamed of a short fairy-like creature who had wanted him to dance a childish dance he didn't know to amuse the queen. When he had told her he didn't know the steps, she had grown to eight feet tall, her clothes had darkened and lengthened to black hooded robes. Her beady red eyes stared and she hissed at him from the dark depths. It didn't matter anymore. The party was over. His time was up, and this time he was going to die.

Cayden jerked awake this time to complete darkness. He tried to raise his head but found the effort more than he could manage. He stifled a groan, attempting to roll over, but his legs and arms were bound behind his back. He gingerly moved them to test if they were operational and a quick exploratory showed no obvious injuries or broken bones. He was lying on his right side on a stone floor. A green glow emanated from the rocky floor, walls, and ceiling, giving a faint but ghostly light. He lifted his head a fraction, trying to observe his surroundings, for he had no doubt where he was: in a prisoner cell deep under the castle of Cathair.

He was in trouble—big trouble—and this time there was no one around to help get him out of this jam. There was complete silence in the dungeon. He was unable to tell if there were other cells or other prisoners around him. The silence was complete. He attempted to move, to wiggle his fingers and toes as they were numb with cold. The ropes were tight, cutting into his skin, restricting the blood's circulation to his hands and feet. He did not know how long he had lain in one position. Cayden tensed and relaxed his muscles slowly and methodically, bringing circulation back into their lengths. His toes and fingertips burned as oxygen moved into muscles stiff from lack of use.

As he wiggled, his head bumped into an object placed on the floor. He strained around and found a ceramic bowl with some kind of gruel mixture and a second bowl with water. He wiggled his way around and lifted his head and slurped the cold water, much like a dog would. He lapped eagerly and then halfway through, stopped as a thought hit him. What if there were more drugs in the water? He grimaced and continued drinking. He would have to risk it. The bowl tipped as his head sagged against the rim and then clanked back down, spilling precious water onto the stone floor. He lapped it all, eager for every drop. Afterward, he relaxed back on the floor, resting for a second, letting the water soak into his parched throat and soothe his dry mouth. He felt the drugs' effects weakening their hold on him as the water flushed the remaining drugs from his system.

He reached out with his mind to Ziona. *Ziona, are you there?* He felt a stirring in the bond as though she was also asleep. *Ziona. Wake up, Ziona. Come on…*

Ziona's consciousness blurred and sharpened as she struggled against sleep. "Cayden?" Suddenly, her mind snapped into focused reality with the force of a bow string. *Cayden, you're alive! Where are you? Wait!* He felt her stop the communication with him for a second and he imagined her rushing from her tent to call the guards. Just as quickly, she re-entered his mind. *Cayden, can you tell me where you are?*

I think I am in a prison cell in the dungeons under the castle in Cathair. It has the look of a cell.

Are you hurt? Is anyone there with you?

No, I am alone, but I am bound hand and foot. I woke up a few minutes ago.

OK. Please do not do anything stupid. We are coming for you one way or another. Take care of yourself as best you can till we get there. OK?

I will. Are you OK? You seemed to be in a really deep sleep.

What you experience in the waking world affects me also. Did they have you drugged?

Yes. That is how the Charun took me.

Charun! He felt her shiver through the bond. *At least you are still alive. We are missing two guards here.*

Yes, they were felled by black arrows. Darius shot them. He betrayed us, me, to the Charun.

Darius! When did he arrive?

It was while you were resting. He was going to take me to Ryder, or so I thought. He said something about him being at the village on the outskirts of Cathair. I think that much of it was true.

We will see if we can find him. Stay safe, Cayden! Alert me should anything happen. I can hear your thoughts and will know. He felt a flood of warmth that felt a lot like love, flow through the bond. He sent it back to her.

"Cayden, are you awake?"

This voice was not in his head. It was whispered.

"Who are you? How do you know my name?"

"Finally," the voice whispered in relief. "I am Mordecai Ben-Moses. It has been I who has been calling you in your dreams. We have much to talk about," the disembodied voice said.

"Are you the one who can give me answers? Aossi said there was one who could help me located here in the castle."

"Ah, I see you have met Aossi already. Good, good. You are strong with your mother's blood I see. That is important, you know."

"My mother was born in Sanctuary-by-the-Sea. She died many years ago. You could not possibly know her? How long have you been here?" Cayden growled suspiciously.

"Oh…I would say for around seventeen years, give or take a few months. How old are you?"

"What does my age have to do with it?"

"A great deal I am afraid, seeing as you are the reason I have been here all these years."

"What foolishness is this?" Anger and a splitting headache sharpened Cayden's tone.

At that moment, the sound of boots scraping on stone reached their ears. "Play the fool, Cayden," Mordecai whispered urgently. "You know nothing and we have never spoken. You do not know me."

Cayden slumped back onto the floor of his cell and pretended to be sleeping again. He was facing away from the door. The boots drew closer and stopped at Cayden's cell. A light shone through the metal bars of the small window set in the door. Cayden could see the light swing crazily, the shadowy bars moving from one side to the other as the light moved.

The light receded and paused. Cayden wondered if—what was his name? Mordecai?—was faking sleep too.

The light followed the boot sounds back up the hallway and eventually faded away.

"Mordecai?" Cayden whispered.

"Yes, Cayden?"

"Who are you?"

"I already told you…just not in detail."

Cayden paused, and then said, "What you mentioned earlier, about my mother. What did you mean by that?"

"Exactly what I said, I was present at your birth. I assisted your mother when she gave birth to the pair of you. She was in need of magical assistance at the time."

"Why would you have been at my birth? What kind of assistance?"

"Not only yours but your sister's too."

"As she is my twin, how could it have been any other way?" said Cayden in an aggrieved voice.

"Cayden, we have much to talk about, but for now it is best that I do not reveal to you more than you need to know, at least until we are out of this mess, which will be quite soon. I am rather tired of this cell and the rats that frequent it. I will enjoy seeing the sun again."

Cayden pondered this silently from his cell. *What would it be like to waste away in a prison for seventeen years?* He shivered. He did not want to know.

"What do I do, Mordecai? I cannot continue to fake sleep"— Cayden's stomach rumbled—"and I am hungry."

"Eat, my boy, eat. First rule of any resistance is you must keep up your strength."

"OK, but this is going to get messy," Cayden said. "How about you talk to me while I figure this out?"

"Sounds good…yes…it's been so long since I have had someone to talk to. Tell me, can you see that green glow on the rocks? No, wait you should not speak with your mouth full, very bad for digestion. Hum, do you see that glow? It is more than a phosphorescent microbial. See how it pulses? Alas, another foolish question. It's quite impossible to answer while your mouth is full. I am sorry. I am rusty in the fine art of intelligent conversation after seventeen years of speaking to the same guard day in day out who has, unfortunately, run afoul of our dearly beloved queen."

Cayden snorted and licked at the bowl's meager contents. The man was really quite humorous and Cayden would have enjoyed his company if his situation hadn't been so dire. As Cayden licked his bowl clean, he let the old man ramble on. The food settling in Cayden's stomach stilled the spidery fingers that had been tickling his insides in hunger.

Licking his lips, Cayden relaxed back onto the floor. "I am finished."

"Oh, and in the nick of time, too! Tell me, what is your predicament there? I assume you are bound?"

"Yes, hand and foot."

"Dear me, that is quite unfortunate. I could be of assistance, but untying you would give the game away, certainly."

Cayden frowned again. He sensed he might do that a lot around this man. "You still haven't told me anything more than your name. How is it you know mine?"

"Once again my manners are appallingly lacking. My name is Mordecai Ben-Moses, First Wizard of the Fell."

Silence greeted these words. So this was the wizard Aossi had spoken of. Cayden had believed they were extinct in the realm, that they had been eliminated during the revolution.

"How can you be alive? I was told all the great wizards were dead."

"Alas this is true, for the most part. I, fortunately, was captured immediately after your birth, stripped of my powers, and imprisoned in this cell. My compatriots, they were not so fortunate."

Cayden found the mixture of being "imprisoned" and "fortunate" a very strange combination.

"So you have super magical powers, then?"

"Something like that, I suppose."

"So...how are we getting out of here?"

"The young are always so impatient. Jumping from one thought to the other. Patience, my young friend, I counsel patience. Your companions need time to prepare and spring their surprise."

"I am tired of surprises," Cayden grumbled. "That is how I ended up here tied like a holiday pig ready for the spit."

"Ahh...well as to that, it was prophesied."

"My betrayal by a friend was *prophesied*?" Cayden was stunned by this news. He was destined to suffer at the hands of a friend?

"I'm afraid so, Cayden. This is the beginning of troubled times for the world. You and your sister are being pushed along a path you were destined to travel since your birth. You know this to be so at least in part or you would never have found me."

Cayden fell silent. What reply was there?

Chapter 48

ZIONA RODE FROM CAYDEN'S CAMP with Tobias at her side and four more soldiers. The number of volunteers had soared with the news that they had discovered where Cayden was being held captive.

Riding into the capital with all of the men in tow would be tantamount to a declaration of war on the capital and they would tighten security around Cayden perhaps making it impossible to reach him or, worse yet, outright kill him before the band had an opportunity to rescue him.

Reaching Ryder was paramount and all she had to go on was Cayden's clue from Darius. Together, they might be able to mount a rescue that wouldn't endanger his life.

It was nearly noon when they reached the village of Lower Cathair. Men and woman tended their crops, cultivating the soil and picking produce for market. Children chased other children through the village square, laughing, while dogs nipped at their heels and raced ahead of them.

Ziona dismounted in front of the inn, flanked by quaint stone cottages that made up the majority of the dwellings of the village. The inn appeared to be the social center of the village as evidenced by the chatter that flooded over them as they pushed open the door to the common room. Ziona's glance around the room took in the two roaring fireplaces and the bustling staff, eventually pausing at a table, where a group of four men and a woman sat. From the breadth of the shoulders, there was no question that she had found Ryder.

She marched up to the table, interrupting their conversation. The others fell silent at her approach, studying her closely, but Ryder jumped to his feet and moved quickly to embrace her. "Ziona! It's great to see you! Where is Cayden?" She glanced back at his companions and frowned. "It's OK, Ziona. These are friends, Kingsmen of old."

"I need to speak privately, away from sharp ears. Is there such a place?" she asked of the men at the table.

Nelson stood up. "You may use the private library, my lady. This way please."

They all rose and Ziona followed Nelson to a comfortably furnished room off of the common room with padded chairs and shelves lined with books.

Ziona's companions remained standing, taking up positions to watch the door and the windows of the room. Two remained in the hallway to make sure they were not approached.

Denzik walked up to Tobias and stared him directly in the eye. Tobias never blinked. "Tobias Townsend. I never thought to see you alive."

Tobias's face broke into a grin. "It's good to see you too, sir!" He saluted the old general.

"You would be a Primordial Seeker...unless I miss my mark." Denzik said to Ziona. "I assume you are the one who has been assisting Cayden?"

"That is correct. Ryder has told you about Cayden? Or at least what he understands of Cayden?"

Denzik nodded.

"Cayden has been captured. He is being held in the prisoner cells of the castle as we speak." The blunt words galvanized the men, who were beginning to seat themselves. They shot back to their feet, all speaking at once.

Ziona held up her hands to quiet them. "Cayden is fine, at least as fine as he can be. We have formed...a special connection. I can sense what is happening to him. He is fine for the moment. I do not believe they are certain who he is or he would already be dead. We must reach him without delay. I can lead you directly to him."

"We have been preparing and planning for this moment for seventeen years, my lady. I assume you have acquired a following during your journeys?" Denzik nodded to the men standing guard.

"Yes, Cayden has managed to attract a large group of former Kingsmen, who have sworn allegiance to him. They are a few hours back, camped out of sight and waiting for our command."

Nelson nodded as did Fabian.

"Gentlemen, ladies, I believe it's time to implement our plan." Denzik walked over to the desk located under the window and pulled a small key from his pocket. Fitting key to lock, he opened the long flat drawer slid under the desktop. Inside were several long rolled scrolls, which he gathered up and brought over to the reading table in the center of the room. Everyone gathered around to view the scrolls.

Denzik selected one and then carefully unrolled it to show what appeared to be a maze of twisting lines that intersected in unpredictable ways.

"This is a map of the underground tunnel systems of Castle Cathair. This, my friends, is how we are going to retake the castle and drive out the queen forever. I would like you to go back to your respective camps and gather the ten most trusted men or ladies from your established captains. We need to familiarize them with the plan and move our troops into position. All the supplies we need are already in place for this attack.

"We are waiting for the heir to arrive and his men to gather. I must say, you both have done a fine job in pulling in the men. Our eyes and ears report that Kingsmen are streaming toward the capital in various disguises. Fabian, here"—he nodded at the plump baker—"has set up a series of distractions inside the castle itself and Nelson"—he nodded to the innkeeper—"will be redirecting the forces as they arrive into the tunnels."

At Ziona's look of confusion, Denzik quickly brought her up to speed about the tunnels dug between the river and the castle foundations. *Impressive that they planned and implemented such a grand design over the years, based on nothing but their belief that the king would return,* Ziona thought. They grinned at her surprised stare. "Very resourceful, gentlemen, I have to wonder who set these plans in place." She raised an eyebrow enquiringly, but the men all shook their heads refusing to speak of it.

"Meet back here in six hours with your captains."

Chapter 49

A BUCKET OF ICY WATER emptying over his prone form jolted Cayden awake. Gasping, he blinked his eyes and squinted against the sudden glare of the lantern held above him. The guard kicked Cayden in the ribs, and he cried out.

Cayden tried to clutch his stomach but, of course, this was impossible as his arms were still tied behind his back. He attempted to curl into a tighter ball, but then he felt a sharp knife slip between his wrists and ankles, slicing through the ropes holding him captive. He groaned as he rolled onto his stomach and moved his fingers and toes, trying to restore their circulation.

The guard reached down and hauled him to his feet by his hair. Cayden cried out again and then his eyes fell on the man holding the lantern. He was a tall steely-eyed man with short cropped hair and a grey goatee trimmed to a sharp point below his equally pointed chin.

"Lord Cyrus, this is the prisoner, my lord. He is awake now as ordered."

Cayden found his legs were weak after two days bound hand and foot. He wobbled and very nearly collapsed back onto the stone floor, but the guard's tight grip on his hair kept him upright. A spikey prickling ran from his feet and up through his legs as he put weight on his limbs. He was glad of the distracting pain on his scalp as the returning blood made his extremities burn.

The lord walked around Cayden, examining him. "I am to believe this skinny boy is to be feared? This poor farmer is the great prophesied threat to my queen's reign?" He stopped in front of Cayden and addressed him. "What is your name boy and where were you born?"

Cayden couldn't see a reason to lie so he answered truthfully.

"Cayden Tiernan. I was born in from a village called Sanctuary-by-the-Sea, on the northeastern coast of the realm."

"You have lived there your entire life?"

"Yes, I am born and raised there."

"Why do you travel to the capital?"

"I joined the legion when it came to our village, but the legion was attacked and everyone perished. I was out of the camp at the time of the attack and survived. I thought to join another legion if I could locate one."

Cayden wondered if his partial lie was convincing. He hadn't actually lied, at least until the end. He had only left out important parts.

The high lord stared at him. Cayden locked his legs and arms to keep them from trembling and betraying his nervousness and then met his eyes.

"You know what I think? I think you are a clever liar and a fraud. I think you do not have the brains to orchestrate a rebellion. Lord knows how many of your type have been tossed in these dungeons over the years, betrayed by beggarly men eager to claim the queen's bounty."

He walked around Cayden one more time and then paused in front of him, a puzzled expression on his cruel face. "And yet…there is something *familiar* about you…as though we had met on a previous occasion." He studied Cayden's features, searching them, and then turned away, tugging on gloves he had pulled from his vest pocket.

"Bind him in chains. I will have Queen Alcina inspect this one."

He left the cell as Cayden was dragged over to a set of leg and wrist irons affixed to chains imbedded in the stone exterior wall.

Chapter 50

THEY WRAPPED UP THEIR PLANNING SESSION around four o'clock in the morning. Birds were beginning to stir, sleepy twitters occasionally disturbing the silence in their wake. The captains rode off to their respective assignments, breaking camp and beginning the march back to the village.

Denzik's plan was to approach the village in units of ten Kingsmen from the dense woods on the opposite bank of the back of the inn. Once there, they would sneak men into the tunnels in small groups. Hopefully, their movements would be missed by the locals busy tending their fields and off to trade in the capital for the day.

Nelson's network of tunnels had expanded to include a riverside entrance, cleverly disguised to blend into the bank. While only he and a handful of trusted men needed access to the tunnels, hiding the entrance in the inn had made sense from a security point of view.

But as the tunnels expanded and the rumours from the ears heated up with whispers of the chosen one approaching, having only one entrance seemed foolhardy. *After all, how can I sneak in an entire army through the middle of my inn?*

As a result, three separate entrances had been established leading into the tunnels, all joining at different points along the underground passageways. Denzik had utilized some of those abandoned corridors and lengthened them. Now in addition to the river entrance, one was also to be found near the well on Denzik's land and a fourth in the storm cellar of the grain barn that Fabian used to store his flour sacks.

Nelson set up sentries posing as gardeners or workers doing repairs about the grounds to steer people away from the back of the inn. Sentries were also posted at the three other entrances. As they spied the men approaching, bluebird whistles would give the all clear signal to the units as they approached.

In the meantime, Fabian brought supplies in through the back door leading to the inn's kitchen plus an assortment of swords, arrows, and bows, all tucked neatly into the bottom of baskets of freshly baked bread, apples, and jerky. The baskets disappeared down the trap door and were hauled to the various staging areas within the tunnels, so that the men and women who arrived with no weapons would leave the tunnels armed.

Tabitha was the last line of defence, as she would disguise the inn's trap door once they had descended into its depths, standing guard with a cook's best tools, cleavers and knives, at the ready.

The first groups arrived, peeking over the horizon with the dawn, creeping through the trees as silent as a stalking mountain lion. They whistled the bluebird call to announce their presence, and the sentries whistled back confirmation that it was safe to approach. He motioned the first group of ten down into the tunnel entrance. Men and women scrambled down the inn ladder, dropped into the riverside stone shaft, slithered down a rope into the well, crawled out the side tunnel six feet above the floor of the well, and crawled into the space under the old mill stone, all intent on joining with their fellow Kingsmen.

The men continued to arrive all day and into the night, ten minute intervals between the groups, sixty men an hour. Twenty-four hours later, one thousand four hundred men in total had descended into the caves and settled into their assigned bands in the caverns and tunnels beneath the castle.

Denzik closed off and hid the riverside entrance, disguising it with an old wooden rowboat he pulled up in front of the entrance, leaning it on an angle and obscuring all the tracks. When he left, it appeared that the boat had been in storage there for a very long time.

He then returned to his home and removed the rope slung from the overhead crossbeam of the well and swept the area with a tree branch to erase the signs of booted traffic.

Denzik met Fabian as he entered the inn and together they wandered nonchalantly back to the library, which had become their makeshift command post over the last two days. The twenty captains, Ryder, Ziona, and Tobias stood or leaned against furniture, studied the maps pinned around the room on the walls, or conversed in low tones. Denzik felt their suppressed excitement, their eagerness to get on with the overthrow of the government and Cayden's rescue.

Denzik cleared his throat and the room fell silent.

"Tonight, the world changes forever. For seventeen years, we have planned, prepared, searched, and waited. But even more so, we have hoped. For seventeen years, we have endured the tyranny of a queen who murdered the royal family of Cathair down to the man, woman, and child. She attempted to wipe them from the earth…but she has failed."

Denzik reached for a box under the desk that had once held maps. He placed it on the tabletop and opened the lid. Inside were folded uniforms bearing the insignia of captains of the Kingsmen. They had been carefully folded and wrapped in bleached paper, the emblem of the Kingsmen stitched boldly onto the royal purple fabric. The men stood taller and snapped to attention at the sight of the uniforms.

"Tonight, we reclaim that which was taken from us. Tonight, we reclaim the throne for the rightful heir. Tonight, we throw off our disguises for tomorrow, and we declare our allegiance in battle." He gazed around at the men and smiled. The men cheered, saluted, elbowing each other aside as they rushed forward to collect their uniforms.

***

Mordecai lit the candles he had hoarded over the years with a flame conjured by his magic. The flames of twenty candles pushed back the gloom and spilled over into Cayden's cell.

Hanging on the wall as he was, Cayden could not immediately see the source of the light, but he was grateful for it nevertheless. The soft scurrying sounds of rats magnified in the dark until it sounded like there were hundreds of them in his cell. His imagination running riot, Cayden discovered a fear he never knew he possessed.

"Mordecai, get me out of here." A tremor of panic made Cayden's voice come out in a squawk. "There are rats here, Mordecai!" He shuddered and twisted in his shackles. "Hurry, please!"

"Just a minute, my boy!"

Cayden heard rustling from the cell across the way and a shadow moved across the wall, Mordecai passing in front of the candles.

Something ran across Cayden's foot, brushing against his pant leg. His leg shot out a whole two inches, in an attempt to kick off the rat, but instead of dislodging the creature, he felt its needle-sharp claws pierce the flesh of his calf. With a choked screech, Cayden thrashed in his bonds, the metal shackles cutting into his exposed skin.

"Mordecai!" he screamed, taking deep gulps of air to stem his rising panic.

"There, that should do it." With a popping sound, the cell door across from Cayden's swung open on squealing hinges.

"Mordecai!" Cayden gasped, as a second rat joined the first, its whiskered nose sniffing at the blood now trickling down from the abrasions on Cayden's leg from the manacles.

Mordecai's thin pale face flashed in the barred window of Cayden's cell, as he reached through the bars and stuck a guttering candle on the lantern shelf beside the door. In the weak light, the floor writhed and bubbled with small bodies that scurried here and there across the floor. Cayden found that actually seeing the rats, was far worse than fearing them in the dark and Cayden began to thrash again as his horror broke free. He screamed as a rat began to climb his pant leg.

"Oh my," said Mordecai. He pulled his focus stone out of his pocket, his balled fist clutching it tightly, and then thrust it back through the bars and murmured a few words that Cayden could not make out. There was a flash of brilliant white and the rats collapsed, slipping off of Cayden's legs as the life left their bodies.

Cayden, his heart pounding, sucked in several breaths, trying desperately to regain control.

Mordecai replaced the stone in his pocket and fished out the master key that he had stolen off of Wendell the last time he had visited his cell. He fit it into the lock, turned the tumblers, and hurried over to Cayden's limp form.

"Nasty business, rats," he said, gazing around while he worked on unlocking the manacles. "They are not normally active this time of day." He released Cayden's hands and then bent to release his ankles. "Ahh, I see now why they came in such numbers, look."

With a click the last shackle fell away and Cayden scrambled off the wooden platform on shaky legs, careful to not step on a dead rat. Rubbing his wrists, Cayden bent over to see what had attracted Mordecai's attention. Under the platform he spied a wooden trough full of rotting refuse. At either end, a hollow stone tube was visible. It connected to a long vertical drain in the floor of the kitchens many stories above. The garbage of the kitchens washed down and emptied into the trough.

"Ingenious," said Mordecai, examining the device. "Obviously, this particular cell is used to torture prisoners. The poor kitchen staff would have no idea that they are innocently aiding in this torture." He straightened then put his hand on Cayden's shoulder. "Are you ready to go? We need to hurry. I can't imagine we have much time. They will be back very soon to see what effect the rats have had on loosening your tongue."

"Let's get out of here," Cayden said fervently, shuddering, eyes averted from the floor.

He followed Mordecai back to his cell, locking the cell doors behind them. Mordecai tapped on a rock at the back of his cell. The sound of an answering knock filled the air.

Chapter 51

QUEEN ALCINA SLAPPED HER MAID'S HANDS AWAY impatiently. "I told you, stupid woman, to fetch the emeralds, not the pearls."

"But, Your Majesty, the emeralds do not compliment your lovely dress." The maid smoothed the black silk and resumed buttoning the high-collared back.

"I care not for your silly opinion, woman. Finish your duties. *Quickly*! I do not have time to waste on your useless dribble."

The maid curtsied and quickened her movements, head bent to hide the bloom of embarrassment on her cheeks. She fetched the heavy silver collar set with emeralds and settled them around her mistress's throat, fastening the heavy clasp at the back of her neck. Next, she placed her thin pearl-studded crown on her hair and secured it with combs. The combination was hideous, but she clamped her lips shut, struggling to keep silent. With the queen's current mood, voicing her opinion now would find her on the way to the guillotine.

Alcina left the ridiculous woman behind, entering her sitting room where Cyrus waited. He blinked at the combination but also wisely said nothing. He knew Alcina was in one of her moods and heads usually rolled when she was in a foul temper.

"Well? What is the news? You have a new prisoner in the cells. Speak up, man. I have no patience for evasions this evening."

"We have an interesting prisoner below, my lady. You know I would not impose on you to perform an inspection, but there is something about this one. I can't put my finger on what it is, but he seems familiar somehow." He frowned in thought.

Alcina raised her severe eyebrows, like a hawk sighting a mouse attempting to hide. "That does not sound like much to go on, but I will humour you this time. Beheading that useless wizard might be just the thing to raise my spirits. Yes, I believe it is exactly what I need to relieve my stress." Her eyes glinted cold chips of blue ice in her pale face.

Cyrus opened the door and stepped back with a bow to let her pass. They made their way from the queen's apartments on the top floor of the main tower, down winding staircases, and through adjoining tapestry-draped corridors until they reached the upper walkway above the parade grounds.

They crossed to the other side of the castle housing most of the guest suites and the various meeting halls for dignitaries or noble petitioners. The kitchens were located in this section of the castle. They descended a broad-curved staircase to the pillared welcoming hall. The queen's coat of arms in a break with tradition was the sole decoration displayed on all the walls of the hall, all former monarch symbols having been removed.

They entered a hallway leading to the kitchens and then took a side corridor to a curving staircase that wound down deeper into the depths of the castle. Arriving at a landing, they spied two guards sitting at a table, playing cards. They snapped to attention on seeing the new arrivals and then bowed deeply at the waist.

"You are dismissed for ten minutes." The guards bowed again and left as ordered.

Cyrus pulled a key ring from his pocket and fitted it in the lock.

"Why did you choose to come down the main stairs this time, Your Highness?" Cyrus asked.

"That nosy maid is why. Unlike the other maids, she likes to hang around my apartments. I am suspicious of the reason why. The other maids are quick to leave my chambers. They understand that I do not want them around once they have performed their duty." She touched the emerald collar at her throat. "That one is too nosy by far. I do not want her to stumble on the secret passage entrance in the back wall of my closet. Secret passageways should remain secret, especially as that one leads all the way down to the cells—handy when I do not wish to be seen, but it would not do for others to know of its existence."

Cyrus lit a splint in the lamp hanging by the door and brought it to bear on the wicks of two unlit lamps. They flared to light, pushing back the shadows. He handed one to Alcina, the light flickering over her features. She stared back at him, a cruel twist of pleasure on her lips.

"Besides, it was a wonderful treat, surprising that servant who was currying favour with the wizard. Ahh, the look of surprise on his face when we popped out of the wall! That was to die for! Hanging him for his crimes was the only answer, of course. Smuggling supplies to the wizard is one thing, but failing to cut his hair was an unforgiveable mistake. One I intend to correct shortly."

Alcina preceded Cyrus down the hall, taking up a lantern from the wall and holding it aloft with one hand and picking up her skirts with the other. A cool breeze blew down the hall, bringing with it the odor of unwashed bodies. She wrinkled her nose in disgust but continued on to the end of the main hallway and then descending the curved rough-cut stone to the lowest of the dungeons. The *click-clack* of her boot heels echoed off the walls as she strode the short distance to the end where two cells flanked the stone corridor. Holding her lantern aloft, she let the light of it flood the interior of the cell.

It was empty.

Swinging the light around to the other cell, she flooded the interior with light, peering into it.

It was also empty.

At that precise moment, the alarm bells sounded. The castle was under attack.

Chapter 52

ZIONA GRABBED CAYDEN AS HE CRAWLED through the hole, pulling him out of the dusty passage, then hugged him, while Tobias crowded close, determined to not let Cayden out of his sight again.

Mordecai popped out of the hole behind him, surprisingly spry for one who had just been released from a seventeen-year imprisonment. He pulled out his focus stone and with a few murmured words, lessened the weight of the limestone block, thus assisting the rescue crews with the realignment of the stones into their original positions. They trowelled the mortar over the thin crack visible around the blocks and blended it seamlessly with the surrounding stones. When they were finished, it was impossible to tell the breach had ever occurred.

Nelson grinned pleased with the way the stones had slid out so easily with the lightest tug. The stone to Mordecai's cell had been used as an escape route in times past, secrets within secrets held silently by the ancient walls. Nice of them to mark the right stone, as it had sped up the process considerably. The dissolving paste was really quite the find, and the mortar had liquefied in a matter of hours. Now with the stones back in place, there was no evidence to show where the escape had occurred. Nor would the queen know where they had gone. They were safe…for now.

Ryder walked up and bear-hugged Cayden. Cayden groaned with the pressure on his sore ribs. Cayden's eyes wandered over the vaulted ceiling of the cavern and then onto the rescue team. "Where are we?" he asked.

"In caverns below the castle," Ryder said with a pleased smile. "Denzik here"—he waved Denzik over to him—"and his cronies have been mapping these passageways for years, ex-Kingsmen all. I think they expected you to come although I am not sure they expected to rescue you." Ryder bent over and whispered for Cayden's ears only, "Who's the old man?"

"A wizard and an old friend; a very old friend, if truth be told," Cayden said.

At that moment, Denzik arrived, and Ryder introduced him to Cayden. He bowed to Cayden and then shook his proffered hand. "Sire, I am so pleased to meet you! We have waited for a very long time for you to come, a lifetime, really. But we have not been idle, as you can see. You are pleased?" Denzik asked, just as the faint sounds of warning bells reached their ears, echoing through the cavern.

Ryder's head swivelled toward the sound and he glanced over at Nelson.

"We need to get back to our teams," said Ryder. "They have begun their assault through the Traitor's Gate. Anthony unlocked it from the inside and the teams are spreading out through the castle. Damn! The alarm has sounded too soon!"

Nelson walked over to Cayden, peering up into his face, as he towered above him.

"Sire, you are the spitting image of the late king, may the gods have mercy on his soul. It is an honour to serve under you once again." Nelson knelt before Cayden, head lowered.

Mordecai's eyes twinkled at Cayden's discomfort. Cayden reached down and pulled Nelson to his feet. "There is no time for this right now!" *I seem to say this a lot lately!* The thought flashed across Cayden's mind. "Didn't you say battle has commenced? Let's move!"

Both Nelson and Tobias snapped a salute as did Ryder. They gathered up the rest of the men and raced back to their respective units.

Ziona slipped back over to Cayden's side and held up a water flask for him to sip from. *More of her magic elixir*, he guessed and took a long swig. Ziona grinned up at him, hearing his thoughts. She slipped her hand into his.

Mordecai's smile broadened.

"Well, my boy, we now have a decision to make. The fight to retake this castle will rage above. But what truly concerns you at this moment in time is down here under the castle, under your ancestral home."

Cayden could feel it. The incessant tugging sensation on his soul made him restless, like his body was pumped full of adrenaline with no ability to burn it away. He now realized there had been a double pull happening, one to Mordecai, yes, but also another…deeper…somehow connected to him personally.

"How do you know this, Mordecai?"

"I was with you when you were born, but more importantly, I was with you before you *died*."

"I died and then was born?" Cayden stared at Mordecai in confusion as did Ziona.

"Actually, you died and were born twice." Mordecai hummed to himself in satisfaction. "Cayden, what do you know of the prophecies? Ziona, perhaps you can help him with this? Your people must have similar ones."

She nodded, understanding. Mordecai closed his eyes, reciting the prophecy by memory.

"And it shall come to pass in the end of days that the Lord of All shall weep with sorrow for the destruction of his creation. Darkness shall cover the land and the Mother Spirit shall be crushed. Her tears flood the mountains, yet who listens? For her tears are consumed by the fires of Helga. Who can stand before her gates? The world is burning. Weep you souls of the earth for he must die and live again. On the wings of an eagle so shall your salvation be carried."

Something stirred with in Cayden awakening in him. A distant memory flashed across his mind…or had it been a dream?

Ziona tilted her head, a puzzled expression on her face.

"Come," said Mordecai, "there is something you need to see."

Chapter 53

MORDECAI LED CAYDEN AND ZIONA down a rocky path that narrowed into low ceilinged sloping tunnels and bent toward the center of the earth beneath the castle. The sweeping curves dug relentlessly into the dark, dank underground, deeper than anyone had ever gone before, if the layers of undisturbed dirt were any indication.

At first, a faint greenish glow seemed to seep from the rocks, but the closer they came to their destination, the colour became aqua and then took on deeper shades of blue. The blue intensified and Ziona, glancing at Cayden, suddenly gasped aloud. Cayden was glowing with the precise same colour that was emanating from the cavern ahead of him. His skin flickered, absorbing the blue, creating a celestial aura around him. He looked at her questioningly and then followed her eyes to look at his own hands. He stopped abruptly, shocked. Blue flames danced and swirled off his skin. Mordecai, hearing him pause, stopped walking also.

Cayden's skin glowed with the light of ten lanterns, dimming the light of their lamps to nothing.

"I suspected this would occur," said Mordecai. "It is nothing to worry about, Cayden. Come."

The cave mouth opened into an oblong cavern. Walls, slick with the dripping of ancient waters, morphed into quarried blocks of marble imbedded with heavy veins of quartz. The unpolished stone of the anteroom glinted dully in the light exploding from Cayden's skin. On the other side of the anteroom, an arched opening pulsed sympathetically with Cayden's glow, and crackling tendrils of cool flame flickered across the opening. Cayden felt his hair try to rise, as the blue lighting drew him forward. He was unable to resist the pull and his feet crunched across the anteroom to the main chamber. Mordecai and Ziona followed Cayden, their steps cautious.

Cayden reached out with his hand and touched the opening. Lighting snaked up his arm and wrapped around his body then melded with the blue mist emanating from his body. He stepped through into a cathedral of marble. The walls towered three stories above the chipped and cracked floor. Soaring buttresses ran from columns standing in each corner, meeting in the middle of the ceiling, where an inverted bowl clung to the ceiling, carved out of the marble of the cavern, and decorated with faces of men, women, and children. Windows that opened onto nothing dotted the walls, and long black scorch marks streaked across the marble. On one wall, a large crack spidered up and out of sight.

It was the simple limestone well directly below the inverted bowl of faces that drew Cayden forward. Perched on a rocky platform and decorated with runes, mist swelled and swirled over the sides, interspersed with more flashes of blue lightning, the source of which was the depths of the well. Cayden stepped up onto the ledge and peered into shimmering surface. The basin was fathomless. Cayden gripped the sides of the well, knuckles whitening, so strong was his grip on the lip. He swayed as a wave of dizziness washed over him. From the depths, faces twisted into the air and shimmered into a three dimensional shape then collapsed back into the foggy surface.

Cayden's eyes widened and he extended a hand toward its shimmering surface. Ziona stepped up beside him and gazed into the well.

The mists stirred and churned in reaction to his proximity and more and more wisps detached themselves from it, forming shapes.

One such shape pulled essence from his body, and steadied, rising out of the well and solidifying into the reflection of a beautiful woman with long curly brown hair and emerald Primordial eyes. Cayden and Ziona gasped at the same time, stumbling back from the well and slipping off the platform. Both recognized the woman, although for different reasons.

"Who are you?" Cayden croaked.

"Princess Gwen?" Ziona peered over Cayden's shoulder.

"My son," the image whispered. A ghostly hand curled toward Cayden's face, as though she longed to touch him. "I cannot maintain this form for long, so we must speak quickly. So long have I waited for your return to your ancestral home. You and your sister are the only hope for this dying world. The evil goddess has stretched out her hand to smother it. Even now, she squeezes the throat of the Primordials in a vice grip that pits family against family, clan against clan."

Ziona gasped audibly at this news.

"You and your sister are the key to stopping a war that will engulf both lands. You must go to the land of the Primordials and meet with the high elders. Time is short, my son. Do not delay! As always, our souls are yours." Her form faded back into the mists of the well.

Ziona, stunned, sank to her knees on the cold stone floor. Mordecai followed her lead.

"You are more than a king. You are the Lord of the Mists, the Seer of Souls!" Ziona gasped as she bowed to the floor, touching the cold stone with her forehead. Cayden looked at them both, a memory stirring at her words. He knew that title. He had been called it before, but it was in a different place, a different time.

"Ziona is correct. This is the Well of Souls, Cayden. You are the Lord of the Mists and the caretaker of the souls within it." Mordecai straightened from his prone position, still kneeling. "You placed these souls here, Cayden. Do you remember?"

Cayden rubbed his head. Vague images flashed through his brain, but he found it impossible to make them settle into an actual memory.

He shook his head. "I do not know. There is something there, but I cannot seem to access it." He stepped back onto the ledge and peered over the edge, suddenly realizing the voices of his dreams were before him. They had not been dreams at all, but real souls calling out to him in his relaxed state. He dipped his hand into the pool and the mist clung to him, enveloping his arm and then his entire body in a lover's embrace.

"How many souls are in here?" Cayden asked, gazing unfocused at the surface as he listened to the whispering of voices only he could hear; the faces of tens of thousands of souls glimpsed in the swirling mists.

"These are all the departed souls who have ever lived, Cayden, at least all those who have not been snatched away by the shadow and not now inhabiting living bodies. You are their guardian, Cayden. You guard their rest until they are reincarnated, until they are blessed to be reborn as infants. That is why they are attracted to you. I think you see why this place had to be protected," Mordecai said. "I have been guarding the Well of Souls until your return, keeping the minions of Helga from discovering its location and from snatching away the future of mankind. Though they have searched long and hard, they have not found this place. It was for this reason the tunnels were created under the castle.

"The Royal Family of Cathair has ever been its protectors, the Spirit Shield of the Cathairs providing a blood shield and a spirit shield for the souls of humanity. Now I give this sacred duty back to you. This is why you must fight for this castle. It is your heritage and your birthright, but beyond that it is a sacred trust to protect, not only for you but for the entire world."

Chapter 54

CAYDEN, MORDECAI, AND ZIONA entered the castle through the Traitor's Gate and slipped up the passage to the parade grounds where the battle was at its fiercest. Soldiers from both sides lay bleeding and dying on the field. Cayden was shocked at the carnage, bodies broken and twisted, some barely recognizable as human.

His footsteps slowed and he hesitated. *This is insanity. There is no reason for this bloodshed. These people fight each other when they should be at peace. They are not each other's enemies. The queen is the enemy; she is the one who pits friend against friend, human against human. I must put an end to this.*

Around the injured and dying soldiers, auras pulsed, as they teetered on the cusp of death. Cayden walked out into the sea of bodies and knelt beside one such man from the Queen's Guard. His eyes were glassy and clouded in pain. Cayden gripped the man's hand. Cayden felt a shiver in his arm and the man went limp. A bright glow formed around Cayden. He visited soldier after soldier, friend and fallen foe alike, giving comfort and solace with a touch at the last moment of their existence on earth. Their souls passed to him like a feathery sigh. Instinctually, he sent them to the Well of Souls to their rest.

Mordecai walked behind him, anxiously scanning the various battles going on around them, searching for signs that someone was taking an interest in their proceedings. Ziona gripped her knife tightly in her hand and scanned the milling crowd of soldiers, spinning when the battle stumbled too close.

Cayden stood and Mordecai grabbed his arm, steering him to the other side of the courtyard and out of harm's way, ducking into the open doorway at the base of a tower leading to the very highest point of the castle. They launched themselves onto the skinny spiral staircase, the clash of steel and screams of the wounded pursuing them as they raced up the stairs. Occasional flashes of battle were glimpsed through arrow slits in the block, but they did not pause.

At the first landing, a shadow detached from the wall and a guard stepped forward to challenge them. "Halt!" he yelled, drawing his sword. Mordecai raised his hand and with a blast of magic, sent the man flying backward to strike the wall on the other side, sliding to the floor. More palace guards spilled from either end of the hallway as Ziona grabbed Cayden by the sleeve and hauled him up the stairs. Fear gave their feet wings, spurring them to greater speed, the whoosh of air and muffled thumps from Mordecai's fight, chasing them as they fled.

It had been a bold plan. They had been outnumbered, their success in no way assured. As he climbed, Cayden caught a glimpse of Ryder battling two opponents who, due to his size, made it a reasonable match. His tunic was torn and multiple cuts to his face left blood dried in patches on his cheek. Cayden paused, wanting to call out to him, but Ziona grabbed his sleeve and tugged him back into motion.

"Don't stop," she hissed. "They are battling for you. Your fight is not their fight. Keep going!"

As Cayden ran up the steps, Ziona heard steps echoing on the staircase behind them. Someone must have slipped past Mordecai. She turned and ran back down the staircase to confront the new threat.

Reaching the top, Cayden spilled out onto a flat-topped spire with a wide stone walkway circling the finial, rising another twenty feet into the air. He panted, hands on knees, catching his breath. Grey stone gargoyles, evenly perched on the waist-high stone wall, caught his eye. Cayden walked slowly around the circle, the wind whipping his tunic and tugging at his sleeves, as he surveyed the entire battle playing out below…a battle being fought for him.

He leaned out over the merlon to check the progress of the battle below when suddenly he felt the cold touch of sharpened steel at his throat.

"Careful now," she *tsked*, "don't want to lose your pretty head, now do you? Move slowly back from the wall. That's it."

Cayden eased away from the merlon, moving so as to not accidently slit his own throat on the fine edge. Beads of blood swelled against the sword despite his careful movements. As he straightened, head arching back away from the sword, Queen Alcina curved around him, inspecting him.

"Is this the upstart from the cellars, Cyrus?"

With his eyes pinned on Cayden, Cyrus said, "Yes, my queen. He is the one I was bringing you to see." His eyes glinted with anger. "Slit his throat right now and we can be done with this."

"Wait!" Alcina raised her hand to stay his swing. "Where is your sister?" She stopped in front of Cayden.

"My sister?" Cayden thought furiously. "I have no sister."

"Liar!" the queen hissed. She grabbed a hand full of hair, pulling his head back and further exposing the taut flesh of his throat. "I merely need to give the word and your head will be bouncing down this wall walk like a child's toy. Where is she?" she hissed again.

"I do not know. I haven't seen her in weeks," Cayden gasped, trying to swallow without moving his Adam's apple, the sword moving with the action.

"Bind his hands, Cyrus. We will take him with us. The castle is lost, but we have our prize. The Great Mistress will be pleased."

Alcina handed her sword to Cyrus and pulled a short knife hidden inside a pocket of her cloak then tightened her grip on Cayden's hair. "To make sure you do not run again, I am going to gouge out your eyes." She raised the short dagger and brought it flashing down. Cayden closed his eyes, shuddering with the anticipated impact.

At that moment silvery fury, in the form of Sheba, flashed through the air. Howling with rage, her paws landed on Cyrus's chest, knocking him back across the merlon. The sword clattered off the top of the wall and spun out into the air, falling to earth. Cyrus slipped between two of the stone teeth, great canine tusks missing his throat by inches as the wolf rolled past.

Ziona's battle cry was no less intense. She screamed and launched herself from the stone archway at Alcina. The queen spun around, ducking Ziona's blade and slashed with her own catching Ziona's arm as she passed. The cut was not deep but blood oozed all the same. Ziona flinched back from the next slash and then both Cyrus and Alcina were dashing for the staircase, disappearing into the opening. Sheba chased after them, snarling and snapping in full blood lust.

Cayden gasped for breath as Ziona reached him. She ran her hands up his arms over his shoulders and finally cupped his head to turn it gently, inspecting the sword cut at his throat.

"Thank the gods! You are OK," she gasped, fear etched into her beautiful face. She sagged with the release of adrenaline and hugged him tight, trembling. Cayden wound his arms around her and folded her close to his body, taking deep breaths to calm his fear.

"It's OK. We're OK. We're OK," he murmured into her hair.

Gently pushing her away, he looked down into her fear-soaked eyes. "Come, we have a job to do. Let's end this."

Chapter 55

THE CASTLE WAS IN AN UPROAR. Armed men fought battles on every level, insurgents against Queens Guard, farmers against innkeepers, milk maids against kitchen staff.

Marcia, Queen Alcina's maid, silently cheered the rebels on from her hiding place in the closet of the queen's chambers. The soldiers had materialized out of nowhere in spots throughout the castle. They were not attacking any servants, not that she noticed anyways. Those they came across they ran straight past without a glance. If servants raised a hand against them, though, they were quickly dispatched. She witnessed one of the cook's staff attack a soldier with a cooking knife and the soldier had not hesitated to run him through.

After that, the invading men gave fair warning, asking the staff to stand down and stand aside, this was not their fight.

Marcia heard the door to the queen's apartments open and stealthy footsteps sounded. She peeked through the keyhole to see who had entered. Alcina ran across the room, grabbed a travel bag and started shoving a random assortment of things into it. Clothing followed shoes followed jewels. The door opened again and Cyrus entered, his jacket sleeve torn, blood running down his arm from a deep jagged wound. His sword dripped onto the hand-knotted silk carpet at his feet. He grabbed the queen roughly by the arm and shook her.

"We don't have time for this, Alcina!" In his panic, he forgot the royal honorific. "If they capture you, they will behead you! We must leave *now*!" he hissed. Grabbing her by the arm, he pulled her toward the closet.

Marcia's heart leapt to her throat. *If they discover me, they will run me through with a sword!* She knew it. She shied back into the gowns and crouched in the corner. The door next to her opened and Cyrus and Alcina pushed past her to the back of the tall storage closet. They pried open a panel on the back wall, which swung open on hidden hinges and disappeared into the black hole beyond the closet wall, leaving it ajar in their haste.

Chapter 56

CAYDEN STILL DID NOT UNDERSTAND the complete how and why of it, but he did understand his aid was needed.

He reached into his pocket and pulled out his flutes. They warmed in his hand, a comforting joyous reunion with his trembling fingers. Ziona had retrieved them from his tent and brought them along. During their walk back up from the Well of Souls, she slipped them into his pocket, reverently, seeming to understand their purpose for the first time.

He hoped she was right. He hoped he understood them half as well as she did.

He selected the one he had carved the day Aossi had appeared. He placed it to his lips and began to play. The air around him shimmered and warped, the sky a rippling sound wave.

At first, the sound of battle drowned the sound of the flute, but as he played, it grew louder and louder. The other flutes in his pocket warmed and vibrated in sympathy. Suddenly, sound burst from those flutes, a chorus of music even though he was not directly playing them. The songs melded into one and swelled like a trumpet call, blasting out over the grounds below.

Soldiers from both sides took startled notice, pausing in their battles to gaze up at a sky suddenly in turmoil, boiling and bubbling with silver grey clouds laced with rainbows. Then a piercing shaft of light split the nighttime sky, blinding the soldiers on the field below.

At the same time, bright spots randomly popped onto the field below. The glowing spots resolved themselves into wolves and snakes, running out of doorways and around the corners of buildings, spilling through archways, slithering and skulking out of drain pipes, sliding out of cracks and crevices in the stone, and rising from the ground in answer to the call of Cayden's song. The men paused in mid-battle, great cries of alarm rising and falling from all who spotted the creatures.

The wolves snarled and snapped at the men; the snakes hissed and danced, rattling tails and flaring hoods, drawing the battling men's attention away from each other as friend and foe turned as one to face this new, unknown threat. Confusion reigned in the milling crowd below.

Thunder boomed and rumbled. Forks of brilliant lightning split the sky, cracking open the clouds.

The soldiers cried out, falling to their knees and clasping hands over ears ringing with the concussion of the thunder. They squeezed their eyes closed against the blinding brilliance of the lightning.

The thunder, the lighting, the snarling wolves, and the slithering snakes were nothing compared to the ghostly forms that rode into the commons, phantom souls riding rainbow-hued chariots pulled by great white-winged Pegasus, their shining armour blinding, commanding the allegiance of the soldiers below.

The great generals of old, Kingsmen whose faces were familiar to all, paused to gaze at the combatants. As one, they pulled flaming swords from sheaths and raised them into the air. The message was clear. Cease this battle now or we will finish it, permanently. Denzik spied Captain O'Reilly and grinned.

The combatants cried out and confusion reigned. Some, crazed at the sights before them, tried to fight the ghosts. On contact, their swords became a flaming inferno that spread from weapon to clothing. Screaming, the flaming beacons of rebellion ran through the crowd, panicking the balance of the Queen's Guard. Some scrambled for the exits, only to find the exits blocked by wolves and Kingsmen. No one was leaving the area.

Cayden lowered his flute, aghast at the stampede that was occurring below. He could not discern friend from foe. All he knew was that people were dying. To his vision, a misty blue fog rose from the ground as more and more men and women departed this life.

"Help me, Ziona! I don't know how to stop this! They are going to kill each other to the last person! Help me stop this madness!"

Mordecai put a gentle hand on his shoulder and squeezed it. "Now is the time, Cayden. Now is the return of the king, the true heir of Cathair, the true Spirit Shield. Claim your heritage. Claim your birthright. Speak to them."

Ziona slipped her arm around his waist from the other side and leaned her head against his shoulder. "I believe in you, Cayden." She gestured to the milling people below. "They believe in you too, if you will allow them to. Speak to them."

Cayden looked from one to the other. "I do not know what to say." he murmured, his eyes roving over the scene below him.

"Speak what is in your heart. They will hear it," said Mordecai, stepping back out of sight of the crowd. Ziona returned to the staircase, guarding his back as he mustered the courage to speak.

Cayden stared sightlessly at the scene before him, blocking out the scene as his mind wandered back over the events since leaving Sanctuary-by-the-Sea. He sorted and slotted his experiences, turning them over, examining them. He thought of Avery, how she had looked the last time he had seen her, the concern in her eyes at his decision to leave. She knew nothing of what had transpired since joining the legion nor did he know what adventures she had stumbled into. Surely her path was a smoother one than this? He smiled slightly, thinking what her reaction would be when they could finally sit down and talk as brother and sister again. *I miss her so much!* he thought, his heart lurching painfully in his chest in that part he reserved just for his twin.

His mind wandered down familiar paths, back into his earliest childhood memories of the pair of them, playing in the pastures around their farm. They had always known they were special, accepted that they were unique. They shared an ability to talk to each other telepathically, but they had innocently believed it to be part of that special, indescribable bond that twins share. They had never thought of their magic as dangerous or deviant, but Queen Alcina had thought it so and she was correct. Her fears had turned out to be a real and justified danger to the queen and to her reign. They'd been physically hidden from the world. *Now the world knows about my magic, and soon it will know of Avery's too, at least amongst the Primordial clans.*

He had not heard the Primordial Prophesies as a child, but the children's games they'd played with the other villagers' children and stories told by the villagers themselves had hinted at the belief in a saviour of souls; that the Lord of the Mists was a real person, a Seer of Souls. *I am a true heir of the powers that belong to a Spirit Shield of Cathair, of this there can be no doubt...but Avery must also be a Seer of Souls.* He tested this newly minted thought in his mind and knew it to be true in his heart of hearts. *We are both Seers of Souls, the pair of us, twin Seers.*

If this is the truth of the matter, then the rest must also be true. With a grimace, he tucked the flute in his pocket and resigned himself to his destiny. *Mordecai has a lot of explaining to do, starting with our family line. I will make him cough up those prophesies, even if he chokes on them. I must learn everything I can, for both my life and Avery's depend on it.* He gazed out over the top of the castle walls and to the north, straining his eyes to see the grey haze that was the mountains of the Highland Spine, dividing his lands (his mind tried to shy from the thought) from the Primordial lands. *I am coming, Avery, and I will be armed with information when I do. Stay safe!*

With a deep breath and a sigh, Cayden raised his voice to speak to the milling army of bewildered and discontented men scattered throughout the castle grounds, still looking for a way to escape the prowling animals blocking all the exits. His voice swelled and moved over the surrounding countryside, magnified by the magic of the flutes.

"Lay down your weapons, immediately! This battle is ended. I have returned to claim my birthright, the throne of the Spirit Shields of Cathair. My sister and I are the rightful heirs of Cathair and the heavens bear witness to this. The usurper has been ousted. The royal line is being restored. Hear me now and obey!"

The Queen's Guard quieted during his speech, which could be heard in every corner of the kingdom. Sword arms dropped and a murmuring replaced the screams of moments ago. The ethereal chariots drifting inches above the ground rose into the air, causing the soldiers to shy back. Leading the chariots, in the most brightly coloured one of all, sat Aossi, grinning like a schoolgirl, feet propped up on the felly rim. She winked at him and waved.

Cayden managed a weak smile and lifted his hand in acknowledgment of the greeting.

"The Kingsmen will gather your weapons. There will be no more fighting. Hear me and obey! Choose to disobey and your time on this earth will be an unpleasant one. There are plenty of dungeons waiting to be filled. I know, as I have seen them."

The few soldiers who remained on their feet slowly lowered their weapons and as one raised their hands in surrender. The wolves prowled the edges of the battle, tongues lolling, giving every appearance of grinning. Snakes slithered onto rocks and back into the crevices they had exited.

Slowly, the fighting ended. A silence fell over the scene, broken only by the moans of the injured. Suddenly, cheers erupted from the Kingsmen, a great ground swelling roar of victory. The Kingsmen moved amongst the Queen's Guard, securing weapons and herding those of the former Queen's Guard still standing into the center of the battlefield, ringing it with the steel of their swords,

"The Kingsmen will escort you into the holding cells on the first level of the dungeons. Once there, you will be offered proof of my lineage and an opportunity to swear allegiance. Those who refuse will be tried as traitors to royal house of Cathair. I suggest you ask many questions of the Kingsmen. Satisfy yourselves as to the truth of this matter."

One belligerent guardsman yelled up at Cayden, "Where is the queen? Where is Queen Alcina! You cannot be king while she lives."

Murmurs broke out from the circle, and the Kingsmen tightened their grips on their swords, in warning.

Ziona crossed back over to stand beside Cayden and he slipped his arm around Ziona's shoulders, giving her a squeeze. She hugged him and stared down at the scene, mouth open in awe.

It was done...for now.

***

In the woods outside of the castle grounds, two figures in heavy travelling cloaks hurried away from the battle. Suddenly, the skies opened up and a piercing ray of light flooded the area. Rays of pure energy pierced the gloom of the forest canopy, silhouetting the trees. Alcina saw ghostly chariots materialize and slide through the solid castle walls. She swore a very un-queenly word and ducked behind a tree. Cyrus paused.

The gaunt trees writhed as light flooded the forest driving back the gloom and stabbing into Charun hiding amongst the trunks of the trees like a red hot poker. The light scoured the forest and the Charun burst from cover, screaming with the touch of the light as it sliced through the darkness. Flames leapt from their withered skin as they writhed and thrashed and burned. Exposed to the light's purity, they shrivelled and smoked as they died.

Cyrus and Alcina bolted, the shrieks lending speed to their flight. *What power was able to destroy a Charun?* Alcina shuddered. She wasn't about to wait around to find out.

Chapter 57

MORDECAI LEANED BACK ON THE CRENELLATED WALL and crossed his arms under his bushy white beard studying Cayden. Cayden sighed and turned his flute over in his hands before tucking it back into his pocket. His mind was spinning with all that had transpired in the past twenty-four hours.

"Cayden."

Cayden lifted his head in response to Mordecai's call, meeting his eyes. He was surprised to feel tears welling in his own. He swiped a sleeve across his eyes to disguise their wetness.

"Was she really my mother?" The question burst from his lips, unbidden. Of everything he had seen, everything that had happened, this was the one piercing thought, the one overwhelming need he had…to know the truth.

"Yes," Mordecai said softly.

Ziona passed a hand across his back in comfort.

"Tell me now. Tell me it all. I want to know the truth. And now, before I have to face everyone below."

Mordecai sighed. He pulled Cayden over to sit beside him at the base of the wall. Ziona eased herself down beside him, to listen in.

"Seventeen years ago, a Primordial princess fell in love with a handsome young prince of Cathair. Tall, blond, and fair, he sat his stallion with a bearing that commanded attention, as the prince and heir to the throne of Cathair should. This was at the peak of the Daimonic wars, which I am sure you have heard of?"

Cayden nodded his head, still staring at his hands.

"The battles between the kingdom and the Primordial forces at Daimon Ford were long and protracted affairs with heavy raiding occurring back and forth across the river and many casualties on both sides.

"During a break in one of the skirmishes, a raiding party was sent out on a mission to kidnap your mother. They sneaked into the Primordial lands and managed to get right into the sacred capital city of Faylea, a feat accomplished by few. It was a bold but desperate attempt to end the fighting. I think the original plan was to merely hold her for ransom and force the Primordial warriors, who are the fiercest of all fighters, to cease battle and retreat.

"Your father, however, took one look at Gwen when she arrived in Cathair as a prisoner and his heart was lost. Rather than return her to her people, he set about convincing his father that their marriage would be best for the kingdom, arguing that it would unite the lands forever more.

"Obviously, the Primordial peoples were in an uproar over the disappearance of their beloved princess and the battles resumed with an even greater fervour. Many, many lives were lost on both sides in the battles that followed.

"Princess Gwen was never mistreated; in fact, she was pampered and given every consideration and freedom to explore the castle at will, but she was forbidden to leave the grounds. Prince Alexander was often seen escorting her on walks, and as their love grew, so did his demands that they be allowed to marry.

"Alcina, your father's sister, secretly harboured the ambition to succeed her brother to the throne. Indeed, the laws of Cathair encouraged her in this, as they state that a ruling king or incumbent male heir must be married prior to ascending to the throne or the next closest married female relative to the reigning king would be crowned.

"As Prince Alexander had not shown the remotest interest in any of the eligible young female nobles paraded before him, Alcina had convinced herself that the throne would be hers.

"Gwen's sudden appearance and the attention lavished by the Cathair prince on the guest captive flared her anger and jealousy. As the next in line to the throne, she was unwilling to see a Primordial princess within reach of the throne. Unbeknownst to the rest of the royal family, she hatched a plan to overthrow the entire royal line, beginning with the murder of her brother." Mordecai sighed heavily, his mouth drooping; his eyes troubled.

"The king's death appeared to be the result of natural causes, but I found traces of heart leaf in his salad the night he died. He had supped in his suite that dreadful night, alone. I could never pinpoint who delivered his meal that evening.

"His son, Prince Alexander, had left two days prior on a routine patrol with a group of young men in training to be Kingsmen. He was killed, once again, under suspicious circumstances and never returned.

"You see, your grandfather had agreed to their marriage, just hours before Prince Alexander left on patrol. The wedding was being arranged in secret via pigeon messengers sent between the Primordial chieftains and the king.

"Your father and mother, so very anxious to be together, had begun to see rather more of each other than is proper for the unwed. Gwen became pregnant and attempted to hide her condition from the rest of the royal family, but Alcina discovered the pregnancy. It was then that I realized the royal family was in grave danger, but I had no proof.

"One day, as they strolled through the secluded gardens near the library, Gwen and Alexander were approached by the fairy Aossi who had been sent as a messenger from Alfreda, the Mother Goddess herself and her brother Caerwyn, the Spirit Shield.

"Aossi knew of the plan to kill the royal family and also of Gwen's pregnancy. She convinced your parents that the only way to save their respective kingdoms and the world was for the godlings, Alfreda and Caerwyn, to be born to humans and walk the world as mortals once more. The catch was that they needed to join with Gwen's babes as hosts.

"You see, the veil, or the shield between the living and the dead, has been weakening, and the minions of Helga are snatching away the souls at rest, and enslaving them in the netherworld. Helga, as you know, is the ruler of the underworld, banished to rule the souls of the condemned in that torturous place by the gods of old with the blessing of her siblings, Alfreda and Caerwyn.

"Fearing for their lives and for yours and Avery's by extension, your father and mother agreed to the plan." Mordecai paused for a moment, checking to make sure that he hadn't lost Cayden along the way. "There are several things that are required to invoke magic such as was being proposed by Aossi.

"Firstly, you need a wizard's Will. This is the essence of what makes a wizard's magic work. Secondly, you need a focus; a tool with which to compact and combine the elements of the spell. I use this stone as my focus." Mordecai reached into his pocket and pulled the smooth focus stone out to show Cayden. It lay flat and smooth, a pearly sheen coating its surface. "With a focus stone, my wizard's Will, and your parent's co-operation, the final element was the soul of a god. With these, we could give human form to the gods. With an archaic incantation not used since the beginning of time, we bound the souls of the immortals to human flesh."

And suddenly, as though buried beneath an avalanche, a memory floated up out of a crack in his being. Cayden's eyes glazed over as he fought to remember, to bring the memory to the forefront of his mind…and then it was gone.

"For an instant," Cayden said, "I remembered…something," he frowned, "but now it is gone." He stood up and started to pace.

Tears of frustration glistened in Cayden's eyes and he did not check them as they slowly made tracks in the dirt on his face.

Mordecai continued the story, politely ignoring Cayden's distress.

"Your mother summoned me to her chambers, the evening after the news of Prince Alexander's fall. When I arrived, it was obvious that she was gravely ill by the deathly pallor of her skin. Her overriding concern was for the babies dying inside her as the poison ran its course. She was desperate to save her royal children, who were conceived to bring peace and a flesh bond between the two warring factions of the earth, a united royal family spanning both nations."

He told Cayden of the magic of the Primordials, how they were attuned to the spirits of the land and the animals that resided in it, of how the mythical creatures of the earth were in tune with the Primordial spirits.

"Your flutes are a conduit of magic that speaks to the spirits of the beasts. The magic you possess calls them and your magic could also act as a trigger for their souls to reincarnate into their mythical form." Cayden nodded, knowing this from his encounter with the werewolf form of Sheba's alpha.

"But what you need to understand most of all, Cayden, is that you and Avery volunteered to do all of this."

Cayden's head shot up at his words. Ziona leaned in closer, to listen.

"If Princess Gwen is my mother and Prince Alexander is my father then who are the people who raised me?" Cayden slipped his hand into Ziona's, seeking comfort. She squeezed his in return.

"The man and woman who raised you, in Sanctuary-by-the-Sea are also your parents, Cayden, in every sense of the word. You are a merging, a blending of both of those babes whose bodies you inhabited. The binding of your godling essence to the physical bodies conceived by your royal parents merged you into a new being. When I triggered the magic that pulled you from your dying infant bodies and into the infants being born in Sanctuary, your mortal and immortal essences merged with those children's bodies.

"As you know now, being the Seer of Souls, no soul had yet been delivered to those infants, so you delivered your own soul to the host baby waiting for this bonding. You and your sister are truly the children of both parents."

Mordecai reached over and grasped Cayden's shoulder in his right hand and squeezed it. "I know you love your parents very much. Surely it is a comfort to know they truly are your parents in every sense of the word?"

Cayden smiled a small smile, the pain of the truth receding from his eyes as he absorbed Mordecai's words.

"I will show you the ancient texts that are stored in the castle library vaults," Mordecai said. "But of this there is no doubt. You are the Seer of Souls, the godling that is the caretaker of the souls of the deceased. You willingly divested yourself of your divinity in order to wage this battle, in order to bring unity to creation. But understand this: as you are now human, it also means that you can die. And for you, young Cayden, there is no rebirth. If you die in this form, you are dead, wiped from existence in any form. For you, death is final."

Cayden shivered. He had suspected that he could die, but not that it would be…forever. Everyone knew about the rebirth of the souls of the dead. It was the basis of their legends.

"What about Avery?" he asked.

"Avery is also a godling. I think you already know who she is."

Ziona gasped. "Is Avery the Goddess Pinesi, the Goddess of the Woodlands?"

Mordecai nodded. "Yes, that is one of many names used by the Primordial people. She is the goddess of the woodland creatures, the mother goddess of nature and guardian of mythical souls. She is also your sister, Alfreda."

"Then she is in danger too?" Cayden asked.

"Yes. Yes we must find her and soon." Mordecai stood up and brushed off his ragged robes, still filthy and torn from his imprisonment. "Now, if you will excuse me, I'd like to find some real clothes and a bath. I haven't had one of those in, oh…seventeen years I believe?" He trotted off to the stairwell and disappeared.

Cayden reached out to Avery with his mind. *Avery, where are you?* He received no response.

Chapter 58

IN THE DAYS FOLLOWING THE RECAPTURE OF CATHAIR, Cayden and his new subjects struggled to settle to a new routine. The town swelled with migrants who flocked in from the countryside on the strength of rumour and a chance to glimpse the new king. The scattered Kingsmen slowly trickled back into the city, bringing their families with them, anxious to offer their services even though many were now past their prime fighting days.

Cayden cornered Mordecai early on and pestered him to teach him his family history, and they spent many long days in the squat, stone library, shaped like a flat topped stone turret, in the center of the walled gardens, pouring over the books contained there.

The royal ascent was on everyone's mind, and both ex-Queen's Guard and Kingsmen alike joined together to celebrate the coronation of the royal missing heir, King Cayden. A simple ceremony was held in the public square the following day out front of the palace amidst great security. It was at Cayden's insistence that all people should be allowed to attend. Commoners crowded the square, hung out of windows and perched on rooftops to cheer as the crown was placed on his head. A week of celebration was ordered, and the festivities lasted for the better part of two before life returned to normal.

Denzik, Nelson, and Fabian were reinstated as captains of the Kingsmen and promoted to Captain Generals. The band was incorporated into the Kingsmen as a new and highly specialized unit, dedicated to service as Cayden's personal guard and allowed to retain their chosen name. Similar units were formed within the Kingsmen, reflecting regional areas and homes, uniting the scattered former guard into familiar bonded units.

Of Cyrus and Alcina, no trail was found to indicate where they had fled. A frightened maid brought to them in the early hours after the cessation of the battle had led them to a hidden passage behind Queen Alcina's closet and gave witness that they had fled through it. A large contingent of Kingsmen ducked inside and followed the hidden passage until it emptied into the tunnels under the castle. They searched but could locate no further clues as to the direction they had fled.

A bounty was set of one hundred thousand gold crowns on the head of Alcina and ten thousand gold crowns for Cyrus for their capture and return. A bounty of five hundred gold crowns was set on Darius's head and Ziona, still furious over Cayden's kidnapping, matched the bounty from her personal purse doubling the sum, so keen was she to capture the traitor. The Kingsmen searched the woods where the ambush had occurred, to no avail.

Denzik was given the charge to map out the underground tunnel system to prevent exactly the type of unseen ambush attack they had engineered on the castle.

Ryder was awarded a knighthood and as his first duty, commissioned to find more like minded people to expand into a full order of Cathairian knighthood. He set off immediately to search the realm for the bravest and most loyal men and women of all the lands, both human and Primordial. His mandate was to forge a unique peacekeeping force, starting with the knights of Cathair. Once the initial shock of his commission wore off, Ryder begged for a training facility. With a broad grin, Denzik deeded his farm to Ryder. Lower Cathair would soon become known as the home of the Royal Knight's Guild.

On the second evening after their victory, Cayden took Ziona for a walk through the rose gardens, hand in hand. He stopped at a secluded stone bench and pulled her down beside him. Once seated, he took up her hand, kissing it lightly.

"We need to talk about this bond. What do you want to do about it? Where do you see this—us going? I know I am attracted to you"—Cayden's ears pinked as his heartbeat quickened—"but how do you feel about us being able to read each other's minds? I mean, what if you want to, you know, date someone?"

Ziona laughed, and Cayden's ears reddened even further.

"You do not need to worry about such things," she said, smoothing his hot cheek with her cool palm, "there is no one here I would consider mate worthy...except for you." She quirked an eyebrow in his direction, and his thoughts instantly winged back to their first meeting in her tent back during his legion stay. "Why don't we take it slowly, see what develops? There is much to be done and I need to return to my people and let them know what has transpired here. There is much to be told that the elders need to hear. I fear that the war between our peoples is about to escalate. Who knows what plans Alcina and Cyrus are about to implement?

"One thing is certain, however. Whether as mates or as very deep friends, we are bonded as no other two people have been in the history of this world. In that sense, we are true soulmates, now and forever."

Epilogue

THE SMELL OF ROTTING EGGS PERMEATED THE AIR as the lava spluttered and splashed over the cracked edges of the pool. The little light shed by the glowing basin was quickly dispersed by shadowy creatures that slithered on the floor of the cavern. The darkness was not threatened by the light, but instead it swallowed the feeble attempt to define the shape of the space.

All of this was lost on the two shivering forms prostrated on the rough stone floor, afraid to lift their faces to gaze on the goddess before them.

"You have crawled here to ask my forgiveness when the stench of your failure has reached my nostrils long in advance of your arrival?"

"Great Mistress of the Dark," Alcina gushed in a rush to be heard, "we hurried all the way to your fortress to bring you the news that the boy has finally revealed himself and we now know which one he is! Surely we can destroy him now if you would loan us the aid of your creatures. We will not fail again." Alcina hazarded a furtive peak out of the corner of her eye at the ethereal shadow swarmed form before her and then, gasping in fear, pressed her forehead back to the stone floor once again.

"What say you, Cyrus? Is your failure as complete as Alcina's? What excuse do you bring to try and persuade me that I shouldn't end your worthless lives right now and feed your souls to my pets here?" The goddess gestured to the mindless, formless milling swarm of minions at her misted feet.

Cyrus stirred and with gaunt face still pressed to the floor, whispered, "Great Mistress, your plan has not yet failed. We know of his weakness now. Our spies report that he will not raise a hand to destroy life, whether that life is for good or for evil. It will be his undoing. He will not be able to stand against our armies or against your greatness. Please lend us the assistance of your servants. I promise when we meet them on the field of battle, none shall remain standing and their souls will serve your glory for all eternity as it is prophesied."

Silence met his plea and he shivered at the icy touch both he and Alcina felt slide into their minds; as a cold and clammy spectral hand clutched at the heart of their souls' essence. They involuntarily cried out at the stroking, empty feeling of the soulless. The goddess stripped their minds bare and weighed their souls, examining their intentions. Shivering uncontrollably, their bodies thrashed on the icy surface of the audience chamber. Suddenly, the touch withdrew and they lay panting, dragging in raged breaths as they fought their terror.

"I find your intentions aligned with mine and so your souls are not forfeit...yet. Do not fail me again. My patience is growing thin. Here is what you will do." The goddess bent down and touched a spectral finger to each of their temples, placing her instructions in their minds.

"Now leave me. Do not return unless you can report success. If you slink back in failure, I promise you will beg for death; a death that will be denied, forever."

Suddenly a sharp cold wind swept the chamber, like a door opening onto a blustery winter's day. As abruptly as the wind began, all stilled. Cyrus and Alcina lifted their faces from the stone floor. Helga was gone.

Soul Sanctuary

Prologue

This is not your fight. Let them die!

THE ARMY ROLLED OUT of the southern plains and into the short hills, a river of red-coated lava swirling through the valley base. The push of soldiers clogged the narrows, splashing up onto the hillsides and coating the passes in a crimson crust of death.

The Primordial runners peered down at the roiling mass of men from their perch high atop an abandoned eagle's nest, wedged in a towering deciduous tree which clung to the northern edge of the pass. The crown of the treetop camouflaged their lookout while providing an unimpeded view of the undulating scene below.

As one, the runners shimmied down from their perches and ghosted into the dense cover of squat pine, the thick carpet of needles providing silent footing as they ran. Of all the passes to approach, this was the worst, the most feared by the Primordial Chiefs, as the civil war left the defending clans stretched to the limit.

Indeed, some defenders had abandoned their posts, their fear over the rumoured fate of their kin overcoming their desire to fight. Whispers of villages emptied and entire families snatched away by unknown forces had caused a swelling defection within the forward units of tribal defenders. It was so rampant that the Chieftains now arrested those who attempted desertion and handed them over to the priests, rather than admit that the Flesh Clan defenders were cowards.

The Primordial priests were only too happy to receive the disaffected clansmen, as they had their own mandate to fulfill.

In a solitary camp perched high on the side of the Wailing Mountain, deep within the pass, the disloyal were marched with hands tightly bound in front, a never-ending stream of clansmen. The guards assigned to this duty delivered their prisoners swiftly and without delay, wishing to be away from the encampment full of shivering, wild-eyed priests. The priests' camp never slept except during the daylight, the time from dusk to dawn alive with the scurrying holy men.

Late into the night, the screams of the sacrifices howled through the encampment, flooding down to the tents below, the souls of the sacrifices dancing in the flames of their campfires, confirming the transfer to those who would continue the fight.

Primordial High Priests, clothed in cloaks comprised of leathery-patched skins of unknown origins and embedded with eagle feathers, raised bloody knives to the sky and chanted. The bleeding of the sacrifices was a delicate thing. Too little bleeding and the sacrifices would go into shock before the transfer was complete; too much bleeding and the soul would be lost.

A bare-chested apprentice with only one eagle feather bound to each tattooed arm dipped a hollowed gourd into a basin of potion warming on hot rocks at the edge of the firepit. Carefully, he carried the gourd, brimming with liquid, over to the naked, blindfolded woman staked out spread-eagle on the ground at the edge of the flickering light. With one hand, he pinched her cheeks so that her mouth was forced into an *O* shape then tipped the contents of the gourd into it. He plugged her nose, forcing her to swallow convulsively while she thrashed in her bonds. The blindfold slipped, and the woman's furious eyes stabbed into the apprentice. Then, with the last of her strength, she spat the remains of the potion back in his face. With a scream, he stumbled away from the woman, frantically wiping it off. Everywhere the potion landed, it bubbled and hissed. Blisters erupted, large red swellings bubbling under the skin. They popped and oozed, drying instantly. Within seconds her skin withered, cracking and curling into drifts that feathered to the ground, even while the woman's eyes rolled back in her head.

Blood bloomed where the curls of skin had been, to run in rivulets that joined larger flows. The High Priests crowded around the woman's corpse and caught the blood dripping from her body in gleaming bone vessels. Once the bowls were full to the brim, the High Priests began a rhythmic chant, waving a hollowed rainstick carved with runes over the bowls, seducing the spirit of the blood sacrifice and binding it to the blood for transfer into a new vessel.

The woman's heart pumped valiantly as the last of its life force seeped to the surface. With a final shudder, she relaxed in her bonds, sagging limply in the ropes suspending her body.

The priests turned their backs on the empty shell, and the chanting rose in pitch, calling forth the spirit of the dead woman. Wisps of movement danced on the surface of the bowls of blood, thickening then dissipating, and formed once again, a shadowed impression of a red face floating above the surface of the vessels.

They walked past the line of shivering men, kneeling at the edge of the firelight, arms bound behind their backs, awaiting their turn to serve the High Priests. All of them averted their eyes, hoping to not be chosen, hoping that they would be executed in the normal fashion. Beheading was preferable to being bled to death in their eyes. A whimper escaped the mouth of one of the deserters, as his courage failed once again. With a jerk on his bindings, he was hauled to his feet by two burly apprentices. He howled as he was dragged toward the sacrificial pit.

The High Priests paid no attention to the commotion, transfixed on the process at hand. Their chanting grew louder, the rhythm faster as they approached a small animal tied to a metal stake driven deep into the ground. On closer inspection, a bear cub peered up at the approaching priests, licking its lips hungrily. The priests placed the bowls before the cub, chanting in a singsong voice that soothed it.

Once the priests backed away, the cub sniffed at the offering and then began to lap up the blood thirstily. The priests' song shrieked assailing the ears of the watchers as the bear drank until all the blood was gone.

Suddenly, the song ceased. A gong was sounded, once, twice, three times. As the sound faded from the third gong, the cub roared.

A vortex formed around the cub, spinning and swirling, dragging soil into its maelstrom as it arose, faster and faster, tiny bolts of energy sparking within the cloud, which grew into a funnel then into a tornado, which picked up the cub and whirled it about. Bolts of lightning stabbed the ground and the priests stepped back, hands covering their faces as the sand stung their skin, whipping their eagle feathers until they mocked flight.

With a great clap of thunder and a blinding flash of light, everything stilled.

As the dust cleared, a body was revealed, curled into a ball on the ground. Slowly, it unfurled and rose to its feet.

A muscular woman stood before them, ten feet tall with a face that hinted at the bear cub, but fully human in form. A ruff of tawny hair curled past her broad shoulders. She was clad in a tight-fitting leather jerkin and leggings with a sheath for a great sword strapped to her hip.

Artio sniffed the air with a feral toothy grin and rumbled in the celestial voice of the gods, *"Bow to me."*

As one, the Primordial clansmen and High Priests fell to the ground, their faces pressed to the earth.

Artio drew her lips back and bared her long incisors in a parody of a smile and then bellowed with pleasure.

Chapter 1

Witness

AT THE TOUCH OF GAIUS'S HAND on her shoulder, Avery Tiernan slowly released her hold on the leafy undergrowth, allowing it to relax to its normal position.

A ringlet of dark hair snagged on a twig, threatening to shake the bush and alert the watched to the presence of the watchers. She peered at the tangle out of the corner of her eye then unwound the stray lock, silently praying the faces would remain pressed to the earth.

Freeing her hair, she took one last peek at the scene and locked eyes with the giant bear-like goddess. Artio bared her teeth, and a chuckling grunt issued from her throat. Avery broke contact and scooted back to her companions, hiding behind a large boulder with their horses muzzled. Sharisha urged her to mount up beside her father, Gaius, who was already seated astride his big barrel-chested mare.

As one they fled, urging their mounts into a swift trot, eager to put distance between themselves and the Primordial encampment. Reaching the mountain face, they slowed to a walk and allowed their mounts to pick their way along the sheer mountain goat trail that crisscrossed the rocky face of the mountain. The trail was even more treacherous with only the moon to light the descent. Loose shale threatened to slip out from under the horses' hooves at any given moment.

Sharisha's mount clattered over the last of the stones at the base and disappeared down a level path just as Gaius's mount slipped, hooves sliding out from under it. With a crash, the horse fell onto its side and slid the remaining ten feet to the base of the mountain. Gaius cried out at the lurch and kicked his left leg out of its stirrup, but before he could push himself clear of his mount, it was sliding down the scree. His leg, trapped beneath its bulk, carried him down the mountainside with his horse.

Avery screamed and reined in her snorting mount, afraid that they would follow the mare's sickening slide. Gaius came to an abrupt stop at the base of the mountain, unmoving.

Avery rolled off of the back of her horse, Sunny, and slid down the mountainside after her father, a shower of pebbles dislodged in her wake. She stumbled over to the still form of Gaius and dropped down at his side.

Gaius was lying on his back, a long smear of blood on the rocks highlighting the path as though the furrow of rubble created by the slide of the horse wasn't enough to show the route. His leg was bent at an unnatural angle, but the steady rise and fall of his chest showed he was alive.

Avery reached out with her senses and detected a feeble fluttering pulse in the horse. It lay on its side, two legs broken and bent. The horse could not stand, even if it had the strength to do so.

Avery examined her father, feeling along his arms, checking for broken bones. All seemed fine except for the large purple bruise blooming on his forehead and a nasty scrape along one arm, blood oozing through the torn sleeve.

Gaius was partially buried in the scree which continued to trickle down to rest against the back of the horse. She scooped away the stone rubble with her hands, scrabbling in the dirt to determine if his limbs were actually trapped beneath the dying horse. As she cleared the last of the stones away from his leg, Sharisha knelt down beside her and placed her forefingers to either side of Gaius's temple and closed her eyes. Avery sensed a mystical power flowing from Sharisha, a quiet stream of healing waters that flowed from her and into Gaius. The swelling receded and the bruise faded to green. Gaius's eyes popped open. With a gasp, he attempted to sit up. Avery pushed him back down onto his back.

"How do you feel?" Sharisha's hands dropped to the sides of her woolen skirt, a tiny frown creasing her smooth features.

Gaius blinked at her, licked his lips and his hand wandered to the bruise on his forehead. "I have a headache. Why can't I feel my foot?"

"It is currently lodged under your dead horse." Avery began digging around her father's foot, using a smooth stone to scrape away the loose soil. "Lay still while we free it."

Avery dug furiously, heart pounding, occasionally glancing over her shoulder to check the lip of the mountainside. If they were followed, they were in grave danger, exposed as they were at the base of the hill. *Capture would be as easy as netting smelt in a shallow pool.* The foot shifted as she scooped the soil back with her hands. Gaius leaned back on his hands and pulled on his leg, groaning with pain, as it popped free of its imprisonment under the horse.

Sharisha bent back over his foot, examining the bones and tendons. "It is broken. This is beyond my limited ability to heal. We will have to set his foot." Sharisha walked back to her horse and began searching her saddle bags for bindings.

Avery felt a nudge at her shoulder. Sunny snuffled her fallen companion. She nudged her with her nose and whinnied, encouraging him to rise. She did not stir. Avery reached out with her senses once again, searching for the life force of the horse. The mare was dying, the barest essence remaining. She gathered it to her, thinking to comfort her during her last moments before death. She stroked her soft nose and ran her hand down her neck.

Suddenly, the mare rippled in her vision. The body stilled and a blue mist began to rise from it, swirling from the pores of the skin, leaking from ears and eyes, seeping from every aperture. The mist rose and coagulated, brightening into a pure white form, which solidified and stepped away from the dead horse on the ground.

Shocked, Avery stood up and slowly approached the shimmering unicorn. It stood about three hands in height and was an eye-blinding, virginal white with dainty pink hooves and a spiral horn of striped ebony, protruding from her forehead. Avery extended her hand, and the mare sniffed her fingers then allowed Avery to stroke her nose. Sunny, not to be outdone, whinnied and crowded in to greet the unicorn, anxious to make her acquaintance.

"Where did you come from, pretty one?" Avery whispered to the unicorn. She glanced back over her shoulder and opened her mouth to say, "Isn't she beautiful?" but neither her father nor Sharisha paid them any attention. Sharisha had returned to Gaius's side and was kneeling beside the foot. It was like they couldn't see the unicorn. Avery frowned and stroked the velvety nose. The unicorn leaned into the touch, and a peaceful contentment flowed into Avery, drowning the anxiety of a few moments before.

The unicorn stepped around Avery and approached Sharisha, who was still frowning over Gaius's ankle, purple and blue and clearly crushed.

"There is nothing I can do for this foot." Sharisha shook her head. "My powers of healing do not extend to this kind of injury. It requires more healing spirit than I possess. I will try to bind it as best I can, but the outlook is grave."

She walked back to the woods where Avery noticed she had tied her mount. The horse's ears were pricked forward, and it watched the unicorn with avid interest, prancing where she stood, clearly as eager to greet the unicorn as Sunny had been.

Avery followed the unicorn back to Gaius and watched as she placed the tip of her horn against the mangled flesh. Avery's father groaned at the touch and his eyes rolled back in his head as he fainted. Waves of energy washed from the horn and encased his foot, sinking into the skin and flickering over it with a cold blue flame. The foot writhed and reformed under the skin, the bones mending, the tendons reattaching, the skin smoothing as the foot was repaired. The blue light faded, and the unicorn raised her head. Gaius's mouth dropped open and he began to snore peacefully.

The unicorn wandered back toward the woods, her tiny hooves leaving no trail.

"Wait!" Avery cried. "What is your name?" She felt silly addressing the unicorn this way, as though she understood her speech, but then a thought pressed against her mind.

You may call me Deva, whispered the unicorn. *It means celestial spirit.*

How is it I can hear your thoughts?

We communicate by telepathy. For you to be able to see me and hear me, you are a rare human. She stepped closer to Avery, Deva's sky-blue eyes shining. *We know you, Mother.* She nosed Avery's sleeve, and Avery's arm tingled and then burned. She yelped and pulled up her sleeve. Burnt into her skin was the outline of a unicorn.

Chapter 2

Legend

SHARISHA RETURNED FROM HER SADDLE BAGS, her healer's kit in hand, and jerked to a halt when she saw Gaius snoring away on the ground.

"Did you provide healing for this foot?" She dropped to the ground and lifted it, examining the formerly crushed appendage. She even went so far as to peel off his mangled boot and sock, gazing at the torn leather then at the perfectly pink, albeit dirty, foot.

"Uh." Avery was unsure if she understood what had happened herself. She rubbed the tingling tattoo on her arm, hesitant to share the experience with Sharisha. It felt personal somehow, as though the tattoo was connected to the unicorn in some form.

Sharisha rose from the ground "Well? It seems you have been hiding talents from my knowledge." Avery did not reply. "Wake your father. We must ride!"

Avery bent down and shook her father gently. Abruptly, the snoring ceased. Gaius looked up at her, startled. Then he sat up, his confusion evident in the way he gaped at his naked foot.

"Put on your boot. We have to move on. We will have to double up on Sunny."

Hearing her name, Sunny ambled over, tufts of grass sticking out either side of her muzzle.

Gaius pulled on his sock and boot, his eyes studying his dead mount. Avery tried to help him up, but he shook off her hands.

Nothing showed of his tumble except for the torn leather of his boot and rips in his right pant leg.

They scrambled onto Sunny's back and followed Sharisha's retreating back down the gloomy trail, hurrying to keep her in sight.

Gaius leaned over and whispered into Avery's ear. "Would you care to tell me what that was all about? Clearly, I should not be walking."

Avery looked back over her shoulder, eyes searching for the unicorn, then hugged her father around the middle and whispered the events to him, as softly as she could, keeping her tone low. Her father knew all about her strange abilities to sense the souls of animals and to sense honesty and integrity in others. She and her brother Cayden had been born with special abilities to see the spirit world around them. For this gift, they had been hunted since before they were born. There were those who would do anything to capture a Spirit Shield and the magic they possessed.

"And why do you not want to share this with Sharisha?"

"I don't know, Father. I just feel uncomfortable around her. I know it's silly, but..." Her voice trailed away as Sharisha glanced back over her shoulder, checking their progress.

"You have never been wrong before, Avery. Trust your instincts. I know Cayden would say the same thing."

Cayden...where are you, Cayden? Avery wondered, as she swayed on the back of the horse. He had reached out to her a little while ago, telepathically, but they had been occupied with the Primordial camp and strange actions of the High Priests at that time. She buried her face in her father's back, trying to erase the horrific images that crept behind her eyelids, images of blood and flesh and bone transfigured into a beast of unknown intent.

Maybe she could contact him if she tried. *Cayden, can you hear me? Cayden?*

It had been two months since she had last seen him, since they had fled their home in Sanctuary-by-the-Sea. She remembered him riding away surrounded by legion soldiers and being scared to death that she would never see him again.

Obviously, he had had a much easier time of it than she, and his powers must have grown for him to be able to telepathically contact her as he did. He must have been able to keep his magic hidden, much as she had, or he would have been dead by now.

"Father, can you hear Cayden in your head? Does he whisper to you?"

Gaius shook his head. "No, I cannot contact him as you do. Have you?"

"Yes. He tried to contact me while we were spying on the camp and then again, about two weeks past. He was safe at the time. As much as I detest being separated from him, he seems to have chosen the easier path."

Gaius patted the arm slung around his waist. "Let's hope so, dear one."

Sharisha partially reined in her horse as it danced nervously. "We must move faster. We might be followed. Come!" She heeled her mount into an easy trot, and they fell silent as they sped through the gloom of the woods, slowly brightening with the dawn.

They rode through a stand of sage willow, leggy branches heavy with dew, hugging the edge of a bubbling brook thick with copperhead fronds and blue-spotted mushrooms right to the water's edge. With a large plop, a bullfrog launched itself into the water. Sunny's ears flicked as she marked the frog's passage, which was soon followed by smaller ripples at water's edge. Her nervous eyes attempted to follow every splash. Sunny snorted then danced sideways as she attempted to keep all the frogs in sight.

They followed the gurgling brook for roughly an hour and then veered north and up out of the valley floor, climbing once again toward the join of two rounded hills that sliced through the cliffs.

"Sharisha," Avery called over her father's shoulder. "Are you going to explain that scene we witnessed back there? What was that thing the bear cub turned into?"

Sharisha slowed her mount, allowing them to catch up and ride side by side. "The cub is no longer a cub."

Avery twitched with annoyance. "I saw that. Would you prefer I said 'who was that'?"

Sharisha rode on in silence. Just when Avery thought she did not intend to elaborate, Sharisha spoke. "As you know, legends are legends because the knowledge of what actually occurred has been lost with time. It is no different for the Bear and Thunder Clans. Some scholars believe that there truly were clans that could harness the magic of the bear and the elements such as thunder. But what remains to us is the stories passed down, not factual account. It is from those brief stories that have we gained what little knowledge we currently possess of the ancient clans.

"According to Primordial legend, in the beginning of time great bears roamed the land, much as humanity does today. In those days, they walked upright on hind legs and it is believed they had developed a rudimentary language. They lived in family units and communities, not much different than we do today. There are sacred caves that record generations of the Bear Clans, familial lines drawn out in detail on the smooth walls. Our High Priests believe that they once numbered in the tens of thousands. The remains of large stone communal dwellings can be found in the hills, some of which are still in use today as way stations.

"When the Great Cataclysm occurred, legend has it that the Bear Clans packed up their families and moved deeper into the mountain to escape the anger of the Thunder Clans. No one is sure what happened to the Bear Clans, but by the time that humans came to be, the great Bear Clans had passed into legend.

"One particular scroll, however, gives account of a she-bear princess pregnant with cub, who braved the open elements and against the clan's wishes, left their shelter to speak with the Thunder Clan Chieftain to plead her people's case that all peoples had a right to the land under the sky. The Thunder Clans, beings of air and water, believed that their powers gave them dominion and that the Flesh Clans were beneath them, lowly as the earthworm is lowly. Unsurprisingly, the meeting did not go well.

"Legend speaks of an encounter of sorts at the Great Waterfall, a waterfall so tall it soared higher than the cliffs, the summit swaddled in misty rainbows which arched into heaven itself; the home of the Thunder Clan. Artio of legend was a humble bear maiden, blessed with a she-cub who she swore was fathered by the Thunders when they came to her one evening, when she had fallen asleep after eating magical gooseberries. The Thunders have the ability to take the shape of flesh beings, and that evening, so legend tells us, they came to be with her in the form of a man.

"To Artio, a human descending from the bear clans, her daughter was a gift from the heavens and a bridge between their peoples. She gave her daughter her own name and believed that if she could get the Thunders to accept her child, then she could bring peace to their peoples.

"So, she started out on a solo quest to the Great Waterfall, hoping to be granted an audience with the Thunders in the sky. The journey was hard, carrying her child on her back in a papoose, feeding her Thunder-cub daughter magical gooseberries that she found by the path side and jiggling her pack soothed the cub to sleep. All the while she planned her words, knowing she would have but a short time to convince the aloof Thunders.

"She arrived at the Great Waterfall just as the sun was setting, and the waters blazed as though lit from within by a fire. She called to the Thunders, but the roar of the waters was too great and no one heard her.

"Finally, in desperation, she began to climb the rocky face of the waterfall, slippery with moss and water. All the while, she called, 'Thunders, hear my cry. Thunders, hear my plea. Come greet our child, the union of our peoples. We can live in peace and harmony for look what nature has wrought? Thunders, hear my cry. Thunders, hear my plea.'

"She climbed and climbed and eventually she reached the clouds. She was afraid that they could not bear her weight, so she put her papoose down to test their strength. Her cub, well-rested from being carried all the way to the falls and up to the sky, climbed out of the papoose and with a giggle, ran across the clouds and onto a rainbow, laughing the entire way as the rainbows tickled her feet. The maiden called to her daughter to return, but the child cub ran on, the tickling colours creating tones that blended into a tinkling song.

"When the maiden attempted to step onto the cloud, however, her foot sank through the mist. She could not follow her cub. Just then, the last rays of the setting sun pierced the clouds and they vanished as if they had never been. In the blink of an eye, the rainbows faded and along with them, her cub."

Avery waited for more. Sharisha rode in silence, her face pinched in a pensive frown.

"And?" Avery asked "What happened next?"

"No one knows," Sharisha replied. "Legend does not tell us."

"And the princess?" *The story could not end there,* Avery thought.

"No one knows."

Avery drew in a deep, frustrated breath. *What was it that was born in that clearing? Or perhaps the better question is who?*

Chapter 3

The Hunt Begins

CYRUS DISMOUNTED FROM HIS FINE CHESTNUT GELDING, handing the reins off to a soldier stationed at the entrance to Alcina's tent. It was easily picked out in the sea of military canvas. The tent was black, slashed with red, displaying the colours of the now-outlawed Queen's Guard and announcing her presence in the camp. It stood tall enough that he could enter the doorway without bending.

The guards saluted and retracted their crossed pikes, allowing entry. A pageboy, dressed in leggings and livery, announced his arrival in a high-pitched voice that cracked on his name. "The Lord Cyrus attends you, my queen."

The first weak rays of the rising sun pierced the tent as he entered, striping the woven red carpet that formed the floor.

Alcina reclined in a sedan chair covered in brightly woven tapestry, a delicate mug cupped between her palms. She sipped at the tea, watching him approach, then placed the cup on a carved bone table and stretched out one lacquered hand.

Cyrus swept his helm from his head, bent on one knee and lightly grasped her hand, kissing her fingers, then released them. "You have need of me, my queen?"

Alcina studied his bent head, observing the thinning thatch forming on the crown. He, too, showed signs of age; time was making fools of them both. Why, she had found a grey hair that morning amidst her own luxurious mane of ebony. A tiny frown creased her brow at the remembrance.

"Rise," she commanded. Cyrus rose then ran his hand over his bald spot as though he could feel her eyes on it. "I understand we have a captive?"

"Yes, Your Majesty. We captured one of the tree-climbing monkeys they use for scouts."

"And?" she prompted.

"He has been placed under guard and will be questioned thoroughly."

Alcina picked up her teacup and drummed her nails on the side, thinking. "I wish to question him myself."

"My queen?"

"I will not have a repeat of the fiasco with that boy Cayden who usurped my throne. I will know what is happening, every minute of every day. I wish to be present for all interrogations." She glared at Cyrus. "In fact, I should conduct the interrogations myself. It is obvious no one else knows the correct questions to ask or how to ask them. I will crush them like bugs under my heel. They will tell me everything they know." Cyrus bowed in acceptance. "When is the interrogation scheduled?"

"At noon, my queen," Cyrus replied.

She nodded and then, stretching, rose from the sedan chair. "There is one other matter I wish to speak to you about." She waved her hand dismissing the servants in attendance. They departed the tent, leaving Alcina and Cyrus alone to speak in private. As the hem of the last skirt disappeared out of the tent flap, Alcina murmured softly, "The Great Mistress spoke to me in my dreams. She showed me a vision of a girl, one with Primordial features. She travels with two companions, an older gentleman and a woman who could be a Primordial Seeker. We are to find this girl at all costs. The Great Mistress warns that she has the power to unite the Primordial factions. She can undo the chaos we have sown here."

Alcina paced to the far side of the tent and touched a shriveled scalp that hung from a canvas tent pole. The hair was silky, soft, and jet black. "While their eyes are set on each other in suspicion, while they attack and kill their own in religious civil war, they are easy to control and eventually eliminate. United, however, they would become a tidal wave that could crush our armies. Continue with the attacks on the outlying villages, and be sure our elite forces leave a trail of clues implicating the other Primordial faction. Be sure that they are so focused on each other that they are virtually blind to our passing."

Cyrus bowed once again. "I will make finding the girl my personal task. I will take a small group of elites and we will find her. Along the way, we will sow seeds of distrust, starting with the Primordial scouts. If she exists, if she is more than rumour, we will find her."

Cyrus saluted, spun on his heel, and marched from the tent.

Alcina stroked the silky black hair again and smiled.

*   *   *

Cyrus straightened as he released the tent flap. The guards snapped crossed-pikes at his back as he strode away. The Great Mistress had also come to him during the night with the same vision. He saw no reason to share this with Alcina, however. He was unsure if the Great Mistress had communicated precisely the same instructions to both of them or if Alcina was aware that the Great Mistress had begun to visit him. Caution meant he was content to keep his own counsel.

For instance, Alcina had failed to communicate that the girl they sought was the twin sister of the boy Cayden, who now sat on the throne of Cathair, the very throne that had been Alcina's. All this time, they had believed they were looking for one heir, when there were actually two. They were twin usurpers to the throne, a throne that he had been promised to share. It was a pretty large piece of information to withhold.

He rubbed his jaw as he strode along, considering his next move. He was content to allow Alcina to sit in the queen's chair, as in truth, the position was restrictive. As a pretty figurehead, she was always surrounded by fawning servants, counselors, and nobles. She could not do as he did: stroll amongst the men to get the feel of the battle, belly up to the bar in a local tavern and hear the latest gossip, or slip between the sheets in a brothel and find out what the local scheming lords and ladies were up to.

Yes, for now, his position allowed him a freedom to move his chess pieces around the board in whatever fashion brought him the best position, the greatest advantage.

He strode through the camp, acknowledging the salutes as he passed with a lazy wave. His destination was the prisoner's tent. Conveniently located next to the horse lines, the black smithy's tent provided a steady supply of red hot irons, a favourite method of the inquisitors of the legion. The closer Cyrus got to the tent, the greater the smell of burning: burning wood, burning coal, burning leather, burning skin, burning hair. The smells mixed obnoxiously with the odours of horse and human manure from the hastily dug latrines located nearby.

A square grey tent swelled into sight guarded by four sentries, one stationed at each corner. At the flap of the entrance, two more guards stood. Cyrus bent to enter the tent, ignoring their salutes.

He straightened then gazed down at the prisoners staked to the ground. Three men stared back at him, stripped to the waist, hands and feet bound, stretched vertically, and tied to wooden stakes driven into the ground. At the sight of him, their eyes widened. Sweat broke out on their foreheads.

The tent flap opened again and an inquisitor, dressed in a boiled leather jerkin and linen shirt, entered the tent. The ties of his shirt hung loose, the mat of chest hair glistening with sweat. Two glowing tongs were clutched in his hands.

Cyrus grinned. How he enjoyed his freedom. Three men…and Alcina only needed one.

Chapter 4

Cathair

CAYDEN WANDERED THE CASTLE, familiarizing himself with its layout. It was immense. Originally it had been a stone hunting lodge, a vacation home for the first noble family of Cathair. Additions had been built onto it over the centuries until present day where it sprawled over a full acre of land and stood four stories tall.

The wall walk was Cayden's favourite place to be, for he could pace around the upper reaches and see the stretch of land in all directions. Up that high, he finally found peace from the whispers of the dead and the demands of the living, a constant cacophony of noise that intruded on his waking hours.

The original lodge now served as the central kitchens. Even at this early hour, the lodge hummed with activity—cooks frying eggs and bacon, pulling loaves of toasty corn bread out of the hearth, and whipping fresh cream into a soft butter blended with honey. Cayden sniffed as he walked past. His stomach growled, but he did not pause. Breakfast would have to wait.

He entered a covered alcove and pulled open the heavy wooden door that housed the Royal Cathairian Library. Generations of Cathairians had collected and stored the most fragile of works in the library, which was rumoured to have existed before the lodge, as a center of learning. Just as the castle was littered with catacombs so the library had an equally elaborate and wholly uncharted underground.

Cayden pulled the door shut behind him and paused to allow his eyes to adjust to the dim recesses. No candles burned in the building, no open flame, no oil lanterns. Instead, the interior was lit by a large parabolic mirror that hung in the dome of the ceiling and reflected the light of the sun, and was mounted on a clever array of gearings that allowed it to be moved and kept in precise alignment with the sun during the daylight hours, constantly gathering the sun's rays, even on the cloudiest of days, and redirecting them into the cavernous room.

The first time Cayden entered the library in the evening, he carried a lantern that he'd used to light his way. Unknown to him, lanterns were to be left on the hanging peg in the portico. The only thing that had saved him from the wrath of the librarian named Brennus was the fact that Mordecai had already preceded him into the library and was able to fend off the broom-wielding caretaker.

"No flame in the library, you foolish boy!" Brennus had shrieked with a wild light in his eye. The fact that his hair stood on end like the ruff of an angry rooster only enhanced his menacing profile. Cayden ducked, and the broom swished over his head before halting mysteriously in midair. It was then that Brennus truly looked at Cayden. He gaped at the royal robes that Cayden was forced to wear. Brennus's jaw had snapped shut with an audible click as realization dawned.

"Brennus, I would like you to meet our new king. Sire, this is Brennus, archival librarian, at your service." Mordecai snapped his fingers, and the broom in Brennus's hands vanished.

Brennus bowed low to Cayden, hands on knees in apology. "My apologies, Sire. I did not realize that it was you."

"It is nothing." Cayden lowered his hands from the anticipated strike. "The fault is mine. I did not stop to think about whether flame is allowed in the library." Cayden frowned. Now that Mordecai had moved, he saw that the library was lit. While it did not have the full brightness of daylight, it did contain enough light should one wish to read. It was Cayden's turn to be amazed. His mouth fell open in surprise.

Mordecai chuckled. "Perhaps, Brennus, you should show your king through your domain and explain why he doesn't need a flame."

Brennus bowed low again. "Sire, will you follow me?" He tentatively tugged on Cayden's arm and pulled him through the library, babbling away about the mirrors and sunlight and the glow bulbs and the gods providing light in the darkest of days.

"What he means, Cayden, is that the wizards of old were rather good at alchemy. It's a simple enough combination, a mixture of basic elements. Strontium and aluminate come to mind and oxygen, a bit of heat, some tweaking of the crystalline, and you have these— phosphorus crystals. For colour, I like to add a pinch of fruit juice. Gives off a nice aroma when it heats up and the colour is truer. It's quite simple, really." He rocked back on his heels admiring the handiwork as though it was his own.

Perhaps it *was* Mordecai's work. Cayden wasn't quite sure.

The dome structure set into the library ceiling was huge and sat on the stone walls of the circular room like half an egg, the top "whites" made of an opaque glasswork and the bottom "yolk" covered in glittering frescos depicting the gods and ancient wars long forgotten. The never-ending scene morphed from one view to another, and Cayden found himself wanting to lie down on the slate floors and gaze up at the artwork. The reliefs were so precise that they appeared three-dimensional.

Crystalized scenes of forests, rushing waters, and towering mountains, of fishing boats and rolling fields of poppies, all scenes from across the kingdom flowed down the walls and framed the stained-glass windows evenly spaced within the stone walls. These were wedged between large bookcases, jammed with scrolls and leather-bound books and blocks of parchment, each bookcase set with its own rolling ladder.

Tables were scattered throughout the library and some reading nooks with pillowed seating placed under the stained glass. On every table and mounted in the nook was a round sphere encased in crystal, glittering with a fresco of the gods.

After that first rocky introduction, the library became Cayden's favourite haunt. He spent a great amount of time in the library, seeking to learn about his kingdom, its history and its people, especially since his greeting on arrival had been less than thunderous applause. Mordecai set him to reading the history of Cathair and its rulers, trying to catch up on seventeen years of education lost to him, an education that would have been provided by his royal parent. His father Gaius, the only one he had ever known, had taught him and Avery to read, but books had been scarce and he found the older texts housed in the library difficult to decipher. While the texts were legible, the syntax of language used had changed, so that he found himself referencing other writings to try to sort out the convolutions of the language structure and word choice in context. It was laborious and grueling work at times simply to get through a text.

Yesterday, however, Cayden had stumbled across a reference that had made his heart lurch. He'd gasped aloud, reading the text five times to be sure of what it said.

He hurried back to the book and pulled it once again from the shelf. It was heavy, the parchment yellowed and cracked, the pages stiff and bound by heavy leather-wrapped wooden covers and embossed with gold lettering. He carried it to his favourite alcove, the stained glass depicting the Well of Souls. While it did not look anything like the real well, it did manage to capture the essence of the place. The flattened angels faced each other, crowded around the edges of the window, golden horns raised in triumphant call.

He placed the book on the table and ran his hand over the embossed lettering, muttering under his breath, *"Na Déithe de Antiquity Cogadh Chéad"* (*The Gods of Antiquity, First War*). Then he opened the book to the page that had caught his eye and ran his finger down to the spot where he had left off reading.

The birth of four children was a strange twist of fate, for the ancient gods normally abstained from earthly entertainments. It was regarded as the height of folly to intercede in mortal affairs, yet one Ancient could not resist the temptation to dabble in mortal pleasures. Morpheus, the God of Dreams, was captivated by woman named Calleigh, who was fair to look upon. Morpheus began visiting her in her dreams, and there they conceived. In one day, the children were born. The Ancients banned Morpheus from their celestial home and cast him to the earth to wander and learn the folly and futility of a mortal life.

Morpheus and Calleigh did not name their four children until their godly gifts became apparent. Artio was the eldest, a lover of the sky and the celestial wonders beyond the earth. One particular constellation, shaped like a bear cub fascinated her and so Calleigh named the child. She was soon followed by the true twins Caerwyn, the fortress, and his twin sister, Alfreda, the mother of the lands. The true twins shared an affinity and some say a shared soul. Unlike their siblings, the true twins could sense each other at all times and read each other's thoughts. They were said to be one person in two bodies. Alfreda would gift a new people to the earth, a people known as the Primordials. Lastly the youngest, Helga, displayed an affinity for the dead, for things that were ready to return to the earth.

In time, jealous squabbles broke out between the godlings. Morpheus, in an attempt to create peace, separated his children into different spheres of influence. Artio was given dominion over the sky, moon, and stars and was tasked with managing the movements of the heavenly bodies. Caerwyn and Alfreda were sent to work with the souls of the earth, each within their affinity. Alfreda was given charge of the souls of the animal kingdom, for their rebirth was as necessary as a human soul. Caerwyn was given carriage of the souls of humanity and charged with caring for them until it was time for their rebirth. Helga was given charge over the recycling of the earth, the plants, the trees, and the bodies of the dead. As the winter witch, she absorbed the decay of humanity and buried it deep in a blanket of white, one season a year. She created a restful environ for the deceased awaiting rebirth. While it was cold above, it was not so in her mountain home where the fires of punishment burned hot, providing a warm core for the awakening of the world in spring. She was also set as the caretaker of the damned, those souls who were beyond redemption and could not be reborn because of the corruption of their natures.

For a time, they were content within their roles and millennia passed, days fading to years, years fading to centuries. Morpheus returned to the gods on Calleigh's death, leaving the godlings to care for the world.

One day Artio, the moon godling, slumped to the horizon, blood red. Helga found her oozing a bloody light across the heavens. Convinced that she was dying, Helga carried her sister into the bowels of the earth. The dark stilled Artio's light. Helga believed that she would be reborn like the rest of the mortals of the earth, but the godling had no one to care for her rebirth, and was forever lost.

Legend had it that Caerwyn and Alfreda banished Helga to the depths of the underworld, never to return, for the crime of slaying a godling.

Cayden lifted his head from the book and pinched the bridge of his nose. *The names are too close,* he thought, thinking about the legend, *especially knowing now what I know about my own abilities.*

He needed to speak to Mordecai. Surely, he knew the legends. It was time for a serious chat.

Chapter 5

Faylea

AVERY WAS CERTAIN she could not retrace the twisting path taken by Sharisha despite the frequent glimpses of the massive tree that was their destination. It sat on the horizon, towering above the swampy plain, dominating the skyline.

The humidity increased as they traveled through the dense swamp, snaking along drier patches of surface roots that clung to the water's edge. The jumbled matting of the thirsty willows created a boardwalk of sorts, wide enough for the horses to traverse safely. Avery's damp shirt clung to her back as did her father's, sticking to his sweaty torso. Avery's head swiveled as she took in the landscape, her mouth opened in awe. The journey had taken the better part of a week even though they had rested infrequently.

The last bridge they crossed extended longer than those previous, rising up out of the swamp and dispensing the travelers onto a wooden platform that ended in an intricately carved archway and an ironwood gate. The gate stood thirty hands tall and was carved straight through the center of an enormous oak tree the crown of which disappeared into the mists. Carved onto the surface of the door were symbols that Avery could not read.

Sharisha rode up to the door and placed her palm on a circular rune on the right side. The rune glowed, and a cloud of blue and white mist swirled around her hand. She withdrew it, and the door swung open. Avery glimpsed a miniature three-dimensional world, like a view through a magnifying glass, before the rune faded back to wood.

"This is the sacred city of Faylea." Sharisha sat straight in her saddle, her bearing regal. "Humans have not been permitted past this door in over a millennium. Not all will be pleased to grant you access."

Gaius tapped the sides of the horse, urging Sunny forward. Sunny's ears swiveled in interest, then pricked forward. "Is it safe for Avery to enter here? I care not for the politics of the land, only my daughter's safety."

Sharisha frowned at him for the interruption.

"You will be safe for you are with me, but I would warn you that to wander off on your own would not be wise. Follow me." She disappeared through the open doorway of the tree.

Sunny frisked through the opening, her nostrils flaring. She swished her tail and seemed excited about whatever she smelled on the other side. The tunnel ran straight as an arrow through the middle of the great tree and at the end, a shaft of brilliant white light illuminated the exit. Beyond the light a dense wood was just visible.

As they crossed the threshold, they drew rein. The sacred city of Faylea spilled from the hillside and lay cupped in a bowl of vibrant green moss that coated every inch of ground. Great purple-spotted toadstools, taller than Avery's horse, towered like trees above twisting paths creating a polka-dot patchwork of shade across the forest floor. Giant ribbed ferns, planted in curving rows, formed the walls of abodes, the leafy reaches interwoven to create roofs. No house was straight but copied the shape of the ferns, gently bending and curving with the will of the greenery.

Avery was mesmerized. *The houses are alive!* She slid off Sunny and walked to the edge of the hillside to drink in the scene. Waves of harmony washed over her. Tears sprang to her eyes as she felt the first tentative touch from the sentient growth before her. The intertwined ferns acted as a group conscience, as a single entity with millions of parts, all working cohesively. Avery closed her eyes to better hear the whispered greetings and peace flowed over her.

Sharisha watched as Avery's mouth quirked and twitched with smiles, staring in the direction of the city. Sharisha did not smile.

"Avery, I think Sharisha is waiting to move on." Avery's eyes popped open, and she broke the telepathic contact she was experiencing with the plant life and walked back to her father, who gave her a boost into the saddle behind him.

Without a word, Sharisha urged her mount onto the meandering path that trailed to the base of the bowl. The trail followed whatever curve the land chose to take, but it did take them down. As they passed the fern dwellings, Primordial children poked their heads out of the round windows, curious at the strangers in their midst. They tumbled out of the doorways and followed them, a whispering and giggling processional that swelled in number.

Avery smiled at them and waved, and a pretty girl not yet to puberty offered her a flower filled with a shimmering liquid. Avery reached down and took the flower, smiling her thanks. The girl mimed drinking. Hesitant, Avery lifted the cup of petals to her lips and took a dainty sip. The girl giggled and clapped her hands with joy. The nectar was sweet and light with a slight strawberry taste and left refreshing bubbles on Avery's tongue. It quenched her thirst instantly, and she passed it forward for her father to drink.

At the edge of a stream, Sharisha stopped and dismounted. "We must walk from this point. Those who approach the heart of Faylea must do so on their own feet as a display of respect for the sanctity of all life. Leave your things. They and the horses will be cared for." She dropped her reins and stepped onto the rose-quartz bridge that spanned the babbling brook. The children did not follow as they stepped off onto a stone path on the other side.

The rose gravel crunched under their feet. Now that she was walking the earth, Avery felt a vibration through the soles of her shoes, the rhythm of a heartbeat. The path widened and ended at a clearing flooded with sunlight. At its center stood a shimmering white temple which rose from the ground in stacked squares and stood six stories tall. At every corner, a legendary beast was carved, climbing up the wall to the floor of the next level.

Every inch of wall was decorated with symbols and pictures. On the first level, the motifs were of plants and plant life, the second of aquatic life, and the third of land animals including depictions of humans. The fourth level showed the spirits of both man and beast, and the fifth was carved with fantastical creatures of myth. The final level displayed only four images; each image was shown only once on its own wall and the deeply carved relief covered the entire surface. An alabaster spike rose from the peak, soaring into the sky.

Avery's eyes climbed the entire structure, taking in the varied images sunk into the marble façade. A matching marble staircase wide enough for four people to walk abreast completed the structure. Ten steps began at the end of the path and ended at a railed landing in front of two wooden doors. A crystal chime sang out, and the doors opened, inviting them to enter.

Avery, her heart beating in rhythm to the cadence of the earth, walked up the stairs, ignoring everyone around her. The call of the temple pulled her forward in a near trancelike state. Sharisha matched her stride to Avery's, mounting the staircase on her left side while Gaius fell in on Avery's right. Avery felt no fear; what she felt was peace. *This is home. I've come home.*

The minute Avery crossed the threshold of the sanctuary, she felt a surge of contentment. A breeze tossed her curls, and she opened her arms to the wind that called her name. Avery breathed deeply and took another step into the interior. In that instant, with a blinding flash of light, the others vanished.

Chapter 6

The Pact

ARTIO SURVEYED THE PROSTRATE FORMS before her. The smell of blood was thick on the air, coppery and cloying, clinging to the waves of heat emanating from the firepit that lit the clearing. She shook her head, stretching newly formed muscles, exploring the motion and connection of her new body. She raised her arm and examined it. Taut muscles flowed from shoulder to wrist, covered in a short, light brown hair that glistened in the firelight. She flexed her fingers, nails rounded and slightly claw-like. Her legs were similarly constructed, thighs strong, calves rounded and corded. She could run for miles. She knew it.

Ah! This is a great body! she thought, dismissing the cub's sacrifice. *For too long, I have been imprisoned amongst the stars!*

Arthmael, the High Priest of the Bear Clan, rose from the ground, bowing and scraping constantly. He peeked from under his headdress and, in a quivering voice, spoke to his god.

"Great One! We are your faithful servants. We have not forgotten. We woke you from your slumber amongst the stars as was prophesied. The elder scrolls promised this day. We alone of all the Primordial peoples remembered the old ways and have safeguarded the secrets of the origins of the gods. We call upon you, Celestial One, to help us in our time of need."

Artio ignored the mutterings of the human, engrossed in the inspection of her new form. As a goddess amongst the stars, she'd observed the scurrying on the planet below, and she had been an avid admirer from afar. Their lives were fleeting. In a blink of an eye, they were born, lived, and died, yet they believed their lives to be of importance and hurried here and there, building this and tearing down that, yet nothing of permanence remained.

Not like me. I am immortal. I could end their pathetic lives here and now, squash them under my heel, grind them into the dirt they were born of…but no, I must learn more. I must understand why they have summoned me now.

Artio spoke with a voice like a rumble of thunder. *"Why have you called me back from my home in the stars? Speak! I will know the truth of it."*

The High Priest cried out at the thunderous clap of her voice, hands over his ears.

"There is great unrest in the world, Celestial One!" he cried. "Our people are divided. The Spirit Clans have blocked access to the temple and to the gods. We cannot approach and pray as we once did or perform the rituals of your people in sight of the temple. They bar our access to the gods."

"Yet a goddess stands before you. I care not for your petty schemes and squabbles. My purpose is set apart from yours," she boomed.

One particularly bold priest, firelight dancing off his shining bald pate, dared to raise his head and make eye contact. He shivered at the ageless depth, the bottomless pit of black reflected in the eyes staring back at him.

"Great One, the temple is only accessible by the gods. There are rumours of one such as you approaching the temple as we speak. If they enter, they will have control and dominion over the temple. Should you not seize it for yourself?"

Artio glared at the man and crossed her arms, considering his words. *"Where is this…temple?"* she rumbled. *"Take me to it! If it is a temple of the gods, I will have it for my own. There you will worship me!"*

The priest turned to the prostrate men, swiping at a trickle of sweat rolling down the side of his face. "Rise! We march for the sacred city of Faylea."

*   *   *

Artio followed the little men, taking one step for every six of theirs. With her superior height, she could see over the top of the priests, who led the procession through the trees. The winding mountain pass through which they traveled was familiar.

She frowned, trying to capture the illusive memory that tickled within her omnipotent brain. She was somewhat disgusted with the bestial form the priests had recalled her to, despite its efficiency. No thunder god would ever be tied to such a menial form. The gods of the sky viewed themselves as a superior life form to the flesh that crawled beneath them. The body did, however, seem familiar. She searched vast epochs of memory, trying to pin down the thought to a time and place. True, she had virtually slept for eons of time, nestled amongst the stars, but it had not always been so.

The Thunder Clan had once ruled the primitives of the land. They had sent the rains and withheld their blessings in punishment. They had controlled the snows in the mountain watersheds and had filled the primitives' wells with water from underground reservoirs. They had been their caretakers until the rebellion.

Artio and the priests climbed steadily for half the day. By noon the sun revealed a sheltered bowl of a valley, nestled between two curving windswept ridges. Large boulders as tall as Artio were scattered about, as though a giant fist had tossed marbles across the valley in a game of chance.

"What is this place?" Artio rumbled, her voice causing a covey of birds to burst from the treetops and the High Priests to cover their ears.

"It is believed it was a bear community long abandoned, Great One. Little is known about the ancient peoples who lived here, as that history is lost to us, but there are curious drawings in caves set against the sides of the valley. Would you like to see them?"

"It would please me to see these drawings."

The priests led Artio over to a section of rock that formed part of the crater wall. A toppled pillar, long and octagonal, blocked the entrance to a cave. Similar columns were scattered around, as though a child played a massive-sized game of pick-up sticks. Artio craned her neck sideways to study the stones. Stood upright and set back in their proper placement, the ruins would create an ancient stone framework for a doorway.

Artio bent down and rubbed at the face of the rock, scraping away moss and lichens that clung to deep grooves. Pictures appeared along with squiggles and lines. Artio pulled away the rest of the clinging growth.

A carving was revealed. It appeared to be of bears walking about on their hind legs much like Artio did, but these bears were purely animal in form as depicted in the pictures. The bears were dressed in rudimentary clothing and carried pouches that might have contained arrows, although the fine lines had been swallowed by time and exposure to the elements.

Artio straightened back up and approached the dark opening in the rock. Two slabs of granite were wedged together, the right slab having fallen against the left, barring entrance. Artio grabbed the right slab and heaved. With a grinding noise, she shifted the door to the side, leaving just enough room for Artio to pass through. She straightened on the other side and took two strides into the cavern.

Her entrance activated a ring of soft glowing lights, suspended at ceiling height around the perimeter of the cave. It pushed back the darkness, and the cavern was illuminated.

The High Priests paused in the entrance of the cave, unsure whether they were permitted to enter a place where a god was honoured with light.

A heavy layer of dust covered every surface, yet it was easy to pick out the objects in the room.

Stone benches were set in rows, facing a raised platform at the far end of the cavern. On the platform sat a massive granite throne, carved out of the wall itself.

The surface was decorated with leaves and trees and animal shapes that once inhabited the valley. Every carving was crusted with jewels: fat emeralds made leaves on vines flash as if moved by a breeze, flaming rubies gilded butterfly wings, yellow citrine graced the bodies of canaries, and diamonds accentuated the spiral horns of unicorns. In the muted light cast from overhead, the chair seemed alive.

Artio climbed the dais and sat down in the throne, running her hands along the arms of the chair. It was sized perfectly.

The priests, frozen in the doorway, gasped and backed away from the opening, bowing as they did so.

Artio had no need of other temples. The Goddess of the Forgotten Temple had returned home at last.

Chapter 7

The Temple

WITH AVERY'S THIRD STEP, she entered a wild forest teeming with plant life. Great trees soared to the heavens, shading the riot of plant life. It flourished and bloomed in every conceivable colour, covering the forest floor. Great ferns and prickly bushes bursting with sweet red, yellow, and blue fruit; toadstools and tender shoots perfect for nibbling; and snaking vines weighed down by large trumpet-shaped flowers dripping with nectar.

Every inch of space was alive. As Avery took another step, the plant life reached for her. Tendrils of roots wrapped gently around her torso, burning her clothing where they touched her. It did not hurt; it felt more like a caress. Mesmerized, Avery pushed on through the undergrowth, careful to not harshly tread on the living presence she felt all around.

With her next step, the forest disappeared and became open skies and a great plain of waving grasses as far as the eye could see. Every type of grain and grass was present and all burned against her clothing as she passed, causing her to lose more clothing to the brushing blades of grass.

With her sixth step, the plant life faded, and she found herself swimming in an ocean. A dolphin swam up to her. Without pausing to think about it, Avery grabbed onto its dorsal fin and was pulled along beside the dolphin. They flashed over barrier reefs teeming with a kaleidoscope of fin and shellfish, eels and sharks—prey and predators alike. As they paraded past her, they touched her hand in greeting or brushed against another part of her and more clothing melted away, even though the water was cool and pleasant. Avery did not give a care for her growing nakedness. There was no sense of shame in this world. She was mesmerized by the vibrant aquatic life surrounding her. Great whales glided into view, and she reached out to touch them as they passed. Bubbles greeted her, and the bubbles glided along her torso as they passed with the sensation of a caress.

The dolphin glided back to shore, and Avery let go as her feet touched the bottom. The scene transformed into a freshwater lake, teeming with brightly coloured salmon and croaking frogs, salamanders and crayfish. They swirled around her, more fish species than she could identify, trout and bass and catfish, all greeting her as the ocean had. She felt their joy at their reunion, and her heart was full of her love for the creatures of the planet she called home.

She took another step, and the scene changed.

The few remaining tatters of clothing left dried instantly and clung to her body as she stepped back onto land. Giraffes and lions, gazelles and cheetahs all flowed toward her, greeting her with purrs and chuckles and lipped kisses, tugging at the remnants of her clothing. Avery touched them all, stepping into all the areas of the earth and welcoming every form of animal life. The vast plains were now full of animal life, including signs of human habitation.

All approached her except the human life. Avery saw them on the horizon, but they did not come close. She tried to walk closer to them, but they were like smoke, slipping away before her steps. Only one man approached her, a grizzled elder, dressed in nothing but a prayer pouch girded about his loins.

"Elder! I am so pleased to greet you!" Avery said to the short wiry-haired man.

The elder tilted his head to one side, studying her. Avery had the impression she was being weighed and judged.

His face split open in a toothless grin, and he reached inside his prayer pouch and pulled out a handful of odd objects. Four knuckle bones; some smooth rocks; several different kinds of feathers, some brightly coloured, some not; a long jagged tooth; and several jet-black claws, curved and razor sharp decorated the palm of his hand. He showed them to Avery then put them back in the pouch. He took the prayer pouch off and handed it to Avery, who strapped it around her waist.

When she looked up from belting it on, he was gone.

Avery took another step and paused at the sight before her. Fantastical creatures of every shape and size surrounded her. They were not randomly arranged. They appeared to have been waiting for her, as though holding counsel and she was the guest speaker. As she thought this, suddenly she found herself standing on a platform made of rock in the center of a natural arena, the glassy slopes rising away from the center, filled with creatures of myth and legend.

A bronze-winged lion, eight feet tall, stood shoulder to shoulder with an emerald-green dragon, puffs of smoke curling from its great nostrils. Both bowed to Avery as she spun slowly in a circle, taking in her surroundings. Proud manticores and hairy leprechauns; grey-feathered griffins and muscled werewolves; shimmering jewelled fae and ghastly ghouls crowded in around the dais, while flaming phoenixes and Pegasuses soared overhead. Avery even spied a thunderbird perched on the crest of a timbered temple as she completed her circle.

"Hello!" she called to the creatures, knowing, somehow, that they would understand her words. "I am so pleased to meet you!"

The crowd of creatures parted, and an unusual sight greeted Avery's eyes. A snow-white unicorn with a long spiral horn of purest crystal stepped daintily toward the platform, each hoof displacing tiny rainbows of light as it pranced towards Avery. On the unicorn's back was an even stranger sight. At first Avery mistook it for a tree, but as it came closer, the figure dissolved into the shape of a man, green of skin and hair and clothed in a moss tunic and living woven grasses, the tassels of the stalks fringing his boots of willow bark. A beard of curly leaves decorated his face and head and wise old eyes of jet black locked onto hers. Avery's mouth stretched into a broad smile, for this was someone she could understand.

"Uncle!" she cried and jumped down from the dais to greet the Green Man.

"Alfreda. It has been too long!" He swung down from the unicorn and embraced her, smoothing her hair.

A memory stirred in Avery at the name he used. It was a name she was familiar with, one she had not used in a very, very long time. She frowned and released her uncle, who continued to smile down at her.

"Remember!" he commanded and placed a finger in the form of slender branch to her temple.

Memories, centuries and eons old, cascaded into her mind. Images flashed before her, and the room spun. The amount of information was mind-boggling, and she cried out at the rush, the pressure of the intense knowledge transfer overwhelming her. With a scream, she collapsed to the floor.

Chapter 8

A 'Wizard's Answer'

ZIONA ROUNDED THE CORNER of the hallway leading away from the kitchens and ran smack into Cayden. A startled *"Ooph"* escaped her lips before she straightened, clutching his shoulder.

"Ziona, I'm sorry!" His arm curved around her, supporting her until she caught her breath.

"Why are you sprinting blindly around corners, Cayden?" She rubbed her stomach.

"Mordecai. I need to talk to Mordecai. Have you seen him?"

"Not since breakfast. He mumbled something about 'exorcising the deadwood' and wandered away with a scone clutched in his hand."

"The greenhouses. He is in the gardens." Cayden grabbed Ziona's hand and pulled her along behind him. "This is of concern to you too. Come on."

"Wait for your guard, Cayden! You know you can't go running off without them anymore." She slowed her steps, forcing Cayden to tow her along, allowing the pair of Kingsmen shadowing them to catch up. Cayden glanced back, frowning at the men. "Are you trying to lose them?" she asked.

"No! Well, not intentionally," he groused, "but I wouldn't be sorry if I did. I never have any time to myself anymore."

Ziona matched his stride as they left the castle through a side door and crossed a short courtyard. They entered the walled gardens via an arched stone entrance, pushing open the iron-wrapped gate which squealed in the damp air. A stone path curved right and left off the main trunk, like the limbs of a very organized tree, leading to various branches of plantings. A muffled buzzing sound reached their ears. With a grin, Cayden strode toward the farthest corner where fruit trees were planted in orderly rows. The limbs of the apple trees were dotted with thumb-sized swellings that would in a few months be bright red apples, ready for harvest.

The buzzing grew louder. The leaves parted, and there stood an old man, his flowing white beard and hair standing on end like a fuzzy dandelion, waving his skinny arms at a cross of sticks that hovered above the ground. It was covered in a light canvas material, stretched tightly, and a breeze created by the wizard accounted for the buzzing sound as it moved over the surface of the canvas.

"What is that?" Cayden's eyes followed the object as it floated into the air.

"It is a kinetic instrument trying to escape." He grinned, watching them mouth out the words, their faces puzzled. "It's called a kite." When they still looked puzzled, he waved them closer.

"Look. The air flows over the fabric, and it creates a wind tunnel which lifts it into the air."

Cayden's brow furrowed deep into his face. "But what holds it up?"

"Air."

"But there is nothing to air! It's not solid like the tree."

"Ah. See the leaves on the trees? Observe how they move. The air pushes the leaves when it flows past them."

"That is the tree spirits," Cayden protested, laughing. "Everyone knows trees are inhabited by spirits. You are trying to trick us, Mordecai. It won't work!"

Ziona stepped up beside the wizard, smiling, and touched the string attached to the bottom of the kite, which trailed back into Mordecai's hand. "Which sprite did you beguile into bewitching the branches for you?"

Mordecai looked from one to the other then sighed. He rubbed the side of his nose, sighed again, opened his mouth to speak, thought better of it, and shut it. Shrugging, he pulled the kite down from the air and tucked it under his arm.

Magic truly is in the eye of the beholder, he thought.

"What is it you wished to speak to me about, Cayden? I trust you found something of interest in your studies?"

Cayden glanced around, noting that they were alone except for the two Kingsmen guarding the pathway to where they stood.

"Yes. I need to know everything you know about the godlings."

"So, you have found the passages. Good. Your education begins in earnest, now. But first, we must return to the library as there are scrolls there that need to be consulted." With a swish of grey robes, he strode away, retracing the path out of the gardens.

On exiting the gardens, Mordecai picked up his pace and crossed the bailey, marching right past the library entrance. Instead, he opened the door that led to the staircase of the right tower.

"Mordecai, where are you going?" Cayden huffed, lengthening his stride. Ziona shadowed their progress.

"There is a particular book we need to retrieve from my rooms. A very rare book, one few eyes have viewed. It is a book of history and a book of magic, but it is much more than that. Yes indeed. It has remained hidden within this castle, concealed under a multitude of enchantments, for over a century. Alcina tried to pry its whereabouts out of me; however, such tactics were doomed to failure. Only one person could retrieve that book, and that person is you, Cayden."

They entered the spiral staircase and curved up to the fourth landing, then approached the wizard's chambers. Mordecai passed his hand over the door handle, and it swung open before them. He held up his hand to the Kingsmen, denying them entrance. They took up posts on either side of the door.

Set in a bartizan that overhung the castle wall, Mordecai's apartment consisted of a large circular room, interspersed with narrow casement windows, tall enough to stand in. The room faced east, and early morning sunshine spilled through, striping the hooked rugs that covered the stone floor. Tables were pushed up against the wall on the north side of the room, and on the south side a staircase curved up to a sleeping loft built above the tables. A squashy, overstuffed chair was set beside the cold fireplace.

Cayden shivered and not from the lack of a fire. The room was a reflection of the royal apartments on the west side of the castle. He refused to take rooms in the bartizans even though they were his if he wished. Mordecai had relayed the story surrounding his and Avery's birth and the murders of his parents and grandparents. He had taken him to the room where his mother had died. Even though Cayden had spoken to Gwen's spirit at the Well of Souls under the castle, he found himself dwelling on her and mulling over what it would have been like to have grown up with her in this castle, as prince rather than as a pauper.

It wasn't that he was unhappy about his childhood home in Sanctuary-by-the-Sea. It was more that he felt a huge gap in his understanding of the peoples of this world. His mother, Gwen, had been a Primordial princess who had been betrothed to his father, a prince of Cathair, at the time of her death. Their intended marriage and the children they would beget were meant to forge a bridge between their peoples. With his royal parent's deaths, the Primordial nation had plunged into a twenty-year-long civil war while Cathair languished under the queen's reign. His mother's desperate bid to preserve her children's lives had been successful but at the cost of her own life, a desperate attempt to head off unrest and a war that now spilled over the borders, setting Cathairian against Primordial.

So Cayden avoided the west towers. He did not want the constant reminder of his dead parents. It was bad enough to feel the ghost of their presence in the darkened halls, as the servants whispered to each other that he was the spitting image of his father.

"Cayden, what do you feel? Can you sense the presence of the books?" Mordecai's voice brought him back to the present.

Cayden looked around the curved room, eyes sliding over tapestries and the ragged edges of very old books, extending his senses. He didn't see anything out of the ordinary.

"No, I do not sense anything. How about you, Ziona? Do you sense anything?"

Ziona wandered through the room, eyes unfocused. "There is something here," she murmured.

Cayden frowned, crossing his arms, impatience stamped into his features. "What do we do now, Mordecai? If I am the one that is supposed to find this book, I must know the key. What could I possibly know that no one else does?" Cayden wandered around the room and paused by the window, which looked out over the gardens they had recently vacated. He could see the apple tree in the midst, and his thoughts wandered to the tree spirits. *I wonder if I could get them to appear if I carved a flute from a tree they lived in.* His flutes were great at making animals and creatures appear.

Wait, I wonder if one of my flutes would make the books appear? Cayden spun around and ran for the door.

"I just had a thought. I'll be right back!" He dashed out the door and down the hall to his apartment. Ziona poked her head out the door to observe the Kingsmen guards bolting after their young king, yelling at him to wait up. Cayden didn't even look back.

Grinning, Ziona returned to the room and seated herself in the chair by the fire to wait for his return.

Five minutes later, Cayden rushed back into the room, his satchel of flutes clutched in his hands. His winded and disgruntled personal guards took up their posts again by the doorway, and Mordecai closed the door.

Cayden upended the satchel over the table and out rolled all the flutes he had with him in Cathair. He sorted them through them then selected a knobbly branch that was mixed in with the finished flutes.

The wood was a gift from the ancient oak tree that hugged the pasture back in Sanctuary-by-the-Sea. While he'd sat on the rocks carving and watching over the sheep, the tree had whispered to him. He had completed the snake flute that day, but several other pieces of the rare wood he had tucked inside the bag to be carved another time.

Cayden picked up the branch and turned it over in his hands, wondering if this was the answer. *Could it be as simple as carving the tool I need?*

"Cayden, come sit here on the rug." Mordecai gestured to the thick rug centered on the floor. Ziona scooted back her chair to give him room.

Cayden picked up his carving tools and sat himself squarely in the center of the rug, sitting cross-legged on the starburst-patterned center.

"Relax your mind, Cayden." The wizard brought out his focusing crystal and clasped it between his palms over Cayden's head. Cayden stared at the branch in his hands. Suddenly, the scene shimmered in his view, the tower fading to be replaced by the field where the ancient oak tree sat. No longer was he sitting on a rug, but on the sun-kissed rocks, his favourite spot for carving. He took a deep breath, breathing in the familiar salty tang of sea air warmed by bright sunshine.

He looked over at the old oak tree, and there it stood, just as he remembered.

"Did you really try to speak to me last time I was here?" he asked the oak. It shook its branches as though laughing at the question.

Cayden smiled. Picking up his favourite awl, he began to hollow the branch. It was tough going, the wooden core hard as iron. It resisted any widening as he burrowed so that in the end the center was the narrowest of openings. Cayden frowned at the branch and peered down the hole, barely able to see through to the other end. With that small of an opening, what sound could possibly escape it?

As he turned it over in his hands the branch began to vibrate violently. Surprised, Cayden dropped it. It smashed against the rock, breaking in two precise halves. He picked them up and checked them over for further fractures but couldn't locate any. The wise old oak tree chuckled…and chuckled some more.

"What secrets are you hiding from me, Elder Oak?" Cayden laughed and began hollowing out the fingering on both of the tiny flutes.

Immersed in the moment, Cayden quite forgot about the others, completely at ease in the illusion.

Or was it an illusion?

Ziona walked around Cayden, watching Cayden's lips move. Obviously, by his reactions, he was deep in conversation with someone only he saw. She saw him pick up the stick and begin forming the flute only to have it snap in two. *Instead of becoming angry, he laughs?* She paused in front of him, the final polish of the flutes underway, just as she had observed all those months ago. How far they had come, she mused, and how far they had to go. The future was so uncertain, even for the Lord of the Mists. As she watched, Cayden put down his polishing kit, checked for flaws in his flutes by running his fingers down them one last time, and then raised the first to his lips. He blew on the flute, fingers flitting over the holes. Ziona detected no sound from it.

Cayden frowned and picked up the other flute and put it to his lips. Nothing happened. He stood up and walked toward the staircase and paused before it. His lips moved, but once again Ziona could not hear anything. Hands on hips, he confronted the staircase.

Cayden spoke to the tree. "I can hear the giggling in your branches, Elder Oak. Who is hiding from my presence?" Elder Oak shook with laughter. It wheezed and sneezed and out popped a couple of tree sprites, giggling and holding over their heads like a serving tray a pair of dusty leather-bound books. The sprites, rather than handing Cayden the books, ran around him and over to Ziona. The minute they touched her skirt, the vision faded and they disappeared with a pop. The books dropped to the carpet at Ziona's feet, just as Cayden swung away from the tree.

"Oh!" Ziona picked up a book from the stack on the floor. "Where did these come from?"

"The tree sprites fetched them from the Elder Oak," said Cayden. Ziona raised an eyebrow at this and peered around the room as if expecting to find the sprites hiding in the shadows of the room.

Mordecai chuckled as he fetched the remaining three books and carried them over to the table.

"Come on, let's have a peek inside. Tree sprites indeed!" His eyes twinkled as he flipped open the cover of the first tome.

Chapter 9

Elder One

MAREA TREMBLINGSPIRIT ROSE from the vine-covered dais, gathered her leaf-green robes about her body, and descended with quick, light steps to the audience chamber floor to greet the weary priest.

"Has she returned from the temple yet?" she demanded before he had a chance to rise from his deep bow, arms spread wide to the side and hands open. The light of the firefly globe dangling from the ceiling on a sturdy woven reed chain danced across his bald pate, encircled by a fringe of wispy white hair.

"No, Most High." Eldrid spoke with a small voice as he straightened. "She has not. The temple is still ablaze with light and colour. The rainbow wards continue to encompass it, barring entry to all. We cannot pass through the bands. The rainbow emits pulses of red in warning when we approach, and all who have attempted to penetrate it have received severe burns. We cannot pass."

Marea's mouth twisted, her thin lips displaying yellowing teeth that clacked together in fury. *How dare that young strumpet enter my temple without* my *presence? The temple of the High Priestess is sacred ground. No one is to enter my temple. No one.*

"What of her traveling companion?" she snarled.

"He has identified himself as her father. We have secured him in the Grass Roots holding cell in Faylea. He is still resisting our questioning," he shrugged, "but it will not be long now before he gives in. If he doesn't, we have other methods of getting the information we need."

"And Sharisha? Where is she? She was to report to me immediately on her return."

The priest opened his mouth to reply, but at that moment the round chamber door swung open and Sharisha strode through, back straight and legs stiff. Seeing who was in the room, her chin raised haughtily. She had changed her clothing back to more traditional Primordial garb. A multi-hued tunic of greens, browns, and purples was belted with woven, purple-dyed hemp. Tan leggings were tucked into soft brown leather boots, which laced up the back to mid-thigh. Flung across her back was a quiver, and she carried an unstrung bow in her hand. Her long hair was tied back by a ribbon adorned with rainbow-hued sequins made from freshwater clam shells.

She strode toward them. Upon reaching the High Priestess, Sharisha gave a deep bow similar to Eldrid's.

"Most High," she murmured on rising.

Marea slowly walked around Sharisha, examining her. "You took your time in reporting to me!" she growled, her anger drawing deep furrows between her narrowed eyes.

Sharisha was not cowed. "Your specific instructions were to return to you immediately, should I have news to share. As your priests had already relayed the news of Avery's entrance into the temple, any 'news' I might have imparted had already been provided to you, Elder One."

If anything, the furrows deepened on Marea's pinched face. "That was only one of my conditions. You have been gone a very long time. You have much to tell me," she snarled, and Eldrid winced at the menace in her tone. Sharisha merely raised one eyebrow and stood tall, refusing to quail or show weakness while waiting for Marea to meet her eyes.

"She is the one we seek," Sharisha said simply, but the words halted Marea's steps. She swung around, her black eyes fastened on Sharisha's, demanding an answer to the question burning in their depths.

"Avery has the gift. She has the ability to read souls. She will be an invaluable weapon." Sharisha smiled for the first time, and Marea's lips thinned even more and curled back into a travesty of a smile.

"Finally, we have captured a Spirit Shield." Triumph rang in Marea's voice as she marched back up to her throne and sat down in the curving branches. "To chain and harness such a one is to have ultimate power. Be sure to collar her when she descends from the temple, and bring her to me. She is destined to serve the Spirit Clans forevermore." She smiled a dark smile, and Sharisha smiled back.

Marea reached under her chair and pulled out a package wrapped in soft deerskin that jingled in her hands. Sharisha mounted the steps and knelt once more, accepting the parcel reverently. She carefully folded back the skins and with a flip of the final corner, a delicate silver collar was revealed, made of fragile, slender links, looping and twisting together into a shimmering rope which caught the light of the fireflies and cast rainbows at the walls. On a smooth bale hung a pendant of polished silver, embedded with a blue stone. The stone flashed and then faded. It could not be looked at directly, seeming to be only partially in this world. Sharisha was careful to not touch any portion of the necklace and thereby interfere with its magic. She gently refolded the cloth and tucked it into the pocket of her shirt.

"It will be done, Most High." Sharisha bowed once more in acceptance of the command.

"Take Eldrid with you. Perhaps he can assist you with penetrating the rainbow." Marea frowned at the puzzle created by this strange event. No rainbow had ever formed around the temple before, not even when she entered it to be raised to Highest. "Eldrid," she commanded in dismissal, "send in the general. I believe he is to be found by the barracks."

"Yes, Elder One." Eldrid bowed low and left the room.

As the door closed behind him, Marea spoke quickly to Sharisha. "Now, before the general arrives, tell me everything that has transpired since you left Faylea. Where is Ziona?"

Sharisha spoke of their wanderings in the human kingdom, the discovery of the twins, the parting of the children by the legion's forces, and her decision to accompany Avery back to Faylea while Ziona went after the boy called Cayden.

"This is a puzzling turn of events." Marea absently ran her fingers over the woven roots forming the arm of her throne. "I never expected to find two children with the gift. What was your impression of this young man? Is he another Spirit Shield? Have their powers been diluted?"

Sharisha shrugged her shoulders. "I do not know. I did not have time to study him. He displayed similar qualities, yet his gift was not the same as Avery's. She has displayed true Primordial bloodlines in the way she interacts with the spirit world. She has a natural affinity for the things of our world." She hesitated, considering her words. "If her brother has the gift, it is a minor talent at most."

Silence greeted her statement, and then Marea's face hardened. "It does not change our plans. We must have a Spirit Shield to champion our fight. The Flesh Clans will come after her, but she is our linchpin. The boy may become a problem, especially if the Flesh Clans learn of his existence." She drummed her fingers on the arm of the throne, a hollow, high-pitched drumming sound accompanying her actions. "I may have to send you after him, in time. We will question Avery closely about him once she is under our control."

Sharisha had risen to her feet as Marea strode toward her. "What of the Flesh Clans? You do know of their plan to recall the goddess Artio back to this world?" Sharisha asked.

Marea nodded. "There have been rumours that the flesh clans have rediscovered an ancient magic of the gods that will bind spirit to animal flesh. It is something that is banned, the knowledge locked away centuries ago. If the rumours are true, then someone has stolen this knowledge and is attempting to resurrect a god. With the return of Artio, there will be two powerful pawns at play in this war. We need Avery to balance Artio's power. She will prove once and for all that the Spirit ways are true, and that Flesh sacrifice is not the only path to appease the gods."

"I had better catch up with Eldrid." Sharisha checked that the collar was secure in the pocket of her tunic and then hitched her bow over her right shoulder. "What would you have me do with her father, the man in the cells?"

"Keep him there. He will be useful as leverage in case our new priestess gives us any trouble. She will not resist us while her father's life hangs in the balance."

Sharisha bowed once more. Then turning on her heel, she strode from the room, pulling the circular door closed behind her.

Marea sat back in her chair and smiled. Soon she would meet Artio. Soon she would meet Avery. Soon she would rule the gods themselves. Her priests were in position and the potions, resurrected from the archives of old, were brewed and tested and working. She would gain control of the Flesh Clans and their leaders without her Clan Chiefs ever lifting a blade against another Primordial. She smiled broadly at her own cleverness then sighed, deeply contented. Soon, the entire world would kneel before her. Soon.

Chapter 10

Cyrus's Plan

CYRUS RODE AT THE HEAD OF A GROUP of twelve legion riders, every man handpicked for his particular skill set. His hands tightened then eased off the leather reins as he pulled his mount to a halt, just shy of the ridge of the mountainside they had been steadily climbing. A mist rose from the ground and swirling opaque fingers intertwined with the horses' legs, obscuring the path.

The last two villages they had entered and "surveyed" had produced only three Primordial males who confessed to having spotted the party he hunted. Not three days back, a group of three riders, two women and a man, had stopped for provisions in their village. With a little *persuasion*, the Primordials had spilled exact descriptions of their quarry and had led him to their aging trail.

Usefulness at an end, Cyrus slew two of them with the curved hunting knives preferred by the Spirit Clans. He was here to sow discord and sow it he would, leaving wounds unique to the curved blades and careful to leave the bodies riddled with arrows fletched with the Spirit Clan's favoured choice of feathers, all of which had been stolen from their villages a few days past. The bodies had been dumped along the path.

The Spirit Clan's villages were to be found in the valleys and open plains where grass was plentiful for their herds of deer and gazelle and the marshes and rivers teemed with fish and frog, while the Flesh Clans favoured hilly and mountainous terrain, prime for herding curly-horned sheep and nimble goats who foraged the steep mountainsides for vegetation. They built stone dwellings that doubled as defensible barriers and outposts to discourage foreign visitors. In the past, the two factions of Primordials worked as opposite sides of the same coin, but now, with the civil war, the Spirit Clans found themselves cut off and isolated by the Flesh Clans, hemmed in by the impassable terrain of the Highland Needle to the south and the Endless Oceans to the north. The few of the Spirit Clans who had created settlements on the human side of the Spine were rumoured to have disappeared without a trace. The Spirit Clans blamed the Flesh Clans, and the Flesh Clans blamed the humans. A few of the elders of both Spirit and Flesh Clan spoke of strange stirrings and signs, but these elders were largely ignored as their traditional views were regarded as not relevant to the modern situation.

Cyrus and his hand-picked legionnaires rode toward their destination under the cover of darkness, a raiding party on the move, with horses shod in the Primordial fashion for silent passage. Reaching the river, they slowed their mounts and allowed them to pick their own path into the swift flowing waters and then headed upstream to rejoin the live trail leading to their quarry. The tracks were fresh. They should reach Faylea and their prey by morning.

The men, halted behind him, waited, the leather creaking as they shifted in their saddles. Cyrus studied the ridge, the undulating landscape changing ever so slightly as his gaze rose to the crest, the vegetation becoming less defined and spookier, its edges blurred as though it was not quite part of this world. Cyrus rubbed his eyes and looked again. It still seemed slightly out of focus and only sharpened when he squinted. Large, perfectly domed tree crowns dotted the horizon, silhouetted by the setting moon, giant feathery pillows resting on a velvety blanket of night. One particularly massive tree towered above the others, its crown sharply defined by the fading moonlight.

"The mists should burn off in the first rays of the sun," the sole remaining Primordial mumbled, his wrists bound to the horn of the saddle, his heavily bruised lips barely able to part to allow the words to escape. He sat tall and proud despite the obvious distress caused by his various injuries. His black shoulder-length hair, matted with blood, stuck to the right side of his head while the left side gleamed in the reflected moonlight. "The mists of the dead only rise in the dark."

Cyrus glared at the man as his men muttered to each other, staring around suspiciously at the mists. Some of the older, superstitious men made a sign to ward off evil. Soldiers they might be, but superstition was a large part of a soldier's life. Few would openly defy the gods and mock the dead. Cyrus nudged his horse forward with his heels. Once alongside the man, he backhanded him with the fingers of his steel-tipped glove. Blood sprayed from the barely crusted lips, and the man's head snapped back with the force of the blow. Slowly, he straightened, returning Cyrus's glare, not a trace of fear in his eyes.

"You will speak when I ask you, not before." Cyrus wiped his gloved hand on a cloth he pulled from inside his tunic. Splatters of blood shimmered brightly for a moment on the dull red fabric with a polka-dot effect before dulling. Cyrus swiped at them, and they faded into the cloth. "We do not care about your mystic Primordial ramblings. The dead are the dead. Mist is mist. Fullmer!" he barked, and a balding pale man with one glass eye nudged his horse from the collective and trotted up to Cyrus's side.

"My lord!" he saluted.

"Take this Primordial popinjay with you and check out the mists. It may not be the dead, but it is a great place to lay an ambush. I want to know all that moves in those mists, and I want you back here before the coals are hot for breakfast. Take two others with you."

"Yes, my lord!" Fullmer saluted once again and with a wave, collected two other soldiers, and trotted away into the mist, leading the captive's horse into the brush. They disappeared within seconds, the mists on the ground rising just high enough to obscure horse and rider. Above the mists, the elongated swelling of a new day blushed across the horizon.

*　*　*

The soldiers, despite their armour and skill sets, scanned the rising mists with apprehension, pulling their knees up higher and leaving their stirrups behind so as to not have their feet touch the ethereal fingers of fog rising around them. A low moan issued from the ground and a collective shiver passed through the battle-hardened men. They had no fear of facing down another man or an army of them, but how does one fight spirits, if that is what the mists truly were?

The Primordial did not react in any way to the mists. They swirled over his feet and wrapped around his legs, encasing him in a shroud of cloud that hid his lower body from view. The mists drifted higher until only the tips of his shoulders were visible, swallowing him and his horse and his surroundings. Then with a final moan, the mist covered him completely, and he vanished from view.

The men, still leading the Primordial's horse by a rope, paid no attention to him, as they were preoccupied with keeping their own bodies and mounts in visible range.

They urged their horses to the crest of the rise. As the sun breached the ridge, the mists vanished, but so did the Primordial. The lead soldier hauled in the bridle rein, but it ended in nothing. Horse and captive rider had disappeared into the fog.

*　*　*

Achak urged his mount forward, keeping to the mists, working at the ropes tying his hands to the pommel. He slipped a sharp piece of stone from his pocket. The rock was a form of shale that chipped in sharp layers perfect for arrowheads, but this piece was not as sharp as a true arrowhead, as he had not had time to refine the stone. Rubbing his bonds furiously against the leather restraints he slid the leather back and forth across the dull edge, but the thick leather held, refusing to part.

"Thank you, ancestors, for your protection," he prayed as he rode silently through the trees. "Phoenix, aid my blade," he said to his Spirit Guide, not expecting an answer and was shocked when he felt the rock grow hot in his hand. He sawed into the leather and it started to smoke against the glowing edge. The leather parted like melting fat and fell from his freed hands. He clenched and unclenched his fingers, working the circulation back into them as the stone cooled, guiding his mount with only his knees. He pointed her into the dense underbrush thick with the spirits of his ancestors, feeling their welcome and their shelter, as he wound his way toward the ancient entrance into Faylea, an entrance long forgotten by the world.

A stream wound along the base of the cliff and caves dotted the edge of the stream, natural occlusions that swelled with water during heavy storms but now were hollowed vertical depressions in the rock with a trickling stream bed for a floor. He chose a tall, thin cave to enter, the spirits around him brightening, providing him with a glowing blue light to illuminate his way. They whispered at his mind as he rode. He felt their concern and also a great joy that infused their presence. The spirits were very active today, more so than he had seen in a very, very long time. He had a sense that something wondrous had occurred although he could not tell what. Still, it was obvious that they wanted his help, for they guided his horse's steps and showed him the direction they wished him to travel.

Achak followed the cavern for roughly two hundred yards before the cliff face appeared. As he rounded a curve in the cave wall, broad stone steps were revealed, crisscrossing back and forth toward the lighter grey of the exit. He dismounted at the urging of the spirits and began the climb, leading his horse. The stone steps were etched to provide a sure footing in the damp climate. The spirits pulsed around him, cocooning him and his mount in their soft shield. Clicking on the stone, they steadily climbed, passing walls covered in frescoes, scenes of people and clans and animals long forgotten. Some of the animals were clearly creatures of myth, as Achak's eyes had never seen them in the flesh. The elders had sworn they existed and during festivals would call on their particular guardian spirit to share in the celebrations with the clan and commune with the people.

I did see a phoenix one time. I swear it was dancing in the flames of the campfire. It is my guardian, my mother had explained, and a powerful one too — a special guardian to come to one so young. Achak had seen it on his eleventh birthday, when he became a man. But he had not seen it again. Now at nineteen, he longed to know if it really did guide him. Perhaps the phoenix had protected him this day, as he was still alive.

When the queen's elite legion squad descended on the village of Antigonish, the residents at first expected a peaceful trading session with their border village, as was the norm. Many a legion division had passed by their collection of huts at the mouth of the Spine and had traded for goods and supplies to supplement their reserves while conducting their patrols. This time had been different. The elders of Antigonish had been carried away by the men, and the women and children slain. Achak was the only one left that could bear witness to the slaughter at the village. The weapons they bore were of the Flesh Tribes, and yet not one of them accompanied the soldiers.

Where were the Flesh Clan warriors, and why did the legionnaires have Flesh Clan weapons?

Have the warriors been slaughtered, the same as the people of my village, and their weapons stolen? And if so, which village has fallen? I must give warning to my people that the legions are coming. I must warn the High Priestess that the Flesh Tribes may be aligned with the men of the kingdom. If I do not warn them, who will?

Achak reached the summit of the cave wall and stepped onto a stony trail that led to a cut in the rocky ceiling. Light spilled from the crevice and blinded him after the soft glowing of the spirits. As he walked toward the light, he felt ghostly touches along his back. They whispered in his ear. *"Avery…Avery…Avery…"*

Chapter 11

Transformed

AVERY CAME TO, face down on the floor, just inside the door of the temple. Her cheek was pressed against the cold stone, the rough surface biting into her cheek. She blinked. The sideways tilt of the room was disorienting. Slowly, comprehension dawned, and with it a rush of memories that made her head ache. She gathered her strength and rolled over onto her back and promptly screamed as it came in contact with the floor. She sat bolt upright and flapped her arms to put out the sensation of flames dancing across her back. Then, she noticed her biceps. Tattoos covered ever visible inch. As she drew her arms back around and straightened them, she could see the tattoos did not stop there but continued down over her wrists and hands, to the tips of fingers. As she rolled her hands to inspect her palms, it was then that she noticed her legs were also covered in tattoos. Alarmed, she jumped to her feet and hurried over to a floor-length mirror halfway down the ornately carved walls, limping as she walked. She stepped up to the mirror and gasped at her reflection.

She was naked. Naked, but every inch of her skin had been inked with vividly coloured tattoos. They were not random tattoos, however. They marched across her body like a moving panorama, scenes and images flowing from one concept to the next.

It's like the scrolling backdrop for the puppet plays, she thought, remembering the troupes of caravan actors that used to stop at Sanctuary-by-the-Sea during Beltine. She could follow one image of a fellow in battle gear from his house to a great battle scene. Slowly,

Avery turned in front of the mirror, trying to follow his journey, but it was difficult to see every bit of the scene as other scenes intersected with it.

Avery lifted her leg and displayed the sole of her right foot to the mirror. Not even her sole escaped images, although these were of people, seemingly writhing in pain, their mouths open in screams. Avery shuddered at the image and put her foot down. Perhaps it was better that that particular image was on the ground. She frowned, a thought bubbling to the surface and then popping before it fully formed. Frustrated, she continued her inspection.

As her eyes traveled up her body, the reason for the chill on her head became evident. Her hair was gone, as though it had never existed. Not a single strand of her former silky curls remained. Instead, her scalp was etched with images of celestial import, familiar stars and planets that traveled the skies.

She met her own eyes in the mirror and that was the greatest shock of all. Her eyes stared back at her from a silver base. Before, her eyes were set in white orbs, but now they rested in liquid mercury. The effect was frightening, and she blinked several times to reassure herself that her eyes were working properly, rubbing her fists across her closed lids to clear her vision. When she reopened her eyes, nothing had changed. She blinked again and stepped closer to the mirror. Faint lines ran through the silver, and they pulsed in time with her beating heart. She stepped back from the mirror and considered the problem. She could hardly stride around looking like this.

What is happening to me? What am I going to do? Avery leaned in closer to the mirror, tracing a finger over her cheek, examining the swirling patterns that now decorated her skin. *Runes. They look exactly like runes, and they are everywhere. My skin has been imbued with magic, the magic of the temple. These are the markings of a High Priestess,* she remembered. Avery straightened away from the mirror. *There will be no hiding from the world. Friend or enemy, every person I meet will have an agenda. They will seek to control me. I am truly alone now.* She shivered, scared to face the future beyond the temple doors. *It is likely that my entrance into the temple has not gone unnoticed. Who waits for me on the other side? Can the Primordial people be trusted?* Avery thought back to her instinctual distrust of Sharisha and she shivered again. She longed to have Cayden with her. She had never been separated from her twin before, and scared as she was, she missed him intensely at this moment.

At least Father is here with me, she thought in comfort. *It is time to face the waiting crowds*—(for she had no doubt that they waited beyond the double sealed doors)—*but first I need clothes!*

Her eyes wandered over the room, and she noticed another door covered in carvings. She strode over and wrenched it open. A large walk-in closet was revealed, and wooden pegs dotted the wall from which hung robes of varying sizes and shapes. Along the back wall, shelves were stacked with folded clothing, and the bottom row contained boots. Avery strode to the cabinet and wrenched open several drawers. Inside were small clothes, belts, bracelets, and other artifacts. The carvings on the jewellery matched the tattoos on her skin. She disregarded the jewellery and pulled out some soft cotton underthings and slipped them on. Next, she pulled a silvery sleeveless shirt from a stack and slipped it over her head. It fell to her hips and hugged her form like a glove. Avery did not worry about whose clothes they were. The fit was right, almost as though they were made for her. *Perhaps these belong to the High Priestess of the temple? But, if they are clothing meant for the High Priestess, then the Faylea High Priestess should be decked out in this clothing already. Obviously, she is not, which means…these clothes were meant for me, for if she had had access, then the clothing would be gone. I must be the true High Priestess.* The thought rang true in her mind and with it, fear surged causing her heart to race.

Another quick search of a stack of clothing revealed soft black leather leggings with fringes. She donned them and then pulled a belt from the drawer, leather embedded with thick silver links. Charms dangled from the links and tinkled as she pulled it though the loops and tugged the end through a heavy silver buckle in the shape of a bear.

Next, she found a black leather vest with silver buttons and slipped it on over the silver shirt.

From the drawers, wide silver bangles caught her eye, wide enough to cover her forearms from wrist to elbow. She picked them up and saw that they were cleverly jointed with tiny hinges that allowed her to slip her arm inside. They closed with a snap and she was pleased to see that she had full range of movement while they covered the tattoos. All that was visible were the twin birds that ran from wrist to fingertips.

Twin phoenixes? she wondered.

She closed the drawer and then knelt down to inspect the boots. The pair closest to her size, tall boots of black leather, was tooled similarly to her belt with silver buckles and adjustable straps. She pulled them from the shelf and took a closer look. The reason for the buckles became apparent as she opened the boot to find hidden sleeves and pockets built in. The intended use of one set of the pockets was clear as they were already occupied by a pair of matching knives, one per boot.

Avery sat down on the floor and tugged on the boots, buckling them up over her knees. She sighed with pleasure, partially because the ugly images on her feet were finally covered over and also with relief as the cool leather soothed her burning soles.

Strange, none of the other tattoos burns, she thought, *only the images on my feet.*

She stood up gingerly, settling her feet in the least painful position. She was several inches taller in these boots and smiled. *Now, to find a coat that fits,* she thought and tested out her new footwear by walking back and forth before the hanging cloaks. A black one caught her eye, and she slipped her arms through the sleeves as she pulled it down. The cloak was fitted across her chest and fell to her hips. She buttoned it up and then walked out to the main room to the mirror and stopped in front of it.

A woman stared back at her, but this woman was a stranger. A woman in sleek leather stared back at her with silver eyes that imitated the silver on her clothing. The cloak's black hood draped down her back to a point, just shy of her waist and the coat split and cut away over her hips and then dropped to the sides in long sweeping tails that swirled as she walked. The cuffs of the sleeves turned up in a similar fashion, and two large silver buttons held the cuffs straight. More hidden pockets were glimpsed in the cuffs. From the front, her boot tops mimicked the cuffs, with rows of silver buttons marching down the side. She tugged up the hood of the cloak and her face disappeared within it except for her glowing silver orbs.

If I didn't know it was me, I would be petrified! she thought, wincing at what her father would say when he saw her.

She wandered back into the closet, but none of the rest of the garments seemed to be the right size. It was almost as though these particular garments had been waiting for her to come and claim them. She was drawn back to the drawers and touched the face of a thin one that she had not noticed earlier. This drawer whispered as it opened, sliding out and unfolding at her touch. On a bed of softest linen sat a silver necklace. Avery saw at a glance that it was very old. The chain was silver and very long with a flat oval-shaped pendant that glowed. She picked it up and ran a thumb across the polished surface and images sprung to life. Mists swirled and resolved into faces and images of places she had never been to, flashed across the surface. Murmuring reached her ears. As she gazed into the stone, the image of her brother Cayden floated to the surface. He was in a stone library surrounded by books.

"A Seeing Stone!" Avery exclaimed, the first audible words she had uttered since rising from the floor. Her voice was dampened by the magic of the closet. She slipped the pendant around her neck and dropped it inside her shirt to nestle between her breasts. Her eye fell on a matching ring that had been hidden beneath the pendant. She picked this up too and slipped it on the middle finger of her left hand. It molded itself to her finger as though made for her. The phoenix tattoo ended where the ring settled, the flat surface glinting like a fiery eye on her finger.

As she left the closet, the door swung shut with a loud click and, glancing back, she saw that the outline of the door had disappeared, becoming just another arch in the paneled wall.

Avery stretched out her hands to the double doors and grabbed the twin carved handles. This threshold she had crossed *moments? hours? days?* before. Did they still wait for her on the other side? It was time to find out. With a mighty shove, she pushed open the doors.

Chapter 12

Heading for Trouble

CAYDEN LEANED BACK IN HIS CHAIR and stretched his arms over his head, his stiff back popping as he worked out the kinks. He then flipped the thick book closed with a boom that sent the early morning dust motes swirling in the first rays of sunrise to light his apartment. He had rearranged the central room into a proper study, complete with overstuffed chairs, long tables on which to spread out books, and ample lamps to light the interior.

He squeezed the bridge of his nose, the strain of studying all night long resulting in a steady throb behind his eyes. It seemed he always had a headache now. At first, he had put them down to his obsession with reading every work, every tome relating to the history of Cathair and the kingdom, the history of the peoples of both his and the Primordial lands, and back even further to the creation myths woven through the histories of both peoples. Clarity was emerging from the chaos, and he began to understand the motivations of his enemy. But now, Cayden wondered if the headaches had another cause.

He glanced down at the couch located under the brightening window and gazed fondly at Ziona's sleeping form. She was curled into a ball on the soft surface, her toes just peeking out from under a tapestry he had "borrowed" from the wall and draped over her in the middle of the night. Even deep in slumber, he felt her nestled in his head, a residual effect of having saved her life. He smiled at the sense of wonder he felt in her dreams.

He walked over and gently shook her awake. "Ziona. Wake up. It's morning."

Ziona's long lashes slowly fluttered open, and then she peered up at him. "Is it dawn? Did you study all night?"

"Yeah." Weary crescents of darkness painted Cayden's eyes and stubble shadowed his chin. He held out a hand to help her up. She placed her slim left hand in his as he pulled her to her feet. Then, she reached up and trailed her right hand across his burgeoning beard.

"You must rest. You cannot push yourself so hard. What is it you are looking for?" She glanced down at the stack of books. The tree sprites had continued to drop books every few hours, great dusty tomes with a woodsy smell, appearing out of nowhere to thump to the library floor right next to wherever Cayden stood or sat until great stacks covered the table and floor. It had been a few hours since the last book arrived, and that was about the time she had fallen asleep on the settee.

At first, Ziona had been surprised every time a book magically appeared out of thin air, jumping at every deep thump, but after Cayden paused several times in midsentence to speak to the sprites, she had come to understand that he could see what she could not, despite her Primordial heritage. Now that they had been summoned, it seemed that the tree sprites were determined to retrieve and return every book they had ever pilfered from the library for safekeeping. Indeed, it seemed to Ziona that they were determined to return every tome immediately when in actual fact they were only fetching those books on subjects that Cayden specified.

Ziona turned to the stack and ran her thumb down the cracked leather spines, tilting her head to read the embossed gold lettering on them.

Cayden massaged the ache in his neck as he sat back down, arching away from the books. "I don't know, something to help Avery. I have this feeling she is in trouble." Restless, he rose to his feet again and walked over to the window to peer out at the pink candy blush spreading across the horizon above the trees. "She pulls at me through this." He pulled a golden chain out from under his tunic from which dangled a stone. "She always said we would be connected by this stone." He rubbed his thumb across the rough surface, and broken images flashed across his consciousness. He saw an emerald city in the bowl of a valley, a shining white temple and wild images of beasts. Some he recognized, having met a few of them himself via his flutes. "We need to go to her. I feel it."

The bond Cayden had with his twin sister, Avery, had existed since the day they were born. They shared a telepathic bond and could speak to each other over vast distances. It had something to do with their heritage, although he had never heard of the Primordial people being telepathic. Whatever its source, he was sure it was tied into their birth and the magic performed to save their lives...or perhaps the magic that they both possessed. The bond had sharpened suddenly during the night. It was more defined, more tangible than in the past. Something dramatic had happened to Avery.

Cayden studied the castle grounds, watching the servants hurrying and scurrying, going about the never-ceasing chores required in a typical day of running the castle. One thing was for certain. All of his study in the dark hours confirmed his suspicions. The gods were playing a game, and the mortal beings that filled the world were pawns, pieces on a giant chessboard, being pushed to and fro at the whim of the gods. *And where does that leave me as a child of the gods? Am I a pawn or a player? Am I a pusher or being pushed? I would rather be a player and not at the whim or beck and call of the gods. But how? How do I get in the game?* Cayden's face hardened and his hands clenched the window frame, whitening his knuckles with the strength of his grip.

Ziona stepped up behind him and placed her hands on his shoulders and began to gently massage the tight muscles in his neck and shoulders. Cayden groaned with relief, closing his eyes, as she worked out the kinks.

"I will go. She is with my people, and I need to report to the head of my order what has happened here. I will check on her and make sure she is safe. No harm will come to her with my people." Cayden stiffened and grabbed her hand.

"No." He spoke before thinking, his knee-jerk reaction to keep her close. He opened his mouth to say more, but Ziona pressed a finger to his lips, pausing his words.

"The danger has passed for you. You are protected now, safe with your people within the castle and its grounds." Ziona gestured vaguely to the room surrounding them. "And I am needed elsewhere."

Cayden grasped her other hand and pulled her close. "Ziona, I don't think..." Cayden broke off as a knock sounded on the door and it creaked open. A young woman backed into the room, carrying a tray covered in a cloth, chattering away as she ducked under the arm of the guard holding the door open. "Sire, time for you to take a break," she chattered. "Your breakfast is piping hot, and you should eat it before it grows cold and lumpy." She broke off as she swung around and caught Cayden and Ziona in a near embrace. She averted her eyes to the floor and stumbled. "I apologize, sire. I should have waited for you to bid me enter. Forgive me."

Cayden and Ziona broke reluctantly apart, Ziona kissing Cayden on the cheek with the lightest brush of lips. She touched her fingers to her lips, then touched his, transferring the kiss. Her eyes softened with a liquid warm, hinting at a promise unfulfilled. Cayden's eyes widened and, with a grin, Ziona swung away, marching to the door. Ziona spoke over her shoulder as she passed the serving girl, eyeing the woman. She knew that the gossip would spread through the castle like a wildfire. In no time, every servant would know she had slept in Cayden's chambers. Ziona smiled, secretly pleased to stake her claim to Cayden, to send out an emotional warning to all to stay away from him. "We will speak of this later, sire. Enjoy your breakfast."

The door closed behind her with a click, and the serving girl straightened from her curtsy, hurrying over to a side table to put the tray down.

A rapid knock sounded at the door once again. It swung open to admit Mordecai, who did not wait to be invited. The serving girl squeaked at the appearance of the wizard and scurried out through the door before it had time to close behind him.

"Good morning, my boy!" Mordecai boomed, a wide smile creasing the sides of his leathery cheeks. He looked robustly healthy, still skinny, but the pallor of the dungeons had faded from his skin. He walked with a spry step as he strode over to peek at Cayden's tray of food. "What do we have here?" He flipped back the dangling sleeve of his magenta robes and swept the cloth cover off the tray, revealing a pot of tea and a mug, a bowl of porridge and berries, a pot of thick sweet cream, and three buttery croissants. Mordecai picked up a steaming crusty croissant and a knife, slathering it with creamy butter before popping it into his mouth. "Ahh." He rolled his words around hot mouthfuls of food. "You really should try these, Cayden. They are quite delightful. I do believe that Fabian is supplying the castle now."

Cayden's stomach did a funny lurch at the thought of putting food in it. *I still haven't got over that stomach flu*, he thought. Instead, he reached for the pot of tea, pouring a liberal quantity of honey into it, and then took a sip of the blueberry-flavoured brew.

Mordecai *tsked* and wandered over to the table to inspect the recent arrivals. "Well? What have you learned, my boy, for all your nightly vigils?"

Cayden sank into a soft leather chair with a stifled groan and leaned his head back against the cushions.

"I have learned that our true opponent is likely Helga, the goddess of the underworld, goddess of the dead." His head swiveled to Mordecai. "How, good goddess, do we defeat an immortal?"

Mordecai grinned from ear to ear at his words. "Why, with another god, of course!"

Cayden felt the temporary relief from Ziona's massage evaporate as he squinted at Mordecai. "With another god...of course. Why didn't I think of that?" Sarcasm dripped from his tongue. "I will summon one with my flutes. Perhaps Aossi is up to the task." Aossi was a spirit of the world between worlds, an immortal that traveled between realities. She was also a tiny childlike entity that had an annoying habit of showing up just to tweak his nose with what he didn't understand.

"No, no, my dear boy. No need for Aossi, as charming as she is. She really isn't up to the task, in any event."

Infuriating! thought Cayden as he peered blearily at Mordecai's smug grin. *Completely infuriating!* "So, what do you suggest?"

"I suggest you sleep on it. Your brain is stuffed so full of information. You cannot begin to process it all." He walked over and pulled Cayden from the chair and then marched him to his bedchamber, pushing him onto the feathery surface and pulling off his boots. "Sleep," Mordecai commanded, "and we will talk when you are awake enough to process the information."

Cayden's heavy eyelids drooped before Mordecai even reached the doorway. By the time the door closed, Cayden was fast asleep.

*   *   *

Ziona fell into step beside Mordecai as he left Cayden's quarters. Mordecai had snagged another croissant from Cayden's tray and was happily devouring it with quick bites while he strode down the hall, his shoes making a clicking sound on the checkered marble flooring.

"I must leave before he awakens. Cayden is becoming more and more reluctant to let me out of his sight. He will not tell me what is bothering him, but I think it has to do with that last prophecy tome that the pixies dropped. I couldn't read the script, but Cayden picked it out right away. Somehow, he is able to read books written in long extinct languages, languages dating back thousands of years. I don't think he even realizes he is doing it."

Mordecai nodded, swallowing his last mouthful. "I believe it to be a result of his birth lineage, the unique blend of his human royal parents, mixing with his immortal bloodlines. Strange abilities surface when gods and humans mix, and I do not believe this has occurred since the very foundation of the world. A remnant of his immortal existence has been pulled through and merged with his mortal existence. It would explain his natural affinity for runes and his instinctual use of them." Mordecai made to take another bite of croissant and frowned disappointedly at his empty hand.

"Well, so far, he has refused to tell me what he has learned. It's almost as though he is afraid to tell me. There have been times when I have seen him sitting there, shaking with grief. I cannot tell if it is because of something he has read or if it is something he has figured out. Either way, he believes that he must go to Avery, but we both know that would be foolish. He would have to go through Alcina's troops to get there, and that is way too much risk for a monarch." She shook her head at the foolishness of the thought. "What would happen if he were to fall into their hands? He is safer here." She followed the statement with a sharp nod of her head, as though that settled matters once and for all.

Mordecai frowned. "I doubt that you can keep him here against his will."

"That is why I must leave now. I have had the essentials packed for a week." She stubbornly crossed her arms.

"He will not be pleased to find you gone. What will you do to get around the legionnaires' encampment?"

"You forget, Mordecai, that the Primordial lands are my homeland. I know of routes through the Highland Spine that few men have traveled. I will find a way around the legion to Avery."

"Be very careful, Ziona. Alcina is likely with them and she would love nothing more than to capture someone close to Cayden. Be very, very careful."

Ziona patted Mordecai on his shoulder and left him at the next corridor, heading off at a brisk walk in the direction of the castle stables where her horse, Seeker, waited, saddled and ready to ride.

Chapter 13

Power Struggle

BLINDING FLASHES OF LIGHT pulsed from the tiered temple, drawing the eye of every villager in Faylea. Crowds of Primordial clanspeople thronged the edge of the sacred grounds, striving to catch a glimpse of what was causing the sky to flash and dim. Those lucky enough to have a front-row view took it upon themselves to yell out a running commentary on the scene before them.

The carvings that adorned the building were no longer still, but writhed on the sides of the temple, resurrected by the flow of spirit within the temple walls. On the walls themselves, visions scrolled, a diorama of the land and the seas and the creatures that lived within them. Scene after scene played itself out. As one level went dark, the one above it lit up until the front-row viewer's commentary was no longer needed. As the images moved up the temple, a great murmur rose from the throng. Some people wept for joy while others screamed with terror. No one in living memory had seen such a display as the temple was putting out that day.

Darkness descended with the setting of the sun, but the temple did not stop projecting its images. The crowds pulsed and thinned as they gradually drifted away to their homes.

Only the elders remained and with them a contingent of Primordial warriors, who ringed the temple. No one could approach the temple or mount its steps since Avery had entered. An invisible force repelled all who attempted it.

At the foot of the stairs, the High Priestess marched back and forth, scowling at the temple. The elders watched her pacing, secretly amused by her annoyance.

"Marea, why don't you relax? There is nowhere for the young woman to go. There is only one door in and that is at the top of the stairs. She will have to come out the same way she went in."

Marea glared at Elder Hania, her scowl deepening so that he took an involuntary step back from her. "She mocks me. The temple and its secrets belong to the High Priestess. She should never have been allowed to enter it on her own. Obviously, she intends to usurp my authority. I will not allow it for the good of our people. Prophesied One or not, she will obey me." She flung out an arm at the glowing temple. "Look what she has done! She has tripped some ancient safeguard and now the temple is out of control. Maybe she never comes out. She may even be dead. *Baw!*" She resumed her pacing, and Elder Hania opened his mouth to respond, just as the temple went dark.

The darkness was complete and eerie after the display that had lasted the better part of a day and a night. As he furiously blinked away the remaining light image, he noticed the beginning blush of dawn creeping across the horizon as the sun prepared to rise in the east.

Everyone stared at the door, and a hush fell across the watchers. The warriors pulled bladed weapons from their leather scabbards and others notched arrows to the long bows common amongst the clan. A nervous tremor ran through the group. Suddenly, the double doors whispered open, ghostlike. A diminutive figure stepped across the threshold to the balcony railing, just as the first rays of sunlight broke the horizon. The sun flashed over her and the blue glow that initially surrounded her faded in the harsh morning glare.

The archers drew back on their creaking bows, arms straining with the resistance of the wood and sighted on Avery's heart. Marea raised her left hand imperiously, halting the bowmen. She cautiously approached the steps of the temple, feeling for the powerful spirit force, the field of spirit that had been humming throughout the day, but it had vanished. Avery's head rose as she approached, her face masked by her heavy hood, and then she moved to stand centered on the staircase. Marea ascended the stairs, eyes intent on Avery. Halfway up, Avery reached back and drew the hood off of her head.

A collective gasp sighed around the crowd, and then fresh murmuring broke out and a few shouts echoed over the grounds. The elders closed in on either side of Marea, who had paused in midstep.

Liquid silver. Her eyes are liquid silver pierced with celestial blue. What is this creature? Cautiously, now, Marea approached Avery, making no sudden movements. Her eyes narrowed at the tattoos covering her skin.

"Hello, child. I am Marea, the High Priestess of the sacred temple you have been enjoying for the past twenty-eight hours."

Avery stared at her, and then her head swung around to take in the weapons pointed in her direction. "Is this how you usually greet guests? With bows and swords?"

Marea shook her head. "No, child, but none of our guests have commandeered a holy site on entering the city either. They do not know your intentions and are correctly cautious, but no harm will come to you as long as I command it."

Avery's strange eyes swung back to Marea, and Marea shivered, masking the thrill that raced along her pulse as the silvery orbs settled on her. The gaze felt ancient, as though an older soul lived behind the silvery window, a presence older than the temple itself, the age of which had passed into legend. No one knew when it had been built or how or by whom. It had simply always existed, as did the mountains around them, ancient and permanent and unmoving.

"I commandeered nothing. I was bid to enter and I did so." Avery's eyes scanned the crowd, but she could not locate her father. "Where is my father?"

"He is safe. What concerns me is what you were doing in the temple for an entire day and night? Come, we must talk, and you need to be seen by our healers."

"I am perfectly fine. I do not need to see any healers. I want to see my father."

"I'm afraid I cannot permit that right now." Avery's eyes swung back to Marea and their silver centers pulsed angrily. "Come, we will talk," implored Marea. "I do not even know your name. What do they call you, child?"

"I am no child!" Avery struggled to restrain the urge to stomp her foot…like a child. Her eyes glazed for a moment, and she struggled to remember her name. She rubbed a hand over where her eyebrow should have been, now permanently inked to match her body.

"Avery." She tested the name on her tongue and found it to be familiar, if not quite true. "I am called Avery in this age." Memories assaulted her with the thought of her name, and sweat broke out on her forehead, a pulsing pain accompanying the effort it took to remember.

"Come, you need rest." Marea held out her hand, indicating that Avery should join her. Avery stepped down the remainder of the steps, pulling up her hood, joining the High Priestess. The clansmen surrounded them and led them away from the temple and back into Faylea proper, crossing over a second bridge that led directly into the heart of the city.

Two sets of eyes, unnoticed by the Primordial guards, followed the retreating group. One was hostile. One was not. But both followed, slipping through grey early morning patches of shadow, pursuing the assembly.

*　*　*

Elder Hania fell into step beside Avery. "Hello, Daughter. It is pleasant to meet you at last. Sharisha has told us of your journey and the trials you have endured along the way."

Avery nodded but did not reply. She took in the buildings as they passed, larger than the homes that had lined the street from the south. This paved stone road was more westerly, and the buildings had the feel of shops or perhaps meeting places. However, it was difficult to tell as no signs decorated the exteriors to advise of their intended usage. The majority were built from saplings, bent and tied and intertwined as they grew. By the number of stories involved, the age of the buildings became apparent. The deeper into the town they walked, the thicker the trunks became until the houses took on a wooden appearance not that different from the log cabins that were popular in Sanctuary-by-the-Sea. The main difference was that instead of lying stacked on their sides, these trunks stood fused side by side.

Eventually they arrived at an immense central square, which was actually an octagon, each side another road departing the central area.

At the focal point of the octagon rose a spire that twisted into the sky and down into the earth. As the sun struck it, the light bounced off and was sent down one of the darker streets that would have remained in perpetual twilight due to the height of the buildings and the trees involved had this feature not have been present. As they approached the spire, a grinding noise met their ears. A mirrored disc halfway up the tower rotated into alignment with the sun's rays and sent a secondary shaft of sunlight down another street. With a series of clicks and whirls, the remaining mirrors aligned themselves and lit the side streets with morning sunlight.

Avery stared at the contraption. "That is incredible. How does it work?"

"We do not know." Elder Hania watched the machine click over to the next setting. "The knowledge of its construction has been forgotten. It is very old, perhaps as old as the temple or the gods."

Avery's head swung around to look him in the eye. "You know of the gods?"

"Of course. I am an elder. Come, we can discuss more of this once inside the spire." He led the way to a curved arch carved out of the base and onto a spiral staircase, which they climbed in dizzying circles until it emptied onto a landing before a door. The door was carved from a huge alabaster clam shell, and the surface rippled with rainbow hues. It swung open silently at their approach. Inside, arched buttresses soared to disappear into the murky gloom of the ceiling. The pale arches reminded Avery of the bones of a whale she had discovered on the beach one summer, washed up and decayed long ago. Only the bones had remained, and she had wandered around and through the ribcage trailing her hand along the arch of bones in awe that such a creature could exist.

Elder Hania and High Priestess Marea led Avery to a trestle table set with matching chairs and indicated that she should take the chair opposite them. The warriors lined the walls, but they did not put away their weapons.

The door opened again and Sharisha entered, striding up to the table and taking a seat on the other side of Marea. Directly behind her entered a woman bearing a tray with a pewter pitcher with a great curved handle and four pewter cups. She set the cups in front of each of them and poured crimson juice into each cup. Setting the pitcher in the middle, she bowed and left the chamber.

Sharisha met Avery's eyes across the table. Shocked at Avery's transformation, she struggled to keep the fear from her face. She studied the tattoos visible on every inch of skin as Avery lowered her hood to her shoulders and then folded her hands in her lap to keep them from twitching.

I must appear strong and confident. I must not give away my insecurity. I must not show weakness. They do not know what happened in the tower. They do not know who I am. Avery's lips curled into a sneer. "I assume you wish to question me? I will only answer what is appropriate for you to hear."

Marea's glare was quickly replaced by a condescending smile that did not reach her eyes. "Child, what could you possibly say that is inappropriate for us to hear? Simply tell us why you entered the temple and what you found in there." Her eyes travelled over Avery, and she was unable to hide the disgust that flickered in her eyes. "Obviously, you borrowed several artifacts of clothing...which, of course, you will return, as they belong to the temple. Where did you find them?" In all her years as High Priestess, Marea had not found the secret closet, despite searching the temple extensively. *How did she find it so easily?* "You also triggered a dangerous display within the temple. What did you do? I must know so that others do not trip over this trigger by accident."

Elder Hania leaned back in his chair and folded his arms, watching Avery closely. He frowned as his eyes examined the visible tattoos on her head. Whirls and symbols followed a pattern that was familiar to him. He stood up and walked back around the table and stopped beside her chair, his frown deepening, drawing his greyed drooping brow almost into a straight line. Avery watched him approach and pause by her chair, and then she clenched her hands, hidden under the table into fists of anger. The elder did not touch her. He simply studied the array of tattoos, moving slowly around her until he paused on the opposite side.

Marea harrumphed and the elder's eyes flickered to her and then back to Avery. With a sigh, he sat back down in his abandoned chair and waited for Marea to resume her interrogation.

Marea swung back to Avery and did not attempt to hide her displeasure this time. "Well, child? Speak up!"

Avery rolled her tense shoulders and took a deep breath. "I don't know what happened. I entered the temple and after that I passed out. When I came to, I was in need of clothes and there was a doorway in front of me. I opened the door, found some clothes, and put them on."

The silence stretched following these words. Then Marea, in a voice so heavy with sarcasm that it hit the floor with a nearly audible thud, sneered, "And? Is that it? Surely you do not think I believe that story, You were in there *for twenty-eight hours—a full day and night!* You want me to believe you *saw and heard nothing?* That you did not explore the temple? You locked the doors! Why? I will have answers, and I will have them now!" This last came out just shy of a screech.

Elder Hania shot a look at Marea out of the corner of his eye but did not speak.

Avery flushed and stared back at Marea, her eyes glowing with emotion. Her gaze switched to Sharisha, who sat expressionless, watching Avery like a cat who had cornered a mouse, after a long chase.

"Well, obviously, you are not meant to know, if you as High Priestess have never had a similar experience." Avery's smile widened, even as her heart raced. *This will not end well*, she thought. "Perhaps you are not meant to access the temple but merely be a caretaker of it? Hmm?"

Marea's face flushed as bright as the ruby liquid in her untouched cup. She leaned forward across the tabletop toward Avery, and her lips drew back into a snarl. "You, young one, are the one who is sadly mistaken. To enter the temple without permission is an offense, punishable by death. You will tell me everything that transpired in the temple, or you will find yourself staked out as food for the vultures. Chosen One or not, you are still human and die just as easily as the rest of us. Your father thought he could resist us too. He came to understand the truth of the matter…in the end."

Avery shot to her feet, lunging at Marea. Before she could do more than lean forward, strong hands grabbed her arms to restrain her. Weapons were drawn, and Avery was surrounded by the Primordial warriors. A knowing grin spread across Sharisha's face.

Elder Hania frowned deeper and shook his head, displeased at the turn of events.

"Take her to the cells until I choose to question her again. The cell beside her useless father would be a good one. Guard her closely, for if she escapes, you will be very, *very* sorry." Marea stood up, eyes glinting at Avery's struggle as she was dragged out through a side passage.

"You will fail, High Priestess!" Avery yelled over her shoulder. "You were never more than a caretaker!" she spat as she was hauled over the threshold and the door boomed closed behind them.

Chapter 14

Artio

ARTIO ROAMED THE FORGOTTEN TEMPLE, examining the throne room and the attendant chambers beyond the main audience hall. In the private rooms she claimed as her own, she located several trunks with rusted padlocks that broke with a swift tug. Inside the trunks were articles of clothing wrapped in silk. The trunks had been preserved with a spell that kept the ravages of time from harming the contents. Rummaging through them, she found several sets of soft chestnut robes that fell over one shoulder, leaving the other exposed, and dropped to just above her knees. She tossed open the lid of an oaken chest banded with iron and found a sleeveless leather vest and leather-plated skirt with interlocking folds of armadillo shell. Her lips stretched into a feral smile at the discovery. It was more armour than clothing, and she was pleased. She also found leather greaves studded with cabochons of emerald, ruby, amethyst, and tiger's eye. She strapped the greaves on her downy arms and, as a crowning touch, settled a rough circlet of hammered gold on her dirty-blonde curls to complete her transformation.

A bubbled mirror on the far wall reflected a distorted view, but it was enough for Artio to see the warrior goddess in her true form. *I am truly a blend now, thunder-bear and goddess wrapped into one lethal package.*

As she had rummaged for the clothing, pieces of long-buried memory surfaced. Memories of a forgotten past and people, of sibling wars and banishment amongst the very stars she was to maintain. She snarled at the image in the mirror. *I will never be banished again. This time*

I will prevail. My sisters and brother have a lot to answer for, especially the twins. I will hunt them down, and this time I will not fail.

Artio re-entered the audience chamber to find the High Priests exactly as she had left them, standing in the center of the hall with their eyes rolling in their heads. On the floor, scorpions scuttled everywhere, blackening the floor in the circle bound by her magic. One priest whimpered as a scorpion crawled over his naked foot, poised with its poisoned tip raised as if to strike.

"Please, Great One! Release us so that we may serve you. We will find the people you seek. We are sworn to your service!" He shuddered as the scorpion began to crawl under the hem of his robes and out of site. Sweat rolled down his cheek, and his eyes widened at the movements that were now not visible, but that he felt nonetheless.

Artio bent and picked up one of the scorpions, which curled up on the palm of her hand like a dog settling to sleep. *"My pets will not harm you, provided you mean me no harm. Think on that this evening, and in the morning, if you are still alive, you may serve me."*

She strode out the temple doorway and into the night. None followed her. None could, for where she was headed only the dead could go.

*   *   *

Artio's long legs carried her through the woods. She began to climb a twisting trail that led up to the jagged peaks forming the tip of the spine of the world. The location of the place she sought had come back to her while she'd searched the trunks for clothing. As though awakening from a long sleep, the clouds had lifted and fragments of memory reorganized themselves, solidifying into a solid plan. If the twins did indeed roam the earth again, as the weak priests had suggested, Artio needed to level the playing field. That meant it was time for a little family reunion.

She snarled once again, annoyed at the time lost. Multiple millennia she had been chained. True, she had been unaware of the passage of time (she was immortal, after all)—but still. She checked that the weapon she'd strapped to her left thigh as she left the temple was secure. The long thin blade of obsidian was set in a creamy bone handle that she had been especially pleased to find right where she had left it before her banishment. The blade was impregnated with the deadly poisonous slavering of Cerberus, a very effective poison both in this life and the afterlife.

Memories of her existence as a thunder god blended and merged with her memories of the godling child called Artio. Artio had been a weak creature, barely aware of the world around her. She had been fascinated with the constellations and with the one she had been named after in particular. The irony was not lost on her. Now returned to a physical form, they were bound as one. She should have anticipated that the experiment harnessing the moon that was her home could have dire consequences. She could not remember her name as a cub. Artio would do.

She strode through the night, swifter than a horse could travel the distance, enjoying the journey after eons of time spent watching the world turn. She increased her pace into a ground-eating lope that took her from one end of the Highland Spine to the other. As she walked, steadily climbing, she plucked ripened gooseberries, discovering an intense liking for the juicy red fruit.

Licking the sticky syrup from her fingertips, she paused at the ridge of the great divide and surveyed the lands before her. The vantage point of being at the peak of the world, combined with her extraordinary sight, allowed her to see the entirety of the world. To the south, the foothills of the Highland Needle melted into the grasslands where the Battle of Daimon Ford had been fought. The plains were interrupted by a large swamp enshrouded in fog and then continued on to the coast, where the capital city of Cathair squatted against the edge of the cliffs, the stone fortress flying the king's flag.

Artio's head swung to her left and her eyes followed the coastline to where the great pine forests began, the trees growing taller and taller the further northeast her eyes travelled. When they collided with the eastern terminus of the Highland Needle, a flyspeck village was detected. She growled at the site. The air shimmered with the residual presence of magic in that area. *The home of my now mortal brother and sister, no doubt,* she thought. She turned once again, looking back the way she had come, across the eastern edge of the Spine and down into the lands of the Primordials. She felt a strange affinity for these barbaric people and not only for the fact that they had called her back from her imprisonment amongst the stars. No, she felt a connection to them physically, another mystery to unravel, another puzzle piece to set in place. Her eyes took in the leafy canopy of gumwood and the rounded tops of the mushroom trees, looking ever so much like ruddy faces staring back at her.

As she completed her inspection, her luminous eyes fixed on a convergence of peaks from which issued puffs of steam, cooling and condensing into clouds that drifted away on the breeze. *That's the spot, the entrance to the abyss my dear sister calls home,* she thought. *It's time to knock on the door.*

Ten more minutes of walking brought her to the base of a waterfall that rose impossibly into the sky. The top of the waterfall disappeared into the clouds so that it appeared to be suspended from the sky. It tumbled down the sheer cliff to a frothing pool before flowing away to the south. A tributary wandered away at the base, and she followed the shore of the errant stream. As the water flowed away, it slowed and finally spilled over into a basin of red rock, hissing as it hit the surface. Steam rose from the contact, creating a curtain that she could not see beyond.

Being of thunder blood did have its advantages. Artio threw back her head and roared at the heavens, invoking the air and the water to blend and gather, swirling faster and faster, more clouds forming and thickening overhead. Lightning flashed and the maelstrom darkened, twisting into a thunderhead above the pool. From the midst of the clouds, a funnel dropped, whirling with ferocious winds that whipped the tree trunks, tearing off leaves and branches and sucking them into the vortex. Yet the tornado did not touch Artio. Her clothing did not even stir. The mists parted, and the open maw of a cave was revealed with jagged teeth, glowing red in the flickering light spilling from its mouth. Silhouetted against the opening was a figure encased in long black robes. The hood was drawn up and the face hidden from view. Its arms were crossed, hands tucked into the opposite sleeve. A crow cawed its raucous song from a nearby tree. The figure held out its arm to the bird, which flew down to perch on the outstretched appendage.

"Welcome, Sister. Welcome back. Will you join me in hell?" Helga chuckled loudly at her own joke, then disappeared back into the waiting chasm. Artio followed, leaving the tornado spinning impossibly in the pool devoid of water.

Chapter 15

Alcina

ALCINA, THE FORMER QUEEN OF CATHAIR, strode through the encampment, ringed by her guards. Her cape of blood-red silk fluttered behind her as she marched along. Her heeled boots kept her hem from dragging through the mud, but she grabbed a fist full of skirts and pulled them higher, just in case. She hated soiling her dress in such filth. *No queen should have to live in such primitive conditions. I will have my castle back if I have to eliminate each and every savage, one by one.*

Trotting at her heels was her new Lord General. The departure of Cyrus and the discovery shortly thereafter of the two dead captives had put her in a very foul mood. Her specific instructions had been to leave the captives for her to interrogate. What information they had told Cyrus, what secrets they had shared as they had screamed out the last few moments of their existence on this earth she would never know. It bothered her that Cyrus had done this against her specific command. Furthermore, he had not come to tell her what he had learned before he left, and that was extremely disturbing. Beyond disturbing. It bordered on treason.

One captive was left. Only one. She would have answers from this one or…

"Darius!" she snapped.

"Yes, my queen?" Darius was a young man, barely a man by most accountings. He bowed low, hands on knees. She surveyed his shock of red hair on his head and the line of freckles that trailed down his neck. The lad had proven his loyalty to his queen by befriending the usurper. Then, in an act of betrayal befitting one of her own, delivered the traitor into her waiting hands. Her mistress's pets had dragged the unconscious boy to the cells. If it had not been for that meddling wizard, she would still be safely ensconced within her castle. She had rewarded Darius by granting him a permanent position in the Queen's Guard. His thin frame was now encased in the uniform of an officer, and the only thing identifying him as a Lord General was the insignia that had been hastily sewn onto the breast of his tunic. His pimpled face was partially covered in a thin scruffy beard. Alcina had the impression that he was growing it in an attempt to look older to the men he commanded. He held himself rigidly as he strode beside her, eyes flickering over the men of the camp and back to her. He swallowed, and his Adam's apple bobbled in his throat.

"You were successful in getting close to the usurper as our spy. I want you to perform a similar miracle here. I want you to get to know the Primordial captive. I want to know everything he knows. You are to become his best friend."

"My lady?" Darius frowned at her words.

"I want you to go undercover. I want you to pretend to be a captive alongside him. See if you can gain his trust and find out what he knows."

"Ah, I see." Darius's frown slid into a speculative smile. "The best way to do that would be to have me hauled in and tossed into the same cell."

"Yes, my thoughts exactly. Listen, do you think your men could rough you up? Give you some bruises and such to make it real? How about a cut or two, as though you were in a fight?"

"I can get those on the training field. No need to stage injuries."

"Excellent. Then I expect you to be deposited in his tent before dark. Now, what do we know about this captive? Has he given any information?"

"The only thing we know at this point is that he is some kind of a holy man. He wears strange robes and talks to himself a lot. I am not sure he is completely sane."

Alcina considered the information. "If he is a holy man, he knows a great deal. Did Cyrus question him? Is he damaged?"

"No, my queen. It seems Cyrus chose the men he interrogated at random as far, as we can tell. I believe that he was not questioned by Cyrus."

"A strange stroke of luck," said Alcina, as she paused at the edge of the tent containing the prisoner. "One I intend to exploit to its fullest." One of Alcina's elite protectors stepped between the two legionnaires manning the entrance to the tent and swept aside the curtain. A second bodyguard preceded Alcina into the tent, followed by two additional security guards who fanned out around the fabric walls, but Darius remained outside.

A man, dressed in nothing but the skin he was born with, sat cross-legged in the middle of the room. His hands were resting on his knees, palms up and his eyes were closed. Red abrasions ran around his wrists and ankles where the hemp ropes had cut into his skin when he had been tied to the stakes driven into the dirt floor. Curly white hair flowed over his shoulders and down his back. His upper torso was covered in tattoos that started at the join between neck and collarbone and spread out over his chest and back then encircled his upper arms. He did not stir at Alcina's entrance nor did he acknowledge her presence. His chest barely moved.

The guard, who had preceded Alcina into the tent, raised a gauntleted hand and swung it at the seated Primordial priest with such force that the man was knocked sideways to sprawl on the ground. A trickle of blood bloomed across his cheek and from the split in his upper lip.

"You will acknowledge the queen when she enters a room and bow to Her Highness," the guard bellowed. "There will be no further warnings!"

The priest raised a hand to his cheek, gazing at the blood left on it as he pulled it away. He sat up slowly and then knelt, bowing from his knees to Alcina.

Alcina walked around the priest, examining the tattoos that decorated his skin. "They say you are a man of importance among the Primordials."

He lifted his head from the tent floor and risked a glance at her. "I am a servant of my people. Nothing more."

"Which clan are you?"

"I am of the Flesh Clans."

"And what is your purpose to your people?"

"I am a spiritual leader. It is our duty to serve."

"I am interested in the spirits of your people. Will you tell me of them? And your faith?"

"I would be pleased to speak to you about my people's faith."

"You would?" asked Alcina, so surprised by his words that she stopped circling, pausing between him and the guards at her back.

"Yes, Your Highness. We have much that we need to discuss."

"What is your name?"

"Hototo. I am a priest of the Flesh Clans. I was sent to help you."

Alcina folded her arms, studying the man.

"Well, Hototo, how about you wash up, put some clothes on, and join me for dinner?" Her guards' heads swiveled as though pulled by the same string to stare at her. "There is more than one way to get business done." Hototo bowed his head once again.

Alcina vanished from the tent in a swirl of flame red silk, and Darius fell in beside her as she made her way back to her tents. "You heard?"

Darius nodded silently. "Perhaps he will be cooperative. Maybe Cyrus did us a favour in torturing the other two, helping to loosen his tongue."

"Bring him to me as soon as he stops stinking like a pigsty. And, Darius, I have changed my mind. You will not be spending the night getting cozy with the prisoner," said Alcina. "I wish for you to sit in on this meeting. If all goes well, I will have a mission for you. If not, I will have a body in need of disposal."

"Yes, my queen." Darius left her in the presence of her guards and returned to the prisoner tent.

Alcina entered her quarters, her attendants curtsying low as she passed. "Bring refreshments, enough for three. I am about to entertain," she commanded. More curtsies followed, and then the servants scurried away. Alcina paused by the basin of water under her mirror and dipped in her hands. It was stone cold. "*Water!*" she screamed. *Once again, they have let my water grow cool. Someone will pay for this incompetence. They know the penalty for failure.*

She smiled with grim pleasure. Someone was going to bleed today. Oh yes, indeed.

* * *

Darius re-entered the tent and stood, arms folded, looking at the little priest. Hototo's clothing had been returned to him, and he was in the process of pulling on the pale leather-like garments. The clothing had the look of leather and fit the priest like a second skin. Darius's head whipped back, and he squinted to take a second look at the clothing, which disappeared under a cloak made of fur. It was skin, but of no animal he had ever seen on his father's farm. A shiver danced up his spine. *Human skin?* His mind danced away from the thought, not wanting to examine it too closely. The Primordial priest pulled on some soft boots of deerskin and straightened.

Thank the gods I know what that skin is! thought Darius as he studied the priest.

"I have a medicine bag that was taken from me when I arrived. May I have it back?" The old man held out his hand as though he expected to be obeyed.

"I doubt you will need it," said Darius with a smirk.

Hototo dismissed Darius's words. "Oh, I need it all right, and so does your queen. It contains the very articles I was sent to deliver into her possession."

Darius grunted and signaled over his shoulder with a snap of his fingers to the waiting guard. The man left the tent and returned a few minutes later with a satchel covered in seed beading. Some of the designs matched the tattoos on Hototo's skin.

Darius opened the bag and rummaged around inside it, looking for a weapon. Inside was a child's straw doll, a pair of them in fact, along with a couple of broken feather quills that were not useful as weapons, cloth that he took to be articles of clothing, and a pot of clear paste like beeswax. Rolling around at the bottom were several coins, the like of which Darius had never seen before, and some polished stones.

He closed the satchel and tossed it to the priest. "Let's get going. She will be waiting for us."

Hototo shuffled to the door and bent to pass through and was greeted outside by four guards who towered over his barely five-foot height. Quietly he stood, allowing a search of his person. He then followed the entrance guards (another pair closing rank behind him) across the camp to the queen's tents. At Alcina's doorway, Hototo was searched once again and then allowed to enter, followed by Darius.

Alcina was ensconced in her sedan chair, her crown perched on her head. She sipped a steaming cup of tea, recently poured by a trembling maid who attempted to blend into the tapestry hanging between two tent poles behind Alcina, close enough to respond instantly to her summons but far enough away that she hoped the queen would forget her presence. Two places had been set on a low table at her feet. They would be sitting on the floor to eat.

The Primordial stood in front of the table and, with a shove from Darius, sank to his knees.

"Now, now, Darius, show our guest the respect due a dignitary." Alcina gestured to the cushions on the floor. "Sit, relax, and eat. You must be hungry."

On the table before them was a bowl of freshly washed dates, slices of cheese and sausage, peppers, and a crunchy, edible green that grew in the shade of the boulders along the trail, and flat-trail bread baked on open grills. Pitchers of water, beading on the surface of clay with the humidity of the tent, sat next to two squat clay cups. "Come, eat. I assure you none of it is poisoned, or she" —she waved vaguely at the cowering maid behind her—"would already be dead."

Hototo did not need to be told twice and fell to the food with enthusiasm. He rolled meat and cheese and peppers in the flatbread and hungrily bit off large chunks, totally engrossed in his food. His free hand drifted to the pitcher and he poured water, gulping down the contents of a mug as his other hand popped the last of the flatbread into his mouth.

"My, my, one would think you haven't eaten anything in several days." Darius barked a laugh but did not take his eyes off the priest.

Hototo slowed down on his third meat roll and only ate half of the fourth, pausing for another drink of water and then settled back on the cushions, sighing with satisfaction.

"I thank you for your hospitality, Your Highness. Let me present you with a gift from my people." He reached into his satchel. The movements brought the guards and Darius to full attention, their hands on their swords. At the sound of steel being drawn, Hototo looked around and stilled his hand, still buried in the bag.

"I will bring it out slowly. It is a doll...just a doll," he said in reassurance. Darius gave a tense nod for him to proceed. A muscle twitched in his clenched jaw. Hototo's arm moved, drawing out his hand and bringing with it a straw doll. It was about a foot tall with short, cut straw sticking out from the top and woven through the folds that made the head of the doll. String had been tied around the neck, and halfway down the straw was split to form legs and partway up to form arms. The doll was dressed in royal purple robes, and the figure carried a stick that resembled a baton. Along the surface of the baton, small dots were placed.

"A doll? You set yourself up to be captured, endured torture, and have beggared yourself into my presence to give me a toy?" Alcina snapped her fingers, and her guards were instantly at Hototo's side and reaching down to grab his arms and haul him away from the table.

"Wait!" he held up his arms to fend off the grasping guards. Alcina held up her right hand, halting the guards.

"Speak now, and it had better be good, or your head will shortly be bouncing down the side of this sorry mountain." She glared at Hototo as he offered her the doll, which she grudgingly took from him.

"It is not a simple doll. It is a Soul Fetch."

Alcina turned it over in her hand, examining it closely. "What does it do? And why is it dressed in royal clothing?" Her hawk-like gaze pinned the priest to the spot. "If your answer pleases me, I will spare your life. I may even reward you. Now speak."

"A Soul Fetch is a soul-seeker. It is empowered with the ability to search out the soul of an enemy and trap it within the doll, enslaving them to the wishes of the possessor. With that doll"—Hototo poked one crooked finger at the straw figure—"you can control the soul of another and thereby his actions, his thoughts, and his dreams. With that, the victim is your puppet, completely within your control, regardless of where he is in the world."

Alcina's greedy gaze returned to the doll, and the ghost of a smile passed her lips as she considered his words and their implication.

"Go on," she said slowly. "I am listening. Why is this doll dressed in royal colours?"

"That is because, Your Highness, that doll is bound to the current king of Cathair. That doll will control the soul of one Cayden Tiernan, once activated. He is someone who has been a thorn in your foot, if the rumours are correct."

Alcina turned the doll over once again, examining it closely.

"How does it work? And why would you offer it to me so freely? What is your price?"

Hototo's lips peeled back into a toothless smile. "Our price is this. You will help us wipe out the Spirit Clans and their leader Marea, the High Priestess. You will help us establish rulership over those who survive, so that the true faith, the faith of the flesh, is no longer suppressed. Do this, and you can have the doll and your kingdom back. Do this and you will have a true ally to the north. Do this and you will never be challenged again." Hototo stared off into the corner of the tent, for a moment absorbed in some vision that only he could see. His face broke into a huge smile, his eyes shining with the fervour of blind devotion. "With the elimination of the Spirit Shield, we will rule supreme! Forever at one with our goddess, Artio. Refuse to do this and you will never learn the secrets of the doll. Without my help, the doll is but a doll."

Alcina's smiled a cold smile. "A tempting offer. Now show me how it works."

Hototo reached into his bag a second time and this time withdrew a doll with no clothing. "Fetch me a scrap of cloth from the servant's dress," he commanded. The guards hesitated. With a twitch of Alcina's hand, a legionnaire with a shaved head marched over to the cowering maid, snatching a fist full of skirt in one hand and drawing a sharp knife in the other. He sliced off a chunk of the rough-spun cloth of her skirt. The servant squeaked in response, cowering behind Alcina's throne-like chair, then resumed her quivering.

The soldier handed the cloth to Hototo, who wrapped it around the doll like a skirt. Next, he dug into his satchel and removed a smooth stone that glowed with a summer sky blue and tucked it inside the chest of the doll so that it disappeared under the woven strands. "May I borrow your hairpin for a moment, Your Highness?"

Alcina reached back and pulled a long bone hairpin from the back of her hair and handed it to the priest. All heads swiveled to the maid, who was now wringing her hands, eyes darting frantically around the room, looking for a way to escape.

The priest began to chant in a singsong voice that slowly rose in pitch. The stone glowed and the maid's arm blurred as an azure blue mist rose from her skin. The stone pulsed and the mist surrounding the girl throbbed as though the stone carried a heartbeat. She felt the pulsing mist and swiped at her arms, scrubbing at her skin. When this did nothing to halt the binding, she screamed and abruptly bolted for the doorway despite it being blocked by the big burly guards favoured by Alcina.

Before the maid reached the doorway, the priest stabbed the doll where the heart would be in a human. The maid shrieked and stumbled, clutching at her chest. The priest stabbed the doll again, and the maid collapsed to the ground, writhing in agony. He stabbed a third time. She cried out, her body spasming on the floor and then it stilled.

The closest guard bent over her and felt for a pulse and then straightened. "She still lives."

Alcina was transfixed by the doll. The doll was no longer straw but had transformed into a perfect replica of the girl with eyes that glowed with an inner blue light. The priest handed the doll to Alcina.

"She is now yours to command. You carry her soul in your hands. Crush that doll, and she is instantly dead. You need but command, and she will do as you ask. She cannot refuse. Total control."

Alcina's gaze travelled between the transformed doll and the straw doll in her other hand. A cold, malicious smile froze on her face.

"And there is no release from this spell?"

"There is no release short of death. Only a Primordial priest will know how to undo the enchantment."

Alcina's smile widened. Her small pearly teeth glinted in the dim light cast by the lanterns.

"I will pay your price," she hissed, as she tucked the two dolls inside pockets sewn into her skirts.

Chapter 16

Drawings in a Cave

CAYDEN BOLTED UPRIGHT IN BED, eyes wild, and stared around the room at the fading grey light of predawn. He shoved the sweaty covers off his body and swung his legs over the side of the bed, scratching at the itch on his chest caused by the clothing twisted around his torso. What was it that had awakened him? He cast a glance around his room examining his surroundings, but all was still and silent. He frowned and, standing up, strode for the door and wrenched it open.

There, sitting at his study table, sat Mordecai. He sipped his cup of tea. With a tiny clatter, he placed it back on the table and then turned a page in the tome. A toothpick twirled in his mouth, as he worked it side to side, engrossed in the words in front of him.

Cayden ran his hand through his silky hair and wandered over to Mordecai, feeling anxious and out of sorts, having just awoken. Something was bothering him, but he couldn't put his finger on it.

At his approach, Mordecai looked up from his studies and smiled. "Ah, so the king rises from his slumber. Good morning, Your Majesty!" He chuckled as Cayden made a face. While it was the proper form of address, Cayden had spent the weeks after his coronation running about the castle trying to impress upon his subjects that they needn't be bowing and scraping to him constantly and that his name was Cayden, pure and simple. Of course, none of the staff listened. If anything, his constant reminders of what not to do only spurred on the opposite.

So popular was the new king that several entrepreneurial peasants started creating trinkets to sell to the constant stream of pilgrims who now flowed into the castle to see the marvel at the return of the king. Of course, they wanted his royal patronage, and Cayden had spent some initial time blessing this amulet or adding his royal seal to that commemorative coin. The trade was so brisk that the tribunal of judges who had been set up after Alcina's hasty departure, now also had to decide how to place a value on the items Cayden had put his royal seal on. Cayden no longer gave his seal of approval for items, as the furor created by this seemingly innocuous event was way out of proportion to the good he had intended.

Mordecai spun one of those coins between his thumb and forefinger as he watched Cayden's sleepy progress across the floor.

Cayden dropped into the chair beside Mordecai, his eyes on the coins. "Were you able to find them all?"

Mordecai shook his head. "No. The judges did a good job at buying them back from the people, explaining that they would go into a museum for all to enjoy. But ten coins are still unaccounted for."

Cayden grunted. "What are you studying? That looks like the book I was going through yesterday."

"Yes, and a curious tome it is. When your mother died, I asked the tree sprites to gather all the books of magic and any books that referenced you or your sister in any way and hide them where no human could find them. They did an excellent job of it, did they not? I did not know that they had snatched this one from my private library, but it is just as well, as Alcina later stormed the place and burned it to the ground."

Mordecai flipped to the next page and then paused. "See this?" He jabbed a skinny finger halfway down the left page. Cayden leaned in and saw it was the passage he had been reading yesterday when Ziona had awakened.

"Yes, I wished to talk to you about that passage, but then Ziona woke up and I fell asleep." His voice trailed off as it suddenly hit him, what had awoken him. It was silence. The silence of a vacuum, only this vacuum was in his mind. He shot to his feet. "Ziona! Where is she?"

He spun on the spot, looking for her familiar form. He strode to the adjoining room where she sometimes slept when they had late night sessions. He grabbed both handles and flung them open. The chamber was empty, the bed linens undisturbed.

"Mordecai, where is she?" he demanded as he returned to the table. "She has left, hasn't she?"

"Yes, Cayden. Sit down."

He sank slowly back into the chair and cast out with his mind. He sensed she was on the fringe, the link stretched thin. Avery was an even slimmer thread, but the threads were similar. Ziona was travelling in the same direction he sensed Avery to be. She was headed back to the lands of the Primordials.

"Why would she leave without me? I need her. I would have gone with her! I need to join Avery too!"

"She knows your duties are here, Cayden, and she did not want you to leave your people and your responsibilities as king. She felt she was interfering and that a clean break was for the best."

"That is ridiculous and you know it, Mordecai!" he hollered. "I have fulfilled my duties here. The Well of Souls is safe and secure. You heard the spirit of my mother. I have to go to Avery. She needs me!"

"Yes, she does, but not yet. Not now." Mordecai pushed the book to the side as a knock sounded at the door and a Kingsman leaned into the room, holding the door open for the maid who had delivered Cayden's tray the previous day. She backed into the room with a fresh tray of steaming food.

"I have your breakfast, Majesty!" She curtsied, and Mordecai gestured for her to approach. Cayden ignored her. She placed the tray in front of him, removed the covers and curtsied, then left the room. The Kingsmen pulling the doors closed behind her.

Mordecai's stomach grumbled, but Cayden felt nauseous the same as the evening before. He grimaced and picked up the tea, thirsty more than anything.

"You must eat, Cayden. Here, try some of this porridge with the raisins and apples." He pushed the bowl in front of Cayden and added a heavy dollop of cream and a scoop of honey to the top. He filched the crusty roll decorating the edge of the plate and slathered some butter on it then sat back, happily munching his way through the crumbling bread.

Cayden picked up his spoon and shoveled porridge into his protesting mouth. He forced himself to swallow four mouthfuls before pushing the tray away, feeling decidedly green.

Mordecai frowned at him. "The headaches are back? And the nausea?"

"It never really left," answered Cayden.

"Maybe we should have a healer look at you." Mordecai placed his hand against Cayden's forehead.

"Ziona is my healer, and you sent her away."

"I didn't send her away. You will be joining her soon, just not right now. Your place is here, Cayden. There are things we must discuss and plans that must be made. She knows this and understands it. You are the king. Your duties lie here, whether you like it or not. Now come. It is time we added to your education." Mordecai pulled a heavy book entitled *A Comparative Study of the Gods and Goddesses of the Pre-Daimon Epoch* back across the table and began to read aloud.

"Helga, the youngest of the godlings, was perhaps (at least historically) the godling who was most in touch with the mortal world. Ancient cave drawings discovered in the Highland Spine and predating the Battle of Daimon Ford clearly depict the goddess Helga attending funerals of the mortals and assisting the grieving with the passage of the souls of the dead into her brother's care. The drawings illustrate a side to Helga that is rarely reflected in the annals of the gods. This illustration, which has been dated to the earliest epoch, displays Helga in her funeral finery carrying the body of a dying child into the blue mists of the Thunder Falls, one of the most sacred of places of the current day Primordial races. Indeed, to be carried into the falls is seen to be a direct conduit of the soul to the spiritual realm."

Cayden sighed, sliding a hand over his sweating face. He loosened four buttons on his fine red tunic. "Yes, I read that already. So, my godling sibling, Helga, is my nemesis. I figured that out yesterday. It's frustrating that I cannot remember more of my own history. Do you know why I cannot unlock it if I put my own soul into this body? Why is it that I have forgotten everything?"

Mordecai sat back and studied Cayden. Dark half circles formed crescent moons under his lashes, a sign of his exhaustion.

"I think it had to do with my magical interference, or assistance, if you will. When we had to take such desperate measures to save the pair of you, somehow the memory link with your soul was disturbed. Ordinarily, when a soul is delivered to a newborn babe, the memories associated with that prior life cease, as the person they were before no longer exists. As you saw, the memories of that prior life can linger on while they are part of the spirit pool, but it does not carry forward to the new host.

"But you and Avery are unique. Neither of you died to give up your souls, at least not in the traditional sense. I believe that the disruption is temporary, but I do not know how to restore your memories. What you proposed originally, through Aossi, had never been done before. It is magic of the gods. Something I am not.

"You will find your answers, Cayden. I am sure of it. If not you, then Avery will, but I think the knowledge is within the pair of you. You just have to unlock it."

Cayden abruptly stood up and began pacing. "Well, I am not going to sit here and wait for it to pop in my head. I will go mad, Mordecai! I cannot shut down the tug at my soul. I need to go to Avery. I will not delay much longer. The counsel is set up, the courts are working, the people are safe and happy, and the knights Ryder has recruited now guard the Well of Souls. My Kingsmen have swelled in number as the guard of old, and now their adult children have returned to service. There is no need for me to stay here." He paused by Mordecai's chair and stared him in the eye. "I must go."

It was Mordecai's turn to sigh.

"All right. We will go. I can see you are not to be dissuaded from it, but first, let's bring in your captains and plan this venture, rather than bolting out the door on whim and adrenaline. Call them in, and let's find out the lay of the land and what the scouts have to report."

Cayden smiled for the first time that morning. "Now you are talking!" He sprang to his feet and strode to the door, wrenching it open. The two Kingsmen on duty saluted. "Find me Denzik, Fabian, and Nelson. Ask them to report to me in the Shield Room in one hour." One guard peeled away from his post and tapped the shoulder of a companion as he passed him in the hall. The second Kingsman took up his spot at Cayden's door.

Cayden closed the door and pulled on a cord dangling from the ceiling. A bell chimed and a maid slipped into the room and curtsied. "Bring me water to bathe, please." She curtsied again and hurried back into the hallway and off down the corridor. Mordecai had not moved.

"Well? What are you waiting for?" Cayden strode off into his bedroom and slammed the door behind him.

Mordecai frowned, muttering words under his breath that sounded suspiciously like "stubborn" and "pig-headed" and then ran his finger down the page of the book to where he had left off and continued to read. *"Other drawings, discovered deeper within this same cave, depicted a darker, less benevolent goddess. In these drawings of the same age as the first set, Helga is depicted as standing over the bodies of a man and a woman. The symbols painted on the foreheads of these people suggest that they are flesh representations of the goddess Alfreda and her brother Caerwyn. They are depicted as mortals and a blue mist surrounds their bodies. Both historians and scholars agree, that the imagery suggests that Helga is harvesting the souls of the twins, her immortal sister and brother. Why they are depicted in a mortal form is a fine point of debate yet to be resolved."* Mordecai sighed a greater sigh than Cayden's and closed the book, pondering the meaning of the words.

Chapter 17

Remember

AVERY PACED THE NARROW CONFINES of her cell with her arms crossed over her chest, boots scraping across the cold stone surface. A weak light spilled in from the street from a window set high in the cave wall. She knew her father was next door, but she was unable wake him no matter how much she called out to him.

The guards had attempted to remove her jewellery and clothing before depositing her in the cell, but it was as though there was a forged link between her and the garb. It refused to come off regardless of how much they tugged. At first, they thought she had resisted, but after a few good slaps and pinning her to the ground with a knee in her back and lots of tugging that arched her back to painful levels, they saw the light. She could not resist, and they quickly discovered that the clothing was fused to her physically and would not come off. The same held true with the jewellery and the lone weapon that she carried. In fact, when they tried to remove it, the blade cut them despite their precautions. It was almost as if the blade had a mind of its own, fighting back against capture. Avery shivered and gingerly touched the knife, which grew hot in her hand now and seemed to hum. She sensed it was *happy*. She felt a welcoming warmth from the blade. *It almost seems alive.*

The end result of this unfortunate discovery was that triple the normal guard was placed around her cell, but she was grudgingly allowed to keep all of her acquisitions in the cell with her. What else could they do short of killing her to take it?

Marea will be thrilled to hear about this! She is probably planning my execution by morning.

Avery grew tired of her pacing and sank down on the stone bench that doubled as a bed and shivered from the dampness of the cave. Discouragement washed over her in a wave. *Some welcome this is. I did not ask to come here. Why is the magic of the temple working in this fashion? What is so important about these things?*

Curious, she shrugged out of the coat. It slid easily from her arms, and there was none of the prickling and pulling and biting of the cloak that had accompanied the tussle of a few minutes ago. *Interesting. It seems to know to whom it belongs. Now how to figure out why it's decided it's me.* She stood up and rummaged through the pockets, seeing if there was anything in them she had not noticed before. The pockets on the outside were extraordinarily deep but yielded nothing. She laid the coat open on the bench beside her. She ran her hand over the smooth, seamless interior. To her surprise, she felt a lump in the armpit stitching. She felt along the seam, and there, tucked where no one could possibly find it, was a small pocket. It looked like a spot where the stitching was missing. In the pocket was a piece of parchment. Gingerly, she pulled it out, checking over her shoulder to be certain she was not being watched.

The parchment was furled so tightly it was nearly impossible to unwind. She carefully unrolled it on the stone bench, using her knife to weigh down the one edge as she flattened it for reading. The script was in her personal handwriting. The ink was faded with time but still legible.

Avery's heart leapt into her throat and started to race. She scanned the letter but quickly became lost and had to force herself to slow down and go back to the beginning. She fetched the stub of candle sitting on a wooden tray and carried it back over to the stone bench to better illuminate the fragile parchment. A thin edge crumbled in her shaking hands as she attempted to position it better. She leaned in and began to read.

If you are reading this, then you have successfully entered the temple and found the secret closet containing the garments of the gods. If you are reading this, I have to assume you are me, for no other could enter this room. It is for the offspring of the gods only and has been set aside for time without end for our use. You are one of only four godlings who can enter the true temple safely, for it is not located in the physical mortal realm but in the celestial. No true mortal could cross its threshold and trigger its secrets. You have visited the realm of the gods.

I ramble, and time is short. I fear that with the plan we are about to instigate I may forget my heritage, so I write this note to my future self. I— that is, you—and my brother Caerwyn have, after great debate and weighing of the odds, decided to become mortals. If you are reading this, we obviously succeeded, which probably makes this letter moot, but I write it for my (our) peace of mind and as a safety precaution should something go wrong with our plan. By the time that I (you) read this letter, Helga will have had eighteen to twenty years to solidify her hold on the world. The mortals, both animal and human, who have been Caerwyn's and my charges since our father died, are in grave danger of being enslaved by Helga for all eternity.

Helga has set in play a plan to capture the Well of Souls in Cathair, which the royals of that land have long guarded through a combination of physical presence and through Caerwyn's influence. I have heard rumours of an assassination plan, but we have been unsuccessful in uncovering its details. Needless to say, to lose the physical Spirit Shield of Cathair would give Helga the opening she needs to seize the capital and take dominion over the souls of the dead awaiting their rebirth. These souls have not been condemned to her realm. My sister grows more and more greedy and jealous of our positions over the earth's inhabitants.

But for me, personally, the stakes are even higher, for the lives of the non-human population are also at risk. The great spirits of the animals are disappearing. Daily, I stroll through my beloved Faylea and the surrounding forests, and they grow quiet. The animals are disappearing, their voices silenced. But even more shocking is that their spiritual forms are also growing quiet. I (we) are their caretakers and yet, they are not coming to me to pass over. I can only conclude one thing, that they are being snatched away before death and enslaved in the underworld. Twisted to Helga's desires, it can only bode ill for the world, for they could be unleashed as powerful weapons against all mortal existence. Soon, all life within our dominion will cease to exist.

We are Spirit Shields. We maintain the River of Souls. We are the guardians of the rebirth, the reincarnation of all mortal kind. This is our fight: to free the captured souls in Helga's clutches. We can do nothing for those already twisted and turned to evil, but I cannot abide the idea that all souls are lost. I have set certain plans in place to slow Helga down, but they will not last forever. I pray that they will last just long enough.

I dare not say more in this letter, lest it fall into the wrong hands, as even in Faylea, I fear that Helga's spies are in our midst. I have been forced to abdicate my position as High Priestess amongst great discord. I believe that Marea will be the next High Priestess, yet only a godling can be a Spirit Shield. I (we) have worn many faces over epochs of time, but this time I see Helga's handiwork. Beware of the Flesh Clans, for they worship a dark spirit that can only be Helga.

I go into exile now and will travel to our brother, Caerwyn, to prepare for the transformation. There is a wizard named Mordecai, who can be trusted in all things. He is but a child now, yet he is the only one that Aossi has spoken to, other than the prince and princess whose twins will become our host bodies.

Something desperate is about to happen, and I am powerless to stop it. I can feel the storm approaching. The only one who was ever able to control Helga was our sister Artio, but she has been lost to us for a long time now. Her focus is on the stones and the experiments that she conducts with the moon. I do not believe her plans to be harmful, yet she will not hear a word against Helga.

You must bind the Primordial people together. Civil war is inevitable, and I fear what will have transpired by the time you find this letter. Understand that Helga will stop at nothing to divide all peoples. Her plans work best when humanity is fighting against one another. Divided, they are easy pickings for her minions of the underworld. Remember always, those souls she enslaves are possibly enslaved forever. Twisted over time, they could become an army impossible to defeat in the human realm. We must succeed in our mission.

As mortals, we have a chance to save this world. As mortals, we can have an influence that was not possible as godlings where our influence could not be known. But as mortals, we can take control and lead the living back to the light and into war, if it must be. We are their caretakers, their Spirit Shield.

Choose your path wisely. I say this as a reminder to myself. Although I cannot see into the future, I can see that much death and pain lie along the path before the end. Remember our bond. Remember our people. Remember our strengths. Remember that we are godlings. Remember.

The last word reverberated inside Avery's skull like a thunderous gong. For the second time that day, she found herself on the floor. The enchanted word sprung the hatch of her memories, and a closed compartment in her mind burst open like a flash of lighting in a stormy sky. The crush of eons of memory made her cry out, and she let go of the paper, which rolled back up and flashed into flame, burning instantly to a fine white powder.

She remembered...she remembered *everything*.

*   *   *

Achak leaned against the wall of the potter's studio and studied the prisoner cell building, counting the number of guards and patrols. So far three had entered the building but only two had come out, so one guard remained inside and possibly more. He would be wise to assume there were other guards within the building.

It was strange to see any guards, for the Primordials rarely imprisoned anyone. In fact, when Achak had left Faylea a few months ago, this building had been used for grain storage. The Primordials were a direct people. Punishments for crimes or infractions were dealt with immediately and publicly and then forgotten. They considered it barbaric to cage anything, including animals. It was the highest of insults to imprison a person, a severe slight that did not escape Achak's notice.

It was probable that there was only a single guard left inside, as there was but one exit from the building. The stone exterior was periodically pierced with small round windows, too small for a child to squeeze thorough. *No possibility of escape from those,* he thought as his eyes continued to study the structure. On the top of the building, grass thatching provided a waterproof roof, yet he knew the ceiling of the cells were thick-beamed timber and mud plaster. Maybe with years to work on it, one could chisel out enough wood to create an opening, assuming one was allowed a knife or other sharp tool. No, he would have to break the woman out by going through the cell door. So, the only question that remained was how to get that door open.

His eyes ran over the thatch once again, and suddenly an idea came to him. He stood up and glanced at the sun, judging the hours left until dark. He would return when it was night to implement his plan. He shoved his hands in his pockets and with stomach rumbling strolled away in search of a meal.

* * *

Cyrus pulled the hood of his robes tighter around his face as the Primordial who had recently been his prisoner walked by within spitting distance. At least he thought it was the same one. To his eyes, they all looked the same.

The woman who had come out of the temple was now being held prisoner inside the stone hut, and that interested him greatly. Regardless of who she was, she was important enough to hold in a cell. He recalled the adage from his early legion training: "The enemy of your enemy is your friend." Whether or not she was a "friend," she was certainly a form of leverage. *How can I use her? That is the question,* he thought.

"Do you have any idea who the woman is?" he whispered to his second-in-command. Fullmer grimaced painfully through the disciplinary injuries he had received after allowing the Primordial to slip away from him in the mists.

"No, Lord Cyrus. Although I have seen her before."

Cyrus's eyes narrowed at the words. "How could you have seen her before?"

"She was in that flyspeck, sheep-loving village out on the cliffs. Sanctuary-by-the-Sea I think it was called. I remember seeing her there when we rode into town."

"She comes from the same village as the usurper? Cayden Tiernan?"

"Yes, my lord, I am sure of it." Fullmer glanced around to make sure they were not being watched.

"Well, isn't that interesting. I wonder what a Primordial would be doing in Sanctuary-by-the-Sea." Cyrus rubbed a hand across his jaw, considering the possibilities.

"I believe she lived there. She was dressed like the rest of the commoners."

"Even more interesting. Now I definitely want her. Come on. I don't want to be noticed in the area." He slipped between two buildings, heading for the woods with Fullmer at his heels.

Chapter 18

Captured

CAYDEN RACED DOWN THE STAIRS, taking them two at a time. The maidservant in the hall at the base flattened herself against the wall, soapy water sloshing over the side of her mop bucket and a bemused expression on her face as she watched the young king run past her like a child in a game of tag.

Ryder's sword clanked against the railing as he launched himself over the side, rather than taking the last few steps, hoping to gain on Cayden's retreating back.

"Cayden, wait!" he bellowed, his boots pounding down the flagstone. He rounded the corner where Cayden's flapping coat had just disappeared to see the door at the far end of the gallery hallway swinging shut. Shouldering the partially closed door aside, Ryder took the next five steps in two giant leaps. Landing on the sunny gravel path leading to the stables, he crunched the remaining distance to the barn, halting just inside to allow his eyes to adjust to the dim interior.

"Cayden!" he bellowed. In response to his call, a head poked out of a stall midway down the length of the barn.

"Yes?" Cayden's head turned in his direction for a second and then disappeared back inside the stall.

"You're mad, you know that?" Ryder walked up to the stall and leaned his arms on the railing, watching as Cayden tossed a blanket onto the back of a deep-chested stallion with one white sock. "There is no way you are going to be allowed to leave alone. We are going with you."

"Fine, but you better be ready when I leave because I am not waiting for you. You will just have to catch up." Cayden tossed the saddle onto the back of the chestnut and tightened the cinch, eliciting a grunt from the horse as he tugged it tight. Cayden tugged on the girth strap once more when it exhaled.

"You won't leave without me." Ryder smirked over the stall wall. Cayden glanced up at him, and his eyes caught on an object in Ryder's hands. Ryder was holding his satchel in his beefy grip, swinging it back and forth. "I know you don't go anywhere without this."

Cayden made to snatch it from his hands, but Ryder stepped back, grinning. "I will be back in thirty minutes, and you will be right here." Ryder walked out of the barn, whistling for his knights, who materialized out of the shadows. "Thirty minutes, gentlemen, and then I expect you saddled and ready to ride!"

Thirty minutes later, the clop-clop-clop of horseshoes on cobblestone and clanking armor announced the knight's arrival. Cayden stood by his mount, impatiently twitching the reins back and forth in his hand. He peered between the stone buildings to where the knights' horses were housed, the stable located at a side gate out of the castle grounds. Spying Ryder, he barely restrained himself from running over to him. Instead, he crossed his arms and glared at him, Ryder rode up beside Cayden, refusing to meet his eyes. Cayden swung up into his saddle and said, with a low growl, "You know, Ryder, you can be a royal pain."

"Of course, Your Majesty, it is my duty." Ryder bowed low, hiding his smirk. He held out Cayden's satchel to him. Cayden took the satchel then clouted Ryder on the back of his head. Ryder's yelp followed him as he walked the big chestnut out into the courtyard and he smiled. Ryder rubbed the back of his head and, still smirking, heeled his mount to follow Cayden.

At that moment, Denzik appeared with twenty grizzled, battle-hardened Kingsmen. As soon as he saw Ryder and the newly minted knights assembled looking as though they intended to ride with them, he pulled Ryder off to the side. The two men began to argue, hands waving and pointing at both the castle and the distant mountains, each man frowning and shaking his head until finally Ryder rolled his head skyward as if praying, cracked his neck to each side and then nodded his acceptance of the instructions with a grimace.

Satisfied, they rode over to the king. "Sire, a change in plans," said Denzik. "Young Ryder here believes the knights could use more training and are reluctant to leave the castle with minimal fortification. They have volunteered to stay behind and continue their training and see to the defence of the castle in your absence."

Cayden studied Ryder's sour expression as Ryder grimaced then echoed Denzik's words. "We cannot leave the castle undefended, and Denzik and his men know the hills better than I, having fought many a campaign in those mountains. They will be of better service and protection on this venture."

Cayden nodded acceptance of the change in plan, his thoughts already drifting back to Ziona. "Where is Mordecai?" he muttered, impatiently. His words seemed to produce the wizard as Mordecai sauntered around the edge of the garden wall, leading an old mare as grey as his beard. She was painted with symbols that Cayden could only wonder at. The saddlebags bulged with large square objects. Mordecai refused to be parted from his books.

Cayden refused to show curiosity and studiously ignored them all, staring off into the distance in the direction he sensed Ziona to be. She was headed directly for Avery. Ziona was not answering his silent call, but perhaps Avery would.

Avery, can you hear me? Where are you right now? I am coming to you.

He waited a moment, and then a voice whispered in his mind: *Cayden! It's so good to hear your voice! Do not come to Faylea! They are not friendly to outsiders, and I fear your reception will not be what you expect. I am being retained by the High Priestess right now, although I do not know why…well, maybe I do…but she is no friend to us.*

Where is Father? Cayden asked through the bond.

He is here but hurt. I will take care of him. Do not fear. I have so much to talk to you about, but we need to meet face-to-face. Do you remember the path leading to the Thunder Falls? There is a wayfarer cabin there. Meet me there in five days. I will figure a way to get out of this…place.

Are you sure you do not need help escaping? Why would they detain you? What is going on?

I cannot say, Cayden. Not now. There is too much to tell. I will find a way out. They will not hold me forever. They do not dare.

OK. Be careful! There are enemies everywhere.

I know. See you in five days.

Ryder rode up beside Cayden and examined his blank expression. "Talking to Avery? Or Ziona?" Ryder had learned of the bond from Ziona during one of their discussions after the battle and had been amazed to know that a form of telepathy existed between them. His childhood friend had morphed into royalty and something more. They had all changed. "Sending her telepathic love notes?" he ribbed, chuckling. "Just imagine, you could say anything to her, and no one would know what you said unless you gave it away by blushing." The colour rose in Cayden's neck at the thought of saying anything suggestive to Ziona. The very thought heated his blood. "See? Just like that. You are turning as red as a—"

"Ryder, shut up."

Laughing, Ryder gripped Cayden's shoulder. "Be very careful, Cayden. Watch for enemies. It is difficult to tell friend from foe right now."

Cayden looked back at him and squinted against the glare of the sun. He raised his hand and rubbed at the persistent headache. Ryder noted the darkening circles under his eyes and the fine lines of strain in the creases.

"Avery. I was talking to Avery, not Ziona. She is in some sort of trouble. It follows her like a swarm of mosquitoes." Cayden's head swung back to where he thought Avery to be. "We will meet up with her in five days at the wayfarer cabin by the path to the Thunder Falls. Let's get going," he said in a louder voice. He nudged his horse into motion, and the Kingsmen fell in beside and behind him, the gates to the castle grounds opening at their approach. They clattered over the drawbridge and into the cobblestone streets of the city proper. A great cheer arose as they trotted out into the city. Ryder watched them depart then swung back toward the castle, dragging his feet to his duty.

Cayden did not look back. His concern was all ahead. Ziona had a three-day head start on him, but he would find her. *Nothing will stop me, short of death.*

* * *

Ziona crept through the bushes, silent as a hare, and froze at the snap of a twig nearby. She listened, cocking her head to one side, slowing her breathing, and lowering her heart rate. After a time, she resumed her stealthy retreat from the edge of the Flesh Clan's encampment.

Why are they so deep into this side of the Spine? she pondered as she slunk silently back to her cold camp. When she'd left Faylea with Sharisha three years ago to search for the prophesied children, she'd not believed it would take so long to find them. Much had changed since they'd left their home. Ziona had heard rumours about the unrest between the two Primordial factions, but if this was any indication of the severity of the split, it was more like a chasm.

Reaching her camp, she checked on her mount, finding him tied where she had left him, munching happily on the sparse grasses at his feet. She stroked his nose and then rummaged in the saddlebags for some dried fruit for a quick meal.

Taking a bite, she examined her options. *Should I stay and observe the camp longer, or should I push on for Faylea?* The decision weighed on her mind as she considered the problem. Knowing what the Flesh Clans were up to would be handy information, but she was not sure it outweighed her need to report to the High Priestess in Faylea and inform her order of the return of the Spirit Shield, of the return of a god, albeit in human form. She still marveled at this, that a god now walked amongst them.

And then there was Avery. Cayden would be angry with Ziona for leaving this way. He had wanted to accompany her in the search for his sister, but his place was in Cathair as the current monarch. He could not be traipsing all over the known world like some common courier.

She felt his pulse in the corner of her brain where the bond nestled, protected by blood and bone and tissue, that ethereal essence that was the blended portion of soul they shared. She had tried not to think of the bond and what it meant for them. In very un-Primordial fashion, she had hidden from the truth. In very un-seekerly form, she had avoided confronting the issue. Instead, she'd taken this excuse to flee, to put distance between them and the overwhelming desire to move past a sisterly relationship to something more...adult. As she pondered the situation, the bond surged, and she physically took a step back from the wash of emotion that flooded her. She stepped back again and abruptly halted as she bumped up against something solid…and warm.

Instinct drove her to her knees, and at the same time she tucked and rolled, pulling knives from her boots. Springing to her feet, she froze in mid-throw.

She was completely encircled by Flesh Clan Primordials, each clutching the wickedly curved knives they favoured. Ziona spun on the spot, trying to keep all eight men and woman in sight at once. She half turned, and froze. The pair closest to her horse parted for a tall, straight-backed woman in a burgundy wool dress that hugged her curves. A cape of black silk, trimmed with ermine, topped the dress, the hood framing an austere face, set in a frown. She held up a regal hand, freezing the combatants.

"Well, well, what do we have here?"

The circle closed on Ziona, tightening the ring, narrowing her focus until the only person she could see was the woman standing directly in front of her. Rough hands relieved her of her knives and others grabbed her arms, winding a rope around her wrists and binding them in place in front of her body. She did not resist. It seemed ill-advised, given the fact she was alone and surrounded. The jute ropes bit into her wrists as the man tying them gave a sharp tug.

"A Primordial woman, all alone in the woods. Spirit Clan too. Now tell me, what would possess such a person to wander unattended through heathen-infested forests?" The Flesh Clan warriors surrounding her shifted their feet at her words. "A foolish one, I think." She drew the finely woven riding gloves off her hands, revealing a large signet ring on the middle finger of her right hand that flashed in the fading light.

Ziona's heart sank at the sight.

Alcina walked slowly around her, examining her. "You would be the Primordial woman I have heard so much about." Ziona's eyes widened in surprise. "Oh yes, I know of you. You are the seeker who left to look for the usurper, and it seems you found him before I did." She laid a lacquered finger up against Ziona's cheek, turning her face to look directly into her eyes. "You have inconvenienced me greatly." Her eyes glinted with malice as Ziona's locked onto hers. "And finally, I have someone who will answer for this crime. You do know that the penalty for treason is death?" She cocked her head to one side, waiting to see what affect her words would have on the woman before her.

"Although you are Primordial, your treacherous actions occurred within my realm. You will be tried as a traitor and hung, as is the penalty for such crimes. *Take her away!*" She dragged her lacquered nail against Ziona's cheek as she flung it away, and the nail cut deeply, leaving a stinging, red tear that welled with beads of blood.

The rope tying Ziona's hands was jerked tight, and she stumbled to keep her balance as the holder of the rope mounted up on his horse. Heeling it into motion, he trotted off toward the camp. Ziona was forced to run or be dragged all the way to wherever they were going. Twice she stumbled in the darkening woods and was roughly pulled to her feet then made to run again. Maintaining her balance was difficult given the uneven terrain, but still she ran as she had been trained to do.

The last rays of the setting sun disappeared just as they arrived at the camp, cooking fires guiding the way to the Flesh Clan encampment just as full dark descended. Eyes followed her as she was dragged and shoved along the pathways to the center of the camp.

They came to a halt in front of a tent clad in skins and reserved for prisoners. The guards pulled aside the flap and shoved Ziona inside. She tripped over the threshold and fell to the floor, catching herself on her bound hands just before her face struck the ground. When she raised her head, a familiar face greeted her.

"Hello, Ziona. Welcome to the combined legion and Flesh Clan camp. Being as you are Primordial, you must already know that they eat their prisoners here." Darius's pitiless eyes were as cold as Helga's dark hearth.

Ziona straightened to her knees, her eyes impaling him with hatred. "Traitor!" she spat. "Cayden trusted you! I trusted you! I hope you are fed to the Charun someday. You are not fit to die a hero's death in battle." Darius snarled. He could not prevent the memory of the Charun, the shadow-formed monsters that had attacked Cayden's escort six months ago, from flashing into his mind. The grizzly aftermath of their rampage through the legion was not easily forgotten. Darius shivered involuntarily. Then, angry that she had witnessed his fear, he back-handed Ziona, with a vicious clout that sent her toppling onto her side. This time she smacked her head on the ground, hard. Darius bent down and pulled her upright by her hair, bending her neck painfully.

"Alcina is the queen, and you are nothing but a dirty Primordial. If you wish to retain those teeth for another couple days, I suggest you shut your mouth." He shoved her back to the ground and retied her bonds so that her hands now stretched behind her back and fastened them to her bound feet. He then ran the length of rope through an iron loop welded to a stake in the ground. Satisfied she was secure, Darius stood up, gazing down at her prone form. "Maybe I will get a chance to enjoy your charming company before you are executed." His gaze wandered across her body, leering at her feminine curves. "I'd keep a civil tongue, or I will cut it out in advance of your hanging."

He left the tent without a backward glance.

Ziona shivered on the cold floor, flexing her fingers to encourage some circulation into her cramping fingers. She closed her eyes, consciously closing off the connection with Cayden, placing a mental wall between them. She did not want him to feel her fear or her pain. She did not want him coming after her. It was her own foolish lack of attention that had gotten her into this, and she would have to figure a way out on her own. *I will not become bait for a trap for him. I will end my own life before being used in that way. My duty is to protect Cayden, now and always.*

Chapter 19

Descent into Hell

ARTIO MATCHED HELGA'S STRIDE, her damp footsteps flashing to steam as the heat of the stone floor evaporated the moisture on contact. Helga led her along a twisting path, lit by glowing fissures in the stone that made their shadows dance wildly on the slick walls as they passed.

A low moan whispered around them, then faded away. Artio's head swiveled in the direction of the sound, and she sniffed the air. It smelled of sulphur and ashes, acrid in her nostrils. The sound of running water echoed oddly around the chamber, the noise coming from the deep cracks and crevices in the rock. Some glowed red and some glowed blue, but the sulphur smell predominated. She rubbed at her nose then refocused on her sister.

"Why do you persist with using that foul odour? Don't tell me you are still pretending that this place is roasting the remains of people?"

Helga chuckled as she reached up and pushed back the hood of her cape. "It amuses me. I push the smell out the exhaust ventricles, and the smell of roasting flesh keeps the mortals from coming too close. It feeds their superstitions and discourages the curious from investigating too closely. Of course, a few well-timed disappearances never hurt. This mountain is cursed. Did you not know? *Tsk, tsk.* You really should have tried harder to escape your starry prison."

Artio glared at her.

"Tea. I think a nice cup of tea and some of those tasty salmon sandwiches you always favoured are in order. Yes, tea on the promenade. Come."

Helga took a fork to the right, and the path pitched down into the center of the mountain. Five minutes of walking brought them to the end of the tunnel, which opened abruptly into a cavern flooded with sunlight. At first it appeared that there were multiple suns, but upon closer inspection, the suns were revealed to be parabolic mirrors suspended around the curvature of the opening to the sky.

The cavern was immense, and a riot of tropical colour assaulted Artio's eyes from every direction. Pink roses climbed the rocky walls, and purple, red, and yellow hibiscuses grew in clumps along the pathways. Date palms heavy with fruit flashed with hyacinth macaws, jumping from cluster to cluster to gorge on the bounty. Their red and green cousins soared around the cavern, alighting on nests wriggling with fledglings. Lovebirds whistled and chirped, and canaries sang joyously from the shrubbery as they passed.

Artio sniffed again, and this time smelled the heady scent of jasmine and honey orchids and the earthy smells of growing things. The air was heavy with mixed perfumes, so strong they made Artio's senses swim. Helga smiled and gestured for Artio to precede her into the hidden paradise. The path twisted here and there, a meandering route that emptied onto a springy moss floor. A river passed through the center of the cavern. Bright blue, it glowed as though lit from below. Fog floated just above the surface.

Helga led Artio to a wooden table set with tea for two, tucked against the stone wall and giving an unimpeded view of the cavern.

"How do you like my garden? It has been millennia in the making, acquiring the seeds and soils and eggs of unhatched birds. They have no natural predators here, so they live long lives in their volcanic home." She picked up the pot of tea and poured two cups from the bone china pot into large mugs. "Honey? But, of course, you want honey!" She dropped a dollop of honey into one cup and stirred it with spoon before passing it over to Artio.

Artio picked up the cup and took a drink. It was as good a tea as she had ever tasted. The smell of the salmon sandwiches made her stomach rumble.

"Sandwich?" Helga passed a plate of sandwiches but did not take one herself. She sat back and studied Artio as she wolfed down several, smacking her lips in satisfaction.

Artio wiped a sleeve across her lips, dislodging a few crumbs. "Still not able to taste food?" she sneered, eyeing the lone sandwich remaining on the tray.

"No, nor can I smell the flowers in my garden. Sometimes, I think I can. I feel it tickling the edge of my memory. What I wouldn't give to smell flowers or taste the tea. I remember I didn't like honey, but I cannot remember what honey tastes like." She sighed and put her tea down. "You did not come here to talk of tea and my gardens. What do you want, Artio?"

Artio leaned back in her chair and considered her sister.

"First, I want to know what happened, millennia ago, when I was locked away in the stars. And secondly, I want to know where to find the twins...to kill them." Her fierce eyes flashed yellow for a moment, the bear rising to the surface. "And thirdly, I want to know why you did nothing to rescue me. Answer all three well, and I might let you live. Answer poorly and your garden will shortly be absent an owner."

Helga threw back her head and laughed. Her blatant display of unconcern did not fool Artio. The sibling godlings all knew it was possible to die as she had. It was not possible for a mortal to kill a godling—the feat was beyond a mere mortal's capabilities—but another godling or one of the gods themselves could accomplish the task. *The twins killed me, and I will have my revenge! Helga will not stand in my way.*

"You were always one to bite first and later wonder if the prey might have told you something useful," said Helga, holding up her hands to hold Artio back. "I will answer your questions. Yes, I will! But first you must answer some of mine. What do you remember of your banishment?"

Artio frowned, thick brows drawing together in concentration. Her nose wrinkled, while she sifted through the memories that were slowly returning to her.

"It was a cold, clear night. We were experimenting with the moon, trying to harness the latent power of its orbit and bind it to the stones. With the moon's power and the healing set up in the medicine wheel, we believed we had found the key to lengthening the normal lifespan. We—well, I—wished to prolong my time with the mortals or one particular mortal. How they fascinated us both! Especially the man named Genii. So tall and so dark! Do you remember him?" Artio stood up and began to pace, suddenly annoyed with the tea-time setting, and prowled around the enclosure, restless. Startled birds squawked into flight. "Genii was special, unique amongst humans. Handsome, broad-shouldered, and brooding, I think his dark features set him apart. He could have been descended from the gods. Could have been, but wasn't. The resident bad boy!" She barked a laugh. "He was always getting into trouble in any town he passed through. I remember him being quite the ladies' man. I adored him. He had two friends who were always with him." She frowned, dragging the names from her memory. "I think the blond one was named Julio, and I can't remember what the weedy one was called. Do you remember them?" Artio glanced over her shoulder at Helga and caught a fleeting look of smugness fade into pinched concern.

Artio frowned, wondering if she had imagined the flashed expression. Helga's face was studious, as though she was hanging on her every word. Artio stopped pacing and planted her feet, crossing her arms. She would not give Helga further opportunity for evasion.

Helga picked up her cup of tea and took another sip, her cup rattling on the saucer as she returned it to the plate. "I remember him. Genii," Helga stated flatly. "He was indeed quite beautiful to look at, but in the end a mere mortal, unworthy of our attention."

"What happened to him?" Artio demanded. "We were trying to harness the power of the moon. We were trying to bring them a sampling of immortality, elongating the span of their lives. Something we have done a thousand times before with lesser creatures."

Helga tilted her head to one side, clearly considering how much she should divulge to this fierce version of her sister. The bear combination had certainly given her a backbone she had not possessed before. "You have changed since you merged with the bear cub. I do not remember you being this aggressive in the past. In fact, you acted more like the

Thunders than your bear heritage. Clearly, your time amongst the stars has aged you." She dismissed the thought with a flick of her hand. "What does it matter? It is ancient history at this point. They were mortals and are long gone from this earth."

Artio didn't hold back the snarl that curled past her lips. She growled and her nostrils flared as her red-hot temper coursed just below the surface of her skin, heating her blood. Her fingers curled into claws as she fought to stay in control. She would have answers or Helga would live to regret it.

Helga stood up and walked around her sister, examining the changes. "If you must know, they all died when the link to the moon's energy snapped and rebounded. They were incinerated on the spot, but you would not know this, for the rebounding knocked you senseless. The twins were responsible for the feedback problem as they disrupted the transfer that you had initiated. Then, believing you to be dead, they sent you to the very moon you were harnessing to be kept in limbo forever."

"Just like that? That's everything? You stood around and did nothing? *We were in this together! These were our boys!*" The last words came out in a roar and more brightly coloured birds took to the air and began to circle high above the trees, a swirling mass reminiscent of bats leaving a cave to feed. Artio grabbed the front of Helga's robes in clenched fists, jerking her to a halt and immediately, darkness fell in the cave and black-hooded beings melted out of the crevices of rock, their forms wreathed in black mist that made it impossible to look directly on them, as though they were not quite in this world. Artio saw them coming and released Helga, who stepped back and straightened her robes, her eyes flashing with anger. The swirling figures crept closer, and Helga halted them with a raised hand.

"Touch me again," she snarled, "and my Charun will kill you. You are here because I allow it, but my pity only extends so far. Touch me again and it is you who will die, dear Sister, and this time it will be forever."

"Tell me where to find the twins, and I will leave you, never to return," Artio hissed.

Helga picked a pen from the tea table and scribbled instructions on a piece of parchment impressed with flower petals. She rolled the parchment and handed it to Artio but did not let go. "You will find them in two different locales, but both are headed this way. You see, I have something they want very badly. They were foolish enough to become human, thinking they would be better equipped to stop the wars occurring amongst their beloved humans, but they are fools. Humanity belongs to me." Releasing the parchment, she sat back down and poured more tea. "I have one last gift for you." She reached under her robes and withdrew a heavy gold chain. Hanging from the chain was a slender bone carved with shapes. She drew it over her head and handed it to Artio. "A piece of your love to carry with you."

Artio reached forward and took the chain, her eyes locked on the slender knuckle bone. She stroked it with one finger and then slipped it over her head.

"My pets will escort you out. Do not return here, Sister. If you do, you will die."

Helga did not notice the person who watched her intently from the shadows. Tall and dark, his eyes followed her retreating figure, unseen. His brow pinched into a brooding gaze. He did not look away from her vanishing form until she had faded from view, then silently retreated back into the obsidian recesses of the underground fortress.

*   *   *

Helga watched her sister's retreat until she disappeared from view over the rim of the bowl and then stood, clapping her hands together. Tea, cups, and table instantly vanished to be replaced by a waist-high stone basin perched on stone columns carved with faces. Liquid silver danced across the sheen of refracted sunlight reflecting off the mirror's surface. Helga peered into the basin, and the face reflected back at her morphed into a serpent, eyes narrowed and tongue flickering, testing the air. Annoyed, Helga swiped the surface, and another image appeared: that of Avery astride a fine golden mare with creamy mane and tail, following a Primordial man through the deep jungle undergrowth. Helga smiled as she watched them push their way through the thick plant life.

It would be fun to watch everything unfold from the basin and even more fun to watch the meeting in person. She was bound to the cavern, however, and could not step out into the real world, a backlash of her and Artio's experiment all those years ago. Artio had been imprisoned in the stars, and Helga in her underground fortress. Try as she might, she could not leave the confines of her gilded prison. She was every bit as trapped as the birds swirling about the bowl. That did not mean she could not touch the world, however.

Abruptly, Helga marched back through a cleft in the rock and down the tunnel, lit by glowing rocks along the ceiling. The tunnel sloped downward, ever downward, into the bowels of the earth. Heat began to rise in waves, and Helga sighed with satisfaction. The caves were cold and damp, but once she reached this depth, they warmed considerably and became moist and humid. She fed this air into the bowl, which accounted for the growth of the plants.

Side tunnels branched off periodically, maze-like, with nothing to distinguish them from the branches before them. After about ten minutes of walking, the floor of the tunnel flattened and widened, and a fresh humid breeze laden with the scent of the sea wafted past her nose. She waved a hand in front of her face to chase away the offensive odour and then raised the front of her tunic to cover her nose.

She paused to glance over the side of the short stone wall that opened into the cavern. A set of steep steps had been chiseled into its side, winding down and around, clinging to the wall like moss to a tree trunk. The staircase emptied onto the floor of the cavern, a thin oblong sliced in half by a ribbon of quartz from which a bluish glow emanated. The cavern stretched as far as the eye could see, and skeletal figures with elongated pickaxes chipped away at the surface, their glowing faces covered in sweat and grime.

Men, women, and children—all were bound in groups of three and four, chains shackling their feet to the person next to them. The slaves of Primordial birth lined the ribbon, pecking away at their section of rock while Charun floated above them, keen eyes watching the slaves and the lack of fervour for their work. Incentives to work harder were plentiful. Whips whistled through the air and snapped, eliciting a cry from the unfortunate Primordial on the receiving end. Here and there, Primordial children scurried, dragging large leather bags of water to the slaves. The Charun carried away the weak with no more regard than for a beast of burden whose usefulness had ended. Most of the slaves who collapsed in the heat, died.

At one end of the cavern, the surface of the quartz had cracked and a faint wailing hiss slipped from the fissure. Helga strode down the steps on the wall with an assurance of long practice and over to the crack, her black robes fluttering in her wake. The workers fell away as she approached, kneeling on the heated floor and pressing their foreheads to the stone, trembling. She knew that they would not gaze on her.

Helga knelt down at the edge and ran her hand over the crack. The wails increased, and the blue swirled faster and faster under her hand. She closed her eyes, the fingers of her right splayed over the whirling mass, ruby lips murmuring soft words. Her hand closed into a tight fist and she pulled. Up through the crack, blue mist melted around her hand and stretched like thin taffy, following her hand as she stood.

With a piercing wail, it snapped away from the crack and the swirling soul bound itself to her hand. Eyes still closed, she chanted and waved her left hand over the closed fist. The celestial blue darkened to indigo then to midnight until all colour fled. The blackness remaining expanded, and a shape twisted in the air, expanding beyond Helga's five-foot nine-inch frame. Helga's eyes snapped open, her eyes dancing with a remnant of blue flame that faded back to black. Her lips curled in satisfaction. "Welcome, my pet. Take your place amongst your kin. Serve me well." The newly born Charun drifted over to join the others swarming around the edges of the cavern.

Chapter 20

Jail Break

AVERY WOKE TO THE SOUND OF…well, she wasn't sure. At first, her dreams had interpreted the tapping as a woodpecker in a tree, high up in her beloved woods out back of the farmhouse in Sanctuary-by-the-Sea. But as she fully woke, her eyes told her the truth and the dream faded.

"*Tat-tat-tat…tat-tat-tat*" went the sound, and her eyes travelled up toward the ceiling of her cell. Small bits of dust and dirt puffed from the ceiling with the impact, creating a fine dusty rain of debris. She walked underneath the spot and, shading her eyes, peered up at it. A hole roughly the size of two fingers appeared immediately above her, large enough to slide an object through. With a pinging sound, the object dropped to the floor. She bent over and picked it up. It was a key.

Startled, Avery looked up in time to see a scrolled parchment drop through the same hole. It dropped to the floor, and then the hole disappeared, covered over once again.

She picked up the scroll and walked back to her bed to read by the flickering light of the candle once more, the key disappearing into an inner pocket of her tunic.

The message was short and sweet. *Second hour. Be ready.*

She glanced at the height of the full moon out her cell window and the angle of the patterns on the floor. She judged it to be first hour or a little after. She got up and crept over to her cell door and placed her ear against the thick wood, listening for sound on the other side, but all was silent.

If someone was going to break her out, why give her a key? What did this mean? And who had it come from? Nervous about the implications, she began to pace. *Is this someone aiding me or setting me up to be killed?* Either way, she had little choice in the matter. She had to get out and she wanted to be ready. She packed her few meager belongings and checked the placement of the weapons she could not be relieved of. Everything was in order. She strode back to the door and bent down to check the keyhole. She saw the dim light of a flickering lantern, and then something blocked the light. A guard paced back and forth just on the other side of the door. She considered putting the key in the door, just to be ready, but if the guard decided to put his in to check on her, then he would discover she had a key.

She glanced at the window once again, judging the time.

Suddenly, an explosion rocked the ground. With a roar and a brilliant flash of light, a powerful fist of wind blew bits of stone and thatch through the bars of the window. Avery was knocked to the ground by the concussive air and threw up her arm to shield herself from the heat of the flames that roared just outside of her window, licking at the wall. Avery smelled the thatch on the roof as it began to smolder. She pushed herself to her feet, rubbing her bruised shoulder. She could either wait to see if someone came for her or use the key clutched in her hand. She chose the latter and leapt for the door, jamming the key in the hole and twisting it viciously. She prayed silently that the guard had not slid the wooden bars in place. The lock scraped and then clicked, and she wrenched on the handle, dragging the door open. She nearly tripped over her guard. The guard she had seen pass the keyhole earlier lay in a pool of his own blood. His throat had been cut, and blood seeped and puddled on the stone floor.

Sickened, Avery ran across the hall to her father's unguarded cell and pushed on the door in a panicked attempt to reach him. She was surprised when the door swung open easily, and she rushed inside. His cell was empty. Avery spun on the spot, double-checking the shadows, but her father was not there. Avery dashed outside and then quickly searched the other cells. All were equally vacant.

Alarmed and close to panic, Avery coughed and threw a sleeve up in front of her nose. The smoke was thickening and the air turning toxic. She had to get out. She heard distant screams and shouting and knew that a crowd was gathering at the entrance to the cells, attracted by the flames. She dashed toward the back, racing down the stone steps that led to the rear of the building. At the end of the hallway was an old wooden door that opened into a broom closet. As she ran up to it, the door swung open and a man stood in the opening. Avery reached for the knife tucked in her boot and then paused when she saw who it was. Elder Hania stood in the doorway, a finger pressed to his lips warning her to be silent. He motioned for Avery to follow him, then turned and lifted a trap door in the floor. He disappeared into the opening without a second thought, dropping down into the dirt cellar and pulling the trap door closed over her. Darkness descended, but the air cleared immediately. Avery sucked in a great lungful of the blessedly clean air. Without a word, Elder Hania strode off down a low passage, lantern bobbing in his wake, leading the way. Avery followed without hesitation. Smoke curled around the edges of the trap door, drifting down toward where she crouched in the passageway.

They ran, hunched over like a pair of armadillos, keeping to the shadows lest they come across another Primordial. The tunnel was short and emptied into a cellar of a building across the road from the cells. The owner was a weaver and seller of carpets, as was evidenced by the bales of yarns and large vats of dyes and shelves stocked with shuttles and weavers' needles of varying sizes. They slowed and slunk through the bales until they found a staircase, then cautiously crept up the steps into the silent shop.

As Elder Hania stepped out from the top of the steps, a youngish voice said in an urgent whisper. "Did you get her out?" Elder Hania stepped aside to reveal Avery standing in the opening at the top of the staircase.

"Thank the gods! Come, we must go." The hooded figure tossed a large cloak at Avery which she caught and pulled on over her own clothing, drawing the hood up around her face. It was deeply cowled and hid her from inquiring glances, but nothing could dim the glow of her eyes. The men ran off toward the rear of the shop, and she followed, slipping out the door behind them and pushing up against the wall to gain her bearings. She was in a narrow alleyway behind the store, rather well-lit for the time of night due to the glow from the flames. She glanced over her shoulder to where a bright glow lit the sky. As they ran down the alley, Avery glimpsed crazed shadows cast by running villagers backlit by the glow of the flaming thatch. Men and women ran back and forth, tossing buckets of water on the inferno, which hissed angrily and flared anew as they ran back for more water.

Avery pulled her hood tighter to her face and glided from shadow to shadow, following the tall elderly Primordial through twisting alleys until they reached a barn on the edge of Faylea. Elder Hania paused under the overhang, checking to see if they were being followed, and then pulled open the door and pulled her inside.

She found herself facing ten Primordial men and women of varying ages. They were all dressed in white tunics embroidered with images of birds and beasts climbing the hem of their garments and twisting around sleeves. Avery recognized many of the images from her journey in the temple, flaming phoenixes and rainbow-hued thunderbirds, werewolves and sabre-toothed tigers, unicorns and Pegasuses, creatures of myth and legend. Except she now knew they were real. Very real.

Elder Hania eased the hood from his hoary head. "Welcome, Ancient One." He bowed over his hands.

Avery's voice, still winded from their run through the dark streets of Faylea, came out harsher than she expected. "Did you kill the guard to get me out? Why would you do that? You could have just knocked him out. Why did you kill him?"

Elder Hania bowed once more over his hands. "An unfortunate accident, Mother. I intended to do exactly that, but he struggled and the knife slipped. I regret the loss of life. All life is sacred. He would likely have died in the fire in any event, as you saw, lighting a thatched roof is usually fatal for all inside the building. It burns so quickly and so hot, most do not make it out alive."

Avery glared at him, but the elder turned her attention to the others in the barn. "I would like to introduce you all to Avery Tiernan, who comes to us from the village of Sanctuary-by-the-Sea. Avery, may I present to you the elders of Faylea, the Spirit Temple guardians."

The elders bowed, hands pressed together. Avery returned the ritual greeting, straightening just as the door of the barn opened again, admitting the young man who had aided her escape. Elder Hania caught sight of the man and smiled. "And this is my son, Achak."

Achak stepped forward into the light and Avery's eyes widened. The light glinted against straight black hair that framed a rugged face with high cheekbones and hollow planes. A straight pointed nose ended at full lips, which were curved in a smile of greeting. Avery met his eyes and a thrill passed through her. Keen intelligence was reflected in his eyes. Broad of shoulder, his cloak was slightly parted and displayed a tattoo of a phoenix in full transformation, a flaming herald of rebirth. His shirt was tucked into soft deerskin pants that hugged his body as though made especially for him, and likely were, now that she came to think of it.

Avery jerked her head in greeting, not trusting her voice to speak, and his smile widened at her reaction.

"We wish to welcome you to Faylea properly," yelled a woman from the midst of the crowd. Avery refocused on her, glad for the interruption, as she blushed slightly. "Marea believes we are traitors for supporting you in your quest, but we know that the spirits have spoken to you. It is obvious that you are the chosen one." Heads nodded, and Avery sensed from their words that they did believe.

Avery smiled in return and lowered her hood. The collective eyes of the elders widened, as did Achak's, taking in her fully tattooed form and glowing eyes.

"May we approach?" the woman asked. "I am called Sarea, and I am a guardian of the equestrian spirits."

Avery nodded. As the woman approached, the other guardians quickly followed. Avery shrugged out of her coat so that her bare arms were revealed. The guardians crowded around Avery, exclaiming at the number of tattoos that covered every inch of skin.

"You are blessed beyond women, Avery Tiernan," said Sarea. "We, who are guardians, are blessed with one or maybe two tattoos when we go through the trials. I even heard of one elder who had three. But this"—she gestured to the landscape of tattoos marching up Avery's arms—"is unheard of. Legend tells us that the only people so blessed were of the gods." Murmurs arose at her words and heads nodded.

Avery shrugged back into her coat and then raised her eyes to meet the gazes of the elders.

"You are correct, Sarea. I am of the gods. I am born as Avery Tiernan, but my true name is Alfreda."

The elders gasped at her statement, their eyes widening in shock and sudden fear. As one, they dropped to their knees, palms pressed together, heads bowed.

"Forgive us, Mother! We did not know!" They bowed, pressing their foreheads to the straw-covered wooden floor.

Avery, embarrassed, quickly reached down and pulled Sarea to her feet. She did the same with Hania, helping the elderly man back to a standing position.

"Please! Stand! I have only just learned this myself. My memory had been lost all these years since my human birth. I am still absorbing the truth. Believe me, it is as much of a shock to me as it is to you. Please stand."

They regained their feet but refused to meet her eyes.

"I need your help," said Avery, "if you are willing to give it. I and my brother Cayden willingly chose to be reborn as hybrids. You see, our mother was the Primordial princess Gwen, and our father, the human prince Alexander. Hunted since the beginning, we nearly died before we were born. It was only with the aid of a dear friend that we survived. Our souls transferred to these bodies just before birth.

"We have returned to stop the war that has been brewing between the nations, Primordial and human, but even more there is a blackness that is creeping across the land. I can feel it. Can't you? It spreads like a plague, the sickness creeping into the minds of men and turning them against one another. Jealousy and greed follow in its wake. Tell me, why are the Primordial people fighting each other? Why is there this divide between the Flesh and Spirit Clans? How did this come about?"

"It started with a legend, as all things do." Elder Hania gestured for them all to sit, and they sank onto bales of hay set in a rough circle, others sinking to the floor, all eyes focused on Avery and Elder Hania. "Legends are the children of myths, and myths are birthed from partially forgotten truths. And truth, well, that is tainted to reflect the perspective of the storyteller. Nevertheless, I will aim to be truthful in this retelling.

"This legend involves two warriors, who both loved the same woman. One warrior was of the Spirit Clan and one was of the Flesh

Clan. In order to win her hand, she set them both a task to perform, to prove their love and show her how much they desired her. She set them a task that was known only in myth and legend. She set them the task of capturing a ray of moonbeam, for love born under the moon is eternal.

"The Spirit Clan warrior, being a spiritual fellow, desired her love not just for this life but for life eternal. So, by the light of the moon, he captured the spirit of a dying caterpillar, knowing that the spirit of the butterfly is beautiful and free, as was his love for her. The moonbeam immortalized the transforming caterpillar. He placed the spirit butterfly in an enchanted cage and carried it proudly back to the maiden.

"The Flesh Clan warrior, being a man of the flesh, desired her to see him as the mighty warrior he was and that he could provide for her for all time. He captured a wild, pure-white mare, and, by the light of the moon, sacrificed the poor beast. As he bled the mare, the spirit of the horse arose, a shimmering soul of a unicorn at rebirth. He captured the spirit of the unicorn in an enchanted cage and brought the spirit to the maiden at the appointed time.

"By a full moon of the vernal equinox, the warriors presented their gifts. The maiden burst into tears and wept for the poor souls trapped within their gilded cages, for she had not believed the warriors were capable of such cruelty. She broke open the cages and absorbed both spirits into her own soul and vanished. You can find her still, wandering the world by the light of a full moon, searching for her true love.

"This legend explains the split of the clans. The Spirit Clans believe that the way to approach the maiden, the Mother Goddess herself, is through spiritual communion. The Flesh Clans believe that physical sacrifice is the path to pleasing the Mother Goddess. The division of beliefs between the clans has ever been a sharp divide, but of recent date, a dark presence moves through the Flesh Clans. They have rejected the preordained right of the Spirit Clan to choose the High Priestess. The Flesh Clans no longer abide by the rules and precepts of the temple. They have resurrected the old ways and now practice open sacrifice and the harvesting of souls as a way to appease the gods. *To appease you.*"

His dark-eyed gaze pinned Avery. "Perhaps now that you have returned to us, you can tell us who is correct."

Avery stared at her fingers, which she had twisted together during the course of the story. She looked up, meeting eleven pair of eyes, all staring at her keenly.

"I cannot tell you what you want to hear, that the Spirit Clan is correct. The truth falls somewhere in between, but I do not believe you are yet ready to hear it. What I do need to know, is where I might find the ancient scrolls? Sharisha mentioned them many times, and I believe there are truths to be found in them that may shed some light on how to bring peace to the Primordial peoples."

Sarea spoke up. "They are hidden in a secret cave deep in the Highland Spine. We have a map that will take you there." Sarea rose from a bale of straw. "Now, you must go—quickly! You are sure to be pursued. I can hear them hunting for you right now." The cries of the searchers were indeed coming ever closer to their location with every passing moment.

"We cannot show you the way. We would be missed immediately," said Elder Hania, "but Achak can accompany you and provide you with protection. We have prepared provisions." Another elder separated from the group and strode over to a pair of saddled and waiting horses, tucking a packet of parchment into Avery's saddle bag. Elder Hania stood and gave Avery his hand, pulling her to her feet. Achak sauntered over to Avery, smiling down at her.

"The sooner we depart, the better." Achak motioned to the rear of the barn where the two horses stamped their hooves, impatiently. Avery nodded and followed him, eager to mount up and to put distance between her and Faylea.

"Ride with speed, Mother. And may the gods protect you!" The barn doors flung open. Putting heel to side, Avery and Achak leapt out into the night, chased by the flickering light of the burning jail.

Chapter 21

Ring of Shade

AVERY AND ACHAK RODE HARD down the narrow trail, under the bright light of a nearly full moon, afraid to stop for the night. Safety lay in creating distance between the searchers and themselves, so they kept a steady pace. They also rode silently, neither one venturing into conversation as the stillness of the night carried sound like a trumpet blast. The pounding hooves of their horses rang in their ears, inordinately loud despite the soft earth of the path.

They climbed higher into the evergreen threshold, leaving behind the tropical paradise of the Spirit Clans. The trail at this altitude was covered in soft pine needles, and other than the occasional click of a hoof on a loose stone, their passage was virtually silent, even to Primordial ears. Non-human eyes followed their passage, the nocturnal scurryings of the forest dwellers the only sounds to reach their ears.

At first, Avery was content to let Achak lead, but toward dawn, she heeled her mount and rode up beside him. "Where are you taking me? What is our destination?" The words came out in a croak. She lifted her waterskin to her lips, taking a drink to ease the dryness in her throat, then let it drop back beside her saddle. Achak glanced over at her, his perfect teeth glowing in the waning moonlight as he smiled.

"We are going to a crystal cave, known only to the priests of the Primordial people. It is a holy place, a depository of sacred things."

"The Shakra Caves?" she asked, the memory floating to the surface of her mind.

"Yes!" Achak jerked with surprise. "You know of them? I thought you were new to Faylea." His eyes travelled over her face and head, examining her tattoos.

"It is true. I have never been to Faylea before, at least not as a human." Achak frowned at her and opened his mouth to ask a question, but Avery cut him off. "And not recently either, as a Primordial. It was a very long time ago. We can chat more about my history once we are out of danger. How much longer till we reach the caves?"

Achak's head cocked to one side as he examined the night sky. "Dawn will be here in about an hour. It is three more hours to the caves. When the trees end, we will have to leave the horses as we will be climbing to reach them."

They rode along in silence for a while and then Avery asked, "Why is Marea so hostile to my presence? I thought that I was expected. Sharisha originally told me that she and Ziona had been sent out to find me. I felt the truth of her words when she spoke them."

Achak shifted in his saddle. "Marea was appointed High Priestess after the assassination of the previous High Priestess. Her predecessor was a Flesh Clan guardian and much beloved by the Flesh Clans who had not had a High Priestess chosen in hundreds of years. They had great hopes that their High Priestess could bring back some of the old ways and give them an equal voice amongst the Primordial people. For as long as anyone can remember, a Spirit Clan High Priestess had been chosen. They proposed that Princess Gwen be sent to the humans to negotiate for peace along the border with the humans. When she was captured and not returned despite repeated requests, the Flesh Clans blamed the Spirit Clans. They saw treachery in the negotiations. They accused the Spirit Clan liaisons of not trying as hard as they would have, had the High Priestess been born of the Spirit Clans. When the assassination of the Primordial princess and High Priestess occurred, the tribes fractured and began to fight amongst themselves. They blamed each other for the assassination. You see, she was born of the Flesh Clans, and on her death the Flesh Clans took it as proof of the treachery of the Spirit Clans, in not guaranteeing her safety. The Spirit Clans, on the other hand, were angry that they were set up in such a fashion and outraged at the accusations. The assassin was never revealed. Her body was not returned to her family. There were rumours that she was to be married to a human prince. But they were only rumours."

It was Avery's turn to frown, digesting the information. "So Marea…she volunteered? How are they normally chosen?"

"It's something like that but not quite. This time, the Flesh Clans were not consulted. They were not invited to present another candidate. They were shut out entirely from the process. You can imagine their reaction when they were shunted aside. Marea was a young priestess who had surprising access to the temple when for many years the doors had remained frozen and inaccessible. No one understands exactly how the temple chooses. But she was the only one who could get past the front doors. There was really no other choice. A High Priestess must be able to enter the temple to contact the gods."

"So, the infighting between the Primordials is a result of the choice of High Priestess?"

"In part. That was the triggering event, I think, but things had been brewing for a long time due to their ideologies clashing." His eyes slid to look at her out of the corner of his eye. "But now that you are here, you can fix things. I saw you enter the temple. *You were gone for days!* Only a chosen one could have done that. Marea is jealous as she has held the power for the last twenty years and has been very vocal about her chosen status. Then suddenly you show up and without so much as a by your leave you march in and occupy the temple."

"Then why search for me? Why send seekers to find us? She would have been better served to leave us lost."

"Well, from what my father has told me, it is precisely because of the prophesies that she wanted you found. I think she intended to control you, use you as puppet to enhance her own power and position. Sharisha has been her right hand ever since she rose to High Priestess. It is not a coincidence that she was the one to find you, I think." Achak twisted to check their back trail, examining the trees. "We are entering the Ring of Shade."

Avery peered around at the trees. The straight-backed trunks of the lower valley were now bent and twisted, as though a large hand had pressed down, squashing them towards the earth ages ago. Yet even in their twisted form, they towered above her, a curly leafed labyrinth of shade and shadow. An owl hooted. From the corner of her eye, Avery saw an ethereal form pass between trunks.

She reined in her mount, curious but somehow unafraid. The woods were calm, and a peace rested on the forest unlike any other place she had passed through. Achak, realizing she no longer followed, halted.

"This place is ancient," Avery whispered, breathing deeply. She felt the body of the woods and the bones of the forest, the spirit of the trees, wise and all-knowing. She also felt the spirits that dwelt in the woods. "Can you feel it?"

Achak nodded and slid off his horse, walking back to her. "I can feel my Spirit Guide. He is near. Would you like to meet him?"

"Very much." Avery dismounted also, and Achak took her hand to lead her off the trail following a path known only to him. He pushed through some waist-high ferns, the early morning dew dampening his coat and slapping wetly against Avery's shorter frame, leaving her dripping from neck to knees. Her ears caught the sound of a brook bubbling over rocks, and she licked her lips, suddenly thirsty. The ferns petered out, and the stream came into view, cascading over rocks in a meandering path. Avery knelt by the water and scooped it up in her cupped palms, bringing the cool liquid to her lips, and drank deeply. As she lowered her empty hands, she noticed Achak standing, eyes closed but lips moving silently. As he mouthed his words, a red glow from the region of his heart pulsed to life and then travelled down his extended arm until it swirled around his curled fist. The suspended flaming glow brightened, and then from the night sky appeared a flaming phoenix, spiraling out of the moon to alight on his outstretched arm. Avery rose from the stream and approached the bird, which flickered with fire but did not burn. Achak nodded his head in introduction.

"My Spirit Guide, Pyrrhos."

Avery heard Pyrrhos's thoughts although his beak did not move. *Greetings, Mother. I have heard whispers of your presence here in the shade of the mountain.*

And I have felt your presence and that of your companions, Avery thought in greeting. *Why do the others still hide? Bring them forth so we can become reacquainted.*

Achak tilted his head, aware that a nonverbal exchange was occurring.

Faint rustling met their ears as the shadows solidified into creatures of every description. Legendary creatures. Achak gasped and gazed around him in wonder.

A werewolf, tall and tawny parted the ferns and knelt to drink, eyes reflecting in the moonlight. A great mane of grey flowed from muzzle to chest and down its forearms, tapering to muscular thighs and calves, which ended in paws with curved grey claws. It straightened upright like a human, towering over them, fixing his gaze on Avery. The werewolf spoke aloud, the human speech partially swallowed in growling tones. "Greetings, Mother. I have met your brother."

Avery's eyes widened in surprise and then crinkled with joy. Achak started at the human-like voice issuing from the creature, and then his mouth dropped open when he realized he understood the werewolf.

"You saw Cayden? Where? Is he well?" Avery touched his arm and stared up into his furry face. "Tell me. Where is he?"

"He is well, Mother. Can you not sense him? He travels this way. My she-alpha shadows his human companions."

Avery nodded, knowing it was truth.

Avery greeted the other creatures emerging from the shadows. Fae folk peeked out from around rocks and roots of trees, male and female, wings a whirl of emerald and ruby and their motion a tinkling song. A kelpie poked its head out of a deep pool, amethyst mane and ears flicking her direction. As she climbed out of the pool, her body shifted into a human form to greet Avery. Her skin cast a pearl reflection on the surface of the pool.

"Greetings, Mother. We are glad of your return. The woods grow silent. Our kin are disappearing. A great shadow moves through the forest, and any who fall under it are not seen again. We hide continuously for this shadow moves in both the day and the night. It is never seen directly. There is no warning, no sense of where it comes from, but..." She gestured to the mountain, wreathed in clouds, just visible above the trees. A continuous cloud of vapour billowed as though a volcano slumbered beneath the rocky tip. "I believe the shadows are from the mountain." The pixies nodded, chiming their agreement.

At that moment, the ferns parted and a familiar form entered the glade. The pristine white unicorn picked her way over the rocks, her horned head bobbing, but it wasn't the horned head that caught Avery's attention but the figure seated on her back. A small child sat astride the unicorn, her rainbow-ribboned skirt fluttering in an imaginary breeze and a large orchid nestled in her tight blond curls and tucked behind one ear.

"Aossi!" cried Avery. She ran over and plucked her off the unicorn's back, swinging Aossi round and round till they were both dizzy. They collapsed, giggling.

A bemused smile tugged the corners of Achak's mouth as he watched their childish display.

Avery sat up and Aossi stood, their heights about equal, and they hugged.

"It has been too long, Mother. It is so good to see you again, although you are much changed from your days as Alfreda." Aossi grinned, deep dimples creasing her cheeks. Surrendering to an impish impulse, she tweaked Avery's nose. "Welcome home!"

"It's been too long. I am still sorting all my memories, but it is wonderful to be home, to remember everything. What news do you bring?"

Aossi's smile faded and an uncharacteristic frown settled on her cherubic face.

"Dark news, I'm afraid. Time grows short. Helga extends her powers further into the world, and it is she who is behind the shadows that have been stealing the living." She waved her hand toward the waiting magical creatures. "They are correct. The shadow looms, and they are taken without warning. Neither the souls of the living nor the dead are safe. Cayden has done his part, but now you must do yours."

"You have seen Cayden? How is he? Where did you see him?"

"He was well when last I saw him. I dropped in on him to enjoy the music of his flutes. His ability is truly magical." Aossi grinned, thinking herself clever at her own joke. "He has secured the Well of Souls in Cathair, but that is only one outlet, as you know. Helga moves to capture the souls of the dead awaiting rebirth and enslave them to make them her own, a part of her dominion. If she can take control of the souls awaiting rebirth, it will spell the doom of humanity and Primordial kind. She hunts the good, those souls worthy of a rebirth, worthy of another chance at a mortal life. She strives to enslave *all* mortal existence. I fear her plan is nearly complete."

"Can you see what is happening, Aossi? Where is she going to strike?" Avery tried to keep the note of pleading out of her voice. "You maintain the veil. What do you see? What do you feel?" Avery shifted onto her knees in front of Aossi and caught a glimpse of worry in her normally gleeful face.

Aossi sighed. "I cannot see unless she touches the veil directly. But holes are appearing, and the threads are weakening. It's like moth's larvae are chewing at the weave, but the hole doesn't appear until later when it's laundered. But eventually, the holes appear, and when they do there is no predicting what comes through the holes. She is planning something." Aossi placed her hands on Avery's shoulders, and she gathered Achak in with her glance. "You must go to the Crystal Cave and recover the box hidden there. The cave is protected by magic that you should be able to defeat, but be warned, Helga is also watching the cave. She will have spies, or worse, waiting for you to approach it." She reached into her pocket. Picking up Avery's hand, she pressed a small crystal bottle with a cork into her palm, curling her fingers around it.

"This potion will hide you from view should you need it. There is only one dose, and the effects will wear off within five minutes, but that may be just enough if the situation is dire."

Aossi turned to Achak, who knelt in front of Aossi with his head bowed. She placed her hands on his head and murmured, "You are now appointed as Avery's guardian. You are her protector. This is a grave charge. Swear to me, on your belief in death and rebirth that you will guard her life as your own."

Achak swore his oath. When Aossi's hands lifted, he looked up. "You have magic at your command. Use it in her service. Your phoenix will add to your strength."

Aossi stepped back, and her impish smile returned. "This will be a *great* game! Play well, and you might just save the world." With a skip and a jump, she sprang onto the unicorn's back. "Farewell and good luck, Mother." Aossi and the unicorn left, their images blurring and fading within three steps.

Avery stood up, brushing leaves from her knees. She walked over to Achak. Taking his hand in hers, she led the way out of the glade and to their waiting horses.

Chapter 22

Sleepwalker

CAYDEN WOKE WITH A POUNDING HEADACHE. His rest had been disturbed and troubled, filled with dreams he could never recall upon waking but that still left him sweaty and shaking. His muscles were stiff, locked up tighter than a saddle girth and he only managed to relax them after a few minutes of stretching in the tent. None of it touched the pain of his headache. He grimaced and pulled on his clothes, stamping into his boots and then belting on his sword before flinging his cloak over his shoulders.

The dawn was cold and crisp as an apple but already warming as the sun crested the horizon. Restless, he stepped out, intent on a walk around the camp. Four guards dropped in behind him before he could take two strides. He ignored them. He was getting good at that. He had no place in mind to go other than he wanted to stretch out the remaining tightness in his thighs and hips before spending the day confined to a saddle once again.

He had walked about a quarter of the distance around the perimeter of the camp when his head throbbed with pain so intense that it felt as though a white-hot iron was thrust into his temple. He cried out, clapping his hands to the sides of his head and fell to the ground writhing, screaming at the top of his lungs. His guard rushed up, hollering for help and tried to restrain him, but Cayden jerked out of their grip in a spasm of agony. His eyes rolled back so that only the whites could be seen. His screaming went on and on, and suddenly Mordecai was there. The guards parted, allowing him to kneel beside Cayden. Mordecai took Cayden's head in both of his hands and gripped it tightly, chanting in a singsong but commanding voice. Cayden arched his back, and drool dribbled out of the corner of his mouth. Mordecai did not let go. Gradually, Cayden's twisting slowed and his body stilled. With a final sharp command, Cayden sagged, body limp and still on the ground.

Mordecai took one hand away and retrieved a polished stone from his pocket and placed it on Cayden's forehead. Still chanting, he drew a line with both hands from temple to stone, repeating the motion three times to establish the link. He stopped chanting and then removed the rock. Cayden's eyes popped open, confusion evident on his face. He turned his head to see the crowd of Kingsmen bending over him and tried to lift himself. Mordecai helped him to sit up. Cayden grimaced and placed a hand on the swelling lump on the back of his head. It came away red, slick with blood. Cayden said nothing but motioned for Mordecai to let him up. Two Kingsmen stepped forward and helped Cayden to his feet. A Kingsman reached into his pocket and handed him a fold of cloth, which he took gratefully, pressing it to the abrasion on his scalp.

"Thank you," Cayden said. The Kingsman nodded and stepped back. *So much for loosening my muscles,* Cayden thought. *I think I know why I did not get any rest last night.*

He hobbled away, Mordecai at his side. "What happened?" Cayden asked. The headaches were increasing in frequency and strength.

"Another attack. I was able to repel it. It is a powerful magic. Cayden, I have been doing some research."

Cayden rolled his eyes. "When are you not doing research? Never mind. What is it you wanted to tell me?" he said, rubbing at his temple. The headache was always present.

Mordecai shook his head and grabbed his arm to stop him from walking away. He lowered his voice. "Listen to me. This is serious!" he hissed. "I believe that it is a form of Primordial magic being used against you! I think someone has created a Soul Fetch."

He snorted. "A Soul Fetch? I have never heard of such a thing. Besides, I have had these headaches ever since I moved into the castle. I think it is more likely that someone has been trying to poison me."

It was Mordecai's turn to frown, then he raised his hands and delved Cayden's body with a quick spell designed to determine the health of an individual. His brows drew together when he detected poison in his body.

"It would appear that your instincts are correct. I do detect a small quantity poison, although it is fading now. As it is weakening, that would confirm your theory that the source of the poison is at the castle. However it does not explain the headaches that are occurring now."

"What is a Soul Fetch?" Cayden asked, his eyes clouded with worry and the residual pain of the attack.

"It is an ancient magic held by the High Priests of the Flesh Clans. I think someone is trying to build a link to you and the link is getting stronger." Mordecai paced off ten steps, feet kicking the hem of his robes, hands clasped behind his back as he thought. "The possessor of the doll is trying to take control of you and I fear they may be able to do it. I am researching ways to block it, but until I find a way, all I can do is assist you when an attack comes. For that I need to be close."

"I don't believe it," snorted Cayden. "I have some headaches, a residual of the poison in my system. That is all. It's probably stress." Mordecai shook his head, negating Cayden's theory. "So what if I have been feeling sick. Everyone has times of illness. Besides, I have never even heard of a Soul Fetch."

"All the signs are there, Cayden. Soul Fetches are extremely rare. Think. The headaches started up just after the recall of the coins. Remember how you could not locate them all?"

Cayden laughed. "Coins? You want to blame the coins? There were not enough missing to bribe a guard."

"The coins are not a bribe. They are a connection to you, a solid connection. A Soul Fetch needs something personal, something important to the victim, in order to bind them. Not only do they bear your likeness, but you imbued them with your will, by making them the objects of such an intense search. It is precisely the type of magic that a Soul Fetch utilizes." Mordecai paused in front of Cayden, knowing his next words would not be received well. "I do not think it wise for you to sleep unattended any longer."

"What? I am not having the entire camp standing in my tent when I am trying to sleep!" As Cayden's voice rose in anger, the guards behind him dropped back a pace. When a king and a wizard argued, it was never good to be close by.

"Well, what do you suggest, Cayden? I could sleep in the same tent with you, and then I would be there to assist you immediately."

"And listen to your snoring all night long? And those spooky eyes that never close? It won't matter if I am attacked. I won't fall asleep with you there." Cayden rubbed his temple, grateful that the headache had lessened with Mordecai's assistance and annoyed at feeling grateful at the same time.

Mordecai sighed with frustration. "Cayden, this is for your own good. Someone wants you desperately, and we do not need to form a long list before we arrive at the most likely culprit. Alcina must be in possession of the doll. She will know you are near. This is why I counseled you to stay in the castle to remain safely away from her machinations."

"It would not have mattered if I was here or in the castle, she would still have attacked me."

"True, but there, it would have been easier to care for you."

He is treating me like an invalid, like I am sick or diseased. Cayden's heart hardened despite his gratitude. He would not be controlled by Mordecai, or anyone else for that matter. He knew that Avery needed him. He felt the pull of her soul. He had to reach her and Ziona. Somehow, that bond was muted, fuzzy as though it had been tossed under a heavy cover of blankets, muffling the connection.

Mordecai sighed and put out an arm, stopping Cayden. "If you will not allow anyone within your chambers, then I insist you take this." He reached inside his robes and pulled out a simple stone and placed it in Cayden's upturned palm. Cayden examined it, turning it over in his hand. It was exactly what it appeared to be, a smooth stone embedded with clear crystal, covered in dirt as though Mordecai had just plucked it from a river bed.

Cayden looked up, puzzled, and in a flat tone said, "You want me to have a rock."

"Yes, I do."

"Did anyone ever tell you that you are a bit strange?"

Mordecai chuckled. "Oh yes, I have been told and by stranger men than you."

"Do you mind me asking why you want me to have a stone?"

"Ask away." His eyes twinkled, enjoying the game.

"So I can remember you always?" Cayden's tone dripped sarcasm.

"Yes! Yes! Very good!" Mordecai clapped his hands together, gleefully.

Cayden rubbed a hand across his forehead as it gave a painful throb. "So I can remember you? I do not see any engraving."

"It's not a party favour. It is a memory stone."

"A memory stone," Cayden said in a flat voice.

"Yes, a memory stone. This is how it works. Before you go to sleep at night, tuck it under your pillow. The stone will remember everything in your head right up until you fall asleep. In the morning when you wake, put it back in your pocket. You will pick right back up where you left off the night before.

"So…what happens if I forget to put the stone in my pocket?" Nervous about the answer, he shied away from Mordecai's gaze.

Bleak clouds drifted across his eyes. "Then…you will be lost."

Not reassuring, Mordecai! Lovely…just lovely. Now I am supposed to trust everything to a bloody stone?

* * *

Cayden tossed and turned and his blankets twisted around his sweat-soaked body.

Cayden, come to me. Rescue me.

Cayden mumbled, his head thrashing on his pillow

Cayden, rescue me. Rescue me.

Cayden sat bolt upright on his cot. His eyes, glazed and unseeing, were wider than a full moon. The memory stone tumbled from his fingers to the floor of the tent, forgotten.

He rose with the jerky motions of a puppet and pulled on clothes and then, taking up his sword, he slit the back of the tent. With the silent but sure tread of a sleepwalker, he disappeared into the night.

* * *

Cayden struggled to wake. Vaguely, he knew that something was wrong. The dream would not end. It was as if he were peering at the world through a spyglass, everything distorted and blurred around the edges. The tents of the camp faded away and trees overtook the narrowed view. He floated through a hazy but amazingly pain-free world. That, in itself, was a vast improvement from the last week. *Maybe now I can get some real sleep…if only I'd stop dreaming. Or maybe I am asleep and this is part of the dream?* He reached out to the horse that swam into focus in front of him. It felt real enough under his hands.

An undeniable force clamped down on his mind, steely and commanding. "Get on the horse."

Obediently, he put his foot in a stirrup and swung onto the horse. It started off, and the swaying of the beast pulled him. He fell into a deep sleep, rocking gently in the saddle.

*   *   *

Cayden woke with a start. The forest of his dream had vanished. In its place, striped canvas walls filled his vision. He was kneeling on a plush carpeted floor on which sat the legs of an ornate chair. The chair was not empty. Groggily, he lifted his head to see Alcina, dressed in a low-cut green gown that clung to her curves, seated in a throne-like chair. Cayden blinked and shook his head to clear it, trying to gain control of his senses, but it was like trying to grab the shifting sand of an hourglass. Thought and memory trickled through his fingers until Alcina spoke.

"Look who we have here. The mighty king of Cathair." She stood up and walked around him in a circle, twitching the drag of her hem out of the way of her pearled boots. "How I have waited for this moment. You have done well, my pet." She stroked his hair, trailing her fingers through it as she passed behind him. "You have come as called, as I commanded."

Cayden's low ebb of panic bubbled ever higher, struggling to free him, but he could not take command of it to make it his own. It shifted away and drowned, leaving him groggy and semiconscious once again.

"I will enjoy controlling you, I think." She completed her circuit and sat back in her chair once more. "Before I kill you, I am going to use you to regain my throne and take control of this miserable world. Before I kill you, you will restore me to my rightful place. I will squeeze your mind and your soul, until you beg for release. The torture of your mind will be delicious! In your lucid moments you will remember what you have done and weep for it. The first place to start is with these pathetic Primordials. You, my pet, will be the key to their failure and to their surrender."

The words registered in Cayden's brain, but somehow, he could not muster the will to care.

Alcina reached over and picked up a doll that resembled Cayden in form. A crude approximation of his clothing dressed the straw. A pin was jabbed into the temple. "See this? I am now your master. When I locate the other doll, I will also control your sister. Soon you will be my playthings, and those you love will never see it coming. Not one of your Kingsmen would lift a finger to harm you, and it will be your undoing." The fingers of her left hand tapped on the arm of her chair, head tilted to study Cayden. She bent over and grasped his chin in her hand, tilting his face up. His eyes flickered with the wild element of a trapped animal. With the other hand, she twisted the pin and Cayden's eyes widened and crazed with pain. He gasped, a scream ripping from his hoarse throat. His hands gripped the sides of his head, and he toppled sideways on the lush carpet, tearing his head from her grasp.

"You will obey my every order without hesitation, my pet. You can't imagine the torture I can inflict on you by this lovely doll now that I have control of your mind." She released the pressure of the pin, and Cayden squinted through watering eyes, trying to bring the swimming doll into focus.

"For your first task, I'd like you to meet an old friend. I promise you will enjoy it," she purred.

Chapter 23

Deepest Desires

ZIONA SAT UP, rubbing the itching abrasions on her wrists from the fibrous ropes. The thin blanket they had left for her slid to her lap as the heavy wooden door of her makeshift cell was flung wide open with a crash. There was no light in the decrepit stone hut, nor was there a source of heat. She shivered with cold, blinking at the sudden glare of light from a lantern held aloft, and her eyes fell on a man stepping across the threshold. Tall and broad-shouldered, his sky blue cloak was flung back to reveal a royal purple tunic was matched with tan pants, tucked into tall suede boots. His face was hidden by shadows as he paused while her two guards pulled the door tight and locked it from the outside.

He raised the hand holding the lantern higher, the light pushing back the dark and illuminating his face. Even without the light, Ziona knew who this was. Cayden stepped toward her. As his face became fully revealed, she saw that his brow was pinched with pain, deep furrows of strain puckering his skin. He swallowed heavily, Adam's apple bobbling. A trickle of sweat rolled down the side of his face from a forehead beaded with moisture. Her momentary spike of joy at seeing him flushed away, replaced by a feeling of dread. He was in pain. Great pain.

He appeared sick, but from what, Ziona couldn't tell.

Cayden, what is wrong? She spoke through their link, only to find that the link was damaged. She could sense him there, but it felt as though a solid brick wall had formed between them. She sensed cracks in the emotional mortar, allowing occasional glimpses of the man she knew, but always the wall repelled her attempts to breech it. She could sense him struggling to find a way around the wall and reach out to her but to no avail.

Suddenly, he jerked into motion as though someone else controlled his steps. He hung the lantern on the peg on the stone wall then removed his purple cloak and hung it beside the lantern on a second peg. He shivered as the cool of the cave touched his fevered brow.

Ziona stood up and walked over to him, placing a hand on his chest. *Cayden, can you hear me? Come on, Cayden, fight it! Speak to me! Use my strength through the bond. I am here. Reach for me.*

Cayden shuddered at her touch, and she felt the burning heat of his body against her hand. Ziona's eyes caught his fevered gaze and recoiled at the wild look about them, as though he was teetering on the edge of madness. His crazed eyes frightened her, and she nearly backed away, but then she remembered how he had saved her and that he did love her. They were bonded mind, spirit, and soul.

Whatever comes of this, I trust him. I swore that my life was his to do with as he chose. Ziona took a deep, shuddering breath to slow her racing heart, then reached out and enclosed one of Cayden's hands in hers. Gathering his wild eyes with her warm, welcoming ones, she spoke to him aloud in a soft voice. "Cayden, you know that I trust you. Do not be afraid. I am not afraid. I am yours, remember?"

Cayden's green eyes flickered with the memory, and just for a second, the madness receded. He gasped, "Alcina! She...she is controlling me...by a doll! I cannot fight it for long. Ziona! I don't think I can stop her from doing what she wants with me. I cannot get past the doll." He grimaced with pain and cried out, clutching at his back and stumbling, falling to his knees at the stab of pain that pierced his back. "She is taking control again, Ziona, bond with me, quickly!" Ziona grabbed his hands, and they merged their minds before the wall closed again. The madness returned to his eyes, but the core of him, the gentle man that Ziona had come to care for so deeply, remained.

Cayden stood back up and jerked Ziona into his arms, his mouth coming down on hers in a crushing kiss that forced her lips back from her teeth. She did not resist but instead wrapped her arms around his neck and melted into his hold.

His tongue darted into her mouth, the kiss thorough, long, and sweet. He pulled apart and then scooped her up into his arms and carried her back to her cot. He placed her on the bed and then began to remove his clothing with jerky, halting movements as though he still fought the control of the Soul Fetch.

Do not resist, Cayden. This is not a bad thing, Ziona whispered to his mind. She held up her hand to him. "Come to me."

Naked and shuddering with relief, he followed her down onto the bed. In a corner of Cayden's mind, the part that realized what he was about to do, he was ashamed. Not for the act of loving Ziona. Never that! But that he was being forced to make love to her in this fashion. He had dreamed of this privately, of being with Ziona, but not in this way. He was revolted that he could not fight back and that a part of him didn't want to. Guilt raged in him as he pulled her shirt off and slid her small clothes from her body. His eyes widened as his eyes slid over Ziona's perfect body, and he groaned aloud as he struggled to resist Alcina's command. She was the most beautiful thing he had ever seen. Suddenly he had no desire to resist Alcina's manipulation, as it was perfectly aligned with his own desires. Pleasure raged in him, and the combination became a different type of agony. A tear he did not know he'd shed, rolled down his cheek as he kissed her.

Ziona wiped the errant tear away and kissed the corner of his eye. She trailed a hand up his strong arm, the muscles rigid with tension, and then let it wander over his bare chest. Cayden shuddered violently. Ziona's last coherent thought was if she was to die in the morning, there was surely no better way to go.

*   *   *

Alcina looked up as Darius re-entered her tent and bowed deeply. "Well?" she barked, ignoring him in favour of adding an extra dollop of honey to her tea.

"He has been placed in the Primordial's cell. We have doubled the guard on the tent door as commanded." Curiosity flared in his gaze, but then his face blanked. Alcina smiled knowingly. She knew he was dying to know what she had planned.

"You are wondering why I put the two of them together, rather than letting you have your way with the seeker wench? Perhaps you resent it?" She picked up her cup of tea and studied him over the rim, eyes taking in his lithe form, the breadth of his shoulders, his narrowed hips. She took a sip then placed the cup down on the small spindle-legged table beside her chair.

Darius stood, hands clasped behind his back, freckle-faced and red-haired, a slight sunburn brushing his cheeks. He strove not to fidget under the queen's intense gaze, but he felt a blush creeping up out of the collar of his uniform despite his tight control.

Alcina's smile widened as she witnessed his embarrassment. "Perhaps I have better uses for your talents." Darius kept his eyes fastened on a point beyond her chair up and over to the left.

Alcina stretched, observing the way his eyes unconsciously followed the arch of her body and the way the tightening of her dress outlined her breasts. She stood and walked around him, trailing a finger across his chest and up over his bulging bicep and then along his back as she slowly inspected him, like a prime cut of beef in a butcher's shop. Darius gulped and shivered slightly when her finger trailed up over the exposed nape of his neck where the blush betrayed his desire.

Alcina laughed at the shivering shudder that wracked his body. "Yes, I can find better ways to test your talents. Let Cayden rut with the Primordial wench. He will despise himself, for his honour will not allow him to seek simple pleasures in the arms of a woman. And as for the Primordial, she is nothing more than an object on which to test my control over him. Pleasure can also be torture. A sweet kind of torture, but it is still torture for those who it is inflicted on. She will hate him, and it will crush his will. He still fights the Soul Fetch, and I will have his soul fully in my grasp before I unleash him on his people. Now, I tire of politics. Come entertain your queen." She tugged on Darius's hand and led him back to the secluded room at the back of her tent. He did not resist.

Chapter 24

Genii

HE WATCHED HER CLIMB the stone pathway to the entrance to Helga's lair, careful to remain hidden in the shadows, even though he knew there was no way to hide. The dark of the cave was as daylight to the dead. For those like him, the undead, well, it was perpetual twilight wherever he went. Yet, he longed to rush after Artio, to grab her hand like in days of old; to hold her and kiss her like he once had. Occasionally, a flash of poignant memory would surface, usually prompted by an emotional trigger. Those very human longings were still a part of him, part of the memory of who he once was, who he had been before the change, before the betrayal of the moon.

He could not disobey his mistress though, for she had bonded him body and soul. He could not run after Artio. His mistress had forbidden it. He vaguely remembered the desire of his mortal days, the longing to be with this godling yet he was held by another, her sister. He'd managed to cage away a small section of his mind and of his heart, and when he was truly alone, he would take it out and examine it, turning it over and over. The pull was still there, deep down.

He watched her vanish over the lip, and he twitched, his body actually taking a step in her direction before the impulse abandoned him, submerged under his mistress's command.

He felt a presence, and then Helga materialized beside him with a purr. "Doesn't she look fantastic? Why, my sister is lovelier as a bear goddess than she was as a human hybrid." Helga drifted around in front of him. Reaching up, she pushed back his dark hood to reveal his still classically handsome features, unmarked by time.

Genii remained silent, accustomed to the leading questions, the digs in an attempt to get a rise out of him, to make him respond. Helga had tested him from day one, and initially he had resented the questions. How could his mistress doubt his loyalty or his devotion? In the early days, he could think of nothing else but how to please her, how to win her favour. There had been nothing he wouldn't have done, including dragging the body of his former love out of the circle of the sacred stones and staking it out for the vultures to pick clean. There had been no one to compare with Helga's magnificence or with her beauty.

Eventually, he had come to see that she was driven by fear, a fear that he would no longer love her, that he would somehow walk away from her love. Absurd as it was, he knew she still harboured these thoughts and so she once again tested his loyalty, and he once again gave her the answers he had learned by rote.

"She is nothing compared to your beauty, my love. She was never anything but a lover of humans, too weak and paltry to be a goddess. Yours is the only face I wish to see. You are my moon, my universe." He reached down and took Helga's face in his hands and kissed her, deeply. Helga wrapped her arms around his neck and pulled him to the ground with her.

"Time to reinforce the reasons I command your loyalty, and pleasure is so much more effective than pain." She nipped at his earlobe, biting down until a moan rose in his throat. "Come, forget the outside world." And for a time, he did.

* * *

Genii took the right fork, and the path began to ascend, twisting this way and that before eventually widening, spilling out into a cavern dimly lit by twitching flames flickering on the eddies of fresh air drifting by. Genii felt a refreshing breeze stroke his cheek, cooling his blood and bringing sanity and self-awareness to the surface of his mind. He paused for a moment and pressed his fevered cheek against the moist stone wall, then drew a deep steadying breath.

When the insanity took over, he lost all sense of himself. His fractured memories were commandeered by Helga's will and drowned before they had a chance to float to the top. He came here, to this special cave, as the distance from her lair weakened her hold. Sometimes he'd surface enough to grab a gasp of air he did not need and regain a fraction of his lost soul.

Well, not his soul—*he was undead, after all*—but a fraction of his consciousness as a human. Flashes of distant memories teased his mind, and snippets of images rushed along the long disused pathways. The urge would occasionally overtake him. When it did, he climbed the final passage that emptied out into the light of the outside world. But his steps always faltered at the last moment. The light was blinding and he was unwilling to test what it might mean to be exposed to it. Yet he longed to try. Artio was out there. For some reason, that was important to him. Gut-wrenchingly deep, the truth of that bubbled inside of him, although he could not say why.

Genii pushed off the wall and strode down the long passageway, firming his resolve. A circle of light shining on the far wall showed the exit to the light of day. He walked to the circle, careful to keep out of the direct rays reflected on the stone floor. The brightness made his eyes water, or at least they would have watered, had there been any moisture to form tears. He blinked but his eyes could not process the light. He looked away and instead stared at the distorted reflection shimmering on the water-slicked rock wall.

A wriggling reflection of trees just outside the shadowed opening zigzagged up the wall, impossibly green and brown and alive. He ran his hand over the image and suddenly a memory of striding under trees—real trees—floated to the surface, and a voice, tinkling on the breeze, laughing.

"Genii! Isn't it a glorious day? Look at how the sun makes the seeds sparkle in the air! Dance!" she commanded, giggling as she spun on the spot, dislodging more seed pods that burst with the force of a mini-explosion, tossing more winged seeds into the air until she twirled in a feathery maelstrom. Genii laughed out loud, both in his memory and for real. The sound was odd in the dark cave, his voice rusty from disuse.

Unbidden, her name rose to his lips. "Artio, my love," he rumbled. He clutched his chest, fingers curling into his shirt at the sharp spike of sensation where his stilled heart lay. Pain lanced through him with the acute throb of longing and despair.

* * *

Artio stood at the base of the falls and recalled the tornado. The mists parted and the swirling mass of water collapsed into the rocky pool. The falls resumed their normal coursing, tumbling into the basin and splashing over rapids as they roared away, destined to join the meandering River Erinn. Artio plucked a leaf and tossed it into the waters and watched it bob and spin, thinking over her encounter with Helga. She had thought to find an ally, not an enemy. She had thought that Helga would champion alongside her, but something was off. Artio looked back at the dark mountain fortress, and a crease formed between her brows. She strolled along the bank and gazed at the rock, willing answers from its stony face, but it remained silent—silent as the grave. She stared at it for several long minutes, arms folded across her chest. With a growl, she opened the furled note and read the words scrawled on the paper.

You will find Alfreda riding toward the Crystal Caves, formed when the moon collapsed. She rides with a mortal you should find interesting. Caerwyn is a guest of my puppet, Alcina, and it amuses me for him to stay with her for the time being.

Artio crumpled the note and tossed it into the waters. The second it hit the water, it flashed into flame then sputtered, sinking below the surface and out of sight.

So, I must return to the scene of my demise, but is this by accident or by design?

It bothered Artio to blindly follow Helga's instructions, but the desire for revenge overshadowed her caution. She turned her back on the cliff face, and a shadow slid across a cave opening several stories above her.

Friend or foe she did not know, but it was past time for lingering. She strode away from Helga's realm without looking back.

Chapter 25

Decisions

MORDECAI PACED THE CONFINES of the squat circular tent set up as the meeting hall for the Kingsmen. In one hand, he held a book and in the other, his focus stone. It glowed softly and provided the only source of light in the otherwise dark tent.

In the early morning hours after Cayden's disappearance, they'd searched the surrounding woods for his trail. Scouts followed his faint path until the trail became unmistakable, trampled by the hooves of many horses. It was a simple matter to follow the all-too-obvious trail to the outskirts of the legion before turning back. No attempt had been made to disguise their passing. There was no sign of a struggle, no sign that Cayden had not joined up with them willingly.

Denzik stood on a raised four-square wooden platform that put him about half the height of the crowd taller, his hairy forearms folded across his chest, and stared impassively at the milling, muttering Kingsmen. The scouts fidgeted, their feet shifting at being the center of attention in the camp and the object of their fellow Kingsmen's displeasure.

"But, Captain, if the king joined them willingly, would he refuse to leave if we mounted a rescue?" They knew where he was being held, but how to get him out was still a point of argument amongst the Kingsmen.

"Don't be daft!" snapped Fabian, brandishing a towel snatched from over his shoulder where he had flung it as he dashed away from the camp kitchen. "Cayden would no more join them than I would volunteer to cook for the former queen." He smirked, as he had done that exact thing to originally assist in rescuing Cayden, but it was unlikely to work twice. Denzik's lips twitched at the comment and then settled back into their straight line.

"Then he was taken!" shouted another from the crowd.

"There were no signs of a struggle," volunteered a red-haired scout, "and no one came into the camp. No one got past the guards. He simply walked away."

"Maybe he was invisible!" shouted another.

Nelson growled deep in his throat. "Listen, you lump-heads! Cayden cannot turn invisible any more than you or I can. He is as human as any of us and can die just as easily. He would not give himself willingly to the enemy, especially an enemy that wants him dead. He wouldn't do it." Nelson divided his silver-browed glare equally amongst all present. He brandished a long-handled spoon as he would a sword, challenging anyone to doubt his words.

Muttering arose from the Kingsmen, each man talking to his neighbour and waving his arms to make his opinion heard, divided on how to approach the rescue of the king. Denzik heard snatches of "guards asleep on the watch" and "the king has magic—I saw it" and "Alcina is a witch and can turn herself invisible"; but the most outlandish one of all was "Cayden became the eagle. He can transform, you know."

Denzik unfolded his arms and held up his hands, shouting over the din. "If you will all quiet down, there is someone here who knows what happened." The murmuring trailed away. Once silence descended, Denzik motioned Mordecai forward.

Mordecai sensed Cayden through the stone. He had found it in Cayden's tent, whether abandoned or forgotten he did not know, but it had performed as expected. The stone was meant to provide interference against the Soul Fetch to allow Cayden to retain control of his mind, but now that he had been taken and the stone abandoned, it provided a perfect beacon, a link that only he could trace. Mordecai had no need of the Kingsmen to locate Cayden. Since the beginning—*the real beginning*—he had been able to find the Spirit Shields by the stones. It was not because of any special ability he had, but because of a stone he'd possessed.

Once, Mordecai had owned many such stones, but the very first stone he had found as a child, he'd kept inside a special box, black as coal, from which light did not escape. The rarity of such a box had escaped his understanding as a child, having been passed down from mother to daughter, daughter to grandson. He had always had it but had never seen its like in the kingdom in all the hundreds of years spent serving the royal family of Cathair. His father was long dead, and all of those who now lived had forgotten that he was also of the royal house, a sidelined branch of the family tree.

One can always locate family.

Mordecai mounted the platform and stood before the assembled Kingsmen, expectant faces staring at the rarity of a wizard. Silence fell.

"My good fellows! Locating the king is not the difficult part. Rescuing him is a possibility, yet it is fraught with danger which you do not understand. Cayden is a captive of mind and soul, not of body. What you seek to free is his person, yet what holds him captive is his mind. This is not a foe you are equipped to battle. Swords will not free him, nor will stealth be able to sneak him away. He is enslaved. To free him, we must break the bond that holds him. But mark my words, the breaking of that bond could kill him as well as any blade."

The Kingsmen shifted their feet and more than one face crinkled in bewilderment. Men of action rarely knew how to respond when the foe was not brandishing a sword in their face.

"Alcina knows this and made no attempt to hide their actions for this very reason. If we are foolish enough to challenge her hold on Cayden, to boldly attack her and the legionnaires, she can snuff out his life before we set the first blade to throat. We would never reach him in time, and we would find a lifeless corpse when we did."

Angry, frustrated voices flashed between the men, fingers flexing on sword grips as they fought the urge to draw blade and dash out to engage the enemy.

"No, we must be very wise in what we do." Mordecai held up his hands to indicate silence, but Denzik bellowed, *"Quiet!"* and silence fell once more.

"We are working on a plan to rescue the king. Do not worry. We will get him back and safely too. But for now, we need to turn our attention to one we can help. General?" Mordecai stepped back, and Denzik stepped forward once again.

"Avery is the king's sister." Heads bobbed in acknowledgement. "She is still out there, and every bit as much of a target as Cayden. Alcina hunts her and will stop at nothing to capture her. I suspect it is why she has stationed herself as she has, knowing that she has travelled to the Primordials with the other seeker. You all know Ziona. Well, there were two seekers sent to find the Spirit Shields, and one returned to their holy city with Avery. We will focus our efforts on finding and guarding Avery, lest she suffer the same fate as Cayden. We know the king was on his way to his sister, which was his primary purpose in leaving the castle. We can pick up his quest where he left off and be the physical shield as we always have been. We *will* secure Avery's welfare. We will reunite Cayden with his sister. While you are aiding Avery, know that we have a plan to rescue the king and will ensure he is returned to us." Expectant faces stared at the general.

"We will leave in two hours. It is time to break camp. You are dismissed." The men filed away in groups of twos and threes, talking softly between themselves.

Mordecai and Denzik stepped down from the landing and joined Nelson and Fabian.

"Somehow, I do not believe that you intend to join us in locating Avery," said Nelson, as he paused beside the wizard.

"Indeed, I do not." Mordecai gestured toward the retreating backs of the Kingsmen with a bony hand. "They need to reach Avery as soon as possible, or we will lose her too. She is vulnerable, and she does not know it. That is, if she has been successful in reaching the Primordial leadership. She is even more dangerous in the wrong hands. You must protect her with your life. *All* of your lives." Mordecai's blue eyes flashed around the circle of faces with the intensity of a bolt of lightning. "When you reach her, give her this." He pulled an object the size of the palm of his hand wrapped in a soft cloth. He folded back the cloth and revealed a Soul Stone, identical to the one he had given to Cayden a short day ago. "Tell her that it works in the same manner as the stone from Daimon Ford. She should understand if she has been reunited with the temple." He folded the soft cloth back around the stone and placed it in Denzik's hand. Denzik tucked it into a pocket sewn inside his shirt, against his chest.

"You will find Avery in the Highland Needle. You will need to get past Alcina's legion and into the mountains. Look to the Primordial forests where the creatures of myth are said to dwell. You will find her there. I will go after Cayden. Only magic can save him now."

Denzik grabbed the elderly wizard's hand in his and shook it, and placed his other hand on Mordecai's shoulder. "Go with the favour of the gods, Mordecai. Rescue the king. We will find Avery and protect her with our lives."

"I will prepare food for your departure. I might even find a sticky bun or two to lighten the journey." Fabian's eyes crinkled at the look of pure joy that lit the wizard's face.

"Oh yes, that would be a delectable twist in what is sure to be a nasty-flavoured journey."

As Mordecai strode away, the Kingsmen were already forgotten. Cayden's stone pulsed angrily in his pocket, flaring with heat. This time, it was Cayden calling to him, rather than the other way around. *Hold on, dear boy. I am coming.*

Chapter 26

Sharisha's Hunt

SHARISHA RODE AT THE HEAD of a long column of Primordial warriors, the High Priestess Marea at her side. Of all the warriors of the Spirit Clan, the dedicated of the temple were the fiercest, bound to the High Priestess by oath, both verbal and physical, the magic of the binding rune running deep under the skin. The seekers were the highest level of the dedicated, their lives bound to the will of the High Priestess.

Sharisha smiled a dark smile. *The strongest soul binds are not made by blood, but by spirit.* Imbibing of flesh and blood created mindless drones, creatures who could no longer think for themselves. But a true spirit-binding bound *the will* of a soul, and left the recipient a thinking, reasoning individual, his will aligned to the purpose of the binder. This kind of soul-binding was unbreakable; a soul-binding was for life.

Sharisha had been bound to Marea as a child, and her feet set on the path of a seeker from the earliest of days. Her purpose had always been to search the world for the Spirit Shields, to find the prophesied children, and bind them for all eternity to the High Priestess, as she herself was bound.

Word arrived from Alcina's legion camp by their spy's pigeon in the early hours, reporting that the alleged king of Cathair was now soul-slaved to a Fetch, a spirit doll.

With that news, a force of forty warriors, Sharisha, and the High Priestess set out on the trail of the fleeing Avery. Marea's singular focus was to catch up with her and bind her in a similar fashion, once she was within her grasp. This time, it would be the necklace stored in their saddle bag that would assure Avery's allegiance. She would soul bind her and bring her to heel at last, in service to the High Priestess, as was her duty.

Sharisha, riding at Marea's side, frowned and glanced back over her shoulder at Elder Hania slumped over in his saddle and tied in place by thick ropes. *He should not have betrayed Marea. He should have obeyed. He should not have resisted. Now look at him.* A dark bruise bloomed on his temple, and the cheek below was split open and hastily stitched. Blood seeped between the stitches and trickled down his slack face. A strand of his white hair stuck in the oozing, stained pink. His right arm was bound, having been broken in two places. They had hastily healed it, but neither of them had the power to fully mend the break. One other man accompanied the elder, slung over the saddle of a second horse. Gaius lay on his belly, tied in place so he did not slip off. He was unconscious.

It had been a simple matter to track the fleeing fugitive to the barn at the edge of Faylea and a simpler matter yet to determine she had fled with assistance. But no matter, if the trail faded, one of the pair would be able to provide the answers they needed to track Avery to her final destination.

"If you are correct, and Avery is headed towards Helga's realm, how do you plan to gain entry? It is deep within Flesh Clan-held lands, and Helga herself does not encourage visitors. Even from those who profess loyalty," Sharisha said softly, speaking for the High Priestess's ears only. She peeked at her from the corner of her eye, trying to gauge her reaction to her statement to gain a hint of Marea's thoughts.

Marea ignored Sharisha, her eyes scanning the path ahead, searching for any sign of movement amongst the trees. Seeing nothing of interest other than a couple of lovebirds flitting from one branch to another, she finally rewarded Sharisha with a glance. "The former queen believes she is in control, that she steers events, but she is as much a puppet as is the young whelp Cayden," she sneered. "This journey will net both Spirit Shields and never again will anyone doubt who rules the Primordials. The Flesh Clan will be brought to heel. The Spirit Clan will take its rightful place in the world and push back the Cathairian infidels. The Spirit Shield's blood will be purified by fire, and their wills harnessed for all eternity." She sniffed and glanced back at the unconscious elder. "Even amongst our own, traitors are discovered."

"Do you mean to march right into the main Flesh Clan encampment and demand their surrender? There is no love lost between Flesh and Spirit Clans. They will not bow to a Spirit Clan leader, even one in control of a Spirit Shield. It is true the main force battles Alcina's legion, but they will not have left their priests undefended," said Sharisha. "Besides, there is nothing to say that the boy is still in Alcina's camp."

"Of course not! But a small strike force can be enough to steal a prize with the right distraction. I want those dolls and the priest who makes them." Marea smiled a grim smile. "The boy is a bonus. If I have the doll, I control him regardless of where he is. He will come to me." *I will recover the boy and his doll, all of the dolls. I will see Spirit and Flesh Clans united under my reign.* Marea smiled grimly, and a vision of the Spirit Shields kneeling before her in the shadow of the temple amused her thoughts for the next few minutes.

There were only three people important to her plans: Avery, Cayden, and Hototo. Alcina was an annoyance. The puzzle was Hototo. Marea did not understand why Hototo had given away the dolls in the first place, unless he thought he could not get close enough to the boy to place the binding. But if that were true, why give them to Alcina? Surely, she would not have had access to the boy, or he would already be dead. No, something else was at play here.

Alcina would have to be disposed of as she possessed knowledge of at least one of the dolls, an additional complication. The knowledge of the dolls in non-Primordial hands was a crime punishable by death. Marea snarled under her breath. Hototo's treason was nearly as deep as the bouncing elder behind her. How could he give away Primordial secrets to an outlander?

Marea rode on in silence, and her introspection made her blind to the details around her. Had she turned her head and looked back, just once, she would have seen the faint smudge of dust in the sky. But she did not.

Marea was not alone in her interest in the prophesied children. The Spirit Shields, now returned to the world of men, were sought by many parties, and one such party shadowed the Primordial clansmen at a discreet distance, biding their time.

*   *   *

Hototo's escape from the prisoner tent was a silent but non-bloody affair. Despite the queen's promise, she'd immediately returned him to the prisoner's tent and promptly forgotten about him. She had spared enough energy to double the guard but left instructions for him to be left unbound, given clean clothes, food, and water.

But Hototo did not have time to waste waiting on Alcina.

Close to midnight, with the camp quiet around him and the campfire coals banked toward morning, Hototo rose up silently and went to the tent door. There, two guards manned the entrance, swaying as they fought sleep in the quiet of deep night. One raised a hand to his mouth to smother a yawn.

Hototo took a reed from his pack, which had been returned to him as part of the agreement for the handover of the Soul Fetch. He prepared several sleeping darts, by dipping a sharpened bird-feather quill into a small pot of paste then slid the drugged quills into a hollowed tube pulled from his pack. Spying his first target, he put his lips to the other end of the reed and blew. The dart flew from the end and struck the neck of the guard with no more force than a mosquito bite. The guard swatted at his neck and yawned again.

Hototo repeated the process and shot a second bug bite into the neck of the other guard, who jerked and slapped the spot.

Less than a minute later, the guards were sinking to their knees and then gently slid sideways to ground, snoring softly.

Hototo returned the reed and the darts to his pack, slung it onto his back, then slipped from the tent on silent feet. He disappeared into the dark, carefully stepping over the sleeping guards, then sliding from shadow to shadow through the main camp to the horse lines. He paused to let a patrol pass then crept up to the horse line, untied the rope of the last horse, and led the animal away at a slow, quiet pace into the trees. Once out of sight of the camp, he swung up onto its back, twisting the horse lead into a makeshift bridle.

With a gentle touch of heels to flank, he urged his mount deeper into the forest and began to climb. He left behind the foothills of the encampment with the fading of the night, and the path became steep and slick with loose scree from the mountain face. The sky lightened with the blush of dawn. As he rounded a corner of the cliff face, he halted abruptly.

The trail was blocked by a recent stone fall. Only the narrowest portion of trail remained passable. He dismounted and continued on foot, leading his mount around the fall, acutely aware of the precipitous drop of hundreds of feet to his left. He glanced down as he walked along, and his eyes were caught on the body of a horse, lying on the rocks far below. There was no sign that the horse had come from the trail, but rather it appeared to be partially buried in scree that had swept past his ledge and down into the beginnings of a shallow valley below.

Hototo frowned at the bloated carcass. His eyes swept the scene below, still partially cast in the gloom of night. The horse was either white or pale grey, or he would not have detected it at all.

It has been there for days, maybe the better part of a week...and the timing is worrisome, he thought. This was the valley bowl where the Flesh Clans had been camped. The presence of a dead horse indicated the presence of spies. Spies who may have witnessed things they should not have seen.

The blockage ended, and Hototo regained the main path. The Crystal Caves were still a day's ride away. The mountain rumbled, and the scree shifted, pebbles and rocks slipping over the side of the trail behind him, to disappear below.

The god who resides in the mountain is stirring. The souls of the mountain call to me. It is time to seek out Dark's Mistress, to warn her. It is time to prepare the Shakra Cave, for her enemy approaches. Artio will be pleased. Serving two mistresses was a fine line to walk, but walk it he did. The Flesh Clans must be victorious. With the power of two goddesses to throw at the Spirit Clan, there was no possible way to fail. They will be crushed once and for all, the temple returned and the true faith restored. He would see these things happen, or die trying.

Chapter 27

Freedom

CAYDEN AWOKE WITH A SPLITTING HEADACHE and groaned as he unstuck his eyelids. He blinked, stirred, and attempting to stretch, only to find himself curled around a soft body. Not simply curled, but spooned together in the most intimate of positions. His eyes shot open, and his groan became audible, the soft something stirring in his arms.

With a stretch, it sat up, blanket dropping to waist. Ziona rubbed sleepily at her eyes, and then they wandered slowly over the astonished man at her side. She smiled and leaned down to kiss him full on the lips.

"You are having a lucid moment, I assume? You have the eyes of a startled fawn."

Cayden passed a hand over his chest then glanced down at its naked expanse. "If I were to peek under the covers, would I be embarrassed at the state of my undress?"

Ziona grinned, her gaze growing bolder. "You are as naked as a tree in winter. Thankfully you are not as cold…although the heat you generated last night would have sparked a forest fire!"

Cayden's face reddened right on cue, and Ziona laughed. He grimaced as a sharp spike of pain flashed across his temples, and his hand rose to the side of his face.

Ziona's mirth fell away, and her mouth sagged in distress. "The pain, is it back?"

"It is always there, a dull throb that turns white hot until it wipes away all ability to think consciously, to react, or take any independent action. Ziona, she can get inside my head, and she steals my thoughts and replaces them with her own. She sabotages my will."

"Tell me." She slipped into his arms and placed her ear on his beating heart. "Tell me what happened."

Cayden filled her in and when he got to the spot about the straw doll, her hand clenched into his chest so hard that the nails bit into his skin as she sat up.

"*Ouch!*" he cried, pulling her hand away.

"She didn't!" Ziona hissed, fury thinning her eyes to catlike slits. Her irises glittered with anger.

"What is it, Ziona? Tell me!" Cayden sat up too, facing her.

"She has a Soul Fetch! Where did she get a Soul Fetch?" Ziona shook her head and then flung her feet over the edge of the bed, pulling the lone blanket with her and draped it around under her arms, tying it off in a twisted knot over her chest. Cayden shivered in the sudden cold and reached for the blanket, but she stepped out of reach. "Your people know nothing about the making of a Soul Fetch. It could only have come from a Primordial. My people have betrayed us. The question is, was it someone of the Spirit Clans or the Flesh Clans?"

"You mean *our* people. I am half Primordial, remember?" She grunted in agreement. "What is a Soul Fetch? I mean, Mordecai did tell me, but I thought you might know more."

"It is a doll that uses magic to bind the soul of the person to the possessor. It captures your will, your very soul." She gazed at the tiny window of her room. "I must get out of here. I cannot protect you from a cell."

She spun back around then bent and picked up his discarded clothing, tossing them onto his lap. "Get up. We have a short window to prepare for the next possession. We must get that doll."

Cayden picked up his pants and pulled them up his legs, standing to complete the process. "And then what? I smash it? Burn it?"

"*No!*" she shouted, and her hands rose in panic. "No," she said in a softer tone. "Whatever you do to the doll will happen to you, even to death. No, we must break the bond...and that comes back to..."

"Mordecai." Cayden finished the sentence for her.

She nodded unhappily. "Yes, Mordecai is the only one we know of that we can trust to break the spell and not kill you in the process. Everyone else is suspect, I fear. We must get you back to Mordecai."

"I would not be surprised if he is on his way here already," Cayden mumbled through the fabric of his shirt as he pulled it down over his head.

"But we cannot rely on him to get us out of the middle of a legion with you bound to the doll. Come here," she commanded, the Ziona of old, now the seeker, the lover of the evening before vanishing. "We have the Soul Bond from when you saved me back in the spring, but now, I am going to put a tracer on you that Mordecai can follow. The only drawback is that any Primordial seeker will be able to track you with it too. I am going to put a seeker bond on you as was placed on me by the temple."

She dropped her blanket and stepped up to him, naked as the day she was born. She seemed unaware of her nakedness and completely at ease, but sweat broke out on Cayden's brow at the sight and he dropped his eyes. How he wanted to ogle her! Cayden fought the urge to stare. She laughed then put her hand under his chin, forcing him to look up. Once his eyes had travelled the distance from toes to her eyes (a journey that took much longer than it should have taken!) she raised her right hand. He had never noticed it before, but just inside her palm at the fleshy join where the thumb connected to her hand was a tattoo of an oak leaf, shot through with an arrow. It looked strangely similar to the oak leaf on the banner of Cathair, the royal seal.

"Place your right hand flat against my hand. That's it." She placed her other hand against his cheek. "Now reach out to me with the bond, Cayden. Merge our minds. Keep your eyes on mine. Do not close them. I must be able to see through the windows of your soul."

Cayden locked his eyes on hers (a tough thing to do with so much flesh available for viewing) and reached out for her soul with his. She was the most beautiful woman he had ever seen. Now that he had really seen her, *all of her*, it was all he could do to concentrate on her instructions. He wanted to forget the war and where they were. He could almost ignore the danger they were in. He wanted her so badly. Yet the constant throb in his temple warned him that time was short. He stamped down on his longings and concentrated on her instructions. They merged with a tingling sensation, and then he heard her voice in his head.

Hi, there, she whispered softly. *Now, I am going to transfer the magic of the rune along our bond. When it is complete, you will bear an identical rune on your palm. It will burn, but do not pull away until the transfer is complete.*

I understand, he whispered back as his temple throbbed painfully, *but hurry!*

The link flared and magic coursed along the ethereal connection, like steam on ice or lava on snow. The ice smoothed the path and the lava burned, his palm burned, skin to skin, until he wondered how she did not flinch away. It took every ounce of focus for him to remain locked in the transfer, but he held himself rigidly and did not move.

Someone moved him.

With a jerk and an inaudible screech, he was flung backward onto the bed and his mind snapped, as the haze of possession rose within him with a sickening lurch. His vision blurred, and Ziona vanished behind a white haze of pain. Cayden jerked upright and walked toward the door, knocking once. The door was flung open and the guard standing in the light of the open door leered at the sight of a naked Ziona before Cayden blocked his view. Squeezing out a last act of defiance, he grabbed the door handle and slammed it shut behind him, smacking the guard's nose as he leaned around him for a better view.

The guard snarled and clouted Cayden across the back of the head in a glancing blow. Cayden grunted and stumbled forward. He did not pause. He could not pause. His will was not his own. He stumbled toward Alcina at her command.

A sensation like a whip slashed across his torso. He cried out, his back arching in pain. His feet sped up, and the guard behind him chuckled at his jerking, faltering jog, amused to see him dance on hidden strings.

Cayden stopped resisting, and the pressure lightened until he could walk normally. The scenery around him was blurry as though he peered through infected eyes. But this time, he felt Ziona, nestled in the corner of his soul, her heart beating alongside his. Their merged souls kept him grounded and kept him sane. His will was not his own—Alcina controlled that—but his heart belonged to Ziona. It would have to be enough until help could come. *It will have to be enough.*

He was pulled along, past tents of guards and legionnaires, past tents dedicated to the kitchen and medics, past smithy and farrier. No one approached him. No one guarded him. Yet he could not flee. He could not turn from the path his feet trod.

His legs carried him once again to the entrance of Alcina's tent. He bent, pushing aside the flap of canvas serving as a door. His feet carried him to the carpet in front of her grand chair, and his knees sank onto the medallion as they had the night before, the first time he had visited this tent. His head bowed, and he panted with the exertion of running and resisting. A lock of hair fell into his eyes, and he didn't bother to swipe it away. He stared at the carpet, trying to make sense of the pattern in shades of crimson and periwinkle.

A slender hand with red-enameled nails reached down and gripped his chin, tilting it upward.

"I trust you had an enjoyable evening?" she purred, searching his eyes. "Every condemned prisoner should have one last pleasure before facing the ferryman. Don't you agree?"

Cayden stared at her, consumed by an overwhelming desire to please her. The command seeped into his head, and he found his lips moving. "Yes, mistress." He licked his dry lips. The words caught in his throat.

"She is going to die...but not quite yet. I sense that you need more incentive to do my bidding. She may have a use yet. If you are a good puppet, I will keep her alive. I might even allow you to visit her again. You now know of her charms. It would be a fitting reward, yes?" She dragged the forefinger of her right hand down his cheek, and it made a rasping sound under her nail. "You are quite pretty with a day's growth of stubble." She dragged her nail down his cheek once more, but this time it curved under his chin and across his throat. Cayden swallowed as the sharp nail scratched across his bobbing Adam's apple.

"But, if you disappoint me, I will end your life and hers by personally cutting both of your throats. You will watch each other die, spilling your life's blood onto each other. That is a promise, my puppet."

"Yes, mistress," Cayden rasped as she dropped his chin and straightened.

"Now, I have a task for you." She bent down and placed her lips against his ear, whispering her instructions.

Cayden's eyes glazed over. The next thing he knew, he was no longer in Alcina's tent. The fog lifted from his brain, and he was startled to see he was standing outside of Ziona's door. There were no guards present. Alarmed, he shoved open the door and stumbled into the room. "*Ziona!*" he screamed, eyes frantically searching the room. He found her bent over her satchel, packing her few possessions into its depths and then tugging the leather thongs tight to close it. She straightened at his sudden appearance and smiled. Relief flooded through Cayden.

"You're safe!" He strode over to her and dragged her into his arms and kissed her, hard. Suddenly, realizing what he had done, he pushed away and mumbled, "Sorry," as colour crept up his neck.

Ziona laughed, eyes sparkling. "Will you ever stop blushing around me?"

The colour crept higher still.

"I have been released. Do you have anything to gather?" Her smile wilted, seeing his surprise. "They told me that you had been released too. Alcina has pardoned both of us. You know nothing of this, do you?"

Cayden shook his head.

"Alcina said all we had to do was swear allegiance, and we could leave. She indicated you already had."

Cayden frowned. "I do not know. I was kneeling in front of her on the carpet and...I don't know. Perhaps I did and I don't remember it?" He shifted, looking around the chamber as though something there would jar his memory.

"Well," Ziona brow wrinkled into a worried frown "you must have convinced her somehow. We are now free. Let's get out of here before she changes her mind."

Ziona took his hand and led him out of the tent and down to the horse lines where they found their horses saddled and awaiting them.

"Wait till Mordecai sees us! He will be so surprised!" Ziona swung into her saddle.

Cayden mirrored her movements then shifted in his saddle as he gathered his reins. Something did not feel right, but damned if he could figure out what it was.

With a slap of reins, they trotted away from the legion encampment.

From high on the hill under the arch of canvas of her tent, the queen watched their departure, an amused smile on her lips.

Chapter 28

Love Lost

THE BOULDER-STREWN VALLEY was filled with Primordial warriors, their tents dotting the ground between the rocks. A clear space like an invisible barrier curved around the entrance to her temple, Artio was glad to see. With a snarl, she left the mountain pass and entered the valley and a wave of Primordials prostrated themselves, arms straight and extended as she passed. Mutterings reached her ears, prayers offered to the gods mixed with an occasional sob, so soft only her ears would have heard it.

She ignored the warriors, her focus on her temple and the High Priests gathered at its entrance. They bowed as one and offered her trays of succulent blueberries, strips of salmon, and a shining goblet of crystal clear water in welcome.

Artio strode past them and into the temple, and they followed. She mounted her throne and sat, motioning the priests to place the food on a table at her right side. Picking up a plump pink slice of salmon, she tossed it into her mouth and chewed.

"Well?"

The High Priests shuffled their feet, uneasy and puzzled by the question. No one wanted to be the first one to answer such a vague question, lest they be in error. The silence stretched.

"What is happening? Where is the girl? Do not tell me you are not spying on the Spirit Clans. Has she taken the temple?" Artio roared in her celestial voice.

The priests fell to their knees, and Arthmael raised his head, lips trembling. "Yes, Holy One, the girl known as Avery has taken the temple. Our spies report that she has left Faylea where she was imprisoned after taking the temple. They say she escaped."

Artio popped another slice of salmon and a handful of blueberries into her mouth and chewed, considering. She picked up the goblet and drank half of the icy water then placed it back on the table, swiping her arm across her mouth.

"Where is she going?"

Arthmael gulped. "Holiness, she is headed toward us. She is coming this way. I do not know her destination. She is followed by the High Priestess of Faylea and a guard. One of the seekers travels with her."

"I know where she is headed. You will give orders to break camp in the morning. Your warriors now serve me and me alone," Artio rumbled. *"Leave me!"*

Arthmael bowed low and backed away with the other priests and left the temple to pass along the orders to their recently assembled camp.

Artio stood and walked back into her rooms. *There is only one thing my sister could be seeking…and it belongs to me…but first I need to eliminate those who follow. This false High Priestess chases a prize to which she has no right. It is time to deal with the temple puppet priestess, so that I can confront the true one.*

And then there is Helga.

She frowned, perplexed at her sister's reactions when she visited her in the grotto. *She may believe she is the master of the mortals on earth, seeing as Alfreda, Caerwyn, and I have been absent for so long. But Helga is not in control of events. She has not considered the heat of my anger.* Artio wandered over to the chest and flipped back the lid. Her eye fell on a velvety bag of softest deerskin, a bag that had once contained a box. That box had carried her hopes and dreams. Dreams she had shared with the image of a man, taller than she, with ebony hair touching his sun-heated flesh, corded muscles straining against a massive stone. *Genii.*

Shock froze her to the spot, her body locking as realization flooded through her. She remembered the fleeting shadow that had watched her depart. *Helga has Genii!* White hot anger surged within her, unlocking her limbs. She struck out at the chest, pounding it with her fists. She did not feel the pain, for it was overshadowed by the pain searing a hole in her chest, in her heart. The heat of the betrayal burned along her nerve endings, raw and searing. *Helga will also pay,* she snarled. *I will slay them all. This I swear on the soul of my lost love, Genii.*

Artio spoke the name aloud as the name floated to the tip of her tongue. Memories long buried resurfaced and with it the anguish of a pure love lost for not simply for a lifetime but *for eternity*. Images flashed into her mind of a former time, of hands clasped and knees touching, bodies cradled in the soft grass of the sacred clearing, minds blended, souls touching, bodies uniting. And then a searing, wrenching pain as her soul was torn from his—then the empty nothingness of space.

Artio sank to her knees, bloodied hands clasped in her lap. She threw back her head and roared at the heavens. Her bellow of anguish brought the camp to a complete standstill, and silence fell. After a moment of frozen silence, they crept back into action, resuming their tasks, but they walked with the softest of tread, lest they bring the full fury of Artio down on them all.

*   *   *

Artio did not leave her chambers, nor was she seen at all, for the remainder of the day. The food brought by the priests remained untouched. They tiptoed in and tiptoed out, not wishing to disturb their goddess when she was angry.

Instead, they oversaw the packing up of their potions and instruments and gathered together the supplies for their dolls. They would not leave behind anything to fall into the hands of the Spirit Clans, should they rediscover the Bear Clan temple.

Just before dark, Artio summoned Arthmael, and he entered the temple on trembling knees. They gave out just as he reached her presence. He let them carry him to the floor, kneeling with his bald head lowered.

Artio was seated in her throne, absently turning over a deerskin bag in her hand. She did not seem to notice his presence.

He remained silent. Artio looked up from the bag, and her eyes fastened on him.

"How many dolls can you make, and how quickly can this be done?" she demanded.

"Highness, we can make as many as you want. We can make about fifty a day if we concentrate all of our people on the task. Forgive me, but may I ask what you intend to do with them? I might be able to provide some guidance as to their use." He bobbed his head, lowering his eyes.

She studied him for a moment, and then her voice boomed, echoing strangely in the throne room, *"I wish to control a large group of people. Can this be done?"*

Arthmael bobbed his head once again. "The dolls work by the trigger of a binding object, usually something of the person you wish to bind. The soul binding works between the doll containing the object and the person it belonged to. But to bind a large group of people, you would need a very special object of great personal value to them all. It would then have the strength to bind all those sworn to the possessor."

"An object of great personal value," she rumbled, considering the trembling priest. *"Bring to me the swiftest and stealthiest person in the camp. There is a service I require."*

"Yes, Your Highness. Right away!" He stood up and, still bowing, backed to the entrance and left.

Chapter 29

The Sacred Slopes

CYRUS STEPPED OUT from behind the rock watching the dust plume drift away, a cloud of dirt borne on lazy winds as the last of the Primordial force dropped below the horizon.

Marea was leading him directly to the primordial, blindly assuming that she was the only one interested in Avery's whereabouts. They did not check their back trail, a mistake they would soon regret. Cyrus was outnumbered three to one, but his elite force was more than capable of handling the rabble of Primordials.

Ahead the mountains of the Highland Spine stretched toothily toward the heavens, a wreath of dark clouds obscuring the summit. Shadows slid down the face of the peak, as though a mountain giant stood blocking the sun. A rumble of what he took to be thunder reached his ears. The giant frowned down at him, angry at their encroachment on its sacred slopes. Cyrus shook his head, squeezing his eyes closed, then looked at the mountain again. The shadows were only shadows once more. *Stop giving into Primordial fancies! You are allowing them to bewitch your mind!*

"Do not look at the mountain!" Cyrus commanded his force as they joined him, leading their horses. "The Primordials are laying their lures and traps. If we are not careful, we will ride off after an illusion. Everyone take a partner, who will ride by your side. If you see anyone acting strangely, it is your responsibility to stop them before they get into trouble. Count off!"

The men divided themselves into pairs and mounted up. Cyrus swung into the saddle, and Fullmer took his place beside him, eyes averted from the mountain.

"Follow the trail, but ignore the mountain." Fullmer put heel to horse, and his mount broke into a fast walk. An eagle soared overhead, circling on updrafts. They crested the ridge, the trail sloping gently down toward a break in the dense evergreen forest that hugged the base of the mountain. As they rode, the path of their quarry narrowed as the brush became shrubs and the shrubs were swallowed by the trees. The dirt track became stony, and the boughs overhead blocked out the sunshine. As they entered the forest, the sound of birds vanished and the woods were silent. The soft needles underfoot deadened the sound of their mounts. Nothing stirred.

The forest holds its breath, waiting to see if violence will be done this day. The grim thought floated through Cyrus's mind. Out of the corner of his eye, a face slid behind a tree trunk. He stared at the spot, and out of the corner of his other eye, the figure reappeared, only to vanish before he could swing his head back around.

Fullmer swiped a hand down his arm, then slapped at it. The sound cracked the silence.

"Stop that," Cyrus commanded.

"Ants! There are ants under my shirt sleeve." Fullmer hauled up his sleeve, but there was nothing there.

Cyrus glanced back at the other men and then reined in sharply.

The men were gone. Not a track showed that they had entered the forest.

Fullmer's eyes widened in shock. "My lord! Where have the men gone?" He swung his horse about and started back down the trail but Cyrus's hand shot out and halted him.

"Stop!" he commanded. "Do not move!"

Fullmer froze, eyes darting frantically to locate the missing men. His horse stood placidly, tail swishing, and reached out its nose to snuffle at...nothing.

"Close your eyes, and slowly open them," commanded Cyrus.

Fullmer did as he commanded. When his eyes focused again, everyone was there, pair by pair, staring at him in a puzzled manner.

"My lord!" Fullmer gasped. "Where were they hiding?"

"They were right behind us, all along. The illusions are strong in the trees. It is part of the warding of the mountain. It is designed to keep strangers away. The Primordials would say non-believers, but what they really mean is non-Primordial folk. Come."

Cyrus guided his mount back to the trail and continued on up the path, a nervous Fullmer riding tight to his side.

They rode in silence for a period of a half hour or so, the forest oppressive and forbidding.

The evergreen trees grew taller and widened until six men linked hand to hand could not encircle the trunks. The lower limbs, long-shorn by age and a lack of sun light rose higher and higher until they were riding clear under the great trees, devoid of any brush and thick with pine needles and cones of every shape and size. Sticky resin ran down the trunks and along the branches, and brown ropes stretched from the tree limbs, drifting softly in the silence.

A soldier riding three rows back brushed against one of the dangling cords as he rode under a tree. With a violent thrash, the tree came to life and the resinous ropes snaked around the rider, jerking him and his horse into the air. Shocked, his partner grabbed for his horse's hoof, a gut reaction, attempting to hold him down as more resinous ropes twisted around him and his mount. Additional ropes dragged the screeching soldiers higher and higher into the trees, and then they vanished.

The shocked soldiers froze, afraid to move a muscle. Resinous trailers swayed innocently, seeking the next victim.

"Touch nothing!" spat Cyrus harshly, then jabbed his mount into motion.

Frightened of attracting the attention of the great trees, the men cowered in their saddles.

"Let's move!" Cyrus heeled his snorting mount and pushed on deeper into the forest.

Signs of the passage of their quarry surfaced as the great forest thinned. Cottonwood and birch saplings sprouted here and there in the soft soil, and burgundy ferns thickened and replaced the pine needles. The air moistened; humidity increasing as the sound of running water reached their ears. The horses pulled eagerly at the reins, hoping to dip thirsty muzzles into the approaching stream. Their riders, however, kept a leery eye pasted on the trees as they passed.

The trail led straight to a bubbling brook, tumbling over rocks and splashing into tiny rapids. Smiles broke out on the men's faces, and they slid gratefully to the ground and dropped down to their knees at the water's edge, cupping the crystal-clear liquid in their hands and splashing it over their faces and hair, allowing it to drip back into the swift stream. The horses' muzzles sank into the froth, and they drank deeply from the cooling waters.

Standing back up, the first batch made way for the second set of soldiers, who happily splashed into the water, knee deep.

"Look!" A soldier named Billy motioned frantically to his partner urging him over to where he stood. "There is gold in here!"

"Where?" Billy's partner splashed over to where he pointed. Sure enough, scattered on the bottom of the brook was a glittering ribbon of gold with nuggets as fat as a thumb.

"Good Lord!" Billy plunged his hand into the water, and his fist closed on the largest nugget he could find.

Suddenly, he jerked and was pulled into the clear water. His fist was pulled into the bottom of the bed, and his arm was swallowed. With a strangled scream, his head was pulled underwater, followed by the rest of his body. Before their very eyes, he disappeared under the surface. A stream of bubbles broke the surface and then they too, stopped.

"Billy!" his partner called and began to scrabble amongst the shallow waters. His hand brushed up against the glowing nuggets. Suddenly, a great jaw rose up from the bottom, the gold sparkling off knobs on its pebbly head, and a pair of glowing green eyes blinked once at him before the jaws closed on his arm. His shriek of pain and panic ended abruptly as he was pulled under the water, the creature sinking back into the stones, pulling him with it. A stream of blood pooled on the surface of the water for an instant when it stilled then was swept downstream by the current. Within the space of few seconds, there was nothing left to show anything had occurred, except for the fact that both men had vanished.

"*I said, touch nothing!*" roared Cyrus from the shore. He drew his sword and spun around to the men, brandishing it at their faces. "The next one of you lump-heads that *touches anything* in this accursed forest will die by *this*! Mount up!"

They mounted again and crossed the stream, continuing down the trail, towing the two empty-saddled mounts behind them. The forest thinned and a sheer rock face came into view, forcing the trail to swing around its base. Another rock rose on the left, and the trail narrowed until it was impossible to ride two abreast. They dropped into a single file, keeping nose to tail, every soldier afraid of being left behind. The last soldier in line glanced back over his shoulder so many times that he mimicked a metronome.

The walls of stone pressed ever closer until their legs brushed both sides as they rode. One barrel-bellied mare caught her rider's leg against the stone, and the man swore and lurched in his saddle, dragging his opposite leg up across his saddle just in time to keep his legs from a dual crush between horse and rock.

With a growl, a grey-and-white sabretooth, the size of a small pony, launched itself from a cleft in the rock overhead and landed on the final rider. Great jaws with long fangs that extended well past the lower lip sank into his throat and, with a shake of its head, the unfortunate soldier's neck snapped. With its second bound, the cat launched off the back of the panicked horse, which reared and came down on the horse and rider in front of him. His partner's scream was drowned by the screams of the crazed stallion, and he was trampled under its hooves. His mount kicked back at the deranged horse and the rest of the mounts also panicked as more snarls and yowls echoed down the passage. Cyrus kicked his horse savagely, driving it forward, and it raced down the narrow passage, heedless of its rider. The panicked legionnaires heeled their mounts, and the narrowest stampede in history ensued. Cyrus glimpsed other cats of different colours with long dripping fangs, swishing tails, and yellow eyes picking out their prey. He did not stop to see how the others faired. He gave his horse its head and let it run.

Suddenly, he spilled out of the cleft into a grassy bowl, and his mount plunged three-quarters of the way across before Cyrus could pull it to a quivering halt. It hung its head, sides heaving, eyes rolling, as the surviving men gathered around him, some calming bucking mounts. Cyrus's eyes scanned the survivors. Horses with long, ragged claw marks shook with shock. One limped, favouring a rear leg dangling from a flank with a chunk of rump missing.

Equally bloodied men, whether from direct injury or from their wounded mounts, he could not initially say, staggered around, eyes darting in every direction in search of the next attack.

Half. Cyrus counted half of his original force. He swore loudly, shook his fist at the mountain. "You will not defeat me!" he screamed at the skies.

The wind chuckled as it swept through the valley, carrying the collective laughter of all creatures mythical and magical, who called the forest home.

Cyrus was not amused.

Chapter 30

Friend or Foe?

ACHAK TWISTED OUT OVER THE EDGE of the trail, leaning precariously to the side to peer around the edge of the curving rocky slide blocking their path. Craning his neck, he saw that the ledge was blocked for a good two hundred paces, to a height taller than his stature while mounted on his horse. There was no possibility of crossing it, even walking the horses.

"We must go back," he said, taking his reins back from Avery's hand.

Avery's stomach rolled. Reluctantly, her eyes slid over the side of the mountain. She hated the thought of passing by the bloated carcass of her father's dead horse. The odour of decaying flesh was heavy in her nose, coy and clinging. Not for the first time, she wondered where Gaius was and what had happened to him. Although she knew he was her mortal parent only, it did not stop her from loving him. Fear pricked her heart. *Surely Marea would not have killed him! If she has harmed him…!*

"Then we must go back," she sighed. She dismounted and leading her horse, doubled back to where the cliff-side path split into a *Y*, the trail zigzagging down the hillside a little more than a goat path. She led her horse, testing her footing as she descended. Loose shale and tenuously anchored vegetation made it too treacherous to ride, as she knew by recent experience. They picked their way slowly, stones slipping and sliding underfoot, the temperature of the air increasing the deeper into the depths they travelled until, an hour later, they reached the bottom. A hot wind gusted down the ravine, carrying with it the odour of putrefying flesh.

Avery wrinkled her nose and pulled the flap of her cloak over her face to mask the smell. Anxious to get by the area, she swung up into the saddle, but her mare tossed her head, dancing nervously, balking at the direction she asked her to go. Avery kicked her mare into a trot and then a run, as anxious as her mount to clear the area. They rounded the base of the rock face, Achak riding tight to her side. Avery closed her eyes as she passed past the dead horse, allowing her live mount to choose the path ahead. The horse ran well past the carcass then slowed as the sharp odours faded. Avery opened her eyes…to a wall of Primordial warriors.

Swords drawn, men and women with painted faces spread out in a wall. Avery hauled on the reins. From the corner of her eye, she spied more men coming out of the trees, circling around behind her and Achak. She recognized the masks, Spirit Guides personal to the bearer, and many of the masks were reflected in the images that covered her body. She pulled her hood tighter around her face to hide her tattooed features. She had no intention of displaying them to the warriors.

The Flesh Clan warriors tightened the circle and then one stepped forward, separating himself from his companions. He was garbed as a Flesh Clan Primordial priest in leather comprised of dried human skins. Avery's mind flashed back to the scene she had witnessed during her first journey through this area. The priest bowed deeply. As he rose, a dart gun appeared in his hand. With two quick *phuts*, he shot a pair of darts at herself and Achak. One pricked the skin of her arm and the other pierced Achak's thigh.

Drat, she thought, as she slid off her horse. She was out before she hit the ground.

* * *

With a jerk of his arm, Hototo ordered several warriors to pick up the unconscious woman and her guard. They slung them over the backs of their horses like sacks of grain. Following Hototo's lead, the guard led them into the valley at the edge of the Crystal Caves. It was a bowl-shaped, verdant-green clearing with gently sloping sides surrounded by steep cliffs on one flat side, and a semicircle of scrubby brush on the other, before emptying into the trees of the Sacred Forest. The narrow path they traversed was the only entrance or exit. Tight up against the cliff a series of cavernous openings dotted its face.

They laid Avery down in the shadow of a circle of tall stones, ancient and knowing, that graced the pasture. Her hood fell back, and the Primordial who had carried her yelled as though burned. The stones by which she lay bore symbols that matched those revealed on her hairless skull. Murmuring broke out. The warrior backed away, afraid to touch Avery, afraid to be near her.

A second warrior placed Achak on the ground beside Avery, and then his eyes fell on her.

"A goddess! She bears the markings!" he gasped, stumbling backward, and grumbling ignited and spread amongst the circle of warriors. "Is she a goddess? A goddess! Where?"

Hototo pushed his way through the crowd to the front of the circle and halted abruptly when his eyes fell on the sleeping woman. He walked around her, gazing at the tattoos, and then examined the pillar above her, comparing the symbols. He did not answer the warriors.

"Pick up her and her companion and follow me," he snapped, striding off toward the caves. The warriors looked from one to another. No one made a move. "Now!" Hototo roared over his shoulder. The men who had originally carried Avery and Achak gingerly picked them up again and followed the priest.

Hototo strode well ahead of them and disappeared into a rift running vertically up the face of the mountain. It was barely wide enough for two people to walk side by side, yet the shade of the bowl disguised the opening. Only by training their eye on where Hototo disappeared could they see the spot. They entered the crack, staring uneasily at the tilted stone that towered above them. After about one hundred paces, the crack widened and flattened into a cave glowing with a soft internal light. The mouth was encircled with jagged stone teeth that caught and absorbed the muted light of the passage, leering at the intruders with a frosted, rocky grin, as they crossed into the cave. The great maw seemed poised to snap shut at a moment's notice.

Shivering, they carried the pair to a stone table at the back of the cave, beside which stood Hototo, gesturing anxiously for them to hurry with their delivery. Gently, they deposited the still forms on the slabs of unpolished crystal and, bowing, backed out the cave. As soon as they were past the mouth, they ran, as fast as their moccasined feet could carry them.

Hototo ignored Achak, his attention focused entirely on Avery. He studied the runes and, lifting a finger, traced the swirls and patterns on her head and over her ears, murmuring to himself. Blue light followed his finger, and the runes glowed. Then with a gasp, Avery sat straight up. Her silvery eyes fixed on Hototo.

Hototo stepped back, shivering in reaction to her unusual eyes, and bowed, palms pressed together, and arms raised so that his fingers steepled, dividing his face. "I apologize, mistress, for our treatment. We saw intruders. We did not know."

Avery swung her legs over the side of the stone slab and swayed as the last of the paralyzing dart faded from her system. She slowly surveyed her surroundings. The walls were a smoothed milky white with shallow pockets as though the walls were made of cheese. Inside the glowing pockets, objects of various shapes and sizes were displayed: glass vials and small leather-bound books, carved wooden trinkets, a bracelet of twisted copper strands with charms, and the mummified bodies of what she took to be small animals. Even an ebony box graced one alcove. The box absorbed all light that touched it.

Avery's eyes drifted down to Achak and then to Hototo. "You have attacked us. Wake him!" she commanded, and Hototo bowed once again then hurried over to the prone form. He traced his temple in a similar fashion to how he had awakened Avery, and Achak's eyes drifted slowly open. Groggily, he rolled onto his side and pushed himself up on one arm, head hanging.

"This is the Crystal Cave. Why are you guarding it? And from whom?" Avery demanded.

"We have always guarded the cave, mistress. It has been our sacred, secret duty for longer than any of us can remember. From the beginning, it has always been so. No one may enter the caverns except the chosen ones. Similar to how the Spirit Clan's High Priestess is the chosen one for the spirit temple, the Flesh Clan priests serve the Crystal Cave. We guard the cave and keep it safe for the return of the Chosen One of the gods. It is here, look." Hototo pulled a scroll from amongst the books in the alcove that housed them. He unrolled the parchment and held it in front of Avery. "See here? The prophecies state that the Chosen One will bear the markings of the temple spirits and will be a priest above all High Priests." He let go of the parchment with one hand, and it rolled back up. He lifted his hand to point at her tattoos. "You are marked by the spirits." Hototo returned the scroll then tugged at the ties of his shirt, pulling it open to display his chest, covered in tattoos. "And so am I. The prophecies say that when the Prophesied One appears, the gods will be reunited with the people. One has already returned to us, and now you appear, mistress."

Avery stood up, frowning. "Who is this other?" she asked, her tone sharp and demanding. "Who else has come to the cavern?"

Hototo shook his head. "No one, mistress; the Chosen One I speak of was returned to us by the gods themselves. She has descended from on high. Artio is returned to us, blessed of the goddesses."

"Artio!" Avery shot to her feet, and Achak, seeing her alarm, forced his knees to straighten, wobbling over to Avery's side. "That's impossible. Where is she?" she demanded, suspicious that a trap may have been laid for her and Achak.

"She is in her temple, mistress. Surely you know of the Bear Clan temple? I must admit, the knowledge had been lost to us, but with the return of the bear goddess, all is being restored, and the timeline reset, as prophesied." He frowned at Avery, hesitant to challenge her.

"Bear goddess?" Avery and Achak's eyes met and then Avery walked over to the alcoves, letting her fingers trail along the wall as she strolled by them. Some of the objects brightened as she passed, others darkened, but all reacted to her presence.

Eventually, she paused at the last of the objects. The black box hummed and rattled, as though a beetle scrabbled inside it. She reached her hand forward, but Achak caught her wrist before she could touch it. "Mother, let me retrieve it."

She shook her head. "You don't know what it will do. Hototo, can anyone touch these objects? Come on, man, speak up!" she demanded in an imperious tone.

"We do not handle the objects, Mother. They were placed here by the gods eons ago. They are not for humans. We would not dare."

Avery tsked. "You mean to say that no one has ever been tempted to handle these things?"

"You misunderstand, Mother. We cannot touch them. See?" Hototo strode over and reached out for the black box. Along the vertical plane of the front of the alcove his hand abruptly halted. An invisible barrier prevented his hand from entering the cavity.

Achak reached out his hand, expecting resistance, but instead, his hand sunk through the barrier. Startled, he stumbled forward, thrown off-balance, and his hand settled on the box. It was cool to the touch and all vibrations ceased. He grasped the box and withdrew it. Behind the box, pushed further back into the cavity was a black leather purse. Achak pulled it out too and slipped the box inside it. The box caught on an object already inside it and would not go in. Achak gave it an extra hard shove, and it slid partway but would move no further. When he looked up, he saw they were both staring at him.

"Well, that is resolved then." Avery swung back to the priest. "I still do not understand the reason you are here. Why are you not with the Flesh Clans? Are they not at war with the men of Cathair?"

Hototo shifted, eyes jumping from one to the other, and then his eyes focused on a spot over her shoulder. "Yes, they are. I had business to attend to elsewhere. I returned here," he gestured at the cave, "to retrieve an object, just before warriors alerted me to your presence."

The runes on Avery's scalp danced as she shook her head, lips flattening in dissatisfaction at his answer. "You cannot touch the objects. What could you possibly have expected to recover?" Avery's eyes shifted to the box in Achak's hands and opened her mouth to speak once again when the light of the cave darkened as though a dark shelf cloud rolled overhead and the ever-present glow of the cave dimmed. Shadows formed in the rounded corners and the temperature dropped. Alarmed, Avery drew her knife just as a slimy hand clapped over her mouth from behind. Strong arms wrapped around her torso and she bucked angrily, fighting to free herself.

Achak found himself similarly restrained, as a pair of Charun slid from the shadows. Thick strands of black stretched like warm taffy to warp an underworld portal into the cave. The box tumbled from Achak's grip and bounced away across the floor, falling clear of the leather bag.

Hototo bowed low to the Charun, backing away from of the spill of dark ooze that was the magical passage to the netherworld, as it spread slowly across the cave floor. He was afraid to touch the soul-sucking blackness. He bent and scooped up the bag as he backed away. Once he reached the doorway, he spun around and ran from the Charun, fleeing the cave, racing down the narrow passageway. He had his prize. He shook the bag as he ran. Out tumbled a straw doll. The last doll. He grinned then stuffed the bag back under his tunic.

Once clear of the passage he slowed to a walk. He had all the time in the world now. No need to hurry. The Charun had the fake High Priestess now. *One problem solved. My mistress will be well pleased. I will be rewarded above all others.* His cheeks creased into a fleshy grin.

Chapter 31

Mordecai's Plan

MORDECAI WAS A PRACTICAL WIZARD. He was also a patient one, and prided himself on his ability to wait out any problem. Often a solution would present itself without having to actually formulate a plan.

So, when he spied Ziona and Cayden riding out of the legion's camp spread out in the valley below him, he was only mildly surprised at the turn of events. He stepped out from behind the big tree he had been hiding behind, observing the comings and goings of the camp, and hollered down to them, waving his arms in the air to attract their attention. His sleeves flapped like the wings of a bird, his grey wizard robes shot with silver thread sparkling in the sunshine.

Ziona spied him first, and tapping Cayden on the arm, pointed up the hill to Mordecai. She reined her horse in his direction, trotting up to his location with Cayden on her heels. As they approached, Cayden swayed in his saddle, slipping sideways as though drunk.

Mordecai frowned and grabbed hold of the bridle, halting the horse as it moved past him. Cayden patted the horse's neck and grinned at Mordecai. "Alcina freed us with a pardon. Wasn't that kind of her?" Ziona frowned back at him, twisting in her saddle.

"Kind? Alcina is never kind." Ziona grimaced. "Focus, Cayden. Fight the doll." She had grown more alarmed the further they had ridden from the legion camp. While they were free, Cayden was obviously not. Strange phrases and thoughts spoken aloud that would never have come from him normally proved that Alcina still controlled his mind. *I do not know what to do about it. While I am with him, I can monitor his activities, but what do I do if she takes him over? What is Alcina's plan?* Mordecai's face echoed the expression on hers, as he frowned at the young king. "She did release us with a pardon, however," she said.

"A pardon, you say? A pardon. I have never heard of Alcina granting pardons, unless they were posthumously. You both look to be alive. So, the only conclusion, my boy, is that she did not pardon you. But now is not the time for that discussion. You are free and away from her camp and that is what matters, for now."

"How did you know we were being freed?" asked Ziona.

"I had no idea."

"So why are you here? Surely you were not intending to come rescue us alone?" Her eyes searched the trees but located no one else with Mordecai.

"I am quite alone, Ziona. I am not powerless, you know. Sometimes one can do what an army cannot, especially when stealth is required. I came to recover the doll, not to free you two." He waved a bony hand at the pair of them.

Cayden snorted, glaring at the wizard. "I suppose you brought the stone too? Fat lot of good it did."

"Actually, it did a lot of good, Cayden. It has led me directly to you."

"Anyone could follow the trampling of two thousand legionnaires. That did not require the stone."

"No, but it still points to you and only to you."

Cayden shrugged, unimpressed.

Mordecai ignored Cayden's grousing. "Ziona, I want you to join up with Avery. Can you still find her?"

Ziona nodded. "She is not far away."

"I thought so. A day's ride at most I would say. Go now." Mordecai's attention swung back to the legion camp. "I am going after that doll."

"The odds of you being successful are low," Ziona muttered. "She keeps it with her at all times. She never puts it down. And there are at least two dolls, not one."

"She will have them together and on her person. No matter. I will figure out a way to recover them."

Ziona gathered up her reins, and her head swiveled in Avery's direction. Her sense was vague, but then Cayden spoke up. "I can ask her where she is."

He closed his eyes and reached out to his sister, mind to mind. *Avery, I am coming to you. Can you show me where you are?*

He felt her touch his mind. Into his vision swam an image of a narrow trail with tall mountains and around and in the distance, a smoking summit. "She is in the Highland Needle, near the Thunder Falls."

"Then let's go. Good luck, Mordecai. Be careful. Be very careful."

"You forget that I have been a guest of Alcina's in the past. I do not fear her. But I also do not underestimate her desire for revenge. I have no intention of falling into her clutches again."

Ziona smiled and, with a slap of the reins, set off, Cayden at her side. Mordecai watched them until they were swallowed by the trees, and then his attention shifted back to the encampment.

He would wait till nightfall and then slip in at the perimeter where the guard was thinnest. They patrolled the edge of the camp but did not venture any further than a couple spans from the set perimeter, and always patrolled as a pair. One hundred paces, square the sword, bow, pivot, one hundred paces back. But in that time when they bowed, there was a point when all eyes were pointing at the ground. That was his window.

Mordecai settled down under the tree, pulling a couple apples from his pocket. He shined one on his robes then took a big juicy bite. *Nothing to do but to wait till dark. Wait and observe.*

* * *

Cayden took the lead as the terrain became rockier and the trail less sure. Birds twittered and cawed and occasionally a squirrel chittered at them as they passed, scolding them for disturbing the quiet of their forest dwelling. Ziona relaxed as they rode. The further away from the camp they travelled and the deeper into Primordial lands, the more relaxed she became. By midday, the trees changed to evergreens, the leafy deciduous of the lower foothills thinning as the soil turned poor.

"Soon we will be entering the Sacred Lands. Here the magic of the mountain will take over, and the guardians who walk it allow only the worthy to pass." Her eyes darted in his direction. "I believe your father tried to enter with the Kingsmen, back before you were born. They were turned away. Sometimes it is done gently. Sometimes it is deadly. It depends on the perceived threat. But you"—she looked at him fully this time—"are a god. I have no fear that they will let you pass."

Cayden yawned and rubbed his eyes. He was having difficulty focusing on her words.

"Cayden, are you all right?"

"Yes, but the doll is still working on me. She may have shelved it, but I think she takes it out to play with it like a child. I think she can't resist. I need rest." Another yawn cracked his jaw. "Where do you suggest we bed down for the night?" He blushed when he realized what he had said.

Ziona grinned at him. "So eager! Don't worry. I have a place in mind."

Several hours later, at the edge of the Sacred Forest, Ziona led them to a clearing containing a small pond. Sunlight sparkled on its surface and bugs skimmed across the surface. Every once in a while, a fish would jump out of the water and snap at an insect, then fall back with a splash. A third of the circumference of the pond was edged with a tangle of raspberry bushes, the branches bending low under the weight of ripe berries.

Ziona dismounted with Cayden, and they hobbled the horses then pulled off their saddles. Retrieving their bedrolls, they made a rough camp. Ziona knelt by the water's edge and gave a blessing to the waters, asking for them to share their bounty. She placed a hand in the water and caught a fat trout with her bare hand, tossing it up on the shore where it flopped and flailed.

Ten minutes later, the trout was grilling over an open fire and they gathered berries to complete their impromptu feast. Before the sun was fully set, they snuggled in each other's arms. Ziona smoothed Cayden's brow with tiny kisses that trailed down the side of his cheek. Cayden gasped and rolled Ziona onto her back, as his hunger for her ignited into a more robust version of her kisses. The stress of the day vanished, and passion flared white hot as they fell under the spell of their love.

*   *   *

In a camp, a long way away, Alcina grinned as she stroked her doll. She ran her finger down the side of the doll's neck and could feel the doll trembling in her hand in response. *What a wicked boy you are, Cayden! Who knew such passion ran through your veins? Maybe I should keep you for myself.*

The bond was just as strong as it had been when he was in the camp. Alcina was pleased with the total control she still had over him, at any distance.

Now, lead me to your sister, like a good soul slave.

Chapter 32

Brimstone

A MIST DESCENDED INTO THE CLEARING, shrouding the pond and creeping across the ground. Fingers of fog ghosted the trees, wrapping around limbs and clouding the space between trunks. The mist cast a bluish hue in the rays of a nearly full moon, filtered and weakened by its passage through the mist overhead.

Cayden rolled over in his sleep, twisted up in the blanket he shared with Ziona, and his face smacked up against a soft muzzle that snuffled and snorted, ruffling his hair.

The horses...have wandered over, he thought in a sleep-drugged stupor. He pushed the muzzle away. The horse snuffled him again then took the blanket in its teeth and tugged it off.

With a shiver, Cayden woke, as the cold vapour touched his exposed skin. Cayden's eyes popped open, and he sucked in a surprised breath. It was not the horses.

Slowly he sat up and the creature stepped back, eyeing him steadily with pitch black eyes that shone in the filtered moonlight. A mane of thickest black curls flowed from sharply pointed ears. Cayden's eyes slowly followed the flow of its neck to its body, from which sprouted long, feathered wings tipped in white. The Pegasus snorted once again. As Cayden rose to his feet, it nudged him hard in the chest with its velvety nose. Cayden stroked the muzzle, hand curving around his lower jaw.

"Brimstone!" he breathed, knowing the name to be right, running his hand down Brimstone's sleek neck.

A hidden lever in his mind clicked, and with it, a rush of memory assailed him. Eons of memory of ages past flooded his mind, and he cried out under the crushing weight of the images flowing through his mortal brain. He sank to his knees, clutching at his head. This pain was not like the doll, which was external. This pain was the pain of memory, the pain of loss and remembrance. Tears streamed down his face, and Brimstone snuffled him once again, smearing the tears with his nose.

Ziona sat up abruptly, woken by the sound of Cayden's sobs. Her training kicked in, and knives appeared in hand as though she had slept clutching them. She sprang to her feet, then paused at the sight of Cayden and Brimstone. "Oh, Cayden!" Seeing his distress, the knives disappeared, and she knelt beside him, putting her arms around him to hug him. "Shhh," she mouthed. "It's OK. I know it hurts."

As she rocked him, she examined the Pegasus. She had never seen one, but the ancient texts spoke of the Pegasuses that the godlings had ridden. They had disappeared with the godlings themselves. No one knew why, but she suspected they were tied to the gods in some way.

Cayden calmed and wiped his sleeve against his eyes, drying them.

"*I remember*," he boomed, then paused, startled at the sound of his voice. The voice was of a distant Cayden, the voice of a godling. Ziona's eyes widened and she backed away in surprise. "I'm sorry, Ziona. Don't be afraid." He stood up, rubbing a hand across his temple and then strode over to the Pegasus who tossed his head, nostrils flaring and flapping his silky, ebony wings.

"Hello, Brimstone, my old friend. Thank you for the gift of my memory."

Brimstone bowed to him.

"Brimstone has returned my memory," Cayden said in his normal voice. "All of it." His gaze swept around the clearing. With eyes suddenly ancient, he focused on her still form. "I remember everything, Ziona." He reached out a hand to her, and hesitantly she took it.

"Mordecai said this day would come. Brimstone carried the key to my memory block. He was waiting for me to come to him in the Sacred Forest to be reunited with him."

Cayden stroked the sleek neck. "Where are Moonbeam and Sandstorm?" he asked Brimstone.

Brimstone shook his head, tossing his mane, and then whinnied and from the mist two more Pegasuses approached. Cayden smiled at them, greeting each of them in turn as they crowded in. "Moonbeam was Alfreda's—Avery's—and Sandstorm was Artio's. Although at the time of the cataclysm, they were with me. They were a gift from our father..." He trailed off, exploring the memory. When his eyes refocused, Ziona was on her knees again before him.

"Ziona, I thought we had settled this. Do not kneel before me." He reached down and pulled her to her feet.

"You are a child of the gods. I am mortal kind. I must worship you." She kept her face downcast.

"No, you are my soul mate now. You will not bow to me. Worship the gods, but not me."

He raised her chin with a finger, and Brimstone crowded in to nuzzle her cheek. She laughed and stroked his soft muzzle. The other two, not to be outdone, shoved their noses in for pats, trampling their blankets in the process.

Cayden and Ziona both laughed, and the laugh was echoed by fairies that flashed out of the reeds at the edge of the pond and flashed around them, jewel-coloured and chuckling with a tinkling sound as they flitted above them.

"Caerwyn! Caerwyn!" they called, their tiny voices the peeping of baby birds.

Cayden reached up, and a turquoise fairy with snow-white hair lit on his finger. "Aossi said you would come soon," she pipped, her iridescent wings sparkling in the moonlight.

Delighted, Ziona said, "Do you have a name? I am so happy to meet you!"

"Laila," she squeaked.

"Laila, Laila, Laila," the other fairies tinkled.

Brimstone tossed his head, and the fairies scattered, bringing attention back to him. He nudged Cayden with his shoulder.

"I think he wants you to go for a ride," said Ziona. Brimstone snorted agreement.

"Oh! Well..." Unsure, Cayden patted Brimstone on his shoulder, and Brimstone sank down on his forelegs, making it easier for

Cayden to mount. With a shrug, Cayden swung a leg over onto Brimstone's back, just behind the withers where jutted the massive wings, and tucked his knees under the huge muscles. He then twisted his hands in the thick black mane. Brimstone stood up and within a couple of strides launched him skyward. Cayden yelled as he cleared the trees, the beats of the wings stirring their leaves. Sleepy birds twitted angrily. Then Cayden was above the trees, above the mist, and soaring in the pure light of the moon.

The ground below sank away as the Pegasus flew. There was only the sky and the moon. If it were not for the cold night air streaming past his face or the heavy beat of Brimstone's wings, Cayden would have thought they were standing still. The peace of the flight helped him sort through the tumbling images in his head. He took a deep breath, settling himself, sorting and filing the information. *I am transformed. I finally remember who I am.*

It was not as comforting as he had thought it would be before he knew. With the return of his memory also came the return of the worries of the world, a return of ancient anxieties and problems. While it cleared his focus, it also complicated his path. With a sigh, he patted Brimstone on the neck. "We need to go back down, Brimstone, and rejoin Ziona. Can you find her?" Brimstone twisted his neck, and a snort of disgust issued from his throat. Cayden smiled. "That's my boy."

Brimstone banked and sank back into the mists, touching down with a lightness that disturbed nothing on the ground. He trotted back to Ziona, who was stroking the other Pegasuses and feeding them leftover raspberries from the palm of her hand. She looked up as they approached, a huge grin of pleasure on her face. Her eyes sparkled.

Cayden slid off and walked back to her. "I know what we need to do."

"I'm glad," she said simply. "I will follow wherever you lead, Cayden."

Cayden smiled at Ziona, shoving his hands in his pockets. Brimstone nudged him hard in the back, pushing Cayden into Ziona. Cayden's arms came up around her. Ziona laughed and hugged Cayden back. Brimstone tossed his head, as though saying, "Now, that's better!"

Cayden eyed Brimstone. "Don't you start getting cheeky with me!" he growled in mock anger. Brimstone shook his head, curly mane flopping into his eyes. Cayden's lips twitched with amusement.

Cayden checked the position of the moon, which was sinking below the crown of the trees.

"We need to get some more rest…if these great louts will let us. I would like to be on the trail as the sun rises."

As he and Ziona crawled back under their blankets and settled in, the Pegasuses wandered over to greet the horses. Cayden's last thought as he drifted off was how happy Avery would be to see Moonbeam once again.

Chapter 33

The Second Doll

MORDECAI WAITED UNTIL THE DEEP OF NIGHT to slip into the legion's camp. As the guards neared the end of their shift, they stifled yawns behind hands. Their paced patrolling slowed as the night crept on. Keeping to the shadows, Mordecai drifted from one dark trunk to the next with each pass. Now fifty feet of grass separated him from the comforting blackness of the nearest tent. He counted…sixty-five, sixty-six, sixty-seven…and on the stamp of seventy, he ran, crouching low across the open space. He slid into the overhang of the tent, which turned out to house supplies for the horses, and paused, listening for any hint of alarm. Hearing none, he stealthily made his way toward the ornate tent located at the center of the camp. He avoided the low-burning firepits that dotted the landscape, and none saw him pass, night-blind by the flickering flames. His hand drifted to the breast of his robes. Yes, the package, his backup escape plan, was still there. He would use it, but only as a last resort, should his escape be…impeded.

Alcina's tent rose up out of the encampment, twice as large as any around it and heavily guarded. Like a moss-covered rock, it was draped in guards, sprouting here and there. It was separated by a cleared circle of trampled grass that left the tent isolated, even though it was surrounded by a legion full of men. The sounds of the encampment around it were muted, and the croaking of crickets filled the air.

He paused, crouching down beside a tent at the edge of the circle and checked the placement of the guards. Two helmeted men stood at attention at the entrance to the tent, and Mordecai counted four others around the exterior; one leaned up against a tree, another lit a cigarette with a splinter of wood from a firepit. Two more played cards by the light of the low flames, and coins jingled as one laid out his wager.

Mordecai pulled the stone from his pocket and clutched it in his right hand and closed his eyes. His lips moved, and a thin probe of spirit whispered up from the stone attuned to Cayden's will. It drifted across the intervening space and then slipped past the guards and through the crack of the tent opening without attracting notice. He commanded the probe to explore the tent, searching for the doll that held Cayden's will. The probe melted around the tent, searching until it paused beside a sleeping person. Cayden's will pulsed, a strong throb that warmed the stone in Mordecai's hand. Mordecai urged it to look for the second doll, and it moved on, wandering around the tent, but it could not find the doll. Frustrated, he recalled the wisp, opening his eyes to break the spell. He had not expected it to. Without the tie of a soul, there was nothing to sense. It was just a doll, after all.

Mordecai made to stand. As he attempted to rise to his feet, he bumped into a solid object. Scarlet-slippered feet peeked from the hem of a grey, rough silk gown. Mordecai's eyes travelled upward to meet Alcina's victorious ones. In her hand, she held a doll, dressed in grey robes. Attached to its chin were several strands of beard, his beard. She picked up a long needle and locking her eyes on his, stabbed the doll in the chest. Pain shot through Mordecai, and he grabbed at his chest, his eyes widening and his mouth opened in a silent scream. His nerveless fingers dropped the stone clutched in them, and he toppled sideways, writhing on the ground while Alcina stepped around him, snapping her fingers to call her guards.

"So," she purred in a soft voice dripping with menace, "we meet again, Mordecai. This time, you will not escape. This time the only possible escape is death. It was useful to cut your hair all those years ago. I kept them, you see, as the mage promised me there was magic to be had in your graying locks." She reached down with a knife and cut a strip of cloth free of the sleeve of his robes and draped it around the doll. "Your will is mine. Your soul is mine. You will obey and serve me until death releases you. But first, I will enjoy torturing you. Oh yes, this time I will find the time." Her pitiless blue eyes stared down into his. "Finally, the will of a wizard is at my command." With a predatory twist of red lips, she commanded, "Pick up this filth and carry him to my tent. I intend to have some fun with him. Gag him first. I do not want to disturb the rest of my troops."

The men bent down and shoved a soiled cloth into Mordecai's mouth, tying it roughly behind his head then pulled back his arms, binding his wrists behind his back. They hauled him to his feet. Still bent double in pain, he sagged in their arms.

Alcina withdrew the pin and scraped it along the chest of the doll. Mordecai groaned, as his chest registered the sensation of a sharp knife slicing across his chest. Blood bloomed under his shirt and trickled down, fine rivulets that quickly soaked through.

Alcina was panting with pleasure as the blood blossomed on the grey robes. A powerful lust consumed her, flaring in her eyes as she called over her shoulders, as the guards hauled Mordecai into her tent. "Darius, attend me," she purred, and followed the soldiers inside, the flap dropping back as the guards released it after she had passed.

Darius grinned and, strutting like a prized peacock, followed his queen into the tent, already loosening the ties of his shirt, sweating with the heat of anticipation. He grinned at the jealous stares of his fellow guards. *They should be jealous,* he chuckled to himself. *Oh yes, they should be jealous.*

Clearing the entrance of the tent, Darius saw that the guards had dumped the wizard on the gaudy carpet, so recently decorated by Cayden. He had laughed at his former friend, the "king" of Cathair reduced to a drooling puppet. Now he grinned at the old man, his queen's nemesis, a rival she had fought her entire life. He walked up and kicked the old man in the stomach, and Mordecai jack-knifed around the blow, his air going out with a whoosh. He thought he heard something crack and shook his head. "He will not last long under torture. He is too old." Darius spoke the words aloud as the guards left the tent, leaving just the three of them.

Alcina placed the doll on the table beside her judgement chair, as he had come to think of it, and then sank down onto its overstuffed surface.

Steepling her fingers, Alcina studied the wizard. He lay panting on the ground, groaning softly.

"Well, Mordecai? You never did have any tolerance for torture. Do you remember the old days? When the Queen's Guard went at you with those hot irons? You would faint as soon as the iron touched your skin, then I would have to wake you to heal yourself. It's no fun torturing an unconscious person. I finally had to give up and forget my plans to extract information out of you. Instead, I left you in that dungeon to die. But you refused to, you stubborn old goat." Her grim smile widened and her teeth gleamed, feral and deadly. "But with this doll, I can fine-tune it, can't I?" she paused, but Mordecai did not answer. He could not answer. With a slippered toe, Alcina dragged the gag from his mouth and down onto his chin.

"As much as I like seeing you bleed, that is hardly going to work with you, is it? No, the torture I intend for you is of a mental nature. You will not be able to shut it off or escape because it will be all in your head. I intend to force you to listen to your friends screams as they die...at your own hand. When I eventually release your mind, you will kill yourself. It will not be of my doing or by my hand."

"You know that I have Cayden under the same control, or you would not have come here. You hoped to recover this." She twitched a doll dressed like Cayden in front of his face, then tucked it back into a pocket in her skirt. "He did not escape. I set him and his seeker free. But he is still completely under my control. From where I send him, he will not return. He has a mission to complete that he has no knowledge of. It will be triggered when he reaches his destination. And then he will die, after he chokes that useless seeker to death. You will never see either of them again, wizard."

Mordecai straightened, fighting the pain of what felt like broken ribs and took a shallow, tentative breath. "Once again your delusions lead you into realms of impossibility. You cannot control me with that doll. *I...will...not...submit!*" he ground out through clenched teeth. "I will stop my own heart before I hurt either of those kids. And as for Cayden, he is stronger than you can possibly understand. He will find a way to undo the damage you have inflicted on him. You will lose again, Alcina."

Alcina reared up from her chair, her temper flashing to the boiling point, then ran at Mordecai. She snatched up the doll and stabbed the pin into the straw head. Mordecai's temple exploded with pain. He screamed, clutching at his head, and collapsed to the floor, thrashing as crushing waves of pain washed over him from head to foot, so strong his toes curled in his boots. He cried out once more then stilled.

Disgusted, Alcina tossed the doll back on the chair and stepping around the unconscious wizard, then grabbed Darius by the arm and dragged him unresistingly back into her private chambers.

Bright red blood dripped from Mordecai's right nostril and puddled on the floor under his right cheek. They left Mordecai on the floor in the spreading pool without a backward glance.

Chapter 34

Fates Align

THE SCREAMS OF THE WOUNDED soared above the clang of metal on metal, a high-pitched counterpoint to the near rhythmic metronome of battle. The high mountain pass had opened into a sparse valley that clung to the side of the mountain, a saucer of greenery in a great stone cup. The verdant green was quickly turning to rust, as the churning of the horses' hooves trampled the grasses and flowers. A metallic taste hung in the air as blood was spilled, the blood of men and horses mixing with the anxious odours of sweat and urine.

Sharisha pulled her own short sword and dug her heels into the flanks of her mount. Her horse shot forward into the mix of Primordial warriors and legion soldiers. The men from the other side of the mountain were already blood-covered prior to the commencement of this surprise attack, and they'd hesitated before launching themselves out of the woods into battle. At first, she'd mistaken their wild shouts as cries of pain, rather than a war cry.

But now, she fought for her life. Soldiers fell on every side of her, but Sharisha's sole task was to protect the High Priestess, to whom she was bound. Her mount trampled two men trying to pull Marea out of her seat, and Sharisha stabbed a third through the throat as he grabbed the bridle of Marea's mare. The man's eyes widened in shock, and then he fell, slipping off the blade, hand frozen on the bridle, pulling the horse's head down with his collapsing body. The horse snorted in fear and bucked, clearing more men from the rear.

Sharisha reached over and pulled Marea off her mare onto the back of her horse, leaving the bucking mount to its crazed dance.

Sharisha sawed on the reins. Marea gasped and slumped against her back. Bright crimson ran down the High Priestess's arm, which encircled Sharisha's waist. With a snarl, Sharisha reared her horse, forelegs flailing, bringing it down on the two men in front of her. Then, she dug in her heels once again and her horse shot forward, bowling over men like stones on a game board. She cleared the main circle of fighting and whipped her horse with the loose ends of her reins urging her mount to greater speed, focused on the resumption of the path ahead. Her only thought was to get Marea away from the battle to find a safe place to tend to her wounds. Sharisha glanced over her shoulder and saw Marea clinging grimly to her, eyes flashing with fury. Her arm bled freely, but it did not look to be a critical wound. Sharisha dashed down the curve in the road, the cries of the battle receding. Just as she reached the edge of the clearing before the relative safety of the woods, a man rose from the bushes. Triumph glittered in his narrowed eyes, and then he grinned, lips stretching into a victorious, toothy smile. Raising his bow, he drew, sighted, and released the arrow with one fluid movement.

The impact was jarring, the arrow piercing Sharisha's right breast and driving straight through. Were it not for the fact that Marea clutched her around Sharisha's waist and held her upright, she would surely have tumbled from the saddle. Sharisha's horse ran on into the trees, now completely out of control, as Sharisha could no longer feel the reins in her hands. She tried to take in a breath, but it was agony. She coughed and blood bubbled to her lips. Spots danced in her sight and she sighed. *So, this is death,* she thought, watching as the light of the world shrunk smaller and smaller until it vanished completely. *I did want to see Avery one last time. There is something about that child.*

Sharisha slumped over the neck of her horse. A blue mist rose from her body and hung in the air, waiting to be claimed.

*　　*　　*

Cyrus lowered his bow and watched the Primordial women ride off into the woods. A clear trail of blood splattered behind them, obvious even to the poorest of trackers, of which, he was not. He gathered his horse, tucking the bow back into its scabbard and then remounted, following the trail. He cared not if his men survived. He only wanted the High Priestess, and now she was his.

He followed the trail for about half an hour, surprised to see that they had kept their saddle. He was sure he had killed the first woman, probably the High Priestess's bodyguard by the way she had come to the woman's defense. The High Priestess was also wounded. Would she stop to bury her guard, or would she shove the body aside and continue to flee? From what he knew of Primordial belief about the dead, he thought she would pause to offer prayers to the gods for the safe passage of the soul. How long she would pause, he was not sure, but it would afford him the time to kill her, if he was swift enough.

Sure enough, ten minutes of hard riding brought him to an ice-cold glacial stream. The trail led straight toward it and stopped at the edge of the water. He dismounted beside a hastily built mound, and laid out in Primordial fashion was the dead seeker. She'd been buried in the loose sand of the river's undercut bank, beneath a cairn of hastily scooped river rock, leaving her face uncovered, so that she could continue to commune with the spirits of the forest even in death. Her eyes were propped open, all the better to see the spirits when they paused to visit. The first of these ancient burial mounds he had come across had been in the foothills on a previous campaign, but he'd thought the bizarre practice had been long abandoned.

He placed his hand on the dead woman's forehead. The body was still warm. Cyrus shivered. *How barbaric! These heathens never change. They are an anthill that should be ground underfoot and stamped out of existence.* The Flesh Clans, at least, had adopted burning the bodies of the dead, if Alcina was to be believed, properly freeing the spirits from the imprisonment of the flesh, as was the way for those of Cathairian origins.

His eyes left the mound and he walked around, searching for the new trail. Horse tracks entered the stream, but due to the thickness of the undergrowth which hugged the shore, the path was obvious.

Crushed ferns provided a guidepost, and he picked out the continuance of the trail on the other side of the stream. The woman was alone now and easy pickings. He remounted and left the dead woman behind. She was nothing. His true prize still ran, and he would not rest till he caught her. With her as his prisoner, he would have all the bargaining chips he needed, especially if he caught up to the other woman they'd been following. He suspected it was their prisoner, escaped from the fiery hut. He would deliver two important gifts for his mistress of shadow. First, he would take this one, and then go after the other. If his men caught up to him, so be it. If not…well, they were a stupid lot and not worthy of accompanying him. Eventually, he would have had to dispose of them for learning what he was up to. He would overthrow Alcina or he would die trying. Too long he had laboured in the queen's shadow, while the goddess whispered to him of the rewards he would receive if he were the one to hand over the prophesied children. Alcina's blundering had cost them the boy. They had had him chained in the dungeon, for spirit's sake! Abruptly, Cyrus jerked his thoughts back to the search at hand. *Focus. I need to recover the woman. That is what I need to do.* With that grim thought, he booted his horse into motion and trotted swiftly down the trail, marking the dots of blood that occasionally dropped onto the forest floor.

*   *   *

Marea clutched at the bandage slipping down her arm. She'd wrapped it hastily with cloth torn from her underskirt and tied it off, but the knot had loosened with the hauling of the rocks she had used to bury Sharisha, and she had lost valuable time. Sharisha had been a loyal seeker though, deserving of the cairn for her final journey. She had protected her and honoured her in life, and now the bond had driven her to protect Marea from certain death. Sharisha deserved to be given the Welcoming Ceremony, the sacred sharing of the soul with the gods, and so Marea had halted beside the stream to let the horse drink, clean her wound, and bury the seeker.

The cut by the blade was deep but not long; however, it was jagged and located in the crook of her elbow. Every last movement of the arm opened the wound afresh, so that it continuously bled. It needed stitching, something she could not take the time to do, and impossible while jouncing on the back of a horse.

Marea pulled out an amulet tucked under her shirt and clutched it in her right hand, the hand of the bleeding arm. It helped to rest the arm across her chest and clutching the stone gave her something to cling to, to keep the arm as still as possible. The amulet of the High Priestess connected her to the temple, to the spirits of the temple, but it remained cold and lifeless in her hand. It had only sung to her one time, when she'd been granted access to the temple on that first occasion. She had picked up the necklace where it lay on a tray just inside the door. It had flared to life and forms had emerged from it, swirling around the common room and around her before fading away. It had not spoken to her since. Yet, she clung to the memory, to the fact that she could still enter even if the temple did not light up like it had for the girl.

Marea swayed in the saddle. Blood loss, she knew it instinctively. She would have to stop to rest soon, but there was no safety here. There was no place to hide. She was weak from lack of blood and weary, her body slowing down. She could not keep up the pace, yet she knew the soldier was still on her trail—she could sense it.

She closed her eyes and prayed to her ancestors, prayed as she had never prayed before. She reached out to the gods of her people. "Temple of the ancestors, I know I have not prayed to you in a long time and I have been negligent in singing your praises, but I pray to you now. Ancient Ones, if I truly am the anointed one, if I am truly chosen, then show me your will. Am I to die to make way for the girl? Help me…please show me my path! Show me your will!"

The amulet trembled in her grip and waves of energy vibrated so sharply through the stone that Marea's fingers numbed and she dropped it with a gasp. The amulet had never done that before. The crystal flashed a ball of blue flame which enveloped her, horse and all. With a clap of thunder, she was gone.

Chapter 35

Answered Prayer

AVERY FOUGHT THE DARKNESS that pervaded the room as she struggled within the Charun's slimy grasp. The stink of death surrounded the Charun, and she fought against the tug of the underworld. It pulled at her soul, at the essence of her being, dragging her down with the dry rattling breaths of one long dead. Avery fought the drag and the pull with every ounce of her strength.

Achak kicked and squirmed in the grip of the second Charun. Suddenly, it was enveloped in a skin of blue fire that slid Achak's entire body, encasing it.

Avery screamed as she writhed in the grip of the Charun, but Achak did not. Instead, he stilled, and the blue flames solidified and parted from his body to reform in the air above his head as a pure spirit phoenix. Its talons, beak, and eyes were ice blue flame. The feathers of the spirit guardian danced in an invisible breeze as the bird lifted into the air. The Charun gripping Achak hesitated, its focus distracted by the spirit bird.

The phoenix began to sing a mesmerizing song that froze the pair of Charun. They began to sway in response to the song, bewitched by the melody, and their grips loosened. With a jarring screech, the guardian dived at the Charun holding Avery and tore at its face with talons of ice that hissed and steamed. It screeched, the noise of good steel sharpening on a grinding wheel. Sparks flew from the Charun, and then it imploded, sucking the blackness back to the hell of its home.

Avery fell to the floor of the cave at the sudden release, and the phoenix swung back to the remaining Charun. Avery raised her head just in time to see Achak picked up by clawed hands as dark as night. The Charun raised Achak above his head and flung him at the glowing phoenix. He passed straight through as it had no corporeal substance. He struck the wall on the far side with a sickening crunch and a howl of pain. The phoenix flickered, then dived at the Charun, grabbing it by its exposed throat, and pulled. Black sulphuric blood bubbled and burned as it spilled onto the floor of the cavern and with a second bang, the Charun imploded.

"Achak!" Avery stumbled over to his side, avoiding the flashing ooze that pitted the marble floor.

Achak moaned, clutching at the leg crumpled and twisted impossibly against the wall. He looked at it and then swiftly away, as bile rose in his throat. He clung to consciousness by a thread.

"Shh!" commanded Avery, as she gently felt along the length of his leg. The femur was twisted under her hands, the sharp edges ridged under her fingers. It was broken in one, possibly two places. "Lay back. I need to splint this." She searched the interior of the cavern, looking for something to use, and her eyes fell on a several carved wooden staffs leaning against a wall in the corner. A straw mattress provided an aged blanket riddled with holes that separated easily in her hands. She tore it into long strips of cloth along the grain of the weave. Once she had enough strips piled in her lap, she retrieved a pair of staffs and ran back to Achak, who now slumped against the wall, unconscious. Avery dropped the staffs and wrappings, then laid Achak out on the stone floor. Straightening his leg, she coaxed the bones into alignment then placed the staffs alongside the break to judge the proper length. She pulled her knife from its holster and sawed at the wood, shortening staffs to the right length. The strips of cloth wrapped the leg from hip to ankle. Avery bound it so tightly that it could not shift. She crisscrossed the strips and tied off the tails, then stood to look at her work. Something about the cave prevented her touching the healing she was capable of. It was like there was a blanket over the cave, isolating it from the natural world around them, smothering her connection with the natural world from which she drew her power.

Rising to her feet, Avery walked to the entrance of the cave and peered out into the rift, to see who might be around. The passageway was empty. Silently, she moved along the path, listening for any indication that a guard remained, slowly edging her way to the opening of the bowl. A contingent of Flesh Clan warriors with their backs to her stood guard at the gap in the rock. Quietly, she withdrew, then spun around and ran back down the rift to Achak. She was about halfway back to the cave when suddenly the runes on her skin flared hot, and she cried out as the power of the temple surged within her skin. She lurched to a halt when with a flash of energy that made sparkling motes of light dance in her vision Marea appeared, swaying on the back of her horse. Marea gasped with shock at the sight of Avery, then slipped sideways and fell from her saddle, slumping onto the ground. Avery shuddered, rubbing her hands over the prickling tattoos to soothe her skin, then ran over to Marea and knelt beside her. She placed her hand on the woman's fevered brow. She was abnormally pale-faced, anemic with blood loss. Avery ran her hand over Marea's forehead and murmured under her breath.

Marea's eyes fluttered open. When she saw Avery, she reached up with her bloodied right hand and grasped the front of her tunic. "I beg your forgiveness, Mother! I have betrayed you! I was jealous. I wanted to hold onto power when I was only a caretaker. I realize that now. I prayed to the gods to save me, and they brought me to you." She sobbed. "Forgive me. You are the true High Priestess. Forgive me!"

"Shh, hush now," said Avery, prying Marea's stiff fingers off her tunic. "Shh. We are one people. Unity is what is needed. The past is done. I need your help to unite the people. Now lie still, and tell me what has happened."

"Sharisha is dead! We were attacked by a legion squad, and she died defending me. He shot her with an arrow." Her lips trembled. "I do not know how many have survived. Perhaps they are all dead but if not, Mother, they are coming this way!" The blood from the cut on her arm dripped onto Avery's lap as she helped Marea to a sitting position.

Avery grimaced. She had not trusted Sharisha, but she had not wished her harm. She had taken care of her in her own way. "Let me try to heal you. Here, lie still." She placed her hands over the wound and closed her eyes. She sensed the jagged edges of the cut where the flesh was torn and reached out with her mind to pull the raw ends together. Then with a flash of her own soul, she knit the flesh back together. Without conscious thought, she willed it to be whole. The skin wriggled and stretched, and then it was still. Other than the dried blood, not a hint of the wound remained.

Avery opened her eyes and sighed, tired from her struggles with the Charun and the exertion of healing the deep wound. Marea stared at the arm, a bemused but sad twist to her lips. "Sharisha was the most powerful with healing, but she could not hold a candle to you, Mother. Thank you."

Avery stood and pulled the older woman to her feet. She led the way back to the cave. Marea ducked under the threshold and gazed around with reverence. "No one has entered the Sacred Caves except for the guardians in eons. I've never been in the caves. The war with the Flesh Clans prevented any such thing." She wandered around the cave, a childish wonderment on her face. "I do not know what these objects do. Do you, Mother?"

"Yes," said Avery simply. "These objects of magic were placed here by my sister or sisters, a long time ago." Her eyes flashed. For a moment, an ancient knowing entered her gaze, as though she looked at the objects through a different pair of eyes. Marea dipped her head and did not inquire further.

"We are trapped here at present, Marea. There is a Flesh Clan contingent at the end of the passage." She gestured toward the bowl. "We need a distraction to draw them away from here. Do you think you could do this? It will be very dangerous. You have the advantage of them not knowing you are here. They will be surprised to see you exit this sacred place, when they did not see you enter." She reached into her tunic and pulled out the vial that Aossi had given her. "Perhaps this will help. It will hide you from your enemies. You must lead them away from the valley. Do not return for me. There is something I must attend to in here."

"What of Achak?" Marea wandered over to look at the injured man.

"He is needed here. I will heal him in time."

Marea nodded. "Then let me depart. I will create an illusion, a trick of the mind. They will follow me, thinking it is you."

"Go with my blessing, Marea, and thank you."

Marea lifted Avery's hand and kissed the back of it and then left the cave.

*   *   *

Marea exited the cleft of the rock and did not bother to disguise herself. The Flesh Clan warriors, on seeing her, quickly surrounded her and ordered her to halt. Marea reined in, and with an imperious tone commanded, "Take me to Hototo, now."

The warriors exchanged looks over their drawn swords. Clearly, they did not expect to be commanded, nor did they believe that Hototo wished to speak to a Spirit Clan priest. They made no move to lead her to her requested destination.

Marea sat on her horse like a queen, regally surveying the men as though they were her escort, part of her entourage. "Better yet, take me to whom Hototo serves. I would speak to his master."

A tall red-bearded man stepped forward, motioning toward the grey stones at the far end of the valley. "Follow me." He took the lead and Marea urged her horse into a quick walk, following Red Beard, the balance of warriors trotting at her side, easily keeping up to the pace of her mount. Her thoughts drifted back to the cave, and she glanced down at her blood-stained tunic. A flash of sorrow for the loss of her seeker—for the loss of her loyal companion, Sharisha, drifted across her thoughts—but then her will hardened.

You are far too trusting, Avery. I will not bow to you so easily. You know nothing of the politics of this world or who serves whom. You will kneel to me in time, as a chained and controlled servant of the temple. Spirit Shields should not be allowed control of world events. They are servants of the people, not rulers...not even one descended from the gods.

As she rode, her hand slipped inside her pocket, and she pulled out the vial given to her by Avery. With a derisive snort, she tossed it away onto the grass of the meadow. It tumbled and rolled and then made a *clunk* sound as it hit the base of one of the tall upright stones in the grass.

Chapter 36

Genii's Vision

GENII BENT OVER THE STONE SCRYING POOL, the waters dancing with internal light that bounced and shimmered off the stone walls and ceiling of the windowless room. He was watching a battle between the Charun, sent to restrain two intruders within the Crystal Cave, a woman and her companion. They struggled in the grip of the Charun, the woman familiar to him somehow. But it was the runes that covered her head and neck and the exposed portions of her arms that intrigued him. They were runes of power, runes of healing, runes of time and distance. Runes of nature and balance. He had never seen so many runes in one place, let alone on a person.

The man seemed to ripple and then a phoenix rose into the air, a spirit guardian of such rarity that it took Genii by surprise. Those creatures born of flame were usually associated with his mistress. To see one attuned to a mortal was highly unusual. Times were changing; Genii felt it in the air.

The phoenix attacked the Charun with blue-bladed talons of spirit. Spirit was the soft underbelly of the Charun, their one vulnerability. Being created from the souls of the dead, they could only be slain by another soul. *The phoenix is a worthy opponent, and my mistress would be pleased to hear of this.* But he did not call her. Instead, he wiped away the scene and returned to the image he had been watching earlier. He had not been sent to spy on the cave, but he had been curious where the Charun were being sent, seeing as everyone had been recalled and tasked to the creation of a lava idol. With the solstice only a day away, there was no time to lose and to spare even two of the Charun was startling.

The surface of the scrying pool calmed and reflected the image of Artio, riding at the head of a column of men and women, clad in Flesh Clan warrior garments. A covey of priests flocked around her, keeping a respectful distance from her side. Genii leaned in to better study her features. They had softened since the last time he'd seen her, some of the wildness of the bear fading into a hearty, healthy young female, but more muscular and shapelier than the Artio that stirred in his vague and scattered memories.

Straight-backed and fierce, she led her servants through a hilly terrain that resembled the early reaches of the sacred slopes. By nightfall, they would be nearing his mistress's realm. He felt a stirring in his chest that he associated with the human condition called fear and another that he associated with...love. He disliked the feelings intensely, yet he knew it was not for himself that he feared. Artio's return would not be greeted with warmth. He knew his mistress intended to slay the bear goddess once and for all. His fear thumped in his chest, gripping his imaginary heart in a tight fist. He could not let that happen. Artio must not be harmed. And yet, she walked into a trap. She did not know of his mistress's plans. But how could he warn Artio? He couldn't leave the caves. Frustration overwhelmed him. Angry at himself, Genii snarled at the image in the pool. At one point, Artio's head swiveled. For a moment, he thought that she saw him, that she was staring straight into his eyes...but then she looked away, expression unchanged.

His hand slapped the surface of the scrying pool, and the image transformed once again. This time his mistress came into view. Helga sat astride a midnight-black horse at the edge of the legion encampment, hidden by the deep shade of the tall pines. Face hidden in a matching-coloured cloak, she was indistinguishable from her mount. For one moment, she was barely visible, but then the illusion faded as black curls of smoke obscured her. She vanished, only to reappear without her horse inside a large tent. Fine furnishings decorated the tent, and a tall straight-backed chair with cushions sat on a raised dais. She stood frozen for a minute, observing the room, and then glided forward on feet that did not touch the ground to hover over a figure lying prone on the floor. Dressed in grey robes and laced boots, the man sported a long white beard. Blood trickled out of his nose and stained the rare and expensive carpet beneath him.

Helga lifted her imaginary skirts and walked around the wizard, examining him, then she paused and straightened, hearing activity in a curtained-off room of the tent. She smiled maliciously, then took her boot and roughly rolled the unconscious wizard over. A small bag with a drawstring tumbled out of his robes. She bent down and picked it up, loosening the fastenings to peer inside. A stone and a crystal were the only objects in the small bag. She pocketed them for later inspection.

On the ornate chair, she spied one of the items she had come for. She plucked the straw doll from the cushions where it had been tossed, and it followed the bag of stones into a deep inside pocket of her cloak.

Helga silently approached the partition of canvas that drifted softly in the air currents of the tent interior, and paused just outside the room. Inside, bodies writhed and danced in the age-old pagan ritual, entwined and absorbed and oblivious to the outside world.

Helga raised her hands and summoned a wicked obsidian knife, the blade twisted and razor-sharp, the glass formed of the very fires that fed the furnace under Genii's feet. Helga paused for a moment longer, listening for the guards, and then entered the room. She was still wreathed in shadows.

When she paused by the bed, a woman ceased her activities and cried out in shock, "Great Mistress!" She scrambled to separate herself from the man, but before she could move, the blade flashed and buried itself between Alcina's breasts. Alcina's face froze in shock, and then she crumpled sideways on top of the man. The man caught her, but before he could do anything further, before he could utter a sound, the blade slashed across his own throat. With a great gushing, Darius gurgled his last, his eyes rolling back into his head.

Helga stepped back to avoid the blood now flowing freely onto the feathered mattress and then wiped the blade off on the coverings pushed to the end of the bed. Once all blood was removed, she began to search the room.

She spied the other doll, her brother's doll, sitting on a table beside the bed, underneath a discarded garment. With a pleased chuckle, Helga picked it up and pocketed it, then left the room without a backward glance.

When she reached the wizard, the knife vanished, and she reached down to touch his shoulder. He became wreathed in the same smoke and both vanished, only to reappear on the back of her horse in the entrance to her abode.

So, Alcina has outlived her usefulness. Genii straightened and ran a hand over his nonexistent beard, a habit left over from his mortal days. What was Helga planning for the legion army? Surely, they would be thrown into disarray with the slaying of the former queen. Or maybe that was the plan? He pondered the events he had witnessed as he walked away from the pool and off to prepare chambers. It appeared they would have a guest...or two, very shortly.

Chapter 37

Stony Silence

HELGA SLID OUT OF THE SHADOWS at the edge of the Thunder Falls, a wraith transformed to human form once again. The unconscious wizard was draped across her saddle, but she would not remove him. She slung down from the saddle and, grabbing the reins, pulled Diablo into the mouth of her home.

"Genii! You have prepared accommodations? I have an unexpected guest, one I cannot say I am sorry to encounter! Where are you, Genii?"

"Here, mistress!" answered Genii as he came around the bend of the long hallway, hands tucked into his robes. "I have a cell prepared, mistress."

"No, no, a cell is no place for so great a personage." Helga dropped the reins and brushed past Genii. "Put him in the guest quarters overlooking the gardens. He is no threat to us now."

"Yes, mistress!" Genii bowed once more and then moved over to the side of the horse and hefted Mordecai's still form over his shoulder like a sack of potatoes. *Skinny wizard; he weighs no more than a starving rabbit.*

Genii straightened with his burden and headed down the side passage that had been travelled not long ago by Artio. Once he reached the bottom, he pushed his way through the dense copse of trees to series of doors that stretched along the stream. He entered the third one and then carried the unconscious wizard to the bed and rolled him down onto it. A bowl and a pitcher of water sat on a washstand under a dusty mirror. He picked up the pitcher and strode outside, dipping the pitcher into the stream and bringing it back filled to the brim with sparkling fresh water. He pushed aside a curtain that allowed light to filter in from the outside and lit a lantern hung on the wall. With one last look at the wizard, he left, pulling the door closed behind him.

*   *   *

Helga stirred the objects on the table with a long-nailed finger, pleased with the outcome of her raid on Alcina's camp. She had only intended to dispose of the woman, to sow seeds of confusion and chaos in the armies of men, but as luck would have it, she had also acquired control of two of her enemies. She chuckled as she picked up the doll of the wizard. To have control over one such as he, was a boon beyond measure. *You serve me better in death than life, Alcina. Your soul was already mine.* But what to do with the wizard? Helga pondered his uses, turning the doll over and over in her hands, examining how it was made. In the back of the doll, a coin was wedged. Although she could not see the significance of this, somehow it was tied to the wizard.

Helga set the doll down and picked up the second one, this one resembling Cayden, her dear reincarnated brother—but a human, no longer a godling. She snorted, amused at their attempts to play at being royalty and at being godlings. They had given up that power to her long ago. If it were not for the wizard's dabblings, their rebirth would have been impossible, but such as it was, they were nothing but annoying gnats that she would eventually swat out of existence, crushed beneath her will.

With this doll, I can make you dance to my tune, Little Brother, and dance you will, before the end. Before I am finished with you, you will wish you had never been reborn.

She flipped the doll over, and a quick search revealed it also had a gold coin tucked in the back of it. *So…the wizard and the boy are linked by the coins…how interesting.* She put the doll back down and then picked up the two other objects taken from the wizard. One was a clear crystal, oblong-shaped and smooth, and it fit easily in the palm of the hand as if made for it. She picked it up, and it immediately darkened. Grey clouds swirled through it, occluding the crystal, and it grew hot, very hot. Hastily, she dropped it, sucking her fingertips. Immediately, it cleared; so fast she blinked, unsure if her mind was playing tricks on her. She stretched out her hand toward the stone, caution slowing her reach, and as her hand hovered over the crystal it flashed again in warning. She frowned at it and instead reached for the second stone, a simple river rock, smoothed by water.

Leery of a similar reaction, she thumbed the rock. Nothing happened. She picked it up and turned it over in her hand. There were no special markings. There were no runes or painted symbols. She scraped a nail down it. Nothing happened. It seemed to be a rock and nothing more. She put it back down, puzzled. Why keep it in with the other crystal if it was of no importance? She frowned. She did not like mysteries, not at all, especially when they were related to magic. What she didn't know had the ability to become annoying and to interfere with her plans.

At that moment, Genii returned from depositing the wizard in the guest room. He stood hesitantly in the doorway, waiting for permission to enter, a good and loyal servant. Helga studied his body, silhouetted by the muted light of the hallway. So tall and handsome, he had been her mate for eons now. She could have asked for no better.

"Enter, my love." She beckoned him forward with a crook of her finger. "What do you make of these objects?"

Genii paused at the edge of the table, studying the objects. He did not touch anything. "The dolls are of Flesh Clan make, possibly Soul Fetches. The stones…they are wizard rocks. The crystal one is a focus stone, which tightens the will of the wizard when performing spells, amplifying his powers. The second…" His hand reached out to the rock but stopped short of touching it and let his hand hover above the rock. "This is a memory stone. I cannot tell whose stone it is, but it carries the unadulterated memories of someone. Possibly of the doll's hosts, but it could be anyone's. I cannot tell. Only the person whose memories reside in the stone can retrieve them. It is also an object of spirit and will."

"Thank you, love. You are such a good pet." She patted his arm as one would pat a good dog. "You will watch the wizard and stay with him at all times. I want to know everything he knows. Perhaps you can persuade him to cooperate with this." She picked up the wizard's doll and handed it to him. "But if you can do it by conversation, that would be better. He will need his strength for what I plan to do with him. His powers will be tapped to their fullest." She stroked the silent stone one last time. After a moment of consideration, she tucked it back in the bag. "Perhaps this stone would help to persuade him, but first I will see what I can learn from him. Work on him with the doll. Lie if you wish, use force if you wish, but find out what he is up to."

"As you command, mistress." He bent over her hand and kissed it. "So it shall be."

Helga patted his cheek, and he left like a good hound. She watched him go and a tiny frown wrinkled her brow. Genii was…different lately, ever since Artio's visit. At times, she thought he might have had a stirring of memory at the sight of her, that something of that distant past may have surfaced, but he never spoke of it. She wondered, not for the first time, if she should be watching him more closely, but then she dismissed it. He was the only one she truly trusted. *Paranoid—you are becoming as paranoid as the ones you manipulate,* she thought, as she picked up the focus stone with the bag it was carried in and then tucked Cayden's doll inside the bag for safekeeping. *But still, caution is warranted.*

Maybe I should not have trusted him with the wizard's doll. Caution is warranted. But what can he do with it other than torture him? Her frown deepened. She did not think he would be careless with the doll.

And she had other tasks requiring her attention.

Dismissing Genii from her mind, she stood up and wandered to the railing overlooking the grotto. A plume of smoke drifted cross the peak of blue sky that shone from the skyward opening, temporarily darkening the grotto. There was no way to mask her machinations beneath the mountain, no way to hide the tremors and quakes as they dug ever deeper into the earth. This time Helga meant to rule all, and no one would be able to resist, not even a skinny boy, now turned elderly wizard. There was no one left to resist. She smiled grimly down at the nearly pastoral scene below and then pushed away from the stone window and marched out the door.

Chapter 38

High-Flying Rescue

CAYDEN SOARED ABOVE THE TREES, scouting the landscape below for activity that might mean enemies lay ahead. Brimstone flapped his wings once, twice, and then spread them full, glittering black wing tips fluttering in the wind. He glided over the trees, hooves brushing the highest tips. Bursts of fragrant pine filled the air, and Cayden laughed. He felt *so free,* something he had not felt in a very long time. But the feeling of freedom was short lived. Memories crowded in, both happy and sad, triggered by his return to the air on Brimstone's back. The past year had changed his life completely. While he now knew the why and the how, it had also brought the weight of ancient responsibilities crashing down on his young shoulders.

They had made so many mistakes. They had originally gone about the investigation of the disturbances in the Highland Spine with an arrogant nonchalance *and innocence* that was shaming. Brimstone had fully restored Cayden's memory, complete with vivid flashbacks of that awful evening when *he had died…when they had all died, everyone except for Helga.* He could still feel the ripping pain of having his soul dragged from his being, of losing his immortality. If it had not been for Mordecai, that sweet boy of Hud's, darkness would have swallowed the world and all would be soul enslaved to Helga. Mordecai was an elderly man now, long-lived for a human as all wizards were, provided they survived the trials of the magic to live to full adulthood. It seemed strange to remember the boy who had been Mordecai. Cayden had so many memories to sort to reconcile with his current life.

As he flew, his eyes drifted toward the heavens to the planets of the distant cosmos where he knew the gods resided, his father Morpheus among them, having returned to the gods. Did he know what a mess his offspring had created on Earth? Probably not. Cayden doubted if his father ever looked at the world he had lived in so briefly. He certainly didn't check on them. Without their mother, he had no interest in the world. Helga had a point when it came right down to it; the gods cared little for the world. Although Cayden didn't agree that the worship of the gods should be completely abandoned, he could see Helga's point. Unfortunately, the power of the gods was necessary to keep the natural world in harmony and the spiritual world in balance. The power of the gods was the sticky and often-hated glue cementing the world, keeping it whole. Without the gods, it was possible to destroy the world from the inside out. Without the gods, the world would decay, rot from within, until all was consumed by the belly of the world, enslaved to the underworld and Helga's dominion.

Perhaps, if they contacted the gods and asked for their intervention, things could be different. Would they respond to the prayers of the people if they prayed? Would they even hear them? *Would they hear mine?*

From the vantage point of Brimstone's back, the peaks of the Highland Spine were ringed in smoke, reminiscent of that day so long ago when the world had nearly ended. The fiery hearths deep down inside the mountain stirred a caustic warning of doom's reawakening. And to the east, an army stirred, clouds of birds rising from the trees, heralding their passage. The Primordial clans were on the move. Cayden's eyes traced the path that would lead him to them, located deep within the Sacred Forest.

As Brimstone skimmed over a break in the treetop, his eyes fell on the remnants of a battle. The bodies of men littered the field below him. By virtue of the fact that there were no crows or ravens or vultures present, the battle could not be that old. *Maybe someone is still alive down there!* Blue mist rose from those who had recently died, their lost souls calling out to Cayden from the clearing. "We must land, Brimstone. Put us down, boy, but away from the worst of the carnage if you can. I don't want us to be shot down." Memories of Brimstone screaming in pain as his wing tore flashed across his mind. He gritted his teeth to stem the flashback. "Keep your eyes sharp!"

Brimstone circled, and Cayden kept a sharp eye, but nothing stirred. With a flap or two of wing and a light gallop Brimstone settled back to Earth at the edge of the forest. Cayden slid off his back and then pulled his sword, examining the scene before him. He grimaced at the sword, knowing he could not kill anyone even if they attacked, but perhaps he could incapacitate them.

The better part of one hundred bodies lay in the clearing, some Primordial, some bearing the insignia of the legion. He walked the battlefield as he had done a thousand times before, gathering the souls of the dead and sending them to the stream of souls that fed the well in Cathair. He was not even sure how he did it; it was just who he was. He could sense the stream of souls that fed the well, the conduits who ran in a hidden stream back to that central point under the castle in Cathair. He could sense the streams wherever they were, for they were a part of his soul and he a part of theirs. It was as if he was the heart and they the veins keeping him alive, and vice versa. He could feel the flow and as he focused on the stream closest to him, he frowned. It was a sluggish stream, as if it was blocking up, the walls narrowing.

Alarmed, he searched the killing field once more. He must find them all; they were his to gather, his to guard. Only the truly evil, the unredeemable, were sent to Helga's realm. They would not be reborn. Cayden cast around to check that he had gathered all the blue pinpoints of light. A blue light flickered on the edge of the clearing, and Cayden walked over to the fallen man. *Not quite passed from this life*, he thought as he approached the stricken man. He wound in and around the corpses, but when he reached the dying man he found two men, not just one.

Cayden tossed down his sword to gently roll over the first man and froze, shock tingling down his body to his toes. Cayden stared into Gaius's heavily scarred face, matted with blood from a sword cut across his forehead.

"*Father!*" he gasped aloud, and pulled him into his arms. "Father!" he repeated and then ran a hand down his arms checking for additional injuries. He couldn't find any, other than the forehead slice that was serious but shallow and had already stopped bleeding. He looked a mess, but Cayden didn't think his father was badly hurt.

Cayden took the sleeve of his tunic and wiped his father's face, clearing the blood from his eyes.

"Move one inch and this sword will have your head bouncing through the grass."

Cayden froze at the prick of a sharp blade against the side of his neck. *Not again!* he thought. *When am I going to learn to look before I leap?*

The blade circled around his neck as the man came into view. Cyrus stared at him, his gaze as cold as death. Pure, unadulterated hatred shone on his sweat-soaked face. His tunic was splattered with blood and torn by one too many blades that had come too close, slicing through the sleeve and breast of his coat. "Well, if it isn't the boy from the dungeons of Cathair. What a pleasant surprise. The Primordial bitch I chased escaped me, but instead I get you." He chuckled. "This is even better. You've caused me a great inconvenience. In a few short months, Alcina would have been dead by now and the throne mine, the last of that family line extinguished. With you out of the way, I would have had her murdered in her sleep, leaving my path to claim Cathair clear and unobstructed...but you had to ruin that, didn't you? You and that straw-filled scarecrow of a wizard. I should have strung the both of you up, not just chained you to the walls. Hung you from the belfry for the ravens to pick clean no matter what Alcina commanded." He paused in front of Cayden, blade sinking from throat to just over his heart. "But it matters not. You will never leave this clearing...and I will deal with Alcina later." He looked down at the two unconscious prisoners, and a look of malicious glee spread across his face. The stare made Cayden shiver to his boot soles. "But first, a taste of what it means to lose what means the most to you." He swung around to plunge his sword into Gaius's chest.

Cayden shouted, "*No!*" but before he could launch himself in defense of Gaius, Cyrus was snatched off his feet by Brimstone's teeth. He clamped on to Cyrus's cloak and jerked him with such force that the sword tumbled from his grip as he was swept screaming into the air. Brimstone screamed a counterpoint through his clenched teeth, the sound high-pitched and heady. His great wings battered Cyrus as he soared skyward, still gripping the struggling would-be king's tunic, climbing and climbing until they were but a pinprick in the sky. Brimstone banked then dived, flying directly at the stony face of the mountainside, diving as a kingfisher dives for fish. Cyrus's screams cut off abruptly as Brimstone released him, dashing him into the cliff face. He smacked the stone hard and plummeted hundreds of feet to the rocks below.

Cayden sank to his knees beside his father in relief and shock, sucking in great gulps of air as he slowed his racing pulse. His large hands trembled. *Too many shocks. I am becoming a nervous wreck! Get control of yourself, Cayden!* He took two deeper, steadying breaths, then pushed himself shakily to his feet.

Brimstone circled the clearing then landed a few paces away. It took Cayden three tries to finally gather enough moisture into his mouth to whistle to Brimstone. Crouching down, he scooped up his father and stood, only to find that his right wrist was shackled to another man's, a Primordial man who lay nearby. They were chained together. By the juxtaposition of the two men, they must have tumbled off their horses together. Cayden put his father back down and went to examine the second man. His chest rose and fell with his shallow breaths, but he appeared to be unhurt.

Brimstone danced excitedly over to Cayden and forcefully nudged him in the chest, snorting at the smell of death all around him, then snapped his wings, his black eyes narrowed and wild.

"Steady, boy," soothed Cayden. "We have a couple of passengers to take away with us. Can you carry us all?" Brimstone snorted again, and Cayden had the impression that he was being laughed at. Brimstone tossed back his head and pipped a high-pitched whistle, then started pawing at the ground.

The wait was a short one, for within a couple of minutes, Sandstorm and Moonbeam dropped down from the sky and trotted over to Brimstone's side.

"A much better idea!" With a rueful twist of lips, Cayden put his father back down on the ground and began a search of the fallen for a guard or someone who might hold the key to their prisoners. After ten minutes of grim searching he discovered a set of keys in the muddy grass. (At least, he hoped it was mud.) They had spilled out of the pocket of a Primordial warrior. It wasn't the only thing that had spilled out, but thankfully the keys were clean and dry. Cayden swallowed heavily then hurried back to his father, slipping in his haste. He fumbled the keys with shaking hands, presenting key after key to the locksets until finally he found the right one, and slid the key into the lock with a twist. It snapped open and the chain fell away. Cayden repeated the process with the second man, dropping the keys twice in the process. Once they were free, he scooped up his father and placed him on Moonbeam's back then returned for the second man and put him up on Sandstone.

"Now be careful, you two," he scolded the excited Pegasuses. "Don't let them fall off." The Pegasuses rolled their eyes, clearly annoyed with his mothering. They pawed at the ground, anxious to be away from the stench of death.

"Yes, I quite agree." Cayden sighed in relief, then swung onto Brimstone's back. "It is time to be gone." With a final searching glance around the field of death to be sure he had gathered all the souls remaining, he sent them on to the well in Cathair. Then with a light squeeze of his knees, he launched Brimstone into the sky.

Chapter 39

Tracks in the Sky

THE FLESH CLAN WARRIORS WALKED AMONG the bloating bodies, checking for survivors. Their Spirit-Clan brethren had lost a bloody battle, with no survivors. By the insignia on their vestments, they were of the temple guard, those bound to the High Priestess herself. But they could not locate her among the dead, nor could they locate her seeker. The rest of the dead were legion soldiers. Murmuring rose from the men. How had the legion soldiers slipped past their posts? How many more might be nearby? And where was the High Priestess? Searching for her made for a grim but necessary task.

"Marea is not here, immortal mistress. Whether she lives, I can't know for sure," Hototo, with forehead pressed to the dirt, informed Artio's feet as she strode by, knife in hand.

"Whose doing is this? Tell me all you know!" She gestured sharply to the festering corpses. "You've been gone far too long. I will hear all you have done since you left my presence. *Now speak!*"

Hototo kept his face pressed to the dirt, and his nose filled with earthy scents mingled with the stench of death.

"Mistress, I was on my way back to you when I came across this battle." He shuddered. "I arrived here shortly before you. If Marea has survived this battle, she will be on her way to the Shakra Caves. No High Priestess could miss the signs. The solstice approaches!"

"The Shakra Caves? What is this place?" Artio glared toward the smoking mountain, convinced she already knew.

"It is a cave of crystal, mistress, and full of sacred objects not touchable by human hands. The scrolls state that when the heir returns, the cave will give up its treasures and the secrets frozen in time. It is also said that only the gods can utilize the treasures within. We are simple guardians, mistress."

Artio snarled. *So that is what my sisters are up to. They are trying to steal my beloved's betrothal gifts.* Genii had showered gifts of magic on her, during their courtship. Rings and bracelets, music boxes and enchanted feathers, and she had kept every one of them in their special, secret cave. *Curse you, Helga! You sent me on this fool's trail when you know perfectly well that the answers lie where it all began. Caerwyn may be nearby, but it's Alfreda who holds the key...and by now my beloved's magical gifts!*

Not for the first time, Artio wondered at how much she still didn't understand about what had transpired that night, so long ago. *What were you up to that night, Helga? Somehow, all of you are tied together in this, and that leaves me with little choice but to go it alone. I will have my revenge! For myself. For Genii.*

"And you?" she snarled. "Did you reach the caves?"

"Yes, mistress, and the impostor you warned us about, the lady Avery, showed her face just as you predicted, but I captured her and sent her to the underworld! She is no longer a threat to you, mistress." He peeked out from under his arm at Artio. His back ached and he longed to sit up, but he had not been granted this boon.

Artio glared at the priest. "How could you accomplish such a feat? You have no powers except what we grant. What connection do you have with the underworld? Do not lie to me, Hototo." *Disgusting worm,* she thought.

She stamped down hard on his outstretched hands. He cried out as the bones ground together.

Gasping with pain, he blurted, "Mistress! They come to me in my dreams, mistress! The Charun! They are as black as night! They come and whisper things to me! It's how I knew how to summon you back from the stars, mistress!" Artio ground her heel on his hand, and he howled. The warriors searching the grounds glanced nervously over at the pair and then studiously ignored the goings-on. It was none of their business. "*She* told me!" he screamed as a finger snapped. "The great mistress of the dark! But I swear I only wanted to serve you! *Ple-e-e-ease!*" he cried as a second finger popped.

"She, being Helga?"

"Yes, mistress!" he sobbed. "The goddess Helga!"

Artio lifted her foot from his hand and strode off toward her mount. *As I suspected, none are to be trusted. Not one.*

As she crossed the ground, her eyes fell on a set of chains cast aside and almost hidden by the tall grass. She bent down and picked up the chains, and then her eyes fell on a long black feather. *A Pegasus feather! But where…how?* She straightened up, and her eyes searched the canopy, examining the sky, but found nothing. *So, Brother, you are closer than I thought. Good. It is time we met once again. Very good.* Artio's lips pulled back in a growl, teeth flashing, and she sniffed the air. *I smell you, Little Brother. I smell you on the wind. Do not think you can hide!*

She mounted her horse as the warriors scrambled into their saddles, and they fell into line behind her as she left the clearing, the bodies forgotten as soon as they faded from sight. She followed the unique scent of the Pegasus. They smelled like the rarefied air after a thunderstorm. It lingered in the treetops. If a smell could have a colour, it would have been golden. Artio's grin widened. She twisted the reins, pulling her horse around and followed the scent, tracking Cayden on the air.

*   *   *

Brimstone touched down in the clearing, followed closely by the other two Pegasuses. Ziona was crouched by the pond filling water bottles for the continued journey when she heard the whisper of wings announce their arrival. She stood abruptly and hurried over when it became evident that Cayden was not alone.

"Cayden! Who…? By the gods, is that your father? And an elder! Where did you find them?"

Cayden filled her in on his gruesome discovery as he slipped from Brimstone's back. He hurried over to his father's side, and together they eased the pair off the backs of the Pegasus and laid them gently on the ground. Ziona checked them over, running her hands over their limbs, thumbing back an eyelid, sniffing at their breath. "They have been hurt, but not fatally. Mostly they are drugged. Fortunately, I have just the thing." She snatched up her satchel and pulled out a packet of dried flowers. "Sharisha said this would cure anything." She took out a pestle and her bowl and ground some of the flowers up and added a bit of water to make a thin soup. "Cayden, lift their heads, one by one, and open their lips. I don't want them to choke. I need to get this potion into them." Cayden did as instructed, and Ziona fed each man two spoonfuls until the bowl was empty.

At first nothing happened, and then slowly their eyelashes fluttered as the cure counteracted the sleeping potion. Their bruises faded, and the gash on Gaius's head mended, now looking several days healed. They stirred, lifting hand to head with groans, the first movements they had voluntarily made since Cayden rescued them.

Gaius blinked once, twice, and then narrowed his focus to Cayden, who was bent over him staring anxiously into his face. Gaius's eyes widened on seeing his son, and he struggled to sit up. Cayden slipped an arm around his shoulders, steadying him.

"Cayden!" he gasped and tears sprang to his eyes. "I am so happy to see you!" They hugged as Elder Hania woke and slowly rolled over on to his side, pushing himself to a sitting position.

"Elder," greeted Ziona, "I am glad to find you alive, if not well."

"Seeker, it is equally pleasing to see you," he replied. He peered around at the campsite. "It appears our captors are no longer in control."

Cayden let go of his father. "They are all dead."

"Including Marea? Sharisha?" Elder Hania's voice was as hard as a stone.

"I didn't see them there. Were they trying to free you?" asked Cayden.

"No, they were our captors."

"What?" said Ziona, sharply. "Why would they restrain you?"

Elder Hania relayed the details of Avery's arrival at the temple and her subsequent reception.

"She is in grave danger then!" Cayden's fists clenched in anger. "We must find her and quickly!"

Ziona laid a restraining hand on his arm. "We need a plan, Cayden. We can't go running off without thinking this through. There is too much at stake. We know they are going to the cave. We can join her there, but who else might we encounter? We need help, some backup. We need Denzik and the rest of the Kingsmen. Then, we will have the might to confront whatever armies harry Avery."

"She has a young man with her. You remember Achak?" At her nod, he continued, "He has been sent as her protector. She is not alone."

Cayden stared at nothing, thinking. "She...Avery is going after the box...," he mumbled aloud.

"What box?" asked Ziona and Elder Hania in unison.

"It is...something of our past, a box of great evil. But there is only one who can control the magic of the box, and that is Mordecai. We need the wizard." Cayden stood up and walked away from them, thinking. *Mordecai said he could always find me via the stone. I wonder if works in reverse? He had it with him.*

Cayden closed his eyes and reached out to Mordecai. *Yes, I can feel him. It's faint, but I can point to where he is.* His arm raised of its own accord and he pointed. When he opened his eyes, it was pointed directly at the smoking mountain. "He is there. Why is he there?"

Ziona came up beside him and slipped an arm around his waist. "If Mordecai is there, it can't be good news. That is Helga's realm. No one comes out of there alive, not ever."

Cayden looked from the mountain to his companions and opened his mouth to speak. His words were interrupted by a whooshing sound, and the trees exploded above him. Debris rained down on them as the treetops burst into flame and fist-sized chunks of lava fell from the sky.

"*Go!*" Cayden shouted, grabbing Gaius around the waist and tossing him up onto Brimstone's back. He slapped Brimstone's rump, sending him skyward, then grabbed his satchel and flung himself onto the back of one of the pair of horses and dug in his heels, bolting for the uncertain safety of the woods in Mordecai's direction.

Ziona took to the sky on Sandstorm. Elder Hania grabbed the mane of Ziona's horse and swung onto its back, then bolted off after Cayden.

Moonbeam reared and followed the other Pegasuses into the sky. As the floor of the clearing caught fire, the grasses bursting into flame, Artio galloped into its midst. She caught a fleeting glimpse of the Pegasus disappearing into the smoke and saw two men on horseback swallowed by the trees.

"Helga!" she roared, cursing. Then she heeled her mount and took off after the two men on horseback. One was a young man and her brother would certainly look young at this time. *It must be Caerwyn*, she thought, following their trail on the ground. "He is mine!" she screamed aloud to the skies at Helga. For a second, back in the clearing a rippling reflection of Helga's face danced across the surface of the pond. The face laughed, watching Artio's furious passage out of the clearing with amusement. Then, the pond stilled and she vanished.

Chapter 40

A Matter of Age

MORDECAI WOKE WITH A START. The carpet on which he had recently lain had been replaced by a soft mattress, and a fluffy down-filled pillow cushioned his head. He frowned and cracked the lids of his eyes open the tiniest of increments in order to assess his whereabouts without alerting his captors of his consciousness. Instinct warned him that he was still a captive, regardless of the cushiness of his cell. Oil lamps with wicks trimmed low hung on wooden staves driven into chiseled holes and solid stone walls devoid of any human shaping draped with tapestries greeted his skinny-eyed appraisal of the room.

Definitely not a camp, then. So, if not a camp, then where am I? He could not see any guards in his room, which did not mean that he was not being watched. His hand twitched, and he opened his eyes wider and then sat up. No one came into the room. He swung his legs over the side of the bed then stood up on wobbly knees. He felt the doll's presence. It was nearby. But no one interfered with him right at the moment.

On a wooden stand under a cracked mirror stood an empty stone basin and a pitcher of water. Gratefully, he poured water into the bowl, then, dipping his hands in, drank thirstily. Next, he washed his face, scrubbing off the dried blood reflected in the cracked mirror above the stand with a rough towel hanging on the side. He rinsed the towel and then dabbed at the cut on his scalp that had bled.

Once his ablutions were complete, he followed the scent of food, his nose twitching at the smell of hot rolls and honeyed ham. He did not remember smelling them when he first awoke, but now hunger drove him toward the platter resting just inside the door. He picked it up and then headed back to the bed. He perched on the side while he wolfed down the contents of the tray. A brimming mug of ale accompanied the meal, and he drank it down in one long gulp.

Feeling much more human, he pushed the tray aside and decided to test the door. He reached inside his robes to touch his focus stone…only it was missing. Of course, whoever was responsible for his current lodgings had removed any objects of power they had found on his person.

I have a pretty good idea of who my host is…or hostess. Time to test the theory.

Mordecai strode over to the door and pulled on the handle. It swung open easily, and he stepped into a verdant green grotto. Bamboo and palm trees swayed in a gentle breeze. Bright parrots and lovebirds flashed from branch to branch, singing to each other. A stream burbled past, cutting the grotto in two. An arched wooden bridge crossed the span, and there, at a small table, sat a woman. On the table sat a pot of tea and two cups. The chair opposite the woman was empty, an invitation to sit implied in its positioning.

Mordecai sighed. *Out of the frying pan and into the fire.*

"Come, join me!" Helga gestured elegantly at the empty chair. "We have much to discuss, Mordecai."

Mordecai straightened his robes and then drew himself up to his full six-foot-plus height. *She is only a woman, if a godling. It does not make her a god. So what if she is older than you but looks like she is barely out of her teens. So what if she could snuff out your life just by thinking about it. Think, man!* Mordecai tucked his hands in the ends of his opposite sleeves, and his face stilled into the tableau of a wise one. His white mustache drooped and curled over his white beard, and his twinkling blue eyes, wrinkled with smile lines, darkened as he approached the woman.

"Tea? This is the last of my supply of oolong from the marshes. This was a particularly good year. I have had this tea for oh…about twenty-five years." A bitter smile creased her mouth and was gone. "I don't get out much, as you know, and all of those who would bring me such gifts have…faded from this earth. Mortality ends the most loyal of servants." She poured tea into his cup and then refilled hers, studying him as he eased himself into the chair opposite her. Her eyes travelled over his wavy white hair and the deep creases and the occasional scar, then drifted down to his hands, thin-skinned and heavily veined. "Age would appear to agree with you, but age, you do. Tell me, Mordecai, what is your plan for immortality? Do you pander to this reincarnation dribble, or do you strive to obtain a higher existence?" She took a sip of tea, sighed with remembered pleasure (for she could not taste it), and then returned the cup to its saucer.

Mordecai lifted his cup and took a deep draft. The tea was wonderful, full-bodied and fragrant. "Deep questions you ask, right off the top. Philosophers have pondered this question over the ages. In fact, my library back in Cathair is stuffed with volumes by wiser sages than myself. Why, I'd hardly know where to begin with such a subject. May I also compliment you on your apparent good health? I dare say you have not aged a day since we last met, and I was but a child."

Helga's dark eyes narrowed briefly, and then her face smoothed. The subtle reminder, that she was older than he sat like a burr under the saddle of a good horse. She struggled to keep the annoyance from showing on her face. Her lips widened into a smile that did not quite reach her eyes.

"Come now, you must have some theories of what immortality really looks like, immortality as enjoyed by the gods? For me, I have as close to immortality as one can have on this rock, but you?" Her eyes swept over him once more. "You are aging, Mordecai. Your body decays around you. Even with the fact that your life has been magically elongated due to being a wizard, you too will eventually die. You never married, did you?" She tsked as though he had overlooked the obvious solution. "No heirs? No one to carry on the wizarding gene? A trifle absent-minded, were we? What have you been doing all these years if not working on a way to elongate your mortal existence?"

Mordecai smiled and took another sip of tea. "Oh, a little bit of this and a bit of that. There is a lot to learn when you are one of the only remaining wizards in the world. There is a lot to record, a lot of information to preserve. Time does not exist in a vacuum. There must be ebb and flow for time to exist. As long as there are mortals, there is time. Time to learn what must be learned; do what must be done, undo what has been done, and take a stab at sorting out the future of time-marking mortals. Enough to keep me busy for another lifetime, I suspect." He drained his cup and set it down on his saucer.

"But I have found that when truly evil times exist, the fates provide for what is needed. It is never one man's victory or courage that wins a war. It is a hundred or a thousand small acts of bravery that carry the battle. No man is an island and their souls combined are stronger than any one foe. The ant surely knows this. Nature is a simple teacher of the complexities of life."

"You waffle, Mordecai. As always, you fill your mouth with useless words that buzz in the ear but say nothing." Helga reached into her pocket and withdrew two objects, placing them in the middle of the table. "I assume you know what these are?"

One was Mordecai's focus stone, his crystal. The second was the smooth river rock.

"A second direct question. Of course, I do. One is my favourite crystal, and the second is a stone I took a fancy to. I do love odd rocks. I have a whole collection back at the library."

"Liar." Helga picked up the crystal, and it glowed, heating rapidly. She dropped it before it could burn and the red blush vanished, returning to a nondescript crystal once again. "This crystal is a Soul Stone, a focus rock, commonly used by wizards to focus their own will. If I can make it glow, one wonders what it will do for you." She reached out and placed it in front of him. "I have no use for it, so I return it to you."

Surprised, Mordecai picked it up and put it back in his pocket. As he assumed he was not just a guest of Helga's, she could take it back at any time, so he did not challenge her on her choice of words.

"What I don't know is why you have this rock." Her finger stirred the grey stone.

Mordecai shrugged. "Occasionally, I pick up interesting stones to test. As I said, I thought it was an interesting rock."

Helga squinted at him, clearly not believing a word of what he said. "So, you would not care if I tossed it away, say, into my lava flow? It could be destroyed with no more interest than any other rock?" She slipped it back into her pocket, out of sight.

Mordecai reached out involuntarily before retracting his arm. "I would prefer to have the stone. They are difficult to find," he muttered weakly. Helga grinned back at him.

"So, it is more than a simple rock. Of course it is. I will keep it for now, for *safekeeping,* but should I decide that your answers and cooperation are less than stellar, we will see what happens with the rock.

"Now, there are these two precious bundles." She reached into her other pocket and withdrew the straw dolls. "Soul Fetches unless I mistake my eyes. One would appear to be yours. And the other…well, I can only guess. Perhaps you will enlighten me?"

Mordecai swallowed heavily. He'd feared that they were in her possession. His mind frantically searched for an answer, for a response that would waylay her suspicions. He settled on the fact that she could not know he knew who the doll was for.

"Alas, I cannot help you there, Helga. Alcina had just captured me with the doll, as you no doubt saw if you took me from the floor of her tent. I assume the other was taken from her tent? I have no idea who that doll binds." He kept his face still, eyes locked on his own doll.

Helga frowned at him, then twitched Mordecai's doll. "If you are lying, I will know it. You are going to be very useful to me going forward, Mordecai. Why, I might even grant you immortality if you please me well enough. You are now my soul slave, and you will do as I command or I will break you. One…bone…at…a…time…" She snapped a thread on the hand of the doll. Mordecai howled as his pinky finger on his left hand snapped. Pain shot up his arm. Tears sprang to his eyes, as he cradled the swelling digit. "Mine to command." She smiled, pleasure and promise in the threat.

"Genii!" Helga snapped.

Genii stepped from the shadows, or rather the shadows pushed him forward until he stood solid in the indirect lighting.

"Take our guest to the scrying pool. I want him to provide intelligence reports. He can begin to repay his lodging debt in this fashion. You will report back to me anything of significance he sees. Take this, and be sure he does not touch it." She handed the doll to him once more.

"Yes, mistress." Genii bowed, tucking Mordecai's doll into his robes, then grabbed Mordecai by the arm and dragged him from the room.

Chapter 41

The Task at Hand

AVERY SHOOK ACHAK, waking him. With that consciousness, he cried out, gasping as the pain of his broken leg overtook him. Avery tipped a cup of water, into which she had crumbled some powdered white willow bark, to his lips, as she murmured, "Drink this. Shh." He drank it down, some slopping down his chin at the angle. As she lowered the cup, his eyes darted anxiously around the cave. "They are gone," she said, lowering his head back down to the bench. "The phoenix did the trick. That is some Spirit Guardian!"

Achak groaned as he attempted to move his leg.

"I'm sorry," said Avery, grimacing. "I can't heal it within the cave. There is some shield that keeps my power from flowing here. I must move you outside to heal you. The guards should be gone now. Marea was here—Hey, lay still! It's OK," she said, restraining him as he tried to sit up. "She went to distract the guards away from the entrance. But first, I want to look over the other objects in the cave here. What can you tell me about these objects, Achak?"

Achak's eyes wandered the cave. "I am no elder, Mother. Elder Hania is who you want to speak to. The objects in this cave are rumoured to be usable only by godlings. They were created with the power and magic of the gods. But they are dangerous objects and so have been ever in this cave under magical protection. It is said in the ancient prophesies that these objects were placed here against man's most desperate hour. When war covered the earth, these gifts of the gods would hold the key to the salvation and preservation of the world." He peered around at the various alcoves and shivered. "I do not like being this close to the gods, even if they are no longer present."

"I do not believe these objects are of the gods, but only one god, my father, Morpheus." Avery wandered around the cave once again, peering into each alcove. "Yet I do not know what they do. To remove them would be to risk them falling into hands that should not have them. But to leave them is also to risk them being taken by those who should not have them. Which is the greater evil, do you think? Can we protect them if we take them?"

Achak's forehead wrinkled with thought. "There is only one place I can suggest that would be safe for these objects where we know no one else could access them—the temple. We should take them to the temple."

Avery swung back to Achak and smiled. "Yes! That is a fantastic idea! There is a room in there, and that is the safest place on Earth. That is what we will do."

Avery walked back over and sat down beside Achak. She pulled the box out of her pocket and sat it on her lap. It was as black as midnight, and all light appeared to be sucked into its depths.

"Tell me, can you hear anything?"

Achak frowned at her. "What do you mean? I do not hear anything. You mean from the box?"

"Yes."

"It's a box. What is it supposed to do? Play music?"

Avery shook her head. "No, it's...whispering to me. I can hear voices, but I can't make out what they are saying. It's very strange." She frowned at the box and went to put a finger on it but then changed her mind. She was loath to touch it. "I know this box. I have seen it before, but it was in the possession of a wizard last time I saw it. A young boy." Her eyes glazed as she pulled up the memory. Although it was the most recent of her past life, it was still a different existence and she found it difficult to reconcile. "I died the last time I saw this box. It is a god-killer."

"*A what!*" Achak struggled to sit upright, and his hand went to snatch the box away, but she grabbed his wrist, halting him.

"It was necessary," she whispered, her eyes still glazed in memory, "to stop a great evil. But we died that day. We must return this to the wizard. He will know how to use it. But I don't know where he is. Mordecai should be with Cayden, but I do not know where Cayden is. We are able to talk to each other telepathically, though. Let me see if I can reach him."

She closed her eyes and reached out to her brother. *Cayden, can you hear me? Where are you? I need you to come to me.* She sent the thought to him, praying it would find its way to him. The answer came back faster than she expected.

Avery! Where are you? I am coming to you! I have so much to tell you! Tell me where you are.

I am in a cave near…well, you will recognize it if your memory has returned, Cayden. It's at the end of a highland meadow, above Daimon Ford. Do you think you could find me if I described it to you?

I can find you easily. I can fly once again! Excitement tickled Cayden's voice in her head. *Give me an image of where you are, Avery.*

You can fly? Wait, how can you fly? What do you mean? Avery sent over the image of the caves and the meadow with the tall stones and waited for his exclamation of horror when he saw it, but it never came.

Cayden replied, *I'd rather show you!*

Avery had the impression that he was chuckling with amusement, like a kid with a new toy. *Fine, come show me,* she sent back.

You are in the sacred meadow with the monolithic stones, the place where we died. Yes, my memory has returned.

Avery shivered. *Yes, the place with the stones,* she sent back to him.

We are on our way, he sent back.

Is Mordecai with you?

No, but he should be along shortly. He had a…task…to complete.

I need to find him right away, Avery sent back to Cayden.

I think I can locate him.

All right, but hurry! A vague sense of acknowledgment reached her and then the link was broken.

Her eyes opened wide, slightly out of focus. "He is coming."

"Who?" said Achak.

"My brother."

"The new king of Cathair?" His eyes widened in surprise.

"He was my brother long before he was the king," she said ruefully, "but yes, one and the same."

Achak struggled to the edge of the platform and slid his wrapped leg out over the side, using both hands to ease it down to touch the floor.

"Help me up! I need you to heal my leg so we can begin packing up these items."

Avery slung an arm around his waist and he grabbed her shoulders for support and then stood. Achak's teeth clenched in pain, but he said nothing. He hobbled to the cave mouth then out into the passage. It was slow going as darkness was descending and little light filtered down to the base of the narrows.

As they came to the mouth of the passage, they slowed, and Avery crept forward alone to check that the way was clear. The clearing appeared quiet and peaceful, the sinking sun casting long shadows across the meadow. The ancient grey stones, missed on her trip into the cave due to being unconscious, now grabbed her attention. She could not suppress a shiver of fear that ran up her back at the sight of them. Tall and unmoving, they cared not for the scratching of the mortals that stirred the grasses beneath the stones, neither slug nor bear nor human. They grimly stood at attention, waiting patiently for the next chapter, the next page in the annals of mankind. Long fingers of shadow stretched from the bases, pointing toward them as the sun sank into the west.

Nervous of being exposed in the open, Avery dragged Achak into the closest copse of trees. Once far enough away from the cave and the rocks to feel relatively safe, she set him down on the forest floor.

"This is a serious break. I do not know if I can fully heal this right here, but I can get the process started." She laid her hands on the leg and closed her eyes once again, feeling her way along the leg. The break was severe, the bone splintered internally. Fractures spiralled within the bone. She drew on her will and the runes on her skin began to glow, pulling on the healing power of the temple. She moved her hands along the leg, her fingers twitching to pull at the sections of bone and align them. Sweat broke out on her forehead and began to run down the sides of her face. With a gasp, she opened her eyes, panting in exertion. The healing had caused Achak to faint, as it drew on his strength to cement the healing.

Avery manipulated the bones, and while it was not completely set, at least it was aligned. Rest would heal it the rest of the way; but the debilitating portion of the break had been fixed. It was all she could manage for the moment. Exhausted, she flopped onto the ground beside him.

The box vibrated in her pocket.

She lifted her head and stared at the stones. In the center of the ring, a light glowed. The light called to her, called to the box. A distant rumble echoed across the valley like great stones grinding together. The valley shook and lava burst from the mountaintop, small flaming pinpricks flashing into the clearing and then winking out.

Time is short. I must begin the healing of the land and its peoples before Helga breaks free, if that is what she is trying to do. But do I wait for Cayden? Do I dare wait for him? I cannot fail. This time the healing must be complete. Artio designed this circle to be a healing focus, and not just for physical injuries. The circle is linked to the temple and draws its power from the temple, and the celestial elements.

Avery read every level of rune carved into the great stones. As the last rays of the sun fell below the horizon, the top level of runes began to glow softly. The light of a full moon on the rise waxed as the sun waned. It was time.

Chapter 42

Anarchy

THE CAMP WAS A FROTHING SEA OF CONFUSION. The legionnaires woke in the morning to a numbing sense of having been asleep for many days and weeks, if not months. They rolled out of tents and began to wander around the main camp, not recognizing anyone. Strangers surrounded them, men who a few days ago they would have greeted as comrades.

One young officer entered the tent of the queen to find her and her lover dead in their blankets. They had been slain in the night, and whatever enchantment had lain over the men evaporated with their deaths and the rising of the morning sun. No one knew who she was or why they were there or who was supposed to be in charge. Their ranks meant nothing to them and the biggest and the strongest began to assert themselves, pushing and shoving at the weaker, taking whatever they wished and filling their pockets with supplies and loot.

Shouts could be heard and fights broke out over what belonged to whom. No one could remember, so each man grabbed what he wanted and tried to keep it from others. Before noon, several men had been left to die on the hard-packed dirt, each with a blade in his gut.

The men slunk into groups for protection. By midafternoon, those who were able to fight their way to a horse had left in mobs of ten or twenty, headed back toward Cathair. Roving bands of angry legionnaires on foot left the camp shortly thereafter, and by sunset the main legion camp was completely abandoned and empty except for the dead.

By nightfall, they had made their way to the plains with only one goal in mind: to return to Cathair and the homes they remembered to be there.

The only problem with this is that the homes they remembered were twenty years in the past, if they were not a recent addition by way of Alcina's recruiting parties.

Like a wildfire, they swept onto the steppe, crazed with flashes of memory, like a badly performed play of a past life they barely remembered. Wives and children and homes, fields and crops left behind. Disoriented by their incongruous thoughts, they marched for an unsuspecting Cathair, a plague of traumatized, battle-weary soldiers returning to homes that no longer existed, to families that had grown, to wives that had moved on to new husbands and lovers.

Lightning had struck suddenly and swiftly, in the form of Helga, and flames of trauma and revenge and need licked the heels of the deranged as they charged toward...home.

*   *   *

Artio sat her horse and watched the bands of roving ex-legionnaires descend onto the grasslands and set off toward Cathair. She held her hand up to prevent the Flesh Clan warriors from loosening arrows on the unsuspecting men.

"Let them go," she growled. Hototo cancelled the order to release arrows, and the men relaxed their draw on their long bows.

"As you wish, mistress. What is your command? I could send a team of assassins to wipe them out. They would not even know we were there." He bobbed his head as her eyes fixed on him, and his fingers throbbed in remembered pain.

"They run like children seeking their mother's pap. They are nothing, a mere distraction, which was no doubt my dear sister's intent. Ever she liked to sow anarchy. They are my dear brother's problem now." She twitched in her saddle, eyes dismissing the legionnaires, great head swinging back around to the forest into which her brother had fled. "Cayden, however, is here and headed straight into Helga's loving embrace. I am sure she has set a trap for him, a lure of some sort," she mused aloud.

Hototo, surprised that she would speak to him directly of her thoughts, bowed his head in acknowledgement but remained silent. He did not think she meant him to hear or cared about his opinion.

By holding my tongue, I might just keep it, he thought.

Artio checked the height of the sun in the sky and then swung her head back toward the mountainside. With a vexed snort, she brutally yanked her horse back to the trail and to the climb, past boulders and along thin ledges to the clearing she knew all too well, shrouded in low-lying clouds. *Which path should I choose?* She checked the height of the sun in the sky once again and cursed, tightening her hands on her reins. She did not have enough time to chase after Cayden and be at the clearing by nightfall. He had a head start, riding that cursed Pegasus and it would easily outrun her four-legged mount. Artio lifted her arm and stared at her hand. It was a curious thing how her body was reverting to her original appearance. A blessing of the approaching solstice, no doubt. She snarled. Time was of the essence. She needed the Primordial warriors and could not leave them behind.

Even though Cayden was on horseback, Brimstone was never far from him and could snatch him from the saddle at any moment. Artio shook her great mane of hair, arguing with herself. No, it was time to push on for the clearing of sacred stones she had erected so long ago. She walled away the tragic events of that day. They belonged to another Artio, another woman, another time.

She stared down at her arms and clenched hands, covered with light fur and grimaced. *This Artio, this half-breed godling, seeks only one thing. Revenge.* The beauty of her youth was gone. The woman she had been, was gone. In its place was this beast formed from her rebirth. Even if Genii lived, he would see nothing but a monster. It was a blessing that he had died. She no longer cared if she lived on, for she had lost all and being brought back had reawakened the pain of that cursed memory. While suspended amongst the stars, imprisoned by their failed experiment, she had neither felt nor remembered. But in being dragged back to this semi-human body, she was forced to endure the agony of a broken heart and mind once more. *This time though, others will feel it too. They will suffer with me for all eternity.*

The sun sank toward the horizon where no doubt her sisters were gathering. She yanked her horse's head around and set off up the trail, the Primordial warriors falling in behind her. They rode silently, following their goddess up the narrow, twisting path.

Revenge will be mine. I swear it on the departed soul of my love, Genii.

Chapter 43

Mordecai's View

MORDECAI BENT OVER THE SCRYING POOL and examined the scenes that rose into his view. A sheltered pond, encircled by tall trees and waving grasses, graced his sight, and a group of people suddenly launched themselves onto the back of Pegasuses. He tensed involuntarily in surprise then stilled, unwilling to give away the game to his companion.

I know those Pegasuses! Brimstone! And Moonbeam and Sandstone! They are alive! Mordecai could not make out the faces of the people in the clearing as they dodged the flaming tree embers and rock that fell from the sky. But where Brimstone was to be found, Cayden would not be far away. The Pegasus launched into the sky, and two men took off on horseback. The outline of a familiar mountain flashed by as he attempted to follow them in the scrying pool, and a peak wreathed in smoke slid through the image. *No! You must not come here, Cayden!* Alarmed, he sat back abruptly, breaking contact with the image and drawing Genii's attention. *What is that fool boy doing?* Mordecai thought furiously, concern for Cayden straightening his back and causing him to break contact with the pool.

"What did you see, old man?" Genii leaned over his shoulder, but only his own reflection stared back.

"This 'old man's' back is stiff from leaning over a scrying pool. It's time for a break. We have been at it all day." Mordecai punctuated his lie by standing and arching his back, then reached up over his head and stretched, letting out a long, relaxing, whistling groan.

Genii pushed him roughly back down onto the stone bench. "Visions, old man. Concentrate on the pool, and continue gazing into its depths. My mistress commands it. You will continue to scry until you provide some useful information." Genii reached over and rapped sharply on Mordecai's purple, distended pinky finger with the switch he carried in his hand. Mordecai flinched with pain. "I can stay here day and night. Time does not affect me. You can also stay here day and night. The choice is yours." He slapped the surface of the pool. As the waters stilled, a vision swam into view of a tall woman on horseback, rushing into the clearing Mordecai had seen before.

Genii gasped and tried to pull back from the pool, but Mordecai grabbed his arm and held him still. "You know this woman?" he rasped, now the one in command. Genii could not pull his eyes from the pool as the woman came into clearer focus. "She calls to your heart. I can feel it. Who is she?"

Genii shook his head and pried at Mordecai's fingers. "No, I do not know. This is your vision."

"It is not my vision. It's your viewing." Mordecai released him, but Genii could not pull away. He was frozen over the pool, staring at the majestic woman.

"She appears to be half-human. You have seen her before, haven't you?" Mordecai said softly. He straightened and crossed his arms across his chest and leaned back from the pool, eyes studying his companion's features. His white-winged brow frowned. "Have we met before?"

Genii's eyes snapped to his then back to the pool as though afraid the image might disappear, which was a real possibility. "I have no memories beyond this cave."

"We may not have met before," said Mordecai, "but I have seen you before, a long time ago."

This time Genii's eyes did leave the pool, and the woman vanished. "Where?" he demanded.

Mordecai began to speak, telling him of a time when he was but a child and of events that had transpired in a clearing not far from where they were currently sitting, of a man and a woman in love, but barred from being together forever by a small thing called mortality, of an attempt to circumvent death by binding the life of a mortal to the immortality of the moon, and a desperate attempt to beguile the heavens by a couple in love. Of a battle between godling sisters for the love of the same man and the battle that ensued, and of one godling left standing but bound to the underworld for all eternity in the backlash.

"What is your name?" Mordecai asked in a quiet, still voice, barely more than a whisper.

"Genii," he whispered back and put his hands to his face feeling the contours, the form he presented as the template of his body here within Helga's realm. As a wraith, he had no need of a solid form. Yet why he felt the need to project a form, he could not remember. "I have…small patches of memories…that may be what you speak of, but not enough to know it for truth."

"You would be of the right age in appearance," said Mordecai. "I was but a small child. But I witnessed the event." His eyes drifted back to the still surface of the pool. "I think that was…Artio?" His eyes caught the flash of recognition in Genii's eyes at that mention of the name. "Although how she has come to be in a mortal form again, I do not understand. She is not quite as she was, yet you recognize her, don't you?"

"Yes." The single word escaped on a sigh.

Mordecai leaned back over the pool, and Artio slid into view once more. "Well, it seems we are both interested in her, but I think for different reasons." Artio watched the Pegasus wing away and screamed silently at the air. "I have a suggestion." Genii frowned at her then passed the gaze to Mordecai. "I suggest we both bind our tongues in relation to this interest. I also suggest that maybe our interests are aligned closer than with your mistress."

"What makes you think I have any interest in anything outside of my mistress?" Genii hissed, pulling away from Mordecai. His face darkened like a thundercloud. "Helga commands my loyalty, old man, not you, and certainly not some vague vision of a forgotten past. Now, unless you wish me to snap a few more fingers the old-fashioned way, get to work."

He gripped Mordecai by the hair on the back of his head and pulled it back, stretching his neck as he tilted his face up. His other hand slid into a pocket of his tunic and pulled out a small vial of a dark amber liquid. A cork popped, and he emptied the vial of potion into Mordecai's open mouth. He continued to stretch his neck, and Mordecai was forced to swallow or drown. He swallowed the bitter liquid then Genii released his head with a shove. Mordecai gagged, leaning over the basin.

"Prophecy, wizard," commanded Genii. "Show us your visions."

Mordecai's vision swam, and the surface of the pool seethed and became a wild red tempest that sucked him into its swirling depths. Events past, present, and future jumbled together, and he was tossed from one event to another without any anchor and with no way of knowing the timeline. The pool was no longer a flat tableau but an angry three-dimensional funnel. The visions came fast and furious, and he cried out as heat washed over him like a wave. Fingers of flame licked his skin and crisped his brows, flashing them to dust on his face. The cry of battle assaulted his ears, and a sea of men and beasts clashed and writhed on the ground below him, the red of the flame surrounding him reflecting off rivers of blood. With a splash, he hit the quagmire, which flowed around his ankles, sucking him down into the river spilling over the edge of a cliff. He grabbed for anything to stop his tumbling progress and the only solid object became another body, and another, and another, until the surface roiled with the dead. With a cry, he was tossed over the edge, and he shrieked as he fell, a sick swooping tickle bringing his stomach into his throat.

The ground rushed up at him, and Mordecai squeezed his eyes shut. Before he struck the bottom, a Pegasus picked him out of the air and flew off with him toward Cathair, following a trail of men. Mordecai gasped and clutched at its mane, squinting down at the remnant of an army, screaming their madness to the plains. Burned farms and looted villages littered their path and ran straight as an arrow toward the heart of the kingdom, toward the capital.

The Pegasus disappeared, and suddenly Mordecai knelt in a tower room beside a Primordial princess, heavy with child.

"*Noooooo!*" he cried out and squeezed his eyes tight. He could not stand to lose her again, not like this.

When he opened his eyes again, he was in complete darkness. There were no windows, no door, and no light to define the space. He was laying spread eagle on his back with a stone floor beneath him:

cold, damp, and hard. He lifted his right arm and was jerked to a halt, inches off the floor. His wrists were encircled with manacles that fed into a set of heavy chains that rattled as he moved his arm. A similar set ran from his ankles. A rat squeaked…or at least he thought it was a rat. He could not remember ever being in such a predicament. He felt a pinch on his toes and kicked out, but the rat did not let go of his toe. It bit down harder, and Mordecai cried out with pain.

"Good, good. Now we are getting somewhere." The voice floated past his consciousness and was gone.

The scene shifted. A great bone temple, multiple stories tall, glowed as though alive, each of its frescoes flowing with movement. The temple groaned and the earth shook as it lifted from the ground and rose into the air to hover about the tops of the trees. The frescoes writhed and detached themselves from the walls, forming bodies of beasts and people and vegetation that could move under its own power. Blinding blue light shone from the windows like great fingers and stroked the air around the temple. Then two people stepped out onto the balcony at the very peak and walked to the edge of the railing, just as a bolt of lightning struck the temple. The flash of light blinded Mordecai, and he was flung back by the force of the vision, soaring through the air for real this time to land in a heap several feet away from the scrying pool, unconscious.

Genii bent and picked up Mordecai's wrist in his fingers. A thready pulse beat in it. He scooped up the wizard for the second time that day and carried him off to his chambers.

The scrying pool relaxed, and the surface stilled. Red and blue flames danced across the surface, and then were gone.

Chapter 44

Sheol Animus

CAYDEN'S WILD RIDE through the forest on his spooked mount brought welts and bruises from slapping tree branches whipping his arms and legs as his horse made the shortest possible dash away from the flaming debris. Burnt horse hair still wafted into his nostrils despite the movement of his horse. His horse was also of a mind to put as much distance as possible between him and the flaming forest.

Cayden's only thought at the time had been that he could not lose his father again, and the safest place for him was on Brimstone. Now he wondered about the wisdom of that decision, but done was done.

As the mountain calmed, Cayden was able to rein in his panicked mount, pulling it to a snorting, shivering halt that allowed Elder Hania to catch up to him. The sides of the horses moved under their legs, great bellows pumping as they pulled in lungful after lungful of air, shaking with exhaustion. Cayden's grip on the reins did not slacken. His head swivelled as he checked the progress of the Pegasuses in the air. It was just as dangerous to be airborne as galloping through flaming woods as he knew only too well. Memories of another flight flashed across his mind, a flight that had ended in the worst possible outcome. This time, at least, he was well aware of what the flaming balls of rock meant. Helga had a lot to answer for. How dare she disrupt the harmonies of the world? Gritting his teeth, Cayden glared at the mountain. Helga also held Mordecai, he could feel it. The how and why of it, he did not know. What he did know was that he needed the wizard. He had always needed the wizard, and this time, he would do the rescuing; this time he would be the one to spring him from his imprisonment. He could still feel Mordecai's pull.

"Where are you heading, my lord? Sire? I believe you are the king of Cathair?" Elder Hania gripped his reins as tightly, slumping slightly in the saddle, still weary from his recent abuse.

Cayden's nodded tightly in acknowledgment, and his frustrated glare swung to the elder and then softened. "I apologize, Elder." He bowed from his saddle. "You should be safe on the back of a Pegasus and winging your way back to your people." He frowned again, then his gaze swung back to the mountain. "I am about to pay a visit on a...relative. This is no place for you." His voice echoed weirdly, as he thought of Helga.

"You would be seeking the goddess who calls the mountain home, the goddess of the underworld. She is called amongst my people Shadow Soul, mistress of the dead." He nodded as if reaching a conclusion and straightened in his saddle. "I will aid you as I was aiding your sister Avery. You have returned as prophesied."

"You have seen Avery!" At his nod, Cayden exclaimed, "Is she all right? When did you see her last?"

Elder Hania shook his head. "No, she did not tell me. She was on her way to the Crystal Caves the last time I saw her. She may even be there by now."

Mordecai or Avery, who should I go to first? Who was the most urgent, the most important? Cayden pondered his choices, knowing that time was short and that possibly the fate of the world hinged on his decision. What was Helga's plan? Avery was free and Mordecai likely imprisoned. Avery's soul was free, and Mordecai's soul was imprisoned somewhere. Cayden prayed that Mordecai had been able to free him from the doll, but until such time as he was sure, he had to secure Mordecai's freedom, and that meant following the trail to Mordecai to get him back. That meant Helga's realm.

Elder Hania watched the play of emotions flit across his face. The struggle was a familiar one.

"We are wasting time, sire." He glanced at the skies and gestured at the sun, low on the horizon. "The day wanes. Time is making fools of us. What is the plan?"

Cayden's mount danced beneath his hands. "We free a wizard." His eyes locked onto the hazel eyes of the elder. "Failure is beyond comprehension. To be captured means death…for all. Are you sure you want to do this?"

"Yes." There was no trace of fear in the elder's steady gaze.

Cayden's eyes swung skyward. "Then come. Ziona tracks us from the sky, and my father is with her. We will see if four can storm an underworld fortress."

The elder squeezed the sides of his horse, riding up beside Cayden. "Just curious, have you ever been there before?"

Cayden glanced at him out of the corner of his eye. "Not even for tea," he said grimly and urged his horse forward onto the twisting path leading toward the summit of the mountain.

A raven circled overhead and with a sharp cry, wheeled back toward the mountain flapping furiously to stay ahead of the Pegasus on the same path. Gaining the shadow of the mountain, it dipped low over a stovepipe opening on the rocky face and disappeared inside.

*　*　*

Helga chuckled, as the raven settled onto her outstretched arm and she withdrew from sharing its gaze, releasing her control over the bird. *Come to me, older brother, come. It will be easier to instruct you once you are safely inside and ensconced as my guest. Why, it will be like a family reunion! You, me, and our dearest sisters once they arrive. How will I ever prepare? I don't think we have all been under the same roof since we were babes-in-arms. I might even find a place for you in my realm, once the peoples of this godforsaken rock bow in acknowledgment of me.*

Helga strode up the hall and called out to Genii. "Genii, come to me. A guest approaches." She paused at the top of the staircase, listening for his approach. She was greeted with silence. Where was the fool man? She leaned out over the short wall and noticed that the scrying pool below was still and abandoned. She continued along the hall, following its twisting path to the break by the waterfall. Cayden would arrive soon at this spot. She looked skyward. No winged shadow blocked the light. She settled herself onto a bench cloaked in darkness and waited, mulling over what she would say to Cayden when he arrived.

At that moment, Genii appeared, sliding out of the twist of twilight like the wraith he was.

"You called, mistress?" He bowed his dark head.

"Cayden approaches with another man. Prepare rooms for our 'guests.'"

"As you command, mistress." He faded back into the shadows and was gone.

Helga pulled out the mystery Soul Fetch and bounced it in her hands, thinking. She had a feeling that the doll was attuned to Caerwyn—Cayden, as he was called in this age.

I will rule supreme, Brother! The souls of the dead need not be tortured with a return to human mortality. They can serve me. Serve us. I am a patient goddess, and I will have your allegiance. We can be family, once again under my rule. There are enough souls for all of us, as long as you bow to me.

And if you refuse? Well, that is for you to decide what will be your fate. You and Alfreda—Avery, as she likes to be called in this age—hold the fate of the world in your hands, at least as it is currently configured. Without their Spirit Shield, there is no possibility of rebirth. Once your meddling is ended, the souls will truly be mine. I will choose who is reborn, and I will decide for how long. You may serve me and live or be converted into a loyal servant. I can always use more souls for my Charun army.

With one finger, she stroked the glossy feathers of the raven still perched on her arm without seeing it. It bobbed its head and cawed, flapping its wings, then it took off into the air to its roost in the tallest tree, closest to the rim of the opening. She watched it join its companions, the flock that scouted on her command. A shaft of sunlight blazed along the stone rim, announcing the hour, and she turned her back to the opening. The clatter of horses' hooves on rock sounded over the murmur of the falls. They were here.

The shrubbery parted and in rode two men on horseback. One was young, barely an adult, and the other an elderly man. They rode around the rim of the pool and toward her and then reined their horses at a safe distance.

Cayden swung down from his saddle and handed the reins to the elder man. His gaze fixed on the falls, and, staring straight at her, he called out in a firm voice, "Helga, I know you are there. Part the curtain, and let me enter." The elder slid out of his saddle and stepped up beside him, his eyes scanning the curtain of mist but seeing nothing.

Helga chuckled and waved her hand. The mist parted, swinging back on both sides like a curtain in truth. It created a dark tunnel of walled water, but the ground underfoot was completely dry. "Welcome, Caerwyn, welcome. It has been a long time."

Cayden gave his horse a quick pat on the neck and stepped forward into the tunnel, followed by the elder. However, when the elder attempted to step into the tunnel, he met with a solid force that would not allow him entrance.

"Your friend cannot enter. Only the dead or those who have the power over life and death can enter."

Cayden paused and looked back at the elder. "Sorry. I must go on, alone."

Elder Hania bowed and stepped back, worry wrinkling his brow. "Be careful, sire."

Helga chuckled from the shadows. Her voice echoed eerily down the passage. "I will take good care of him, elder. Return to your people. You have no place here amongst the gods."

Elder Hania gave a start at the sound of her voice. It was a cold voice, a howling moan, which reminded him of open graves and restless spirits. He'd not heard the original welcome to Cayden, and the sound of her voice sent a shiver down his spine. He clenched his teeth together then stepped back with a quick bow before returning to this horse. He mounted quickly, a touch of panic in his movements.

Cayden strode the rest of the way under the falls. With a wet slap, the curtain closed, and the fall resumed its normal flow. Cayden paused, allowing his eyes to adjust to the near dark. Helga stood up, filling the doorway to her home.

"So. The king returns. Welcome to Sheol Animus. Welcome to my home." She stepped aside to allow him to enter, then stepped up beside him. "I know why you are here, Brother. The wizard lives. He is bound to serve me now, as are you. There is no returning to the outside world, except as I command."

Cayden stiffened at her words, and his hand drifted to the sword hilt at his waist.

Helga laughed, amused. "There will be none of that. We both know that you cannot kill a soul. You may think that I have no soul to kill, and you would be right, so striking me down is impossible with such a weapon. Besides, it is a rude way to greet your sister. We are family. Come, we will have tea and chat about old times and what you have been up to since we last…met." Her lips twisted into a smile that did not reach her eyes. "We have plenty to talk about, you and I. And when we are through reminiscing, we can chat about these." She reached into her pocket and pulled out the two Soul Fetches. She saw his eyes widen with shock and recognition, then Cayden licked his lips nervously.

Cayden's mind spun furiously. Doubt and fear twisted his gut. *What have I done in coming here? Forgive me, Ziona! Forgive me, Avery! I have failed you both.*

*   *   *

Denzik and the raft of Kingsmen with him studied the Primordial host trotting along in the wake of the overly tall woman on horseback. That she led the band was clear by the deferential distance formed around her, as though she physically repelled them from touching her somehow.

Denzik scratched at the scruffy beard on his chin, thinking. They were headed in the same direction that they had tracked Avery—to the clearing where she and a companion's trail ended. They had been slowed by the disintegration of the legion, having run into band after band of half-crazed former soldiers. The first few instances had resulted in fierce battles that had wounded and weakened his men, a few had even died. Finally, they decided they would avoid any further confrontations and had begun a stealthy sneak through the thick forest, avoiding all forms of human contact. They could not avoid the creature contacts, but the creatures seemed to know that they aided Avery or were attempting to and left them alone for the most part. The legion soldiers were not so lucky and were harried out of the forests, which may have explained in part the crazed look in their eyes.

This band of Primordials, however, was neither crazed nor scared of the woods and moved with a purpose to where Avery was holed up. The tall woman bothered Denzik. She did not appear to be fully human. If not human, then what was she? It all smacked of the gods, and Denzik was no fool to stick his head into an immortal wasp's nest. If she was indeed of the gods, then he could best help Avery by choosing the time and location of the battle with care.

So, he continued to watch, and wait. The sun was setting, and the beginnings of a moon were in evidence on the jagged skyline. It looked to be a full moon. He and his men settled into hollows and into crooks of trees, with a view of the magnificent stone ring and the long valley. He pulled his curved pipe from his shirt pocket and clamped the stem between his teeth, but he did not light it. His thoughts organized themselves better when he had his pipe clenched between his teeth. Something was about to play out, and they had front-row seats. He just hoped it would be a show he wanted to see.

Chapter 45

Focal Point

BLOOD DRIPPED FROM AVERY'S FINGERS as she crawled through the brambles, the sharp points snagging her clothing and biting deep into the flesh of her arms and face. For once, she was grateful that she no longer had hair to tangle in the clinging vines, but that lack also meant that the rune-infused cap of skin covering her skull was shredding in equal measure. She blinked away a trickle of blood that insisted on pooling at the crook of her nose, and drew a sigh of relief on reaching the edge of the clearing. The brambles fully encircled the clearing. There was but one way to approach the clearing undetected. From this angle, she could creep over to the stones, their height and width hiding her approach from watchful eyes.

She hated leaving Achak behind. In truth, she hated being alone back in the woods where she had healed him, but there was no way he could keep up with a broken leg. She also did not want to expose him to what lay ahead. As he was unconscious, he should not be discovered.

The clearing was roughly two hundred paces in width, and about three hundred long. Four tall sentinel rocks ringed the clearing, each massive stone like a grey guardian towering over it. Each was decorated with a series of symbols, which Avery recognized, although some were faded to the point of being barely legible. The etchings themselves were not required, as the magic was set into the stone. It was equally obvious that they had not been used in a millennium. The glen smelled of decaying memory and stillborn traditions, abandoned by time and the mortals confined by it.

In the past, this glen had shuddered with power. Originally, this green meadow had been a gift from the heavens to the mortals they loved so dearly. This sacred clearing had once been the portal to the gods.

Now, the clearing was empty except for the stones. Long grasses swayed in the gentle breeze that sifted through the clearing. Buttercups dotted it, and a sense of peace pervaded the air. Avery sniffed the breeze and smiled. Relaxed, she walked up to the closest monolith, examining the carvings. The stones grew out of the soil, as much alive as the plants surrounding them, and indeed the bottom of the monolith was covered with carvings of vegetation. Sacred plants, plants long used in healing and nurturing. Great stalks of tobacco decorated the stone, and she ran her hand along the deep grooves. A waft of pipe smoke drifted to her nostrils, and she smiled at the memory it invoked. She glanced around and noticed that the other stones also carried carvings of plants, thin stalks of sweet grass, leafy sage, and fragrant cedar.

Stacked on top of the sacred plants were deeply carved reliefs of animals, all familiar to her. An eagle soared over the sweet grass; a buffalo chewed contentedly above the tobacco; a she-wolf stalking prey with her cubs above the sage; and a bear scratching at the ground where the cedar grew. Each animal was carved in a position of peace or contentment. Avery ran her hand over the buffalo. The face of the image looked at her, jaw ruminating.

Chiseled above each animal, an elemental was drawn, connecting through to the carvings below. The sun shone down on the buffalo and the tobacco; softly swirling currents of air carried the eagle over the sweet grass and encircled it; gentle rain bathed the wolf and cubs and watered the sage; and dark loamy earth fed the mighty cedar and the bear, scratching into the soil.

As Avery looked closer, she could also see the seasons carved into the four pillars. Spring, summer, winter, and fall were reflected in progression around the circle. Crocuses dotted the meadow of sweet grass; a thunderstorm threatened on the horizon behind the buffalo; the sage was partly covered by fallen leaves; and the earth had a slight crust of snow that contrasted with the russet ground.

The final carvings were spiritual and interpretive. The faces of the gods, those who were the elders in ancient times, stared down from the crest of the stones. A Spirit Guardian perched, overseeing the eagle, surrounded by a halo of carved eagle feathers. The second guardian's face was laughing and crying, the emotional guardian of the Primordial people. The third face was wise and caring, a consummate reflection of the guardian of wisdom and intellect. The final face was youthful with strong cheeks and a clear gaze, the guardian of the physical.

Avery swiped at the trickle of blood that once again attempted to block her vision, leaving a smear across the bridge of her nose.

This is the spot, the place I remember as a child. Papa used to bring us once a year to renew our vows to the gods.

Avery stepped into the center of the stones, memory guiding her to a spot equidistant to them, and knelt down. It looked the same as every other overgrown section. She grabbed great handfuls of the meadow grasses and pulled, uprooting them, and she pulled out the matted soil pack created by the webbing of roots, peeling back the sod like the skin of an orange.

When she had cleared an area roughly the size of wagon wheel, she stood up and dragged her boot across the partially cleared spot, pushing dirt back with it. Half an hour passed and the sun shifted along its axis, sinking closer to the horizon. Avery glanced up from her work and frowned. She had but an hour till the appointed time, until the rays of the setting sun were aligned as prophesied.

A niggling sense of panic wormed its way into her consciousness and she ran to the side of the clearing to search for a tool to use as a shovel, the box giggling in the inner pocket of her tunic. She cast her eyes over the ground, eyes searching for something to assist her with digging. A twig snapped in the woods and she froze, melting into the grasses to stare at what approached the clearing. One hand curled around the flat stone she had spied just before the sound. The other slid into her coat to clutch the handle of her throwing knife. Her eyes studied the edge of forest encroaching on the chest-high brambles. There was but one path into the site. All other approaches were on hands and knees, as she had entered, if one was to remain unseen.

No one could have followed her. No one would dare try. And if no one followed, that left one possibility. If someone was spying on her, they were already here. They already knew the location of the

Sacred Meadow. And the only one who would know this...she shivered at the thought. Avery suddenly felt very, very alone.

Cayden? she whispered in her mind. It did not matter that she knew it was in her head, the habits of a lifetime made her whisper, even there. *Are you coming?* She waited in silence, eyes still roving over her surroundings, searching for anything out of the ordinary.

Silence greeted her. Her mind remained silent too. *Cayden?* Her head swiveled. Tamping down her rising fears, she grabbed the stone and headed back to the center of the clearing. What choice did she have? The sun was going to set regardless of whether anyone was watching. It was now or never. Another solstice would not occur until after the doom had fallen. *No choice. None whatsoever.* Avery gritted her teeth and pushed aside her fear of whatever watched from the trees.

She knelt once again and took the stone in both hands, scooping the loose dirt toward her, moving around in a circle to drag back more and more soil all the time. She worked steadily for twenty minutes, sweat dripping off her forehead and mixing with the blood, stinging through the cuts even as it washed the blood away. She dared not swipe it away with her hands covered in dirt, and endured the stinging sweat.

The stone clunked and scraped against something solid. She paused, then dropped the stone and began to scoop away soil with her bare hands, clearing the area. Gradually, a white disk emerged, which glowed faintly in the waning light. Avery tossed aside the stone and began to scoop out handfuls of dirt, tossing them over the side and brushing the remainder off to the sides, smoothing her hands over the surface.

The disk was about three paces in circumference and made of a smooth stone-like substance that glowed softly in the fading light. The buttery texture was soft to the touch yet hard as steel. The scraping stone had not marked the surface, yet Avery swore she could have marked it with the edge of her fingernail.

Avery snapped her fingers and a flame danced to life. She held it over the disk and swept away the last of the dirt then bent to examine its surface. It was completely smooth and unmarked except for a hollowed-out bowl in the center and eight sectional lines, like small troughs that ran back precisely to where monolithic guardians stood.

The bowl was patterned with dots, some larger, some smaller. As Avery studied them, she realized they were a reflection of the heavens; the planetary bodies and the stars that would be visible at this time of day if the sun's light had not obscured them from human view.

Avery sighed with satisfaction, pleased that she had found the celestial bowl.

She glanced up to mark the placement of the sun. When she raised her head, it was met with the cool press of a blade at her throat. She sucked in a quick breath and froze.

"Hello, Sister. It is about time we met." Artio's blade forced Avery to her feet, and with a casual flick of wrist, she pushed the remainder of Avery's hood off her head. Their eyes locked for the first time in a millennium, sister to sister.

Avery's eyes widened in shock at her sister's bear-like appearance, and Artio's reaction was similar, if less intense. Artio's bladed knife dropped, while she studied her sister's tattooed form. She gripped the curved blade tightly in her right hand as though uncertain whether she was dangerous. The thought flashed through her mind that she should finish her right then and there.

Avery's eyes ran around the stones, searching for a path to freedom, but the Flesh Clan warriors surrounded them three deep. "Thank you for guiding us to the Celestial Temple," Artio growled. "I knew you remembered where it was. You were the one who worshiped Papa, you and…what does he call himself now, Cayden? You both worshiped the ground he walked on!" Artio chuckled as she strode around Avery, looking her up and down. "Of course, Morpheus was a god, but even so, I found your fawning quite revolting. But look at you! My, what a puny human you have become." Artio's hand shot out and grabbed Avery by the throat, lifting her up with one hand, so that her feet dangled inches from the ground. Avery gasped, choking, and grabbed Artio's hands with her own, pulling herself up to relieve the pressure on her throat, to little avail. Her eyes widened in fear, then flashed back to defiance. Artio threw back her head and laughed while Avery writhed in her grip. "I do believe I could snap your neck by simply squeezing, but you fight on! So, there is a remnant of the stubborn little girl in there." Artio tossed Avery to the side, where she bounced and tumbled through the grasses, coming to rest face down.

Avery sucked in a lung full of air and dirt, her hand rising to touch the bruise already forming around her throat from Artio's crushing grip. Avery heaved several gulps of air into her lungs and then sat up, only to be met by spears and knives before she could fully sit.

"Let her up, my pets. She has something of mine. A trinket box, promised to me by my beloved." Avery froze at the words. *How does she know? Have I been betrayed?*

The spears withdrew incrementally, and Avery sat up, gazing warily at her sister.

"You do not speak. Come now, Alfreda. This is a reunion! You should be rejoicing in our reacquaintance."

Avery stood up, testing her various wounds. Her head ached and her throat was on fire, but both of those she could deal with. With alarm, she found that her right foot tried to buckle under her. She had not even realized she had twisted it in the fall, but now it was well and truly sprained. Pain flashed as she tested it for weight, and she bit her lip to hold in the moan.

"I do not understand why you do this, Artio. You are Artio?" Artio nodded. "Cayden and I have never caused you any harm. We were your champions always, and especially after your disappearance! What has happened to you?"

Artio snorted and walked closer to her sister, her feral eyes absorbing the setting sun and glowing golden in the refracted light.

"Lies! You try to distract me from my purpose here tonight, but it will not work. Time is of the essence, and you would like to see the sun set on this day, true?" Avery's eyes widened involuntarily. "Yes, I know of the solstice prophecy, a prophecy that arose from my demise. From our demise, is it not? It promises that on this evening, the circle will be completed once more, and the healing of the stones unleashed. The Flesh Clan priests chatter on about how I will bring back the gods and that they will rule supreme under me." Avery shook her head but remained silent. She knew there was more to it than simply triggering the stones. "And I also know that my trinket box is key. You will now hand it over to me." The warriors grabbed Avery's arms and held her tightly, swords coming to throat again. "Go on. Remove the box from your pocket. My warriors have heard the stories of your cloak and know they will not be able to remove it from your person." Avery started defiantly back at Artio, not moving a muscle to comply with the order. Her hands clenched into fists, and she had to consciously relax her white-knuckled squeeze. She quivered with suppressed anger.

Artio's grin widened. "Oh yes, that is the Alfreda I remember. Defiant and stamping her feet to get her way. No worries, I have the perfect incentive for you." Artio snapped her fingers, and a man was dragged, screaming with pain, down the path and into the meadow. Achak was dumped, bound hand and foot, at her feet. He flopped face-first onto the ground, smacking his head on a rock, breaking his nose and gushing blood. He did not move.

Chapter 46

Daimon

ACHAK'S ARMS BENT to hands tied behind his back. His crumpled face pressed into the dirt, lips askew. His tunic was torn, and the wooden splint Avery had strapped to his leg with such care and attention was nowhere to be found.

Artio stepped forward and grabbed Achak by a fistful of hair, yanking his head back. One eye was swollen shut and his lips were split, blood dripping from his nose to join the blood flowing down his chin to. Artio pulled the obsidian knife from her leg and placed its shining edge against his jugular.

"Now," she spoke slowly and precisely, enunciating each word that followed, "you will place the box in the celestial bowl. If you do not do as I say, you will still place the bowl in the box, but it will be joined by pieces of flesh we carve out of his body. When we are done with him, we will start on you. If I put enough pieces of you in the basin, the box will be there too. This is your first and only offer, Sister. Shall I start sawing?" Artio lightly dragged the blade against Achak's skin, and blood blossomed along the cut, coating the blade edge with glimmering droplets.

"Wait!" Avery shouted. "What is your interest in the box? Why do you care about the healing of the world? You abandoned us to care for it. What does it matter to you if the world lives on? Why have you come to stop me?"

"Stop you?" Artio threw back her head and barked a laugh. "What do you think is in that box, Little Sister? I don't want to stop you. *I want to use you.* Only you can trigger what I need." Avery stared at her hard, reaching out with her mind. She could sense the truth in her sister's statement. That alarmed her more than Artio's threats that she was determined she use the box. Dread settled into her belly, a roiling cramp of fear sharp as a knife. *What has Artio done to the box? Or has someone else tinkered with it?* Not for the first time, she wished she knew what had happened after she'd died. *But what choice do I have? If I refuse, Achak is dead.*

"Enough delay! The sun fades." Artio's hand moved, and Achak swayed in her grip.

"*Stop!*" Avery shouted. Artio's eyes gleamed. Without another word, Avery limped over to Artio, reaching into her pocket and withdrawing the box. Artio released her hold, and the unconscious Achak slumped back to the ground. Artio took the box from Avery's hand and gently examined it. Avery's eyes darted to Achak. She could see the rise and fall of his chest, despite the blood staining his neck.

Artio's eyes glistened for a moment and then hardened. Avery thought she saw tears, but in an instant they were gone.

Artio handed the box back to Avery. "Place it in the basin, and speak the words."

Avery took the box and hobbled back to the disk, placing it in the center of basin. She closed her eyes and pulled from deep within her most ancient of memories, words she has spoken long ago, during a ceremony in this very spot. Their father, Morpheus, had been with them that time, holding both girls by a hand, one on either side.

He had thrown back his head and prayed to the gods as the box flashed with a wild blue light. Avery echoed those words, only now understanding their power, sending her prayer to the heavens.

"Blush of blood, barely born,
Sacred spirits eternally sworn,
Flesh of man's fading form
Magic's bonding, magic torn.

Torn from time, never mended
Crumbling oaths of faith upended
Abandoned of the gods descended
Shield of spirit, creatures blended

Time eternal, gods forsaken
Reign of man, dominion shaken
Sibling wars, the cause mistaken
Runes align, the world awakens

Strife consumes, unwary foe
Minds controlled, a killing blow
Long forgotten, flaming woe
Time divided, slowing flow

Carry away the cursed one
Bring an end to father's son
Wild magic's cast begun
Sacred creed, moon undone."

With an audible click, the lid popped open, just as the last rays of the sun settled into the clearing. The beams struck each pillar precisely on a guardian that began to glow, then the light travelled internally down through the columns of stone lighting them from within. The stones trembled and from each level, triggered by the guardian, waves of healing shot out from the monoliths and encased all who were within the circle. The beams touched everything and everyone, and every physical injury healed in that instant. Aging ceased and time rewound and flesh mended. But something more than flesh and blood began to heal.

At the same time, whispers of shadow snaked from the trinket box, twisting and gathering into dense black ropes that thickened and rose into the air. The ground shook and the ropes became a coil that expanded and solidified at an alarming rate. The healing waves rebounding around the clearing collided with the smoke, and the twisting forms resolved into bodies, both human and animal.

At first Avery though she recognized them, but as their features grew sharper, more defined, she knew she did not. Grotesquely deformed creations were being mended, healed back into existence by the healing portal. But these creatures were never meant to be. They were the result of an experiment gone wrong, the creation of a sick mind. Banished by the gods, torn apart in defeat and ashes scattered to the netherworld, they were never again to see the world of the living. Yet Avery could not deny the evidence before her eyes. *They are here!*

Someone has gathered the remains of the Daimons and secured them in the box! And I have released them right over the heart, the source of their strength, Daimon Ford. How could I have forgotten the events of that night?

And now, they were reforming. Not just released, but *healed and alive*!

Artio threw back her head and roared her pleasure. The Primordials at her side shied back, muttering amongst themselves in confusion and fear. A keening cry rose from the swirling mass, the horrible screech that was the ancient speech of the Daimon hordes. The sound was the last straw, and the warriors raced from the clearing, abandoning Artio and Avery to the dervishes forming in the night. Artio did not even acknowledge the abandonment, so focused was she on the rebirth of her true army. She raised her arms to embrace the daimonic spirits, the firelight dancing across her body, flickering in the depths of her eyes. Her only thought was of the revenge she would wreak on the world. How she would avenge her true love. *I have stolen your army from you, Helga! They are mine to command! I will have my revenge at long last!*

Avery dropped to her knees and crawled away from the portal, over to the still form of Achak. She ran her hands along his leg, checking the break, but she already knew he would be fully healed. She rolled him over and shook him awake, wincing at the high-pitched squealing that ramped higher and higher behind her, all the while keeping an eye focused on the hellish rebirths. Their non-corporeal bodies blurred into a tornadic swirl as the sun dropped below the horizon.

The energy of the sun's rays was no longer needed, for now a light glowed from the center of the swirl, blood red and volcanic. The white disk at its center flared a blinding white, and then melted into a blinking morass before her eyes. A rift opened up along the fault lines leading back to the monoliths. Magma pulsed up out of the fiery cracks and bubbled, hissing, into the bowl. The figures drew on the coursing lava and thin fingers of flame trailed up and over their bodies, igniting muscle and bone. Wings unfurled from backs, and demonic faces began to glow, their eyes a burning flame.

"Achak! We must go. *Now!*" Avery hissed, tugging on his arm. His eyes snapped open, widening in horror at the hellish vision greeting his groggy mind. He scrambled to his feet, swaying, and his foot kicked a glass vial. Avery spied a bottle rolling away, full of potion and quickly snatched it up, amazed at their luck. *Aossi's potion!* She popped the lid off, drank half and then passed the other half to Achak. He tipped it back, and they both faded from view. Hands linked, they both bolted for the cover of the brambles, caring not for the fresh scratches and injuries inflicted as they crashed through the underbrush. The earth quaked, and they staggered as they ran. Their one thought was to put as much distance as possible between themselves and the abyss forming in the sacred clearing and the monster rising from its midst.

A great keening rose on an unnatural wind, spawned of the blistering breeches, as the formerly peaceful meadow flashed into flame. The tall grasses were consumed with the ferocity of a grasshopper plague, and onto this crackling inferno stepped a hideous obsidian Daimon of unbelievable size. Twenty feet tall, the shining rocky goliath towered over the burning carpet. Its clawed feet puffed swirls of sparks into the air as it took its first steps out of the circle. In its massive hand, it gripped a flaming sword as tall as Avery. More rock Daimons followed it, spawned of the goliath, but Avery was no longer paying attention.

Avery dragged Achak behind her. "Move faster!" she screamed, launching herself over a log in their path. Achak's laboured breathing assured her that he was right behind her as they reached the cover of the trees, fleeing from what was surely death.

Artio's chilly laughter chased them as they fled. "You can run, Little Sister, but there is no place to hide."

Avery and Achak dropped behind a rock as Artio's words reached them, pressing their backs against the stone and gulping air. Avery peered around the side of the rock, horrified at the monsters erupting in the clearing. The flames of the meadow reflected off of the varied planes of their obsidian bodies and refracted in all directions, multiplying the crazed dance of demons so that was impossible to track with the eye. She could not count them because her human eyes could not focus on one long enough to register it as an individual. Only the tallest one, with glowing pits in its face where its eyes should have been, gave it away as a sole being, that and the great horns curving from its skull. It was similar to the Daimon from Artio's demise, and yet unlike the original beast of Daimon Ford. This version was refined, its face hot with an intelligence that flickered in its fiery gaze. This Daimon had been altered; improved, blended.

Avery shuddered and grabbed Achak's hand once again and started running. As they dashed away, Artio's words chased them. "We will meet again, Little Sister, on the plains of Daimon Ford. There, you will meet your doom. There, you and Little Brother will face Asag, champion of the underworld, and there, *you will die.*"

Asag! Avery shuddered. How had the Daimons been summoned? This had all the hallmarks of Helga's doing, but how had Asag come to be bound to the box? Avery did not pause to challenge Artio's statement. She knew they would die now, if they stayed any longer.

They ran.

Chapter 47

The Plan

IN A CAMP FAR AWAY from the sacred clearing, Avery sat on a log in front of a small fire, sipping at tea from a large pottery bowl. Across from her sat Denzik and Achak, both men mirroring her actions, letting the silence stretch.

Nelson appeared out of the dark, carrying three large bowls of steaming stew—goat, by the aroma—with potatoes and a wild edible orange root that was native to the area. He set the bowls down in front of them and straightened. "Two Primordial strangers have approached the camp kitchens. They are friends. I think you know the one woman, Avery. Her name is Ziona. The other is an elder. Your father Gaius is with them."

"My father! Is he all right?" Avery gasped and began to rise to her feet, but Nelson pushed her back down with a firm hand on her shoulder. "Stay and eat. They are bathing and will join you shortly. Eat!" he commanded and then disappeared back into the dark.

"Amazing news! What luck that they have found us! Or is it luck?" Denzik shovelled a mouthful of hot stew past his lips and chewed vigorously at the tough meat. He waved his spoon at Avery. "If you don't eat your meat, you won't get any dessert." His mouth twitched with a smile. "And around here, no one wants to miss dessert."

Avery pouted but complied, eating the hot stew as quickly as the heat would allow. The warmth of the meal spread through her belly and dispersed the chilly horror that had dogged her ever since their narrow escape from the clearing.

Her connection to Cayden was silent, as though he was no longer in this world. She frowned at the thought, and worry paused her spoon part way to her mouth. "Why doesn't he answer?" she murmured, unaware she had spoken out loud.

A hand fell on her shoulder, and her father said, "Because he cannot."

Avery bolted to her feet and flung her arms around him, hugging him, her face buried in his chest. A tear slipped out from between her tightly scrunched lashes as she choked back a sob.

"Avery, I'm OK. There, child, do not cry." He rubbed her back as he had when she was a child, passing a hand over her bald head. He sighed and hugged her tight, then placed a kiss on the top of her head, a father comforting his only daughter. She was still his child and always would be, regardless of the demands of the gods. After a couple minutes, she pushed back, swiping a hand across her cheek to dry her tears. Avery's eyes searched him, checking him over, looking for injuries.

Gaius smiled. "See? I am in perfect health. Ziona took care of me."

"I thought I'd never see you again." She hugged him tight once more, just as Ziona strolled into the firelight, followed by the fat baker Fabian, balancing a tray of sticky buns on his shoulder.

Sniffs and sighs greeted his arrival as he placed the tray next to the tea and settled himself to a cup of the hot brew. Nelson returned with the remnants of the stew and settled himself down too, filling a cup with the fragrant tea.

Once everyone was assembled, they shared their collective experiences, bringing each other up to speed on the events of the last few weeks.

When silence descended once again, Ziona cleared her throat and stood. "Cayden is there." She pointed, straight as an arrow toward the summit wreathed in smoke, the underside a red glowing smear. "He went after Mordecai, so Mordecai must be there, also. I can feel him, weakly, like the brush of a breeze on my mind. He is there one minute and gone the next. That"—she pointed at the smoking mountain—"is Helga's realm. I can only assume he is in Sheol Animus, the underworld." Her voice hitched and then firmed. "No one returns from the underworld. No one."

"Nonsense." This time the voice was Elder Hania's. All eyes swivelled to his. "You only say that because no one ever has…and because those who go there are usually dead. Do you think he is dead?"

Ziona frowned, examining the feeling in her chest, then shook her head. "No, I do not think he is dead, but we must be realistic."

Denzik spoke up, "The king is not dead. I can't believe it. He has a plan, and he has the wizard."

Gaius smiled weakly. "That wizard is too stubborn to die anytime soon. I also believe they are alive."

Fabian shoved a sticky bun into everyone's hands, and they stared at the dripping sweet in bemusement. Fabian waved his through the air and said, "Then we are decided. We carry on with our plans. Nelson, the Kingsmen, and I will return to Cathair to sort out the former legions and regain order. We will return with a bigger, better army. I know that there is a well-trained force of knights waiting to avenge the king's honour, Ryder will have seen to that training and be chomping at the bit to see some action, especially when he learns of Cayden's capture.

"Avery, Achak, and Elder Hania will return to the temple of the Primordials and explore ways to fight the Daimon running loose under Artio's command and see to the uniting of the clans. We must have unity if we are to take on the underworld." Heads nodded in agreement.

"Ziona, since she can still sense some of Cayden's essence, will join Gaius and Denzik to go after Cayden and Mordecai. They can figure out a way to assist them in their escape from Sheol Animus. Only freed can they fight for the souls of the world, for the preservation of the souls of the living, and for life as we know it.

"With luck, we will see each other once again." Fabian raised his sticky bun in salute. The others mirrored his movement. "Let us toast to the end of Helga's interference, once and for all." His eyes swept the flickering faces. One by one they nodded and raised their buns in a sticky toast to success.

"I promise a dozen sticky buns a week for life to the one that brings me the rock Daimon's head!"

Denzik chuckled. "A reward worthy of a king. I accept your challenge!"

"Hear! Hear!" they shouted, challenge accepted, their hearts lighter than they had been for a long time.

Trials lay ahead, but they went to their beds with the focus of a plan settled, with goals set. The path would not be easy. In truth, the real trials were about to begin. But they had hope, and hope could make all the difference between good and evil.

Epilogue

DEEP UNDER THE HIGHLAND SPINE lay Sheol Animus. Miles down in its dark depths, a second scrying pool ripped with images. This pool did not show current events however, like its cousin at the lip of Sheol Animus. This pool was located beyond the boundary of the living, bound to the souls of the dead, and as such reflected the future from the perspective of the dead. With the accuracy of a mirror, those who looked into the pool would see deaths to come, deaths in the future. Only those who were about to die could see their reflections.

Helga rarely used it for obvious reasons. Everyone around her was already dead, until now.

Four Charun dragged two unconscious men down to the poolside and dropped them on the slippery rocks at the edge of the steaming water then drifted back into the shadows at the edge of the circle of weak light. Curls of vapour drifted off the surface of the cloudy, sulphur-smelling water. The odour of rotting eggs dragged them back to consciousness, and they gagged, choking on the stomach-curdling smells.

Cayden rolled over and dragged his torn sleeve across his mouth and nose, attempting to block out the smell.

Mordecai did much the same thing, only he had no robe to use. He pressed his bare, bony arm to his nose, eyes watering.

Helga stood over them, disgust evident in every bend and curve of her face. "Look into the pool and tell me what you see."

Cayden eyed the putrid pool, suspicious as to what it held.

"What is it you expect us to see?"

She shook her head, bemused. "Look into the pool," she commanded again.

Cayden glanced at Mordecai, who was weak beyond belief. The years were catching up to the old wizard.

Cayden stood up and cautiously approached the pool and bent over the edge.

Grey clouds rolled across the scene. Rocks and landscape were obscured by what they took at first to be a huge storm. Lightning flashed and the ground shook, but the closer Cayden looked, he could see the rocks were actually men and beasts, dead for as far as the eye could see. The storm clouds roiled and flashed and suddenly he realized that he was flying toward tall plumes of smoke. Whole villages and towns were burning, along with their associated crops, and the fire was everywhere—every town, every village. He began to recognize the landscape the closer he flew to Cathair, until the great walls that had withstood every external siege ever thrown against it came into view. A glow, like an early sunrise, rose from behind the walls, and more smoke rose from the interior. He was swept along in the vision. As he came closer to the outer crenel wall, he was swept up to a tower he knew all too well. There, at the top of the tower, stood a figure. Tall and imposing with his back to him, he flung fire down on the outlying villagers and back into the castle keep, casting a ring of flame and death.

"No!" Cayden gasped as he swooped closer and closer. At the last minute, when it appeared he must collide with the figure, it twisted to face him. *"Nooooo! By the will of the gods, no!"* Cayden wrenched himself away from the pool and collapsed to the ground, weeping.

The man atop the tower wore his face.

"This has gone too far! All will perish!"

Soul Sacrifice

CHAPTER 1

The Village

THE CHARUN DRIFTED ALONG THE PATH, enrobed in a veil of darkness, the trailing edge of its garment stirring eddies of dust as it passed. The spectral beings, spawn of the underworld, owned the dark and were indistinguishable from the surrounding shadows. In one gore-slimed hand, it grasped a decapitated head, bony fingers twisted in the straight black hair. It swayed toward a window of moonlight spilling onto the path, illuminating the first few rows of the otherwise solid wall of blackened tree trunks.

Silence greeted its passing. The normal nocturnal sounds of croaking frogs and chirping crickets faded, then stilled. As it reached the ring of moonlight, the tree trunks extended and sharpened into the shapes of additional Charun. The shadows rippled as they joined their brother by creation.

In the middle of the clearing, a mound of rocks rose up from the ground, the pyramid a lighter grey against the harsher black of the grass. The Charun slid toward the pile of rocks and paused beside it to toss the severed head onto the pile.

Achak sucked in a hard breath. He lay in the brush at the edge of the clearing, his head peering around the side of a small cluster of boulders that hid the rest of his body. He dared not move a muscle, for as the usual night sounds faded away with the approach of the Charun, an anxiety he associated with impending death swept over the clearing. Nature itself rebelled against the unnaturalness of the Charun, and his own soul twisted in response. Achak knew without a doubt that any movement, any twitch, would alert them to his presence.

Dragging his eyes away from the Charun, he squinted at the pile of rocks around which the Charun had gathered. *Why pile rocks in the middle of a clearing? It was strange behaviour even for a Charun.* The moon cleared the covering cloud, and a brilliant beam fell on the rocks, illuminating them clearly for the first time. Achak's mouth fell open in shock, and he bit down on his tongue to still his own cry of alarm. What he had at first thought to be rocks were not rocks at all. It was a pyramid of skulls. Primordial skulls. He had found the missing villagers. All of them.

*   *   *

Avery marched back and forth, her arms crossed over her chest, boots clicking on the tiled floor of the once prosperous inn. On reaching the end wall, she repeated the pacing, gnawing at her lower lip. The inn was empty despite it being dinnertime, a time when it should have been packed to overflowing with hungry people. But the hearth was cold. No fire had been laid, and no smells of cooking came from the kitchens. Flies buzzed around a bowl of decomposing fruit sitting in the middle of a table. Avery waved her hand at one that buzzed too close to her ear.

It had been this way in every building she had inspected. The people of the border village were simply gone, swept away as though by a tornado. *But all of them at the same time? Why would they leave? Or were they taken?* She was careful to not touch anything that was personal. She knew the imprint of their owners' souls would bring flashes of visions of their last moments. She'd had visions like those in similar villages to this one on her ride to Faylea with Sharisha, and this time she refused to leave without finding answers. She would learn the truth of the mysterious disappearances once and for all but not until Achak returned. She would not enter those visions alone. She sensed a great danger in entering their soul streams.

Evening was falling. Avery picked up one of the full oil lanterns she had retrieved from a ledge where they had been stored during daylight hours. She had lit it earlier and carried it over to the stout oak door, wrenching it open with her right hand. She stepped out into the cool night. The village around her was as silent as the grave. Not even a dog remained to bark at her presence.

With a determined step, she marched to the end of the main street, passing a tin smithy with samples of the wares available inside nailed to the faded ship lap siding. Next to it, a whitewashed building with peeling paint and a series of steps mimicked the temple in Faylea. A weathered sign painted with faded images swung above the entrance. It bore faces she took to be representations of the gods.

On the other side of the street, a barbershop and dentist's office were combined into one space and a large sign in the window advertised a two for one special. She dragged her eyes away from the distracting message as she reached the intersection of roads that gave the town its name, Crossroads.

She put the lantern down in the middle of the intersection and slowly rotated on the spot, searching for any sign of what had taken the villagers. By the meals left on tables and the closed signs flipped in store windows, she knew it must have occurred around the supper hour, at dusk or close to it, when most people would be in their homes or settling to their evening repast. People grouped in familiar settings by family units or with friends. Why this would make any difference, Avery was not sure. *Maybe I am trying to find significance where there is none.*

If her hunch was right, the phenomena should show if it was a natural occurrence. If it was not, then she would watch the sun set. Of course, there could be a more sinister reason for the disappearances.

She knelt to trim the lantern flame to its lowest setting then placed it behind her on the road. She was counting on her mortal presence to lure back whatever had attacked the villagers. As she straightened, the tattoos on her hands glowed blue as her spirit pulsed with nervous energy. Not that the tattoo was unique. In fact, she was covered from head to toe in tattoos, a gift of the Primordial temple and the priesthood of her heritage. She was marked so that all would know she was the true High Priestess of Faylea.

She pulled the precious bone knife, also a gift of the temple, from her boot as a precaution. It was at times like this that she longed for her twin brother, Cayden. He had been missing for a week now, ever since the confrontation in the sacred clearing with Artio, their sister in truth. Born of the gods, Cayden and Avery shared a bond that they had yet to fully comprehend. Ever since the clearing, she could not hear his voice. His voice had been with her all her life, a telepathic connection forged of their common ancestry she was only now beginning to understand. Bereft of that security, her loneliness threatened to overwhelm her. Cayden's absence highlighted her sense of vulnerability. More and more, she leaned on Achak, not only as a companion but also for support and counsel. She was growing quite fond of him. *Hurry back, Achak. I don't want to face this alone.*

The only warning she had was a slight creeping chill that raised the hair on the back of her neck. She dropped to her knees and slashed out with the blade wrought in the mystic temple of Faylea. It sliced cleanly into the inky cloak that materialized in front of her then slowed as it became mired, stuck in a gelatinous mass. The Charun staggered, as though suddenly made of flesh. It howled. The sound was like fingernails on slate, a high-pitched screeching wail. Then, it staggered back, bucking in the air. With a pop it exploded, black flecks sparkling in the lamplight, then vanished. Taking advantage of the moment of surprise, Avery quickly thumbed the light higher on the lantern, revealing three more Charun descending from a black slash in the night air through which she could see flickering fires and a river of lava. The portal closed behind them, and the three remaining Charun surrounded her, their eyes locked on her bone blade.

They shied from the light, preferring to work in darkness.

Avery wished she had brought more than one lamp, but she would not have been able to thumb the wick to a high enough flame simultaneously on multiple lanterns. She'd feared that the distraction factor of lighting multiple lamps would prove fatal. One would have to do. The light would not stop them, but having a ring of lit lanterns might have warned them away. No, she wanted to attract them and now she would have to deal with the threat, alone.

With a growl, she cried, "Shadow-cursed minions! You have no place here! Go back to the abyss wherein your dwells your mistress!"

The Charun on her right hissed in a bone-shivering whisper that grated along her nerves. "Daughter of Morpheus. My mistress will be so pleased. Long has she wanted to see you. She has your brother, you know. I can hear his howls day and night. He feeds us. Delicious, the soul of a god."

Avery spat at the hem of the Charun's cloak. "You lie. Cayden is stronger than you know. He will kill you all."

The Charun chuckled, the sound reminiscent of angry monkeys. "Now who lies, godling? He cannot kill. To do so would be to stab himself. He will die. He will die because he will fail to kill my mistress. It is his fatal weakness. Perhaps if the need is great enough? But he will never have that chance, will he? And then there is the wizard. Such long-lived souls...so delicious! They will feed us for all eternity." Its voice faded into a lisping hiss.

Fury swept over Avery. With a blood-curdling scream, she hurled herself at the mocking Charun, knife flashing. The Charun drew their blackened blades and met her advance, tightening the circle to cut off her escape, but Avery dropped and rolled past them. From the corner of her eye, she caught a flicker of motion as Achak launched himself out of the woods. Grasped in his hands was a heavy wooden axe. He raised it high over his head and throwing his weight behind the effort, launched it at the closest monster.

"Get away from her!" he roared as the axe left his hand. It spun head over haft through the air to land with an audible thud, pinning the sword-clutching hand of the nearest Charun to its chest. The axe buried itself deep into the floating body.

Achak could not sense a reaction. Possibly because it was already dead, it did not use body language as did the living. The Charun simply stared at the offending weapon. Then, a skeletal hand emerged from the opposite sleeve, and it pulled the axe out of its body. The damaged hand fell to the ground with a rattle of bones, the sword clutched in the severed appendage rolling away across the grass. None of this impeded the Charun. It rotated, spinning on the spot to face Achak, and then whipped the axe through the air to send it spinning toward him. He dived behind a tree trunk just in time, as his own axe imbedded itself in the timber by his head. The injured Charun staggered, toppling over with a screech as Avery buried her blade in its back. It twitched then stilled, but Avery did not hang around to see if it was dead. Wrenching her bone knife loose of the putrid body, she ran to Achak's side just as he pulled twin swords from his back strapped sheaths.

The two remaining Charun hesitated. What had been easy odds was now an even challenge. They silently conferred, and then the air shimmered. A blast of scorching heat forced Avery and Achak to back away, throwing up their arms to shield their face. The slash in the air opened once again, and the Charun slid through the opening, retreating into the underworld. The smell of sulphur wrinkled Avery's nose, and she buried it in her sleeve but still she coughed. Achak took a step forward intent on giving chase, but with a blinding flash and a clap of sound the rift closed. Silence descended as Achak and Avery swung around to the bodies of the slain Charun, intent on examining them, but they shimmered and vanished before their eyes.

"By the gods!" Avery swore. "All that fighting and the corpses vanish? What are they, Achak? How are they connected to Helga?" She knelt by the spot where the slain Charun had lain, running her hand over the soil, searching the ground. When they faded away, the axe had simply toppled over and lay in the grass. No sign that something had died there remained. No blood, not even a crush to the blackened shoots of grass revealed in the weak lamplight. It was as though they had never existed. "Surely I did not imagine that battle."

Achak bent over and picked up his axe and ran his finger along the flat of the chiseled blade. A smear of black ooze appeared briefly on his finger and then flashed and vanished. "They are called Charun. I think they cannot exist in this world except by enchantment. As soon as they are parted from the enchantment, they are pulled back to the underworld, which is surely where they are spawned, being Helga's creation." He pulled a cloth from his tunic and wiped down the axe head, then sheathed it back into his hip belt. "Good thing I stopped to grab this," he gestured with the axe, "in that farrier shop down the street. It came in handy."

"You look like a walking butcher." Avery eyed him and his broad shoulders as she rose, dusting off her hands. "Not that I am complaining, mind you." She let her gaze wander around the empty village. The chirping of crickets had returned. "Should we stay the night? They know we are here."

Achak's answer was to pick up the lantern and walk down the street. "They also know we are not easy prey. I do not believe she will not send another attack tonight. It isn't her way, is it? Helga likes to win, and what fails, she abandons. Isn't that what you said?" Avery followed the bobbing light back to the heart of the village but did not answer. Achak pushed open the door of the inn, grabbing a second lantern off the shelf. He fed a splint into his flame and lit the second, then headed into the kitchen, shouldering the door open. "There must be food in here somewhere."

Avery pulled open an icebox set into a wall. The block of ice that would have cooled it was reduced to a third of its normal size, not having been replenished with blocks from the height of the mountain. But what was there still cooled the interior. She pulled out cheese and sausage and a basket full of tomatoes and edible pea pods and carried them to the wooden prep block in the center of the kitchen. "Grab that crock of pickled onions on the top shelf there," she said, pointing at an earthenware jug.

Achak pulled it down. Written across the side in grease pencil were the words "pickled onions—first crop." He placed the crock on the butcher block. Avery scooped out a sizable portion of onions, slicing them in half. A quick search of the cooler produced some flatbread and a further search unveiled a crock of spicy pickled eggs, which she quickly mashed into a spread.

They placed everything on a tray and then wandered back to the common room, pausing only to pull a jug of ale from the cooled cask sitting on the bar. Then they slid into a booth. Silently, they fell into the food, ravenous after the hard day's travel and the ensuing fight.

As the munching slowed down, Achak sat back with a satisfied sigh. "I found the villagers," he said as he dragged the last of his bread through the egg mixture and topped it with sausage and tomato. He popped it into his mouth and chewed, watching Avery's reaction.

She paused, a tender pea pod halfway to her mouth. "You did?" She frowned at the food, as though it had offended her on some deep level. Her hand returned it to her plate, and she picked up her glass of chilled ale. She watched, fascinated, as a drop of condensation rolled down the side of her mug. "I take it that none were alive."

"You could say that." Achak raised his glass, somber eyes locked on her downturned face. "To the departed souls who have left us this bounty. We will avenge you."

Avery raised her glass. A smile curved her lips but her eyes remained troubled, clouded with worry. "To departed souls. *We will avenge you.*" She drank. "Now, let's plan our takeover of Faylea."

CHAPTER 2

The Cave

DEEP WITHIN A CAVE, carved into the side of the tallest mountain, set on the Cathairian side of the Highland Spine, a butterfly flitted. It soared from flower to flower, dipping its proboscis into the bell-shaped trumpet vine encircling the opening in the ceiling of the cave. From flower to flower it flew, intent on its task, but it did not see the danger of the lurking darkness, the oozing shadow that waited just below the lip of the crater, the only opening that was free of enchantments.

But it wasn't, really. Death shrouded the opening, allowing nothing to enter and nothing to leave. The thin layer of the underworld would only allow passage in one form, as a spirit, a soul. The butterfly had no soul.

When its wings inadvertently touched the black mist, it flashed into ashes in an instant. The black mist sent out tendrils, searching for a soul to steal, but this time it went away hungry. With a whine, it sank back below the rim to wait for the next unwary soul.

Cayden's eyes followed the drift of ash as it fell through the opening, and a great sadness arose within him. Another life lost because he sat within the underworld arguing with his sister. A sister who did not know mortality as he knew it, who did not appreciate the frailty of life, the flash of human existence and, yes, of animal existence. She did not understand how precious those lives were to the owners of those souls. How could she? She had never been mortal.

He ground his teeth in frustration. *How can I get through to her? Impress upon her the crime she is committing? I don't know the half of her plans, yet what little I have seen scares me.*

There, he had admitted it. He was afraid. He felt no shame in being afraid. He was apprehensive, though. He had already died once. This time, if he died, he knew it would be forever. *I don't want to die. I have too much to live for, even in this form.* He shivered, thinking of Ziona. *Ziona,* he sent to her via their telepathic connection. *My love, please stay away! I beg you!*

He did not know if the link was broken or disrupted. Ever since he had entered Helga's realm, which he knew to be a gateway to the underworld, his soul connection with Ziona was intermittent at best. He still lived, but it was as though the connections of their souls were being smothered. *Perhaps I am dead. No, that is not possible. I would not feel her at all then. I must still live. It's this place.* His fists were clenched as tight as a spring in a wound clock. He forced his fingers to relax, taking a deep breath.

Focus on the task at hand.

Ziona, do not enter. I can feel you coming. You must listen to me. Do not enter. He paced the chamber, reaching out with his soul, cursing the limitations of his all-too-human body. Yet it was all he had to work with. Their merged souls could transcend the barrier; he was sure of it. What he was not sure of, was the risk to their mortal bodies. *I have a plan. Ziona. Can you hear me?*

Frustrated at the silence, he strode over to Mordecai and peeled back his swollen right eyelid. "You look like hell."

Mordecai squinted back with his usable eye, blue and sharp as ever. "You do not look much better, my boy. Is that a leftover from Helga's rejection of your plan?" Cayden looked down at his torn sleeve, the gash deep and hastily bound with strips of cloth torn from his shirt. The blood had oozed through for a long time, eventually trickling to a stop. Crusty dried flakes fell from his arm as he bent it. With the other hand, he absently brushed off the last of the blood.

"Yeah, well as to that, she seemed to take offense to the idea that we were equals." Cayden shifted the bloodied bandage and winced as the stuck hair on his arm pulled. "Helga has lost the charm she once had. She was famous for her tea parties, back in the day." His voice trailed away, and his mind shifted focus as a long distant memory floated to the surface.

* * *

He and Avery (Alfreda as she was named then) were maybe ten years old. Artio was eleven and Helga nine. They had been sitting on cushions on the floor of one of the chateaus of the gods. A lacy tablecloth had been spread over a low table, and a child-sized china set graced the table. Helga had placed every cup and saucer just so. The cup's curved handle pointed at four o'clock. The child-sized luncheon silverware precisely lined up under the cup, equidistant from the other cutlery. A tri-layered sconce tray with a golden handle occupied the center of the table, each layer loaded with a selection of dainty finger sandwiches.

Cayden — *I was called Caerwyn then* — remembered his hunger and fidgeting on the cushion, impatient to dive into the food. The gods, including their father Morpheus and his human wife (their mother) could be seen through the tall glass garden doors, thrown open wide to tempt in a breeze. They reclined on loungers, and servants moved amongst them, topping off goblets of wine. They were deep in conversation, the rumble of voices a distant thunder.

Caerwyn rose to go ask his father if he could eat, just as Helga backed out through a side door, clutching a tall teapot decorated with unicorns. She walked slowly and carefully, afraid that she would slosh it over the sides or out the spout, which was slightly steaming.

Caerwyn threw himself back down, fanning his face. "Hot tea? Why did you bring hot tea? I am already hot!" he whined.

Helga glared at him, placing the teapot precisely on the coaster decorated with pressed flowers.

"Because this is tea time, you dolt. You have tea at tea time. If you want milk and cookies, go see Nana." Caerwyn glared at her.

Alfreda piped up, "It looks lovely, Helga, and I'm starving!"

Artio, as usual, ignored the proceedings, her nose buried in a book about the movement of the planets. She flipped a page, completely engrossed in the words and pictures.

Helga placed her hands on her hips and with a murderous glare said, "Why is it that everyone ignores me when it's tea time? Artio!" she snapped, in a tone that was a near perfect imitation of their mother. "Put the book away!"

Artio looked up, blinking owlishly. "Is the tea ready?"

Helga rolled her eyes then poured tea for everyone.

Caerwyn pouted. Artio started reading again. Alfreda with a bright smile said, "Oh! This is so much fun! I love it when we all play together. Can we do this again tomorrow? Helga?"

Helga slammed the teapot down glaring at Caerwyn and Artio who were ignoring their tea and all her careful preparations. Alfreda's chirping syrupy voice only accentuated her anger. "Play? I never play...except to win." Helga stomped over to the doorway beyond where the gods sat, stopping short in the opening, in the lee of the shadow created by the balcony overhead.

She melted against the frame, listening hard. Caerwyn's eyes followed his sister, and it was then that he heard the voices drifting through the doorway.

"No, it cannot be. The mortals do not know how to rule themselves. They are celestial children. They do not have the lifespan to acquire the wisdom needed for self-governance. They do not have the lessons of the ages as a resource. One century maximum, maybe part of a second, but not nearly enough to mature into a race capable of self-governance."

"Then let me set my children as their governors. They are of both worlds. They will have the knowledge and experience of the gods and of mortals...no wait! I know you disagree, but there are things to learn from the mortals. Their mortality grants them clarity of sight that is often lost in long debate. I know this because I have lived amongst them."

The gods' voices rose, angry rumblings that rolled out of the temple as thunder.

Aegir leaned forward around his wife, Ran, sloshing some ale over the side of his tankard. Red-nosed and red faced, Morpheus's brother burped then glared at him. Ran stretched her willowy body, encased in a seafoam gown that clung to every glorious, goddess curve. Her eyes scanned the city below, watching the labours of the people, especially the men. Those she studied intently.

"Then you are a fool" said Aegir. His eyes flickered past Morpheus to his wife, Groa, a lesser mortal supposedly with the talent of a seer, although no one had ever heard her prophesy anything. *What good is an oracle who doesn't receive viewings?* Aegir thought, a sneer creeping across his upper lip.

Morpheus's face darkened at the insult. He rose in his chair, his hands clenched tight.

Helga shrank back further into the shadows, ambling slowly to the tea table, lost in thought.

*   *   *

Cayden jerked back to the present as his arm seared with pain. He clutched it for a second till the pain passed then bent low to scoop Mordecai's arm around his shoulders. He hauled the old wizard to his feet.

"We need to keep going. There must be an exit out of this hellhole somewhere. Let's keep looking."

Cayden grabbed the lantern in his other hand, and they shuffled off together down the closest dark tunnel.

CHAPTER 3

Plans Within Plans

HELGA LIFTED HER KNIFE from the scratch drawn across the arm of the Soul Fetch, her lips stretching into a tight smile. *So, this doll is connected to your soul, dear brother! How very useful. I think it's time to send you on a little journey. Flee if you want. Run even. But in the end, you will serve my purposes. Let's see where you go if I open the door for you. But first, to plant a thought.* She straightened from the scrying pool then picked up the doll connected to Mordecai and jabbed a pin into its temple. She leaned in close, whispering into the imagined ear of the doll. "You will return to Cathair, and you will take Cayden with you. You will forget that I have instructed you to do so." She jerked the pin out of the doll then placed both items in her pocket and sauntered way down the darkened hall.

Red light flickered around her, bouncing off the shining walls and rebounding, encasing Helga in an aura of crimson. Even her eyes flashed red for a moment. She cared not who saw the aura. It had been a small price to pay for the power to have dominion over the Daimons. Now she ruled them too. The Daimons burned with a similar desire to conquer and become omnipotent, but their burning was a wild heat, that of the untamed and untameable. Being the essence of death, they did not fear it. With their will chained to hers, harnessed and brought to bear, Helga would fill the vacuum left by the abandonment of the gods. *There can only be one ruler, one god, and it will be me for all eternity. When the will of mortals fails, I will gain the strength to break free of this prison. I will crush them so thoroughly that they will beg for death. When I absorb their souls, there will be none to challenge me, ever again. I will rule all, and they will serve me for all eternity. If the gods return, I will crush them too. I will rule supreme!*

She took a side passage that spiraled into the rock, dizzying circles of stone around a center abyss with no railing to stop a sudden slip. The inky blackness moaned with a phantom wind, and she shivered despite the muggy heat of the chimney. To slip would be to fall for all eternity. She had once kicked a stone over the edge and not heard it hit bottom. For all she knew, it was still falling endlessly into the bottomless chasm. Once a Charun had tumbled over the edge, and its shrieks had bounced and echoed up the shaft long after it had fallen beyond the deepest depths they had explored.

Fifteen minutes of descent brought Helga to a ledge that sliced through the side of the staircase, a stone platform that stretched out finger-thin over a crack. She walked across the tiny bridge and through a new opening in the wall and into a low hallway that contained cells, each one barricaded by what at first appeared to be iron doors, but on closer inspection the metal moved. Within the cell was a bear of a man with a heavily bearded chin and a massive chest that flowed into heavily muscled arms. He was slumped against the moist wall, his purple and sky-blue tunic filthy and torn. A dented chainmail covered the tunic from shoulder to knees and glowed red to match the door. The man lifted his head and glared at her as she paused outside his cell.

"Clever of me to power your cell door with the strength of your loyalty to your king. You cannot escape unless you abandon your liege and swear loyalty to me. You must betray your friend and king. The stronger your loyalty, the stronger the prison and the weaker you become. Your cell is feeding on your will. And when it is all used up, you will become one of my pets. I could use a muscular Charun such as you." Ryder lurched to his feet swaying, and his hand instinctively moved to his sword hilt. Helga had seen no reason to remove their weapons, as they were bound. Ryder pinned Helga with a heavy-lidded gaze, burning with hatred. "Such a fine knight," Helga said with a tsk. "Cayden chose well. Too bad he never discovered your existence here. It will be such a shock when you are not where you are supposed to be, guarding the Well of

Souls. But you see? You are not needed there. Cayden will fetch them for me. He is already my pet, he and Mordecai both. Soul slaves that can walk freely across the Earth, not bound to the underworld as I am." She tapped a finger to her lip. "I might even let him live if he serves me well. I might have need for one who can control the souls who escape me. There are always a few. But the wizard," her face hardened as she turned away, "him I will torture for all eternity for trapping me in the underworld in the first place."

"You will fail!" Ryder spat through cracked lips. "The king is stronger than you know. For every person you oppress, another will rise in rebellion. The people are loyal to the king. Alcina learned as much the hard way."

Helga chuckled. "She did indeed, but she was never a goddess as I am." Her eyes roved his body, and her smile widened "You could live forever, you know. It would not be…unpleasant…to serve me, body and soul. Think on it before this cell drains all of your will. If you refuse, perhaps one of the others will take up my offering."

Laughing, she sauntered off down the hall, hips swaying. Every cell door was glowing.

As she exited the hallway, she was joined by Genii, drifting out of the shadows to match her long steps in response to her silent summons. The hood of his cloak was up, shadowing his face. His hands were tucked into the openings of his sleeves. He looked every bit the wizard that he was. Helga peered at him out of the corner of her eye as she walked, her black skirts drifting around her legs.

"I think it is time to give you the ability to leave the underworld," she mused aloud. "I need someone to accompany Cayden and Mordecai. I've given them the urge to return to Cathair. I want you to accompany them."

Genii bowed his head in acceptance. "How can this be done?"

"It will require a merging. You will need to take over a body and become mortal once more. Are you willing to give up immortality, my sweet?"

"It will be as you command. My soul is yours do with as you please."

She studied him out of the corner of her eye. "You will live a mortal life going forward. Your days will be numbered. But on death your soul will serve mine for all eternity, just not as you do now, as a shade. This does not bother you?"

He shook his head. "I have lived longer than I ever expected to already. Most wizards die before reaching adulthood. The only ones to live longer than me are the gods and the wizard Mordecai. If my days are as long lived, it is more than I expected and more than I deserve."

Helga nodded. "Then come. We have a potion and a body to prepare."

* * *

"See that light? I think that is an exit, a breech in the wall of the cave." Cayden struggled to drag Mordecai up the steep slope toward the faint glow peeking around a curve of wall. "Yes, it's an opening. I can see the edge now!"

"Not so fast, my boy!" Mordecai groaned as his feet slipped on the slick surface. If Cayden hadn't been half-carrying him, he would have fallen. They struggled up the last of the sloping tunnel and, rounding the corner, stopped abruptly as the light spilling into the opening was a glaring white sheet that overloaded their eyes. They blinked, and Cayden lowered Mordecai to the ground to rest. He walked over to the opening, careful to not step beyond the lip, remembering the butterfly and the inky ooze.

"The barrier is thin here. I can feel Ziona more strongly than before." Cayden closed his eyes in concentration and reached out to her.

Ziona, love, can you hear me? Joy flooded along the bond.

Cayden! You're alive! Where have you been? I have hardly been able to sense you! Are you OK? We have been frantic with worry! There is so much to tell you.

I am where I set out to be. I am in Helga's realm, the lip of the underworld. You cannot come in here. You would die instantly.

We are almost there. We are coming to rescue you. I am not alone.

No, stop! Listen! No ordinary mortal can pass, Ziona. If you enter, you will die. We will free ourselves and join you shortly. Do not enter.

Frustrated silence filled the bond. *Fine! Where can I find you?*

Mordecai and I will meet you at the Crystal Cave. Wait for us there.

Are you sure? We could wait for you by the falls.

No! You must stay away from here. We have found a way out. We will join you shortly.

Annoyance flitted along the bond, then a surge of love.

Be careful! Ziona messaged back, and then she was gone.

CHAPTER 4

The Return

CYRUS RODE TOWARD CATHAIR at the head of an invading army, not for the first time. Fullmer was the only surviving legionnaire of the original detachment that accompanied him into Faylea. He rode tight to Cyrus's side, his eyes flickering over the terrain ahead, searching for signs of trouble. Cyrus paid equal attention to the countryside, aware that an arrow shot from the cover of the trees would kill him as easily as a sword thrust.

Although he had not returned with the ultimate prize of a Spirit Shield in tow, he had accomplished much. He had eliminated one of the seekers, severely wounded the Primordial High Priestess, and, by good fortune, now found himself where he had set out to be, in control of the armies and set to rule when the usurper was eliminated. His mistress had disposed of the former queen, leaving his ascent to the throne clear of obstacles. Now all that was left was for him to secure the castle and the grounds.

So, he'd spent the last few weeks tracing the whereabouts of his men, gathering in the scattered legionnaires. They were not hard to find, really. He just had to follow the trail of raids and the tales buzzing on every tongue of every person they encountered. Soldiers were like sheep. Without someone to lead them, they broke off into smaller flocks and ran wild, but as soon as someone showed them leadership, they fell into step rather quickly. Those without the toughness to survive had already been weeded out.

Something had changed the men. They were no longer uninterested in what occurred around them. Before, they had obediently done whatever was commanded with no thought of the consequences or whether it was a good plan to follow. Cyrus suspected that some enchantment had broken with Alcina's death. Now, they stepped warily without the mindless obedience of the past. They struggled to understand the world around them. Released from the bewitchment, they discovered as much as twenty years had passed. Alcina's hold over them had begun with the passing of the Primordial princess and the fated twins, a by-product of the magical treachery bestowed on her by her mistress. As the trigger was one set of deaths, so the enchantments bound to her life lifted as her soul was recalled to the underworld. In the confusion and disorientation of awakening, the legion had sunk into anarchy, feeding off of suspicion and fear. Fights broke out and before they ended, the carnage was widespread and bloody. Former friends had turned on each other in an instant. Those who had led became the hunted in the mindless confusion. Legionnaires slew their former comrades. The desire to return home became obsessive and, alone or in bands, they had returned to their homeland. But the journey back had ground away the soft edges of their minds and polished their mental survival skills. Now, they moved as an injured wolf moves, snarling and dangerous.

A rougher, tougher legion was the result, battle-hardened and weary, with a sharpened edge and focus that made them more mercenary than legionnaire. They would not blindly follow orders any longer. Each village they passed, they plundered, taking gold, cattle and women in equal measure. The men were slain. They did not see this as attacking their own. They saw it as their due, battle pay owed for all that had been taken from them by the very people who had never volunteered or been conscripted, who had sat back on their lands and in their homes while the legionnaires fought and died with no thought to return.

Thus, the legion grew daily, swelling in size, fattened by the taking.

Cyrus did not care as long as they obeyed.

He had a kingdom to win.

He rose up in his stirrups as they crested the rise, and the final approach to Cathair was revealed. The short hills rolled steadily downward before flattening into farmers' fields and orchards, encircling the approach to the castle which stood at the furthermost tip of a peninsula. Tall, sand-coloured, and flying the flag of the king, the turrets pierced the blue sky like a javelin. Assailable from only one direction, the castle had never fallen in modern times until Cayden and the Kingsmen had discovered a secret network of tunnels that led under the castle walls. Cyrus's gaze shifted to a flyspeck village, filled with stone and mud mortar buildings tucked under tightly thatched roofs. They hugged the street, feeding to a main square with a central well for watering horses. Lower Cathair was perched at the outer boundary, as close as it was possible to be without trespassing on the castle lands. It had been a thorn in his side for too long. Cyrus had never discovered the beginning point of the tunnels that had allowed the usurper to gain entrance through the castle walls, but he suspected it had something to do with that village.

"Fullmer!" he snapped.

"Yes, my lord!"

"Take a squad of men and turn out that village. I want every man, woman, and child gathered in the village square by the time I arrive."

"Yes, my lord!" Fullmer sawed at the reins and galloped back to the captains of the legion.

Cyrus snapped his fingers, and an aide trotted up beside him, a weedy man on a dun gelding. He also doubled as an advance scout.

"What is your name?"

"Patrick, my lord"

"Well, Patrick, I have a mission for you."

"Sir?"

"I want you to take two other men down into Cathair. You are to engage no one. You are to observe fortifications, manpower, and the general lay of the land. You are to note weaknesses. Then you are to return. I expect you back before nightfall."

"Yes, my lord." He also wheeled around and took off in a different direction where the men designated as scouts rode together in a group of eight.

A third man replaced the scout, awaiting orders.

"We will remain behind this hill for the night. Spread the word to make camp."

"It will be done, my lord."

With a short blast on a horn, he announced that the legion was to halt and make camp, the sounding repeated by other horn bearers down through the ranks.

Cyrus turned and walked his mount back toward the area where his tent would be erected. As he rode up, he could see the command tent rising into place. With barely veiled impatience, he swung from the saddle, handing the reins of his grey stallion to a guard. Then, he made his way to the entrance. His attendants were still setting his furniture in place when he ducked through the entrance.

They bowed as he entered, hurrying to finish their appointed tasks.

Fullmer returned, just as Cyrus settled into a chair behind a table, pulling out maps from the chest set on the floor by his feet. Fullmer saluted. "The men are on their way to the village. They will send a runner when the villagers are gathered, as ordered."

"Good. Now bring me the witch."

"Yes, my lord."

Fullmer ducked out of the tent. Cyrus unfurled a map, weighting it down with two identical knives pulled from the sheaths on his belt. Both had been gifts from his father on reaching the two stages of manhood. The first was a traditional gift given from a warlord to his first-born son on his sixteenth birthday. It was also the time when a man was expected to bed his first woman. The second was given at the age twenty-one when it was expected that he would have made his first kill as a soldier. Cyrus had received both gifts at the same time when he was fifteen.

The map was not of the land but of the tunnels under the castle. He was sure that this was how Cayden had gained access. But none of the tunnels on the map left the castle grounds. So that had to mean that there were passages that were missing. They had to be deep indeed, for he and Alcina had never known of their existence. Absently, he traced a finger from Lower Cathair to the dungeons. It was a long way to go. If a tunnel had not originally existed, it would have taken years, decades to dig. Yet it was the only explanation. And if it existed, it was his ticket to entering the castle. Even if the passages were guarded, once he was into the warren reflected on his map, he could work around and past the current residents of the castle grounds. He smiled, grimly. *It will be a pleasure to turn his plan back on him.*

The tent flap opened, and Fullmer dragged in a bent, elderly woman, her wrinkled hands bound before her, her eyes covered in a thick black cloth that allowed no light to pass. Yet as she paused inside the tent, her head swivelled toward Cyrus and gave the sensation of pinning him to the spot. *Bloody witches!*

She smiled a wide smile, displaying a mouth devoid of teeth. The gummy expanse was creepy in a way only witches can be. Cyrus had hold of his knife before he even realized he had grasped the handle. Her smile widened at the sound.

Cursing under his breath, he motioned for Fullmer to bring her forward. He pushed her further into the tent then forced her onto her knees. Secretly, Cyrus was amazed that the old knees would bend so without snapping.

"The swamp witch, as commanded, my lord."

She threw back her head and cackled at the ceiling.

"Lord Cyrus wants Calleigh's help. Calleigh knows it! But will he be willing to pay Calleigh's price?" She laughed again and wriggled her fingers. "Calleigh is old, and the bindings chafe. Bring Calleigh's thinking chair," she commanded, "or do not. Calleigh's days are at an end either way, and she would prefer to be comfortable before she dies."

Cyrus stared at her, nonplussed. Shaking his head as though awakening from a spell, he gestured for the chair to be brought. One of the guards ducked out of the tent.

"Remove the blindfold and release her," Cyrus commanded. The guard behind Calleigh pulled the blindfold from her eyes and pulled a knife through the thick rope tying her hands. The flap of the tent opened again and a carved chair was dragged into the room and placed across from Cyrus. Calleigh pushed herself to her feet and sat in her chair, straight-backed and regal as a queen addressing her court.

"Now what do you wish to ask of Calleigh?"

"It is not what I ask. It is what I command! You will tell me everything you know of the whereabouts of the boy Cayden."

"I do not know the location of the king."

"Liar. There is not a thing that escapes your notice. You seek to aid him, do you not?"

She stared back at him, one eyelid drooping onto her cheek, giving her face a wild, crazed appearance. Cyrus found he could not hold her eye and grimaced, looking away.

"The king of Cathair is not your concern. Calleigh gives you this one piece of advice free of charge. The one you should fear is the wizard. Calleigh prophesied long ago that he would be your downfall and your doom. Alas, he is beyond Calleigh's eye at present."

"What does that mean? Is he dead?"

"No...not dead, but the netherworld cradles his soul. Calleigh senses a great evil poised to be loosed on the world. It is a plague no man can stop, for no sword can harm it." Her head swiveled in the direction of the smoking mountain and tilted it as though listening to a voice only she could hear.

"Useless dribble," Cyrus muttered. Abruptly, he stood and motioned to the guards. "Get her out of my sight." The two guards dragged Calleigh from her chair and dragged her out the tent door, Cyrus following them to the entrance.

As she stumbled away in the guard's grip, she cackled and over her shoulder he heard the words, "Be warned, Lord Cyrus, your doom is nigh!" She cackled until out of earshot.

Annoyed, Cyrus motioned to another soldier, who snapped to attention. "I want the three of you to follow her back to her hovel in the swamp." The soldier nodded and turned to leave. Cyrus grabbed his leather clad arm to halt him. "Make sure she never leaves it again," he growled.

"Yes, my lord. It shall be done."

CHAPTER 5

Human Again

MAREA TREMBLINGSPIRIT APPROACHED the floating temple in awe, her eyes drawn up to where the peak of the structure was highlighted against the pinkish blush of dawn. It wasn't really floating; a thick early morning mist coated the ground thigh-deep and billowed around the base of the structure, opaque fingers drifting up the alabaster steps in soft curls.

Ever since her investiture as High Priestess, she had been in awe of the temple. The magnitude of the responsibility weighed heavily on her to this day. She had been the first in three generations to be granted access by the temple, the first chosen in her lifetime. It was her heritage, her home.

When she'd sent the seekers out on their mission to locate the prophesied children, the Spirit Shields who by their very blood protected the souls of the dead, it had been at the temple's bidding. The prophecy had leapt off the page of the scroll she had been examining, accompanied by a blinding headache that had made the cursive swim as she'd sat in her chair in the inner sanctuary. She liked to think of it as her office, a sign of her power and authority, as much as her robes were a symbol of that authority. Only she could cross the threshold to the inner chamber. It was her sacred place. Until *she* came.

A permanent frown now creased Marea's forehead, crinkling in vexation as it always did when she thought of Avery. That the child was unique, that she had been gifted with special powers by the gods, was unquestionable. However, the ability to heal wounds did not make one a god. If she was to be believed, she had accessed beyond the inner sanctuary of the temple. She had actually plumbed its depths. Was that even possible?

Only for a god, her inner voice whispered back. Marea shoved the thought rudely aside.

Marea was about to find out the temple's will, and she would to do so alone. A niggling doubt tickled her stomach, and her jaw tightened in response. She did not want any witnesses should she fail to enter where Avery had been permitted to cross.

Marea paused at the base of the steps, her eyes taking in the magnificence of the temple floating above her. The ivory-carved figures stared down at her from their perches on the walls. Each layer of the temple was a diorama of life, the animals and people climbing from one level to the other in their trek to ascend to the gods. Great serpents twisted around columns and lizards and dragons crawled up the corners, twisting around the corners and peaking onto the balcony of the next level. Birds morphed into their spiritual twins, as they hopped from one twisting alabaster vine to another, the carvings so lifelike Marea thought she saw an eye blink.

It was symbolic of the circle of life. Strive to attain the spiritual perfection of the gods, and they would ensure the passage of one's soul to the next life, qualified to live again in a new body. To fail was to remain imprisoned forever in the depths of the underworld. These were basic beliefs, whether Primordial or Cathairian. How to attain the perfection of the gods was the great divide between the peoples of the world, a belief that even split the Primordial people.

Marea peered around at the retreating gloom once again to be sure she was alone. Then with a deep breath, she mounted the steps. The mist swirled and parted as she walked up the steps and onto the first landing.

Movement out of the corner of her eye made her jump, but as she peered at the corner of the temple where she thought she had seen it, all was quiet and still. She shook her head and lifted her chin slightly in resolve. Marea walked over to the door and placed the palm of her hand on a glowing flat disk on the front of the door. The disc brightened and warmed, the bones of her fingers clearly defined as her skin became transparent. With a click, the door swung open. Marea exhaled heavily, not realizing that she had been holding her breath. She stepped across the threshold, the orbs on the walls casting a flickering light in the room as they flared to life. The door swung closed behind her, the lock clicking in to place.

This much was normal. She was still allowed to enter. *Maybe she isn't the mother goddess after all!* With a small smile, Marea walked over to the desk against the far wall by a small fireplace and examined its surface. Nothing had been disturbed on the polished walnut desk. The piles of reference books were still stacked on the table and scrolls were tucked into cubby holes along the side. Quill and paper sat as she had left them. She looked around the rest of the room and could find nothing out of place. *What had Avery done for all those hours in here?*

With a sigh, Marea sank into her chair, staring around blankly at her incomplete work. She had no enthusiasm for it. She pulled out the scroll that had started the journey to find the prophesied children and unfurled it, thinking to look for further clues or insight.

It was blank. Smooth and clean, there was not a hint that any quill had ever traced its length forming cursive into words.

She flipped it over. The back was the same.

Yet the seal remained. Even as she looked at it, it reformed.

Shocked, she pulled out the next scroll and the next. Some contained full passages, yet where the subject matter turned to the prophesied children, blank spaces now remained. Marea counted fifteen scrolls that now had blank segments that ranged from a couple of lines to full pages.

She relaxed her grip, and the scrolls sprung back to their normal tightly furled curl.

Frowning, she stared at the offending scrolls. Her eyes wandered the perimeter of the temple room. Plain, blank walls stared back at her, the contrast sharp to the busily carved exterior. The walls mocked her.

Suddenly, the cold fireplace sprang to life, and the shadow of a woman stepped from its confines. She was dressed in a floor-length white gown with a pure white cloak, the hood pulled up to hide her face.

Marea gasped and stumbled from her chair to kneel before the projection. "Mother! I thought you had abandoned me! Where have you been? The child! We had the child! I knew she could not be a real goddess. But she has escaped, and I cannot find her now!" she babbled. "The scrolls! The prophecies are gone! I was just reading them, but…someone has erased the prophecies! It had to be the girl." Her voice trailed away as the hood turned her direction, raised an arm and halted her speech.

"Silence, woman," whispered the voice. "You know not of what you speak. All is as it should be. Those prophesies have been fulfilled so they are no longer part of the enchantment placed on the scrolls. They will be filled with new prophesies when the need arises. Until then, I have a task for you."

"Yes, Mother. What do you command? I live to serve!"

"Listen closely. You are to go to the forests of the sacred mountain."

* * *

Helga let the illusion drop as she faded from the fireplace. The High Priestess was so biddable. Ambition combined with fear was a powerful mind trap, and she reeked of both. The bigger the ego, the easier it was to manipulate humans. Marea was a useful tool to throw up against Alfreda. The more obstacles she could put in her sister's way the better.

Genii stood silently behind Helga, waiting patiently.

Helga took his arm and pulled him beyond the fireplace and over to a paneled wall in her chambers. She touched a rosebud carved into the wood, and the bud sank into the paneling and disappeared. A click sounded, and then the wall swung sideways revealing a secret room. Frigid air blasted them as Helga stepped through, Genii following without question. Icicles hung from the ceiling where water had dripped through the rock and frozen. The floor was covered in slick icy puddles. The wall whispered closed behind them as they walked down the hallway. Helga picked up a vial of orange fluid as she passed the narrow table against the right wall then strode to the glowing room beyond.

Genii came to an abrupt halt as he crossed the threshold into the room. There, lying on a stone slab was a body. *His body.* A thrill chased along his arms and down his back, not related to the cold. He shivered and licked his lips, the first physical reaction he had displayed in her presence in a long time. Helga studied him.

"This pleases you, yes?"

Genii nodded, speechless.

"I preserved your body in case we had need of it in the future. This," she held up the vial, "is a binding elixir. A handy potion for times such as this. It is the last of the potion, at least until I locate Calleigh and have her make more. Unfortunately, I cannot do that until I am able to leave this wretched dungeon again." She frowned at him. A flash of doubt crossed her sharp features, then it was gone. "I trust you as I trust no one else on this sorry rock." Her hand curved around his cheek, her thumb under his chin. She tilted his face to look into his eyes. "I trust you to not betray me, but hear me now. If you do betray me, you will suffer a thousand deaths, a thousand rendings of your soul. It will be torture beyond comprehension. Know this for truth, Genii."

Genii met her gaze with a blank, steady stare. "I have served you faithfully for centuries. You doubt me now?"

She searched his eyes then smiled and pulled his mouth down to hers. When the kiss ended, she turned back to the body encased in ice.

"The transition from shade to mortal will be a painful one. Come sit beside your body."

Genii did as instructed, sinking onto the stone bench beside the...his...body. Of all the shocks he had endured while bonded to Helga, this was the worst. With the physical reminder of his once despised human existence came fear, fear of a death not quite realized and fear of a loss beyond endurance. His mind reeled, and he was afraid beyond belief. His hands began to tremble in his lap, and he found that he could not look at the...his...body. He forced his eyes to look at it, noting partially healed wounds frozen in time. Nothing life-threatening, yet wounds they were.

"Drink this," commanded Helga, proffering the vial of potion.

Genii tore his eyes off the corpse and took the uncorked vial, tossing it back like hard liquor. It burned the same, although the sensation was vague and peripheral, being a shade.

His eyesight began to shimmer, and he held up his hands before his face. The vial slipped from suddenly nerveless fingers, which also began to shimmer and fade.

Helga held up her hands and began to chant a spell that Genii did not know, even as his body faded completely into mist. His consciousness floated on the air. He was spirit, nothing more a soul drifting in eddies of a cold breeze.

Suddenly, the air scooped up his essence and sank into the body pulling him with it, merging his soul with the frozen, ice-cold corpse. He shuddered, or would have shuddered if he had the ability to do so, his mind screaming at the sudden imprisonment within the numb brain.

Helga clapped her hands, and small fires began to burn: one, two, three, four of them dancing in chiseled alcoves. The flames melted the ice and lit wicks fed by pockets of gas. The walls, slick and shiny, reflected the glow, and slowly the chamber warmed. She walked over to the body and bent over the still form, placing her hands on either side of him. Her face lowered, and she placed her lips on his frozen ones and kissed him, breathing into his mouth. Slowly his chest rose then fell three times. Helga paused and rubbed his arms, massaging his skin. Then she repeated the kiss.

As his temperature rose, his body warmed and thawed. Suddenly, Helga sat back and thumped at his chest once, twice, three times then bent her head to listen. A slow heartbeat sounded in the once still chest. She continued her ministrations until with a sudden cough Genii stirred and began breathing on his own. Helga took off her cloak and spread it over him, trapping in the beginning of heat within his body.

A finger twitched, and his eyelid fluttered. Slowly his eyes opened, and Genii stared at the ceiling, unblinking.

"Welcome back, my love."

Genii's head fell sideways toward the direction of the voice. A flood of memories, as intense as an avalanche overwhelmed his mind. The key had been turned, opening a compartment of memory long locked away. He squinted, trying to clear his vision. At the sight of Helga, he screamed a scream of pure terror then promptly fainted.

CHAPTER 6

The Meeting Place

ZIONA, ORDAINED SEEKER of the Primordial people, bound by the sacred temple of Faylea and commissioned by the High Priestess herself to search for the prophesied Spirit Shields, woke with a start. She twisted in her blankets and sat up, peering around at the canopy of trees just visible past the curve of the rock face where they had taken shelter for the night.

She had been dreaming of Cayden and had felt the touch of his mind against hers. She could still sense where he was, in the underworld, but she could not speak to him through the bond. The loss of that presence had made her weepy of late. She hadn't realized how dependent she had become on the connection, how she drew comfort from his presence. To this day, she marveled at it, to be not just physically but soulfully connected to a godling. Her hand drifted to her belly where the faintest stirrings of new life tickled. She shivered, amazed and at the same time anxious, the gravity of the situation robbing her of sleep on most nights. Yet, her primary calling was as a seeker. She rubbed her hands over her arms to warm them, and then stood.

The dream had been real. She was so sure she could have stepped from one dream to the other and met him there. But he had warned her, quite loudly to not come to him.

The dream was fading, but it left a residual echo in her mind, an urge so strong it amounted to a command to go to the meadow that emptied into the Shakra cave.

She stepped over the two sleeping men and walked into the woods. There, she found the Pegasuses, Brimstone and Sandstorm, lying with heads tucked under their large drooping wings, dozing in the shelter of the trees. Both heads rose in unison as they spotted her movements. They whickered softly to her as she approached. Moonbeam drifted down through the trees toward them at the sound. Ziona reached into her pocket and pulled out three small orange apples, feeding one to each of them.

Patting Brimstone on the neck, she whispered "Is it time to go find them, Brimstone? I want to go to the Thunder Falls to find Cayden, but I am commanded to meet him at the Shakra Caves. What do you think, boy?"

Brimstone tossed his great silky mane then tensed his wings, the pose suggestive of launching into flight. He danced sideways and snorted. Ziona laughed as he eyed her impatiently. "Yes, we will go soon. He needs our help."

Moonbeam nudged her under her arm, and Ziona turned to the mare to stroke her velvety nose. Moonbeam's nostrils flared, and she snuffled the front of Ziona's tunic, rubbing her nose over her belly. Moonbeam's right eye stared at her, maternal knowing in her gaze.

Ziona stroked Moonbeam's silky pointed ears. "You are a smart one, aren't you?" Moonbeam tossed her head as if to agree. Ziona laughed once again. "We can't worry about that right now. That is for another day. But, yes, I will take care." Moonbeam's ears flattened in disapproval. "I can't tell Cayden, Moonbeam. He is soul fetched. I do not know how much Helga can read of his thoughts or desires. What if she were to learn of the baby? What might she do to him when he is suffering so already? Could she break him? What if I were to fall into her hands?" Brimstone crowded in at this point and shook his head, baring his teeth and then he whinnied shrilly. "Oh, I know you would protect him and Avery too, but the risk is too great. This needs to remain our secret, OK?" Brimstone eyed Ziona's resolve then snorted and pawed the ground before bowing his head in acceptance. Moonbeam copied the form. Ziona's eyes glistened with unshed tears. "Thank you, my friends."

Her seeker instincts tugged at her to follow Cayden to the falls, but his command rang in her ears, demanding that she go to the caves. So, to the caves she would go. She trusted the bond, however weak.

Swiping away the threatening tears with the back of her sleeve, she returned to the camp and shook Denzik and her father, Gaius, awake. Both men's eyes opened and flashed to their sword hilts, before relaxing.

"A change in plans. We are going to the Shakra Caves. Cayden will meet us there." They nodded and rolled out of their blankets and began packing up their bedrolls.

Denzik had ceased to be surprised at her sudden announcements, once she had told him about the bond and how it worked and more importantly why. Now he simply obeyed and went where she commanded.

Ziona frowned as she parceled out dried berries and a chewy jerky, worried about the swiftly diminishing state of their staples. At least grass and water were plentiful for the horses and for the Pegasuses. They would need to forage for food soon or replenish supplies at a local village, but danger lurked in the villages scattered throughout the area. They were likely Flesh Clan and would be less than welcoming of them. So far, they had avoided the settlements, choosing to err on the side of caution, rather than engage a potential enemy. Their first priority was to reach Cayden.

Ziona rewrapped the remaining food and tucked it in her saddlebags. Then, she carried it over to her picketed horse and saddled her. As she tugged the girth tight, Gaius spoke.

"When we get to the caves, what are we going to do there? Why does Cayden want to go to the caves?"

"I don't know. He spoke to me in my dreams."

"There must be something there he wants to get. We should arrive first to make sure there are no enemies lying in wait," said Denzik. "It would not do for him to escape the underworld to be captured by forces outside of it."

"My thoughts exactly. We must cover a lot of ground today." Gaius swung into his saddle, eager to be off.

Ziona spoke to the Pegasuses. "Scout for us from above. Do not reveal yourselves. We ride for the sacred caves." Brimstone tossed his head and launched into the sky, followed by Moonbeam and Sandstorm.

They rode hard, slowing only fractionally for a drizzling rain that slicked the rocks and made the passages treacherous. The deeper they travelled into the sacred forests, the darker the forests became. Shadows slid behind trees, stirring the underbrush and rustling leaves overhead. They were being followed by the spirits of the forest, but they did not attack. Ziona took comfort from their presence and began talking to them aloud. At first the men stared at her, thinking she was going daft, but she rebuked them with a severe look. After that, they kept their eyes forward and watched the shadows from the corner of their eyes, backs stiff and twitching when twigs snapped.

"Tree spirit, you know all who pass through the sacred forests. Aid us in our quest. We come to save the Spirit Shield, to aid him in his time of trial. Forest spirit, it is for you that he went into the underworld to confront his sister. But he is a mere mortal now and needs our help. Aid us as we aid him. Give us your protection now."

The rustlings followed them the entire way, ceasing at the edge of the clearing where the trail ended.

Denzik slid from his horse and dropped the reins, drawing his sword as he crept toward the edge of the clearing. His head swiveled as he searched the treetops for scouts and watched for anything that moved. Eventually, he dropped to his hands and knees and crawled over the last section to the very edge of the clearing. Parting the bushes, a grassy bowl was revealed with tall angular monoliths set in a circle. Buttercups dotted the meadow, a yellow flash waving in the tall grasses interspersed with an occasional pink-petal daisy. There was no other sign of life and no Cayden.

Denzik crawled back from the edge and walked back to Ziona.

"He isn't here."

"He isn't here, yet," she corrected him.

"He isn't here, yet," he acknowledged.

"Then we will make camp deep in the woods and wait. He will come. The forest spirits will protect us. And they will alert us to what comes, friend or foe."

Denzik exchanged glances with Gaius, who shrugged.

Ziona turned her mare off the path. "Come, you can forage for supplies while we wait."

Obediently, they followed her into the woods with the guardians of the forest close behind.

CHAPTER 7

Bowls

ARTIO SNIFFED THE AIR. Rank fear oozed from the men kneeling at her feet, foreheads pressed to the black soil of the farmer's field. The Primordial villagers quivered, their outstretched arms shaking as they pledged their vows to serve her. Artio stepped over the first row and the second, before pausing beside a man with jet black hair and a muscular build. He was larger than the rest by a lot. He reeked of magic, rather than fear.

"You! Rise to your feet," she rumbled. The man's head lifted to meet her gaze. He did not shake nor did he flinch at being centered out of the crowd. Warily, he rose onto sandaled feet and stood as a soldier would stand with feet shoulder-width apart and hands clasped behind his back.

"You will be my manservant. You will relay my commands and follow me."

She marched away from the quivering mass of people with a long stride and entered a tall narrow building that she had taken over as her own. The tall paned windows were broken out, shutters askew, some clinging to the window frame from one twisted hinge. She'd tossed the previous owner out the window when he had refused to give up his house. The force of the impact had broken his neck and silenced his objections permanently.

Inside the shadowed interior, the heat of the day was muted, but sweat ran down the backs of the assembled priests, only due in part to the humidity of the still air. They turned as one when Artio entered and bowed low, hands on knees as she passed. Her new manservant walked behind her, drinking in the obedience of the priests.

Artio went to the back of the entrance hall where three large bowls stood on waist high plinths. Each glowed with an inner golden light that spilled over the sides, casting a circle on the weathered wooden floor. Artio stopped in front of the first magic bowl, staring down into its contents. The glass bowl was half full of a shimmering liquid that shot tiny sparkles of light into the air. Just below the surface, a skeletal hand rested. The second bowl was pewter and empty except for the etching of runes on the face of raised squares that covered every spare inch of space, spiraling to the flat base that mimicked a vortex sucking the ancient black ink into oblivion. The third clay bowl was fired with a chipped blue glaze. A significant crack ran from rim to base. It was filthy, as though it has been dragged for miles then placed on the pillar. A storm, complete with billowing clouds, flashes of lightning, and sheets of grey rain, continuously circled around the sides of the bowl. Every time it crossed the crack, splashes of rain dripped onto the floor.

Artio walked slowly past each bowl, pausing for second to gaze into them. At the end of her tour, she swung back to the man with the features reminiscent of her beloved Genii. "Come!" she commanded. He approached her, feeling the gaze of every High Priest in the room as a hot poker in his back. "You will guard the bowls. They are sacred and of the gods. You will guard them with your life. No one is to touch them. No one is to approach them."

He bowed as he had seen the priests bow, hands to knees, back straight. He would not lower himself further. "As you command, mistress."

"What is your name?"

"Dagan, my lady."

Artio stiffened at the name. *The translated name means "son of magic," or "born of magic."* Artio shook her mane of hair. *How is it that just when I need someone with magic, he is here? I do not like coincidences. I do not believe in them.*

"Do you have magic?" she rumbled.

"I believe so, my lady, but I am untrained."

Artio spun on the milling priests, some of whom had crept closer in an attempt to eavesdrop on the conversation. "Leave me, now!"

she commanded with a growl, her voice booming around the room. They scrambled, pushing and shoving each other to reach the door. When the last one had disappeared, Artio swung back to Dagan.

"Where are you from? How did you come to be here?"

"I...do not remember."

Artio's eyes narrowed at the pause. "What do you remember?" Undisguised menace filled the silence. Her hand fell to the bone-handled knife, fingering it as she tilted her head.

His eyes rose to meet hers. Not a stitch of fear showed in their dark clear depths, twin stones of polished tigers eye. Tawny flecks decorated the shiny brown disks.

"I woke a few days ago in the woods over there." He waved in the direction of Cathair. "I have no memory of how I got there. I woke with a satchel full of supplies and in the clothes you now see." He gestured at the tall boots, slim pants tucked into their tops, and a black tunic embroidered with symbols. Around his neck hung a leather cord. A stone hung from it, visible in the V of his shirt.

Artio walked around him, examining him. His clothing *was* different from that of the Primordial people around them. It could be from her time...*from their time. Genii had worn clothing similar to it.* "How is it you know your name?"

Dagan shook his head, curly hair bouncing. "I do not know. It is the one piece of information I have retained. But I can read the words on my tunic and on that bowl" He pointed to the simple clay bowl on its plinth.

"You are meant to serve me," Artio said, reaching a conclusion. "Study this bowl, but do not touch it. I need to know what it says. I can read parts of it but not all. It is vital that we decode it and the other two bowls. That is your task."

"Aye, mistress. It will be done." He bowed once again and walked over to the bowls.

Artio folded her arms and studied the man. The resemblance was uncanny. Perhaps the gods had been kind and returned a part of her life that was stolen. Perhaps.

But she could not be distracted by memories of the past. She had a future to secure. Having stolen a tentative control over Helga's Daimon, she needed to shore up her efforts. The key was with the bowls, she was sure of it. And if this version of Genii had magic, she was one step closer to her ultimate revenge.

Watch your back, sister. You may think you are safe from attack and in control of events, tucked away in the underworld, but there are worse things than dying. I should know, I have already lived that particular hell.

Artio left Dagan to his musings and walked over to the reading chair she had selected because of its size, placed beside a sagging shelf piled high with books that she had acquired during their recent raids. She'd pieced together the significance of the bowls from the text in one very old tome she had taken from a Flesh Clan temple. After that, it had been a simple matter to gather the three bowls from the three temples where they had sat as sacrificial vessels to the various gods. Artio sensed the magic of the bowls. The foolish priests had no idea what they were truly for. However, the sacrificial blood had preserved the ancient bowls. Artio was sure they had been left behind by the gods, and she intended to fully decode their use.

She flipped open the book where she had found the clues. The book was entitled *A Comparative History of the Ancients: Gods at War.* She dismissed Dagan from her mind. *The key to the knowledge of the bowls is in this book. I am sure of it. Both the knowledge of how to use them and the proper order. I will have this knowledge. If I cannot use the bowls myself, I must find the one who can. That one will serve me.* Artio's lips curled back into a grim smile and began to read.

CHAPTER 8

Legendary

AVERY AND ACHAK WATERED THEIR HORSES at the trough out front of the inn, the crisp morning air leaving floating wisps of frosty exhale on the slight breeze. The sound of horse hooves clicking on stone carried on the air long before the rider became visible. Elder Hania appeared at the end of the street, wearily slumped in his saddle. He kept his horse to a slow walk as he approached them.

"Father!" Alarmed, Achak ran over and grabbed the bridle as Elder Hania slid from the saddle. Avery caught him mid-fall and helped him over to the boardwalk to sit.

"You look awful" she said "Did you not stop to rest at all?"

"I couldn't," he said, wincing as he adjusted his sore backside on the solid planking. "I picked up a hunter despite my care to stay hidden. I fear to say he will follow me here. I dared not rest for he would have surely have caught me."

Achak straightened at his father's words, his back rigid, and scanned the edge of the woods for movement, checking anything that stirred, leaf or limb. "Stay here, Father. I am going to check your back trail." Achak slipped off between the buildings, taking a shortcut back to the forest.

"Come. I will help you inside." Avery placed his bony arm around her shoulder. Together they made their way into the inn where she lowered him onto a cushioned chair in the sitting area.

She fetched a pitcher of cold tea and poured a cup and brought it back to the elder.

"Drink," she offered, pressing a glass into his hands, and watched while he took a deep drink of tea. When he lowered the cup, she continued "Now, tell me what you saw."

He shook his grizzled grey head. "Every village was empty, as though someone had gone through and scooped up the villagers and carried them away. In some, the livestock was gone too. In others, just the people were missing. I rung the necks of a few chickens and brought them back to keep us fed for the next few days. They were wandering around on the loose with no one to care for them. So I packed them in my saddlebags. But the people...they are all gone. The Flesh Clans are no more, at least not as they once were."

The door opened, and Achak returned, shaking his head at Avery's inquiring gaze. "All is clear for now."

Avery's gaze swung back to Elder Hania. "What do you mean, they are no more? Why do you say that?"

"I fear some are in the grips of a great evil, a life-threatening terror." His gaze swung in the direction of the mountain they knew contained at least one godling of old. "The godling of the mountain stirs. We would be foolish to not suspect that Helga is responsible, at least in part. As for the other half of the people, I believe they have been pressed into an army of sorts. In those villages, every edible thing had been removed. Someone is gathering the people—men, women and children—for some purpose." He shook his head again, disbelieving what his eyes had shown him. "Children have little strength for battle, but they could be useful in other ways. I am afraid of what their ultimate purpose may be in such an army."

Avery's hands curled into fists, her nails digging into the fleshy part of her palms. Anger flared, and she abruptly straightened and marched over to the now cold fireplace. The log had burned down overnight until only ashes remained.

She stared into the blackness, thinking. If the people were taken, then they were being imprisoned and used against their will. They were not the enemy. They were her people. *But how can I help them? We are but three people and not the strongest or the fiercest...but we are clever! If Helga has snatched one set, then it stands to reason that Artio controls the other half. The Flesh Clans are being squashed between two goliaths with little recourse. Time to think outside of the box. Where can I find an army just as powerful as anything Artio or Helga can conjure that will not harm the world in the process? Where?*

And then it dawned on her. She knew where there to find an army ready and waiting that no one even knew existed. A silly grin spread over her face, and her hands relaxed.

"I know what to do," she said aloud as she pushed away from the fireplace, pinning Achak with her gaze. An answering grin spread across his face. Achak picked her up and spun her around.

"The forest?" he said. Avery laughed clutching his shoulders, nodding.

Elder Hania harrumphed and cleared his throat. "Care to enlighten me?"

Achak put Avery down. She adjusted her cloak before answering.

"The Primordial forests are teeming with life. You know this to be true, right?" Elder Hania nodded. "Well, we need to enlist the help of the legendary creatures that live there. They have just as much of a stake in this war as does humanity. And they live in the spirit realm, so they can move between realities, something a mortal cannot do." The legendries were the spirits of the animal kingdom, who on death passed over and transformed into their immortal kin. Only the wild animals could transform on death. The domesticated ones, for reasons not know by anyone living, did not carry on into spirit form. Or maybe they were just a different breed of animal. While their souls did not move from host to river to host as humans did, they lived for all eternity in their legendary state unless they were killed in the spirit world. If they died in spirit form, they died and faded from existence forever.

Elder Hania slowly nodded his head, his finger tapping his lips as he considered the idea. "They have not been inclined to take sides in the past. They keep themselves separated from the world of mortals. They refuse our call."

"They will not refuse mine. I have already spoken to them."

"Then it is worth a try. What would you have them do?"

Avery began to pace as she thought through the plan. She traced a worn path on the inn floor, pondering her next move. "I believe their best use would be as spirit spies in the beginning. They can bring us intelligence and help us see what is currently hidden. Seeing as they can move behind the veil, they might be useful for a darker purpose too, but we will see about that when the time comes. For now, I would be grateful to know what Helga is up to. She is always one step ahead, it seems. It's almost like she can see our movements."

"Some will agree. Some will not," said Elder Hania. "But I think that for the most part they will agree."

"I know my guardian will be eager to join the fighting," said Achak. "He likes nothing better than a good tussle. I think we should lay out our needs and let them decide how they want to help. Do you have one of the legendary immortals in mind to assist in organizing them?"

"I certainly do. And she mostly appears as a child. Aossi will be thrilled to hunt down the missing children."

"Aossi? You have seen Aossi? She hasn't been seen for thousands of years," said Elder Hania, amazement in his voice.

"Until now." Avery smiled. "She bade me to call on her if I needed her aid. We are in need, desperate need."

Elder Hania pushed himself to his feet and smiled. "Then I see no reason to waste time sitting here. Let's travel while we have daylight to guide us. I must admit, I am keen to meet the legendries who not only reside but guard the Sacred Forest. It would be such an honour."

"You do not need to rest?"

"I slept in the saddle. Besides, that tracker will be catching up to us soon. It would be best to not be here to see what it brings with it. It won't be anything pleasant." To punctuate his point, he headed for the door."

Achak held it open for his father then held out his hand to Avery. "Time waits for no man or woman it seems. We can plan from the saddle."

Avery crossed in front of him. As she passed, she tweaked the week-old beard beginning to stretch from his chin. "Your wisdom astounds me."

Chuckling, Achak followed her through the door, and it swung back with a click. From the shadows of the narrow alley between the buildings, a pair of eyes followed their path to their horses and watched as they rode out of town.

With a wheeze and a sneeze, the eyes melted back into the woods and followed their retreat from the shadows.

CHAPTER 9

Abaeterno

THE FEELING OF BEING FOLLOWED was an itch that could not be scratched. Achak glanced surreptitiously over his shoulder, his eyes scanning the brush along the trailside. The birds had long since stopped singing. The deeper they travelled under the heavy canopy, the more eerie the passage became. They were being followed. He had felt a presence since the village. Whether it was the same person or thing who had tracked Elder Hania to the village, he did not know. Yet he knew that the creature was there, pacing them. It watched from the shadows and, therefore, had to push through undergrowth while their path was clear. Neither a twig nor a branch stirred in the woods, yet he could nearly point to where it was. That it moved neither stone nor weed worried him more than the fact that the usually loud forest had gone silent.

Achak had encountered this creature once before. On his eleventh birthday, when he formed the bond with his spirit guide, the presence had been there, creeping along at the edge of the firelight, watching from the shadows. Achak did not think it was his phoenix, but a darker spirit, somehow connected to the phoenix but separate from him.

It was not always present. Only in times of great peril or great need did he sense the presence. He still did not know if its intent was malignant or peaceful.

Avery reached back to scratch at a spot between her shoulder blades, and her head twisted toward the bushes, frowning at the same area of nothing.

Achak heeled his mount to ride up beside her. Elder Hania brought his horse up on her other side to listen in. "You feel it too?" said Achak

"Yes, I have felt its presence since leaving the village. I'm surprised that you sense it too."

"Do you know what it is?" said Achak.

Avery reached out with her gift. The creature was very ancient, attracted to the swirl of time that surrounded the crest of catastrophic events. *They were certainly living in those times.* It lived in the breach created by the swell of souls released around such events, a consequence of battle. It was immortal, yet bound to time and to the flow of the world. There was only one creature or set of creatures that could do that.

"It is of the same species as Aossi. They are called the Abaeterno. They are beings that live in the space between the world of the living and the world of the dead. They maintain the veil between life and death. It is a veil that is thinning dramatically. Perhaps it has torn." Avery's eyes wandered to the smoking mountain that was visible even in the thickest forest. When the mountain could not be seen, she still knew where to look for the reddish light from its numerous volcanoes backlit the leafy canopy overhead. "I think I know what you are up to, Helga," she muttered aloud.

Achak shivered as the words she uttered drifted over to him. "This is really a war of the gods, isn't it?" he said flatly. His finger punched the sky in the direction of the mountain. "It's not about Primordial versus Cathairian. It never was."

"No, it never was," Avery echoed, her voice soft but resonating, her tone other-worldly. She twisted in her saddle to face Achak. "That is why it is imperative that we unite the peoples, as my sister is dividing them, creating chaos where ever she can to hide her true plans. She fully intends to take over everything, and what better way than by enslaving the souls of the world before they are even reborn? And who is there to stand in her way? There is myself and Cayden and those who would aid us. The list is short and the peril extreme. We do not have enough strength in human form to succeed. But there are those who can help us. This is why we are here."

Avery pushed her mare between a large oak tree and a boulder covered with moss, the path just large enough for a horse and rider to access single file. The boulder stretched on and on, undulating with green and yellow mosses clinging to the cracks and crevices. Achak studied the rock. It was an unnatural formation and too smooth to be the result of weathering, and then it dawned on him. It was a statue in the form of a human, toppled and laying on its side. His eyes ran down the length of curving grey stone to where it ended and there, covered with clinging vines, was a squat building. The wooden door had rotted away long ago. Only the hinges remained in the worm-eaten frame. The only thing that gave away that it was a stone structure under all the greenery was the obsidian spike that rose from the very center, its shining black tip glowing with a flickering red flame that kept the jungle from swallowing it whole.

Elder Hania stared around, puzzled. "What is this place? I have read and studied every sanctuary recorded in the Primordial scrolls. This temple is not recorded there. I have travelled this way before too, but no one has ever mentioned this temple."

Avery swung down from her saddle, patting her mare on the nose before turning back to the elder. "It is the Lost Temple of the Abaeterno, otherwise known as the Spirit Shield Temple. It is a gateway of sorts. It sits over the heart of the veil, the place where the two worlds are in closest alignment. See the spike? That flame should not be visible. The veil is indeed pierced."

Avery tied her mount to a nearby tree, and the others followed suit. She slowly walked around the temple, examining its structure. It was as she remembered it from when she was a child, a mini-representation of the Sanctuary located in Faylea. A second statue stood to the right of the doorway, but this one had broken about ten feet up. Its upper structure had fallen to the right. She knew who the statues represented. She placed her hand on one resembling herself.

"The statue on the left is male. This one, here on the right, is female. They are stone representations of the godlings Caerwyn and Alfreda." Avery stared at her statue, remembering when it had been raised and the ceremony that had gone with it. The festival had gone on for a month. Both Spirit and Flesh Clans had rejoiced that day. It had been a dedication to dwarf all others, the sanctifying of the Spirit Shield Temple, originally protected by the guardians of the veil. Until the Spirit Shields vanished. Avery did not know what had happened in the intervening years after that dreadful day.

Avery placed a hand on the male statue in front of Achak. "The Spirit Shield guardians have been gone too long. It is time to correct this imbalance."

She turned back to the door. With a deep breath, she plunged into the dark interior of the temple...and vanished.

Achak yelped and ran into the interior after her, but there was nothing inside. Pitted and worm-holed chairs and tables filled the chamber, much like a library, held up by the choking vines that lent structure to the decomposed wood. Glass and clay vessels sat on solid stone shelves untouched by time. The walls were carved with faces, representations of the guardians. Some appeared to be human and some did not. Achak's gaze scanned all the faces then froze on one that was familiar. His phoenix stared back at him, and he could have sworn it winked at him.

"Avery!" he yelled, frantic eyes searching everywhere for her. "Where are you? Avery!"

Elder Hania ran in behind him and clapped his hand on his son's shoulder. "Quiet, Achak! She has been summoned by the Abaeterno, that much is clear. Do not interfere. They will not harm her." He turned on the spot, examining the temple. "So much has been lost. This temple, had we preserved it, would have kept peace between the tribes and the Cathairians." He shook his head, saddened by the decay around him. "We have lost our way. If we lose it all, it will be of our own doing. Helga would not have been able to drive the wedge between our peoples if we had remained faithful to the gods." He picked his way toward a crumbling chair and, seeing the sad condition of the aged wood, thought better of sitting in it. Instead, he walked to the back of the circular room.

* * *

Avery floated in a dark void, weightless and sightless. She could not see anything around her, yet she felt as though there was an end to the darkness. There. A pinprick of light formed and slowly expanded, giving the sensation of an onrushing object. She could not flee the light, for it was aimed directly at her and simply moved as she did. Faster and faster the pinpoint spun, growing in her eyes until it was everything she could see. She flinched as it passed over her, closing her eyes, then slowly opening them to find herself in a pristine alpine meadow, filled with daisies and pink wintergreen and purple larkspur. Butterflies wandered from flower to flower and bees buzzed lazily. A fresh breeze wandered through the valley, sweet smelling, gently stirring the collar of her shirt. She had forgotten what a breeze not tainted with sulphur smelled like. She inhaled deeply and relaxed. She would be happy to stay here forever, for it was the most incredible place she had ever seen. She sank down into the soft grass and laid back, staring up at the azure blue above. Her eyes drifted sleepily.

"Rest is a wonderful thing. I am sorry I cannot let you nap at present, but someday, you can come back. I will string a hammock for you, under the trees. You will have that well-deserved rest."

Avery sat up abruptly to find a pretty child with long bouncing red curls and a dress made of tiers of rainbow-striped cloth, sitting cross-legged on the ground across from her, smiling impishly. Beside her sat a boy of maybe ten, dressed in leopard-print shorts with long leather straps that crossed at the back over a loose fitting white shirt, embroidered around the V-neck with green and burgundy vines. He scowled at her, his lower lip pouting.

"Aossi!" Avery gasped. "It is so good to see you!" She hugged the girl, and then her head swung to the boy. In more formal tones, she said, "Actaeon. It is good to see you again."

"You bring war and grief once again, Alfreda. I am not happy to see you." Actaeon plucked at a flower, examining its ethereal beauty. "You always bring pain."

"I do not. It is not my fault that Helga is jealous of the world. It is not my fault that she is power hungry. It is not my fault that she is angry with the gods. And it certainly is not my fault that we were all slain by her," Avery finished with a whisper. Here, in this place, she could feel the ripping of her soul as her body had died. Here, in this place, where the Spirit Shield was maintained by the link to immortal souls, the pain was intense and she clutched at her shirt between her breasts where her all too human heart beat, the agony of the memory causing physical pain. Here, the Spirit Shield's immortal souls dwelled, tied to the shield sometimes known as a veil. The veil that created the barrier between the living and the dead.

"Come," commanded Aossi with a frown at the boy. "Let us walk to the river. I need to show you something."

Aossi popped to her feet as did Actaeon. Avery rose to follow them to a babbling brook no wider than three spans. She could easily have stepped across it in the human world, but it was not its width that created the obstacle. It was the height of the mist that rose off its surface, a rippling ribbon of blue. Or it was supposed to be blue. The screen of blue was dotted with red pinpricks of light that flashed and sizzled, as though under attack by tiny shards of lava. With each strike, the mist quivered and the peaceful vision around her shook.

"Our home is under attack. The veil is weakening," Actaeon whispered. "Our sanctuary is compromised. We have to leave." Avery's mouth opened in shock, but no sound came out, as she stared at the ancient child. Actaeon's lower lip was drooping again and a quiver shook it. "The very fabric of the world trembles. If you cannot stop Helga, we will all die."

Aossi stepped in front of him and smiled, but it was without mirth. "It is not as bad as that...yet. But it is serious and you and young Cayden as the Spirit Shields must stop her. As prophesied, you are the only hope for this world. To help, we are returning the magical creatures to the forests to fight for not only their lives but for all existence. They have lived alongside us for a long time in this peaceful dominion.

"I overheard you speaking to the elder, Alfreda, and you are correct. The world is in dire need of the aid of the legendaries, for only they can cross the veil without harm. It is our hope that Helga will ignore their presence as she does not see any value or advantage in magic, or the creatures transformed by it at death."

Aossi reached into a pocket and pulled out a flute. It was the ugliest flute Avery had ever seen. Avery smiled at it, for she knew where it had come from.

"I believe I should give this to you. I retrieved it from the old oak tree where Cayden hid the first flutes he had made. This one...let's say I have enhanced its abilities. It will call one and all of the magical creatures. Guard it with your life, for they will come to whoever holds the flute." She placed it in Avery's outstretched hands and closed her fingers around it. "If the need is dire enough, it will also cleanse a soul of enchantments. But many will die to give strength to the spell, so do not activate it unless the need is dire."

"One more thing," Actaeon said with a slight hitch to his voice "Artio is searching for a bowl located in this temple. It is plain clay and inscribed with runes. She must not be allowed to take it. It is one of three and useless without the other two, but if she was to find all three, she will be able to access the celestial temple of the gods. You know that the temple is only for the Spirit Shields. She must not enter without a Spirit Shield at her side. Enter without you and she will trigger the traps hidden there. Find the bowl and safeguard it, or we are all dead, forever." A tear escaped as he bit his lip to stop its trembling.

Aossi patted Avery on the sleeve. "I have every faith in you, Alfreda. Go with our blessing." She clapped her hands together, and meadow and brook vanished. Avery popped back into existence with a crack that startled Achak and Elder Hania. The snap back to reality was so sharp that Avery's gasp was audible, echoing around the temple. Dizzy and disoriented, it took her a moment to locate Achak and Elder Hania in the dim interior. They stood in front of a stone ledge, scattered with artifacts. Every object was covered with cobwebs and dust inches thick except for one area. That spot was clear of cobwebs. A circle, devoid of any dirt, sat in stark contrast to the surrounding artifacts. Something had been there and was now gone. Someone else knew about the temple and had taken an object from it. It could not be good news…not after this long.

The void drew her eyes. The bowl was missing.

CHAPTER 10

The Way Out

CAYDEN AND MORDECAI STOOD STARING out at the marvelous sight of the outside world, pausing in the shadows to study the bright sky and lush greenery visible beyond the opening. After the illustration of the butterfly, they hesitated to move beyond the threshold of darkness. Mordecai physically restrained Cayden with a hand to his chest as he took a step toward the opening. Mordecai moved his other hand through the air, testing for traps.

"There is something there," Mordecai said with a heavy sigh. "This exit is also shielded."

"Of course, it is," said a voice behind them. They spun on the spot, Cayden reaching instinctually for the sword he carried at his hip. Genii stood in the narrow hallway, blocking their retreat. "There is only one way out of the underworld. By the river. Would you like me to show you where it is?"

"Why would you show us a way out?" Cayden said, his eyes narrowed in suspicion.

"Because I want out too, and there is safety in numbers, especially when travelling amongst those bound to hell."

"You are a shade. You cannot leave the underworld." Cayden spat the word "shade," it being the foulest creation of Helga's cruel imagination. And he had a personal reason to dislike this particular shade. "And you are Helga's minion. I wouldn't trust you if you were the last hope for the world."

Mordecai moved his hand to Cayden's arm and gripped it hard. Cayden started at him for a moment then went silent.

Mordecai stepped between them and pulled his focus stone from his pocket, running it up and down Genii.

His eyes widened at what the inspection revealed. "He is human again," he said in a breathy voice filled with shock. "He has been returned to his body. I have never seen the like!" He walked around Genii, studying the auras generated by the focus stone, sending tendrils of magic into the device. "Why?" he said simply, stopping in front of the man.

He shrugged. "Helga wants me to accompany you. I think she wants a spy, someone she can control on the outside, someone to do her bidding. I am not completely free." He held up a sleeve which dropped back to reveal a rune of the underworld tattooed on the inside of his wrist. "She left me with this. But at least I can no longer hear her in my head day and night. It would seem that mortality has its benefits." He smiled a weak smile, as though the expression was foreign to him.

Cayden stood with arms folded, clearly not trusting this strange twist of fate. Yet they needed a guide. They had searched for days to find this pathetic opening only to discover it was also a dead end.

Dead ends in the underworld, he barked a laugh. The other two looked at him quizzically.

"It's your call, Mordecai," Cayden said instead.

"We need a guide. I don't think we have any choice, my boy."

Cayden nodded and then held out his hand in invitation. "Lead on, Genii, but know that I do not trust you and neither does Mordecai."

Genii smiled a grim smile. "I can hardly stay here, now can I? I already feel the drag of death. I am as eager to leave as you are." With that, he turned and headed back down the passage. They followed tight on his heels.

Mordecai relit the floating orb of light he had conjured to illuminate their way, and followed Genii's silver trimmed black cloak down the twisting maze of passages at a pace considerably faster than they had been moving. Genii marched as though he had the passages memorized. Perhaps he did, having been imprisoned there for centuries. The path descended sharply, and then leveled out, opening onto a tall but narrow cathedral of rock. It was hot in the cavern, due to a fissure in the floor through which a bubbling lava could be seen, a steady stream flowing just under the cooled crust. They traced a wide path around the stream and headed for the far end of the cave where mist rose into the air and billowed against the cold ceiling, creating a dripping slow motion waterfall with no apparent source.

Cayden eyed the scalding water apprehensively, but at the last minute Genii took them behind a cleft in the rock that shielded them from the steam. The sauna-like passage was clinging and cloying. Cayden likened the sensation to the proverbial frog being slow cooked in water as the temperature slowly rose around him. The passage fogged temporarily as a cloud of steam drifted down the tunnel. Cayden panted in the heavy moist air.

Then the passage began to rise and the air cooled so much that Cayden's sweat turned to ice and he shivered in the fresher air. His damp clothing clung to his body and his feet squished in his sodden boots. It was nothing compared to Mordecai, though. His long white beard now resembled a rat's tail, and his snowy hair clung to his scalp in ropes, dripping onto his robes. He swiped the dripping tendrils out of his face and grinned. His grey robes were nearly transparent, clinging to his bony frame. "Ah I do like a good sauna. They are so beneficial for the skin."

Genii shot a look over his shoulder and sped up now that the passage had leveled out once more.

The source of the refreshing breeze was a pile of boulders located in the middle of a bubbling spring. The spring burbled, flowing smoothly from a break in the floor and out of the cavity formed by the vacated stone. They crawled up onto the boulders and stared over the lip of rock at the valley that sloped away from the opening.

"Why is there no barrier here?" asked Cayden, suspicious of the seeming ease of the exit.

"Who said there is no barrier?" said Genii, flexing his fingers. "It is just thinner here with the waters of the spring. I think the spring cleanses the opening periodically. It represents life, and the shadow is pushed back. Come, we must push through the veil now. I will go first as I am not afraid. I was already dead." Without a backward glance, he started down the rocky slope, rocks sliding out from under his feet. About a third of the way down the slope a barrier sprang into being as he collided with it. His body jerked. Spasming, he slid through the barrier. The veil darkened and a keening wail rose on the air and then silenced as he slid through. He lay still for a moment and then slowly regained his feet, shaking visibly.

Cayden caught Mordecai's gaze. "What do you think?" he said quietly.

Mordecai frowned, brows pulled tight with worry. "I think we have been a long time in the underworld, and it is going to take its toll on us getting past it. But leave we must. I can do this much though. Perhaps it will ease the passing." He pulled the focus stone from his robes and clasped it between Cayden's two hands, wrapping his finger around his. Mordecai closed his eyes and began muttering a chant. Something stirred in Cayden's memory. A memory of another time when this spell was used to protect the souls of two babes. He closed his eyes and felt the spell settle on them both.

"Now we are bound together. If one soul fails to cross, the other will pull him through. Come. It is time." Mordecai turned back to the barrier. With a deep breath, he launched himself off the rock, sliding toward the barrier, Cayden on his heels.

They hit the barrier at roughly the same time, and the keening wail this time was not one voice but thousands, all rushing to the spot to feed on two of the mightiest souls alive. Cayden screamed as what felt like rough, rasping lips full of serrated teeth scraped across his soul and latched on to his being. Mordecai thrashed, caught temporarily in the net. Then it let him go, and he was flung down the slope, tugging Cayden with him in a tumbling slide. They came to rest against a fallen tree, dazed and unmoving. Cayden was soaked in blood, his skin torn in thousands of places. None of the cuts were serious or deep, but the sheer multitude soon had him coated in a blood-soaked sweat that burned over every inch of his body. He groaned as Mordecai crawled over to him and began passing the stone over him, muttering a spell for healing under his breath. Genii staggered over and sank down beside them, shaking. He had a deep gash across his forehead, a cut that he had received in his tumble down the slope. He held a cloth to it while Mordecai worked, silently watching the proceedings. With a sigh, Mordecai sat back as Cayden's eyes drifted closed, then took a deep breath and turned to Genii.

"Let me see that." Genii pulled the cloth away from the cut. Mordecai frowned. "I do not have the strength to heal it all the way, but I can close it. You will need to be careful until it can fully heal." He placed a cool hand against the cut and drew on his will through the stone. The flesh mended, and the scar faded to a light pink. His eyes examined the area around them. "Do you think it is safe to camp nearby for the evening? We need to rest. That was a more traumatic experience than I anticipated."

"Yes, and I know of some shelter nearby. Come, it's only a short distance away," said Genii.

Mordecai put an arm under Cayden's and hauled him to his feet, stumbling after Genii, who grabbed Cayden's other arm. Ten minutes of walking that felt like a lifetime brought them to a series of caves hollowed out the hillside. Gratefully, they stumbled into the driest of them and collapsed to the ground. Exhausted, they rolled up in their wet clothing and were asleep before their cloaks settled on the ground.

The wispy shadows of night hid a creeping fog that spread out from the pierced veil, the veil where the three men had so recently passed through. The fog slithered through the vegetation free at last. Everything it touched, screamed, but there was nothing that could hear its cry.

CHAPTER 11

The Letter

BLACK CROWS CIRCLED THE ENTRANCE to Artio's commandeered headquarters, screeching and cawing as though to attract her attention. She eyed them, annoyed at their presence. *Spies of Helga, for sure, but why were they acting that way?* She growled at them, flashing sharp teeth at a bold crow that dived towards her, an object clutched in its claws. Artio grabbed the handle of her bone knife. With a flash of steel and a "thunk," the blade impaled the bird in midflight. It dropped from the sky and bounced, rolling to her feet. The object clutched in its claws tumbled away. Artio ignored the bird and marched over to the wrapped parcel, pushing it over with her toe. The wrapping fell away and inside was a box. A trinket box. Shock electrified her, and a thrill ran down her spine. *My trinket box! What is my trinket box doing here? I thought Alfreda had it.*

Artio bent down and picked it up. The box was the same, square with a silver gilded lid carved with stars and a full moon peeking through tall etched monoliths. It was their meadow.

She ran a finger over the lid, and tears welled up in her eyes.

She thumbed the catch, and the lid sprang open. Inside was a small piece of parchment, folded several times to exactly fit the interior of the box. With trembling fingers, she plucked the parchment out of the box and unfolded it.

My dearest Artio,
I could barely believe it was you who visited my mistress a few weeks

past. At first, I had no memory of you, but something pulled at my mind, at my heart, and that small place where my soul should have resided. It must have been some residual echo of our love. I had to meditate on your image because it is different than it was all those years ago. Yet, I knew it was you.

How such a thing is possible after what happened in the meadow, I do not know, but maybe the gods have seen fit to smile on us once more.

In a strange twist of fate, Helga has preserved my mortal body, and I am reunited with it once more. Although I am still bound to her as my mistress, I have hoped that we might meet again and...

Words fail me. What I would hope for, wish for, is in the hands of the gods. Believe me when I say, I will be searching for you and will be overjoyed to see you again. Look for me on the road to Cathair. I will be traveling with your brother and the wizard. Do not harm them. They are not your enemy, despite what you may believe.

Until we meet,
Yours in life and death,
Genii

Artio gently folded the missive and tucked it carefully back inside the box and clutched it to her chest, staring at the dead crow with haunted eyes. *Genii! He's alive!* she thought with a silent wail. She scrubbed the back of her hand across her eyes, wiping away tears that she could not stem. She tucked the precious box into her pocket and tugged her knife free of the body of the dead crow. Then, with a roar of anger and grief long buried, she ran off into the woods. Shocked stares followed her flight as she ran from the pain, ran from all that she had locked away for so long. Sobbing, she stumbled into a cold stream and sank knee deep into its frigid depths, splashing water on her face, shocking herself back to a hiccupping control. She took several large gulps of air and slowly exhaled, slowing her panic and her pain. *He's alive! He's alive!* The thought chased itself around and around her mind. *By the gods, he's alive!*

She crawled back to shore and collapsed against a fallen willow trunk, water dripping and pooling on the ground where she sat. Her head flopped back so it rested on the log, staring up at the heavens and tracing the clouds and the stars above. *Genii, what am I going to do? With you dead, my path was clear. With you gone, all I had left was my hate, my anger, my fear. You have torn the bandage off of an eternity of pain with that note. How can I go on? Why am I here?*

Artio shuddered and wrapped her arms around her knees, imagining that she was lost in Genii's strong embrace once again. She ached to hold him close. Another shudder shook her, and she sobbed, her choking cry caught in the tightness of her throat. Tears rained onto her sleeves, soaking the rough cloth. She threw back her head and roared with the pain of her loss. The roar made early roosting birds take flight, shaking the leaves above her as they took to the air.

Eventually, she quieted. Exhaustion took her, and her eyelids drooped. She dozed off, waking the dream of her memories, the hope awakening once again, as they danced in the woods of old.

She woke with a start to find the sun nearly set. She lurched to her feet, brushing off the detritus of her flight and headed back to camp. Tomorrow she would begin the search for Genii. She knew where he was headed and where to find him. But first, she must set her plan for the bowls in motion. She would have her revenge. Perhaps none of them deserved to live. Either way, she now controlled the destiny of her siblings. She would not waste that advantage. She would set in place safeguards to keep it. She had questions for Dagan, many questions for which she would have answers. She would not be duped again. Her absent-minded, misplaced trust in the past had laid open the door for exploitation. This time she would control the outcome of battle. If all perished in the process, it was only her due.

CHAPTER 12

The Watcher

MAREA LED HER SADDLED MARE out of the stable behind her home and paused beside the four burly temple guards waiting at the rear gate. Each led a mount loaded with provisions. Her dark-green cloak was pulled up over her hair, shadowing her face against the early morning chill. She barely looked at the men who sat waiting, creaking in their saddles, accompanied by the occasional stomp of a hoof and a jangle of metal on a bridle as one of the horses shifted a leg, impatient to be off on the journey.

She was privately annoyed at the prospect of riding the long distance back to the caves, but travel it she would if it netted her the child Spirit Shield once and for all. She paused to double check her saddlebags, reassuring herself that she had everything she needed. Reaching deep inside the lowest pocket, her hand touched a cool silver collar wrapped in deerskin tucked in at its base. She checked the other pocket, and there, wrapped more robustly, were several stoppered vials. Satisfied, Marea fastened the buckle of the flaps and swung herself up into the saddle, settling her cloak over the rump of her horse.

Her hand drifted subconsciously to her arm where the deep sword cut had been healed, and her face tightened.

"Eldrid!" she snapped. The balding elder nudged his horse up beside hers. "What is the fastest way to take control of the temple?"

His face blank, he stared back at her unsure how to respond. "The fastest way to take control of the temple is to take control of the child," he murmured carefully.

Marea nodded, her eyes narrowed like a hawk spotting prey. "That was the original plan...and yet, where is she? Running free across the land and creating all kinds of trouble. She is consorting with the Flesh Clans! She is dabbling in the underworld! If she were to fall into the clutches of the underworld, all life would cease. *By the gods, she is a Spirit Shield!*" Marea yelled. Eldrid flinched back as though struck. "She wanders free when she should be chained and controlled," Marea continued in a quieter voice. "She should be brought to serve our people for all eternity. It is our birthright to control one such as her. We are the Spirit Clans! Is this not the reason why we feud with the Flesh Clans? They understand nothing of the purpose of a Spirit Shield. Care of the sacred temple of Faylea was given to us. I am the High Priestess. It is my duty to guide the child in her duty. This time, I will accept no failures, no excuses. Failure will be met with...unpleasantness." She twisted in the saddle, eyes focused on the cloud-shrouded mountain. Eldrid bowed from the saddle, as did the other three men. "Come! Let there be no more excuses."

She touched her heels to the rounded sides of her mare and led the way out of the clearing.

*   *   *

Hototo silently shadowed the party, keeping a parallel course to the High Priestess. He had been watching her for days, keeping track of her movements. He'd been surprised when he witnessed her ascent to the temple entrance. She'd entered the temple with no difficulty at all. How she could do it when she was not a Spirit Shield he did not know. It should have been impossible the first time, but now that the Spirit Shields had returned, it made no sense at all. The temple belonged to the Spirit Shields. Of course, he could not see what she had done within the temple, but the fact that she could enter at all was worrisome, especially for the bear goddess. Artio would not be pleased.

Now that Marea was away from the protection of Faylea, possibilities blossomed. Her route would take her right past where his mistress was encamped. What a prize she would make if he were to hand her over to Artio. Yet, perhaps it was best to see where she was headed first. She had some purpose for leaving the Sanctuary and the protection of Faylea. He suspected that what motivated her, beyond simple power, was the ability to control those around her. He burned with a similar desire. To snatch his enemy was to take control of the Spirit Shields. With Marea within their control, they could make the Spirit Clans kneel before Artio. *I will be the ruling High Priest over a united Primordial people.* Visions of glory swam in his mind even as his eyes tracked the party. *The Flesh Clans will rule in truth and our ways will be vindicated. Once united, I will abolish the Sprit Clans, leaving only the true faith of flesh sacrifice to appease the gods. No longer will the gods be remote. No longer will we be shut out of the temples. The Flesh Clans will finally see the faces of their gods, for the gods will dwell among us as Artio does now!* Hototo's smile was fevered, his eyes glowing with a fanatical light.

Once their route was determined, Hototo circled back to his encampment to collect his men, decision made. He would make a move. The clans must be united, and Artio's instructions were to clear a path to the temple. With Marea under his sway, they could enter the city with little to no bloodshed. He could force the elders to surrender. Then, they would be forced to join in the worship of Artio, the true goddess. And the Spirit Shields? They would provide him access to the Sanctuary. They would be harnessed to the goddess's will.

He smiled as the waiting Flesh Clan warriors followed him back onto Marea's trail. They easily picked it up and followed Marea's small group at a leisurely pace. The trail was two hours old, and they rode at the same pace, lagging a safe distance behind so as to not be discovered by accident by the ones they pursued. As a precaution, Hototo sent out a pair of advance scouts to spy on their prey's back trail. Marea might have had someone circling, checking to see if anyone followed. Hototo thought it was not likely as she had set out with such a small party, but still caution was part of his nature. He liked to eliminate surprises. She could be meeting up with more Fayleans. It was best to know the lay of the land before committing one's resources.

Two warriors circled ahead of the tracked party with instructions to be delivered to a Flesh Clan warrior lying in wait ahead. The missive commanded them to take up positions on the approach to the sacred forests.

At midday, they paused for a quick lunch and to allow the horses to rest, but soon took up the trail again. Marea was entering a section of forest that bordered Flesh Clan territory where his warriors waited.

Hototo heeled his mount into a trot and then a run. His party of thirty swiftly closed the distance, whooping a war cry as they burst from the trees on the heels of Marea's confused guards.

Marea held up her hand, stopping the guards from engaging the Flesh Clan warriors. She sat, regal and queenly, surrounded by her men. Steel bared and arrows knocked, but they did not release because another thirty Flesh Clan warriors suddenly drifted out of the trees ahead.

"What is the meaning of this, Hototo?" Marea snapped, as Hototo walked his mount forward. "You will recall these warriors immediately. You are interfering with business of the temple. Now get out of the way! I have urgent business to attend to. Do you not know who you are addressing? Now step aside!"

"I am afraid I can't do that." Hototo reined his mount in, just shy of her men. A slow smile spread across his face. "You are to be our guest, Marea. I suggest you inform your guards to put away their weapons, unless you want to be our only guest."

Marea's eyes flickered around the clearing. There was no escape. She motioned to her guards, and they slowly lowered their swords and eased back on their bow strings. With a grimace, they tossed their weapons to the ground. A young Flesh Clan warrior ran over and picked up the discarded weaponry then hurried away.

"Now, if you would follow the warriors ahead of you, there is someone in our camp who would like to speak to you." He gestured with his arm, pointing in the direction they had been travelling. With her head held high, Marea resumed her journey, treating the Flesh Clan warriors as though they were simply an escort. Hototo nudged his horse forward and brought it alongside hers. He could feel her anger rolling off her in waves. It made his smile widen.

That was easier than I thought it would be. Pleased with himself, he trotted beside her mare as the warriors closed in on all sides, separating the temple guards from Marea's side and sandwiching them in the middle.

CHAPTER 13

To Your Health

FABIAN TUMBLED OUT OF HIS BLANKETS, rolling to his feet as the alarm sounded. Three short blasts on a horn and the camp stirred like a kicked anthill. As he stumbled into his boots and out the door, the object of the alarm galloped into view.

The scout lay slumped over the neck of his horse, blood dripping from the two arrow wounds piercing shoulder and thigh. Just as it reached Fabian, the barrel-chested gelding skidded to a halt, its chest heaving. Sweat ran in pink rivulets down its withers where blood had splattered its coat. Fabian grabbed the bridle as the scout slid sideways out of the saddle. He was caught by two Kingsmen and laid gently on the ground. A third wound, an arrow puncture to his belly was revealed, the shaft broken. Blood soaked his tunic.

"Tegan, stay with me, son," said Fabian, pressing a hand to his wound in a vain attempt to staunch the bleeding.

Tegan's eyes opened at his voice. "Forgive me. I have failed. They were waiting for us. They knew we were coming!"

"Who knew you were coming? Where are the others? Are they dead?" Tegan's eyes drifted closed. "Tegan!"

With great effort, Tegan dragged his eyes open and reached up with one hand to clutch at the white sleeve of Fabian's hastily donned shirt. "Cyrus. He laughed at us. He said that you would know where to find him. He's waiting for you, Fabian. He told me to tell you that he will wait for you at the Well of Souls. Then he put me back up on my horse and let me go. Forgive me. I tried to kill him, but I couldn't reach him."

Tegan's breath caught on a painful inhale. He exhaled, his hand slipping from Fabian's arm, leaving a bloody handprint smear as it fell away.

"Dammed to Helga's hell!" Fabian swore, rising to his feet. "Is he the only scout to return?"

"Yes, Captain."

Nelson appeared at his shoulder, frowning down at the dead scout. He knelt on the other side of Fabian and slid Tegan's eyelids closed. He murmured aloud for all to hear "May your soul be added to the Great River. May you find peace and comfort with the souls of those who passed before us and are awaiting rebirth. May you rejoice at the reunion with family and loved ones." They straightened then motioned to two of the Kingsmen. "Provide him with a proper burial." The Kingsmen picked up Tegan's body and carried him away.

To the gathering surrounding them, Fabian barked, "Saddle up! We move within the hour!"

He spun around and stalked over to his tent, Nelson at his side. Quietly, for Fabian's ears only, he said, "To continue on this path is suicide. They are waiting for us. Cyrus has had time to search Upper Cathair. He may have found the tunnels by now. Even if he has not, there is bound to be an entire legion between us and there. If I were he, I would have forces in both Upper Cathair and Cathair proper. We need to think of another way in."

Fabian ducked under his tent flap and over to his saddlebags where he pulled out a map of the region. He unrolled it on the makeshift table consisting of his saddlebag and his boots with a cloak tossed over it. He unfurled the map and picked up several stones from the ground to weigh down the curling edges.

Fabian stabbed a finger at the center. "We are here. Cyrus's forces are likely gathering here," he stabbed to the right, "and here." He dragged the finger across to the left. "See how it's shaped like a wishbone? And we are the snapping point. The only way to keep a wishbone from snapping is to make the pressure equal. It does not matter how much force there is."

"What are you suggesting?" Nelson squinted at the map.

"We give them a target that both sides of the legion want badly enough to disregard Cyrus's commands," said Fabian

"OK," Nelson said slowly. "I can see that. What I can't see is what you think could possibly pit a split legion against each other. What do you have in mind?"

Fabian smiled grimly as he laid out his plan. Nelson nodded, mouth stretching into a grin. *It might work. Yes, indeed, it might work, at that.*

* * *

The cart creaked as they approached the nexus of the two armies. The road was empty and dark, lit only by a watery moonlight that pooled on the road, where the canopy of the trees that lined the road, grew sparse. Fabian kept the mules to a slow walk, hunching over in his seat. His floppy crowned hat was pulled low, the very essence of an elderly brewer on his way to market. Nelson, seated beside him, yawned ostensibly and kept his stubbly chin pressed to his chest. Obviously, the brewer's partner and just as old and weary.

They had located some unburned shabby old clothing in the back of the inn in a stone cellar used as cold storage when the inn had stood. The barrels of whiskey had been a little more difficult to come by, requiring a few days' delay to search out and secure from a nearby town. But now the evening had come.

The cart hit an overturned rock and lurched, throwing Nelson against Fabian. Nelson pushed back into a seated position and grumbled loudly, "Dang it, Pietar, can't you keep the cart level?" He twisted on the bench to pat the kegs, their contents swishing noisily. "We have to get this to Cathair safely! It's the last of our whiskey for the season. You don't want to waste any of this, do you? Best season we ever had!"

Fabian scratched his nose and squinted down the road. "Can't see a dang thing, Tomaz. Not a dang thing. Stupid idea to push on in the dark. You and your stupid ideas," he grumbled, yawning.

Suddenly, a tall man stepped out into the middle of the road, dented armour glinting in the moonlight as it bounced off the creases of his chest plate. The insignia of the legion was impressed into the metal. He was joined by another and then another until twenty men stood in the middle of the road, blocking the way. The lead soldier stepped more fully into the moonlight. Long stringy hair hung from beneath a matching helmet, his thin lip covered in a hairy mustache, curling into a sneer.

"That is far enough," he growled as he drew his sword. Twenty other blades followed. "You will get down from the wagon, and you will run. We are confiscating this wagon in the name of Lord Cyrus. It now belongs to the legion and to my band." The men behind him chuckled, licking their lips, eager to sample the contents of the casks.

"Certainly!" said Fabian, rheumy eyes squinting at the men as though he couldn't quite see who they were. "Tomaz, we have enough to share, right?" Nelson nodded quickly, his eyes darting around, as though looking for a place to hide. "Yes, yes, we will share!"

"You will share nothing," said the tall man. "We will leave you your clothes and your skin and be thankful for that. They have no value to us. Now get out of the wagon."

Nelson bounced to his feet and then froze as a voice behind him said, "Stay right where you are." Fabian turned toward the voice to find a squat, blond man in similar armour blocking their retreat. He had no less than thirty men with him, and they also stood with swords drawn.

Fabian stood up slowly, hands in the air, an arm extended in both directions. "Now, gentlemen, there is plenty of whiskey to go around for both you and your men back at camp. Surely you can share?"

Nelson stood stock still, eyes darting back and forth between the two parties. He licked his lips. "How about we draw lots?"

Fabian stared at him. "Do what?"

"Draw lots. I mean, it would be fairer for them. Otherwise they are going to fight over this premium keg." He patted a small keg by his knee. All eyes were drawn to it immediately, and greed lit their expressions.

"I propose we toast the lottery with this premium keg." He licked his lips again as though nervous they would not accept his proposal. "A small taste of what is to come." He smiled weakly and reached down to pull out a bag of cups that tinkled in a sack.

"Whaddya say? A toast to your good fortune?" he pleaded in a squeaky voice.

Tall man threw back his head and roared. Blondie followed suit and soon they were lining up at the side of the wagon, each man to grab his glass of whiskey while Fabian drew up lots on squares of paper.

Nelson measured out the precious amber fluid from the keg in precise quantities until it was empty, while the soldiers drew lots. As one, they tossed back the whiskey, smacking their lips in appreciation. Then with lots drawn, they picked out the barrels that belonged to them. In short order, the kegs were rolled off the wagon and the victors were hauling the loot back to their respective camps. Most surprising, they left Fabian and Nelson with one mule and the wagon.

In the silence that fell after the last rattle of the kegs had faded, Nelson and Fabian grinned at each other. Turning the mule around they headed back the way they had come. They did not speak for several miles to be sure they were clear of any listening ears.

"Well, that went easier than I thought it would," said Fabian.

"Yes. I guess greed truly wins out," said Nelson.

Another mile brought them to a rocky two-wheeled path. As they directed the mule down the lane, an owl hooted. After about five minutes of squeaking and creaking wagon travel, the rough passage exited the trees onto cleared fields lined with low stone walls. At the end of the lane was a two-story farmhouse and barn set high on a hill. An owl hooted and more owls replied. Kingsmen rose from the field where they had hidden themselves.

Fabian swept his hat from his head and stood. "It is done. Prepare the men."

CHAPTER 14

Two Loves

CAYDEN WALKED THE EDGE OF THE CLIFF, precariously balanced on its razor-sharp edge. His bare toes hung over the gap between him and the other side. A simple step would put him across the chasm, but somehow he knew it wasn't that easy. He wanted to cross but for the voices in his head. Two voices struggled to reach him. One he knew and trusted, but the other was foreign. Intrusive. A rasping sigh on his soul. Yet he could not disobey its commands.

He turned his head, seeking the source of the friendlier voice and there she was. Dark-haired and vibrant, she shone with light and life and love. *Ziona!* His mind whispered, and he reached for her. But she was on the other side. She was across the void. Tears welled up in his eyes, and he glanced back down at his feet. *Why can't I cross?*

The thunder of wings and great sweeps of air distracted him from the brim, his attention caught as a shadow passed overhead. A black Pegasus circled then dropped from the sky to land on his side of the cliff, ruffling his great ebony wings before folding them to rest along his ribs. *Brimstone!* He reached out his hand to touch the soft muzzle and woke with a start when the soft muzzle snuffled through his blankets, searching for the golden apples that were his favourite. He blinked and pushed the heavy mane out of his face.

"Brimstone, you found me!" Cayden mumbled through a mouthful of hair. Brimstone took the edge of his blanket in his teeth and pulled it off Cayden with a toss of his head, clearly of the opinion that it was time he found him some apples. Cayden laughed and sat up, wincing as the freshly healed wounds stretched painfully. He felt as though he had been caught in a fierce sandstorm with no clothes on. As though drawn by the thought, a pale cream Pegasus soared gently into the meadow below, a figure perched on its back. Cayden squinted down the hillside, and Ziona waved then slid from the Pegasus and ran up the hillside toward him. He stared, disbelieving his sight.

"She arrived a day ago while you were still passed out. She and her two companions." Mordecai, a bowl of what smelled like stew in his hand, waved his spoon in the direction of the small camp that had sprung up around a small stream a short distance away. Denzik stood at the entrance to a tent, deep in conversation with Gaius, a curl of pipe smoke wreathing his head. Gaius lifted a hand and pointed in the direction of Cathair, then pointed toward the east. Cayden's heart lifted at the sight of his father. "It will be nice to have company on the trip back to Cathair," Mordecai mumbled around a mouthful of hot food. "There is safety in numbers."

With his foot, Mordecai nudged a pile of fresh clothes that sat on the ground beside Cayden. "I'd hurry and put those on unless you want her to catch you with nary a stitch on!" His eyes twinkled knowingly, and Cayden felt a flush creep up his neck. There was no need to ask who he was referencing, as he could feel her approach through the bond. With a muffled oath, Cayden struggled into his clothes and was just lacing his shirt when Ziona appeared, running out of the woods to throw her arms around him. She grabbed his head and tilted it down to hers, as he pulled her hard against him, kissing her with all the longing of their combined souls.

Mordecai harrumphed. They broke apart but did not let go. Hard-earned was their reunion and neither wished to release the other lest one of them disappear again.

Ziona placed both hands on the side of his face, sharp eyes fixed on his green, searching them carefully. "Promise me you will not leave my side again. I swore to protect you, Cayden. Never again leave me like that." She ran a thumb over his cheek, touching one of the many healed nicks. "I go where you go, even if it's to the grave. I won't have it any other way."

"I promise. I promise we will never be separated intentionally. But I do not promise to let you die if I can save you. You cannot ask that of me."

She kissed him again deeply then grumbled, "It will do. For now."

* * *

Genii watched from the edge of the tents, his face twisted with jealousy. The tenderness, the care they took with each other was a kindness he had never experienced. Passion, yes, but this? This was…love. Yes, that was the word he sought. He tested it on his tongue and found the taste sour, bitter. The bitterness came from his dried tears; tears he never realized had spilled from his eyes while watching the reunion. He reached up with his hand and wiped away the foreign sensation with a hand that trembled. His newly beating heart thudded painfully in his chest, and he was besieged by a longing so intense, it could only be called a craving. Deep and penetrating, it was everything he could do to not pull at his hair and howl his misery.

Helga was not his love. She never had been. What had changed in him was the understanding of the difference. The reactivation of his body, the reactivation of his heart and lungs, and blood, had also reactivated his memory. His soul had been enslaved on death with the transformation to a shade. His true love was Artio. A flood of images swam just beyond reach, stopped at walls of flesh and bone, memory long locked away behind the frozen barrier of stasis. Those that had leaked through were painful enough when he was still a shade, but now the agony of examining them was maddening. He shoved the thoughts aside, back behind the wall, dragging in deep breaths to regain his former control. There they stayed until surprised with a scene such as this.

Artio, my love, did you get my present and the missive inside it? He had discovered the box next to his body and knew it to be the original one, the one he had given to her so long ago. Only he knew the significance of it. He had quietly sent it out to her by one of Helga's crows before leaving the caves. Only the crows could pass through the veil. He longed to know if she received it, but there was no way until such time as they were able to meet. He did not even know if she would remember him, changed as she was.

If anything, she was even more beautiful now. She had a strength about her, a no-nonsense demeanor he found quite alluring. A thrill of excitement ran through his body at the thought. Looking down, he realized that…his body was fully functional. He grinned, but it was a foreign feeling, this upward curving mirth. His hand rose to his face to touch lips and cheeks, to trace the outline of his face. He couldn't remember the last time he was happy or amused or that he had really felt anything.

He took a deep satisfying breath and exhaled.

It was wonderful to be alive again. Truly alive. Not many men ever had the chance to live again. He must not waste it. But what to do with it? He did not believe he was fully free. He could still feel Helga's control in the back of his head, like a sleeping sickness ready to strike when he let his guard down.

And then there was the problem of Cayden and the wizard. Both were bound to the Soul Fetches. Genii wasn't sure that he cared but his fate was bound to theirs, and for that reason he would keep them alive to fulfill his mistress's commands. Freedom lay at the end of the road, freedom for him and for Artio.

He left the edge of the clearing and returned to his tent. He would do what me must, whatever the cost.

CHAPTER 15

Riddles

"ARTIO, I HAVE FOUND SOMETHING. Come look."

Dagan straightened from the table, dropping his hands to his side. The looking glass glowed softly as though lit by an internal light. It hung, suspended from a wooden tripod over the pewter bowl, resting on its plinth. The magnification brought into sharp focus the magic of the bowls, the runes and symbols and pictures taking on a living quality. The images were so lifelike they nearly breathed.

Artio peered over his shoulder, an easy feat as she towered above him almost by a head.

"Do you see this symbol here?" He pointed to a raised square within the pewter bowl. On its rough surface, a series of scratches could be seen. Every tile was decorated with a picture or a series of lines. "That symbol is the beginning, and this one," he pointed to one on the other side of the bowl closer to the bottom, "is the end. In between, I believe we have a riddle."

"How do you know it's a riddle and not clear instructions?" She frowned at the bowl, willing it to give up its secrets.

"This starting symbol here is an image." He jabbed a finger at the coloured square. "Ancient poetry and stories, writings used to entertain used this form of script, while writings relating to business or work detail used sharp symbols. This bowl, carries both forms, see?" Dagan pointed out the different types of symbols. "When used in combination this way, it cannot be poetry—which is solely meant to entertain—or correspondence meant to instruct, but a combination. Poetry meant to instruct. A riddle."

"Very good." Artio walked slowly around the plinths, yellow eyes flickering from bowl to bowl, brows furrowed in concentration. "Can you read it?"

"It will take me awhile yet to be sure that I have the correct translation, but, yes, I will be able to decode it."

"What of the other two bowls?"

He nodded slowly. "Yes, I believe so. The riddles may speak of future events or even past ones. There is no guarantee they will be understandable. It is part of the magic of the bowls. They may even change to suit the bearer of the bowl. A translation now may not yield the answer you want. See these markings?" This time his hand pointed to the outer rim of the bowls. Swirls decorated the outside of each one. Artio nodded. "These are not decorations. They are time inhibitors. They control the flow of time inside the bowls."

"So, the bowls are a prophecy?" Artio asked.

"No, I would say more like an oracle. They are activated by the souls of the dead. The bowls are a literal vessel, but the person would be the true oracle," said Dagan.

"Well, that would explain why the Flesh Clans used them in sacrificial ceremonies." Artio's pensive gaze compared the markings. "I think I know exactly who to consult about the bowls." *Avery would make a wonderful oracle.* She chuckled as she thought out the plan. "Yes, indeed. She is the one. Well done, Dagan. Continue to translate the runes. Perfect your understanding. Anything less and I will be very disappointed in you. You do not want me to be disappointed."

Dagan bowed his head in silent acknowledgment of the threat and returned to studying the bowls.

At that moment, the doors opened to the street, and a High Priest bowed his way into the room. "Pardon, mistress! I beg you forgive me the disruption of your sanctuary, but Hototo has returned. He has prisoners and wished me to relay the message."

Artio stepped away from the plinths. "Take me to him."

* * *

The priest led Artio to a building with a peeling white-washed stucco and a stout wooden door on the edge of the village. It was ringed by Primordial warriors on horseback. Four riderless horses were being held by a pair of junior priests. As they saw her approach, they drew back from the door, a curtain of people being pulled back from the entrance. The door was opened for her by Primordial warrior with more scars than face. His fierce countenance was reinforced by the scarred droop on the left side of his mouth, where a wound had cut the muscle of his cheek. The scar continued up and through his left eye, covered in a leather eye patch.

Artio grinned at the warrior in approval, baring her teeth. The warrior met her stare boldly with his good eye and gave her a lopsided smile back, just as fierce. She ducked under the low door lintel and entered the dim interior. Her eyes widened automatically, adjusting to the dim interior more swiftly than a mere human could have done.

Seated in chairs against the wall were a woman and three companions. The woman's haughty stare faded slightly as Artio straightened in the door frame, clearly taller than a normal human and a woman at that. A trace of fear flickered across her features before she stilled them. Her chin lifted in defiance.

Good, this one has backbone. I can use that.

Hototo hurried forward and fell to his knees, face pressed to the dusty rug that covered the worn floorboards.

"Your Highness, I have brought you a great prize, Marea Tremblingspirit, the High Priestess of the Spirit Clans. She knows how to access the temple, mistress. She is their spiritual leader."

Artio barely spared a glance for the Flesh Clan High Priest, stepping around his grovelling and over to the petite woman. She paused in front of Marea and crossed her arms, staring down at her with an intensity that made Marea shrink back despite her best desires. Marea did not drop her eyes, but it was a near thing. She hung onto her courage by a hair. The intensity in Artio's gaze was like staring into a bright fire. She stilled the urge to blink and look away. She raised her chin a fraction higher.

"*Leave us!*" commanded Artio in the hollow voice of the gods. The boom shattered the quiet and echoed off the walls. Warriors and the priests alike scrambled for the door and the room emptied except for Marea and her three temple guards. They were not bound by anything except fear. There was no need for physical restraints as there was no place to go.

"Tell me about the temple, and do not stop until you have told me everything."

Marea shivered then opened her mouth and began to speak. She left nothing out.

CHAPTER 16

A Werewolf's Tale

ELDER HANIA ROSE FROM THE FIRESIDE and headed out into the bush with a "be right back" wave, indicating a need for privacy. Of course, they would assume that his need was of a physical nature, but in actuality, it was more spiritual. He crept away from the campsite down toward the river and knelt at its side to splash water on his face. He cupped the cool liquid in his palms, then raised his hands and spoke a spell that turned the surface smooth as a mirror. He stared into his reflection for a second then whispered "Mistress, are you there? Helga?" He peered around then whispered again "Mistress?" The water showed the reflection of a grotto and a stream, with brightly coloured birds flitting happily from limb to limb then the image vanished. Silence greeted his summons. He tried once again with no reply. Finally, he let the water drop and got to his feet.

As he turned around, a shadow moved across him, and he cried out in alarm. His blood-curdling shriek of terror was swiftly silenced as the shadow attacked. He was knocked into the thrushes at the side of the pond. The reeds thrashed and then stilled.

Avery and Achak, hearing his cry of alarm, had dropped their plates and bolted into the trees, knives in hand. "Father! Where are you? Father!" Achak tumbled down the slight slope to the waterside and splashed into the murky water, frantically searching the reeds that poked up above the surface of the water. Tiny ripples reflected a wrinkled moon, but nothing else. Nothing stirred.

"Elder!" Avery called, slowly moving over the beach, studying the scuffs and scrapes in the sand by the light of the pale moon. Not a sound could be heard; even the crickets were silent. Avery knelt and picked up a scrap of cloth. It was shredded as though great claws had torn it apart. She handed the piece to Achak, who frowned and warily studied the woods.

Suddenly a howl rent the air, a great bark and then a snuffling sound and the brush parted. A six-foot-tall jet black werewolf paced out of the shrubbery before standing up on its hind legs.

"Mistress Avery," it chuckled in a barking voice, "you are safe now. The traitor is no more."

"What have you done?" Avery gasped, rushing over to the bushes, completely ignoring the werewolf. Avery's lack of surprise at the appearance of the werewolf made Achak's eyebrows rise. Achak was not so complacent and warily watched the shaggy creature of myth.

Avery staggered back out of the bushes, shocked at the sight. "You have slain an elder!" she gasped, "Why?"

Achak pushed his way in front of Avery and at the sight of his father's torn body, he spun on the werewolf, ready to attack. Avery grabbed his sleeve and hissed "No, Achak. Wait!"

"Yes, mistress. I had to." The werewolf dropped to all fours as docile as a pup. His tail curved between his hind legs. "He was betraying you. I have been watching him for days."

"Are you sure? He was an elder!" Avery flopped onto the ground as Achak pulled away. He dashed into the brush to kneel by his father's side, frantically checking for signs of life. He placed his fingers on the side of his neck, searching for a pulse and finding none, lowered his ear to his father's chest to check if his heart still beat.

"Father!" He shook him and his father's head flopped sideways at an angle that should not have been possible. His neck was broken. "No!" screamed Achak, and he launched himself to his feet intent on only one thing, avenging his father's death. He ran out of the brush and Avery, reading the intent in his anguished face, jumped between the pair.

"Achak, stop. Stop!" She grabbed his sword arm with both of hers and threw her weight behind the gesture, as he struggled to draw his knife.

Avery tore her eyes away from Achak and glared at the werewolf. "Why? What did you see? It had better be good. You killed him!"

"He was trying to scry the Goddess of the Dark, Mother. I heard him whisper into a pool of spelled water cupped in his hands. There are very few who work in this fashion and most are of the underworld, as it is a form of prophesy. I heard him speak the dark mistress's name. I am sorry if I have done wrong. I only meant to protect you."

"Why didn't you bring him to me? We could have found out more!" Frustrated, Avery pressed her fingers to her temple, trying to force reason into her whirling thoughts.

"Uh, Avery. Could you introduce me to your…friend?" Achak's voice came from over her shoulder as a menacing growl. Avery heard the snick of his knife being drawn. The werewolf bowed its head low, ready to accept the blow if she decreed it.

"This is Samba. Samba was mate to Sheba, who is a wolf that is friends with Cayden."

"How do you know this?" The muscles in Achak's arm quivered as he fought the urge to slay the creature, his eyes fixed on the werewolf in loathing.

"Cayden told me about the wolves. Or maybe it came to me in the temple." She frowned, tilting her head, trying to think where she had learned of the connection. "I think it was in the temple. Samba, have you been following us since the Spirit Temple?"

"Yes, mistress. Now that we are free to roam again, we are drawn to the Spirit Shields. There is a weakness to the shield, as though something is draining it." The wolf shook his head, tuft of hair flopping into its eyes. "It is disturbing, like a flea that you cannot dislodge. You need our protection. The spirit world is restless and afraid. It is not the peaceful communal rest it once was. Something stalks us. I wish to stay at your side. It is my desire to be close to you." He laid his head down on his paws, brown eyes wide and pleading.

Avery flopped down onto the grass, staring at the sky overhead. "Achak, put that away and sit beside me. We must talk." She looked up into his face and saw the shine of tears behind the anger and her voice softened. "I am sorry for your loss, but if your father really was betraying us, then Samba has saved our lives. Sit, please." Achak, with a great reluctance, sheathed his sword and sank to the ground beside her.

With a weary sigh, Avery said to Samba, "You may stay with us, but," she raised a finger to make the point, "you cannot kill anyone else without my permission. Elder Hania might have been trying to contact the other elders or his wife or someone completely innocent. You chose to judge his actions and execute him immediately. For this, I am displeased."

The werewolf's ears sank with shame. "I saw what I saw, Mother. It was more than what he was doing, mistress. I could smell the evil in the air. Werewolves can do that. They can smell the taint of the underworld. It is one of our gifts, to detect evil magic when it is being performed. I am afraid my instinct took over. I will not overstep my bounds again."

Avery did not reply. Achak continued to stare at the werewolf, a creature that legend described to be as dangerous as a black widow spider. Little was known, in truth, about the creatures as they had not been seen for thousands of years.

"What reason would Elder Hania have to betray us? He was your father." Avery took Achak's hand in hers, and twined her fingers, tugging his attention back to her. "Achak? Can you think of any reason why he would decide to do that?"

Achak scrubbed a hand across the back of his neck, in an attempt to ease the tension there. "I don't know," he said, shaking his head. "I think he was deceived by a lie. We all were at one time. The Spirit Clans have controlled the temple for as long as anyone can remember. To have an outsider march up and claim it as their own and disrupt the High Priestess they put in place over the objections of the Flesh Clans…maybe it was one change too many. And if this deception was being aided by an illusion of Helga's making he might not have seen it for what it really was. He was deceived."

"I found this on the man." The werewolf grunted and held out his paw, dropping an object into Achak's stretched out palm. It was a raven's feather. Achak handed it to Avery. She stared at the feather sadly.

"How long has he been betraying us?" she whispered. Avery reached over and took Achak's hand, holding it gently. She squeezed it, lending him her caring. "I know he was your father. I'm sorry, truly I am."

Achak took a deep breath then with a voice that hitched said "Probably long enough to lead us into a trap. Father knew our plans and what we have been up to, didn't he?" Achak eyes swept the woods around him and then came back to fix on the werewolf. "Long enough to know how we are guarded. We can expect an attack soon."

Avery snuggled into his chest, wrapping her arms around him and nestling her head against his chest. Avery's chest rose and fell in time to the steady beating of his heart as she breathed in the moist night time air, staring at the sky above, trying to calm her whirling thoughts. Ever since she crossed the Highland Spine, she had been betrayed by one after another.

Achak, whose hand had not left the blade at his side, stared at the werewolf, distrust of its intentions deeply etched on his face. It was evidenced in the tautness of his arm and the muscle that twitched in his cheek. Avery studied him for a moment and a sobering thought crept into her mind. *Can I trust Achak? If his father was willing to betray me, why not the son? Is there anyone I can trust?* She hated herself for her suspicions, but what did she really know about him? And yet, she could not believe it of Achak. She could not. He had saved her too many times. She shoved away her suspicion, refusing to give into fear.

Avery sat up abruptly and placed a hand on his bicep, which tightened with her touch. "You can relax. Samba is on our side. He was sent by Aossi."

Achak's eyes flicked to hers, unreadable then he unclenched his fist, but he did not put away the knife. As he rose, he pulled her to her feet, his hands wrapped around her arms. Avery's hand slid from his bicep up to his neck to cup his face. Her azure eyes met his chocolate ones. "I don't want to be alone tonight," he whispered. Achak's eyes searched hers, and his head lowered to brush her lips with a feather-light kiss.

"Neither do I," said Avery with a sigh "We both need comfort. Come. We are safe for tonight." Achak put his arm around her back and steered her to their dwindling fire.

Avery crawled into her blankets and rolled onto her side, staring at the black wall of forest beyond the edge of firelight. "Achak?"

"Yeah?"

"We are not going to win this fight, are we?" Silence greeted her words. She heard a shuffling sound. Suddenly, his chest pressed up against her back. He pulled her head down to rest on his arm, as a pillow.

"Now is not the time to worry about the future, Avery. Now is the time for rest. Tomorrow is a new day. We can worry about what the morning sun will bring all day. For now, you need rest. I need rest." Gently he ran his palm over her tense shoulders, working out the knots and kinks of the day. Slowly, she relaxed and fell asleep.

It was Achak who stared at the woods all night. He would not rest. Not when there was no one else to take the watch. His grief was a dull ache. He had not been close to his father, who had spent most of his time serving the High Priestess and had spent little time with his family. Achak hardly knew him if the truth were known. Yet, he felt the loss keenly. With his mother gone, he was now alone. He had no siblings. All he had, in the world, was the woman sleeping beside him. For all that his father had forced him to go with the Spirit Shield woman, he was glad now that he had not refused the command. His heart was lighter and happier for being able to spend this time with Avery. Even though she was younger in physical years than he was, she was mature in ways that no elder could understand. He brushed his hand over Avery's downy hair, channelling his grief into the need to defend this woman. No, sleep was not on his agenda this night. Instead he watched Avery sleep, watching the soft rise and fall of her chest as she slept, and a smile of contentment stole across his face. He settled in to wait for dawn.

CHAPTER 17

Aid from an Unlikely Source

THE MORNING SUN PEEKED THROUGH CLOUDS of frothy pink, bathing the campsite with the glow of another world as Achak gently shook Avery awake. The werewolf had faded back into the woods as dawn approached, keeping to the shadows. They would not be able to see him by daylight, but Achak knew he was there, watching. Once or twice, Achak thought he had seen other creatures of myth. The veil was truly weakened when the spirits of the animals were able to cross into the land of the living. They should not have been able to touch the world except during very special times. His spirit guardian was only able to come in times of dire need, but perhaps these were dire times. Still, the sun restricted their movements. Its harsh glare was dangerous to them, so they avoided direct sunlight.

Avery stretched and sat up rubbing her eyes for a moment then took the proffered slice of flatbread topped with crumbly cheese. Achak sat back down beside her and placed a jug of water between them to be shared.

"Sleep well?" he asked, crossing his long lean legs.

"Yes, thank you." Avery picked up the jug and took a long swallow before biting into her bread. "You?"

"As sound as a baby." Dark half-moons painted his lower lids and creases in the corners of his eyes betrayed the statement. He took a bite and chewed.

"Liar. I can see the dark circles under your eyes. You sat up all night, didn't you?"

"If you recall, we had just lost a pair of eyes set as a guard. I did not want any more surprises last night." Avery opened her mouth to protest, but he held one up to stop her. "I will sleep tonight. We can take shifts, but I think it would be wise to find a more defensible place to bed down, going forward. Some place that can be defended by one person alone."

"Fine, but tonight you sleep. Achak, I am sorry about your father."

Achak grimaced and took a swig of water before replying. "We were not close. We had...disagreed over how to best help you. Now I know why." Avery reached over and squeezed his shoulder in comfort. When he continued to stare at the dirt, she left him to his thoughts.

Finishing her meal, she dusted her hands off then stood and folded her blankets into a saddle roll. She carried the bundle over to her picketed horse then saddled her mount, tying the blanket behind it. Achak followed suit. Within a half hour, they had erased any evidence that they had camped there. Well, other than the dead body.

"There is one last task here. We need to bury my father," Achak said and led the way to the bank of the stream, the location of the attack. Avery's heart lurched at the thought, and sorrow for Achak's loss washed over her. However, when they arrived at the area of the attack, there was nothing to be found. It was as though the elder had never existed. Not a drop of blood or torn clothing, nothing remained of the man. Puzzled, they searched the grasses for signs of him but could find not a trace of his body.

"I do not understand. Where is he?" Achak rotated in a circle, trying to find a trail of anything to show that the body had been carried off. There was nothing. No broken flora, no crushed grass, no disturbed dirt. He sniffed the air and sniffed the ground. No copper smell. He smelled flowers and moist soil. Nothing more.

Avery turned in a circle and her suspicions grew. "I think we can take this as confirmation that he was one of Helga's. I think he has been taken away by the same forces that took the villagers. His soul has moved on to the underworld, and the Charun have collected the body. He has passed through the veil." Avery closed her eyes and walked through the space where the body should have lain, reaching out with her senses. Moving her hands slowly through the space, she felt the air. Suddenly, they paused. She could sense a tear in space, a separation in the fabric of reality, hot and sharp. She pushed a finger against the jagged edge, and *pain, anger,* and confusion spilled out of the void in such crushing intensity that she screamed and was flung violently away from it, spinning head over feet. A thin ribbon of light flashed like a lightning strike as she crashed into a tree trunk and crumpled to the ground, twitching violently.

"Avery!" Achak scrambled over to her side, careful to avoid the area of contact with the underworld, although it had now faded from his sight. He ran his hands over her body but could not find any sign of physical injury. Avery's injury was internal, an attack on her soul. Achak peeled back an eyelid and caught a glimpse of a red energy flickering across the white of her eye, and then it was gone. The twitching slowed and stilled. "Avery." He ran his hand through his hair, smoothing it back from his ear then bent to place his ear against her chest. Her heart was beating but erratically. Yet it did beat. She was not dead.

I need to get help for her quickly. Where should I go? I could go to a Flesh Clan village, but they would take her prisoner if they healed her at all. And the last thing we need is a run-in with the Charun while trying to get help for her. Ziona would be able to heal her, but I do not know where she is. Which leaves Faylea. Better the enemy you know than the one you don't.

Decision made, he picked up Avery and carried her back to their horses. He placed her in the saddle ahead of him and tied her in place so she would not fall off, then swung up behind her on the horse, snaking an arm around her waist to hold her to him. Leading Avery's horse, he touched his heels to the flank of his mount and took the animal path that meandered beside the pond, then turned and climbed along the stream leading out of the gully where they had set up camp for the evening. As he reached the crest of the hill, it leveled off and he booted his horse to a quick walk, anxious to put distance between their location and the rift in the veil.

Avery felt feverish, one minute burning up with such intensity that she began to sweat. The next second she turned ice cold, her skin pebbling. Occasionally, she would start muttering gibberish through clenched teeth. Once he thought he heard Helga's name on her lips and frowned. Where was Avery? Was she still with him in this form, or was she partially in the other realm? Fear chased him down the road. Fear that she was dying, that he was losing her to the underworld.

Two hours of travel brought him to the main road leading to Faylea. With no thought to caution, he turned to the north, intent on making the distance before dark. Before he could touch heels to flank, a rank of Primordial warriors rode out from the trees, blocking the path. Alarmed, Achak turned to head the other way, only to find that way was also blocked. He sharply reined his horse, and it snorted, dancing, feeling its rider's apprehension.

A man detached himself from the group and rode forward, his fur-lined vest ending in heavily muscled and tattooed arms. His short beard and mustache outlined heavy lips. His head was shaved bare.

"None may pass on this road except on the authorization of Artio. You will come with us. We will find help for your lady."

Achak's eyes darted around the ring of warriors. His options were limited. With a wounded Avery, he could not travel fast. He nodded his acceptance. Avery's hood shadowed her face so her tattoos were not visible. Perhaps news of Avery had not reached this village where they were camped. It was a risk he had to take. *They do not know who Avery is. I can keep that secret, and she does need help.* "Thank you for your assistance. I was riding to Faylea for medical help, but if you can help her, it would be appreciated."

They formed an escort and led the way back the way he had come, deeper into Flesh Clan territory.

Stay unconscious, Avery, please. Do not wake now.

CHAPTER 18

Morass-Fen

MORDECAI FROWNED AT THE MAP. The swamp on the plains sat a mere hour's ride from their current location, but he felt an overwhelming urge to visit the village of Morass-Fen. He had wandered its suspended living bridges once before as a small child of six. But he still remembered it, as clearly as if it were yesterday. Created by the twisting trunks of the swamp willow and matted with vines and ferns, the trees created pathways over the dangerous waters below. Plants floated on the surface of the murky depths. So crowded was the surface that it gave the illusion of solidity until a swamp snake ruffled the surface with its toothy spine.

Times were as desperate now as they had been all those years ago. The difference this time was that they were at the end of the journey, not the beginning, and he was an old man. Longer lived than any on the planet, thanks to the magic that coursed through his veins, but an old man nevertheless.

During his last visit to the village, he had secured the assistance of the village witch, an old hag of a woman who surely was dead by now. But it was not a safe thing to assume. Calleigh had ways of preserving life, ways he had used to preserve the souls of two infants while in the throes of a doomed birth. Calleigh remained the most remarkable woman he had ever met and for this, he would make the journey to the swamp. He would catch up with Cayden, Ziona, and Genii when he could.

Mordecai tugged his hood tighter to his head, the extra depth protecting his face from the constant drizzle that had chased them from the foothills. The muddy road was the hardest surface around them, squelching under the horses' hooves.

He tucked the map back up his sleeve and pulled on the reins, steering his horse down a barely discernible path of sand, riding away from the others. After a couple minutes, he heard a soft plopping sound, and Genii appeared out of the grey gloom to ride up beside him.

"I thought you were going to stay behind?" Mordecai said out of the side of his cowl.

"I have decided I wish to meet this witch. I may have met her before, but my memory is fractured on this part, but I too feel the urge to discover if she is still alive."

Mordecai nodded and rode on.

"You are not as I expected," Genii said into the silence.

"Oh? And how is that?"

"I was led to believe that the great Mordecai was a selfish person, seeking to elongate his life by attaching himself to the gods. You have lived a queerly long time. Why is that?"

Mordecai chuckled. "Only the young find long life fascinating. By my age, you begin to realize that you have left far more behind than there is ahead. Friends. Family. Dreams. Hopes. Aspirations. What little is still ahead begins to lack luster. For three hundred years, I have fought to stay alive for a sole purpose. To return the Spirit Shields to their rightful place and repair the rupture that began with their deaths. To live this long is no reward. It was mere necessity. Yet lately, I feel tired. The flesh weakens. Death comes for us all. The only question will be who will receive my soul? Will it be Helga, who will find no end of tortures to amuse herself for eternity? Or will it be Cayden and a hope of rebirth into a simpler age, one free of war and destruction? One with a return to the worship of the gods?" He slowly shook his head. "Even I cannot tell what the future holds. But there is one who might be able to see a glimmer of the future. Calleigh."

Genii rode along in silence, musing over his words. When he spoke, it was with a soft voice. "Then I am happy to accompany you. I also would know the truth of the future. I admit I am anxious to live since I have been more dead than alive for the last three hundred years. I am not sure what I have to live for, though. Perhaps she will have these answers too."

"I do not know what will be left of the village. It was always the birthplace of magic in the world, but during Alcina's time, she sent raids to the village on a regular basis. Many of those who used to call the swamp home were killed or ran away. Calleigh would not have left. I am not sure she could. She probably died long ago, but I am drawn to find out."

On the horizon, tall drooping trees grew out of the sand and the drizzle became a clinging mist that dripped from their cloaks and the nose of their horses. The trees themselves were weighed down by the weight of the water droplets, slender limbs brushing the ground and in the middle of the wall of greenery roots snaked and twisted over each other, twisting to form a tightly meshed road, nearly smooth because all it was constructed of was rounded roots. The wall of greenery disguised the fact that the trail had left the ground, gently sloping into the air until the roots lost touch with the soil and hung suspended from the trees themselves.

The remnants of a swamp were visible below, heavy with the odour of rotting vegetation and aquatic life. The duck moss on the surface was brilliant green, floating on an oil slick of decay, the contrast so brilliant that it made the still surface a polished mirror, reflecting the weak light that passed through the canopy overhead. The swamp was still and silent. Not a frog croaked, not a bug chirped. Nothing stirred in the inky depths, but Mordecai was not fooled. He had seen what lived in the swamp. Place a wrong foot, and there would be no foot.

"Do not touch the water," he said quietly as they rode slowly across the suspended bridge. "Do not drink the water. Only drink what drips from the trees and is caught in your vessel."

The main bridge into the village ended on a central island, which existed only as a foundation for scores of other bridges that swung out into the trees. There were no roads, just more bridges and more swamp and more inky black water. Genii halted his horse and stared around, frowning. "This place has the feel of the dead. I do not think we will find anything living here."

"I agree, but we must make sure. Come. Calleigh's house is this way." Mordecai took a right bridge that raised high into the air, before twisting in a corkscrew back to a convergence of tree limbs in one of the largest trees in the swamp. Tucked onto the stout branch was a squat hut, made of bamboo reeds and covered in clinging vines. The only thing giving away that it was a house was the door set in an arched frame.

As they rode closer, the true state of the hut was revealed. Large gashes rent the vines and ripped into the fibrous mat of roots that made up the walls of the structure. The door hung on one hinge and was splintered as though struck with an axe. The sap still dripped from the wounds in the walls.

Mordecai halted Genii with an outstretched hand, studying the scene for a moment before dismounting. Genii followed suit, and they silently crept toward the hut, listening for any hint that the perpetrators were still in the vicinity. A low moan issued from the interior, and they cautiously shouldered their way through the shattered opening.

The interior of the abode was unrecognizable. Every piece of furniture was smashed, every jar, every cupboard emptied. Most of the contents had ended up in a heap in the middle of the floor and then had been set on fire. Broken chair legs and piles of books, torn and loose papers, and even a painting hauled off, all doused with the oil of smashed lanterns and set ablaze. The flames had licked up the walls, following trailers of oil, the long scorch marks shaped like blackened teeth. The flames appeared to have been suddenly doused, leaving a damp smoky smell to the room.

Mordecai summoned a light and held the floating orb above his hand as they checked the interior, peeking behind a beaded curtain at the back of the room in which was located a low bed and a pile of blankets, and a smashed dresser with every drawer upended.

Coming back into the main room, they heard the moan again, and the pile of burned debris in the middle of the room moved. Shocked, they froze for a second and then hurried over to the detritus, pulling off the charred bamboo poles.

There, under the remains of the collapsed ceiling, lay Calleigh. Her hair had caught fire and had burned away, leaving aged skin, mottled with moles and now fresh bubbling blisters. Her right arm had also blistered along its entire length, but her face was unscathed. She'd used her arm to cover it. She moaned again as Genii and Mordecai quickly hauled away the debris and freed her from her funeral pyre. Then, Genii bent down and scooped the old woman into his arms and carried her back to her bed behind the beaded curtain.

Mordecai found a mostly intact pitcher and filled it with water from a barrel outside the door, then rushed back inside. Calleigh moaned as they treated her wounds, soothing her burns and easing her pain. Mordecai laid his hands on either side of her face and muttered a spell, seeking to know the extent of her injuries. Slowly he lowered his hands. She was dying. There were too many injuries inside for him to heal in time. Sadly, he blocked some of her pain and then picked up her hand in both of his, patting it, attempting to wake the woman from her pain-induced coma.

"Calleigh. Calleigh, wake up. We need to speak to you. You are not in danger any longer. Come back to us." He massaged her uninjured palm, seeking the pain control points of the nerve, pressing gently.

Calleigh's lashes drifted open, a swampy reflection of green shot with gold and darkened in pain. She drew a ragged breath, her eyes flickering from one man to the other. Her prune-shrunken cheeks creased into a glad smile, as a tear born of pain trembled and spilled out of the corner of one eye.

"My prayer has been answered by the gods." She grasped a hand of each man in hers, squeezing them with surprising strength. "I prayed that in my final days, my sons would be returned to me. And they have been. I rejoice in our reunion." Her arms trembled, and she lost her grip on their hands. "Beware of Helga. She holds more power than you can possibly know. Her Charun are multiplying like rats and infest the world. Genii, there's a lad, reach under my bed. There is a chest buried beneath the floorboards. Take it. It will explain everything. It is my journal and a few other important things I wished to keep from Helga's grasp. It is meant for the pair of you and no one else." Her breath rattled as she wheezed air out to form the words.

"Now go, there is nothing for you here. You are the last hope for magic in the world. Right the wrongs. Guard the Spirit Shields. They have an important task to fulfill, or we are all doomed." She sucked in another laboured breath then whispered on the exhale "I love you." Calleigh's chest stilled, and the light of life fled her eyes.

Mordecai, eyebrows climbing into his hair, tugged on his beard, the shock of her words a slap to his wrinkled face. Recovering slightly, he whispered, a hitch in his voice, "May you rest in the warm embrace of the Mother. May your soul be delivered to the Spirit Shields for protection. Safe journey, Mother." A blue mist rose from the collapsing shell then soared out into the swamp, seeking its way home.

CHAPTER 19

Slave for a Day

THE RIVER OF LAVA that ran through the center of the cave tossed waves of heat into the air that curled and crashed down on the slaves working alongside the Charun. When it contacted the cooler stone surface, it hissed as though alive, leaving a slick trail of moisture that threatened to toss the weariest and most distracted of the slaves into the raging inferno.

Helga had lost thirty more Primordial slaves this week to just that sort of an incident, but the losses were acceptable. Besides, with the fresh blood she had incorporated into the effort, the losses were affordable. The knights of Cathair were a hardy lot, strong and lean and defiant. They would serve her long and hard before they eventually died.

She stood on a curved outcropping of stone that formed a balcony overlooking the pit below, watching her newest slaves herded into position as they were chained to the poles set as spokes on wheel around a central hub. There were actually six hubs, six gigantic wheels laid out a long row parallel to the river of lava to which knights of Cathair were being chained. She had thirty-six new slaves to power her machines.

The central shafts of the wheels sank into the stone, an auger of sharp teeth that ground away at the shale and metamorphic stone, chewing ever deeper into the rock. Two of the six drills had breached the wall of the river below. Helga left her perch and strode down the curving walkway to the pit below and over to the wheel that had the deepest penetration into the substrate. Two Charun poured water from large barrels continuously onto the drill bits. They had snapped many of them in the beginning as the metals overheated with friction and weakened. Now they kept a steady cooling stream of barely melted snow, gathered from the peaks of the Highland Spine, flowing over the heated metal. A long line of Primordial women and children snaked back through the cavern to a stone chimney that opened up through the mountain. Down this chute dropped snow and water in a continuous stream, fed by slaves on the mountain side. The women and children of the villages carried pails of rapidly melting snow to the barrels, filling them continuously.

One knight stood out as the leader, a broad-shouldered and deep-chested youth of an age with Cayden. He glared a challenge as he took up his position at a thick timber pole and was shackled into place. His bare back was striped with whip marks. The Charun had not been gentle in their handling of the knights. As Helga watched, five of his companions were pushed into similar positions and chained to the remaining poles set as spokes on a wheel around a central hub.

Helga studied the dark-bearded man. *He might make a suitable replacement for Genii,* she mused, her thin lips curving into a self-satisfied smile. *Maybe it's time for a new form of amusement.*

As Helga approached, a Charun took up its whip and flogged the nearest Kingsman, who cried out with pain and arched away from the sting of the biting leather. The others pushed harder at the wheel, and it began to rotate faster, the grating noise of metal on stone rising in pitch as it spun.

The Kingsmen were moving at a fast walk by the time Helga reached the wheel. She held up her hand to halt it. They eased off on their efforts, relaxing back to a walk and then slumped over their spoke in exhaustion as the wheel slowed and stopped.

Helga stepped up onto the rim of the wheel and walked across a broad oar to peer down the center of the hub to the surface below. A bluish mist was visible at the bottom of the bore. It writhed and then smoothed, flowing swiftly and then slowly, the light cast by the mist reflecting off the planes and hollows of her narrow face. A grin stretched her lips into a pleased smile. A new breach meant fresh souls to harvest.

She straightened and made her way back to the tallest of the Charun. It had been a commander in the armies of old, back when Cayden had used his true name, Caerwyn.

"Captain Brennan, this hole is deep enough. Have these men dismantle the wheel and move it to a new location further down the line. You can begin the extraction process for this pocket of souls."

The Charun bowed at the waist in submission. "It will be as you command, mistress."

She continued to the next wheel, the former Captain Brennan following behind her to perform the same inspection. Only the faintest glow was visible in the bore.

The breech will be soon. Another day perhaps, Helga thought, tapping a slender finger against her lip then turned to look at the Primordial men slumped over their spokes, barely alive. "Remove these men and replace them with our Kingsmen friends. Redouble the efforts on this wheel. The new slaves should bring fresh energy, and this bore is nearly deep enough. It should breach very soon. This is the next one to move down the line. I want it in place by this evening." The Charun bowed in acknowledgment, its face swallowed by the heavy hood that was never removed, even in the excessive heat. With a snap of its fingers, six Charun floated up behind each of the slumped men and reaching down, grabbed each man by the neck and snapped them as though snapping twigs. The Charun bent and unchained the corpses and carried them over to the river of lava and tossed them into the fiery stream where they flashed and were gone, the bodies instantly burnt to a crisp.

A new set of knights were dragged forward and chained into position. The wheel ground into motion again as whips cracked the air.

Helga didn't acknowledge the activity behind her. She bypassed inspecting the remaining wheels, knowing that they were not even close to a breakthrough. As she walked past the wheel to which Ryder was chained, she paused and then walked over to him. He kept his face averted, ignoring her presence, yet the set of his shoulders screamed defiance and anger tightly held in check. He was a firecracker waiting to burst.

Oh yes, it will be fun to tame this one. He will be a pleasure to bring to heel. She drew a finger down the side of his cheek and trailed it across his mouth. Ryder jerked away from her touch, and his eyes met hers, deep brown with loathing. Helga shivered. *The hatred is so intense that I should be burnt to a crisp right now! Yes, this one is not destined to die here.*

"I have need of a new manservant," she snapped. "Unchain him and bring him to me." The Charun named Brennan bowed low and drifted between Helga and the slave, but she had turned away. "Redouble your efforts! Next time I come to the pit, I expect the holes to be deep enough to complete the extraction. I will take no more excuses. Get back to work!"

A flurry of activity swallowed her footsteps as the chamber ground back into motion. She did not look back. They were already forgotten. Her thoughts dwelt on the young knight Ryder.

CHAPTER 20

Captain Brennan

RYDER'S MURDEROUS EYES followed Helga's retreat as she leisurely climbed the walkways as though this were a simple stroll around the gardens, leaving the pit full of dying men, women and children behind. A Charun drifted up to him and unlocked his shackles, then grabbed him by the arm and dragged him away from the spoke. Ryder did not resist. He knew it was a battle he could not win. He met the eyes of his men and silently promised that he would be back for them. They seemed to understand and quick smiles twitched on their faces. They would do their best to stay alive. That was the plan they had settled on. Stay alive to fight another day. The day would come. Maybe this was the break they needed.

The pit was lost from view as the Charun named Brennan dragged Ryder into a darkened cave that lengthened into a pitch-black hallway. Ryder stumbled frequently, not able to see the floor or walls or ceiling, but the Charun had no difficulty traversing the dark corridor.

So much had changed in the last year since he and Cayden had left their home, the village called Sanctuary-by-the-Sea. *So much has changed since I had slew the legion scout by accident,* and all of it was inevitable in the end. Fate had taken its course. *I can hardly believe it. Cayden a Spirit Shield!* Ryder would not have believed it if he hadn't seen the proof himself. But Cayden was more than that, if he had attracted the attention of the likes of Helga, goddess of the underworld. Ryder wondered what the connection was and how she knew him so well.

When they had discovered the Well of Souls and Cayden had revealed that he was its guardian, Ryder had swelled with pride. When Cayden had turned out to be the missing heir to the kingdom, Ryder had rejoiced. There had never been a question in his mind about leaving and going back home. All he had ever dreamed of was being a knight and serving alongside the king of Cathair.

In the time since Cayden had left Cathair, at the mysterious beckoning of his sister Avery, Ryder had schooled and trained the men recruited to be knights. They had perfected their weapon skills, been drilled in tactics, and had trained for sieges. Everything expected of a knight.

What they had not planned for was an ambush while on maneuvers. Oh, not the fighting kind. It had come in the form of a peddler with goods heading for Cathair. One of the knights had purchased a tonic that promised to give a boost of strength for the coming field training contests scheduled for the next day. Thinking to impress Ryder, the knight had slipped the tonic into everyone's ale that night around the campfire, laughing about how everyone boasted of being superhuman but rarely showed the talent or strength. But instead of giving strength, it had been a sleeping potion and shortly after drinking it, all were slumped around the fire, snoring as if their wives slept nearby.

Only Ryder had not drunk any of the ale. When the hundred or so Charun had drifted into the light of the campfire, he knew they were doomed. He could not save them. He could not save himself. Buried in their midst was a scared, skinny peddler, wringing his hands and begging to be let go.

"I have done what you asked!" he had gasped to the faceless, merciless beings. "Please, let me go! I have a wife and children!" The lead Charun had casually backhanded the man across the face. With the crunch and snap of bones breaking, the man had crumpled to the ground. On the whole, Ryder thought the better plan was to feint sleep. He had relaxed his body, slowed his breathing and waited for capture. It was that or die as swiftly as the peddler had.

A thought struck Ryder as he was dragged down the dark hall. This was the same Charun who had led the pack that had captured them. It was taller than the others. A vertical slice in his cloak caused it to flap in a unique way that was missing in the others. Ryder could always pick him out of the pack. He broke the silence, overcoming his fear of the spectral being. "Why did she call you Brennan?"

The Charun paused fractionally, the hitch so small Ryder wondered if he had really felt it. *I surprised him with the question.*

"I do not know. It is a name she calls me."

"Is it your real name?"

"Charun do not have names. We are made to serve."

"Made? Made from what?"

"From the blue mist in the bore. And from the dead."

Ryder stumbled in earnest this time, as shock thrilled through his system, as the truth dawned on him.

"You are made from the blue mist?"

"Yes, we are born of fire and mist and blood."

Holy spirits! Ryder swore silently. *She is robbing the Well of Souls! That is why she had us removed! To gain access to the well!* His eyes drifted nervously to the Charun at his side. Or m*aybe to make more creatures like Captain Brennan?* Ryder recognized the name. It was an ancient family surname, one that stories were told about. Somewhere inside the disfigured shell was a man that had lived, served, and died as a Kingsman, an early knight of the realm called to service as Spirit Shield defender. Ryder was sure of it. But how much remained? When a soul was snatched and enslaved and transformed in such a manner how much remained of the original? Dare he ask? He sneaked a peek at the Charun beside him and asked the simplest question he had.

"Where are we going?"

"You are to be joined."

"Joined? What does that mean?"

"You are to be mate to our mistress. You are to become a shade."

An electric thrill pulsed through Ryder's body so intense he might as well have been struck by a bolt of lightning. His heart lurched in fear. *A shade! No!* His limbs quivered in the hands of the Charun, and the Charun's faceless gaze swung toward him.

"You should be afraid," Captain Brennan hissed. "A shade never dies. You will serve the great mistress forever."

Ryder fought the panic rising in his throat. He wanted to scream but choked back the urge.

"Captain Brennan, I am a knight and a Kingsman," he pleaded, "and you were a knight and a Kingsman. Do you remember?"

"I do not know that name," he snarled "I have no name."

"You do remember. I can feel it. You have just forgotten. Try to remember. You do not want to do this. I can help you escape. I am here fighting to protect the Spirit Shields, the ones who guard the Well of Souls, that protect the dead from being twisted into what you have become."

The Charun tightened its grip on Ryder and he grunted with the pain.

"I do not know of what you speak."

"Yes, you do. You have seen the other Charun created. You know the process." Silence greeted his words. "Help me, please! You once fought alongside the Spirit Shields. Fight again! Reject this existence. You can make a difference beyond that which you died for originally."

The Charun's grip eased, but he did not slow or stop. "I must obey my mistress. I must."

Frustrated, Ryder tried to think of another angle, some other thought that would trigger the memories he was convinced lay just below the surface.

"How did you get the tear in your cloak?"

The Charun's hood swung his direction, then back down the long, dark hallway.

"When we were sent to collect your knights, one of them was not fully asleep and fought back."

"Why didn't you snap his neck like you have done to all the others? Why hesitate?" Ryder pressed. "Did he catch you by surprise? Somehow, I doubt that was the case," Ryder pressed. "So, why?"

The Charun did not reply. The silence stretched until Ryder thought that he would not answer.

"He reminded me of myself at that age," the Charun whispered, the hiss more a sizzle for being so soft. "He was even missing an eye. I noticed that right before I snapped his neck."

Ryder's heart sank. He knew who had died. He had no further words.

Neither did the Charun.

CHAPTER 21

A Spy or Two

NELSON EASED BACK from the edge of the rock face, grinning, having seen his fill. The tents below were haphazardly arranged with no distinguishable organization. The fires burned low with men passed out by the fireside or within tents. Not a person stirred in the camp. The guard set around the perimeter of the encampment slumped against trees or had slid onto their sides, mouths open and snoring.

The Kingsmen with him waited in the trees, holding the reins to his mount. All were fully armoured and bristling with weapons, ready for battle, but nothing stirred around them.

"Have Fabian's scouts checked in?"

"Aye, they report the same conditions, every man passed out asleep, including the captains. We have detected none awake. Remarkable, really."

"Yes, we have been strangely fortunate that all were greedy enough to partake. But the sleeping potion will only last so long. There wasn't enough alcohol in those barrels for everyone to get drunk. So as an added measure, we added a healthy dose of this to increase the effects of the small shot of brandy they consumed." He bent down and snapped off a segment of a leafy plant with flowers with yellow petals. "Senna has a wonderful relaxing effect on the bowels. I think when they awaken they will find it difficult to do anything other than squat."

He took his reins from the lieutenant holding them and swung up into the saddle.

"That does not mean that the way is entirely clear though. Caution is needed." He heeled his mount and headed away from the camp, the other Kingsmen falling in behind him. Now was the time to run the gauntlet, while the path was clear. Nelson did not want to risk his men in open warfare. There were more important matters at hand. If the knights truly did not guard the well any longer, then he needed every soul alive, not dead.

They kept to the trees and hid as they thinned in the hollows between the hills, conscious of the fact that a long glass or a lookout might be able to spot them. Once they came across a scout hiding in a tree. They would not have seen him except that the soldier's horse whinnied to their mounts as they rode up. An arrow through the chest dispatched the man, but not before a pigeon flashed out of the tree, winging its way swiftly out of arrow range. Bad luck that.

Half an hour after that encounter, they were joined by the Fabian's men at the appointed meeting grounds, a field denuded of grass by a flock of grazing sheep visible at the crest of the hill. The field had belonged to one of the outer farms for Upper Cathair. Nelson's heart lifted at the sight. *This must be a sign that the village was undisturbed and the people intact. Perhaps the farmer was also safe.*

As he rode up to Fabian, Nelson noted the various bandages tied to arms and legs.

"Your reception does not appear to have been as quiet as ours," he said as he pulled up beside the stout baker.

"Oh, they were asleep all right. The lot we ran into were not with the camp. They were returning with orders from Cyrus." He grimaced and flexed his hand, wrapped in blood-stained bandages. "Took a slice to the hand," he grunted, seeing the direction of Nelson's scrutiny and the eyebrows lifted in silent enquiry. "There were not a lot of them but enough to do harm. Ten legionnaires are nothing to sneeze at. But still, not to our calibre."

The men parted, and two Kingsmen pushed through the crowd with a woman, her hands tied behind her back. She was dressed in legionnaire clothing, her black hair cut short and square. She could have passed for a youth. "We captured this soldier, only he turned out to be a she."

Nelson leaned forward and whispered, "You know how I don't like killing women."

Fabian nodded and watched the woman approach. As she saw the captains sitting on horseback, her back stiffened and she glared at them, narrow-eyed defiance in every ounce of her bearing. Her chin lifted, and she shrugged off her captor's hands, standing free of them in front of Nelson and Fabian.

"This is your one capture? A woman?"

"Yes. She was not in the fighting. She hung back from the battle. We found her hiding, slinking away. She is dressed like one of them but does not act like a legionnaire. More like a spy if you ask me. I think she will be useful before the end."

The woman spat at them, murderous glare in her eyes.

Nelson and Fabian exchanged glances. "Put her on a horse. She rides with us."

The Kingsmen guarding her saluted, and one ran off to get her a mount. He was back in a second with a horse, and then he tied her hands so they were bound in front of her. She grabbed the pommel with two hands and climbed into her saddle, taking the reins placed in her hands. Fabian and Nelson moved alongside her and began a slow walk across the field. The one hundred or so Kingsmen fell in behind them.

They rode in silence for a while. Then Fabian said, "Are you hungry?" He reached inside his saddlebag without waiting for a response and pulled out a package of flatbread and offered it to her. She shook her head. "It's not poisoned or drugged, I assure you."

"I am not hungry." Her voice had a musical quality, high-pitched and lyrical. The accent was surely Primordial.

"Is this the first time you have spoken?"

She nodded, clamping her lips shut again.

"A wise decision overall. How did you get along in the legion without talking?"

She mimed a sign language. Nelson grinned. "Clever. A mute would not be able to tell stories, right? So, they trusted you to go places without fear of you spilling your secrets and also hiding the fact that you are a woman *and* a Primordial." She smiled a quiet smile. "Who was your contact? Let me guess, you were reporting to Cyrus himself, or is it to the Primordial leadership?" Her smile widened, but she said nothing.

"A double agent," said Fabian.

"I will neither confirm nor deny. You may speculate all you wish. Just know that I mean the Spirit Shields no harm. But understand this. My aid is crucial to their success. Dare I say it is essential? Without it, they may very well fail in their quest. You do not dare silence me or restrict me in any fashion." Her swamp green eyes stared at him. Gold flecks reflected in their depths.

Nelson and Fabian openly stared at her, confusion and worry chasing each other across the planes of their faces.

"This was not a chance meeting, was it?" Fabian said flatly.

"No, it was not," the woman said quietly.

"Who are you?" asked Fabian.

"What is your name?" asked Nelson right on top of Fabian's words.

She remained silent, staring straight ahead.

"All right, what should we call you?" said Fabian.

"Calleigh." She hesitated slightly, then her face firmed. "You can call me Calleigh."

CHAPTER 22

Duty's Heavy Toll

CAYDEN AND ZIONA RODE SIDE BY SIDE, the silence stretching. The harsh words of their most recent argument hung in the air between them. The abrupt departure of Mordecai and Genii had left Cayden a foul mood, one she was stuck dealing with. Denzik and Gaius trailed a little behind, leaving them space to spar in peace. Ziona did not think they wanted to be near two lovers quarreling. Ziona glanced at the king and bit her lip to keep from speaking what she longed to toss in his face. The quarrel had started out innocently enough.

"Why don't you call down Brimstone and soar above the trees for a while. You know you forget your worries and fears when you are flying."

"I am not going to leave you down here alone!" he said, shocked. "There are enemies all around us."

"I am not alone! We have Denzik and Gaius not one hundred paces behind us. Even if that weren't true, why would that matter, Cayden? I am the one protecting you, remember? And on Brimstone's back, you are untouchable." Guilt flashed briefly when she realized that she had two people to protect now, rather than just Cayden. Nevertheless, she nodded, satisfied with the plan. He would be safer in the skies, and she could blend into the brush land and not be detected as a Primordial rider. She could guard from the woods, and the other two men could act as decoys. Her first duty was to Cayden's protection. She could guard Cayden and the baby at the same time and keep them all safe.

"You are not my protector, Ziona. Not anymore." The flat tone of his voice dismissed the subject as ridiculous. Ziona bristled.

"Excuse me? Did you just fire me? You can't do that you know. My mission is given to me by the temple. As a seeker, my job was to find you *and protect you.* Nothing has changed about that bonding or the one since…other than it has become more…intimate." She blushed slightly, as Cayden's embarrassment slid along the connection. As she said it, she felt a familiar heating along their soul bond. It only heightened the flush of her cheeks.

"I do not need a protector, Ziona. I know who I am now and *what I must do.* There *is* no protecting me. That was *never* the plan." His voice trailed off, and his eyes stared at nothing for a moment, lost in thought, thoughts she could not share despite the bond. Cayden's voice firmed. "Now, I must do my task alone. I will not have you attempting to follow me into a danger you cannot protect me from. I would not have you hurt on my account. That is my final word on the matter."

"*Your final word?* What makes you think I will take orders from you?" Ziona wanted to stamp her foot, but it was firmly wedged in her stirrup. Instead, her horse jumped ahead at the pressure as she reined it around sharply, blocking Cayden's path. "You may be the king of Cathair, but you are not my king and no order you give is binding. You may be a Spirit Shield, but I was protecting the temple long before you knew it existed. You may be descended from the gods, but you are *not a god.* I will do as I please!"

Cayden reined in and stared at her, his face a thundercloud. Ziona struggled to keep from dropping her eyes under his angry glare as his face darkened with fury.

"You think this is a game, don't you? *Do you really think that we are going to survive this?*" he yelled, pushing his horse forward into hers and leaning forward until he was nose to nose with Ziona. "We have next to no chance of making it out of this alive! Helga knows our every step. She has the Soul Fetch, Ziona! Mordecai told us, remember? I had hoped it was safely lost when Alcina perished. *Think, dammit! Helga has the Soul Fetches!* You know what happens to me when it is triggered." He sat back in his saddle, the fight going out of him. Despondence tugged the corners of his mouth down, and he rubbed his aching temple, a muscle twitching in his cheek as pain shot across his forehead.

"Avery and I *must* confront Helga," he said in a quieter voice, "but *I will not be responsible for your death, Ziona.* I nearly lost you once. I could not bear to lose you again. If you insist on this path, you will be a constant distraction, a constant reminder of what could be. What I wish could be, and everything I have to lose. Even if I were to survive, with you gone I would still crave death." He shook his head like a bear with a sore tooth and growled much the same way. "If you are dead, I will lose all will to fight. With you dead, I am lost." He whispered the last words then reined around Ziona and continued down the road, moodily swaying in the saddle.

Ziona touched the flanks of her horse with her heels and rode up beside him, staring straight ahead, pondering the problem. There was no way she was going to do as he asked and stay behind. That was out of the question. With every passing mile, Cayden's mood dipped lower until she feared it would fall so low that he gave up. The headaches had started again. They both knew the source of them. Cayden blamed himself for not destroying the Soul Fetches when he was in the underworld, but he had not known they were there.

Moreover, he blamed Mordecai for not telling him about them when he had had the chance. Another fight had erupted over Mordecai's loyalty. That that the wizard had known of the Fetch's presence in the underworld and not told him rankled Cayden. His trust of the wizard was severely shaken. Ziona did not think that Mordecai would do anything to harm Cayden. She believed him to be loyal to the Spirit Shield, yet she could not convince Cayden. His doubts persisted. Mordecai's unannounced departure a few days back with Genii at his heels had heightened Cayden's suspicions. Fear of betrayal was a rank odour that wrinkled Cayden's nose.

Ziona feared he would not allow the wizard close to him going forward, that his intent was to isolate himself from everyone who had aided him before, including herself.

"What about Mordecai?" She tossed the question into the silence where it dropped like a stone down a well, bouncing off the walls of distance between them.

Cayden grunted and did not reply. She reached out to him through the bond.

"Don't do that." His head turned to stare at her angrily. "Stop trying to pick my emotions apart. I will share what I want to share."

"I'm not...," she began, but he ran right over of her words, as his hand rose to his forehead again. "My mind is not a book for you to read at your leisure. Learn to respect my privacy." The slap could not have hurt more if he had physically raised his hand. She bit down on her reaction, stemming the flood of hurt that she knew he would feel along the bond. "And quit sulking. It's so annoying!"

After that, Ziona did not try to speak to him anymore. There was little sense with the mood he was in.

A fine drizzle had begun, and the damp crept under her cloak. She shivered and pulled her hood closer around her head, but the heavy wool did little to warm her frozen heart. She could not speak her concerns aloud, but she would be dammed if she would leave the Spirit Shield undefended. But beyond that, if the time came and failure seemed assured, she had other duties to perform. Bond or no bond, she would see them performed. Ziona prayed that it would not become necessary. She loved Cayden...*but I will do as I must as seeker. He cannot be allowed to fail.* The rain picked up and soaked through her cloak, but she no longer felt the cold. Her heart was a frozen pond. *I will do what I must.*

CHAPTER 23

Detour

CAYDEN RODE OFF AHEAD of the group, his deep hood pulled forward to fend off the rain, but more importantly to fend off Ziona. His heart ached. He longed to pull her into his arms, not to push her away. It hurt to be so cruel and distant with her, but he could not afford the distraction of her presence, and lately he sensed a mental barrier had been erected, as though she was keeping something from him. That barrier bothered him in ways that a simple secret could not. He did not want to be suspicious of Ziona, yet something was going on. It had been bad enough when Alcina held his Soul Fetch, but it had been a simple twisted pleasure she took in controlling his actions. She'd made him dance on strings of pleasure and pain for personal amusement.

But the news that Helga held his doll had rocked him to the core. Ziona could not understand the horror coursing through him because she did not really believe it, not fully. Mordecai might have some working knowledge, but they did not understand the total lack of remorse that made up Helga's nature. Hers was a soul without a soul. She had long ago surrendered hers to the underworld and merged with it in the cataclysmic battle that had ended all of their lives, one way or another. Mortal and immortal ties cut, each in a different way but no less dead. Even Helga, who had not perished, was not truly alive. Where once she had roamed free across the land, now she pulled strings from behind a curtain, a curtain that was the veil between the worlds.

Yet like a giant spider, spinning webs and twitching threads, she tweaked her influence over the world of flesh. She schemed endlessly. Whatever her plan, she relentlessly strove to extend her control and influence over all mankind, Primordial and Cathairian.

For Cayden, there could be no greater horror than to be controlled by the very one who swore to destroy him, *who has indeed ended my existence once before and was…*he could not come up with the words. A creeping terror slithered up his backbone, and he shivered. He threw back his hood and lifted his face to the heavens, letting the tears of the gods mingle with his own to wash his face. The gods.

He had not thought about his father, Morpheus, in a very long time. In a long distant memory from another time and era, an image flashed into his mind.

He was four years old. It was one of those sparkling clear fall days when the sky was such an intense blue one could fall into it and not get wet. Cayden rode on his father's broad shoulders, giggling and his chubby fists tangled in his father's dark curly hair, hanging on for dear life. His father ran down the hillside, arms outstretched. Cayden (or Caerwyn as he was called then) bounced on his shoulders so badly his teeth rattled, but he did not care. His father *flew*, or pretended to, his voice building to a fevered winded pitch as he recited the last words of the cantata to the gods rather than sing it. (He had a voice like a drowning bullfrog.) His father slipped on the slick grass. With a shrieking laugh, Cayden soared over his father's head into the air. The arc was spectacular. On the downward fall, he was snatched mid-tumble by a midnight black Pegasus, his teeth gripping his tunic. It was his first introduction to the Pegasus Brimstone who was to be his guardian and his companion. A gift of the gods, the Pegasus could exist in the mortal world and in the world of the eternals. They could move from mortal to celestial without harm coming to them.

His mind flashed forward to a different memory, this time of a furious father. Morpheus came over the hillside, dragging a kicking and screaming twelve-year-old Helga by the arm. She was covered in blood. Her hands were slick with it, and her hair was sticking out wildly in all directions, bits of leaves and twigs tangled in her silky black tresses.

Morpheus was yelling at her and shook her hard, so hard that Helga's head bobbed back and forth on her slender neck. She shouted something back at him, angrier than Cayden had ever seen her. She tried to pull out of her father's grip, but Morpheus did not let go. Helga kicked at his leg, but he held tight to his struggling daughter.

"Brimstone! Take Cayden back to the house," Morpheus yelled.

Cayden, wide-eyed, shoved the sticks he had been collecting into his satchel. He had a mind to trying his hand at carving. He loved the feel of wood in his hands. Puzzled, he'd started to walk toward his father and sister, when he was jerked from the ground by the Pegasus.

"Brimstone, put me down!" he'd hollered at the Pegasus as he dangled in its jaws, the ground shrinking below him.

As Brimstone's wings beat the air to gain height, a horrific scene in the forest was revealed. A flash of pure white, splattered in red blood, the ground trampled, the grasses crushed. No blue mist rose from the crushed grasses, rather darkness encircled the scene, a ring of black curling mist that spiraled and bent in on itself. Cayden could not tear his eyes away. A unicorn lay on its side, a long gash across its throat. Its belly had been sliced open, and its entrails removed and arranged in a bloodied circle, forming a pentagram of the underworld. Candles had been set at focal points and a vortex in the center sucked the swirling mist toward it.

Caerwyn screamed for Brimstone to put him down. There was no blue mist. There was no soul left. The unicorn was gone, forever, wiped from existence. Adult Cayden shuddered. The image shimmered and faded.

From that day on, Helga had turned her back on them all. From that day on, she served only the dead. Cayden had tried to talk to Helga about the episode with the unicorn, but she had flat out refused, rejecting every advance he had made. She withdrew into a shell as hard as an armadillo's. When she was sixteen, she had walked away from their family home, never to return. Later, Cayden had heard she was living in the Highland Spine, but by that time their father had departed this world, leaving them to fend for the people as best they could. The sorting of duties had been without pomp or ceremony. Morpheus's last admonition before returning to the heavens was to be very wary of Helga and that she was lost to them.

Suddenly, a white-hot poker jabbed into Cayden's temple, and his head exploded with pain. He screamed and fell from his horse and hit the ground hard. His body spasmed into a tight ball on the ground, his arms wrapped around his head. His scream rose in pitch, and he did not feel Ziona's hand as she threw herself down beside him and tried to pry his arms off of his head. He rolled side to side, splashing mud. Then suddenly his legs shot straight out and his back arched off the ground. Tremors rocked his whole body, causing him to shake and convulse uncontrollably. His arms came away and jerked board stiff beside him and his eyes rolled back in his head. With a final scream, he collapsed and lay still.

Ziona put her ear to his chest and then peeled back an eyelid to see the whites of his eyes only. She felt for his breath, the placed a cool hand against his forehead, searching for his thoughts, searching for their bond. She found it, once again locked behind the wall. She sat back with anger. Foolishly, she had allowed her feelings to get in the way of the mission. She smoothed back his hair and then looked up. The clouds were low and angry with no break in sight.

With a sigh, she stood up and examined their surroundings. The only shelter she could see was a giant pine with low-hanging branches and a dense pine needle ground cover. It would provide protection from the wind and the rain if she could rig some tarps. It would be quicker than trying to set up a tent when she did not want to leave him alone for long.

Ziona fetched her supplies then hurried to build a shelter under the branches, all the while keeping an eye on Cayden. Eventually, she was ready and returned to drag Cayden back under the temporary shelter.

She tended to the horses but left them saddled, then crawled under the awning and settled down next to Cayden. He slept peacefully as far as she could tell. Weary from their travels, exhaustion quickly took her, and she fell asleep before the count of ten.

When she woke around midnight, Cayden was gone.

CHAPTER 24

The Journey Home

CAYDEN TRUDGED ALONG THE RIVERBED, leading his limping mount. The sun was rising. The blush of the dawn spread above the crown of the forest, crowding in on either side of the vertical slice created by the water's passage. The river ran east, and east he would go until it made him go another direction. Time was short and his ability to resist the doll was failing as Helga chipped away at his resistance. The constant battering was slowly but surely breaking down the temporary bond between him and Ziona that kept it at bay. He would not allow Ziona to add her strength to the bond. If Helga found out about it, she would kill her. Of that he had no doubt. *Worse yet, she will force me to kill her, and that would kill us both instantly. I can't keep her near. It is too dangerous!*

When he had awoken from his collapse, he had found Ziona snuggled up against him under a temporary shelter. He had swept the hair off her face to study her profile, and the surge of love that came was so strong that he thought he might be sick with it. She was the picture of health, pink-cheeked and full-lipped, her eyelashes a fan of black on her skin. He couldn't allow harm to come to her. His destiny was set, but her whole life was ahead of her. His path could only lead to death, and he was loath to take her with him.

Silently, he'd packed up and left, slipping into the darkness. She could follow him certainly—there was nothing to stop her from tracking him—but he did not think she would. For one, Mordecai and Genii were sure to catch up to her. Secondly, the direction he was headed was not where she would figure him to go. He was headed home. Home as in Sanctuary-by-the-Sea. If he could not break the doll's control, he could at least gather some assistance to help him resist the commands. He meant to retrieve his flutes, hidden under the ancient oak tree. He knew them now for what they were. Subconsciously, he had begun to carve the flutes on instinct as a way to breach the veil and bring him in contact with the spirit world that his thread of a soul longed to connect with. The flutes with their magical abilities to call to animals created a bond that connected him with the animal kingdom. Although their transformation at death was immediate, unlike their human counterparts, it was no less soulful. In that bonding, that aid he could give to their transformation, he was reconnected to the spirit world in a way he could not be as a human mortal. The spirit world was a part of *his soul, what had been his soul as a godling,* and now the flutes were the only way to touch it short of death.

He needed those flutes.

His original set was lost. He had not seen them since his unfortunate capture by Alcina, but perhaps they were still a part of him. Were they a physical door or only a trigger? He needed to know. He needed those flutes!

Helga was not focused on him at the moment. He could feel the Soul Fetch. He could *always* feel the Soul Fetch, but it did not exert influence on him, so he pushed hard toward his destination. He chafed with frustration over his lame horse and for not the first or even second time, considered abandoning the animal. He rejected it once more as he needed the supplies in his packs for the journey and so wearily kept going. It would take another two days of journeying to reach his destination, but he wasn't sure he had the time. He pushed the thought ruthlessly aside. There was no time for worry. The mental energy it took slowed him down.

The stream broadened into a pond where fat trout swam in the steady current. Cayden paused to gather some breakfast. He pulled a short spear from his pack and several tries later pulled a fish from the stream and set about filleting it for breakfast. He started a small fire in the rocks using some driftwood scattered about on the beach and his flint, poaching the fish, then wolfing it down quickly before it cooled. Just as he was tossing the last bite into his mouth a large shadow swept overhead, temporarily blocking the sun before it swung back toward him. The eagle shaped silhouette dissolved into Brimstone, who dropped onto the beach and trotted up to him, bowing his head.

"Brimstone!" Cayden jumped to his feet and ran over to the stallion, wrapping his arms around his neck. "I am so glad to see you!"

Brimstone snorted then pushed him hard in the chest with his nose, one black eye sparkling indignantly.

Cayden's smile was rueful. "I know I should not have left without you. But you were not around when I left, and I couldn't wait. Thank you for coming." He hugged the Pegasus once again. "We need to go to Sanctuary-by-the-Sea. Can you find it?"

Brimstone nodded his head as if to say, "What a stupid question." Cayden laughed and ran back to the fire, kicking it out and then drowning it with river water. He transferred his saddle to Brimstone and then checked the leg of his horse one last time. It was healing. It could take care of itself. He gave the horse the rest of the oats and then freed it to fend for itself.

Swinging up into Brimstone's saddle, he patted his neck.

"Let's go, boy. From here on out, we will not be parted."

Brimstone tossed his head and whinnied again. Cayden imagined Brimstone saying "About time you came to your senses. We are stronger together." Sometimes, Cayden swore that the Pegasus could talk. Maybe it was a residual effect of the return of his memory, an echo of the knowledge.

"So true, Brimstone! To Sanctuary!"

Brimstone galloped down the riverbed gathering speed, launching into the air with a powerful push of wings, clearing the treetops in short order. Cayden drew a deep breath and shivered in the icy air rushing past him, drawing his cloak tight and leaning into Brimstone's warm body. A sleepy lethargy crept over him at the rhythmic stroking of wings, and he found himself nodding off as he rested his head on Brimstone's smooth neck. His constant struggle to resist the headaches and possession exhausted him.

Into his sleepy semiconscious state a voice whispered, *I know why you left. I am always here for you, Cayden. If you find yourself in trouble, reach out to me. You don't have to do this alone. We are bonded mates you know. Draw on the bond. Fight Helga. Don't give in. We are coming and will join you before the end. I love you.* Cayden quivered then sighed and fell deeply asleep, at peace.

CHAPTER 25

The Bargain

HELGA TOSSED THE WIZARD'S DOLL onto the low table beside her brother's, eyes locked the whole while on the young knight named Ryder. His eyes followed the flight of the second doll to the table. She saw them tighten although no expression crossed his face. He sat with one leg thrown over an arm of the heavily carved and polished chair, as nonchalant as though he sat in his mother's house and with as little regard for the furnishings. He idly drew pictures in the beaded moisture clouding his glass, the very image of a bored guest.

"You brought me down here to show me your doll collection?" he said in a deep growl. "Is this supposed to impress me?"

Helga laughed, throwing back her head. "You *are* delightful! So cocky and self-assured. One would think you were the gatekeeper and I the prisoner." She leaned back in her high-backed chair, stretching out her arms along the padded rests, tapping a manicured nail on the dense wood. "So, tell me, young Ryder, what does interest you? Give me a reason to keep you alive. Come, don't be shy! It has been a long time since I had a young man around to entertain me. Are you a betting man?"

Ryder looked up from his finger-tracing and started at the woman. She appeared to be no more than thirty, yet she had to be centuries old. Raven hair in large curls cascaded past her shoulders, framing a pale oval face. Her body-hugging dress was midnight black and cut in a deep V in the front with black diamonds glittering darkly along its edge. But it was her dark chocolate eyes that held him. Hawk-like, they missed nothing. They were sharp as knives, and Ryder could feel the menace in her smiling stare. He could fatally wound himself on those eyes. One careless misstep and he would be dead, they promised. A panther waiting to pounce.

He affected a casual grin and said, "I like a game of dice or a turn with the cards, the same as any soldier. But I don't think you speak of tavern games, mistress."

"Very astute. No, I do not. What if I were to place a wager with you? No, better yet a wager on you? Would you honour such a debt should you lose? Are you a loyal man or a man of honour?"

"It would depend on the nature of the wager. I would know the stakes before entering such a game, for me and for you." He raised his glass and took a sip of the honeyed wine.

"Certainly! Let's speak of the stakes. You are a knight, sworn to protect the poor reincarnation of my dear brother, the pitiful human you call Cayden. You are a mortal, doomed to die and in time join me in the afterlife. This replanting of souls in infants was a ridiculous scheme hatched by my father. It is against nature to live again, to go from one host to another like some kind of freakish virus. Mortal kind was meant to die and the souls of the living to enter the realm of the dead. That would be my world, the underworld.

"Nature, does it not show us the true path? Why is there soil? Because of decay. Why is there decay? Because it is unnatural to live. From the day that a squalling infant takes its first breath, it begins to die." Helga's hand sliced the air as though to silence the offensive sound. "You can continue to fight for a lost cause, for an unnatural cause and die forever, your soul enslaved as the Charun are enslaved, for the natural order is being restored. There will be no reincarnation. Or you can choose to live at my side, forever and rule beside me, but you must make a choice. I have forced obedience in the past. The outcome of that particular…experiment…was flawed. To force the decision scores the mind. They transform into a shade without memory or personality. All that they were was lost. *You will be lost.*"

Ryder shifted slightly in his chair but kept his face impassive. He did not comment.

"There will only be my world at the end of days," Helga said softly. "It will be the world that I build, an eternal existence under me. There will be no mortal flesh in it to live and to die. All will be eternal in my realm. Whether you choose to live in it as a mindless slave or a co-ruler...well, that is the choice before you, isn't it?" Helga picked up her glass and took a sip, studying him over the rim.

"You make a fine argument," Ryder said, staring off into the cavern, his eyes tracking the birds flitting about in the treetops. *I wonder how she comes to have birds in the underworld?* The idle question crossed his mind as he stalled for time. What choice did he have? He was already in the underworld. They all were. To stay here was to die as surely as it was to die in the world above. Yet he did not feel dead. He still had his mortal body. He could still feel his heart pounding, the coursing of his blood, and the flexing of the muscles in his broad shoulders as he shifted. Maybe his fate was not as sure as she proclaimed. Maybe.

"Tell me, what will keep you from replacing me, should I agree to your terms? Forgive me, but this hardly feels like a wager. It feels more like a persuasion. Where is the risk to you? How do you stand to lose?"

Helga stood and walked over to the edge of the stream that meandered through the jungle stretching toward the circle of light at the peak of the cavern. She stared up at the light, and a second of anguish flashed across her face. "I have already lost," she whispered. "Once I could walk the world, as you do. Now, if the light touches me, this happens." She stretched out her hand into the weak shaft of light that filtered through the canopy. As her hand touched the light, it began to smoke and the smell of roasting meat filled the air. She snatched it back, cradling it against her chest, her back turned to him. Her body spasmed for a second. Then she shook her hand and crouched down and placed it in the cooling stream for a moment. She straightened and whirled around, thrusting her hand out in front of her. It was whole and unmarked.

"If I cannot walk the world as I once did, I will remake the world into one I can walk. This is my promise to you. This world, without end." She flung her arms open wide to encompass her realm. "I only have time left to create one companion for all eternity. You should be pleased that I have chosen you. Honoured, I would say."

"You have given me much to think about." Ryder rose to his feet and found that he towered over the woman. "But it is to my men that my thoughts stray, not to your offer. I have my price too. And my price is their price. Release them. Give them back their lives. If you are correct and we do stand at the fulcrum of time, then I know they would wish to spend it as humans and die as flesh and blood in the world they know. Release them…and I will consider your offer." He crossed his arms and stared boldly at her, unflinching, commanding her by his body language to agree.

"Let the games begin." Her humourless smile stretched, and she crooked a finger to him. "Come here."

CHAPTER 26

A Shaky Welcome

AVERY CRAWLED BACK from the abyss, quite literally, at least in her mind. The chasm of the underworld yawned beneath her feet, but she knew it was not her time. The path she needed to climb was long and steep. She was not sure she had the energy to do it, but a bright white light beckoned a beacon of hope. Sanctuary was at the end of it, and she could not refuse. She needed to reach sanctuary. It had always been about sanctuary, not just for her but for all mankind. So, she began to climb. As she ascended, the light became brighter, illuminating the stairs until they glowed a soft white. The glow increased and brightened until it filled her entire vision.

As Avery took the last step, she woke to a room lit by a watery sun pooling on the floor by her cot. On either side of the doorway stood two guards, Primordial Flesh Clan warriors dressed in sleeveless animal skin and sporting feathered arm bands of rank. She studied the room under heavy lashes, wishing to ascertain where she was before she announced to them that she was conscious. A headache accompanied the inspection. She ached behind her eyes, so that moving them brought thudding pulses of pain. It would not be difficult to drift back into semi-consciousness. With that thought, she drifted back to sleep, this one dreamless and untroubled.

When she next awoke, the guards were gone and Achak sat beside her cot, smiling down into her face. As her eyes fluttered open, he raised a finger to his mouth, warning her to be quiet and not speak. He leaned over and kissed her cheek then whispered softly, "They do not know who you are. I have told them we are husband and wife, and you fell ill while travelling. For now, we are safe. I have heard nothing of them searching for a woman with tattoos from head to toe. Fingers crossed." Then in a louder voice, he said, "You look much better, my love." He ran his hand through the couple inches of hair that now hid the tattoos on her head but did nothing to disguise the tattoos decorating her face from prying eyes. "Would you like something to eat before we discuss our departure? We have imposed on their hospitality for far too long. You have been asleep for a day."

Avery's eyes darted around the room once again. Then, she slowly sat up. "Yes, I would like something to eat. Please, bring me my cloak, I feel chilled." In actuality, she could see that her tattooed arms were clearly visible beneath the covers. She raised an eyebrow in silent inquiry, and Achak smiled a cheeky grin. She smiled back. No need to ask who had undressed her. Achak rose and fetched her cloak and tunic which hung on a peg by the door. He brought them over and opened the cloak up wide, providing a screen to his eyes. Avery swung herself over the side of the cot and stood on shaky legs. She slipped into her tunic, belting it on followed by a pair of leggings supplied by her hosts and her boots. She swung her cloak over her shoulders and hastily checked her pockets, sighing with relief when everything was accounted for. She then pulled on the cloak and pulled up the hood.

A knock sounded at the door, and a guard stuck his head out. He conversed in low tones with the person on the other side. Then with a gesture to his companion, he left the hut. The second guard followed, pulling the door shut behind him, leaving them alone.

Achak quickly walked over to the door and placed his ear against it. A muffled murmur was all he could hear, the words intelligible. Worry flitted across his face. He crossed back over to Avery's bedside and picked up a bowl of cold porridge. "Eat quickly. We need to leave. Every moment we stay, we risk discovery by those who may know who you are." He handed her the bowl and then walked over to the solitary window, peering outside. The window faced the back of the hut. Achak studied the alley for several moments to see if anything moved, but all was quiet.

Avery scraped the bowl clean then placed it back on the table and stood. Her knees felt a little less shaky with food in her belly. "You want to climb out the window?"

"I don't think we have any other choice. Why guard us if we were allowed to just wander out the door?"

"Perhaps they are more of an escort. Or perhaps they are suspicious of strangers." Avery walked over to his side and peered out the window.

"I'd rather not find out the hard way. We need to go." He picked up their satchels and was just about to throw a leg over the window sill when the door opened. Startled, they whirled around just as the guard stepped out of the doorway. Ducking low to clear the door frame, Artio stepped into the room.

Artio straightened to her full height, her glowing eyes pinning Avery and Achak to the wall. She took in Achak with satchels in hand and Avery's robed and shadowed form and a slow smile stretched across her lips.

She strode up to Avery and snatched the hood from her head. Avery stared back with angry defiant eyes.

"Welcome to my camp, sister. The name you use in this time is unfamiliar to my tongue. I think I shall call you Alfreda." At Avery's frown, she said, "Indulge me. Oh look, you appear to be in a hurry. Why, you would not be thinking of leaving so soon, would you?" Artio's smile grew larger. "We have prepared a banquet for you and everything. It is not often a Spirit Shield drops in for dinner." She snapped her fingers, and the two guards took their satchels from their unresisting fingers, clamping a meaty hand around Achak's upper arm. "We have much to talk about, you and I. There is another guest too. Someone you will be familiar with. Come."

She turned and bent back out the door as the guards pushed them forward. Achak shook his arm to free himself from the guard's steely grip, which earned him a clout across the back of the head that drove him to his knees.

"Do not resist, Achak!" said Avery, as she bent to help him. Her guard yanked her away as Achak stumbled back to his feet, feeling for the lump rising on his head.

They were dragged out the door and into a waiting ring of warriors ten deep, who parted way for Artio and her procession, a rippling wave of hardened faces glaring at Avery. Whispers moved through the crowd, and Avery drew her hood up to shield herself from prying eyes, feeling as exposed as a spawning salmon. The hostile stares made her shiver, yet she knew they were not her enemies. They were deluded, lost sheep following the shepherd's crook, not knowing they were being led to slaughter.

Someone spat at them. Achak jerked out of the way, glaring at the crowd.

"Spirit Clan scum!" someone yelled from the back of the crowd.

"Death to the traitors!" screamed another. Suddenly, they were pushing forward, trying to reach them. Avery's hand drifted to her knife, fingers twitching over its hilt ready to pull it, while her guard hauled her along behind her sister's back.

"Enough!" roared a Primordial captain on horseback, riding forward and blocking the way behind them. "Return to your duties! Now!" He uncurled a whip and snapped it above the waiting crowd. The loud crack froze the frenzied crowd. With another snap, he laid the whip across the shoulders of a man who had come too close. He howled with pain and tumbled back into the crowd, which absorbed him then broke up and melted away before the flickering whip could strike again.

Artio led them to a tall building set in the center of the village, the windows lank and empty of glass, the shutters hanging askew. She entered the building, and they were pushed up the stairs and through the open door. Inside, the interior was dim. Heavy curtains were drawn to block out the light, and the only illumination came from several sets of candelabras lining the back wall, attended by Primordial priests. A series of marble plinths glowed in the flickering light and on each plinth stood a bowl. Avery gasped when her eyes fell on the gleaming vessels.

"You have found all the bowls!" she cried in shock.

At that moment, a woman rose from a winged chair with its back to them. She turned around.

It was Achak's turn to growl. "Marea," he spat. "I should have known."

Artio paused by the bowls, running a finger along the top of the plinths as though checking on the housekeeping by inspecting for dust.

"Now that I have all three of you here, you will answer my questions." Artio swung around and straightened to her full seven-foot height, her arms crossing her chest. "You will answer them all. Or you will die, right here, right now."

The door to the house slammed shut. Avery heard a bolt slide into place, shutting out the outside world. The guards released her arm, and she sank into the chair vacated by the former High Priestess.

Marea sank to her knees in front of the goddess and began to babble, words spilling from her lips in a torrent. It was going to be a long night; a *very* long night.

CHAPTER 27

The Truth Dawns

SNEAKING PAST THE SLEEPING and drugged legionnaires was a simple enough procedure for a small force sent in small bands like raiding parties. Hauling the rumbling wagons and support that inevitably attached itself to any army was more difficult, as by necessity Fabian and Nelson had to keep to well-trod paths and roads, which were surely watched. Not every man of the legion had been asleep and skirmishes had broken out along the way. The balance between stealth and security had to be maintained, but which of these was paramount? This was the ongoing argument tossed back and forth between Nelson, driving the lead team, and Fabian, plodding along on his gelding at his side, once again pretending to be merchants on the road, but this time with no cargo. A string of five other wagons rumbled along behind them each with a Kingsman alongside, mercenary guards for the wagons. Nelson and Fabian argued softly right up until they ran into the next patrol party.

They crested the rise of a low-lying hill, the road twisting around a curve and into a wooded area where a path through the woods joined the bumpy dirt road. The wagons rolled down the slope to the jangle of harness, noisily announcing their presence, just as an armed and hooded party of three rode out from the woods.

The Kingsmen eased the swords at their hips. Nelson flipped back the corner of a blanket covering his hilt, resting beside him on the wagon seat. Hearing the rumbling, the party turned and unsheathed swords, clearly as alarmed to find them on the road.

Nelson held up his hand, signaling a halt to the wagons. Fabian rode forward a few paces, then stood up in his stirrups and yelled, "Hail riders! How fare the roads ahead? We hear of bandits, lying in wait along the roads, for disorder and anarchy has gripped the land. What news do you carry?"

One of the riders nudged his horse forward and rode to meet Fabian alone. Fabian did the same, and they met in the dead zone between the two parties. The horseman halted his mount within a horse of Fabian and then dropped his hood. A grey-haired familiar face grinned back at him.

"*Denzik!*" Fabian spurred his horse forward and was gripping the captain's arm in short order, grinning from ear to ear.

The others dropped their hoods to reveal Ziona and Gaius, who rode up to greet the other party. Cayden was suspiciously absent, a turn of events that bode ill for their plans. Cries of recognition rang from the other wagons. Nelson hopped down to join the rest of the Kingsmen in greeting the newcomers. Handshakes and slaps on the back were exchanged. Over the din of welcome, Nelson asked the burning question in his mind.

"Where is Cayden? Where is the king?" Silence descended on the jovial crowd, a wet blanket of concern tossed over the merriment of moments before.

Ziona's head swiveled in the direction of Sanctuary-by-the-Sea, the first place she had laid eyes on the young man, the Spirit Shield who would become the king of Cathair and her mate. Subconsciously, she placed a hand on her stomach then lifted it to point toward the simple abodes. "He is there, headed back to his village. I think there is something there he wishes to retrieve." She stared in the direction for a few more moments, anguish flushing her face before she wiped it clean, before dragging her eyes back to the Kingsmen. "But he will return. He is heading for Cathair. If we wish to be of aid, we will be there when he arrives. I warn you, however. He may not be the man you remember. He has fallen afoul of a Soul Fetch, and his actions in large part are being controlled by the goddess of the underworld." Her face hardened, her eyes flashing around the crowd. "I must do as I must. We must do as we must. Hear this now, we cannot allow this possession to go unchecked. He is too powerful. If he cannot overcome the Soul Fetch, he will destroy us all. A Spirit Shield that is weakened is no shield. It is a leaky boat sinking into the abyss, and at the bottom is an eternity in hell. I will do as I must." Her eyes burned into the assembled men, her grief a blade sharp and cutting. "If you stand in my way, know I will do as I must. I will not see the collective souls of mankind condemned in such a fashion. I will not see the world end because I failed to act. You are warned."

Silence followed as Ziona turned her horse and began a slow walk in the direction of Cathair. Gaius hurriedly mounted and trotted after her, amidst the jangle of armour and clinking of swords. The steady clop, clop, clop of horses and bridles filled the air as the Kingsmen mounted up and hurried to join her retreating figure.

Denzik tied his mount to the back of Nelson's wagon and climbed up in the seat to do a hurried debrief with his captains. The grim telling of events passed back and forth, and an hour later, both faces stared ahead as the grim truth dawned on them. They were in a fight they could not win, short of a miracle. This was a war of the gods, not of mortals, and their champion was no longer a god, even though his chief adversary was. Nelson clucked to the team and urged them into a slow walk. Fabian rode alongside, matching their pace.

"What about Avery? Is she as...*mortal*...as Cayden? Does anyone know?" Fabian dragged his hand through a beard that was far too long. Nelson and Denzik shook their heads, neither having come close enough to Avery even recognize her, let alone know what her abilities were. Grimly, Fabian hauled his hand away from his face. It had begun to itch. *Maybe I need a bath.* "Well, curse the gods! How can they just sit back and let this happen?" he growled. "We have dedicated our lives to making sure the king was returned to power so that he could fight this battle. Are you trying to tell me we are doomed after all this time? Dammit all to hell. Gah! I can't believe it. I won't believe it!"

Denzik pulled a pouch of tobacco from an inner pocket, followed by his favourite pipe. He tamped it full of the fragrant leaf, then clamped on to the stem with his teeth. Next, he scratched his flint on the wagon wheel as it churned, sparking a taper to flame that he held against the flint. A short burst of flame flared as he brought it to the bowl, then he settled back and puffed away on his pipe, hooded eyes watching the activity around him. He puffed a couple more times, the bowl glowing red, then rumbled into the cloud of smoke wreathing his head, "The gods surely know what will be the fate of mankind. What I am unsure of is if they care. When is the last time you prayed? The last time you visited a temple or a shrine? The old ways crumble, and the jungles overtake the sacred places. The old priests have died and with them the knowledge of how to commune with the gods. Instead of a knowledgeable priesthood, a pale imitation takes its place. If we want the gods to respond, to intervene, we must go back to the beginning. That is when they left. That is the closest source." He puffed again, rocking on the bench. "It is also beyond common men to commune directly with the gods. Only the Spirit Shields can. Only they can repair the breach. All hope rests with them."

"And if they fail?" asked Fabian, a deep frown on his face as he rode alongside the wagon.

"Then we are doomed. We will become part of the dammed for all eternity. No rebirth. No chance at another mortal life. The world as we know it ends."

"Then they must not fail." Fabian touched heel to flank, and his horse sped up to a trot. "We cannot repair the breach, but we can protect the king. We can make sure that he fulfills his destiny. We can be the shield to the shield. We can protect his mortal being while he fulfills his spiritual oaths. Come we must be there when he arrives. There is not much time!"

As one, they sped up to catch up to the swiftly moving Ziona. They would all do as they must. There was no other choice.

One horse trailed a little behind the rest. Calleigh rode in silence with the rear guard, forgotten in the excitement of the reunion. She turned her horse and disappeared into the woods. No one saw her go.

CHAPTER 28

The Witch's Plan

MORDECAI AND GENII RODE out of the swamp, the small chest strapped to the back of Mordecai's saddle. Neither spoke, neither looked at the other. The silence was a wall they did not know how to breach.

Calleigh's whispered revelation of their family linkage had rocked them both to the core.

Brothers.

Genii stole a glance out of the corner of his eye at the elderly wizard. *Perhaps there is a way for me to learn more about the magic in my blood, after all.*

"Mordecai, we need to talk."

Mordecai's pale blue eyes flickered, then he said in a slow slur, "Yes. Yes, I suppose we do. It would seem that, since I was a mere boy during the first evolution of the gods, you are actually my older brother?" His eyes crinkled as he attempted to process the thought, so incongruous with the tall young silhouette of a man riding beside him. "But how do we know that Calleigh was telling the truth? That she is our birth mother? Perhaps this is some plot she has hatched."

Genii's eyes strayed to the box. "I suspect that the chest will contain the proof of her assertions. I cannot see her leaving a truth such as this unprovable." The silence stretched again. "The real question is what does it all mean? Why did she draw us to her now and not at any point in the past? Why hide all of this in the first place?"

Mordecai rode on, staring straight ahead, but staring at nothing. "I was told that my mother died in childbirth, that the magic that is passed from mother to son can kill the mother. Yet it would seem that she survived not one but two births. Why did she leave me with my father? That is what I would like to know."

Genii stared straight ahead, also staring at a similar nothing. "And is he my father too?" he asked softly, turning the concept over in his mind. "Somehow I do not think so."

They rode along in silence awhile longer, the constant drizzle reflective of their mood. They did not want to open the chest in the rain, afraid that the moisture would be harmful to the contents. They also did not want to stay in the destroyed village, fearful of the return of those who had wreaked havoc on it. That they sought Calleigh was the only logical conclusion, and she swore they were after the chest. Therefore, it was prudent that they get it as far away as they possibly could from the searchers.

Mordecai set up a vanishing spell that wiped the tracks of their horses, disguising their back trail. Eventually, they reached the comparative shelter of a copse of trees that skirted an upright formation of reddish rock, thrusting out across the plain. Scouring winds and blistering heat had eroded most of the structure away over the centuries leaving only the tall trail of red sentinels, the last holdout of an ancient landform. The rain eased off, and a weak sunshine spilled through the breaks in the grey cloud cover, bent stalks of grass glistening with thousands of tiny beads of water. Mordecai reined his mount in front of the protrusion and peered around, examining the horizon. A rough ramp of reddish gravel spiraled up around one pillar, leading to a suspended bridge of stone

"This looks like a good spot to open the chest. We will be able to see anyone approaching for miles. Let us ride to the bridge." Mordecai pointed up the ramp to a spot at the crest.

Genii nodded and nudged his horse onto the trail and began to climb.

The final curve broadened into a flat wide ledge with an overhang, creating a suspended cave partway into the arch of the natural bridge. Genii slid out of his saddle, tying his horse to a scrubby, stunted shrub growing out of a crack in the rock. "It will be dry under the arch." He walked over to the opening in the rock.

Mordecai dismounted, looping the reins around another branch, then untied the chest and carried the relatively light box into the shadow of the overhang. He set it down on the ground and straightened up, gazing at the chest as though it were a living thing. He ran a hand down his beard as he studied the markings on the lid. Genii marched over and flicked the hasp on the lock with a resounding click.

He flipped back the lid as Mordecai shouted, *"Stop!"* spluttering to a halt when nothing happened. Nonplussed, he bent over and pushed the lid further back. "I thought it might be warded," Mordecai muttered.

Genii grinned at him. "Mother was never that subtle. She would stab your fingers if she found you stealing or put crabs in your bed for lying, but nothing like warding. She believed in swift justice."

Genii bent and plucked out the first object. It was a smooth disk, about four inches in circumference, flat but fat like an oversized coin or a biscuit and made of a shimmering white substance, coarse and gritty feeling like sand, but solid. He turned it over in his hands, then passed it over to Mordecai with a shrug.

Mordecai examined it also. It was blank on both sides. With a shrug, he put it down and reached for the next object. A small flute, barely as long as his hand, presented itself to his searching fingers. It also shone with a pearly coat, tiny rainbows of colour flashing across its glossy surface. The flutes made Mordecai think of Cayden, but he knew this had not been carved by his hand. He handed it to Genii, whose hands were even larger. He also shrugged, placing the flute beside the disk.

"So far, we are coming up empty for proof," he muttered.

The next object, wrapped tightly in a soft brown cloth, had to be unwound over and over before showing itself to the light of day. A crystal orb fell into Mordecai's hand, fat in the center and tapered to points on either end. Inside the orb, the crystal was faceted so that it bounced the light to the center and created an iris of ever-changing colour. The eye followed him as he bent it one way or another. It almost seemed alive. Mordecai handed it to Genii, who yelled and almost dropped the orb when he saw the eye staring at him. He hastily handed it back to Mordecai who wrapped it back up as carefully as it had been unwrapped.

Genii's eyes followed the wrappings as Mordecai placed it carefully on the pile. With a shiver, he reached for the last object, a scroll of parchment contained within a bone tube. He inserted his pinky finger within the tube and pulled the parchment out, careful to not tear the ancient fragment. Once he had it clear of the tube, he sat down. Mordecai followed suit, peering over his shoulder as he unrolled the missive.

My dearest sons,

I have watched over you more than you know. Always I have been there, guiding your steps, helping you to the path you must take. Always I have loved you.

For so long I have craved to hold you both, to comfort your tears, to guide your steps. I have ached to tell you the truth of your birth, Mordecai. Yet to do so would have meant certain death for you and for me. There was only one way to protect you and that was to send you away, to make sure that no one ever discovered the secret of your lineage.

If you are reading this, I know that you have come together at long last, that the end is near and that I have likely passed into the river of spirit, awaiting my chance at rebirth. In preparation for this day, a day I knew would come, I wrote this letter, so that you might know the truth at the end of days.

You see, the world believes that there were four godlings, four children of the gods, four who fought for power and struggled to control the world. Artio, Alfreda and Caerwyn, and Helga, all were children of Morpheus, all the stuff of legends.

What the world doesn't know is that there were actually six.

Morpheus was forced to leave his mortal family and his wife Groa, by the other gods when their judgment was that there should be no more interference by eternals in the affairs of mortals. They decreed that should any god visit the world of mortals, their offspring would be slain for the crime of lying with a mortal. Morpheus was forbidden from that day on to see his family ever again.

The law broke Morpheus's heart. He could not bear it. Oh, he obeyed as far as the Gods were concerned, and made a great display of burying Groa, when she died from an assassin's blade shortly after the decree. But what they didn't know was that Morpheus and I staged this death, in order to bring an end to the searching by the gods. I disguised my appearance and hid in the swamp, hoping to be able to leave it when the god's attentions shifted elsewhere.

Morpheus secretly returned to the world of men to gaze on his family who he could not contact. He was very lonely, and I thought only to comfort him. He visited me on occasion and it was during those wondrous and precious pairings that you both were conceived.

But the gods were suspicious. So to save you two from certain death, I went into exile. Calleigh the crone was born and Groa the Seer was laid to rest. But we are one and the same.

Genii, you were the eldest child of Calleigh, so I kept you with me, but I placed you, Mordecai, with a family in the service of the castle with a witch that I knew from that time. I thought it would be too difficult to hide you both with me, for your magical powers were great, even as a babe. She raised you as her own until she died of a spell gone wrong. Hud always believed you to be his son and loved you as one.

And yet I could keep none of you with me, for the gods were searching, looking for signs of immortal offspring. I thought that hiding Genii with the gods would be the easiest way. When Artio fell for her half-brother, it seemed the easiest thing to do was to encourage the relationship. Before you start judging me for that, know that Artio was not my child. Artio was a daughter of Morpheus but of a witch you never knew, a sister of the mother that raised you until the age of six, Mordecai. By the time I placed you with your adopted mother, the godlings were a hundred years old and the connection forgotten. I know this is a lot to take in, but the truth must now be told, for you both have a crucial role to play in the future of this world.

The objects before you are the keys to defeating Helga's plans. You must join with the Spirit Shields for they need your help to heal the breach. With these objects, you can give them that time. There is a second sheet that explains their use. Read it and memorize it, then destroy it. Do not let the knowledge fall into the hands of others and especially not Helga. She is twisted with jealousy and will show no mercy to the world or to you.

May we meet in the next life. Until that day,
With great love and affection,
Calleigh.

A tear dropped onto the letter. Another plopped beside it, running down the page. They did not come from the same eye.

Mordecai picked up the second page of parchment. With Genii staring over his shoulder, they read the instructions.

"She requests that we split and each go to a Spirit Shield. You are to take this," Mordecai picked up the wrapped eye and handed it to Genii, "and join Artio and Avery at the temple. They are surely headed there already. They could hardly miss the signs. And I am to take this," he picked up the smooth, fat disk, "and the flute and join Cayden at the Well of Souls." He slipped them into his pocket. "So, do we go?

Genii sat, staring at the wrappings of the eye without really seeing it. Finally, he lifted his head and stared at Mordecai. Through the residual shine of tears, a fierce light shone, every bit as brilliant as that displayed by the orb a few minutes ago. "I am looking forward to facing Helga once more. But this time, it will be her downfall, not mine." His head swiveled in the direction of the smoking mountain and the city of Faylea beyond. "And I can finally see Artio again. She needs me. She needs to see me. I need to see her." He tucked the orb back into the chest, snapped the lid closed, then rose to his feet, tucking it under one arm. "If I am truly to die the final death, I'd rather it be as it started at Artio's side, dead forever more."

Mordecai rose and clasped his brother's arm in his, gripping his elbow, then pulled him into a hug. "Go with the blessings of the gods. May they have mercy on your soul."

"And with yours, brother. Guard your heart. Remember the Soul Fetch. Helga will try to use you and your magic before the end. Good luck." Mordecai acknowledged the warning with a short nod, and they separated, riding off in opposite directions without a backward glance. Neither intended to sleep until they reached their destination and set their horses to a ground eating lope. Time waited for no man, not even for a god.

CHAPTER 29

Choose

"COME NOW, SURELY YOU KNOW what these are, dear sister?" Artio stood directly behind her flesh kin, staring at the three bowls. Avery stood rigid, arms and legs locked, unable to move closer to them. There was a barrier around the bowls, invisible yet present, that halted her advance on them. Dagan, however, moved in and around the bowls, humming to himself as he studied them.

"What is this barrier?" Avery raised her hand and moved it across the invisible screen.

"It is a little something Dagan created at my command to keep the bowls safe. You do not need to touch the bowls." Artio bent and whispered into her sister's ear "All those years ago, we had a tea party, do you remember? One of these bowls was in the house. Do you recall which one? Hmm?"

Avery's eyes flicked sideways in response to the voice and then focused back on the bowls. She raised her hand and pointed at the clay bowl with the chipped blue glaze. "It was that one."

Artio's feral grin of agreement elicited a squeak from Marea who cringed up against one wall as though trying to disappear into its depths. "Very good. Seeing as Father made it for you, I assume you know what it does. I would dearly love for you to enlighten me. Dagan," she purred "has figured out the pewter one. But the clay bowl remains a mystery, a mystery that cannot remain. You will tell me what you know.

"I cannot say what it does." Artio's grin turned into a snarl, thinking the slight to be intentional, but Avery turned this time to meet her sister eyes. "I can only say what it did. When Father gave it to me, he said that it was a keepsake to help remember him by. He said whenever I was sad to look into the bowl and I would be able to find him there. I never used it. I placed it in the temple of the Spirit Shields after he left, and there it stayed I assume until you found it. You did find it, right?" Artio nodded. "And the others? Where did you find them?"

"One was in my own temple. This one," she said, jabbing a finger at the pewter bowl etched with runes. "Someone must have placed it there. I do not recall having such a bowl when I was...human." She skirted around Avery and walked through the shield and up to her bowl. "Dagan has cleverly discovered the key to the runes. We know what that one says. But this bowl, it is still a mystery." She stopped beside the glass bowl with the skeletal hand floating in the bottom.

"Where did you find it?"

"In the cave that was our special place...Genii's and my place...by the Sacred Stones. My sacred stones." She turned abruptly and marched back to Avery, stopping in front of her and leaning in, nose to nose. "Now you will tell me all you know. That blubbering fool," she pointed without looking at the cringing Marea, "knows less than a stone."

"I cannot tell you what I do not know. Let me approach the bowls. Lower the shield."

Artio studied her for a moment then motioned to Dagan, who passed his hand through the air and the barrier vanished. Avery cautiously approached the bowls. She did not attempt to touch them, but instead she reached out with her senses. The bowls hummed. It was like a low-grade fever, a buzzing, hot sensation, as if angry bees worked just out of sight. She passed a hand over the bowls and closed her eyes. She sensed that the bowls had stories to tell, that they held secrets—no, riddles—which would unlock the truth. Secrets that could not be solved here. There was an element missing. Avery passed her hand slowly over each bowl, searching for the quiver of intelligence that lay just beneath the glazing. *Yes, there it is.*

Someone has imbued their essence into the bowls. Someone had placed a piece of their soul in the paint, in the glaze, in the magic of the bowls. But it cannot be accessed here. I am certain of it.

Avery opened her eyes and gazed back at her sister. "You want to know the truth of the bowls? Then you must do as I say. There is only one place that the bowls can be activated and their secrets revealed. There is only one place left in this world with the power to activate them. They must go to the Sanctuary in Faylea. They must be reunited with the temple. There and only there can the magic of the bowls be triggered and their secrets revealed. Only there can it be done."

Artio glared at her sister, distrust evident in her every frowning wrinkle, and in the stiffness of her crossed arms and puffed chest.

"Oh, and there is one other thing." Avery walked over to Artio's side, pinning her with an angry crystal gaze. "You must decide who the real High Priestess is. Only the true High Priestess can pass the enchantments of the temple and only she can take the bowls where they need to go." Avery crossed her arms, imitating Artio's threatening stance. "Are you ready to work by my side? Or are you still wallowing in self-pity and plots for revenge?" Artio scowled, looking every bit the rebellious teenager she had been at her death. Avery cocked her head to one side, studying Artio's reaction to her words. "If you care to remember, I also died that evening, so long ago. Perhaps your enemy is the one who survived. It's time you decided once and for all who the real enemy is. Well?" she prompted.

Artio's lips drew back in a scowl, flashing long serrated teeth. When Avery did not react to the feral snarl, she abruptly stopped and threw back her head, howling with laughter.

At least she's laughing. Either way, its progress, Avery thought, grinning at her sister.

"Fine. We will try it your way." She flicked her hand in Marea's direction. "She was never anything but an obstacle to trip you up. You may go," she growled over her shoulder at Marea.

But Marea, instead of running out the door, hesitantly approached Artio. "Are you not my mistress? The one who appears to me?" she asked tentatively. She cringed as Artio's attention focused fully on her.

"I do not work from the shadows. That creeping presence is Helga's calling card." She shook her great mane of hair. "You are delusional and deceived. Now, leave me!"

Marea dropped to her knees and dared to reach out and touch the edge of her tunic with a trembling hand. "I wish only to serve, mistress! To serve you and the temple. I can be of service. Please let me help you."

Artio's harsh glare drove Marea face down on the wooden floor before she realized she had moved. "You can serve the Spirit Shield, as it was decreed in the beginning of time. You can aid her in her quest to prepare the temple for battle. That is why you were given access, was it not? As the caretaker of the temple until the Spirit Shield's return? Serve her," she pointed to Avery, "not me."

Artio's glare swung to her sister. "And you will serve the gods, dear sister. I still haven't decided if I will slay you when this is finished, but for now, it suits my plans to partner with you. You will carry the bowls into the temple. We will see what the will of the gods is concerning this world."

Avery nodded. She would indeed carry the bowls because it was her destiny.

"Time is fleeting. The faster we return to Faylea, the better. I can sense that Cayden is in great distress. We need to prepare the bowls. It is time to go."

CHAPTER 30

Deal with the Devil

THE MOUNTAIN SHUDDERED. The Highland Spine was not normally susceptible to earthquakes, the event rare enough that the scraggly vegetation dotting the steeper slopes had sunk its roots only deep enough to stay attached to the rocky crevices. The mountain shuddered again, this time so violently that a chunk of the southern face peeled away, the grey slab of rock crumbling away from the main block. The slab was as tall as a house and cut like a cheese knife down the slope, slicing through everything in its path. A great cloud of dust rose into the air, obscuring the rapidly building slide of rock, trees, and soil from view as it tumbled and churned down the face of the mountain.

When the dust settled out of the air, a scar was visible from tip to base, an unsightly rent in the verdant covering. A ribbon of lava oozed from the fresh opening and moved slowly down the mountainside, flashes of flame sparking as it burned away all vegetation that it touched.

At the lip of the opening, Helga watched the trail of lava begin its descent to the valley floor below and smiled. *That should keep anyone from approaching my home without me being aware of their approach. No army will be able to cross that lava flow.* She moved back into the darkness of the cave and crooked a finger at Ryder, who fell in at her side.

"See? There is no escape. No one can approach the mountain now to rescue you or your men. No mortal in any event. And

Cayden, your so-called king, he is mine, I'll have you know. Body and soul. My dear brother is worse than useless to you, but do not worry! I have a very special mission for him.

"It was an ill-thought plan that they came up with, he and Avery. Why anyone would want to become *human* I will never know, but to choose it as a path to victory? It was doomed to failure from the moment they conceived it. In the end, they will bow to me. Cayden will obey my command. He has no choice." She patted the pocket that contained the dolls. "Such a wonderful thing these dolls. A deliciously wicked and devious invention."

Ryder did not reply. *The king is her brother?* Ryder's mind reeled at the thought. He let none of his shock show on his face. He simply watched her retreating back, memorizing the passages and what led where, to what opening, creating a mental map and hoping to learn where a crack to the outside world existed, a place for him and his men to escape from when the opportunity came. So far, he had not found anything that would be of assistance. Time was running out. Ryder knew that if he hoped to help Cayden, he must disrupt Helga's plans. As much as he and his men would rather be defending the castle and battling mortal foes, the truth of the matter was they were here in the underworld and perhaps that was where they were meant to be. A battle to the death need not be a spilling of blood. And if they were already mostly dead, then they had the advantage where they were. He could battle from the underworld. *I had better battle and win if I ever hope to be reborn. My soul may very well depend on it, along with the rest of the world.*

But Ryder was the only one walking free. He had to change that and even the odds. *But how? What do I have that she doesn't? What could she possibly want that is denied her on a daily basis? Think!* And then it hit him. Companionship. She had told him already albeit in a more perfunctory method, worded as a command. He could manipulate her heart.

Ryder shivered, rolling the thought over in his mind. He was playing with fires that had their origins in hell itself, but if he were successful he might just free his men in the process.

"You have gone strangely silent," Helga said, glancing back over her shoulder as she paused at the top of the staircase leading to the pits.

"I have been mulling over your proposition. You have given me a lot to think about."

She smiled and trailed a finger down his cheek again, the nail rasping against his beard. She tangled her fingers in its curly length and tugged as a lover would. "I will give you even more to think about," she purred. "An eternity in hell doesn't have to be…hellish. Come, my pet. Let us check on the progress my new recruits are making." Releasing him, she glided down the staircase that zigzagged down the wall of the cavern to the floor of the pit. The rivers of lava still flowed, but here and there a bluish hue was visible through cracks opening in the floor of the cavern, created by the grinding drills. The Kingsmen sagged against their wooden paddles, muscles straining and shirts stained with blood and sweat. Most wore clothing that hung in tatters. The Charun were not hesitant to lay into any back that was not putting their full effort into their assigned task.

Ryder watched as a Charun loosed his whip, a cruel nine-foot length of leather split on the end into three long tongues, embedded with bits of sharpened bone. The weapon rent shirt and skin in equal measure. The whip came up, back and forward, and the Kingsman on the receiving end, a man named Jack, shrieked, arching away from the whip as far as his manacled hands would allow. He staggered sideways into his oar companion, gasping, his eyes streaming with pain.

"Work, you fools!" growled Ryder in a low whisper as he walked past, schooling his face to blankness. The nearest Kingsman gave a barely discernible nod then whispered to the man next to him. The wheels ground back into movement and Jack's groans were drowned by the scraping squeal of the drill as it bit into the stone.

Helga walked over to a deep crevice that glowed brighter than the others, kneeling down beside the chasm. The flickering blue light washed across her face. Ryder knelt beside her and peered into the crevice. "What is it?" he asked, suspicion tainting his words

Helga dipped her hand into the light and her hand became more solid. As soon as she withdrew it, the skin darkened and faded back to normal. "It is a crack in the magical casing that surrounds the River of Souls, the souls that my foolish brother was set to tend and guard. This is what the souls of the world look like when gathered. They combine into a flowing river of spirit, a great miasma of nothing."

Horrified, Ryder backed away from the light. He had seen this light before, deep under the castle in Cathair, but then it had been a joyous thing to see, akin to a miracle. A great well, a shimmering sky blue, full of the souls of the dead awaiting their chance at rebirth. A sacred treasure he was sworn to protect, by protecting the king and by protecting the Spirit Shields.

"No soul is distinct from another. They have no thoughts, no personalities, and no consciousness. They are worse than the simplest life form, not even symbiotic in nature. The greatest minds ever to walk the earth, reduced to a dribble of consciousness, less alive than a parasite. They will serve whoever controls the river.

"I am freeing them from this enforced imprisonment. I am freeing them to serve me for all eternity. You see, in this state, they will serve whoever controls their existence. You have met my Charun. They were once disembodied *ooze* such as this." She straightened and called out imperiously, "Brennan, attend me!"

The Charun who had dragged Ryder to Helga initially, separated from the others and floated toward her, slowing to a halt before them. He towered over them, a slimy ethereal monster. "You summoned me, mistress?"

"What do you remember of your former life?"

The Charun shifted slightly. "I do not remember my former life. I live only to serve."

"What is your first memory?" she demanded.

"I remember you. Your mind in mine, guiding me towards a red light. When I awoke, I was here."

"And what is your wish?" she demanded.

"I wish only to serve you for eternity. My wish is to obey."

Ryder frowned then said, "May I ask him a question?"

Helga's smile was wintery. "By all means, indulge yourself. Ask away."

The Charun's cloaked head swung in his direction. "Where did your body come from, such as it is? Why are you not human again?"

The Charun shifted again, its hood swinging in Helga's direction. "There are no bodies to possess. We are given these vessels to inhabit as there is no flesh in the underworld. These vessels allow us passage into the mortal world, being formed of spirit. They are sufficient for our needs. We live to serve."

"You have said those words before. I do not believe that you have no memory of being a mortal." The Charun did not answer.

"You see, I do not have to leave my fortress to accomplish my goals or to create my dominion," said Helga. "All who die will serve me in time, for I will divert the flow of the river and create a greater well, right here within my domain. All will serve me going forward. If not in life, then in death. If they will not bow to me, then they will die and serve me. It is their fate. It is the future of mankind. My Charun number in the tens of thousands, a great host able to stamp out the mortal existence of mankind.

"In the meantime, the chaos currently sown across the world works to my advantage. While humanity is in discord, they cannot challenge me. They are ripe for the picking and will all surrender in time."

Ryder's eyes tightened, and his lips cracked open to form a grimace he turned into a grin. "Then I suppose I should join with your efforts. I'd rather be in this form," he pointed at his chest, "for all eternity, than as one of them," he pointed at the Charun circling the straining Kingsmen. "So, what duties would you have me perform, mistress?"

Helga placed both hands against the sides of his face, her fingers touching his temples. A thrill shot down his torso, and he cried out with pleasure. The world turned sideways, and they vanished…together.

CHAPTER 31

The Ancient Oak

BRIMSTONE CIRCLED THE MEADOW of the ancient oak tree, slowly descending over the tall grass in a glide, the shadow of his wingspan creating a rippling dark shadow that grew in size as he descended. A stag with a large rack of horn raised its head, watching the shadow approach. Its ears twitched as the Pegasus flapped then touched hooves to earth in a gallop, folding his wings back along his broad flanks. Seeing that the creature was another hoofed animal like itself, the stag dipped its head and pulled at the long grass, losing interest in the newcomers.

Cayden slid off Brimstone's back as he slowed then stopped under the golden canopy of the old oak tree. The first thing Cayden noticed was that the tree was dying. Even though fall approached, more than half its leaves were gone and naked branches reached up into the sky as grey as the clouds overhead. Cayden hurried over to the tree and placed his hand against the trunk, searching for the presence he used to feel when sitting on the rock cluster carving his flutes.

A soft sigh reached him from within the tree, a tremulous voice that quavered with age. Cayden sent his thoughts into the tree, a warm greeting and then asked, "What has happened, Ancient One? Why is your life force fading after all this time? Tell me what is going on?"

Come closer. Druantia is not as strong as she once was. Come closer.

Cayden leaned on the tree. Suddenly, the bark split and opened a passage into the ringed core of the trunk. He ducked his head.

When he straightened, the tree had expanded into a rounded room, complete with carved benches, bookshelves stuffed with books, and several windows that reflected light into the room. It smelled of the natural scents of freshly turned earth and sanded wood with a hint of lilac blossoms. Cayden took a deep breath, inhaling the heady fragrance then wandered over to the bookcase. He ran his thumb along the spines, recognizing many of the titles on display. Some volumes were missing, as if they had been recently taken out for some reason.

"Is this where the tree sprites stored the books? They were fetching them from here, weren't they?" A deep chuckle reached his ears, as the tree laughed in agreement. Cayden took another deep breath, fully relaxing for the first time in a very long time. The Soul Fetch seemed muted within the tree, as though her bark was not easily penetrated.

He wandered over to a carved wooden chair padded by a soft and welcoming woven mat of leaves stuffed with wool. With a grateful sigh, he sank into the chair that shaped to him, as though made with his measurements in mind. "The wool is from my sheep?" The tree chuckled again. "Tell me, Druantia. Why are you dying? What can I do to help?"

I think you know the answer, Cayden. Your soul is as ancient as mine, perhaps more so. As it is in the world, so it is with me. My roots are deep, my life long, but connected to the souls of this world I am. Where once flowed a continuous life force nurturing my seedlings, now my roots are starving and shriveling. The great river is failing, Cayden, and all of our work is being undone. Do you remember how it all began? No? Cayden shook his head. *Then let me remind you.* A sleepy peace stole over Cayden, and he relaxed back into the chair, listening to the voice of the ancient elemental. *In the beginning, when the world was young, it was decided that a life form other than a human should be set as a guardian of the souls of the world as an early warning device should something happen that would interfere with the natural order of rebirth. Rebirth was essential to the evolution of the world and to the maintenance of all mortal life. Without a cycle of death and rebirth, life would eventually fade away. I was planted as that safeguard, as a warning that dire times were upon us, that the natural order was being disrupted. Those times are now upon us,*

Cayden. The souls of the dead awaiting rebirth are being drained from the river. A great evil rises in the mountains and as it grows, so I die. There is not much time left for me. If the breach is not sealed, all mortal life will die, forever. The drain is quickening, I can feel my roots withering in the ground, clogged now with decay. I reached out to you in your dreams to bring you to me, to tell you the truth. Helga is drilling into the river and stealing the souls for her own use. She is building an army with which she will be able to defeat any mortal army thrown against it. They are growing rapidly now. Soon all will be lost.

You must heal the breach, Cayden. You must plug the holes or the entire world is doomed to fall into darkness, its eyes forever dimmed.

Cayden lifted his head, thinking aloud. "But how do I do this? Do you have any ideas? Help me, please!"

Open the door below the bookshelves. Perhaps something in there will help.

Cayden got to his feet and walked back over to the bookcase, crouching to open a knot of wood serving as a cupboard door. Inside, on a soft bed of green sat several flutes. He recognized them. He had carved them, but when nothing seemed to happen when he'd played them, he had put them under the tree, thinking to carve them some more to correct whatever was wrong with them.

Seeming to hear his thoughts, Druantia said, *There was never anything wrong with them, Cayden. They speak to the spirit world, something you were yet unprepared to see when you made them. I can sense that Avery has one too. She carries it with her. I do not know how you can use them, but if ever someone had the ability to call help from the spirit world, it would be the Spirit Shields. Remember that there is more to this world than the humans who walk it. There is a world beyond this world, a world that is the transition to the gods. They are able to help you even though you are mortal. They can help with what you lack, no longer being a godling. It is possible to seal the breach if you are brave enough to do what must be done. I cannot measure the ultimate cost, but I can see that the only hope for this world lies in your hands and the use you make of the spirit world around you. This was your plan and your design. You and Alfreda decided in the beginning to create this fail-safe. It is up to you both now to trigger it. Now, do you see the stoppered bottle sitting on the third shelf of the bookcase?*

Cayden straightened, tucking the flutes into a pocket in his cloak. His eyes caught on a black glass bottle with a heavy orange wax seal, impressed with an oak leaf half shrouded in shadow, on the shelf.

Take the bottle. It contains a potion that will help you to see the spirit world around you. It will aid your vision. I must warn you. You must not take it until the end, until you are ready to do what must be done. Once triggered, there will be side effects, and I do not know how long you will be able to withstand them. It is a potion that Alfreda created and placed with you for safekeeping, knowing you would be drawn here in a time of great need. I'm sorry I cannot be more precise, but as the potion has never been used, I do not know precisely what it does. I can only pass on the warnings you advised me to give, so long ago.

I can do little more for you, than this. You must hurry. Time is very short…for me and for you. Rest for a moment. Take a nap in the chair and build up your reserves. Ten minutes here is like an hour's sleep in the waking world. Rest then continue your journey. You will need every ounce of strength. Sleep.

Cayden found himself sinking into the chair, which had elongated into a reclining bed. Before his head touched the plush back, he was fast asleep.

CHAPTER 32

So Close Yet So Far

THE APPROACH TO CATHAIR became more rolling, the series of hills like the curving back of a sea monster, rounded and smooth. The hills, long denuded of trees to provide grazing for sheep and cattle, acted as a security perimeter. From the vantage point of the limestone walls of the castle proper, the approach of an army could be seen for miles. As they broke the horizon of the first series of hills, the height gave them their first glimpse of the castle that they had seen in over half a year.

Denzik shaded his eyes. Cathair shone like a golden jewel in the late-day sun that had broken through the low cloud cover, washing the limestone with sunlight so intense the castle walls glowed.

Nelson smiled at the sight. Fabian shoved back his hat and grinned.

Denzik opened his mouth and betrayed their hearts. "Isn't that a sight for sore eyes? It's good to be home." The other two nodded as the Kingsmen caught up to them crowding around the hillock, all eager to catch their first glimpse of the castle.

"Enjoy the view, men. It will be awhile yet before you can even think of entering the capital. That," Denzik pointed toward the darkening village that sat to the west, the thatched buildings fading away into the scattering of apple trees that marked an orchard, "is where we are headed."

They studied the distant village, watching for any sign of life stirring in the early evening hours. It was far too distant to see movement, but the coolness of the approaching night should have shown a curl of wood smoke escaping the various chimneys. All was strangely still and silent. Their eyes swept the fields, searching for the flocks and herds that normally fed on the lush grasses, but all was still. More still than was natural. At a bare minimum, the whistles of the farm boys should have been echoing on the air as they called to the scattered sheep. The silence dampened their initial enthusiasm.

Denzik turned to the men, clustered around them. "We will camp here tonight." He pointed to the trees they had just passed through. "But I intend to know what is happening in Upper Cathair. Where are my volunteers?" Hands shot into the air hand he chose four out of the crowd. "You, you…you. And you. Come with me. The rest of you, make camp."

The four Kingsmen flung themselves into their saddles and followed Fabian, riding to another shorter hillock where they dismounted at the base. Denzik pulled out a spyglass from his saddlebags then motioned for the men to follow. The dense brush made for difficult passage. They eased their way past the grasping branches, eventually dropping to all fours and crawling to the crest. Flattening themselves on the lip of the rise, they passed the spyglass back and forth taking in the tableau.

"Maybe we will find the village the same as the others we have passed through." Denzik's stomach tightened at the thought. "But it could be that they have been rounded up, captured and guarded but still alive. They are a smart bunch, our villagers. They have lived for decades on the edge of tyranny in the shadow of the former queen. We must know the status in the village in order to plan properly. I suspect that Cyrus has taken the town. It's what I would do. He will want to deny us access to the tunnels. He will not have forgotten how we sneaked into Cathair the last time, and he will be guarding the entrances so that we do no repeat that feat. The question is, has he located them all?

"So here are your instructions. Two of you," he pointed at a skinny man with a drooping grey mustache and his companion a red-headed man with too many freckles, "will visit all the original entrances. Get as close as you can, and try to determine if they are being guarded or if he has just grabbed control of the village to prevent entry. I want you to report back to me within twenty-eight hours. You two," he pointed at twin brothers, stocky, muscular fellows, "will sneak into Cathair itself and report on the legion positions and how it is being defended. You will also report back within the regular twenty-eight hour day. One way or another we will know the lay of the land before another day passes. Watch the skies. Keep a keen eye out for the winged spies of the underworld. Also, beware of shadows. They are gateways for those who dwell in the shadowy abyss."

Denzik motioned for them to retreat, and they backed away from the edge. Once they reached the base, they mounted up and turned to ride back to camp, but before they could take more than a few strides, the shadows cast by a small copse of trees moved weirdly and coalesced into a half dozen Charun, black, misty, and menacing. They floated forward in the gathering evening gloom, hastening the darkness, riding the shadows into the world of men.

Denzik hauled back sharply on his reins. His horse reared, screaming at the Charun. Blades snickered from sheaths as the Kingsmen drew steel. The Charun spread out, cloaks weaving from side to side as they inspected the humans. One raised its head and sniffed, as though trying to catch their scent.

"Away with you!" shouted Denzik, brandishing his sword. "Back to the abyss, demon spawn! In the name of the Spirit Shield, I command you to retreat!"

A Charun detached himself from the group and approached Denzik, sliding silently across the ground. The Kingsmen crowded around Denzik, but he held up his hand, stilling them. The Charun slid to a halt just past the blade's reach.

"We are not here for you, human," it hissed, its head turning, still sniffing the air. "We seek the immortal one."

"Immortal one? You cannot have the Spirit Shields. We will die defending them!"

The Charun's hood swayed side to side. "We seek the immortal one. You are not immortal. You stink of fleshly decay." With that, the Charun rejoined its companions and dissolved into shadow. With a faint popping sound, they disappeared.

Blades slid back into scabbards as the tension eased and full dark descended. "What was that all about?" Fabian heeled his horse closer to Denzik's.

"I do not know, but perhaps it has something to do with our most recent guest. I think it is time for a further talk with the young woman, Calleigh. The Charun had a purpose in revealing themselves to us, and I do not believe in coincidence. Not now. They must have been commanded to search but not engage in battle."

Fabian knuckled his mustache then muttered, "And there has only been one new person to join us of recent date. Come, let's rejoin the band." They rode back to camp, keeping a careful watch on the enveloping night, nervously twitching at every innocent scurrying. No one took any movement in the dark lightly, especially when Charun were known to be lurking nearby. Even the horses stepped livelier, eager to rejoin their herd as the flickering firelight of the camp came into view. They rode to the horse lines, and Denzik and Fabian tossed their reins to a Kingsmen standing nearby. The four scouts saluted and continued on to their assigned duties, eager to be away.

As Denzik marched over to his command tent, the young woman named Calleigh rose from the fireside, the orange reflection bouncing off of her raven hair.

"You have come to ask about the Charun," she said with a satisfied nod. "I sensed their presence. Come, we have much to talk about." She held back the tent flap and waited for them to enter, inviting Denzik into his own abode. Bemused, they ducked inside.

Fabian couldn't help but think, *This is going to be one hell of a tale.*

CHAPTER 33

Shielding the Shield

"**STOP RUNNING!** Stop swatting at them! Stand still!" Avery screamed at the lead Flesh Clan warriors as a blood-curdling cry ripped from their lungs. The spiders swarmed their bodies, crawling over their boots and up and under their pants, squirming in the gap of their tunics and into the seams of their shirts. Every swat, every twitch triggered a corresponding bite and large swellings bloomed as the venom took hold. Three Primordials had already collapsed and lay twitching on the ground, looking more like great overgrown squash than humans.

Only two stood stock still and controlled their fear, and those the spiders completely ignored, flowing around them as though they were trees.

Avery entered the clearing and dropped from the back of her horse, walking into the midst of the spiders, reaching out to them with her mind. She could hear thousands of whispers and sense their hive-like oneness, controlled by the large adult female hanging from a huge web that stretched from one side of the pathway to the other. It was large enough to snag a horse…or an unsuspecting scout or two.

"Trespassers, invaders! Protect the shield! Protect the shield! Sacred trust!"

Avery stood in the middle of the sacred forest, which they had entered an hour before, amidst dire warnings to the warriors to not agitate the inhabitants needlessly. She held up her hands, palms out, and closed her eyes to the swarm. Then she reached out with her mind to the queen. *Peace, Ancient One, peace. Passage is needed and required.*

The queen arachnid twitched a silk and shifted slightly in the web. *Passage is granted, Mother, may you shield us all,* said the queen with an audible series of clicks and high-pitched whistles. The juvenile spiders swarming the ground scuttled to the side, the clicking of their pincers like the dry crunch of leaves under a wagon wheel. The queen detached a few strands of silk and then swung like a trapeze artist over to another tree, folding the giant web with her. The passage cleared.

Avery whirled around and pointed at Achak and snapped, "Do not allow the Flesh Clan warriors to wander off the path! And *you,*" Avery marched up to her sister, "you were never so cruel. Stop pretending to be this great 'avenging god.' Give over and leave that role to our dear father, should he choose to intervene. You know, Artio, it wouldn't be a bad thing if you prayed once in a while!" Furious, Avery stormed back to her horse and swung back up into the saddle. The rune on her right arm that was connected to the spiders itched, and she scratched at it absently. The closer they got to Faylea, the more her tattoos flared, bringing pain or itching in equal measure. The temple was stirring, and she was connected to the temple in a way not seen since the beginning of the age. The constant crawling under her skin frayed her nerves and shortened her fuse. She could not return fast enough, yet she was constrained by her guard and by the large party of Primordials on the move. Hundreds, no thousands, of Flesh Clan warriors moved into Spirit Clan lands. The only thing that would keep this move from going really, really bad, was the fact that she led them. Well, sort of led them. This was still a delicate point of discussion, if the truth be known. Despite her best arguments, Artio would not be budged on this point. While she acknowledged Avery as the true High Priestess and grudgingly accepted that she had not caused her downfall all those years ago, distrust was rooted in her soul and so she gave up only what power was necessary, as she saw fit, when needed.

Avery gnashed her teeth in frustration. "Artio is a blind dumb fool," she groused to Achak, riding at her side.

He reached over and stilled her hand before she managed to break the skin once again. "Stop scratching, Avery."

She glanced at him then down at her arm and took her hand away. She stretched her neck to either side, trying to ease the tension riding up her spine. "The temple calls to me. We must move faster!"

Achak half turned in his saddle to peer at the long line of Primordials strung out along the road to where it twisted away in the distance. "They can only move so fast. What is this urgency you are feeling?"

Avery stared straight ahead, and her eyes shifted out of focus as she examined her feelings and reached out with her senses. "They are on the move," she said softly, "the Charun and the Daimon. They are coming. I can feel a shift in the underworld. It's like an earthquake but deep underground. They are spreading out. The temple can feel them coming. It calls to me to defend it. I must go!"

Achak took in her pinched face and the slight sheen of sweat on her brow. Her eyes had a fevered gaze, as though she was being possessed from within. *Perhaps that is closer to the truth than I realize.*

Abruptly, Achak swung his horse around and rode back to Artio. "Mistress, may I speak?" he said, as weapons were drawn at his abrupt approach. Artio nodded. He rode up beside her, ignoring the hands drawing bow strings, arrows notched. "You must let Avery move on ahead. She is bound to the temple, and she suffers for it. She is being pulled back urgently. May I suggest that you accompany her with the bowls and a small contingent of warriors? They can move more swiftly through the Spirit Clan lands to Faylea. I will stay with the warriors here and ease their passage. Hototo can work with me. Every Primordial is going to be needed in Faylea, and I will see that they get through. Please, this is urgent."

Artio frowned at him then took in her sister's rigid back, thinking. It was true that they could move faster in a smaller group. She snapped her fingers, and Hototo rode up on her other side. "You will work with Achak to bring the warriors to Faylea. At the first sign of treachery, you will slay him." Hototo grinned and nodded his head, a feral gleam in his eyes, as he accepted his instructions. "Bring them through the valley on the western side of the city. That way is the closest to the temple.

Impress into the army's service all who you encounter. I expect you to arrive by the third morning from now."

"Yes, mistress. It will be so." He bowed in his saddle.

"Do not double-cross me." She held up a rigid finger to Achak's nose. "Avery's life will be forfeit if you do." Achak bowed a bow equal to Hototo's in subservience.

Artio heeled her shaggy stallion up beside Avery, settling in beside her. A contingent of ten warriors, all special guards of Artio's peeled away from the group and followed.

Avery's eyes were still glazed over, as she communed with the temple. "Come, sister, the temple awaits." Avery's eyes swung to Artio's, and Artio saw the shadow of the immortal in her eyes, ancient and knowing. "It is time."

Together, they touched heel to flank. Their mounts shot forward at an easy, ground-eating gallop. Destiny called, and they would meet it head on, whatever their fate. *Besides, I have an old score to settle and the sooner we arrive, the sooner the battle begins.* With a silent snarl, Artio rode.

*   *   *

Hototo paused, blocking Achak's way while the sisters rode away with their escort. Achak's eyes followed them until they disappeared over the rise, then his eyes swung back to Hototo. "We will have your allegiance, right now." Achak's eyes narrowed as he watched Hototo pull a bundle from his saddlebag, carefully wrapped in animal fur. He unwrapped the parcel. A large doll was revealed, the likeness of the face and clothing matching Artio's figure and appearance. Frowning, Achak raised an inquiring eyebrow, confused as to its purpose.

Hototo flipped the doll over and opened a seam in the back. The inside was stuffed with hair. Hototo touched his heels to the flanks of his horse then reached up and yanked several strands of hair from Achak's head. He yelped. Hototo stuffed the strands within the doll and closed the seam tight once more, carefully rewrapping the doll.

"You are now soul bound to Artio as are we. All who will serve her must be bound. This includes all we meet and bring into the fold. All must be bound."

Achak felt the binding sink into his skin, along with the urge to obey Artio's bidding. *Of course, he would obey. What would be the logic of disobedience?* He nodded to Hototo, and together they rode to the front of the string of warriors. *All will be bound when we reach Artio. Our numbers will have doubled. Artio will be pleased*, he thought, and the thought gave him great pleasure.

CHAPTER 34

The Wall Walk

CYRUS MARCHED ALONG THE HEIGHTS of the outer curtain wall, occasionally pausing to lean out through a crenel to determine what lay below. Although he was intimately familiar with the castle, in the past he had not had call a reason to plan the defence of it. His former duties had been limited to finding and eliminating the prophesied one, in order to foul the return of the Spirit Shield. His orders had been to seize the capital of Cathair, the spiritual seat of the Spirit Shield, historically. The planning of the defence of the city was left with the Queen's Guard and Alcina while he hunted the usurper.

He grimaced, remembering all too well that no siege had occurred. Instead, they sneaked into the castle via the catacombs that ran like a rat's maze beneath the foundations. Well, he had stoppered that leak. This time the attack would come from the hills rolling away from the castle grounds. He was sure of it. So he walked the walls and examined the battlefield, not satisfied to believe his captain's reports. This time he would make sure of the defences himself and assure himself with his own eyes that all potential avenues of breach had been removed, and that the castle would do what it was designed to do, which was to stand firm in the face of overwhelming odds.

They had been pleasantly surprised as they rode into view of the castle to find a pastoral setting, empty of defence. Sheep and cattle grazed the tall grasses and were quickly rounded up to feed his men. The farmers had scattered in front of his men, leaving them their pick of lodgings. The few who they had captured, babbled about a dark shadow that had snatched away the knights, leaving the city defenceless. It was a simple matter to push aside the barricades and wobbly defences constructed by the elderly men who had been left behind. With no leader to organize a true defence, they had crumbled at the first touch. Cyrus hadn't even lost a man to the taking of the castle. Before nightfall, the first day, the people of the city and surrounding villages were kneeling in the square, swearing their allegiance.

It was boring, really, this anticlimactic taking of the castle. Little had changed within, and he had moved into his old quarters, which had remained untouched, as the castle was not exactly full. The door had been locked up and the room forgotten. Other than a good layer of dust on the furniture and an evidence of a hasty search, it had been ignored.

The legionnaires, returned from years of wandering the world, took over their former homesteads, kicking out the occupants. Where they found a wife or a lover with another, they slew them both and moved in with the women captured along the way.

Consequently, the evenings were raucous affairs, punctuated by the screams of frantic women and the rough deep laughter of the men who were the cause. The streets were not a place to be if one was not a soldier. Consequently, very little patrolling was needed to keep the Cathairians in line. The local residents stayed behind barricaded doors, anxious to stay out of sight lest their presence be taken as an invitation.

Cyrus cared little about the people of the city. They had turned their backs when the usurper had arrived. Instead of defending their queen, they had swiftly kneeled before the conqueror as they were doing now. Might made right, and right now he was the might. That his soldiers reinforced who was in command was to be expected, and a few spoils was their due.

No, the attack would not come from these peasants. It would come from the Primordials. That was where the power was, and that was why the young whelp had run to them, as soon as he felt it was safe to go. He was gathering the tribes, solidifying his hold over them. When he had them in his grasp, he would lose them against the legion. By the time Cayden figured out that the city had fallen and that the castle was his once more, Cyrus would have his trap laid and ready to spring. The Primordial forces would be wiped out, a thorn in his side no more.

As he finished his survey of the eastern wall, a breeze swept through the crenel-filled cracks, swirling the sand into narrow drifts, borne on a gust of wind from the seashore below. The southern face perched on the edge of the limestone cliff, overlooking foaming rocks and an angry swell of waves that broke relentlessly against them. It was said that on a rare still night, when the Primordial Sea was made of glass, that the silhouette of a woman could be seen walking on the water. The moonlight would sparkle off her opaque gown, and stars would twinkle in her hair. The legend went that the woman was a cast-off lover of the gods, sent to wander the waves in search of the one who had abandoned her. Cyrus believed her to be a siren, one of the sea goddesses seen only by sailors on their way to a watery grave. It was bad luck to see a siren.

Nothing moved on the vertical cliff face other than the constant wheeling of ocean birds, crying and fighting over the best roosting spots for the evening. Nevertheless, Cyrus hurried his inspection of the seaside approach. He was anxious to be away from the wall before dark fully descended, which was not far off. The sun sank into the western horizon and plumes of purple night bloomed in the eastern sky. As he hurried off the wall, the wind gusted over the rampart and he heard laughter on the wind. A faint scent of sulphur burned his nose, and he rubbed at it, clearing his nostrils of the foul air. The laughter chased him down the stone staircase, and he found himself checking over his shoulder for a presence, but nothing was there. Still, he felt an itch between his shoulder blades, as though unseen eyes followed him. He rubbed the back of his neck and was unsurprised to find that the hair was standing straight out.

At the base, he hurried across the flagstone and pushed open the double doors that led to one of the main audience chambers. Two of his captains stood at his appearance, saluting. Spread across the table in front of them was a map taken from the library, tracing the known tunnels under the castle. In heavy pencil, new tunnels were being drawn onto it by a scribe dressed in pale blue robes. The scribe had also been located in the library, and now Brennus's duties included updating the map for Cyrus. At first, he had been reluctant to leave his precious library, but when it was pointed out to him that he could update the maps or rot in a cell in the dungeons, his attitude changed. He hummed as he sketched, absorbed in his work, happily adding in the information brought by a series of legionnaires, all mapping different tunnels.

"Brennus, report." Cyrus dropped his hand from the back of his neck and waved the captains back to their chairs.

"My lord, we have discovered an additional twenty corridors and have added them to the map. See? This one here is the most recent find. It leads directly to the stables outside the wall. The stables used by the inns on the western edge of town. Very useful if you want to sneak in a mistress or two without the whole town knowing it." He chuckled to himself.

Cyrus bent over the map and studied the new additions, analyzing their approaches. "And the size of that tunnel? How many could move through it, in say...an hour or so?"

Brennus looked up and blinked. "That would depend on if they were walking or running? But assuming they were walking, I would say maybe a thousand?"

Cyrus turned to Captain Sengal, a broad-bellied man with thinning blond hair and a large mole on his cheek. Before he could open his mouth, the man rose. "I am on it, my lord. I will have four legionnaires and a runner assigned to the stable immediately. We will know if any suspicious activity happens at that site."

"Good. See to it." Cyrus watched the door open then swing shut behind the captain. Guarding the entrances to all these tunnels was thinning out his men dramatically, but there was nothing to be done for it. To ignore the tunnels would be a disaster. A disaster he knew personally.

A blaze of light, a finger of waning sunlight came through the window and struck a statue in the likeness of the king, standing on a plinth against the wall. The figure glowed in the light, and a bluish aura surrounded it for a moment and then was gone. Cyrus blinked twice, uncertain at what he had seen. The haunting laughter returned, and he shivered. Neither the remaining captain nor the scribe reacted to the laughter.

Is it possible it's all in my head? Cyrus walked over to the statue and picked it up. It was one solid carved piece of stone, cold to the touch. No blue light shone from it now. He put it back on the plinth and shivered once again. *I need a drink badly.*

CHAPTER 35

Sisterly Squabbles

"**MUST I CALL YOU AVERY?** The name is foreign on my tongue. It is a…simple name."

Avery's head swung sideways to peer out of the corner of her cowl at her sister, silver eyes flickering over her face. "None of us are as we once were. You admit to having memories returned. How much do you remember of the past?"

Artio raised her face to peer at the sky overhead, perhaps searching for a particular star. Her horse swayed beneath her, but her head was still, focused. "I remember enough. Who remembers everything? When humanity is reborn it is not natural to remember anything at all. That any memory has resurfaced is strange. What has returned is…broken and fragmented. I can only remember flashes of the past and nothing after a certain point." Artio growled the last, the images flashing across her mind like a falling blade. "In the end, all that matters is revenge. The one responsible *will* pay."

"Pay for what? And how will you determine who is responsible? You can't even remember what happened. Did you ever think that maybe your quest for revenge is flawed?" Avery dropped the cold words into the air between them, Artio growing more frigid and frozen with each syllable.

Artio's back stiffened her grasp on the reins so tight she jerked the head of her horse. It snorted and tossed its head, annoyed. Artio's lips peeled back into a snarl and her long-fingered claws clenched around the handle of her knife. "Genii was stolen from me," she spat, "and I will avenge him."

"How? By killing everyone you meet? You were never that way. You were the gentle one, the brilliant scholar, Morpheus's angelic daughter, doted on by the gods. This is not you." Avery swept a hand in Artio's direction. "This is a form forced on you."

"I like this body. It gives me great strength. I can feel the power surging through me. I can smell the earth around me and the creatures that stir." She sniffed the air. "They make me hungry."

"That is the bear speaking. You are not a bear. You are a godling. And you were once the kind godling who loved science and astrology and looked at the natural world with wide-eyed wonder. You were not a killer. That is the sister I remember."

They rode along in silence, focused on the path ahead, neither one acknowledging the other's existence, the warriors giving them a wide birth.

So far the journey had been one skirmish after another. The Spirit Clans had never taken well to Flesh Clans on their lands, suspicious over their reasons for being there. Now the religious divide over how to approach the gods fed the distrust of centuries, and human sacrifice was an abomination to the Spirit Clans. Any encroachment on their lands was met with open hostility.

When during the first encounter Artio had ordered the execution of a young man not much older that she, Avery had shouted at her sister. They had happened upon him along the road side, examining the hoof of his horse. The man had set off running as soon as he saw them coming, but he had been riddled with arrows before he had taken more than a half dozen steps.

"Why did you do that?" shouted Avery, so furious at Artio that she swung her horse in front of her sister to confront her, and instantly had a dozen arrows aimed at her, ready to loose. Artio glared around at the warriors, and they lowered their bows and backed away. "If one arrow so much as pulls a thread of our clothing, the one loosing that arrow will have their skin removed strip by strip and rewoven into clothes to match the torn," she hissed. The warriors backed off to a safe distance and did not approach them again.

Artio heeled her horse up to Avery's and leaned in, the feral growl rumbling in her throat. "All who run are enemies and cowards. Stand and fight and be accounted amongst the warriors. He was obviously a scout."

"You think so?" Avery snorted, then slid from her horse and wandered over to the lad. She rolled him onto his side and held him there with her boot. Clutched in his hands was a bouquet of wild flowers, crushed by his fall. "A scout gathering flowers in the woods? When did you become so heartless, Artio?" The shaming look she directed at her sister was blistering. "You disgust me," Avery spat and swung back into her saddle, turning her back on her sister. She slowly returned to the path and continued up the trail without a backwards glance.

Artio slid from her horse and approached the body. The fair-haired Primordial was enough of a man to sprout the beginnings of a beard, thin and scraggly. Sixteen or seventeen summers at most. It was true. Clutched in his hand was a bouquet of flowers, the stems snapped and the flower heads torn. He was not wearing armour but the simple clothing of a young lad. A bright flash caught Artio's eye, and she bent over to pick the object up, thinking it to be a knife, to assuage the feelings of guilt that wormed away just under the surface of her heart. When her fist closed over it, she knew it was not. It was a locket, small and dainty, made of silver with a fine clasp. She rubbed the dirt and grass off of its surface then sprung the clasp and opened it up. Inside, a young woman's face laughed, dark ringlets framing a sweet smile that radiated love. The man's face decorated the other side. A betrothal locket, worn when one was traveling, searching for a place to settle down to establish the couple's first home.

Artio snapped the lid shut and clenched her fist around the token, then glared after her sister. Angrier that she had been in a very, very long time, she mounted her horse and roughly yanked him back to the trail. *I will have my revenge and no one—no one!—will change my mind. Not now, not ever!* Yet the memory of the young man lingered in her consciousness as she rode away. If there was something she hated worse than betrayal and treachery, it was being wrong. That hurt like a bee sting, pricking her pride. From somewhere, the memory of a foolish cub sticking its nose in a nest of honey surfaced. She savagely buried the memory, furious at a reminder that was not her own. She had no time for weakness, no time for considerations other than her own. Her path was set.

I will have my revenge!

CHAPTER 36

Escape

MICHALE CREPT ALONG THE DARK TUNNEL, knees shaking. His hand trembled on the short-bladed knife he clutched in his right hand. The candle he clutched in his other hand flickered feebly and threatened to plunge him into darkness, but the intense black was brightening slowly, the further he traveled along dank passage.

A chill that was not cold ran up his spine. He shivered, on the edge of panic. Even as he quivered, he was angry with himself. He had joined the knights after his rescue from the legion camp by Ryder and his men, training long and hard alongside those unique men against the day that he could take his revenge against the Charun that had decimated the legion in such a cold and calculating fashion.

Well, that day had arrived and in spectacular fashion.

For all that he had been indisposed when the Charun had arrived, Michale had not expected to be the only one left behind. Guarding the Well of Souls was a necessary task, if a lonely one, and the tunnels surrounding it were vast and complicated. Despite all their efforts to map out the labyrinth leading away from the castle, new ones were found constantly. What had once seemed like a clever way to penetrate the castle had now become a nightmare for security, as their roles had switched with the taking of Cathair.

It was not until many hours later when his replacement did not show up for his shift that Michale felt the first twinges of concern, and then outright alarm. The oil for his lamps was running low. That combined with hunger drove him to leave his post and investigate what could be causing the delay of his shift replacement.

Early that morning, he had been assigned to guard the carved doorway, backlit by a blue mist that led to the chamber housing the Well of Souls. He'd taken only a few steps away from his post when he sensed a presence nearby. Michale ducked into a side passage and pressed his back up against the wall, peering cautiously around the corner to see what moved.

Flickering light danced across the far end of the passage, the silhouette sliding weirdly across the uneven stone of the wall. The image jiggled then slumped to the floor along with a body as it collapsed onto the floor. A lantern rolled way from his hand and went out.

"Pieter!" Michale gasped dashing down the short passage to where his fellow Kingsman lay sprawled on his stomach. Michale eyes scanned the intersecting passages, which were blessedly silent and empty. He placed his lit lantern off to the side then reached out to roll Pieter over and his hand froze midway. Pieter's tunic was shredded and matted with blood, his back a criss-cross of whip marks, great chunks of flesh missing and oozing with blood and pus. Michale felt his stomach lurch and swallowed heavily. Gently rolling him onto his side, he whispered, "Pieter! Wake up, man! Pieter!"

Pieter's pain-riddled eyes flickered open at the low call. Recognition dawned in their grey depths, and he reached out with one hand to grasp Michale's sleeve. "Charun!" he croaked, swallowing heavily. "Charun…have taken…the knights…must get help!"

Michale's eyes widened in alarm. "Where? Where are the Charun?"

"Gone. Took them all. They took them. I escaped!" Pieter released Michale's sleeve and clutched in his hand was a crumpled piece of paper. "Take it. Find the others. There isn't much time! Map." His eyes drifted shut, and he stilled.

Michale lifted fingers to his neck. A feeble pulse still beat alongside his throat. He shoved the map into his pocket then heaved Pieter to his feet, slinging his arm over his shoulder and clasping him around his waist. He bent and grabbed the lantern and began to drag Pieter up the passageway.

"First, we must get you to safety," he said through gritted teeth as he hauled him up the rocky passage.

Fifteen minutes later, he stumbled into the infirmary door. The bang brought Laurista running toward the sound, furiously waving her hands and her mouth open to release a well-rehearsed tirade about disturbing patients, but then her eyes fell on Pieter.

"Oh my! Bring him in here," she said instead, leading Michale to a freshly made cot in the corner. He staggered under the heavy weight and lowered Pieter as carefully as he could, nearly dropping him in exhaustion.

"What happened to him?" she said as she grabbed a pair of scissors and began cutting off his tunic.

"I don't know. He mumbled something about Charun before passing out. Laurista, the knights are missing." Michale grimaced as he stretched, easing his back after the heavy load. It did nothing to dispel the feeling of being watched. His eyes strayed to the shadows, checking the corners of the room where Charun were likely to appear.

Laurista's head swiveled, alarm straightening her back as she focused on Michale. "Charun! Here?" She straightened then motioned to two of her assistants, who left the cleaning of utensils and bowls and hurried over to the windows to check the grounds, their hands suddenly busy with knives and scalpels and whatever other weapons occurred to them. Michale shook his head, surprised at how quickly the orderlies became soldiers, but then he remembered that was what they were, retired Kingsmen.

"How? Where did they come from?" she asked sharply, barely pausing to check the placement of the orderlies before bending back to tend the injured Kingsman.

"I don't know. I must go back and figure it out." He reached into his pocket and pulled out the rumpled paper, flattening it with the fleshy side of his hand as he bent over the parchment.

"He shoved this into my hand. I think it's a map or a clue as to where the Kingsmen are being held." He peered at the paper, squinting in the low light, trying to make out the scribbled notes and lines. They made no sense, the hasty scribblings of a man in the dark.

Michale held the paper under a bright lamp beside the cot and studied the scribbles in charcoal.

"Twenty-four R, twelve R, fourteen L, twenty-three R, skip, twenty-two R, forty L, seventy-two R…"

The list went on in similar cryptic instructions.

Laurista leaned over his shoulder to peer at the script. "Are they coordinates?"

"Coordinates underground? What would he use as a reference? You can't see the sun or the moon or the stars. It can't be coordinates."

"What about a code? Is it scrambled?"

Michale frowned at the paper. "I don't know the crypt codes. I wasn't taught them yet." He blushed. "I am not a full knight," he said, fidgeting, "but I want to be one! I will figure this out."

He stood up and began to pace back and forth, the paper in his hand. As he paced he subconsciously counted off the steps required to cross the infirmary…one, two, three, four…ten, right turn…one, two, three, four, five, six, seven, eight. His ninth step paused in midair, as it suddenly dawned on him what the numbers and letters meant.

"It's not code. It's the Kingsmen's march, their paces in patrol," he said. "It's a soldier's counts and turns. He has tracked the tunnels as he fled the only way he could, a maze while in a daze. This *is* a map back to the knights!"

He straightened, the parchment clutched in his hands. "It's up to us. We are all the hope they have. The question is, where are they if the Charun are part of it?" He shivered, although no breeze stirred the tepid air. "Is anyone aware that the knights are missing? We need to get word to the Kingsmen, but there are no Kingsmen here. We are defenceless except for the legion and well, they are pretty much useless, aren't they?" Michale grimaced as he thought of his former colleagues, the legion of old reduced to a band of drunken fools. They would panic at the sight of a Charun.

Laurista placed a hand against his arm. "I'll send a pigeon in the morning. Maybe help is closer than you think. For now, you should rest." She pushed him toward a cot in a dark corner. "I will wake you when it is dawn. Rest."

Michale sank back onto the cot. A great weariness crept over him. He didn't think he could sleep. There was too much to do, yet as soon as his head hit the pillow, his eyes closed and he slept.

CHAPTER 37

A View of Home

CAYDEN LEFT THE SECURITY AND WARMTH of Druantia's warm embrace, slightly groggy from waking but feeling more refreshed than he had felt in a very, very long time. As he greeted Brimstone, stroking his hand along his velvety soft nose, Druantia waved her limbs and a shower of leaves dropped around him, a confetti of swirling fall colours. Cayden felt a light touch against his mind, and then it was gone and the tree stilled.

"Come, Brimstone. We need to find a way into the castle that is not known to any others." He swung onto Brimstone's back, and they launched into the air. They climbed well above the tree line. Cayden's eyes were automatically drawn to the farm where he had grown up. He guided Brimstone in that direction, curious to see how the homestead fared. It did not take long to arrive, Brimstone gliding on the currents of air climbing the cliffs of the seawall.

As they cleared the forest and the farm came into view, Cayden's heart sank. Of the house and barns that made up their home, nothing remained. A fire had swept through the buildings, burning them to the ground. Cayden guided Brimstone lower, and they swooped down to glide just above the earth.

The charred stone chimney of the living room was the only upright structure remaining. Even the wooden fences of the sheep's pen were burned. The grass of the pastures grew tall and thick, already overtaking the burn and hiding the scars left by the fire. Cayden frowned at the scene. The fire must have occurred shortly after they had left to be overgrown to this stage. The timing was not lost on Cayden. He knew the burning of the farm was intentional.

Anger flared in his chest. With a curse, he urged Brimstone back toward the cliffs, climbing to gain height. Just as they were about to clear the trees, a rain of arrows burst from the ground, soaring up toward them. Brimstone screamed as an arrow struck his flank, and Cayden felt the solid thunk of an arrow pierce his calf through his pants. Brimstone continued to climb to gain the safety of height, blood streaming from the wound and dropping away into the air as he struggled to maintain his height.

"Easy, boy. Easy." Cayden gritted his teeth against the pain and pointed Brimstone towards the cave where he had once hidden with Ryder, fleeing from a furious remnant of the legion.

This time, he knew his enemy. And this time, there was no sanctuary.

Brimstone's powerful wings beat fast to slow their descent. As his hooves touched the rolling rocks of the cliff, he stumbled slightly, favouring his leg. Cayden slid down off his back and nearly fell as his right foot touched the ground. He clutched Brimstone's mane to remain upright and gritting his teeth, grabbed onto the shaft of the arrow and broke it off halfway along the wooden length with a sharp snap. He groaned low and loud, eyes rolling back in his head and nearly passed out with the pain. He took several deep breaths then hobbled around Brimstone to where the arrow was lodged in his flank. Thankfully, the angle had been wrong and the arrow was not deep. Brimstone snapped his teeth, trying to reach the arrow himself, but Cayden pushed his head back and drew a short knife.

"Stand still, Brimstone. This is going to hurt." Cayden patted his neck. Then with a quick slice, opened the hide above the arrow and pulled. The arrow came free to a fresh gush of blood, and Brimstone shivered with his head down. Cayden pulled a spare shirt from his pack and pressed it against the cut, slowing the flow. It quickly grew tacky with blood. As he took his hand away to tend to his own injury, the wadded shirt stuck to Brimstone's wound. He hobbled over to a rock, easing his body down onto the chill surface, then took the knife and sliced up his pant leg, exposing the gash. The arrow had pierced the meaty part of his calf, missing the bone. The sharp tip was just visible poking out the other side of his calf. There was only one thing for it. He had to push-pull it through. Cayden took a deep breath and shoved at the shortened shaft, driving it further through his leg. Pain roared up its length, a fiery monster burning and licking his wound. He cried out, slumping over his leg, shaking uncontrollably. The arrow had moved about two inches, the arrowhead now clear of the tear of skin that split his crimson-slicked leg. Gritting his teeth, he grabbed the arrowhead and pulled with all his might. This time the pain crawled inside his skull and he fainted, skidding sideways off the rock to the grass below. When he came to, it was to Brimstone's wet nose and rough tongue washing the side of his face. He pushed up out of the grass, shaking with the effort and looked over at his leg, which lay in a bloody pool on the grass. He had to stop the bleeding. With a huge effort, he pushed himself upright and picked up the pant leg strips where he had dropped them, then tied them tightly around his leg to staunching the flow.

When he awoke again, night had fallen. Brimstone kneeled on the ground beside him, a large wing draped over Cayden's body like a blanket, providing a warm and downy shelter under his midnight blue feathers. Hunger crawled in Cayden's belly but so did nausea. In the end, the nausea won out and he fell back asleep.

Dawn was splitting the horizon when he stirred next, weak as a kitten and longing for one of Ziona's elixirs. He crawled over to his satchel and pulled out some food. He slowly chewed on the flatbread baked with berries, washing it down with water from his canteen. Thoughts of Ziona only increased his longing to be with her, and he forced her out of his mind.

Brimstone folded back his wings and stood, testing his flank. The bloodied shirt had fallen away overnight and a dried patch of blood marred his sleek coat. Cayden pulled himself up by the rock and stood, tentatively testing his leg. It shook as he put weight on it. He picked up a stick off the ground of the right length to use as a cane and hobbled to Brimstone's side. He ran his hand over his flank, examining the wound. It had healed rapidly, much more rapidly than his.

"You are amazingly well, Brimstone. I guess that is one advantage of being a magical creature, eh?"

Brimstone tossed his head then butted Cayden in the chest, as if to say, *why are you not healed?*

The force knocked Cayden sideways into the boulder. He winced at the spasm that ran up his leg. "I know, but without Ziona, I cannot fix it. There is no one to help with this injury. You are it, boy. You are all the help I have. Come, we must find an entrance to the catacombs." He awkwardly pulled himself onto Brimstone's back, tangling his hands in his mane and urging him off the cliff.

There must be another way, a hidden approach to the castle. The arrow attack proved that to approach Cathair directly would be suicidal. Cayden feared that much had changed during his time away in Primordial territory, and he no longer knew the lay of the land or the status of his people. He berated himself for not keeping in closer contact with the Kingsmen. While the castle should be secure, to assume so would be foolish in the extreme, given Helga's manipulations.

At his urging, Brimstone launched himself out over the sea, a great soaring shadow, black on grey, in the predawn light. They had an hour at most before they would be visible to the castle occupants. Cayden set Brimstone winging along the coast, flying to the sea side that formed one of the castle's outer defences. As they flew, Cayden's eyes searched the limestone cliffs, the shush of water over rocks below and the peeping of sleepy sea birds the only noise in the still morning air. Silently, Brimstone flew along the cliff face. At first light, the castle came into view. They flew by, Brimstone battling the unpredictable winds that swept the vertical approach, at a height with the castle wall. They hugged the cliff face so as to be not seen then dropped lower on the return pass, following the curve of the cliff.

On the third swooping pass that barely cleared the water, Cayden spied a wide ledge with a scooped hollow of rock, a shadowy recess about ten feet above sea level. The opening was mirrored by a second, similar crevice, a pair of omega-shaped black orbs sunk into the stone. Cayden urged Brimstone to land on the right ledge with a clatter of hooves and scattering of stones. As he touched down, the height of the aperture became apparent. Cayden studied the opening for a minute then urged Brimstone towards the gap. Carved all around the face were runes, weathered and ancient, similar to those on the great stones in the sacred clearing. The entrance was very, very old, from a time long past. A haze covered the opening, flickering shadows of light and dark as though seeing through a mist or a cloud. Cayden drew Brimstone up short, studying the markings. His eyes roved over the runes. Something tickled in the back of his mind…a passage he had seen in a book during his study of the ancient manuscripts in the library.

He studied the runes. A moon hidden by clouds sat at apex of the opening, the clouds flowing into everyday images of animals and people and what appeared to be armies. Always the moon flowed over them. The moon reminded him of an eye. It even had an eyelid, a slit of rock that if one blurred the eye, suggested a blink…or a wink.

A wink.

Cayden narrowed his eyes, and that was when he saw it. He slid off Brimstone's back and hobbled over to the winking slit in the rock face sliding his hand inside the smoothed opening, palm down. The rock shrank around his hand. Panicked, Cayden tried to pull it back, but it was impossible. The rock flared with heat and just as quickly cooled, a blue mist puffing from the opening. With a sigh, the rock released his hand and the eye opened. The screened illusion lifted, and the tunnel was revealed.

Welcome…welcome…welcome, the passage whispered. Cayden limped into the cave. As soon as he crossed the threshold, the veil returned, cutting him off from Brimstone. The way was shut.

One eye of the rock face now glowed with life. The other remained dark, waiting.

CHAPTER 38

Apples

CALLEIGH RODE AWAY through the scraggly brush intent on reaching the castle before the Kingsmen. Her knowledge of where to find Cayden could have been of use to the Kingsmen, who she knew only wished to protect their king, yet she knew she could not delay. Too many people would make for noisy passage, and she had to reach him without alerting his enemies to his presence within the castle. She was in a unique position to be of influence to the Soul-Fetched king. If anyone could reach him in his befuddled state, it would be her. And yet her heart was torn in as many directions as she had children. As much as she knew she needed to be there to make sure Cayden fulfilled his destiny, she longed to aid her other sons. It was time that the forgotten children of Morpheus were acknowledged and given their rightful place in the world of godlings. Mordecai and Genii deserved to be acknowledged, rather than being pushed aside and hidden away as the shameful by-product of a god's lust. Even after countless eons of time, her anger over their forced exile burned with the slow ache of an infected sliver. She had done as Morpheus had asked. She had remained in the swamp quietly raising her remaining son Genii, only to have him taken from her by the godlings she was hiding from. She had managed to hide Mordecai in their midst, giving him up to another woman's care, but with Genii she had not been so lucky.

She'd heard rumours of Genii being alive after a fashion, but the shock of seeing him in the flesh in her hovel had almost undone her illusion charm. She scrubbed a hand across her eyes as she felt the welling moisture of tears. There was no time for self-pity. Her illusion had worked for they were none the wiser and now thought her dead. Her boys would continue on their mission and take their rightful place as the true rulers of the world in the end. But first, she had a vendetta to fulfill. Helga had broken her promise. She would not do so again. The Spirit Shield Cayden was the key, and Helga would use him up. Cayden was her revenge, and Calleigh would be there to see that he destroyed Helga.

She regretted leaving the Kingsmen behind, but the urgency of her task did not allow for plodding armies and chest-thumping strategies. She had not waited this long to transform only to be caged. For far too long, she had been restrained by the swamp in a self-imposed exile, but it was necessary while she hid the children of her affair with Morpheus, the forbidden godlings who were the result of a quick visit back to the world of men. Had they been found, the other gods would have demanded that their throats be slit upon discovery. Exile seemed the lesser of the two evils, and the swamp was a natural barrier to curious eyes. With a special blend of her magic enhanced by a few tricks she had learned from the Primordial priests, the swamp quickly became a place that few visited. The reputation kept them safe, secure, and lonely.

Age had its advantages, she now knew of entry points long forgotten by the generations that had come and gone during her lifetime. She rode out of the woods on the east side of Cathair, skirting around the edge until she was due east of the castle. Pastures dotted here and there with horses, cattle and sheep gently curved upward to the distant seat of power set against the cliff. The town of Cathair spilled out all around it except on one side that was reserved as pastures. Rough mounds rose from the ground in regular patterns, some overgrown and buried with time, others displaying the tip of the stonework that revealed ancient foundations. Calleigh studied the layout and from memory located an intersection of stone that was once a portion of the royal stables that had housed the legendary Pegasuses.

She heeled her horse toward that spot at a slow walk, just a rider crossing the land, nothing to pay attention to. She did not fear meeting any of the rioting legionnaires. They were all ensconced in the towns and villages, not out watching sheep, which was why this forgotten access made so much sense.

The stables of old had been magically enhanced to care for the Pegasuses. Not being a herd animal or even mortal, their housing needs had been more in the form of providing a connection to the spirit world for rejuvenation, so the "stables" had actually been a form of temple of spirit. Although not honouring the gods, it had drawn its strength from the prayers of the people. When the fall had occurred and the temples were abandoned, the Pegasuses had disappeared and their stable had simply faded away, leaving only the original rune-enhanced stonework to show anything had ever existed in the place.

With the passing of the Spirit Shields, the place was forgotten and enveloped into the pasture grounds of the castle.

But Calleigh remembered.

She slid off the back of her horse in the shade of an ancient apple tree. The tree towered over the other trees in a field that had a square foundation wall. It was the only apple tree to be spotted amongst the elm and cottonwoods that were most common in the area. The tree had originally grown inside the barn, as a magical food source for the Pegasuses and was meant to be consumed by them alone. Now, overgrown and tangled, the apple tree produced small, sour fruit, not in the least appealing to humans, and so it was ignored and forgotten. The few who had tried them of recent date had writhed in their beds with such wicked belly cramps that the people believed the tree to bear poisoned fruit. Everyone avoided the tree, including the animals that roamed the pastures.

Calleigh walked over and patted the old bark, murmuring, "Hello, my old friend. It has been a long time." The tree waved its limbs, creaking and a couple of apples fell to the ground with a thunk. "Yes, the Pegasuses have returned. They will be coming for your apples." The tree straightened, and two knots popped open revealing liquid chocolate eyes shot with gold. Calleigh smiled at the hope reflected in the elderly face. "I need access to the tunnels. Could you open a passage for me, Ancient One?" The tree creaked and its roots shifted, the earth between them crumbling away to reveal a set of stone steps descending into the dark. "Thank you, elder. Best put a proper polish on those apples of yours. They will be hungry when they arrive!" The elder tree's smile widened. Calleigh chuckled, shaking a couple of birds from their perch with a squawk.

Grinning, Calleigh descended the ten dark, dank steps, pulling a stick from her pocket. She pulled on both ends, and light flared along its length, as the roots closed over her head, shutting out the daylight from above. Light stick in hand she examined her surroundings, the light sliding over limestone passages with a ceiling of earth and fingerling roots, reminding her of the thinning hair of an elderly man, where the scalp is clearly visible. She moved the light stick over her choices once again then picked a tunnel on the left that headed roughly in the direction of the castle grounds.

At the end of this underground labyrinth was the culmination of years of hiding, of years of neglect, of years of denial. It was time for truth, and she would see it freed, if it was that last thing she did. *It might very well be, for what is to come may not be possible to stop. One thing is certain, without me the Spirit Shields would surely fail. I must get to Cayden in time and do what must be done. But first, I must retrieve my spell book. I instructed Hud where to hide it for safekeeping against a future need, and that need is now.*

Crossing her mental fingers, she chose a path. As the black of the tunnel swallowed her, the odour of sulphur assailed her nose.

Even here, Helga touches the world. Calleigh quickened her pace. *Even here.*

CHAPTER 39

Darkness Spreads

AVERY RUBBED HER ARMS, sensing treachery in the air. Something was wrong, a foul slicking of evil spreading out through the world, coating the living. The forest was no longer safe. She walked in a slow circle, reaching out to the beings that surrounded them, to her friends, beckoning to them with her mind, asking them to appear. Her eyes glowed with the intensity of her gaze.

Artio sniffed at the air, nose wrinkled and teeth bared, sensing the danger. The hair on her head stiffened. A great evil followed them, a swirling black void of despair. The magical creatures fled in front of it so that they crowded around their small party, clamoring for Avery's attention. She sensed their presence, but they did not reveal themselves, cautious of Artio's intentions.

"Come, my friends. There is nothing to fear. Come tell me what you see, what you saw, what you feel, what you felt." Avery sank down on a moss-covered log and crossed her ankles. Then, she reached out a hand in invitation. "Gather around me. We will talk." Her voice hardened. With steel in her voice she said, "Artio, sit beside me," patting the log beside her.

Artio snorted and strutted over to her side, glaring at the hidden creatures. "They are afraid. Afraid of me…afraid of death. They are not warriors. They cower in fear. They are not worthy of me, not anymore." She sat, hands on knees, face impassive and waited.

The first to approach, possibly because of their opaque quality, were the tree sprites, followed by the fae. "Avery, Avery, Avery," they pipped as they flew in a blur, dancing on the air. Their usual merry, twinkling dust was dimmed as though viewed through a filter. "Help us, Avery!"

The bushes shook and a unicorn pushed out of the brush, the pearly sheen of her coat dulled by a grey mist. Deva bowed to Avery, her horn touching the ground before rising. Avery dipped her head in acknowledgment. "I feel a great sadness spreading across the land. What is it, Deva?"

"Helga has implemented her plan. She has loosed a disease-carrying necromancer on the land. He spreads the plague to all he comes in contact with. We must flee! We are no longer safe in the Sacred Forest. We must return to the temple, to the celestial realm, or we will perish forever."

"A necromancer!" A ripple ran down Avery's spine. The shock of one so horrible being loosed on the world was beyond comprehension.

Artio's lips peeled back in a snarl. "Helga!" she spat. "She has much to answer for." Artio stood, hands on hips, staring down the back trail to menace all that approached and failed to notice the werewolf that sauntered into the clearing until it paused right beside her. On its hind legs, he stood as tall as Artio.

Avery had never seen Artio surprised, but this sudden appearance startled her so badly that her knives flew into her hand, and she spun ready to slash.

"*Artio, no!*" yelled Avery. The werewolf grabbed Artio's wrist, freezing Artio's throw before she was able to release the knife. They leaned into each other's faces and snarled, deep rumbling in their throats. Avery jumped up from the log and pushed her way between the two, mindless of the danger. "Stop it! Both of you!" She shoved them apart, daring them to attack with her in the midst. Avery stamped down hard on their toes with the heel of her boot to get their attention. With a sharp stab and a twist that dug the point into Artio's instep, Artio's eyes snapped back to her sister then narrowed with mistrust and suspicion before she sheathed her knives with a final glare tossed at the werewolf.

"We have no time for this! *By the gods,*" Avery swore "*we are on the same side! Do you want Helga to win? She is the enemy, not us!*"

Put aside your natural antagonism. This is not the time for it," she spat. "Save it for the battle to come."

The fae folk whirled around their heads, their anxiety evident in the strobe-like flashing of colours. "Hurry, hurry, hurry," they pipped. "Time is short! Time is short!"

The werewolf bowed and backed up several steps. "It has been a long time since one of the Bear Clan has walked the sacred forests. The world is changing. If you can work with her, Mother, then I will too.

Artio turned and walked back to her horse, climbing back into the saddle. "The temple is a few hours' ride. We can be there by noon. We leave now." She reined her mount toward Faylea and trotted off, clearly expecting to be followed.

"Come, all of you. I need you for the task to come. Stay close."

Avery retrieved her own mount. With a few minutes of brisk riding, she caught up to her sister. They rode in silence for a while, the creatures shadowing them in the green forest, forming an invisible honour guard of sorts. As they rode, more and more creatures joined the throng, fleeing the menacing shadow that darkened the forest floor.

By noon, the sun was a watery disk in the sky, partially obscured by the smoke of the sacred mountain and also by the blackness spreading across the land. They reached the great tree that guarded the entrance to Faylea. As Avery rode up, she immediately noticed the change. The leaves of the great oak were yellowed and curling, as though autumn had arrived early. A carpet of leaves spread out under the tree, and its branches drooped as though carrying a weight of snow. Her horse stepped on a leaf, and it squished under its hoof, the smell of rotten eggs replacing the normally sweet scent of flowers on the air. Avery glanced down and gasped. The leaves were covered in dark blisters, black swellings that bloated them. Her eyes searched the scattering of leaves. They were all the same. Her eyes rose to the massive oak. The leaves still attached to the tree were swollen as a hand swells when injured. One poke and the blackened bubbles would burst. A tarry ooze slid down the trunk to puddle on the ground at its base. The grass smoked as the tar moved across it, slowly consuming everything it encountered.

"Stay away from the leaves," Avery said sharply. "Do not touch them!" She led them on a zigzagging path to the opening at the base careful to not touch any of the squishy blobs herself. Her horse was not so lucky, however. Where the ooze had splashed onto her legs, burns welled with moisture. She whinnied with pain, attempting to lick at the boils. Avery slid from her back at pulled her satchel from where it was lashed back of her saddle, then slipped the bridle from her mount and let her go.

Artio rode up and copied Avery, freeing her horse. "They will not last long. They are dying already."

"I know," Avery whispered, as she watched the two horses limp away. She could feel their pain and confusion. The magical creatures that had shadowed them to the entrance were nowhere to be found, preferring to find their own, plague-free approach to the city. "Follow me." Avery walked off into the tunnel, followed by Artio, whose head nearly brushed the underside of the curve. She hunched to keep from coming in contact with the tree, a difficult feat while the black tar stretched like taffy.

Avery pulled her hood tighter to her head and hurried down the passage to answer the call of the temple. As she entered the temple, the whispering began, rising in volume in a crescendo, the noise knocking against her skull like a gong. She burst from the tunnel to the cliff top. Where on her previous visit a few short weeks ago the valley had been verdant and lush with vegetation, it now appeared to have been shaved. Shocked, Avery froze, her eyes disbelieving, then eased forward, forcing her mind to make sense of the devastation. The lush ferns and bulbous mushroom trees were shriveled dead sticks, devoid of life. The riot of flowers had been replaced by tumorous growths that swallowed the blooms, and everywhere the sickness of black could be seen. Everywhere, except for a lone holdout.

The moonstone temple stood on an island of enchanted greenery, the lone survivor in a sea of death. Yet even it struggled to keep from being swallowed by the dying forest. A cracking sound and a series of pops broke the silence, as the trees toppled from the weight of the blight on their limbs. Artio stepped up beside Avery, snarling. "It seems the sickness not only pursues us but also moves before us. We cannot cross that," she said, pointing to the valley below. "We will surely die. We are cut off from the temple."

Avery's heart sank. Artio was right. There was no away to cross it. But she had to get to the temple! Frustrated, she thrust her hand inside her satchel, searching for she did not know what. What could possibly help to get across that? Maybe an herb? She crouched down and began to rummage inside her bag, and that was when she found it. Her hand closed around an object she had nearly forgotten about. Suddenly, she knew what it was for. She pulled out her hand. Clutched in her fist was a necklace of pearly white beads, long enough to be slipped over the head, and hanging from a golden bale was a moonstone.

"Yes, this will work," she murmured. Closing her eyes, she spoke to the beads. "Moonbeam, can you hear me? Can you feel my call? I need you. Can you find me? I know you are out there. I felt you earlier. Come to me, and bring Sandstorm. Be careful of the bleakness spreading around us. It will hurt you."

She stood up and waited, her eyes fixed on the treetops. It wasn't long until the weak sunlight was blocked by two large-winged bodies. Moonbeam and Sandstorm dropped from the sky and galloped up to them, careful to not touch the plague. Avery grinned and hugged both Pegasuses in turn then turned back to Artio. What she saw in her face shocked her. Tears streamed down Artio's face and with a choking sob, Artio flung her arms around Sandstorm's neck, howling into his soft mane. Sandstorm nibbled the back of her coat, rubbing his nose up and down with a Pegasus's equivalent of a pat on the back. Avery smiled and swiped away a stray tear from her own eye.

Artio smiled at her sister, as she raised red-rimmed eyes to meet hers over Sandstorm's back. "Come. Let's get to the temple."

They climbed onto the back of their Pegasuses, and with a flap of wings launched into the air to soar over the diseased valley floor. It was even worse from the air. The city had been reduced to a seething cesspool, teaming with the kind of creatures that haunted children's nightmares. Once Avery thought she'd spied a great snake sliding through the muck, a dozen feet long, and scaly. Avery's heart pounded with fear for the people of Faylea. She remembered the bright-eyed smiling children who had given her cups of nectar on her first visit. This blistered landscape below could not harbour life forms as fragile as a human's. Where were the residents?

CHAPTER 40

A Change of Leadership

MAREA, FORMER HIGH PRIESTESS OF FAYLEA, limped along at the rear of the column of Flesh Clan warriors, forgotten in the excitement of the godlings' departure. It seemed that the warriors had concluded that since she had spent so much time in the Artio's company that she had been bound to the clan and was no longer in need of guarding.

The simple fact of the matter was that she was neither drugged nor soul fetched and completely her own free agent, a free agent seeing clearly for the first time. She was unsure of what do to about that fact, seeing as she was deeply embedded within the clan's ranks. She rode along and pretended to be one of the enslaved clan, observing the antics of her kin and sorting through the last few weeks of upheaval and change.

She acknowledged that she was not a High Priestess in the ultimate sense of the word. An up close and way too personal view of two godlings had disabused her of that notion. With the clarity of hindsight, she realized she had failed those she had sworn to serve, those to whom the temples were dedicated. Remorse flowed over her and with it a great sadness. Was it too late to make a difference in the flow of time? From beneath her hood, her eyes traced Hototo's movements, her closest equivalent in the Flesh Clan realm. He held the warriors on a path that led straight to the temple, but there was nothing to be done there except wait for the godlings to reappear. In the meantime, the mountain under their feet rumbled and grumbled, small quakes opening fissures beneath their feet and the hooves of their mounts. Her head swiveled to the summit of the Spine, to where she knew the entrance to Sheol Animus was located. The threat was there. As far as she knew, no one was confronting it. Someone needed to stop Helga or at least run enough interference to her plans to give the Spirit Shields a chance to succeed.

Marea's head swiveled back to the fore, and she heeled her mount up beside Hototo. No one stopped her approach. Hototo marked her movement as she rode up beside him on his right then dismissed her presence, focused on the trail ahead. Achak rode on Hototo's left side and was similarly studying the terrain ahead.

With lightning reflexes, a slender-bladed knife slid into Marea's right palm. With a swift thrust under the sternum, she stabbed Hototo, piercing his lungs and heart. With a strangled cry, he slumped forward, and his coat flopped open revealing the doll. Marea snatched it away as he toppled off his horse to the ground, dead before he hit the ground. Marea wrenched open the back of the doll and pulled the binding agent from its back, breaking the connection, then for good measure, tore the straw apart and sliced its head off with the bloodied knife.

That is the one weakness with Soul Fetches. Those bound to the doll cannot undo the enchantment, but someone who is not bound can remove the token that magically binds without harm and reuse it to their own purposes. Risk or no risk, they must be freed. In their current state, they are less than useless. As mindless puppets, they will not see the danger before them. We need thinking, sane warriors. It is a risk I must take!

The Flesh Clan warriors jerked as though slapped awake and blinked rapidly as the bewitchment fell away, staring in shocked recovery at each other and the slain High Priest lying in a sticky pool of his own blood that was soaking into the earth. Blades were drawn and angry shouts rose.

Marea raised the blood-stained knife and doll and hissed, "I have freed you. Choose now. Time is short. Listen to me. *Listen!*" The murmuring lessened but did not cease. The more aggressive of the warriors edged closer to bring her within striking range. "You have been under an enchantment," she shouted, waving the doll. "The world as we know it is ending. You may choose to die here now, fighting each other and me, or you can choose to battle for the future. The temples call to us. Not just the main temple in Faylea, but the Thunder temple and the Spirit temples. These are our temples, not Flesh Clan or Spirit Clan. They belong to all Primordial Clans.

"You ride for Faylea where you cannot possibly aid those you claim to serve, as they will move beyond our assistance. But there is one thing you can do. You can help to buy them time. The legion has returned to Cathair. The Spirit Shields maintain a Well of Souls in Cathair that may have been taken by the legion. Go fight for the Spirit Shields. Engage the legion who is under the sway of the goddess Helga. Helga has been manipulating Hototo, controlling his mind. I regret what had to be done, but I had to break the bond to the Soul Fetch before he betrayed us all, including Artio."

Achak shook his head, vision clearing then swung around to face the hardened warriors. "What she says is true. Avery and Artio have their mission in the temple to complete, but we can help Cayden, who is also soul slaved. Avery needs her brother, and Helga is controlling him. I suspect that Lord Cyrus is also under Helga's influence. If we are to give the king of Cathair a chance, we must tackle the legion's forces. When the battle comes, when Helga moves against Cathair, it will not be from afar. The battle for the souls of the world will happen where it all started, in Cathair. It is there we must go to give aid. It is time to set aside clan divisions and unite as a primary Primordial force. We will gather Spirit warriors as we travel. Who is with me?"

Leather creaked and bridles clinked as the warriors considered his words.

Then a burly Primordial with a livid scar that ran from brow to chin urged his horse forward. "We will fight this battle, Achak. I speak for us all. We will fight for clans and country. You will accompany us and lead the way. It is time to put an end to the legion once and for all."

Achak nodded acceptance of the conditions then nudged his horse closer to Marea and spoke in a soft voice that did not carry. "Why do I get the impression that you will not be accompanying us?"

Marea smiled. Her steely eyes stared up at the mountain once again. "I intend to drop in on the lady of the mountain. Someone needs to trigger her traps and disrupt her plans. I intend to deliver a gift." She smiled grimly and turned in the direction of the smoking mountain. "Do not wait for me to catch up for I doubt I shall return." She caught Achak's eyes and smiled the first true smile he had seen on her face. "Take care of Avery. She deserves your loyalty. She is an amazing High Priestess."

Without a glance back, she heeled her horse into a trot and rode off into the woods, alone.

Achak stirred as Marea disappeared from site then glanced down at the corpse of Hototo on the ground beside him. "Do you wish to bury him before we go?"

"Burials are by fire for Flesh Clans." The wizened warrior snapped his fingers, and a companion rode forward with a tinder box, stoked with coals for starting cook fires. Several other warriors dropped reins and gathered dried brush and wood, piling it over Hototo where he lay. Once enough tinder and wood had been collected, they set the funeral pyre alight and burned the body while chanting prayers to the gods for his soul's safe journey. When the corpse had been reduced to bones and the fire winked out, they remounted, awaiting the next command.

"If you have spirit guides, now is the time to summon them. Their aid will be needed before the day is over." The assembled warriors reached into their packs and pulled out their spirit masks and cloaks and donned the apparel of their guardians, hiding their faces and bodies from the world. Achak resisted the urge to shiver as the macabre assemblage organized themselves at his back and followed him south out of the mountains. His final wish was that the legions would be more afraid than he was. He was afraid, very afraid.

CHAPTER 41

The Old Captain

RYDER PEERED AROUND THE CORNER of the stone wall, watching the Charun sweeping up and down the staircase at the far end of the cavern. A dull red glow reflected off the wall, casting the staircase and the black billowing shapes in relief on the wall behind them. The Charun were already tall, but their shadows reached up and curved over onto the ceiling, a weirdly distorted real-time puppet play. But it was not the dancing shadows that held Ryder's attention. It was the grunting creatures of stone that milled at the base of the pit. The Charun dragged the bodies of the dying slaves down the stairs, most of them barely alive, unconscious and at the end of their time as flesh beings.

Reaching the edge of the pit, they picked up the bodies and tossed them into it, where the grunting and scraping noises surged, only to fall back to a quieter rumbling.

For the life of him, Ryder could not guess what was down in the pit. Whatever it was, the Charun were feeding the mostly dead slaves to it in a steady stream. The things in the pit seemed to have no end of appetite.

Ryder crept closer, keeping to the shadows, timing his movements to the dance on the walls. He was only another shadow in a shadow-filled room. The Charun paid no attention to the cavern. They saw nothing but the task at hand.

A scream suddenly rent the air. Ryder froze, his eyes dragged to the area of commotion against his will. He was now close enough to see over the edge into the flaming pit below and what he saw there made the blood freeze in his veins. The screaming came from a man who had regained consciousness just in time to realize he was in mortal danger. He thrashed in the arms of the Charun like a fly in a spider's web. The Charun showed no more pity than the spider, heaving the man off his feet and flinging him over the edge with a shriek. His screams followed him to the bottom where he hit with a thunk. A blue mist rose from his corpse. With a grinding of boulders, flaming red Daimons nearly as tall as the pit converged on the body. Grey-skinned with curving horns and long snouts, the Daimon snuffled around the dead man and began inhaling the blue mist seeping from the victim, feeding on the soul of the Primordial male. As they scraped across the surface, they crushed the body beneath their heavy stone feet, the blood flashing to powder as it evaporated in the heat of the pit. Within seconds, nothing remained of the man. They sniffed around, searching for some remnant of the soul of the victim. Then as one, their heads swiveled in Ryder's direction. Ryder scurried back from the edge and crawled into the shadows behind a bolder and crouched, waiting to see if the Daimon had noticed.

Stupid! he chided himself. *Of course, they can smell a living soul!*

His eyes roved over the cavern one last time. His feet wanted to flee, but he had followed the Charun for a reason. If the Daimon in the pit were Helga's secret weapon and the horror she was about to unleash on the world, she had to have a way to get them out of the pit.

And then he saw it. A door was set in the far wall, tall as a two-story building and shaped like an arrowhead. The way out.

Ryder's eyes went back to the pit that was swarming with Daimons, and he swallowed heavily. It was the only exit he had found. His eyes travelled around the cavern one last time, but no other door presented itself to him. Cautious of drawing attention to himself, he silently backed into the shadow-filled passage he had taken to reach this point. Once he reached the inky blackness, he felt his way along the wall to the crevice where he had stashed his torch. He pulled the welcoming light from its hiding spot and turned to go, only to find his way blocked by a Charun.

The Charun was the reconstituted soul of Brennan, former captain of the Kingsmen before his death centuries ago. The eyeless slits in its face drooped as they had in real life because he had lost an eye during a battle long forgotten. That much had come forward into this form. Ryder was convinced that more was present. Much more. He had seen flashes of understanding, flashes of what could be memory carried along with his snatched soul.

It was not uncommon for people to have flashbacks to former lives, but the normal process of death and rebirth erased those memories for the most part. But while they waited for rebirth, the disembodied soul remembered their former lives, a comfort that all was not lost while they waited their turn to re-enter the land of mortals.

I am no philosopher, but it seems to me that those memories are being retained in the Charun, at least those who as people had had the moral fortitude to know who they really were, when human. Brennan was a sworn protector of the king and the Spirit Shield. His memories would be long, his loyalty off the scale. There is a soldier in there that I can reach. I have to try!

"Captain Brennan. It is good to see you again." Ryder kept any hint of pity or loathing out of his voice. He was just one soldier addressing another. "How goes the watch?"

The Charun floated back a step and paused. Ryder sensed confusion and familiarity at the greeting. "What are you doing here, human? You wander where you should not be," he grated in a hoarse voice, the sound the scraping of a metal file.

"I wander where I must, and Helga did not forbid any area of the labyrinth to me. There is no place off limits."

"A foolish position, if this is true. My brethren…do not see things as I do. You will find yourself fed to the Daimon, and your screams will be truly terrible, as you are *not* mostly dead." The cowl of his hood swung toward the pit then back to Ryder. "I urge you, little man, to stay away from this area."

"Captain, I need your help." The Charun shook his head as though shaking rain off his hood.

"Do not call me that," he hissed.

"Captain Brennan," Ryder said sharply "I call on you to fulfill your oaths. You swore to protect the Spirit Shield. You swore to protect the king. Those oaths are not cancelled because you are dead and neither are they cancelled because your soul has been stolen. If anything, you have been called to a higher mission. You are in a unique position to battle from the inside, the same as I am."

"I cannot."

"Help me to overthrow Helga. Serve your king one last time. Make a difference, now and for future generations. Help me."

The Charun swayed, hood dipped, hands hidden in its sleeves. "I…cannot. Leave now before it is too late." He swayed once more then seemed to turn sideways as he slid through the rock and back into line with its companions.

Frustrated, Ryder strode up the passage no longer masking his steps. He would figure out a way to bring Brennan over onto his side.

I must, for my men and for myself. If I don't, we are all dead men.

CHAPTER 42

A Price to Pay

GENII RODE AS THOUGH fiery Daimons pursued his back trail, riding with no heed for his personal safety or that of his horse. His only thought was reaching Artio in time. As he rode, his mind distilled the shocking information he now carried. *I have a brother!* He weighed it against everything he had ever known or experienced. That Helga had betrayed them all he no longer doubted, and a great shame spread through him, warming his body. The shame was quickly replaced by anger, the anger of one fooled and of one bewitched. He knew academically that there was nothing he could have done at the moment of his demise, yet the warning signs had been there.

As he reached the foothills, he intentionally took a path that kept him out of the forests that hugged the mountain, for he knew that Helga's spies lurked in the trees and reported all that moved beneath them. The curving route brought him to a mountainous valley strewn with large boulders as though the gods used it as a game board for marbles. The normally tall grasses were trampled, evidence that a large force had camped there, and recently. He rode around the abandoned clearing, reading the signs, mentally counting the force of Primordial Flesh Clan warriors. He estimated the camp followers to number around two thousand men and women. At the far end of the bowl, a series of caves with carved lintels warned of a temple of the gods. He reined up beside the Bear Clan markings and studied the runes, reading the warning. He did not enter as the temple was not for him. He was not of the forgotten Bear Clans or even Primordial. But the evidence was overwhelming that it was active.

Temples are living things. Every wizard knows this. I can hear it humming. Genii carefully skirted the temple, the vibrations making his skin itch like ants under his sleeves. He heeled his horse, following the trampled path to his quarry. The cold camp was perhaps six hours old, which meant they had left in the predawn hours. Genii glanced at the angle of the sun, judging the timing of his arrival at the Primordial camp. He could not reach them before dark unless he moved faster than he already had but travelling in the dark was dangerous for all.

The woods swallowed him once more. He pushed his mount to cover the distance, his eyes studying the trail as he rode and eating from the saddle. The trail freshened surprisingly swiftly, and two hours later he rode out into a break in the woods to find the entire Primordial encampment spread out in front of him about half a mile ahead. He reined in sharply, keeping to the vestiges of shadow and studied the scene ahead of him. His eyes scanned the milling horsemen, clustered around small fires and sprawled on the ground. It appeared they were in the process of setting up tents for evening. He searched, but he could not find any evidence of a royal presence with a tent that was being given preferential treatment. Every tent was a warrior's tent. Artio was not there.

He searched one more time convinced that she was not with the main army. He faded back into the trees and backtracked to an animal trail that skirted the clearing. He dismounted and quietly led his horse along the trail, circling around then sneaking past the encampment on soft needles of pine. He kept a hand on his mount's nose, discouraging her from whinnying at the other horses. Once, twice, he paused as a warrior looked his way, his horse's ears pricked in their direction. Seeing nothing, he settled back to his cook pot. Genii exhaled slowly, relaxing.

Clearing the army, Genii picked up the trail once again, mounted and booted his horse into a gallop. It was darkening swiftly now. Studying the trail, he could see that they were moving as fast as he was. He could not possibly reach them before dark. As the sun set and the trail darkened, he was finally forced to admit defeat and rode off the trail to where he had spied a tall pine with low-hanging branches. It would make a fine shelter for a night. He hobbled his horse on a small patch of sketchy grass, pouring water into a leather-lined depression that he scooped from the soft soil. Then he crawled under the pine with a blanket and was soon asleep.

He awoke with a start, his arm itching furiously. He scratched at it and then fell back asleep. The next time he woke, the black of night had lightened to a dull grey. He rolled out of his blankets, ready to start down the trail as soon as light permitted. He dragged his blanket out from under the pine, rolling it tightly. His arm itched, and he scratched at it absently. His clothing was stuck to his arm. He frowned, dropping the blanket. He peeled off his cloak and then peeled back his shirt sleeve. His skin came with it. It was stuck to the shirt, but it did not bleed. Instead, it peeled back in layers, some with chunks of blackened flesh clinging to the strip. Genii stared at his arm, and a twisting sick welled up in his stomach.

Necromancer skin. He fought the urge to throw up all over his dropped blanket. *I have necromancer skin! Helga's parting gift of reuniting me with my body was not a gift after all. She has cursed me never to return.* Helga's "gifts" always came with a price. In his heart of hearts, he had known she would not fully release him. Instead, she dispersed him as a plague to infect all of those around him. Anyone he touched, anyone he came in contact with would surely die. *Was this your intention all along, Helga? To set me as a plague on your family? To wipe out all the resistance left in the world?* Genii pulled his sleeve back down and donned his coat, pulling the hood up over his head. Had Calleigh known? Why his thoughts should turn to his mother at this point he did not know, but they did. *Mordecai, I am so sorry, but you are now exposed too. Forgive me, brother!* He wondered absently if Mordecai would know how to heal this but dismissed it immediately. His curse was of the underworld. Where would Mordecai learn such a thing?

Artio. His eyes swung her direction and grief clawed his heart, a monster of pain and longing. All the joy and hope and love he had carefully stored, corked inside, now exploded to the surface to mix with his tears of grief, desperate longing and the searing pain of denial. He could not have what he'd lost. Not then, not now, not ever. *Artio!* Genii collapsed to his knees, squeezed his eyes shut and wept.

When he opened them again, the grey had lightened and the trail was visible once more. Woodenly, he picked up his blanket, tied it to the back of his saddle and climbed up. His face was a mask of death, his teeth bared in a rictus smile. He was death. Nothing mortal could harm him. Once again, a necromancer walked the earth. He would spread the plague, but he would make sure before he died that all deserving of death joined him. He booted his horse and rode off after Artio.

CHAPTER 43

The Catacombs

CALLEIGH SHRANK BACK against the cold stone as a shadow danced across the wall. Someone was down in the abandoned tunnels, wandering the same corridors as she was. She frowned at the light. No one knew the passages as she did. No one was old enough to remember, with the possible exception of Mordecai.

Leery of discovery, she crept forward, testing each footfall for silence before committing to the step. Her light sheltered under her coat so as to not allow its beam to cast her shadow. Calleigh reached the intersection and peered down the corridor just in time to see the light vanish around a bend. She followed the bobbing trail, as it was moving in the same direction she wished to go. Her curiosity was stronger than her fear.

Whoever it was moved swiftly, unconcerned about concealment or stealth. The lack of caution indicated a familiarity with the passages and a certain amount of arrogance. Or foolishness.

The shadow slid forward, and then Calleigh heard a scraping sound. She hurried her steps then paused at the corner, peering around it at a short passage that ended in a heavy oak door with rusting hinges and a large old-fashioned lock. The man—she could see it was a man now—pocketed a heavy iron key and disappeared through the door, pulling it closed behind him with a squealing bang that stirred up the centuries-old dust in the passage. She drew her sleeve across her nose to stifle the sneeze that itched to be set free. As the dust settled, Calleigh inched forward until she was directly in front of the door then put her ear to the rough surface. Silence greeted her. She counted to ten, then pulled on the handle. It rewarded her with a softer squeal than before but was still loud enough to make her cringe. She opened it only as far as she needed to slip through then paused again on the other side. Silence greeted her. She counted to ten once more, her ears straining to catch the slightest sound that would warn her she was not alone. Not even a rat stirred. The light was gone. She pulled out her own lamp and started off down the passage. The light did not reappear, and her pace quickened. Whoever the man had been, he had been in an awful hurry and had outpaced her.

Eventually, the passage began to slope upward and the damp lessened, the rough stone lightening to the limestone that was the signature of the castle base. Etchings appeared, words carved into the stone in a language no longer spoken, the meaning of the words long forgotten by those still alive. Calleigh could read them, of course. She paused by a set of words carved above an archway leading into a room built of squared limestone blocks. "Within these hallowed walls, knowledge is bound. Within these sentry stones, eternity rests." Calleigh smiled. She had arrived at her destination.

She stepped across the threshold, intent on the recovery of her magic kit. She had gotten about five paces when a voice said, "Who dares to enter the catacombs? The knowledge of these passages is lost. Halt right there, not a step further."

Calleigh froze, cursing quietly under her breath, deriding herself for her carelessness.

"Turn and face me! Slowly now! Show me your hands!"

Calleigh turned, hands outstretched, gripping the lantern in the right, to face her challenger.

A young man stood before her, tall and slender, dressed in soiled riding breeches and a cloak that looked to have been slept in. His sandy hair was rumpled, and under his eyes deep pools of exhaustion sagged onto his cheekbones. Yet he stood with an air of command. In his hand was a sword, carved with the insignia of the royal house of Cathair.

Calleigh curtsied. "Sire, I beg your forgiveness. I did not mean to startle you." As she rose, her eyes roved over him, noting the weary set of his shoulders and measuring his emotional state. He teetered on the edge of madness, his eyes fevered and bright.

"Who are you? Quickly now. I do not have time for games."

"I am called Calleigh. You would not remember me, sire, but I certainly remember you."

Cayden ran his eyes over Calleigh. "The Calleigh I remember was an old woman who lived in a swamp. A witch of prodigious skill, if I remember correctly. She did not look like you."

Calleigh curtsied once again. "My lord's memory has returned. I am grateful because it will save much time in explanation. You need my help, Caerwyn."

"I am called Cayden in this time."

Calleigh nodded.

Cayden rubbed his temple with his free hand.

"My lord's headaches, they are the result of a soul bind, are they not?"

Cayden nodded again, his eyes weary. "They are, and there is nothing I can do to free myself from it."

"No, there is not. You cannot free yourself, but there is a way to limit their influence on you. That is the help I came to give. Hud hid a spell book here in the castle at my request, down here in the catacombs. That is why I am here, sire. To retrieve my bag and assist you. Will you search with me?"

Cayden lowered his sword and sheathed it on his hip. "Yes. If you can help, I will gladly accept it. There are few I can trust and even fewer that can assist me. Do you know where he hid it?" Cayden peered around the room. It was similar to the room where the Well of Souls was contained, and of a similar age. "These are the chambers below the library. There are four similar to this above us. Where do you intend to search?" Cayden took the lantern from her grip and walked over to a torch hanging from a peg on the wall. He lit the torch with the flame from the lantern then repeated the process with the others hanging around the room. In all, seven lanterns were lit, pushing back the shadows. The brightness revealed hand-painted words and inscriptions on the walls, some above alcoves, some decorating small wooden doors, others bearing pictographs begging for interpretation.

"What are we looking for?" Cayden's head turned as he heard the click of Calleigh's boots on the flagstone floor. She was running her hand along a series of symbols and runes above a rectangular drawer, murmuring the ancient words. The magically imbued runes glowed with power and purpose.

"I believe that what I am looking for is on this level. Hud would have hid it far away from accidental discovery."

"Hud, as in the Hud who was a captain back before the fall?" Cayden remembered the man who had raised Mordecai, who had served in the Kingsmen centuries ago.

"The same. He and I had an understanding. He could see the issues brewing between the godlings. He knew that magic was in danger of being eliminated from the world. His wife was my cousin, and she raised my son, Mordecai." Calleigh carefully kept her face hidden so that Cayden would not see the flash of pain that crossed her eyes. She spat on her fingers and then wiped it onto a rune set in a swirled design within a box shape. She traced the rune murmuring its name then ran her moist fingers along the spirals, following them out to the corner of the box. She did this four times, tracing a different swirl to a different corner. As she touched the fourth corner, the outline of the box glowed then sprang away from the wall, revealing a tray on which sat leather bag, blackened with age.

"Excellent!" She picked it up carefully and carried it over to Cayden. "My brew kit."

"What do you intend to brew?"

"A tempest for all tempests. Something that should have been done the first time you all set to squabbling. It is something to make your tummies so sour you will never ever again think to bring your squabbles to the world. I intend to make a binding." At Cayden's look of alarm, she said, "No, not a binding like to dolls. Primitive things those. No, these bindings are celestial. They will restrict the godlings access to the world. A bubble if you will, powered by will and by spirit. Your spirit, Cayden. You are a Spirit Shield, correct?" He nodded. "Then this will enhance what you already do. Now. I need access to a place to brew the potion."

"The main levels are crawling with Cyrus's men. I cannot take you to the castle kitchens."

"What about the librarian's living quarters here in the library?"

Cayden nodded slowly. "Yes. Brennus should be supportive. Let's see if he is awake."

Calleigh turned toward the staircase at the end of the room, but Cayden's hand on her arm stopped her. She raised an eyebrow in enquiry. "Sire?"

"Do not double-cross me," Cayden's voice hardened, roughened. "I have no intention of failing in my duty, yet there are times when I am not myself, when the madness takes over. In those times, I could kill. Do what you came to do, and do not hesitate to do what must be done. I will not hesitate. Helga will not hesitate."

Calleigh nodded acceptance and curtsied, then followed his tall form as he strode away.

I will do as I must...as we all must...before the end, Calleigh thought, *I just wish it didn't have to be to you...my lost son.*

CHAPTER 44

A Family of Four

MORDECAI RODE IN A DAZE, slumped in his saddle. The truths bestowed on him were not the cause. Helga had activated his doll, and the powerful tugging on his mind was unhinging him. With a wizard's will, he dueled, slashing and mentally weaving looking for an opening to cut down his opponent to break the bond of the Soul Fetch.

He gritted his teeth and fought her command, shaking his head like an old dog. "I will not do it! I won't!" The pain ratcheted up a few notches. He gasped at the agony swelling inside his head till he thought it would explode. He wasn't quite sure it wouldn't. He didn't know the extent of the doll's control or what other effects it might have on the body. Could it boil his blood? Stop his heart?

Yet even as he fought, he subconsciously steered his horse in the direction of Helga's command, the village of Upper Cathair. It wasn't until he broke through the trees and a stone-walled pasture came into view that he knew he had ridden to the village even while he fought the command. Appalled, he tried to turn around and go the opposite direction, but it was as if he were nothing more than a puppet, his body following the commands of the puppeteer. He could see it with the corner of his mind he had walled off from Helga, but he no longer controlled his body's functions. Horrified, he watched as he rode along the fence and then through the gate that led to the farmhouse on the hill. As he rode up, a child ran out the front door with glad cries of, "Mordecai! It's Mordecai! Hey, everyone, Mordecai has returned! Come see!" The girl of ten ran toward him, her golden curls bouncing around her head, her face wreathed in a joyous grin.

Mordecai fought like a Daimon to break the bond, but he could not. *Helga, leave her be! She is but a child! I beg you, leave her alone!*

I must test your obedience, my pet. You must obey instantly and without question. A little demonstration of my control is in order.

No! cried Mordecai as he thrashed in his mental bonds. The rest of her family spilled out the door, the girl's mother wiping her hands on her apron, her sturdy husband carrying a toddler. With happy smiles, they came down the stairs to greet him.

By the gods, no! he shouted mentally to no avail.

Lazily, he raised a hand as though in greeting. He did not lift it; Helga did.

A fiery glow enveloped his hand and grew brighter, then coalesced into a ball. His hand drew back, and a wizard's fireball shot from his hand, striking the golden-haired girl. She screamed as she was engulfed in flames, burning on the spot, her hair a flaming halo around her face. The smell of burning hair and flesh assailed his nose, but he did not pause. He could not pause.

He turned toward the rest of the family who were now screaming in shock and turning away. His next fireball caught the husband as he ran for the barns, trying to shield his son with his body, but there was no escaping a wizard's fire once it struck. They too were engulfed in flames.

Mordecai roared with pain, with grief, even as the next fireball loosed, catching the woman as she yanked open the door. She screamed, and one word escaped her lips before she succumbed to the flames.

"Why?" she wailed then collapsed on the porch, flashing to a crisp.

The flames of the victims winked out.

Mordecai's wizard's fire faded.

He slumped in his saddle and retched over the side of his horse, sickened by what had occurred. Alcina had been right. This was worse than any torture he had ever endured at her hand. He almost wished he was back in her control. But ultimately that control had been Helga's all along. A tear leaked from behind his clenched eyelid, not wanting to see what his nose told him all to clearly. They were all dead.

Are you going to continue to fight my commands, wizard? There are a lot of people in this village. I can make a demonstration of every person in it. Maybe I get to someone you do care about in time. I will break you if I must, but you will obey me, unconditionally. The choice is yours.

Mordecai straightened in his saddle and forced his eyes open. Of the small family, only smoking skeletons remained. He silently prayed for their souls to be sent to the well and to be sheltered from Helga's control. A light feminine laugh echoed in his head as he focused his will, amused by the prayer.

Mordecai swiped the back of his hand across his mouth and considered his options. There were not many, but he needed to know what Helga's plan was.

What would you have me do, Helga?

Why, I want you to help my dear brother, of course. Was that not also your plan? There is much work to do. There is a whole city to take over and a garrison under Cyrus's command that must be dealt with. I fear they are not loyal to me and need to be taken in hand. Kill all that you meet along the way. You are to join Cayden.

I will not kill the common folk! They are not your enemy!

All mortal life is my enemy! What do I want with mortality? It is with souls that my power is defined! See? You are useful to me right now because your soul is mine, not for any power you may possess as a wizard. When you die, you will serve me forever and that is where the true power lies. Do we need another demonstration?

Mordecai shifted his horse toward the village and began a slow walk that his mind fought against to no avail. Struggle as he might, he could not control his actions. Sadly, he thought back to Cayden's similar struggle to maintain control of his very being. The invasion was deeply personal and private, a hijacking of soul and spirit so complete. Mordecai wept. No physical torture could compare, and his powers were useless against this foe. Never had the great Mordecai felt so helpless. The sensation was unnerving.

Stop...stop! I will go to Cathair, but do not harm these people. This is not your fight. Silence greeted his thoughts. *I might be accidently injured or killed before reaching your goal. You would not want to lose me now, would you?* More silence. The horse continued walking toward the village, and Mordecai could see roofs of the first outlying houses. *Answer me, Helga, dammit!*

A soft chuckle brushed across his mind. *Very well, my pet. I will reward you with their lives. Do not expect me to be so generous the next time.* The pressure in his mind eased, and he found he had control of his horse once again. Jerking its head around, he heeled it into a quick trot and then into a gallop, anxious to put as much distance as he could between himself and Upper Cathair.

* * *

Helga leaned back and massaged her aching forehead. *The wizard is strong!* His constant battering resistance had nearly overwhelmed her. How he could feed back on the connection she did not know, but it was an unexpected side effect and an unpleasant one. Controlling both of them was proving to be more taxing than she had originally thought. She had to take breaks to recover, lest she slip up. Cayden wasn't nearly as adept, but he too had a barrier she could not cross. Helga thought it might be connected to the seeker who was sworn to him, but she wasn't sure.

She could not fail now, not at the culmination of all of her plans. Mordecai was set on his path, and Cayden had already arrived. Soon, they would be dead and the world hers.

She stood and turned in the direction of Faylea, now a bubbling pool of death. Genii was performing admirably. She'd hated to lose him, but such are the sacrifices she had to make toward her ultimate goal. Soon, all would be dead, and she alone would rule in peace. The frail mortal plane would vanish and only spirit would remain. She would claim her true heritage, her true destiny, as the supreme goddess of the world. The world finally brought under her dominion. God of all.

I will claim the temple in Faylea as my home and the castle in Cathair as a retreat. She did not recognize the incongruousness of her thoughts, clinging to the symbols even while wiping out what they represented. *I will remake them so that all souls can worship me from their former homelands. All other places and forms of worship will be dismantled and banned.*

CHAPTER 45

The First Bowl

MOONBEAM AND SANDSTORM LANDED on the patch of green within the protective shell of the temple. As they had flown across the threshold, a beam of light had passed over them, tingling on their skin and making the hair on Avery's arm rise. She flinched, expecting a bolt of lightning to strike them out of the sky, but then they were through and circling the temple.

To say that the temple was alive was an understatement. It was in a state of anxiety, the runes and images on the walls agitated and flashing, boiling over the various levels. The exterior writhed. As they crossed the boundary, the excitement increased to a blur.

"Does it always do that?" Artio asked as she slid from Sandstorm's back, patting her friend on the nose.

Sandstorm shook his head, his heavy mane swinging, and then eyed Artio with a thick-lashed look as if to say, *Play nice, now.* Artio grinned the first real smile she had produced for another living thing. Sandstorm snorted.

"No. The temple is agitated. It's...afraid." Avery walked slowly toward the glowing pyramid, their immediate poisonous surroundings forgotten, reaching out to the spirit of the temple. She paused at the base of the steps and her eyes closed. "Hurry, bring the bowls. It is time."

Artio retrieved the vessels in their secure wrappings and had taken one step away from Sandstorm when he snorted a warning. Artio swung around, tucking the bowls under her left arm and a bladed knife flashing into her right hand. Sandstorm danced away, flapping his wings and bellowing. Moonbeam pawed the ground and whinnied shrilly.

Avery broke communications and turned to see a tall dark form pass through the boundary. Hooded and cloaked, the man stepped toward Artio, who snarled in warning. "Stay where you are or die this minute." The figure froze and then lifted spotted hands to its hood, pushing it back off his head.

"Genii!" Artio's words were a barely audible whisper. "Is it really you?"

"Yes, Artio."

"But how? How are you here and human? What is wrong with your skin? Are you sick?"

"After a manner," He grimaced. "It's a present of Helga's. She released me but not before she cursed me." Artio made to move closer, but he held up his hands. "No, stop. Stop! Come no closer. You will die if you do."

"I am committed to death. I do not fear it any longer. To die this time is final. Helga has no control over my soul. Finally, I will be a peace. Let me help you." She took another step.

"No!" Genii shouted, stepping back. "Wait, please." He turned to Avery and bowed. "Mother, I wish to offer my assistance. I bring you a gift from one who wishes to help. May I present it to you?"

Avery nodded, puzzled.

Genii reached under his cloak and pulled out a wrapped bundle which he placed on the ground before them then backed away. Avery picked it up and unwound the wrappings. A crystal in the shape of an eye glinted back at her.

"The eye of the gods." Surprised, her head rose. "How did you come by it?"

"My mother gave it to me. You should remember her. Her name was Calleigh." Recognition of the name shone in Artio and Avery's eyes. "She said to bring this to you and to not fail. But as you can see," he gestured to the blight outside the shell, "It had a cost. I pray it will bring you victory in your quest." He bowed once again. "Now, I will leave you both."

Artio growled and walked over to him. "You will do no such thing, wizard. You are coming with us." She grabbed him by the arm and dragged him forward, Genii protesting as she pulled him along in her wake. "If anything can cure you, it's that." She pointed to the temple gone wild. "So, you will come with us. We live or die together as always." She grinned at the shocked expression on his face. "It's good to see you too."

Avery smiled and swung back to the temple. A humming buzz filled the air as they stepped onto the first step. The temple did not protest as they climbed the stairs, and the doors swung open of their own accord welcoming all three of them inside. Avery stepped across the threshold into a white light with Artio and Genii beside her. The doors closed with a bang and the blinding light faded.

This was not the chamber Avery remembered from her previous visit. They were standing in a vast open field that stretched as far as the eye could see. There was neither tree nor shrub to break the monotony of the sea of grass. A midnight sky full of stars of every colour crowded the heavens and stretched from horizon to horizon, as far as the eye could see. Yet strangely, a pearly white staircase rose out of the grass, a staircase that stretched up into the sky and vanished into its depths. The glow of the staircase reflected Avery's eyes, matching them exactly.

Artio stepped up on one side of Avery with Genii on the other. "It's time, dear sister. The bowls. Tell me what they mean. We are here."

Avery nodded. "The first bowl to be used is the bowl with the skeletal hand."

Artio nodded in agreement. The book had told her as much. "How do you know this?" Artio asked.

"The knowledge of the order and use of the bowls is knowledge of the temple, gifted to me as its guardian and godling," said Avery.

Artio kneeled in the soft grass and unwrapped the first of the bowls, carefully setting it in the grass.

"See these runes?" Avery wrote out the message in the air with a finger of spirit. The words hung in the air above them. "This is what the runes say."

Loyalty is key to gain what you must.
Death is a passage, never to trust.

**Pure of intent, a hand remains. Bring back the dead.
That much is plain.**

**A drink of health, it might contain. But who should drink it?
A mortal slain?**

**Choose incorrectly and all will be lost.
Mankind's doom will be the cost.**

"See? It's a puzzle; we need to solve the meaning of the passage to know what to do. I like to start at the end," said Avery.

"The end? Why would you start at the end?" Artio asked.

"Because that is where the action is. Figure out what the end result is, and you can figure out what needs to happen before it."

"But…no wait. One works into the other so how can going backward work?" said Genii

Avery grinned. "Did you ever spin in a circle until you were dizzy? The best way to counter the dizziness was to spin in the opposite direction. Equilibrium. I thought you would understand this instinctively, Artio. Besides, the best is always saved for last."

Avery read the passage aloud again but slowed over the final two lines. "'A drink of health, it might contain, but who should drink it, a mortal slain?' What do you think?"

Artio crossed her arms in classic Artio form. "There is only one 'mortal' among us. At least one who was mortal in the beginning. Genii."

Genii shifted, uncomfortable with the tag of mortal. He could barely remember *being* mortal. "OK, so suppose it means me. What does the line before it mean?"

Artio frowned at the words then glanced down at the skeletal hand submerged in the bowl. "Hands are used to grab things, pick up things, manipulate. How can a hand bring back the dead? Which dead?"

"I was dead." Genii held out his hands, now covered in so many black blisters as to be not recognizable. "And I will be soon dead again. I am the walking dead. It must mean me. I think I am supposed to use that hand." He pointed to the skeletal remains in the bowl.

Artio snarled then stepped between Genii and the bowl. "You may have been my love, but trust a necromancer to the magic of the dead? We have too long been separated. How can you be trusted?"

Avery tapped Artio on the shoulder. "You forget the first line."

Artio read the line aloud. "Loyalty in death." Her mouth twisted as she glared at Genii. "Have you been loyal to me? Speak, wizard, or here be slain."

Genii, head bowed, murmured softly, "You are the only one I have ever loved, Artio. To be snatched away and ensnared, enslaved by a goddess of the underworld is hardly what I would call betrayal." He raised his head and pain blazed in his eyes. "How could you even ask that? I had no more memory of the passage of time than you did. I could ask you the same thing. But when you came to visit Helga, something stirred within me, something long dormant. I recognized you and memory resurfaced, slowly at first then I remembered more and more. Mordecai helped me to put together the pieces of my fractured mind. I hadn't lost all memory with my death, perhaps because my soul did not return to the pool of souls awaiting rebirth? My loyalty and my love remain as they did on the day we parted."

Artio stared at him and her face softened. "I trust you. I know you were also wronged. Please, forgive me. Help us now?"

Genii nodded and knelt down beside the bowl. Avery and Artio knelt on either side of him. Genii took a deep breath then placed his hands on either side of the bowl, touching the runes with his blistered fingers. They brightened, glowing blue, then red, then blue again. The crystal shield covering the contents of the bowl shimmered and vanished, revealing a liquid in which the skeletal hand rested.

"To your health." Genii picked up the bowl, raising it to his lips and drank the contents of the bowl until nothing remained. He put the bowl back down on the grass. The hand was gone.

Just then his skin began to bubble, the black blisters bursting. Genii cried out in agony, falling back on the grass and thrashing as the blistered skin fell away, rolling on the ground in agony. Artio reached for him, but Avery grabbed her arm and held her back.

"Wait!" Avery commanded, watching Genii with calm eyes.

Artio's arm quivered under her sister's hand but she waited.

Genii's writing slowed and then stilled.

Avery let go of Artio's arm, and she sprang to her feet and ran over to Genii. She grasped him by the shoulder and rolled him over onto his back.

The blisters were gone. Smooth pink skin shone from a youthful face, a face she recognized instantly. With a sob, Artio placed her ear against his chest to hear the steady beat of a strong, young heart.

"Praised be the gods!" she sobbed, cradling his head in her lap. "Praise be!" Tears flowed, and she made no attempt to hide them or wipe them away. "He is healed!"

"A blessing of the gods" Avery said pointing toward the staircase. "Look."

A doorway had appeared at the base of the stairs. It shone as though the moon infused it with its heavenly glow. A black keyhole with a skeleton key embedded in the lock was waiting for someone to turn it, someone worthy.

Genii's eyes fluttered open and met Artio's, locking into place.

"I love you."

"I love you too."

"Then let's do this." He struggled to his feet then staggered to the door and turned the key.

CHAPTER 46

Hell's Fury

THE DAIMONS OF SHEOL ANIMUS burst from the rocks of the hillside in an eruption of fire and smoke, instantly setting the patchy grass aflame. Smoke rose from the burning tips, creating a flickering haze that made the Daimon's silhouettes quiver. The odour of sulphur and burning vegetation filled the air and rolled down in a dense cloud toward the tents in the valley below.

The camp of the Kingsmen roared to life as the monsters were sighted, and warning horns blared. Dinners were abandoned and kettles kicked over in the mad scramble to gather arms and mounts. In less than a minute, the band of five hundred Kingsmen strong were mounted and ready for battle.

The Daimons crawled out of the rents in the stone and pushed themselves to their feet, sniffing the air. Giant horned heads swung in the direction of the humans. Catching the scent of living souls, they ran, lumbering toward the camp. Flaming swords raised high, they screeched an unintelligible battle cry that grated on the ears.

In front of Nelson and Fabian, Denzik reined in, his horse snorting and rearing with nervous energy as the calls of the Daimons reached its twitching ears. Each one wore a coloured band on his arm denoting a general to the men.

"This is a battle we cannot win. We need reinforcements. We need the legion. The enemy of your enemy is a potential ally. We have little choice, now. Even with the legion at our backs, I do not know that we can defeat this enemy. Order the men to ride hard for

Cathair. Within the castle walls, we may have a chance, but out here in the open we are dead men. Split the units and go! Once clear, meet me at the prearranged location. GO!"

With a sharp nod of their heads in acknowledgement, Nelson and Fabian raced away from Denzik, shouting orders to the captains and riding hard for the crest of the next ridge. The columns of Kingsmen fell in behind their unit captains and galloped away toward the walls of Cathair. Denzik prayed that the ancient walls would be enough to save the Kingsmen, but first they had to reach them.

Denzik spurred his mount, and the men assigned to him fell in behind just as Ziona rode up beside him, galloping hard.

Nelson and Fabian crested the rise and reined in, motioning for the Kingsmen to ride past them, watching the approaching flames that heralded the Daimons' advance. Denzik, on a separate rise, counted off his men, making sure that all were accounted for. As the last of the Kingsmen streamed past, the ground beneath them trembled, quaking and rolling under their mounts so that the horses staggered and would have fallen had they not had the sense to urge them into motion. Denzik and Ziona raced down the hillside as the ground exploded and ten Daimons erupted from it. Huge streams of lava were tossed high into the air and then fell to splatter the low shrubs turning them into living torches.

Ziona cried out with pain as a drop of lava fell onto her left arm and burned through the cloth. She shook her arm hard, knocking the lava away, but the blistering wound was agony. Denzik, seeing her distress, grabbed the bridle of her horse and headed for the trees, thinking to slow down the towering terror that pursued them. Their horses needed no further urging, as they plunged into the trees, wild-eyed and whinnying with terror. The denseness of the forest forced Denzik to let go of the bridle.

"Ziona, meet me at the pre-arranged coordinates," Denzik said and then veered away from her, leading a pack of Daimons away from her.

She bolted away on a path of her own choosing was soon swallowed by the trees.

*   *   *

Nelson cursed as the ground in front of him opened up and a blast of heat and sulphur stench issued from crevice. The advance of the Daimons had separated him from the main body of fleeing Kingsmen. His horse shied away from the rent, tossing its head. From the crumbling earth, a Daimon pulled itself out of the pool of lava and straightened, taller than he as he sat astride his horse.

Nelson's eyes widened with fear, as the enormous beast turned toward him, sniffing the air. Great curving horns accentuated the black orbs of its eyes in which flickered the flames of the underworld.

Stark terror gripped Nelson. Never in all his years of battles and confrontations had he known fear such as this. This beast of magic was nothing a mortal could fight. No sword could stop it. He saw no shame in fleeing, and he doubted that he could have stopped his horse in any event. His horse reared then landed stiff-legged and bolted away. Nelson crouched over the withers and urged it to greater speeds as the ground trembled beneath the first lumbering steps of the Daimon.

"For kingdom and Cathair!" he bellowed by rote. There were none near to hear his battle cry. He hesitated, searching for a response. When he received none, he fled.

*   *   *

Fabian's horse lunged forward, struggling to clear the breach that had opened up under its feet, but the soil liquefied and fell away into the abyss opening beneath them. Fabian kicked free of his stirrups and launched himself forward as his horse scrabbled to grab hold of the lip, but its weight dragged it back and with a scream his horse fell into the flaming hell.

Fabian rolled, tumbling, across the burning grass, embers igniting in his hair and on his tunic. He stood, wincing at the pain in the twist of his ankle, swatting at the burning cloth and hair. Then he froze, as a grunting snort reached his ears. An eight-foot-tall Daimon crawled out of the rent, shining horns preceding a snout for a nose, sniffing the air as it clawed its way free of the pit. Fabian's eyes widened, and he ran, as fast as his damaged leg would go, instinctively heading for shelter, eyes scanning for a place to hide, for there was no defeating the beast that now pursued him.

He stumbled into the cover of the trees and slid behind a broad trunk, gasping for breath and squeezing his eyes shut to try to ignore the painful throb of his swelling ankle. A crunching, grinding sound accompanied by the smell of burning wood assailed his nose as the Daimon drew near, hunting him by the smell of his soul, a sweet stench to the Daimon's nostrils.

Frantic, Fabian searched the woods, eyes scanning for an avenue of escape or a place to hide. He pushed off the tree trunk and staggered deeper into the woods, heading instinctually for the rendezvous point he knew he would never make on foot. He hobbled as fast as he could, but the forest behind him illuminated the Daimon's passage as it caught fire with its passing. If anything, the burning illuminated the woods and mocked Fabian with the lack of hiding places, stripping away the false security of darkness.

Fabian hauled himself over a log blocking his flight. He stumbled as he placed his foot on the other side, losing his balance and rolling down the steep incline to the bottom of the hill. As he pushed himself up from the ground, the Daimon appeared with flaming sword in hand. With a howl, it leapt over the log and ran at Fabian.

Fabian rolled to his feet, limping. He hobbled away as he heard the Daimon thrashing behind him and tensed for the sword thrust he knew was seconds away. The heat of the Daimon scorched his back as he half ran half hopped. *At least the end will be swift with no suffering.* He staggered around a trunk just as the Daimon swung the sword and it bit into the tree, slicing through it like butter. The tip of the blade scored Fabian's back, searing his flesh. He cried out in pain. The tree creaked and toppled crashing to the forest floor and sending sparks flying. New fires erupted as Fabian stumbled toward the one clear area remaining. As he hobbled into the clearing, he heard the sound of hooves. Nelson raced toward him, arm outstretched. Fabian flung out his arm and caught the crook of Nelson's as he thundered past and was pulled up behind him onto his horse.

The Daimon roared and lumbered forward, screeching as its prey escaped on their swifter mounts. The Daimon dropped behind as they gained the sanctuary of the unburned forest.

CHAPTER 47

The End of the Line

ZIONA WATCHED FROM THE SHELTER of the trees as the lone rider was swallowed up by the familiar leafy sentinels forming the woods at the far side of the farm. He left behind its smoking inhabitants without a backward glance. Ziona swallowed the hard lump in her throat, sickened by the scene she had just witnessed. She was unsure which terror was worse: the Daimons rampaging through the countryside behind her, or the thought of a wizard not in control of his magic.

That the rider was Mordecai she had no doubt, but something was wrong, terribly wrong. He jerked in his saddle as Cayden had jerked while under Helga's control, stiff-armed and ramrod straight. His face was set in a furious scowl, framed by long white hair beneath his cowl as he rode away toward the village proper, but then he suddenly changed directions and booted his horse in the direction of Cathair.

Once he disappeared into the woods, Ziona slid out from behind the ribbed bark of the elm tree trunk and approached the deceased family. There was nothing she could do for them—she had already known it—yet it seemed harsh to not check. Instead, she knelt beside each and said a prayer that their souls be cradled by the Spirit Shield and delivered to the well, yet she wasn't entirely sure that was a safe haven anymore.

After her prayer, Ziona fetched her horse. It shied as she climbed back into the saddle, skittish and as anxious as she was to be away from the stench of death. But which way should she go? To follow Mordecai was to ride into a similar situation, for there was little doubt that he was being controlled by another Soul Fetch. *Disgusting things! How could the Flesh Clan priests believe that a Soul Fetch would solve anything? It was like setting fire to a forest to combat drought. And I have just witnessed what that spark will do.* She put heel to her horse's side and galloped away. *Perhaps the Kingsmen have found a safe route into Cathair.*

An hour's hard ride brought her to the prearranged meeting coordinates, a place that the sly leaders of the Kingsmen swore no one knew about but them. As she rode into the clearing, whistles announced her approach. In the center, a tilting wooden structure with glassless windows hid the opening below. The building was a common miner's hut of a century ago. Some huts had been intentionally kept plain with little in the way of maintenance, so as to not attract attention. Hundreds of abandoned huts could be found throughout the countryside of Cathair, originally constructed by one prospector or another. They were soon abandoned when the promised vein of gold or silver or crystal petered out.

The best they could do was an abandoned mine shaft? she thought as she dismounted, disappointed. She raised an eyebrow at Denzik who hurried forward to greet her. His jacket was blackened with soot, and his pant leg ripped. "Denzik, have you forgotten already how Cayden took Cathair a little over a year ago? And that your Kingsmen have been mapping the tunnels ever since?"

Denzik grimaced, scratching at his thickening beard. "Ah, but this tunnel was only ever revealed to the squad captains. Not that they were doing anything illegal, mind. It was more a matter of not corrupting the men with bad habits. This tunnel has long been used to smuggle in a late-night nip of fire whiskey, something to foil the grip of a cold winter night spent guarding the castle walls. It might be the *only* way into Cathair now."

Ziona tied her horse and then crawled into the leaning hut, careful to not disturb the timber of the decrepit building. Indeed, several casks lined the walls, narrowing the tunnel once she dropped down into it. The original wooden stairs were missing, yet a faint smudge of wood was still visible where the stringer had originally attached itself to the floor joist of the hut. That the tunnel was that old fascinated Ziona, for it brought it parallel with a time when the godlings were in their original form. It must have been a closely guarded secret and faithfully passed down through the legion commanders to remain in human memory. But then again, whiskey on a cold night was a powerful motivator.

She eyed the casks as she passed them, wondering about the proof after aging for so long, then dismissed them in favour of the sight of Fabian, slumped against the stone wall. Nelson was applying a cold wet cloth to a searing red cut across his back. It blistered and bled, dripping down his back and soaking the dust floor. Both men looked worse for the flight away from the Daimon.

"I have news," Ziona announced as she brushed a cobweb off her sleeve, dragging her eyes away from the pair.

She opened her mouth to tell them about Mordecai, when the world exploded around them. A bright flash of red seared her eyes, and she was thrown, tumbling like a rag doll. A rumble reached her ears and then blackness descended as the light from above vanished with a roar. With the absolute blackness of a tomb, the tunnel walls collapsed and rubble buried her under an avalanche of stone and dirt. A rock struck her head and consciousness fled.

*　*　*

Mordecai sat his horse at the edge of the forest and continued to toss fireballs until there was not a thing that moved. His face was twisted into a grimace of pain and fury, yet he could do nothing to stop the rain of death. His will was commandeered and twisted to the doll's control. In a corner of his mind that he had sectioned away, he knew he had to stop this but agonized how to break through the linking. He did not know what to do, short of ending his own life. He agonized over the decision, not because he cared about prolonging his own life, but because he longed to aid Cayden and help him complete his mission...but it might not be possible. *Ziona! Please be alive! Cayden will fail if you are dead. I tried to hold off until you were safely down in the tunnel!* Mordecai ignored the bodies of the dead

Kingsmen scouts as he rode past them, their throats slit, all men he knew. He jerked his horse's head and rode off toward Cathair, feeling older this day, than he had ever felt in his long, long life.

*   *   *

Ziona woke coughing, hacking trying to clear her lungs of the dust and dirt that filled the air. She could not see the dust and dirt, for there was no light in the tunnel. Instinctively, she delved her body, to check on her condition and that of the babe within her. She sighed with relief when she found the babe unharmed. Her eyes scanned the thick cloud, searching for her companions.

"Denzik! Fabian!" she called in voice edged with panic, desperate to know that she was not entombed alive in the collapsed underground tunnel, the only one alive. "Nelson! Wake up, please!" Silence greeted her hoarse cry, and the dense dust brought on another spasm of coughing. She began to move her limbs, testing arms and legs. Nothing appeared to be broken, although a tacky substance stuck her sleeve to her arm. She touched it with her hand and brought it to her nose to sniff. *Whiskey!* She raised her hands above her head and could not feel a ceiling, although a slab was tilted over her. She got the impression she was in a pocket of stone. She felt around some more and her hand fell on a piece of wood, part of the broken barrel.

Her hand continued to search. As she felt around, her fingers fell on the strap of her satchel, and she grabbed it and tugged. It slid about an inch then stopped. Ziona's hands scrabbled over the satchel, her fingers digging into the debris and pushing it off, freeing her bag inch by inch. She pulled as she dug and it slowly slid out from under the rubble, stones rattling away. She pulled it onto her lap and opened the flap, fumbling with the contents. As her hand frantically searched the interior for her flint, she heard a low moan. Joy and fear flooded her. Someone was alive still, but in what condition? Her hand fell onto the flint and she grasped it in her hand and pulled it out and placed it between her teeth so she wouldn't lose it.

Ziona grabbed the non-sticky sleeve of her tunic and yanked it, tearing a strip out of it then rolled it around a length of the whiskey barrel stave. Tying the ends tight, she plunged the cloth into the alcohol soaking it until it was dripping then she laid it beside her knee. She grabbed a stone and her flint and began to strike sparks, the flash of light blinding in the pure black. It took several strikes but then an ember fell onto the alcohol and caught, pushing back the inky envelope and showing her for the first time their predicament. She picked up the makeshift torch, coughing again and raised it high.

The roof of the tunnel had collapsed down on the men, at the opening, but as she shone the light further down the tunnel, it was intact. She had been thrown by the first concussion nearly clear of the collapse, but not all of her companions had been so lucky. With a gasp of pain, she pushed herself to hands and knees and crawled to Denzik's side, feeling for a pulse. It was thready but present. A huge dark swelling decorated his forehead, and one leg was pinned by a large boulder. She checked out his arms and legs. From what she could determine, he appeared to be alive and intact, although unconscious.

Ziona slithered deeper into the mouth of the collapse where the worst of the cave in had occurred. A foot and part of a sleeve came into view as the torchlight slid over the rubble. Someone had been crushed under the weight of cave in. She scooped away the rubble and uncovered a face. Nelson's vacant eyes stared back her, glassy and unknowing. Ziona swallowed the sour swelling lump in her throat and prayed for his soul, reaching out to Cayden at the same time, begging him to receive it. Ziona touched Cayden's mind briefly, drawing comfort from the contact.

Beside Nelson, she spied a boot that she knew belonged to Fabian, but he was buried so deeply, she couldn't even check that it was him. She peered at the heavy cascade of stone and knew it was impossible to rescue them, even if they were alive. Her eyes shimmered with unshed tears and she desperately cast her light around, searching for any other survivors. Of the men who had stood before her when she arrived, only Denzik still lived.

Ziona crawled back to Denzik, wedging her makeshift torch into a crack between two large stones and then began the ordeal of digging him out. "Denzik! Denzik! Wake up, man!" She shook his shoulder as a tear escaped and rolled down her cheek, then reached back into her satchel to pull out her healing packet. She selected a bitter, papery bark and some poppy seeds and crushed the pair between her fingers. With her other hand, she pinched open Denzik's mouth and shoved the leaves under his tongue. "Wake, dammit!" she sobbed, massaging his arms then moved further down his leg to the boulder. Now that she looked closer, the boulder had come to rest to the side, and his leg was wedged but not crushed by the massive stone. She reached down and pulled on his limb tugging hard. After several tries Denzik's foot slid out of the boot and the sudden release of resistance spilled her backward onto the stone floor. She winced as her head smacked the stone. Ziona sat back up, rubbing the swelling lump.

Denzik stirred, blinking slowly, then with a long loud groan rolled over onto his side. "My head!" Denzik echoed, grunting then he spat out the leaves in his mouth. "Gaah! What is that stuff?"

Ziona scooted across the stone floor and put her arm around Denzik. "Look at me," she commanded taking his whiskered chin in her hand and turning his face to into his eyes. She thumbed back his eyelid before he could make his foggy mind respond, brushing against a swelling, purple bruise. He winced and blinked slowly, trying to stop the room from dancing in his vision. "Good. No sign of internal bleeding." She eased him to a sitting position against the boulder, then tore her other sleeve and wrapped it around another length of busted barrel, dipping the torch in the alcohol and lighting it in the burning torch. "I suggest you take a swig of that whiskey right now," as Denzik opened his mouth to speak. "The others are dead. I already checked."

Denzik's mouth sagged. "Nelson? Fabian?" She nodded.

At that moment, the fall of stone rumbled and shifted.

Ziona grabbed Denzik's arm and helped him to his feet, shoving a torch into his hand. "Come, we have to go, or we may not escape either. The rest of this ceiling is about to come down." She tugged on Denzik's sleeve. "I have said a prayer for their souls. There is nothing you can do for your friends, Denzik. *We must go.*" She turned him in the direction of Cathair and gave him a push.

Denzik stumbled down the passage that blurred before his eyes as his tears fell. He was leaving behind a quarter century of friendship, trials and triumphs shared together. His steps dragged with the weight of his pain and his grief. There was only one hope. His circle was now complete. The only way he could help his friends now was to make sure the king succeeded in his mission. He was the last one, and the duty now fell to him to eliminate Lord Cyrus and even the odds of the Kingsmen retaking the castle. Besides, Denzik had a personal vendetta to repay. Cyrus was the reason they were exiled in the first place. He had sworn to avenge his old captain, and he would do so.

CHAPTER 48

Too Painful to Endure

ZIONA DRAGGED DENZIK down the long passage, their shadows bouncing across the stone walls like a reflection on choppy seas.

"Wait. Let me rest," panted Denzik as he slumped against the wall, one foot booted the other bare. He slid down the wall, groaning, his swollen appendage stretched out in front of him. The flickering torch illuminated hairy pink toes twice their normal size now that they were freed from the boot.

Ziona dropped down beside him and laying her torch aside probed the ankle and foot with gentle fingers. "Nothing is broken. I think it's badly bruised and possibly a sprain but not crippling. The cold air is helping with the swelling."

They'd limped along the passage for the better part of thirty minutes, following the markings that Denzik knew by rote. Kingsmen of old had carved symbols that only a Kingsman would know, symbols of a spirit world long left behind by Denzik's time, as the demise of the Spirit Shields began. The main symbol, Ziona noticed, was one of wings, sometimes alone, sometimes attached to a roughly drawn four-legged stick figure that could only be a Pegasus. Other symbols were drawn on every wall, a decoy to those not knowing the purpose of the passage and where it led. One such decoy promised gold and sent the unwary off into a maze that circled back on itself over and over until it deposited the seeker into a field of golden poison oak.

An itchy end to an otherwise unprofitable journey, Ziona thought with a grim chuckle.

A grim chuckle was all they could manage. The weight of Nelson's and Fabian's deaths tore into the tapestry of their lives, leaving a ragged and raw edge. No amount of thread and needle could bind the severing pain that sliced across their hearts. Critical lives snipped from the pattern of current events, a sudden gaping hole that was impossible to mend. Fabian…with his delectable sticky buns that bound the men together like no glue made in Cathair. Nelson…with his sharp tongue and even sharper wit, the innkeeper who welcomed all to the table despite their ability to pay. Two men, two giants with very big shoes to fill.

Denzik's head dropped to his knee, and his shoulders shook as weariness and grief flooded his body. *Gone. They were both gone! His best and oldest friends…gone!*

Ziona softly ran her hand over his back, her throat tight around the solid lump of pain that was lodged there. She dropped her head back, staring at the ceiling, supposedly to clear her head, but actually to let the few escaping tears to drain away without dripping down her face. *I will not give in. I will not!* Aloud, she said, "Helga must not win! Denzik, listen to me. We all knew the price of seeking out the Spirit Shields. Every one of us knew that we may not live to tell the tale. Nelson and Fabian have died as heroes doing their duty. Better yet, *they have died as they would have wished, serving the kingdom.* Do *not* dishonour them by entertaining the thought that their deaths were a waste. They were not. They saved us by taking the brunt of the attack. *Look at me, Denzik!*" He lifted his soggy, aged face to stare at her. "*They saved us!*" Ziona gripped his arm, locking her eyes on his. He did not look away, silently begging for solace. She reached over and wiped the tears from his face. Her voice firmed. "We will not allow their sacrifice to be for nothing. Come, Cayden and Avery need us. Our mission is not done."

Ziona reached into her satchel and pulled out a couple of leaves. "Chew this as we walk. It will help to control the swelling and pain."

Denzik took the leaves and placed them in his mouth and chewed. He pushed himself to his feet. Grabbing his torch, he began to limp down the passage, their feet the only ones to have trod the path in a good twenty years. No footprints marred the coating of dust that had settled over the intervening time, a good sign that their chosen path remained a secret, at least from the hostile elements they were marching toward. A grand army they made, two stranded people—one a Kingsman, the other a Primordial seeker—injured and weakened with a weapon apiece.

A thought occurred to Denzik as he limped his way toward his death, as he now saw the journey. "Ziona, what is your plan when you reach Cathair?"

Ziona did not answer right away. The silence stretched until Denzik's steps slowed, but then she spoke. "My calling has always been to aid the Spirit Shield in his or her mission. That is my calling, my bond as a seeker. To do what must be done *to be sure the Spirit Shields can do what they must do.* That is my plan. To help Cayden succeed in his quest. To be the steel to his spirit, the blade to his love. If they fail, we all perish. I will do what I must."

"Does that include killing him? Could you kill Cayden, Ziona? I fear it may be necessary, even more so since the cave-in." He winced, his voice wobbling, then it steadied. "That wasn't Cayden. But it was an enemy, someone close. Someone knew where we were. Someone followed us. Someone with access to magic. There are only so many who can wield magic."

"I know, but that was Mordecai, not Cayden. He is in the castle," said Ziona softly. For once, she was glad that Denzik led and did not pause to look at her face. "We must all do our duty, or the world may perish for that lack. Despite our all too human desires, we must do our duty or suffer for all eternity."

"I am glad to hear you say it," Denzik tossed over his shoulder. "I am a soldier, long-forged and tempered. I will do my duty to king and lord, to Spirit Shield and saviour, as I am oath-sworn to do. Our path is clear." *You are mine, Cyrus!*

"Our path is clear," she murmured, scrubbing the back of her hand across her eyes. *Cayden, be safe my love. Feel our bond. Stay strong! Draw on my strength!*

With a snap that struck her as though it had been physically delivered, her message rebounded and running over the top a sneering laugh reverberated down the connection. *Your love is mine, honey, as you will be soon!*

Ziona screamed and dropped to her knees, clutching her head, sobbing. The shock of the connection was too much to bear, the eternal, other-worldly mind of a god pressing against hers, too powerful and out of sync with humanity and time. The laughter scraped across her soul once more, and a high-pitched squeal tore from her throat.

Denzik pulled her close, his eyes searching the shadows for the source of her pain, but all was still. "Ziona, snap out of it." He shook her slightly, his eyes widening in surprise as Ziona's rolled back in her head. A seizure quaked through her body, and her tongue rolled to one side of her open mouth. Alarmed, Denzik picked her up and began to carry her down the tunnel, limping heavily. All he could think of was that they needed to get out of the tunnel and as soon as possible. He had to find help, and there was none to be found here. One torch would have to do. The abandoned torch was quickly swallowed up by the darkness as Denzik carried Ziona toward the castle foundations.

CHAPTER 49

The Second Bowl

GENII PULLED ON THE DOOR HANDLE. It slid into nothingness, absorbed back into the tableau presented by the illusion or dream, whatever this was. He reached back and grasped Artio's hand in his right and then took Avery's hand with his other. In unison, they stepped across the threshold.

Instantly, the grassy field vanished, and they floated amongst clouds that obscured their vision of everything except the structure ahead of them. The clouds flashed as though a thunderstorm approached the billowing expanse backlit with rainbow-hued lightning. As soon as they cleared the threshold, the door vanished. They peered around, but there was no place to go.

Avery stepped forward, and the clouds parted in response to her motion. The kaleidoscope of lightning struck each of them in turn running over their bodies and making the hair rise on their arms and the backs of their necks, but it did not harm them.

"Do not be alarmed. The temple is checking our identities. Stand still," Avery cautioned.

The lightning slid over them. Then, satisfied, it withdrew back into the surrounding storm clouds. When it faded, a glimmering staircase appeared, once again infused with the light and magic of the moon, but this time the steps were tiled in polished crystal. Encased in each icy square was a golden oak leaf the size of Genii's hand. Branded into the center of each leaf was a letter from the ancient alphabet of the gods. Eight letters decorated each step, and the staircase climbed eight risers high to a crystal platform that twinkled amongst the stars above the encircling storm. In the middle of the platform, a spire rose up, as far as the eye could see, stabbing into the sky. The tip glowed blue against the heavens.

"Gather 'round. It is time for the next bowl in the sequence. Artio, retrieve the grey vessel." Avery knelt on the floor and waited for Artio, to comply. Knowledge floated into Avery's mind as they gathered around it, a gift of her first adventure within the sacred pyramid. Instinctively, she understood the purpose of the bowls and their intended order, now that they were within the confines of the temple. As High Priestess, all knowledge was laid bare. She needed only to guide the others.

Artio opened her pack and carefully placed it on the tiles, and then unwrapped the bowl. Made of dull grey pewter, the bowl was dented, concave impacts along its surface made a mockery of the term "bowl." Each dimple displayed a rune. The closer they were to the base of the bowl, the smaller the runes appeared and the closer together they were spaced until at the bottom they blurred into an inky smear that was indistinguishable.

Artio sat back on her haunches, hands clasped across her knees. "I do not understand this bowl. It makes no more sense here than it did back in the Thunder temple." Genii squatted beside her, and neither touched the bowl.

Avery knelt beside them and reached into her pack and pulled out the focus stone she shared with Cayden. If ever there was a time she needed focus, this was it. She placed it between her palms and held it over the bowl. "Clasp your hands around mine. This will require all of our will focusing on the bowl."

"What does it do?" Genii asked, as Artio clasped Avery's hands in hers. He followed suit, encasing both of their hands within his large grasp.

"The bowl is another key, but unlike the first one, it doesn't unlock a door." Avery gestured over her shoulder at the floating staircase. "I think it reveals a path. Now close your eyes and focus."

They closed their eyes, and Avery began to pray, as she had never prayed in this incarnation. "Gods above, we kneel before the stairway that leads to your abode. If we be worthy, grant us passage to climb the sacred stairs. Guide our steps. Judge our path. Show mercy for this world."

The focus stone in her hand heated and glowed, the light piercing their closed eyelids, tempting them to peek.

A breeze blew past them, stirring their cloaks. Avery cracked open one eye and stared down into the bowl. She shook off their hands. "Look."

Artio and Genii opened their eyes to see that the bowl was glowing. It was no longer dull and dark. Runes glowed, seemingly at random, but as they stared, they shimmered. Up to the luminous surface floated a message, a ribbon of red satin across which marched words in a bold black text. Avery translated the message aloud.

Silver squares, runes etched deep.
With utmost caution warily creep.

Every stroke, a lover's kiss.
Guess the name and no step miss.

To change appearance, that is key.
Don't believe what your eyes see.

Monies paid are not the price, but costs it will with prayers suffice.

Lovers reunited be, more of you and you are me.
Now put together, the stairs are set. Tell me now which god to get?

Genii sighed heavily. "More riddles. Why couldn't whoever set these traps just toss a minotaur or a Charun into the path to fight?"

Avery rolled her eyes and struggled to keep her voice even. "Because this is a temple, not a tavern. Only the worthy may pass here. It is not a matter of might but of loyalty and faith to climb the sacred stairs. It is a pilgrimage."

Genii crossed his arms stubbornly, and Artio unconsciously mimicked the attitude, crossing her arms to face Avery.

"Well then," he said. "If I wanted access to the temple, I would kidnap one such as yourself and make you puzzle out all the riddles, then slay you at the end. It is not my faith in the gods that keeps me from slaying you right now but my loyalty to Artio."

Avery raised her eyebrows at the words, but Artio placed her hand on his corded arm, cautioning him. "I think Genii has a point. An invalid could not mount these stairs, so some brawn is called for and possibly needed. What does the riddle say?" She leaned over the bowl "'With utmost caution warily creep.' Tell me, what need is there for caution, if there is no danger?"

"I did not say there was no danger," Avery murmured. "It would appear that the key to the stairs is in the name of the gods. One of the gods needs to be called on in order to safely traverse the staircase."

"One of the ancient gods? Or the lesser gods? There are over thirty gods and goddesses in the celestial pantheon." Artio scratched the side of her nose, thinking. "I think we should list them and then see if we can work out the clues."

"Good idea. I have a quill." Avery reached back inside her satchel and pulled out the quill, parchment, and a tightly stoppered ink jar. She unrolled the parchment, weighting the corner with the jar while Artio and Genii knelt on either side. "Call them out and I will write."

Artio chucked a husky laugh. "This will be like a family reunion!"

Avery eyed her severely out of the corner of her eye.

"OK, OK. Here goes." Artio named off the family gods and goddesses with barely a pause while Avery furiously wrote.

Uncle Erebus—favours the dark in a grumpy, moody way

Aunt Nyx——wife of Uncle Erebus and responsible for his dark outlook

Aunt Asteria —bores you with portends and tries to read your fortune at every party; wife of Uncle Phobeter

Uncle Phobeter — scared of the dark, sleeps with the lights on

Morpheus (father) —the dreamer and schemer

Uncle Hypnos —stares glassy-eyed at nothing; nearsighted

"So, this is the short list of the original six. Are we going to include their mortal dalliances?" asked Genii, studying the list.

"Not unless we cannot find our answer within this bunch. Read the riddle again." Artio straightened and walked over to the bowl and read the floating message out loud.

"'Silver squares, runes etched deep. With utmost caution warily creep.' Yeah, we covered that one already. 'To change appearance, that is key. Don't believe what your eyes see.' To change appearance. To change clothing. Cut one's hair. To colour one's hair. That could mean fake or phobe...no wait," Artio muttered holding up her hand when Avery opened her mouth, the words stalled on her tongue. "Let me work this out." Annoyed muttering drifted over to her ears while Artio tried different combinations of words and syllables. "Nyx could mean null which could be a negative appearance." Genii opened his mouth, and Artio's hand shot into the air, cutting him off without even glancing in his direction. Genii's mouth snapped shut, and he growled low, a growl to match Artio's. "No, that can't be it. Too complicated." At the sound of Genii's growl, she met his eyes.

"You are describing how to change," said Genii. "I think we need another word for the word change, like transformation," Artio frowned at the script, "or a modification. Something like that."

Artio shook her head. "We have no relatives that with names like that." She smirked. "It doesn't work with anyone's name...if it is a name we are looking for."

Avery sat up straighter. "How about metamorphosis?" They stared at her, blank-faced and slack-jawed. "Morph?" said Avery.

Identical surprised noises issued from their lips as they hurried to bend over the riddle. "Morph as in shape, yes! That might be it! Hurry let's work out the rest to see if it works."

Genii murmured, "Monies paid are not the price, but cost it will with prayers suffice. Pay with prayers, not with money. Prayer costs no money. Prayer is free...free? No, that is not a price. It is free. It's less than free...less that free...could it mean only part of the word, 'ee'?"

Avery clapped her hands together, nodding, a grin wreathing her face. "And the last bit, 'Lovers reunited be, more of you and you are me.' What lovers do you know that should be reunited?" She grinned at the pair of them their heads bent together. The face of the bear was fading, and the Artio of old was emerging. Artio's hand crept into Genii's, and she smiled the first genuine smile that Avery had seen cross her face.

Artio's eyes rose to meet Avery's, and she whispered, "Us. The answer is us. Morph-ee-us." Artio eyes locked on Genii's. He smiled, then pulled her to her feet and drew her into his arms and kissed her soundly. The clouds swirled with the intensity of emotion, wrapping around the pair, drawing on the currents of love. For a moment, there was no other "us" in the world but the two of them, reunited.

After several moments, Avery harrumphed. "Could we save that for later? The world is waiting for us to save it." Artio and Genii broke apart but did not drop hands, looking sheepish but satisfied. Artio's cheeks glowed warmly, and the last vestiges of the bear slipped away leaving the young woman of Avery's memory. "Look at the stairs," Avery commanded. "'Now put together, the stairs are set. Tell me now which god to get?' The answer is Morpheus. We are to call on our father," she said softly. Avery took a step toward the staircase. At her approach, the steps began to glow, the crystal brightening to a creamy white glare that nearly obscured the runes etched into their surface. A shuffling sound told her that Artio and Genii had joined her. Without turning around, she pointed at the first step. "Morpheus is eight letters. Step only on the rune that corresponds to the letters of the alphabet. We must spell out Father's name. Do not put the edge of a foot nor a hand on any other surface. Only one foot can be on any given square at a time. You must hop from square to square. If you step on two at once…well, something will happen or why include a warning? Remember, one step at a time." With those parting instructions, Avery stepped onto the first stair, squarely on the rune representing the letter M and vanished from view.

CHAPTER 50

The Gates of Hell

THE FINAL SET OF DAIMON residing under the mountain milled about in their makeshift pen, snorting rings of fire that were slowly melting through the steel that bound the wooden doors imprisoning them in the pit. The tallest and bulkiest Daimon was a great beast known in myth and legend as Asag. It stood upright on its hind legs, multiple stories tall, with massive curving horns sharpened to razor-sharp spikes by continuously scraping them on the rough metal edges of the banding that lined the pit. The other Damion gave their sire a wide berth, experienced as they were with his horn's lethal capabilities.

The Daimons' hierarchy was formed from a herd mentality that drove their animal brains. Creatures of myth and magic they might be, but they did not possess intelligence and any organization amongst them was bestial at best. Only the strongest and the mightiest rose to the top by constant challenges, but none could top the sire.

Helga studied the beasts milling about in the quarried stone cage. Her champion Asag gazed up at the smoke hole above, a natural ventilation shaft that cleared the air of the smoke from the lava pools. By the colour of the thin wedge of daylight visible at the top of the shaft, the twilight was waning to dark. It was time to launch her final set of Daimon on the unsuspecting world. Genii would have spread his plague, and the mortals living on the godforsaken surface should be infected and dying, even if they did not know it yet.

Launching my Daimon on the world will be a blessing, a mercy. They will feed on the carcasses of the dead and dying, consuming both plant and flesh and cleansing the earth in the process. The Charun will gather their wandering souls and bring them home to me. Genii will die. Of course, he will. I knew that when I sent him out into the world. But it was a necessary sacrifice. This time I will bind myself to Asag to lead the charge and take a direct hand in the capture of Cathair and the Well of Souls.

Her mind turned to her new slave. She smiled. Ryder was turning out to be a very amiable companion and so much more interesting than Genii, who had been little more than a shell after his change. Perhaps she would let Ryder retain his humanity. She'd never have thought it, but the human aspects did add depth to their scattered personalities. Ryder dared to challenge her, and she found the interaction stimulating.

Decision made, Helga climbed a set of stairs beside a carved pillar, which led to a platform directly above the gate. It was guarded by two Charun who bowed as she reached the level. She walked past them, ignoring them for they were nothing but servants to her mind's eye, and invisible. At the end of the platform was a golden-handled lever notched into the floor and attached to a hidden gear. Carved onto the handle were images of the underworld, runes of death and remorse. Of all the images carved onto the handle, the lead one was of Asag as the lever controlled his domain. Even Helga would not confront the Daimon. There was no controlling the beasts once they were set free. They could only be destroyed by another immortal, for they were born of the spirits of the condemned and immortal.

Helga strode over to the lever and taking it firmly in both hands, pulled.

The mountain shook. At first it was a low rumble, but then the rumble became a howl and loose rock began to fall throughout the chamber. The Daimon in the pit paused and sniffed the air as a hot sulphur wind swept the chamber, watering Helga's eyes. The rumble grew louder and cracks appeared in the floor glowing fractures through which a river of lava could be seen. With a grinding howl, the massive doors at the end of the chamber separated and began to open, swinging out into a passage beyond. With a howl, the Daimon bolted for the opening doors, fighting each other in their lust to leave the pit, driven by hunger and the scent of the dying. They climbed over one another, jabbing their kin with their horns and opening flesh which instantly healed. They threw back their shaggy heads and howled stomping on the slower beasts in their frantic rush to escape until every Daimon had exited the chamber and disappeared with a roar, into the dark honeycomb of tunnels.

Every tunnel led to a different exit point. Soon the surface would be swarming with Daimon, the fiercest predators of the night. Helga watched as the pit below her began to fill with lava, oozing up through the cracks in the floor like blood from fresh cuts. It trickled and spread to join other cuts until the pool melded into one that covered the floor and began to rise.

Over the next several hours, the lava flow will fill every tunnel, flow through every branch of honeycomb until even the smallest tributary of the River of Souls is eliminated. There will be no more soul stream. The Spirit Shields will have no place to send the souls of the dead. My pets will soon roam on the surface and will wipe out all physical resistance, leaving my path clear to commandeer the Well of Souls in Cathair and bind the spirits of the dead to me for all eternity, including the souls of the twins. They are, after all, the key to rebirth. Soon the plague of humanity will cease, stamped out by the Daimon. Once the Daimon's usefulness is finished, I will send them back to the abyss from which they rose, and I will rule supreme.

As she turned away from the rim, she caught sight of Ryder standing in the mouth of a cave leading to the Daimon pit. Helga frowned as she watched him pull back into the shadows. Although she enjoyed his company, she did not trust him. Perhaps it was time to put some restraints around his wanderings. He could not harm her—no one could—but this close to the fruition of her plans, she did not want to leave anything to chance.

It was time to put a collar on her pet. With a smile that did not reach her eyes, she left the platform to go in search of Ryder.

CHAPTER 51

Brennus's Kitchen

"BUT, SIRE, I SHOULD BE DOING THAT! Here, let me do it. Menial tasks are not for the king."

Brennus scooped up the bag of herbs and dumped them into the stone-mortar basin, grabbed the grinding pestle and crushed the dried leaves vigorously, releasing a minty aroma into the air.

Cayden sighed and placed his hands on his hips, exasperated. The mortar and pestle had been swept out of his hands before he had even set them down on the polished wooden butcher's block. Calleigh chuckled at his annoyance.

"I can grind some herbs. Time is of the essence here. We need to get this brewed silently and swiftly. Look, it's almost sunset."

"Yes, sire, but I can do this much faster. I have ground herbs all my life. I have much more experience. Come, sit in the chair here. We will take care of everything." Brennus guided Cayden toward an overstuffed chair by the fireplace and made him sit, handing him a cup of tea once he was settled. "It won't take but a moment for us to make this brew, sire."

Brennus shuffled back over to the table where Calleigh smirked as she measured wine into one vial and water into another. Satisfied with the quantity, she dumped them into a pewter cauldron that she had set on a metal arm by the fire, ready to be swung over the flames. Next, she tipped some flakes of a leathery substance that glowed briefly then spread out across the brew to float on the surface. Calleigh muttered under her breath and the flakes burst into flame then sank below the surface. She stirred the contents with a glass rod then added some flowers from the third pouch, crumbling them between her thumb and forefinger.

"Larkspur and digitalis," she said as she dropped them in. The aroma was heady, the waves of perfumed air making Cayden slightly dizzy.

Brennus had stoked the fire with fast-burning logs until the heat was almost unbearable. Sweat poured down Cayden's face, and he loosened the ties of his shirt, pulling at the fabric in an attempt to cool his heated skin. The heat accentuated the pounding in his head, the never-ceasing headache that was his constant companion. His shirt clung to his chest as he eased himself out of his coat, his hand falling on the flute given to him by Druantia. It nudged up against the vial of potion hidden there, but he did not speak of it, nor did he pull it out. Some things were best kept to himself, especially when it involved access to the gods. He pulled out one flute that warmed under his hand, curious to see why.

He'd forgotten that he had carved this particular flute, for it was the one not made of wood. It was a lightweight and porous bone, eleven inches long. A bone that should belong to a bird's wing, but no bird this size had ever roamed the earth that he was aware of. He studied it once again in the flickering light of the fire, examining its surface and the holes he had carved so carefully into the pale surface. It was naturally hollow but bumpy inside. It resisted all attempts to smooth the interior of the shaft. In the end, he had left it as was, accepting that this flute desired its own shaping. When Cayden had raised his lips to the shaped mouthpiece and blew, it made no sound at all, which was very strange considering the convoluted interior.

Now, as he examined it, a thought occurred to him. Perhaps it was meant to call creatures that were not mortal. Perhaps this flute was meant to call the spirits.

"What do you have there?" Calleigh asked as she leaned in over his shoulder.

He slipped the flute into an inner pocket of his tunic. "A gift from an old friend," he said cryptically. "Is the potion complete?"

"It will require about thirty minutes of brewing time. What is your plan when it is done?"

"I intend to drink it right away. I must be able to defend myself from the effects of the doll and Helga. If this potion will give me the extra resistance I need, then I want it working immediately. Explain to me what it does," he demanded.

"Of course, sire," Calleigh said as she pulled up a chair beside him. "Give me leave to command your servant?" When Cayden nodded, she said to Brennus, "Leave us now. I must speak to the king privately."

Brennus bowed and left, closing the door softly behind him.

Calleigh rummaged through her pack once again and this time pulled out a dart and a small bow, small enough to tuck into a pocket.

"The potion is not to be drunk, sire. It is not meant to enhance your powers but to negate them. This mix is to be injected under the skin and only at the last minute because the potion is a poison. Should Helga take control of you completely, this may be the only avenue of escape left to you. You need this hand held mini-crossbow to inject the poison."

Cayden's head jerked up at the words, even as Helga's consciousness via the Soul Fetch tightened on his mind momentarily.

"Show me how it works," he said harshly, grinding out the words past his clenched teeth.

Calleigh calmly demonstrated how to tip the dart with the syrupy potion and then how to set the dart in the mini-crossbow. It could be loaded and launched with one hand.

Cayden practiced the motions until he was confident he had the mechanics mastered. Then he tucked the stoppered vial, bow, and quills into the inner pocket of his cloak.

"What is your plan, sire, if I may ask?" Calleigh's ebony eyes held his green ones, noting the lines of tension radiating from the corner of his lids. He winced at the searing pain that flashed through his temples. Cayden rubbed his forehead, trying to ease the pain that never went away.

Calleigh brought out a packet of leaves and plucked one out of the pouch and handed it to him. "Chew this slowly. It will block some of the pain but not all of it."

"Why give me three darts?"

"One never knows who might show up at the last minute. Best be prepared." Calleigh patted his arm.

Cayden heaved himself to his feet and ground into motion. "Thank you. It is time."

Calleigh rose to her feet and curtsied. "May the gods be with you, sire. May they shield you and protect you."

Cayden nodded curtly then strode from the room, slamming the door behind him.

As Calleigh rose from her curtsey, the light reflected off of eyes shining bright with unshed tears. "May the gods bless you…my son."

CHAPTER 52

Flight from Hell

RYDER PEERED DOWN THE TUNNEL to where his men slept where they had collapsed, still chained to the great oars of the drills. The Charun who in its former life was known as Captain Brennan, floated by his side, a dark smudge against the black opening behind him.

"The first thing we need to do Captain, is free my men. Then we can follow the tunnels that the Daimon used to get out of here. Helga has given them paths to the surface. We need only choose one that goes in the right direction, toward Cathair, to get where we need to be."

The Charun's voice met Ryder's ears like a growling hiss, sending shivers down his back. Despite understanding the origins of these creatures, it did not make Ryder any more comfortable with them. "My kin will obey. It is a hive mentality, but they are below me, so they will follow my command. I can aid you only so long as my mistress does not impose her will upon me. We must hurry if I am to be of assistance. I help you now because a part of me remembers old oaths not broken by death. Perhaps it was the manner of my death. I am not sure, but the others hold no such oath. I cannot vouch for their behaviour should I be detained by my mistress." Brennan drifted out of the opening and out over the wall, disregarding the staircase, which was not needed for its kind. Reaching the bottom, it drifted among its companions, gathering the Charun. With the eerie communication unique to the Charun, it delivered the instructions. One by one they drifted back to the sleeping men, unlocking the shackles with great keys that hung from their belts. The rattle of the chains being pulled through the metal loops of the ores woke the exhausted knights. With bleary eyes and hopeless countenances, they raised their heads from their arms to see why they were being unchained.

Ryder did not waste time running down the stairs. Instead he yelled from the platform, *"To arms! Knights to arms!"* and then leapt down the steps, his feet barely touching the cold stone as he took the steps three at a time. Reaching the bottom, he dashed over to a shallow gated storage room that a Charun was unlocking, flinging open the door.

The Kingsmen pushed themselves to their feet and realizing they were free, they staggered over to Ryder's side, grabbing their confiscated swords and belting them around waists that had shrunk a couple notches in size. Many of the knights did not stir, having died in their sleep from their toils. Ryder said a quick prayer for them, but he could not linger.

Ryder took a quick head count. Fifty-two knights of the original eighty gathered around him.

"Right. Divide yourselves into pairs. I want a buddy system here. Once in the tunnels, search the passages for the scrape marks of horns, left by the Daimon. That should provide a guide of sorts to the surface. I do not need to tell you to not engage them. I have no idea where we will all end up, but anywhere has to be better than here.

"We are leaving immediately. I have secured the Charun's assistance, but it is only temporary. They can and will likely be forced to come after us. We want to be as far away as we can get. May the gods bless your flight. *Now move!"* Ryder ran for the nearest tunnel exiting off the ledge and grabbed up stacked torches, lighting them one by one as the knights crowded in. Two other knights picked up additional torches, and soon they were lighting and handing out the torches in a steady stream as the men pushed past them. As the last knight disappeared down the tunnel, Ryder turned to find Helga standing behind him, a bemused smile on her face.

"Did you really think I would not know of your plans? That I cannot read the minds of the Charun and know what they are up to? Tsk, tsk, Ryder. I am a goddess!"

"Then why let them go? If you are 'all-knowing,' why did you not try to stop us? You do not have as much control as you think," Ryder replied, his heart thudding with anxiety, but he kept his face smooth and unconcerned, lest he display his fear.

"The Charun? You think I do not control them utterly? They are bound to the underworld. Always they must return, regardless of where I send them. There is no escape for them. Their souls are mine for all eternity. I chose to let your men go. What I really wanted to see is how far you would go. How resourceful you would be." She stepped up to him and trailed a finger down the side of his face "It has been a long time since I have had someone who would challenge me, and I must admit I find it…thrilling." Her hand curled around his throat, and her thumb paused over his Adam's apple. Ryder swallowed painfully as her grip tightened his Adam's apple sliding up and down under her thumb's pressure. "But," she purred, "if you ever try something like this again, I will crush your throat and feed you to the Daimon. Your choices are simple. Rule at my side beneath me for all eternity or die for all eternity, forever condemned to the life of a Charun. It's your choice, my pet." She dragged her nails across his throat, opening deep gashes that bled immediately, dripping down his neck. "Now come. I believe someone approaches." She turned away, never a question in her mind that she would be disobeyed.

Ryder's hand rose to his scratches, his hand coming away bloody. He turned back to the tunnel to see Captain Brennan barring his access to it. With a heavy heart, Ryder turned and followed Helga away from the tunnels. Perhaps he could not free himself, but he could give his men time. He called over his shoulder as he walked away, "Captain, would you accompany us?" The Charun swayed and then drifted toward him. The rest of the Charun did not. They were still for a moment. Then as one, they turned and disappeared down the tunnels after the fleeing Kingsmen.

Interesting, Ryder thought, *his orders are to guard me or at least keep an eye on me. I can command him. Whatever Helga says, I believe there is still something human within the Charun. I do not believe they are all lost as the condemned are lost. There is still good in them, those Charun formed from the souls snatched by Helga.* As the Charun floated up beside him, he said "I believe that you are still in there, Brennan. I do not believe you are condemned. Trapped, yes. Evil, no."

The Charun did not reply as it drifted along beside him. Finally, the hood swiveled in Ryder's direction, and it hissed, "You are right. My soul is that of Captain Brennan, who served the godling Caerwyn all those years ago. My rest has been disturbed. But there is no release for me, human. I have committed atrocities I would not have done in my former life, but as a soldier then and now, I know what it is to kill and my soul is no longer worthy of rebirth. This is where I will stay, serving my mistress."

Ryder absorbed this information and nodded. "Then I hope I can count on you to aid me when my time comes for escape, for I do not intend to remain here. As one Kingsman to another, will you aid me in my next escape attempt? I will escape or die trying. I'd rather my soul be enslaved than my entire being. There is hope yet for the souls of the world. I place my trust in the Spirit Shields to do their duty by us. My hope of salvation and redemption rests with them, not with Helga."

"I will do what I can," said the swaying Charun. "That I promise."

"It is enough. It will have to do. Thank you."

CHAPTER 53

Parting Company

ZIONA AND DENZIK PUSHED the heavy trap door up a crack, peering through the narrow slit at the tiled floor of the kitchen, past legs of stacked chairs and pickle barrels, listening hard for any sound that would indicate a human presence in the room. After several moments of silence, while they scrubbed at their noses to still the sneezes attempting to escape from the stirred-up dust, they pushed open the trap door and crawled up through the floor into the empty kitchen pantry. The root cellar they had found was attached to the castle kitchens. By the condition of the burlap bags of root vegetables and withered apples, it appeared no one had accessed the cold storage for quite a while.

Ziona pulled herself through the hole and crawled over to the barrel where she rested her back against the cool surface for a moment, then leaned forward to grab Denzik's forearm to help pull the injured general up out of the hole.

Denzik slumped beside her and leaned his head back, staring at the ceiling. "I am getting too old for this," he groaned. "I hurt from head to toe."

Ziona shook her head then reached into her pack and pulled out her last precious vial of healing potion. She had been saving it for an emergency, but she knew that she and Denzik needed it more if they were going to be of any use to Cayden in this battle. With a heavy sigh, she uncorked it, drank half of it down then handed the bottle to Denzik. "Drink this. I had been saving it, but...drink it." Denzik peered at her out of one swollen eye and did as instructed, gasping as the liquid burned in his throat. "We will rest here for a moment to let the potion begin to work."

Denzik nodded, looking around at the cramped cupboard. "I believe this is the pantry off the west castle kitchen, closest to the parade grounds. Provided the grounds are not swarming with guards, I should be able to get us into the tunnels that lead to the Well of Souls easily enough. But is that where we want to go?"

"What do you mean? Of course, we want to go there. That is where the king is or where he is headed, right?"

"Most likely, but is that the best way to aid the king? He has his duty, and I believe that the best thing we can do is make sure he is not interfered with. I trust him. Do you?" Denzik stared hard at Ziona. She swallowed heavily under his scrutiny.

"Of course, I trust him. Of course…but, there is still a chance he may…slip up, fail because he cannot complete his mission. The Soul Fetch, it still holds him. What if he cannot loose himself of it in time to do what he must? Shouldn't one of us at least be there to give aid? My mission and my duty to our peoples are to see that the Spirit Shield entrusted to my care completes his mission, regardless of any personal feelings I may have for him." She twisted the empty vial in her hands, turning it over but not seeing it. "I must go to him, Denzik," she said softly for his ears only. "I must."

Denzik pursed his lips and out of habit, searched his pockets for his long-lost pipe. He thought best with that darn pipe clenched between his teeth. In the end, he settled on a pickle fork lying on the shelf beside him. He picked up the dusty utensil and wiped it on his sleeve, then stuck the wooden end between his teeth like a toothpick while he considered her words.

"Swear to me that you will not harm the king. Swear to me that you will defend his life with your own. Not all failure is a result of a lack of will. Swear you will not confuse the two, as I know you are pulled by two different sets of loyalties. I am adding a third. Swear on your hope and faith in rebirth, that you will defend his life with your own as you swore when you first found him."

Ziona locked eyes, Primordial to human and nodded once.

"Take the hallway out the back of the kitchen into the castle main. You are familiar with the castle layout. By the staircase leading to the cells, there is a doorway that leads to the Traitor's Gate. You remember the way?" Ziona nodded again.

Denzik pushed himself to his feet. "The potion is doing its job. I am going to hunt Cyrus. He must be holed up in the castle somewhere." Denzik drew his sword, examining the blade for nicks and, satisfied that it was undamaged from the rock fall, rammed it back into the scabbard hanging from his hip. "Good luck, Ziona, and thank you. I wish you Godspeed." Denzik walked over to the door, thumbed the latch and eased the door open. The kitchen beyond was deserted, the fires cold. This kitchen had not been used anytime recently, probably not since they'd left Cathair. With one last glance back and a warm smile, he slipped out the door, pulling it closed behind him.

He went over to the closest window and moved the curtain aside far enough to peer out at the bailey. The sinking sun cast long shadows across the open space. The gate to the lower town was just visible to the right and that gate was guarded by no less than ten guards. The library was straight ahead in his line of sight. He thought he saw a shadowy cloak around the corner disappear behind the apple trees, but stare as he would, nothing further moved in the gloom. He put his hand on the latch of the door beside the window. With a gentle squeeze, he eased the door open that led out on the opposite side of the kitchen from the gate. All was still. He slid out the doorway, closing it with a soft click, and then crept along the wall until he came to a staircase in the junction formed against south wall of the bailey, leading to the outer wall walk. Denzik paused in the recess of the stairway, counting to fifty inside his head, quieting his breathing while he observed all that moved. How many guarded the upper reaches? His patience was rewarded when four shadows slid across the eastern staircase wall as he watched. He flexed his hand and was pleased to see that Ziona's potion had relieved the stiffness of his joints. It was only temporary. However, he would have preferred to fight with the limberness he had enjoyed in his youth. Drawing his sword, Denzik crept silently up the stairs and sought out the guards.

The first one was a burly young man with a month-old patchy beard and blotchy skin, who yawned and crossed in front of him without checking the staircase he had just passed. Before he could reach the corner, Denzik was up the stairs and lightly tapped him on the shoulder. As the guard spun around, he swung upward with his sword and slashed him across the throat, catching him as he staggered and toppled forward. He lowered him gently to the ground so as to not make a sound.

Denzik crouched over the dying man, relieving him of a short-bladed knife that he tucked into the turn down of his boot. He scanned the wall walk. As he rose, a guard rounded the corner and froze in surprise. With a bellow, he charged at Denzik who stood up and backed away from the dead guard, preferring to keep him in front. *Rule number one, always choose the battlefield if it is within your grasp.* The guard came on fast, a bull charging down a challenger, and leapt over his fallen comrade, falling on Denzik with a fury of slashes. Denzik parried but was forced back under the onslaught of the younger man, staggering back several steps before he found an opening. He ducked under a chest-high swing then brought his sword forward in an upward thrust that his opponent sidestepped. He came at the man with a lightning swift counterattack that forced his opponent to retreat. The guard stepped back once, twice. On the third step, his heel caught the corpse on the ground, and he staggered slightly to the left, but it was enough for Denzik to find his opening. With two quick twirls of his sword, he cut the tendons in both wrists and the sword fell from the guard's useless hand as he fell back across his dead companion. Denzik stabbed him through the heart, and the guard collapsed on top of the other man.

Breathing heavily, Denzik wiped away the sweat dripping down the side of his cheek with the back of a hand. It came away bloodied from a dripping cut above his eye that he had not felt until now. *Ziona's potion was weakening,* he thought with regret.

Two down, but I do not need to fight the other two. He hurried over to a doorway that was his destination. It swung open to reveal a tower with a circular staircase, ascending a flight to the upper floor of the castle, the royal wing. If Cyrus was to be found anywhere, it would be in these hallowed halls. Denzik hurried up the stairs in search of his prey.

CHAPTER 54

The Map

MICHALE PICKED HIS WAY along the dark passage, his ears sharp for any sound that would betray movement ahead. He held the map in front of him, more properly called a puzzle because trying to think in reverse was proving harder than he had originally thought. Not only that, but fear naturally shortened his steps, and he had to consciously focus on the length of his paces so as to not pause at the wrong fork.

He'd returned to the spot where Pieter had collapsed then squinted in the lantern light at the number at the bottom of the page, *Twenty-four R.* He raised the lantern, peered down the passage, and began to walk, counting off twenty-four paces. He passed no less than five other branches, but he stayed on the straight path, eyes blind to all but the count. Precisely on the count of twenty-four, he paused and turned left, reversing Pieter's instructions. He had decided that this was the proper strategy, as he could not see that Pieter had been strong enough to reverse the instructions as he fled. He would have gone with his instinct, honed through his training with the knights. He would have written down his exact path to where he was found. At least, that is what Michale hoped was the truth.

As he worked his way back, he ticked off a pacing so as to not duplicate the instructions by accident. Counting each footfall in his head, he paused at the next intersection where four tunnels lead off like wagon wheel spokes. Michale froze, his eyes darted between the four forks and sweat broke out on his forehead. *Which fork? By the gods, there are four of them! Which one do I choose?* He held the lantern high above the paper and read the tenth number from the bottom of the page. Panic made bile rise in his throat and he swallowed heavily, panting with panic. He clung to his courage as a leech clings to skin, praying that his tenuous hold would not be dislodged. Michale sucked in a deep steadying breath, feeling the blood pounding in his ears then slowly exhaled.

Four paths. He turned on the spot. Four paths...and then it struck him. Pieter would have been in the far-left tunnel (far right for Pieter). Any other tunnel and he would have turned down the one next to it and away from where Michale stood. Michale scratched the annotation "Twenty-four R" into the right wall of the correct tunnel then took a quick glance at his paperwork and paced out his steps again, heading down the proper tunnel. Slowly his racing heart eased back from the panicked cliff edge of his fears. *I can do this. Ten, eleven, twelve. I can do this!*

It was on the thirteenth stealthy step that he heard it. At first it sounded like a low moan, multiple voices blended into one echoing hum, the words unintelligible. Michale raised the oil lantern higher casting the light as far as it would travel. The din drew nearer, louder and began to separate. Michale could barely distinguish between the sounds of swords and stamping feet and hoarse male voices, echoing down the paths and bouncing off the walls. Swallowing past the dryness in his throat, he peered at his map. It read "Thirty-two L." Nineteen more paces would bring him to a junction. If his suspicions were correct, he was about to meet up with some knights of the realm who had no idea of the path to Cathair.

Michale picked up his pace walking rapidly but not increasing his stride, abandoning caution. He counted out loud to keep his focus despite the shivering howl that filled the chambers, like a mad wind. At the count of thirty-two he reached a crossroads intersection and wrote on the wall "thirty-two L." The knights would appear on his right, if he was correct, followed by who knew what, but he suspected the Charun were loose. Michale took a quick look down the right fork but saw nothing. The sounds echoed through the cavern, bouncing and rebounding. It was impossible to determine from where the sounds originated.

Suddenly, a set of fiery eyes appeared at the far end of the corridor, straight ahead of him. The tunnel ran straight as an arrow and a flickering flame silhouetted a massive beast with great curving horns. Michale's eyes widened in fear and he froze, holding his breath lest the tiniest of movements betray his presence. The beast sniffed the air, grunted, then continued along original path, passing out of sight, but the glow did not dim. The smell of sulphur reached his nose, and he raised his shirt over it to lessen the stench.

To his right, ten men suddenly burst into view running madly with swords in hand. They pounded down the stone floor straight toward him. From his left, an equal number of Kingsmen appeared and as the two sets spied each other, then hollered, thinking they viewed the enemy.

Michale leapt into the middle of the intersection and screamed. "Halt now! Shoulder weapons and prepare to march! Defend the king!"

The familiar command slowed their steps, and their training kicked in, automatically responding to the battle cry. Backs straightened and weapons relaxed as they fell into the stance to quick march to a new target.

As they trotted up to him, he appeared out of the gloom in their midst, sheepishly staring back into the ranking knight's wild eyes.

"Michale! What are you doing here? Do you know the way out? What is the path back to Cathair?"

"Good to see you too, sir! This way, follow me!"

He turned and retraced his steps, following the instructions he had written on the walls, with the twenty-odd knights in tow. Behind them, a Charun wailed, searching for those left behind, but the tunnels were as confusing to them as they were to the knights. Without Helga to guide them, their howls soon blended in with the Daimon wandering the labyrinth.

"This way!" Michale led them back to where it had all begun for him, past the chambers outside the Well of Souls and up the staircase to the Traitor's Gate. Seeing the familiar door was like a homecoming to the knights. They collapsed on the floor, exhausted. It was not until they paused and Michale lit the wall torches of the chamber that he saw the extent of their injuries. Some collapsed and could not rise again, burning fear and adrenaline burned in equal measure to power their escape. Spent, they passed out on the stone floor.

"You all need help. Can you defend yourselves till I get back? I will bring Laurista and the healers."

Three of the knights took up positions of defence, swaying on their feet, but grim in their determination to cut down anything that entered the chambers.

Michale climbed the staircase and wrenched open the door to find the way blocked. Ziona stood on the cusp of the threshold, knife in hand and ready to pounce on whatever stood on the other side. She blinked twice then peered over Michale's shoulder at the injured men.

Michale pushed past and tossed over his shoulder, "I am going for help!" then took off at a run past the dungeons. His only thought was to find Laurista and bring her to the aid of the knights. His mad race down the stone hallway and up the stairs spilled him out into the courtyard. He slowed to a brisk walk so as to not attract attention, hurrying into the infirmary. He burst through the doors, calling, "Laurista! We need you! The knights are back, but they are hurt!" He ground to an abrupt halt as his eyes caught up to his words. Two towering Charun stood with Laurista strung between them, held in their sway. She thrashed, trying to loosen their hold.

With a cry and a surge of anger, Michale drew his sword and launched himself at the left-hand Charun, screaming the entire time "For king and Spirit Shield! For Cathair! For honour!" He stabbed the left Charun in the face where its eyes would be on a human. It screamed, as though the blade had pierced flesh, dropping its hold on Laurista and staggering backward. It writhed, the blade to the eye a fatal wound, and exploded into dust. Laurista, her right arm now free, drew a short knife from her pocket and stabbed at the hand of the Charun clutching her left arm, while Michale's swift down stroke beheaded the distracted creature. The hooded head leaked a tarry black substance across the floor as it rolled. With a pop both body and head shredded into dust. Silence descended.

Laurista tumbled to the floor as she was released. Michale dropped down beside her. "Are you all right? Did they hurt you?" His eyes searched for injury.

"No, the timing of your entry was perfect." Michale helped her to her feet and opened his mouth to ask about the orderlies, and that was when he saw them. Only their feet were visible, behind the screen where they had fallen, but an inky black trail of smoking ooze pointed to another pair of dead Charun taken out by the orderlies before they collapsed.

"Sanchez!" Laurista gasped, hurrying around the curtain. She swept aside the cloth where Pieter was pushing the body of the stinking Charun from the foot of his bed. The corpse rolled and bounced, spewing tar from a surgical slice across its abdomen. The elderly orderly Sanchez had known exactly where to strike the creature as it had advanced on them.

Pieter grimaced and pointed to the second orderly. "Trenton might be alive. He tripped and whacked his head against the fence post, tripping one Charun. Whether intentional or accidental, it worked because Sanchez finished the pair of them before he fell."

Michale pulled Sanchez to the side and sure enough, Trenton's chest rose and fell evenly, a swelling bruise blooming on his forehead.

"Of all the luck." Laurista checked Trenton's pulse and then with some light slaps woke him. "Trenton, wake up. Wake up!" He moaned and his eyes flickered in response but did not wake.

"Pieter, are you able to assist me? The knights are back but need help. We need every hand right now."

"The knights! Certainly!" He struggled to loosen himself from the twist of blankets wrapped around his legs then swung them over the side. "I have strength for this." He pushed himself to his feet, eyes searching for his pants. "I'd rather die with a sword in my hand than in a sick bed." Spying his pants, he pulled them on and wobbled toward the door. "Where is my sword?" Laurista, clicking her tongue, pulled his sword belt from a peg on the wall in a back room and handed it to him.

"Help me get Trenton into your bed." Together they lifted the woozy man onto the cot and then stuffing medical supplies into a satchel, Laurista straightened and said, "Lead the way to the knights, Michale." With a last, sad look over her shoulder at Sanchez, she hurried after the men.

CHAPTER 55

A Gift

RYDER STOOD AT STRICT ATTENTION, a knight on duty, impervious to the taunts of the crowd or the distractions surrounding him. That he was located in hell and standing next to a goddess dressed in a slinky low-cut dress did not escape his attention. Rather, he chose to tamp it down, bury it under duty and routine. He would not allow the distractions to pierce the armor of his will or his mind.

"Come now, Ryder. I have given you a great gift! Immortality can be yours and power as you have never known. The wealth and riches of the world are yours for the taking. You will be king in your own right! I will even allow you to live on the surface in time once your loyalty is beyond doubt as was Genii's before you."

"You would release me on the world as a plague? You call that a reward?" The scrying pool at his side had delivered a catastrophic prophecy. Disease spread unchecked in the wake of a necromancer. The towns and cities of his youth were reduced to ashes as they burned. Black smoke, thick and oily with the smells of the dead filled the air, punctuating the fulfillment in ghastly detail, complete with visions and horrifying smells. Strangely the pool delivered both sight and smells and everywhere the ground cracked. Lava oozed just below the surface of the ground until the plants burst to steam and flashed into ashes. There was nothing left.

Ryder gripped his emotions in a tight knot refusing to give Helga the wedge she sought so ardently, the key to his undoing.

Where are you Cayden? Avery? You are our only hope! He was not a praying man, but he prayed now from the depth of his soul to the gods that protected it. *Gods of old, celestial spirits, hear my cry. I beg you to hear our call before it is too late. I ask, we ask, for a miracle. Please intercede on behalf of your children or we are all lost. Please hear my prayer. Save us!* Over and over he prayed, the litany dulling Helga's words and creating a shield in his mind that rejected her control.

Helga plucked a ruby bloom from a hibiscus bush, observing its perfection before crushing it in her grip and casting it to the floor. She was clearly frustrated. She stopped her pacing and squaring her body to him and slapped him so hard that his head jerked back. Furious, he pinned her with his dark eyes, hatred glowing in their depths. "You will serve me, or I will make your life such a living hell that you will wish for the Charun's tender mercies."

Ryder straightened lifting his chin. "I will not," he said simply.

Helga hissed and drew back her hand to strike him again but froze as she heard the sound of horse hooves clattering on the rocks that led to the entrance of her domain. She stared at the entrance, her hand lowering. "Who dares to approach my home?" She gathered her skirts and strode to the tunnels that lead to the surface. Ryder followed.

*   *   *

Marea slowed her horse then slid from the saddle to ground. There was no sound in the clearing except for the rush of the great falls. Not a bird twittered, nor a squirrel chattered. The hush in the sacred forest was that of a breath held in expectation of violence. Yet the Highland Spine trembled as the entrance to Sheol Animus quaked. *Unsurprising, considering what I just rode through,* she thought wryly. Her horse snorted backing away from the entrance, spooked by the sulphurous vapour that bloomed out of the cracked rocky path.

Marea searched with her talent as High Priestess for the blue-veined mist of the redeemed, those who would be reborn and were the sanctified souls, the hope for the world.

There were none. Frantically, she searched. Where she could normally feel the stream as a steady pulse of spirit, there was nothing but death. The corrupted souls below her feet howled. She sickened, fearful that they would reach through the crust of stone and snatch her feet, so intense was the hatred and murderous intent of their souls.

She shuddered, wanting to flee from the sensations. The wind gusted around her, hot and putrid, and she covered her nose with her sleeve. Her horse reared back, spooked by the foul air. She pulled it down, trying to calm the wild-eyed beast, but it was having none of it. The horse wrenched the reins from her hand, clattering away as fast as it could run back to the relative safety of the forest.

"So…you have come."

Marea whirled and gasped at the apparition that appeared in the mouth of the cave. She had never seen Helga in person before although she was not sure that was the proper term. The edges of her silhouette were blurred, as though she was not quite in the world, which was probably true. This was the entrance to the underworld, after all.

Marea curtsied deeply, her face staring at the ground and did not rise until Helga said, "The question is why have you come? Rise and face me." Marea straightened and took a step closer to Helga.

"Great mistress, I came because I sense the end is near." Another step.

"But you have not completed your mission. You were to bring the girl to me. You have failed." Something stirred behind Helga. *A man. But this man is not blurred around the edges. So, he is not dead.*

"Mistress, I could not bring her. Your sister Artio has taken her. I had no choice. She would have slain me!" Another step.

"Then you should have died. You are useless to me if you cannot complete a simple task when she is delivered into your grasp. You were a failure as a High Priestess, and you are a failure as a servant." Helga glared at Marea. Marea met the man's eyes over her shoulder and understanding passed between them.

"Helga, who is our guest? Do tell me, has the High Priestess of Faylea graced us with her presence? Why don't you invite her in for tea?" Ryder tensed his muscles, readying himself.

Helga spun around ready to let her hand fly again for having spoken out of turn. At that precise moment, he gave her a hard shove. Helga stumbled across the threshold of reality between her domain and that of the physical world and the contact with the barrier seized her in a paralyzing grip.

Marea, seeing her chance, yanked a velvet bag out of her cloak and shook it over her hand. Out tumbled a silver necklace, flashing in the red-tinted light of the lava flows. *I had intended this necklace for Avery, but I believe it is a better fit for Helga.* With a cold smile, she stepped up to the veil and reached up to snap it around Helga's neck. Helga's eyes bulged and Marea, satisfaction dripping from her lips, shoved her back into her realm. As her hands came in contact with the barrier, Marea shrieked, the sensation similar to that of being plunged into an icy river, needles pricking her hands. Her hands withered and she cried out in pain. Helga grabbed the withered hand and tugged, attempting to pull Marea into the underworld.

At the same moment, Ryder launched himself through the barrier. He hung, comically suspended in midair for a moment, his mouth frozen in a scream as the air was sucked from his lungs. In the next minute, he was flung out of the barrier, knocking Marea away from Helga's grip at the same time. He tumbled away, sliding to a halt at the edge of the misty pool, jerking spasmodically. His passage through the barrier released Helga, who tumbled back into her domain, frantically scrabbling at the necklace which now tightened around her neck, a solid ring of metal imbued with spiraling webs of blue spirit. Her hands flew to the collar and she shrieked, the high-pitched sound bouncing off the walls of the cave. Her screams became an earthquake of sound that started a slide of pebbles and medium-sized rocks down the face of the mountain, bouncing and tumbling to splash in the waterfall terminus.

Marea ran over to Ryder, placed her tingling hands on his forehead and closed her eyes, summoning some of the magic of the High Priestess granted to her when she took up the calling. It was the little bit of she had access to. Her lips moved calling for aid. "Mother, heal this man. Bring him back from the abyss. Hear my prayer."

Her hands glowed. A soft fall of mist encased Ryder, settling on the surface then sinking in to disappear under his skin. His convulsions stilled. Marea peered at him, clasping her shaking hands together, for they quivered with aftershocks. She glanced back over her shoulder to where Helga had been, but she was gone from the entrance. An eerie red light pulsed in the opening. *Oh no, that can't be good!*

"Wake up!" Marea tapped Ryder's cheek, trying to rouse him then gently shook his broad shoulders. She bent and placed her ear against his chest and was relieved to hear a steady beating. "Wake up!" She slapped him again, this time harder. Nothing. She slapped him again. Ryder's eyes jerked open and caught her hand in full swing.

"Kindly don't do that again." Ryder pushed himself to a sitting position, trying to steady his sight as the world spun before his eyes. The pulsing light in the doorway was growing in intensity and frequency, a red strobe that put him in mind of a beating heart, only this one was very, very agitated. "Uh, I think we should get out of here right now." Grabbing Marea by the hand, he pulled her to feet with him and they raced for the trees, Ryder staggering like a drunk. The mountain shook, and the resultant earthquake rolled the ground under their feet. They stumbled into the trees but did not pause as the canopy began to quiver and whip with the tremors. Mighty oaks that had stood for millennia cracked then snapped, crashing to the ground behind them. They ran for their lives as the mountain behind them came alive, the top exploding with the force of ten volcanoes. A keening cry wailed overhead, the sound of ultimate anguish mingled with fury and they dived for any cover they could find. An outcropping of rock was the best they could find and as they rolled under it they prayed that it would not fall on top of them. The forest was struck by a blast of wind and heat that laid it flat in a deafening roar of popping branches and snapping trunks. Dirt pelted the sheltering rock and dust flew at the speed of cosmic winds in celestial skies.

It was no accident. Ryder and Marea peeked around the corner of the rock over the wreckage of tree trunks, to the starkly visible mountain. Only it was no longer a mountain, but a hillock, and from its center, a colossus of a Daimon was rising. Helga had poured her soul into the Daimon Asag, merging her consciousness with the Daimon, and forming a better, stronger Daimon, one strong enough to challenge the gods. But this one wore a bright blue collar…and the face of a god. Helga.

CHAPTER 56

Fetched

CAYDEN STAGGERED THROUGH the ancient tunnel under the castle, sweat dripping from his brow despite the cool underground draft. The passages were familiar yet strange. With one part of his mind, the one that remembered a life before this one, he could see the building of the tunnels, great warrens of rocky passages hewn with one purpose: to confuse a potential enemy. The underground maze protected the most important feature in all of Cathair, the Well of Souls, the place that the souls of the deceased were sent to await their rebirth. They also acted as a last defence against the most desperate of hours when all would be lost, a grim and deadly trap waiting to be sprung.

But the tunnels were no longer safe, the passages no longer secure. Because of him.

Cayden bent at the waist and vomited. His stomach heaved. He vomited again then wiped his mouth with the back of his sleeve.

He was tearing apart inside.

At first the commands had been gentle, almost teasing, as though the commander was testing the bond of the doll, working out its limitations.

At first it had been simple things, such as reaching for a peach in his pack and suddenly deciding peaches were horrible and that he wanted an apple instead. Or deciding to take the stone path to the library and at the last minute deciding to go via the gardens. Each decision was so logical, so simple and subtle he couldn't decide if the thought was his or not. And each destination was one that he knew was his own decision, yet the path to the decision was slowly being taken over.

In the three days since he had gone underground, he'd sneaked into the library twice via the hidden door in the lower chambers. Few knew that the library had four floors below the flagstone of the main public structure; a full four floors crammed full of manuscripts and books of account, marriage and death records and every other sort of information that might be accessed once in a generation. He had discovered the door that opened onto the tunnels by accident, the first week of wandering about the castle after his ascension. While searching for a series of temple scrolls referencing the history of the gods, he'd found a door hanging behind a curtain in a back room. Now that same door was proving to be a convenient access to the castle, allowing him to roam without alerting the legionnaires as to his presence underground. He scoured the library's ancient texts, searching for a way to disrupt the Soul Fetch's hold on him, desperate to break the bond. A bond that was swiftly overtaking him.

The voice in his mind was not subtle, nor was it simple, and it certainly wasn't his. It burrowed into his brain like tree beetles seeking the sap-filled core of a tree to eat it from within. The grinding command clamped down on his consciousness, driving all other thought from his head but to obey. But the control was not complete. When the possessor of the doll's attention waned, a semblance of himself surfaced and with it a slowing of his steps as he struggled to regain control of himself and his actions.

It was this struggle that brought on the bouts of nausea, heavy sweating, and the blinding headaches which were becoming more violent. The last bout had left a trail of blood. His physical body could not keep up this level of punishment.

Tears leaked from the corner of his eyes brought on by a wracking cough from a cold he had acquired or possibly the slow-moving poisoning of his body. Angrily, he swiped them away, hardening his heart. There was no time for self-pity. The important thing was that Helga was distracted for a moment and he needed to hurry while she was.

He forced himself to straighten, then half ran, half staggered toward the entrance to the Well of Souls. His heart sank when he realized that there were no guards in the tunnels leading to the sacred chambers. The knights under Ryder's command had been tasked with this duty yet not a one could be found anywhere in the kingdom. It had all the hallmarks of Helga's doing, but how she had accomplished it, he did not know.

The entrance to the anteroom shone with a pale blue flickering light, a high-energy shield attuned to him as a Spirit Shield. He stepped through it easily and hurried across the sandstone room. Vaulted buttresses held up by fluted sandstone columns. Runes and the faces of the gods were painted on the ceilings and halfway down the walls. The flagstone floor was covered in a thick coat of dust. His boots were the only fresh tracks. The only other markings were from his, Mordecai's, and Ziona's boots from that original trip to the well.

But something was wrong. As he approached the inner sanctum, the familiar blue glow was absent. The welcoming, warming touch of the souls did not come. There was no sizzle of energy, no mental buzz of disembodied voices. Alarmed, he sped up his steps and entered the rocky room where the well resided.

As his eyes slid to the dark well, he screamed, "Nooooo!" and ran to the lip of the well. "Mother!" he gasped. "Mother!"

The well was nearly empty. Only the feeblest flicker of bluish light could be seen in the deepest part of the well. There was no answer to his call. The souls were gone.

Cayden screamed and collapsed against the side of the well, hands fisting in the hair on his head, despair knocking the air from his lungs. He gasped as deep in his mind a voice chuckled, amused. For a moment, he considered throwing himself down the well, but then a deep surge of anger tightened his chest.

This close to the well, he knew the source of his headaches. The draining of the well was draining him. His soul was connected to the vessel, powering the shield that encased the great River of Souls. The ripping pain he experienced was the pain of a soul stretched beyond its capacity, shredding as it failed as Helga won.

Helga.

Cayden turned on the connection with anger and a hate so intense it swelled like a blister, until one prick and he would burst. *You will pay for this, Helga. I swear it on my gift of rebirth and on my eternal soul. You will pay! Forever!* He shouted down the bond. *Watch your back because I am coming for you!* he shouted down the connection to Helga, a lightning bolt of fury released at his target.

Helga laughed. *You would not do such a thing, dear brother! Why you cannot lift a finger to harm another. That is why everyone around you always dies. You bring death. I am the true saviour of the world. Once all souls are mine, there will be no need for you. Now go fulfill my commands. Today will see an end to the dominion of the Spirit Shields. I will be the new Soul Queen. I will rule all, and by my blessing they will be permitted mortal lives…or not.*

White hot knives drove not only into Cayden's head, but also sliced into his flesh. He screamed as the cuts began to flow with blood. His body jerked upright, and he stumbled from the chamber, a macabre puppet pulled along on invisible strings, blood dripping behind him as he staggered from the chamber. The pain was so intense that it blocked out his emotional agony, submerging it under a haze of anguish. He forgot once again who he was, what he was, and why he had come down to the tunnels. He had work to do above ground, and it was time to do it. His will submerged under the weight of Helga's control, he picked up the lantern and wove an unsteady path back through the shield of spirit, which flickered and died as he left the anteroom.

He fell several times as he climbed out of the chamber, skinning knees and hands, adding fresh wounds to the ones inflicted by Helga. He never thought her name. He did not know his own. He simply obeyed.

Cayden staggered up the stone steps and at the top pushed open a heavy arched door that exited out onto the moonlit palace parade grounds. The field was still, shrouded in the deathly stillness that preceded great evil. Stumbling to the armory, Cayden wrenched open the door. The lantern pushed back the shadows and glinted off racks and racks of weaponry: swords and maces, pole axes, and bundles of steel-tipped arrows. Helmets and suits of armour lined the wall on stands, his own included. Quickly he donned his chain mail and plating, remembering dimly a time when someone had assisted him in dressing in the heavy metal. Twice he dropped his chest plate but eventually had it buckled in place. It weighed a ton and dragged his injured body down so that he sank down onto a bench for moment to rest.

His head hung, sweat dripping off the end of his nose. Just as quickly, he began to shiver in the cold steel, made colder by the seeping damp night air. Cayden shook his head raggedly, trying to clear his thoughts, but then the pain returned and he jerked to his feet, grabbing sword and pole axe before clanking across the armory to the rear door.

As he wrenched opened the door, his path was blocked by a tall man in flowing black robes, hood pulled up and face hidden in the dark folds.

"Out of my way," growled Cayden.

The man did not move. Cayden drew his sword, bared steel ringing, but a bony hand gripped his wrist. With his other hand, the man pushed back his hood.

Long white hair framed a thin sallow face, lips slack and eyes glowing fiercely. Madness chased through its depths, as the magic within his body was manipulated by another.

His lips parted and words forced their way out in a high, thin voice. "Do not think that you can escape me, Cayden. Mordecai is also my puppet. He will see that you perform your duties…to the end."

CHAPTER 57

The Third Bowl

AVERY PAUSED AS THE DOOR DISAPPEARED. She was alone. The staircase was replaced by a polished marble floor that graced an audience chamber fit for the gods. Fluted pink marble columns ribboned with gold were evenly spaced around the perimeter of the grand hall. Beyond the columns, clouds swirled with flashes of blue sky, all backlit by a sun that could not be seen. Carved cornices supported a ceiling of hammered gold, and central to the space was massive marble plinth with a blunt cut spire. It rose up and up through a square cut in the roof, disappearing into the heavens. Avery knew where she was. She stood at the threshold of an altar, Morpheus's altar.

Her eyes searched the hall for any sign of Genii or Artio but could not spot either one. Avery walked up to the altar and mounted three steps to where a pillow graced a notch in base of the spire. She settled onto the cushion, sitting cross-legged then closed her eyes. Clearly prayers were needed, for her brother, for her sisters and for the world. Prayers long ignored to a temple forgotten. She allowed her eyes to drift shut and began to pray.

* * *

Genii stepped onto the first step then the second, then the third, but the step to the fourth was a long stretch, even for one as tall as he. As he sprung from the r to the p his foot wobbled and his heel came down on the crack between stairs. The incorrect rune plate crumbled and fell away, revealing an inky abyss that swooned into the melting blackness. The pieces of stone step disappeared and hard as he listened, he could not hear them land, nor did they touch sides or make any sound at all. Genii breathed deeply to steady his nerves. Fortunately, the next step to h was directly above the p, and he stepped up onto that rune, which held his weight easily. "Jump to the proper rune and grab my hand when you do. I will not let you fall," Genii called out to Artio. He had no doubt that the rest of the false letters would crumble in a similar fashion, casting them into an endless fall for all eternity.

Artio growled low in her throat then launched herself with abandon at the offending letter. She overshot her target slightly, and the force of her jump nearly pushed both of them onto the next runes inlaid on the stairs.

"Slow down, Artio." Genii pulled her head into his chest (for standing above her, he was taller) and she wrapped her arms around his waist. He kissed her hair then pushed her slightly away, grabbing her hand. "Next letter...e." His eyes searched the runes, only to find there were two runes displaying the symbol for the letter e. Perplexed, he studied the runes above. Both paths led to the completion of the spelling of the word. "Artio, there are two paths. What do you think? Are we supposed to climb separately or take the same path?"

Artio peered around his back at the stairs. "I do not know. Why divide the path? It must be a test of some kind."

Genii snorted. "Of some kind. I am not Primordial. I do not know what was intended here."

"The temple is not Primordial. The temple is of the gods. This is a test of the gods," said Artio, as she studied the two paths. "If you are given a choice, how do you decide? On the merit of the question? Or on the truth of the answer? This was the kind of riddle my father used to place before us when we were children, to test us. I hated them." Artio crossed her arms, glaring at the offending stones. Her gaze drifted up the staircase to the top, where another door peeked through the fog from time to time. "My father would have waited for us to answer the question then take the opposite position to argue the point. We were never right."

"Well, maybe that was the point?" said Genii. "Maybe there is no right or wrong answer because it is a choice." Artio looked at him, eyebrows raised. "Maybe it's about unity of thought, rather than the thought itself. I say we go together."

"When did you become so wise, my love?" Artio smiled.

"Well, they say men mature more slowly than women. Perhaps I just needed to do some aging." He grinned back. "Shall we?" He pulled her up onto the step beside him and then hand in hand, they stepped onto the e runes, each to their own stone then froze, waiting for a response. When nothing happened, they grinned at each other still holding hands.

"Look. The last two letters, u and s. They are together, on the same step." Genii pointed at the broad slab in front of them, the only possible path. Together they stepped on to the last step. The moment their feet touched the doubled rune marker a blue mist rose and expanded between them and the door barring their access to the landing. The mist rose and swirled then broke apart, twisting into shapes that resolved into magical beings, the spirits of the dead and the spirits of the animals in their immortal forms. A vast intelligence pressed against their minds and they spoke as one, although the words came from the mouth of a small girl standing in the curtain of blue.

Daughter of Morpheus, you request access to the temple of the gods. Have you proven yourself trustworthy? Have you proven your loyalty to the gods? For only those who believe can cross to the altar. One has gone before you. We know of your mission and the treasure carried by the wizard, but only the faithful may pass.

Artio knelt on the stair, and Genii followed suit, head bowed.

"Aossi, it has been a very long time since we have met. I am humbled in your presence. My path has been a rocky one, and my return not as I had anticipated, but I have returned both physically and mentally. Confusion greeted the opening of my eyes. At first, I did not understand the nature of my being, but I remember now and I honour the gods. I wish to approach the temple to pray to my father, to beg his help, for without it our world is lost. All will perish as it began, with Helga crushing life out of existence. Time is short, Aossi. Surely you feel it? The veil is torn, and the souls of man are being swallowed by the underworld. Only the gods can restore the balance. I beg you to let us pass. I will crawl on my knees if you insist."

Aossi quirked her head to one side, an inquisitive child fascinated at the grovelling of an adult. A broad smile wreathed her face, and she clapped her hands together with glee. "Stand, Artio! Time is indeed short. Come, come!" Aossi held out her hands, and Artio and Genii each took one and stepped up onto the platform. The door vanished. They found themselves in a grand hall, and there, surrounded by spirits, was Avery. She did not stir. Her body was wreathed in blue as was the spire rising out of the squat plinth, the swirling blue spirit flowing in an unnatural wind, spinning and swirling at a dizzying speed.

"Come, Come!" Aossi repeated, tugging them forward. They crossed the floor to the plinth, and that was when they saw it. A thin white staircase was carved into the side of the spire. Cut from the face of the stone itself, there were no handrails, no grips, just stairs that rose impossibly into forever to the gods themselves.

"You must climb." Aossi pushed them toward the staircase. "You must climb and deliver the eye to the gods, so that they may see why they are so urgently needed. It will take both of you to ensure that you do not fail." Artio opened her mouth to ask about Avery, but Aossi pushed her forward. "There is no time for questions. Avery is doing as she must, as is Cayden. This is your task to complete, together. Hurry!"

"Wait, the last bowl!" Artio dropped to her knees, pawing in her pack retrieve the last bowl while Aossi tapped her foot impatiently. "Here it is," she huffed as she pulled it from the sack. Artio unwound the wrappings and placed it on the floor in front of them. The dirty blue bowl had turned an ugly grey, the clouds inside the bowl now a full-fledged thunderstorm. The storm swirled around the bowl, boiling with anger.

"What do we do?" asked Genii, but no reply was needed for at that moment. Avery's lips opened, but her eyes did not. She spoke in the voice of the gods, the sound reverberating of the non-existent walls.

**"Sands of time, slipping by. Fissure of clay, godling's eye.
Tempest born of Helga's fury. All are former souls, surely?**

**To ring the bell of death's long grip,
at heaven's door souls must chip.**

**Spirit Shields, a god's remains, only answer to devil's bane.
The river breached, souls snatched away.
To conquer now, steadfast must stay.**

**Mother's breath, the skies obey. Before her kneel. Before her pray.
Shield extended, sacrifice combined.
Souls required, eternity's shrine."**

Kneeling beside the bowl, they had a clear view of the tempest inside and with that last word from Avery, lightning forked around the bowl, followed by a sonorous boom. At the same time, the clouds of spirit around the spire darkened and lightning flashed, bolts of lightning arching from cloud to could and stabbing down to strike the marble floor.

Artio met Genii's disbelieving eyes. He said, "We are supposed to climb an open staircase *in that?*" as rain began to fall. They peered at Avery to see if she would say more, but when her eyes remained closed, they switched to the curving stair of the spire.

"I think we are about to pay my father a house call. Let's just hope he is home," said Artio.

She rose to her feet and grabbed his hand once more, then Artio and Genii ran to the base of the stairs. Genii began to climb, followed by Artio. Aossi watched them disappear into the blue, and then her eyes drifted in the direction of Cathair, where she could feel the other Spirit Shield to be. A tiny frown marred her cherubic features, her toe tapping on the marble floor.

CHAPTER 58

The Well of Souls

DENZIK PAUSED BEHIND A SUIT OF ARMOUR, melting back behind it as a man stepped through the doorway between the windows. Finally, he had caught up to Cyrus. He raised his sword, preparing to strike as soon as the man drew level with his position. Blade held high, he gathered his strength, but at the last second he froze as the man hurried past. The cloak was the same, but this was Mordecai, not Cyrus. Denzik lowered his sword, puzzled, as the wizard disappeared around the corner. Denzik was about to step out into the hallway to follow the wizard when the door to the balcony opened again. He flattened himself once again behind the suit of armour, and this time he was not disappointed. Cyrus stepped into the hall, glanced both ways and then turned in the same direction as Mordecai, a self-satisfied smirk on his face. He drew gloves from his hands as he walked. As he drew abreast of Denzik, Denzik attacked.

"Hello, Cyrus. Finally, we meet again, face to face." With a thrust of his sword, he ran Cyrus through with his blade. "This is my thanks, long overdue, for the enforced retirement." Cyrus gasped, but no air was available. He crumpled then slid part way off the sword, leaving a bloody smear on the polished silver. "Give my compliments to the queen when you see her in hell." With a savage twist of his wrist, Denzik shoved hard and Cyrus fell back onto the tiled floor.

Denzik pulled his blade free as Cyrus's eyes rolled back in his head. He checked the hallway once more then quickly wiped his blade on Cyrus's cloak and ran off down the hall after Mordecai.

Mordecai moved awfully fast for an elderly wizard. Denzik paused at a window and saw his cloak crossing the bailey below. Denzik took the first set of stairs and pelted down the circular staircase to the base, then out onto the level and hurried across the grounds. Bodies littered the ground. Denzik stumbled to a halt, shocked at the carnage. He pressed his back to the wall to check for guards, but nothing moved in the killing field. The bailey was as silent as the inside of a tomb. Not even a bird called from the trees.

A flicker of movement by the armoury caught his attention. Denzik hurried after the wizard, sword drawn once again, cautious now and unsure of the old wizard's mental state. He crept up to the door and eased up beside a window, then raised his eyes to see into the room. Mordecai stood in the doorway confronting the king. Both had the glazed look of men not in control of their wits...or their wills. Denzik ducked below the window, hiding himself in the bushes as they left the armoury bristling with armour and weapons. They strode side by side across the bailey then pulled open the door that led to the prison cells and eventually to the Traitor's Gate.

Denzik waited till the count of five then followed. *This cannot be good. Are both under Helga's control?* He placed his ear against the door and then gently eased it open, slipping in to the passage. Lit torch in one hand and sword in the other, he ran down the passage, anxious to not lose sight of the king. The empty cells taunted him as he passed, a tribute to Cyrus's reign. The criminals who had been housed there since Cayden had declared himself must have been set free to terrorize the populace. *For the life of me, will this ever end? I feel as though I have been chasing this dream since the first day I picked up the sword. My only wish is to see the king returned to his rightful place and the Spirit Shields securely in charge, guarding the end of days and the rebirth of all peoples. My life is nothing in the grand scheme of things, but perhaps I can make a difference for them. For the king. For the Spirit Shield.*

Denzik took the stairs to the lowest level, and there he saw it, the Traitor's Gate, wide open. He ran up to it, but it was not the king and the wizard that he found. He found the knights, stretched out on the floor of the cavern in a makeshift hospital, being treated by Laurista. Glad cries of "Denzik! General Denzik! He's alive!" greeted him from the floor as he trotted down the staircase.

Denzik grabbed Michale by the sleeve as he ran past, bandages in hand. "Where did they go? The king and Mordecai? Which direction?"

"They ran off into the tunnels. Didn't even pause to say hello. I'd say they are on their way to the Well of Souls. Why? What's the matter?"

"Nothing," said Denzik "Tend to the men. But have them on their feet ASAP. War is upon us and every sword is needed."

"I know. The Charun are here and worse." Denzik nodded curtly, acknowledging Michale's information.

"They must be on their feet to face what is coming. *What is here.* I must aid the king. Be strong. Keep faith." He clasped the younger man's arm and then hurried off into the tunnel chasing his king and the wizard.

The space narrowed and dark overtook the passage, interspersed by flickering torches. He ran as silently as his old feet could run, not wishing to alert them of his presence. As he rounded the bend leading to the entrance chamber, he ran smack into an invisible shield. The field of energy surged. He hung suspended for a moment before he was flung violently away and into the stone wall. His head struck hard, and he collapsed unconscious to the floor.

*   *   *

The flare of the energy field lit the chamber, but both men ignored the bright light that washed over them.

Mordecai's wild eyes flickered frantically under his narrowed eyelids. Their strange movements were spooky to say the least, especially when framed by the untamed white mane of hair that was a wizard's signature. It stood on end, electrified by the coursing energy crackling through his body. Wizard's fire sparked in his palms once again.

Cayden stood at the edge of the well, resting his weight on his quivering arms, knuckles white with the fierceness of his grip. He shook his head, a bear with a sore tooth. His head swung back and forth muttering under his breath.

Break the seal. Smash the well. Do it! Helga's voice was a cannon's roar. Cayden winced as it impacted his brain. He fought her commands, but the Fetch was too strong, the squeezing pressure both physical and mental. His eyes were bloodshot, the whites greying. He was dying. He could feel it. The poison he had ingested in the castle was catching up to the abuse he had put his body through the last few weeks and months. Combined with the control of his will via the Soul Fetch, he was at the end of his endurance. Cayden coughed and blood splattered the edge of the well and dropped into the dark depths below where the feeblest blue flickered.

I give you this last chance, Cayden. Disobey me again, and the Primordial woman is as good as dead. You don't want to lose her, do you? I sense you have become attached to her. Break the seal. The vise clamped down, and Cayden shuddered and withdrew the war hammer he had retrieved from the armoury. He raised it high into the air. As he made to strike, Mordecai lifted his hands and cast wizard's fire at the weapon. The war hammer blazed with fire just as Cayden swung it. The enhanced hammer crashed into the well with the force of an avalanche and cracked. Cayden swung again and the crack spread through the mortar, the wall tipping inward. The third swing sailed right through the wall of the well and with a groan, the stone fell into the hole, bouncing and crashing into the base. Cayden dropped the hammer to the ground and leaned on it, gasping for breath from a chest filled with congested lungs. He staggered over to the side of the well and brought the hammer down again, over the central seal in the floor. It cracked on the first impact, the crystal shattering like glass.

Excellent! The voice screamed in his mind. *Now poison the stream.*

Cayden reached inside his tunic and pulled out a pouch. He removed the contents and laid them on the ground in front of him.

-A vial of poison, a present of Calleigh's

-A flute given to him by the great tree

-A dagger forged in the flames of Sheol Animus, imbued with the binding for a Charun

-A blue stone that glowed softly, a relic of Avery's

These were the weapons left to him. Something to kill himself with and to kill others. His destiny was not to save the souls of the world but to destroy them. Forever.

Which order should he use them? If he drank the poison first, he could die before disrupting the stream, thus saving the river from extermination. But if he did that, Mordecai would take over and finish the job so there was no benefit in dying first.

He could use the flute to call for aid, but again, Mordecai would kill him first before the spirits could reach him and complete the task.

If he used the dagger and then drunk the potion, at least he would not know about the demise of the world. A coward's exit.

The blue stone. It was a connection to his sister, the only one he had. At least he would not die alone. He picked up the stone on its chain and swung it around his neck, comforted that Avery would sense him in his dying moments.

Cayden bent over the seal, picked up the knife and stabbed it into the crack. There was a blinding flash and a wail as the souls fell away into the river of red below, swept away by the angry boiling stream. Cayden screamed, for as the seal broke, so did his own soul. Agony, such as he had never felt before tore through his being, grabbed his heart and squeezed with the force of a smithy's vice. The souls of the well crowded his mind until he fell to the ground convulsing as they tried to hide within him, seeking refuge. Cayden cried out to Avery, screaming her name, but it was not Avery who loomed over him. It was Mordecai.

CHAPTER 59

A God's Intervention

AVERY'S EYES SHOT OPEN at the touch of Cayden's mind, the cry so intense she jerked to her feet expecting him to be lying beside her.

Cayden! Cayden, I am here! Reach for me. Use my spirit! I will strengthen you! We are nearly there! I will be your rock, brother! Come, come to me.

The spire had changed while she had been praying. The grand hall was no longer empty. An audience had gathered. The souls of both Cathairian and Primordial and of the beasts transformed lined the hall. An army of spirit answering the temple's call, answering her call.

Avery surveyed the crowded room and opened her mouth to send them to Cayden's aid. Before she could speak the command, they disappeared. One by one, they vanished, sucked from her presence in a whoosh.

Aossi, eyes wide with alarm, scrambled onto the dais beside her. "It's Cayden. He has broken the seal!"

"How can we help him, Aossi? What can we do? How can we disrupt Helga's hold on his mind?"

"I do not know. Such a soul bind, the binding of one god to another, has never been done. I fear it will take a god to break it."

Avery's eyes swept the sparking spire behind her. "Then let us pray they are successful," she said softly. She turned back to the remaining spirits. "You know what you must do. Go to him now." The room emptied, and she found herself alone once more. Prayer was definitely in order. She sat back down and reached out to her father.

* * *

Artio climbed and climbed for an eternity of steps, collapsing onto the wind-tossed pinnacle from trembling legs. The climb might have been hours but felt like days. Indeed, the passage of time had no bearing in their quest, having passed beyond mortal reckonings. Panting heavily, Artio swallowed twice before gaining enough moisture in her mouth to speak. "There...it is. The...eye." She pointed directly ahead of them.

The slab of pristine marble they stood on contained but one thing. Sunk into the exact center of the platform was a grey granite head, staring at them. One eye was closed in a wink, the other a hollowed orb waiting for sight. Genii flipped open his pack and pulled out the wrapped present from his mother, gently laying it on the surface. He pushed the coverings aside, revealing the crystal eye.

"Where did you get this?" Artio gasped, the crystal eye moving at her speech, swiveling to stare at her. "An orb of the gods!"

"It was a gift. I did not steal it. It would appear I was meant to have it." He picked it up in one hand and pulled her to her feet with the other. "There is only one possible purpose for this eye. Come, let's do this." Genii hurried over to the face and lined up the eye with the socket, then pushed it in with an audible click.

At first there was silence, then a distant roar filled their ears which grew louder and louder. The spire trembled and the lightning increased, swirling the clouds of true tempest. They rolled over the platform as it vanished into the roiling vapour. Forks of lightning stabbed down, but none touched them.

Then the spire moved. One second it was stone, the next it transformed into the body of a god.

The platform became the palm of the giant's hand, and both eyes stared at the pair of them.

"Your need must be great to call me so. I never thought it would happen, and certainly not by you. It is good to see you again, Artio, although you are transformed, I see." He chuckled. "Ever you were the wild one!" The voice spoke to their minds but filled the gaps around them too. There was no hiding from it.

Artio fell to her knees, face pressed to the curve of his palm "Father, Caerwyn needs your aid. Helga has disrupted the flow of souls and is about to destroy this world. Alfreda prays for your intervention! We need your help, Father. Please help us in our most desperate hour! I beseech you!"

Morpheus gazed at his daughter then his eyes swung to Genii. "It is also good to see you, son. I know that your journey has been especially arduous. A healing of the mind is in order, I think." A gentle wind swept the pair of them, and they gasped as pure joy settled into their souls, euphorically healing.

Genii smiled "Hello, Father."

Artio stiffened as the words sunk in. "Father?" she whispered in a shocked voice, eyes shifting from Morpheus to Genii. "Genii is your son?"

Morpheus nodded. "There is no time to discuss this now, Artio. It is a chat for another time. Perhaps over tea?" When she opened her mouth to protest, he held up his hand, forestalling her words. "I have been gone too long. The world I created has suffered as a result. It is time I corrected this oversight, starting with reuniting my family…all of my family. I will aid you in your time of need. Sacrifice is still needed, for the will to save this world must come from the mortals within it. There is only so much I can do. Are you prepared to do what must be done?" At their dual nods, he continued, "I see Caerwyn is in great distress. I will break the hold of the Fetches. But to do so, you must give me the will to do so. Are your hearts pure of intent? Do you will this to be? Are you ready to sacrifice your will for the greater good of all the souls bound to this planet? As the caretakers you were called to be?" Artio's hand slid into Genii's once more, and together they nodded.

"It does not mean that Helga is restrained. That is a battle that must still be fought. She was ever the wayward one."

"We will go and aid the Spirit Shields, Father," said Artio

"Then be at peace. Come, I will take you to them."

Morpheus's hand closed and his will merged with theirs. With a flash, they were gone.

*　*　*

Ziona felt the tug of Cayden's mind as a wrenching possession, as he gathered strength from her. *Cayden? What is happening? Cayden?* Her hands left the tying of the bandage she was working on. She stood, swaying on the spot at the rush of raw power and emotion flowing through Cayden. "Oh no, he is about to do something desperate." As she turned to speak to the others, howling Daimons came running in from every tunnel, eight in total, emptying into the cavern at the base of the Traitor's Gate. "To arms!" she shouted and snatched up her knife, but she knew their weapons would be useless against the conjuring of the underworld. The wounded knights staggered to their feet, snatching up their swords, but Ziona could see it would be a slaughter. She prayed silently to the gods for intervention then set her feet, ready to engage the fiery monsters.

Three steps from her, when she could feel the monster's breath hot on her cheek, the beast vanished. With a poof and a whiff of sulphur, it was simply gone. Bewildered, the knights lowered their weapons, confusion mirrored on every face.

Ziona reached out to Cayden once more...but he was gone. There was nothing. The bond was gone, empty. Ziona gasped, staggered and collapsed to the floor of the cave, unconscious.

*   *   *

Cayden flipped over onto his back as a surge of pure will soared through him, gasping as a fish out of water, trying to take a breath that was impossible. Mordecai had fallen to his knees also, a trembling aspen leaf in the wind, as the hold of the Soul Fetch broke and fell away. Mordecai slumped onto his side twitching then stilled.

Cayden gasped then pushed himself onto hands and knees and crawled back to the seal, greatly weakened by his struggles. Calleigh's potion still roared through his veins, and now that he was free of the Fetch, the poison was acting as any poison would. He was dying. He knew what he needed to do.

Cayden reached out to Avery and to Ziona and gathered their courage to him. Strengthened, he sat up then snatched up the flute and placed it against his lips.

The flute did not play a sound, but it did not need to, for the music was of the soul and for the soul. As he played, souls winked into the chamber, one, two, four, ten and then so many that they melded into a blue mist that became something more solid.

This time he did not resist the merging. Cayden pulled the souls of humanity, the souls of the magical into him, in a surge of raw power that built under his skin, pulsing with life and will and hope. When he could hold no more, he called on his father's will, and Morpheus's joy flowed into him, a healing balm for his wounded spirit. He smiled even as his skin cracked and blood flowed. What was this mortal body but a vessel to carry the soul?

Cayden took up the knife. Without a second thought, he plunged it into his chest. The flow of the spirits sent by Avery, combined with the souls already coursing through him built to a crescendo so strong, it was a simple thing to step out of his body. As his life emptied, he left the broken shell of his body and poured himself into the seal, pulling the souls with him to join with him in the soul stream. Cayden's will and his soul was more than a simple soul. His soul was the shield, the dense protection that separated the souls to be reborn from those condemned. He was the veil, that barrier between worlds. Without his protection, there was no rebirth and all mortal life would cease to exist. His will was the only way to seal the rift. He knew there was always the chance for rebirth, even for a godling, for he had made it so. What was important was that the souls be protected, forever...even to the grave.

CHAPTER 60

Great Balls of Fire

MORDECAI CAME TO WITH A START. He rolled onto his bony knees and shook his shaggy hair out of his face like an old bear waking from a long hibernation. The action did little to clear his muddled thoughts. The floor swam before his eyes as he lifted his heavy head. Mordecai stared warily about him, unsure how he had come to be lying in the chamber that housed the Well of Souls. A throbbing mass of memories surfaced and with it an accompanying jolt of pain, as though half of his brain had been forcibly removed through his ears. He raised his hand to check for bleeding, the pounding pulse of his blood roaring in his ears. It came away clean.

A flickering blue light drew his eyes to the Well of Souls. Pushing himself to his feet, he staggered to the fractured rim and peered over the side. Deep down in the depths of the well, the River of Souls swirled and danced, thickening before his eyes. Slowly the level of the well began to rise, and it was then that he knew that Cayden was healing the stream.

With a gasp, he pushed away from the rim and ran between the arches leading to the tunnels. "Cayden! Fool boy, what have you done?" he said aloud, his voice reverberating down the hall as he stumbled toward the castle.

The ground rumbled and shook. Loose stones fell with a clatter of rock on rock. The earth groaned around him. Mordecai quickened his pace, hiking his robes up around his knees as he ran. He met no one in the passages. They remained devoid of life.

That is because the battle for Cathair has already commenced, and you slept it away! Fool wizard, you prepared for this moment all your life, only to lay unconscious at the pinnacle of the plan? Please don't let me be too late! Mordecai chided himself for the elderly fool he was.

Memories assailed him, and with every step, the hazy time spent enslaved to Helga came back to him with a crush of grief. *I have a brother! And not just one! And sisters too!* The realization that everything he had striven to do his entire life was nothing more than a family feud was a truth that he was only now beginning to understand. *Father, why did you decide to abandon us so? Surely, you could have made a difference. Was it really so important to keep the peace with the gods? Or were our lives forfeit if you aided us in any way?* The thought, which he sent skyward as a prayer, rang true and he grimaced over the choice. Ultimately Morpheus's abandonment of his family was a testament to his love. He had desired more than anything else to have his family live. Mordecai felt a light brush against his mind, and a soothing calm settled on his conscience. The touch was so personal, he stopped walking. "Father?"

"I am here, Mordecai." The darkness lightened and solidified into a glowing figure. Morpheus stepped from the rift and walked up to his wrinkled, greying wizard of a son. "It is good to see you, son." He folded the old man into his arms. "It is even better to hold you."

Mordecai hugged him back then pushed apart to stare into a face that was an exact replica of his own, right down to the twinkle in his eyes. Mordecai's eyes twinkled in response and a grin split his face then faded as another boom loosened the stone under his feet. "The battle has commenced. We do not have much time, do we, Father? Can we win this battle and right the wrongs we have committed? Your children have made such a mess of things. We have forgotten your charge, to care for the world and the mortals within it."

"All is not lost, my son. But you must intercede or the battle may truly be lost. Helga is even more embittered than I remembered. She must be stopped and to do so, you have a role to play. The others converge even as we speak, but you must halt Cyrus. He has survived the attack by Denzik, by the healing powers of his mage. He is in league with Helga, and he intends to let the legion and the Kingsmen be crushed against the walls of this castle. The blood of mankind will stain the soil forever and the magic of Cathair will fade, should this event come to pass. The land will be salted and unfit for human habitation and the Well of Souls will dry up forever. The task of stopping Cyrus and his mage falls to you, Mordecai. Do what you must."

"I will, Father."

"I must go, but first I wanted to clear your mind of the Soul Fetch's presence. Be at peace, my son."

"Bye, Father!" Mordecai's waving hand dropped back to his side as his father walked away through the stone wall, fading just before he reached it.

We will speak again, my son, Morpheus whispered to his mind, and then he was gone.

The tunnel heaved, throwing Mordecai into motion. He ran for the exit, even as the ceiling collapsed behind him. He staggered up the limestone steps and into the courtyard where the battle shrieked with the cries of the wounded and the clang of armour. The skyline above the walls of the outer courtyard glowed with a red haze. His eyes searched for resistance, but he found none. The legionnaires had gathered at the outer gate leading to the plains, and all eyes were focused on the battle beneath the walls. No one challenged him as he raced up the circular tower access to the outer defense wall.

As he burst onto the catwalk, he spied the tall shadowed silhouette of Cyrus. He was attended by eight guards and two mages who peered down at the scene below. Cyrus stood back from the wall with arms folded, a pleased smile on his face. The fiery glow of the Daimons reflected off his face, turning his cheeks and pointed grey beard a ruddy red.

Mordecai flattened himself against the wall and watched as a mage lifted his hand and began to throw fireballs down into the confusion below. Everywhere the comets struck, men and horses screamed, but the Daimons were unaffected, being creatures born of flame. The grass ignited and smoke billowed across the tableau, obscuring friend from foe and adding to the confusion. Mordecai could smell the putrid oily odour of burning horse hair and flesh. Recent memories surfaced, and he had to force down the bile that rose in his throat, swallowing painfully. Sickened, his hands glowed with his own wizard's fire and as his anger mounted so did the intensity of his fire so that his hands began to crackle with the pent-up energy.

Sensing the disturbance, a mage turned to look his direction. Before he could shout a warning, Mordecai's fireball struck him in the chest. Instantly, he was enveloped. He staggered backward. As he hit the wall, he slipped through a merlon and toppled backward off the wall into the seething mass below.

The guards charged down the wall toward Mordecai. One by one, he sent fine streams of fire at them. Lightning thin, the flaming spears pierced armour and flesh alike as they dropped where they were struck. Mordecai ignored them, his eyes fixed on Cyrus and the one remaining magician.

The mage and Cyrus were now encased in a bubble that reflected a silvery sheen when the light touched it.

He has cast an energy shield over himself and Cyrus, thought Mordecai as he walked slowly forward, hands crackling with pent-up energy. He let the wizard's fire die and instead cast his will toward the trough of water in the bailey below. With a pull, he drew the water out of the trough and sent it swirling through the air, a spinning storm that swept up out of the courtyard and slammed into the pair. The energy shield crackled, but did not fail. It did not matter, for the tornado simply picked them both up and swept them out over the wall. Once they were out over the battle, Mordecai released his will and the tornado vanished. The energy shield vanished with it as the mage frantically worked a new spell, but Mordecai was faster and his hands reenergized, sent fireball after fireball into the falling would-be king and his magician. Cyrus and the mage were engulfed in flame. Glowing like meteors, they hurled towards the ground, only to wink out of existence before impact.

Mordecai ran to the rampart. His family needed his aid. Drawing deep from within, his newly freed will soared out over the battlements and created a wave of interference that settled on the defenders, causing the blades of the Daimons to veer off target as though sliding along a slick coating of ice. He glimpsed Ryder being run down by Asaq, the Daimon of his childhood nightmares. Memory flashed of his first meeting with the Daimon, in the sacred clearing where he had watched Caerwyn and Alfreda die. Mordecai screamed in defiance and joined the battle in earnest, tossing great balls of water down onto the flaming fields below.

CHAPTER 61

The Final Battle

THE KINGSMEN RODE OVER the final rise and straight into the waiting ranks of the legionnaires. Three men deep, they drew swords as the Kingsmen bore down on their position outside the outer castle wall gate.

"Let us through! Give way! Daimon on the horizon!" shouted the lead Kingsman, waving a flag of truce over his head. "We come in peace!"

"Defend the castle! Man the walls!" shouted another Kingsman with a second flag.

Confusion swept the front line. This was not what the legionnaires had expected, seeing the Kingsmen racing toward them under a flag of truce. They had expected a head-on assault to take back the city, a battle for supremacy. Instead, the Kingsmen appeared to be surrendering. They were still too far away to hear the words they shouted, but the meaning of the flags was evident.

"Halt where you are!" shouted a legion captain, pointing his sword at the oncoming flagman. "We will slay you all if you approach any closer!"

"Daimons, you fool!" shouted the man with the flag, "Let us through! We come to aid you, not fight you! Daimons, I say!"

"What is this dribble? There are no such things as Daimons," the legionnaire's voice trailed away as his eyes were drawn to a fiery glow over the rise. "What is that smoke from? Are the grasslands on fire?"

"Hell, no! Are you deaf? *There are Daimons on the loose, and they are coming this way!*"

With no command to attack, the Kingsmen rode freely into the midst of the legionnaires and pulled their sweating mounts to a halt, turning to face the way they had come, pulling their swords to face the approaching storm.

The glow brightened and expanded until it stretched across the entire horizon. Howls pierced the air, at first faint, then growing louder as the glow brightened.

"What *is* that?" asked a young legionnaire, pointing to the glow, eyes widening in alarm.

"Daimon, straight from Sheol Animus. They have been chasing us for miles."

Muttering broke out amongst the legionnaires.

At that moment, the glow broke the horizon in a wave of guttural cries that sent a shiver down every back. Each Daimon brandished a flaming sword and howled with soul lust. They paused for a moment on the crest of the hill, then fell like a wave, crashing down the slope toward the waiting defenders.

A grinding of gate gears tore the attention of the men to the castle wall. The gates swung open and the knights of Cathair spilled out to join the mixed Kingsmen and legionnaires. Ryder led the way, riding up beside the makeshift captains of the Kingsmen and the legion. The gates swung closed behind them, and a hollow boom echoed out to them as the great iron bars were slid into place, barring the doors.

"Glad to see I have not missed the party," Ryder said, nodding at the captains. "I have a personal interest in this battle. Now listen, and listen closely. There is no time to repeat these instructions. Here is what we are going to do."

Hastily whispered instructions spread amongst the ranks of men, and then they spread out into two wedges of horsemen with a thinner band in the middle of foot soldiers. The idea was to draw the Daimon into the midst of the army of men. Runners appeared on the castle wall, and brass caldrons appeared in the toothy gaps of the upper reaches.

The Daimons burst through the last scrubby cover, blazing a trail of destruction. They slammed into the main force of men with the strength of a battering ram. For all that the men tried to fight back, they were swept aside by flame and sword, toy soldiers scattered by a child's tantrum. The only thing that slowed the Daimons was when they stopped to feed on the souls of the slain. In their feeding frenzy, the Daimons began to fight amongst themselves; a pack of fiery hyenas around a fresh kill. The flaming swords, so effective against the defenseless humans, were equally effective against a Daimon.

Ryder, seeing that the swords would slay a Daimon, quickly passed the information to the runners with instructions to capture swords. A group of ten knights attacked a smaller Daimon, slicing and stabbing at the creature. With a swift swinging slash, they cut off the Daimon's sword hand, and the flaming blade tumbled onto the grass. It was as though it had been plunged into water. As soon as the Daimon's hand was severed from its body the flames vanished, leaving behind a blackened corrupted blade. Separated from its sword, it gave an angry screech and staggered, flickering oddly. Ryder scooped up the charcoal blade with a gloved hand, careful to not touch the metal, then slashed the Daimon across its calves, hamstringing the beast. It roared as it toppled, snapping at those closest to it, dragging a legionnaire down even as Ryder cut its throat. Lava flowed out of its neck and congealed as the Daimon perished, solidifying to stone.

"Right!" shouted Ryder in triumph. "We know how to defeat these things!" Ryder straightened and then ducked as a Daimon bore down on him, flaming sword raised high. With a wicked downward stroke, meant to split Ryder's skull, the Daimon attacked. Ryder threw up the blackened blade in a desperate defense and the swords struck like the gong of a bell, black on red, sparks flying off the skidding blades. It was all Ryder could do to keep the Daimon's sword from taking his head.

I am not sure how much longer I can hold him. This beast is strong! he thought as his arms shook, muscles bulging. With a mighty heave, he pushed the Daimon back a step then dove through its legs, scrambling to his feet behind the monster. The blackened blade swung out again, and the Daimon toppled, but this time it still had its sword and continued to fight, managing to take down three more of Ryder's men before it was turned to stone. Unfortunately, the blade was also encased in stone. *Rotten luck, that!*

Ryder stumbled away from the pile of rock and froze as a scream split the air, so high pitched it could only be called feminine. All eyes were drawn to a towering behemoth of a Daimon, twice the height of the other Daimons. Asag had arrived, famed Daimon of legend, and yet it was more than that. This Daimon's features were softer, more feminine, and oddly it wore a bright blue collar that flashed with lightning.

Ryder swallowed heavily. "Damm! Why did you have to come, Helga?" As though she heard him, her head swiveled in his direction. She lifted a hand and pointed directly at him, a portend of his doom. Ryder ducked as a blade whistled past his ear. The Daimon roared their approval of Asag's arrival and with a surge of renewed ferocity pushed the Cathairian defenders back against the castle wall.

The battle raged around Ryder. Helga was on the move, taking giant strides that would bring her swiftly within striking distance. Ryder had no doubt that she planned to finish this battle to the last man. None would survive. Desperate, he grabbed the bridle of a horse wandering lose and swung into the saddle, but not swiftly enough to avoid a burning cut across his knee. He dug his heels into the sides of the wild-eyed horse, and it bolted away from the fray. He hoped to distract Helga away from the main battle and away from his men. He could feel her eyes on him as he whipped the reins against the horse's flanks, urging it to run faster. He felt Helga veer off her original path.

"So this is what a vengeful god looks like," he muttered aloud to the horse, as the ground shook beneath her pounding steps. He rode in a curving arch that would bring him parallel to the castle wall and away from the gates. He took a quick glance over his shoulder to see that she was mere steps away from him and squeezed his eyes closed. There was no place to go and nothing he could think of to stop the inevitable. *Bad choice, messing with a god. I think I am going to regret this for a very long time.*

"Ryder!" she screamed "You will serve me in hell for your betrayal. Forever!" He heard the blade whistle through the air and tensed for the thrust.

At that moment, several things happened.

Horns blared on the horizon, a long, low blast that moaned across the hills. Suddenly, the abandoned hills were crawling with an army, recently arrived. A host of Primordial warriors, their faces shielded by spirit masks, filled his vision. With another long, low wail, they hurtled war cries to the air and raced down the hillside toward the battle, led by Achak with his phoenix on his shoulder. Above the Primordials their spirit guardians soared, racing forward, their transformed spirits of the wild answering the call. The echoing and amplified battle cry bounced off the walls of Cathair, drawing every eye.

The Daimons milled about in confusion, distracted by the spirits of the animals, those mythical beasts of legend called to battle.

Helga slowed her chase of Ryder and twisted to see what the new threat was, snarling. "Attack them, you dumb beasts!" she screamed at the Daimon. "Kill the Primordials before they engage their spirits!" The Daimons sniffed the air then with a howl, left the decimated men at the gate and roared toward the newcomers.

Helga turned back to Ryder, who had also reined in at the sight of the Primordial host. "Now, you will die, my pet." She bounded forward, but before she could take three steps, the air in front of her shimmered and a portal opened, depositing Artio and Genii on the grass in front of her. Hands joined, they pulsed with light and love, a blessing of the temple.

"That is enough, Helga," said Artio, walking towards her sister. "You will cease this now, or you will be banished to the underworld forever."

Helga threw back her head and laughed. "And who is going to stop me, you? And my former slave? You do not have the power to do so."

"No, but he does." Artio and Genii gestured behind Helga where a second portal had opened, but this one did not touch the ground. The soul surge spilled out of the rift, all the souls of the river, those still free and those Cayden freed with his healing. They were joined by the spirits of the animals, the mythical renderings of the physical beasts, snarling and flapping and snapping at the Daimons as they fought for their eternity too, wrapping around Helga in a swirling tornado of life, completely encasing her from head to toe in a pulsing river of spirit.

Mordecai, tossing a blue fire that froze on impact, built a rapid-fire icy cage around Asag, imprisoning him and Helga. She screamed and tried to force Asag to cross the ice, but the touch of the crystals sizzled and froze his flaming flesh and he howled, refusing to cross regardless of what she did to force his obedience.

Avery, riding in a chariot driven by none other than Aossi, descended from the skies, casting peace and love on the scene, cooling the fires of hatred and encasing the lust for blood. "Peace, my children," she said as she landed beside the field of battle.

Cayden's soul surge throbbed and touched the blue necklace, pulsing with life and hope. It convulsed around the Daimon's neck. Helga screamed, and Cayden screamed as his will came in contact with the black, soulless heart of the Daimon, drawing all eyes. It was a creature without mercy or remorse. Cayden tightened his hold on it, suffocating the fires of Asag. Reaching in with the last of his will, he pulled the souls from the beast, those souls who had been sacrificed to its creation. Separated from the living souls, Asag slowed and cooled, turning to stone.

Helga was ejected from the Daimon and fell to the ground at Artio and Genii's feet. Ryder, who had ridden forward as soon as he had seen the soul surge, tossed the blackened blade to Artio, who drew it against Helga's neck, freezing her where she kneeled.

"Do not move," she commanded.

Avery vanished back to the temple, her task complete. She was needed elsewhere and she obeyed the summons. Cayden needed her.

CHAPTER 62

Soul Sacrifice

CAYDEN HAD EMPTIED HIMSELF into the soul stream. Everywhere his soul touched, the veil was healed. Coursing along its length, he'd repaired every breach, every crack and every fissure. He'd coursed the labyrinth of tunnels, halting the lava flows and hardening them to rock once more. Cayden spread his will across the entire world, mending the souls he found and sealing the fissures in the stream to the Well of Souls. He recalled the lost souls those snatched away against their will, and brought them tenderly home. Charun vanished, flashing to ashes where they stood as the soul feeding the blackness vanished. Cayden's will cast a net over the underworld, encasing it, dampening the fires and calming the mountain. He swirled into Faylea, that ancient city of old, pulling the poison of the necromancer's passage from the world and restoring the flow of spirit that fed all living things. As he swirled around the temple, he appeared before Avery as another soul that had come to her.

"Cayden!" Avery cried and rushed to hug him, knowing she could not yet desperate to try.

"It is done, Avery." He was tired, so tired. "I have soul surged the river to heal the breaches. All has been restored. You are safe now." His image flickered, fading slightly.

Tears streamed down Avery's face. "What shall I tell, Ziona? She will be heartbroken."

Cayden smiled sadly. For all that he had been prepared for this eventuality, the reality was gut wrenching. *Ziona! I will always love you!*

he sent to her, along the bond. "Tell her I am with her, always. She will be able to find me in her mind and in her heart. There is no parting when two souls are truly one. Tell her I will love her always."

"I will, Cayden, I will." Avery swallowed painfully. "I will also seek you out that way. Tell her…" Cayden's words faded as his voice failed, choked by his despair. "Avery, tell her…tell her I love her. Maybe this is how Father felt, all those years ago. Tell her, I will always be with her and that I wish it could have been different." He flickered weakly, yet Avery sensed through their bond the anguish he felt. "I can no longer find our bond. It has been lost. I would go to her but I cannot." Avery saw tears in the insubstantial shadow that was her brother. Her tears joined his in a journey down their cheeks.

"I will, Cayden, I promise. I will miss you so!" she cried.

"I know. Perhaps…perhaps Father will leave a gateway for us to communicate. I love you, Avery." She felt the tender brush of a hand on her cheek, and then he faded away. He was gone.

EPILOGUE

IN THE DAYS THAT FOLLOWED, the people returned home.

Not to homes as they were before the cataclysm or even before the reign of the queen, but to their homelands to where their hearts said they should be. There was surprising little loss of life, considering all the rampaging of the Daimon and the warring factions. Most of the suitable housing had burned and needed to be rebuilt, fields plowed for crops, scattered herds gathered, and lives re-established.

But the biggest project undertaken in every village, at every crossroad, in every town, was the building of the temples. In those communities where temples existed, they were refurbished or reclaimed from the jungles that had swallowed them.

The people knew what had happened. Their king had sacrificed himself to save them all.

Mordecai decreed a week of mourning and instructed the knights to hand out blue bands to wear in tribute to their fallen king. Mordecai was also proclaimed interim leader of Cathair until the line of ascension could be determined. There was great news on that front, and the people were happy to have the wizard guarding the well until a Spirit Shield could be returned to the throne. Many had thought that Avery should take over as queen of Cathair, but the High Priestess had declined, explaining that the temple in Faylea had been too long without a High Priestess to care for it and that her duties lie in the Primordial lands. Her newly discovered half-brother was up to the task, as Mordecai had essentially been guarding it for hundreds of years already. Released from the Soul Fetch, Mordecai searched out those families he had harmed and made recompense for his damage, even though he could not have changed a thing. Such is the heart of a godling. In this, the gods had been wrong. The combination of god and human was not to be feared but to be honoured. The combined offspring were smarter, wiser, and overall, a thing to be desired, not feared. Helga notwithstanding, those born of the gods were a boon to both sides and a bond that was to be treasured.

In honour of Cayden, a new statue was erected in the village square, a young man seated on a rock carving flutes with the faces of the fallen staring up at him. Garlands were placed around his neck and around the necks of the fallen by a steady line of well-wishers.

But perhaps the biggest change for Cathair was the village that sprung up on the outskirts of the city. At first, they were only tents, but as time went on, permanent structures rose from the short grasses. Dubbed by the locals "Little Faylea," a Primordial village was built like a subdivision to the main town. Flesh Clan and Spirit Clan comingled and invited the people of Cathair to trade with them. When asked why they had decided to settle around Cathair and not return to their homelands, they replied, "Cayden was the son of a Primordial princess. He was also Primordial by birth. We come to honour the heritage of the king, our king."

The other remarkable thing, which set the people abuzz with rumour, was the arrival of the Pegasuses. For reasons unknown, they had appeared after Cayden's death, panicking the knights' horses, and sharing the field where the ancient stables were located. Once it became evident that they had no intention of leaving, the horses were moved to adjoining pastures and the old stables were repaired and shined up to house them. The magical creatures were another constant draw to the capital and a source of awe and wonder. Why they had not faded away this time with the demise of the Spirit Shield, no one understood. Most gave the credit to Avery as the remaining Spirit Shield, although she had not come to see them, busy as she was with affairs in Faylea.

The Kingsmen and the knights had taken up their usual duties, but there was a lackluster feel to their ranks. Many openly wept for their lost king. A dark cloud permeated their ranks, the loss and grief too fresh.

But time was the ultimate healer. Fall faded to winter, and with the first vestiges of spring, hope sprung anew. With spring came the lambs and the colts and the piglets. With spring came the tender shoots pushing from the soil, budding trees and the smells of life sprung anew. As the rebirth of nature gripped the land newly returned from the dead, so it also did in a mullioned room in the tallest tower.

*   *   *

Ziona's screams rent the air. Sobbing uncontrollably, she pushed once again. It was agony, pure agony. Childbirth was a universal torture, whether Primordial or Cathairian, the pain unescapable. Panting, she clutched at Mordecai's hand, while the midwives attended to the birth.

"The baby! It's coming! It's coming!" Excitement warred with exhaustion, her eyes ringed with black from a long, sleepless night. The first twitters of the spring birds could be heard in the silence of dawn. Mordecai patted her hand and smiled, wrinkles curving into a whiskered wreath of happiness.

"Shhh, Ziona. I know. We are ready. Trust me."

Mordecai reached into his pocket and pulled out a crystal, oblong in shape. He placed it in her palm and closed her fingers around it, then placed his hands on either side of hers. The stone warmed and together they began to chant, Ziona's words punctuated by more screams as the pain of childbirth interrupted her litany.

The stone hummed and a blue lightning shot from the gaps between their joined fingers, bathing the stone walls in a brilliant azure reflection. The tower room warmed as the light shrank and coalesced into an ethereal form, floating in the air. Ziona gasped as it pulsed, tears glistening to life in her eyes. She recognized the spirit that pulsed alongside her own. Another contraction gripped her, and she squeezed her eyes shut, as her body convulsed, striving to push the infant from her body.

One, two, three pushes and the newborn slid into the waiting hands of the midwife.

"A boy!" crowed the midwife closest to her. Moments later a cry was heard.

Ziona's exhausted eyes met Mordecai's and tears of gratitude tumbled from them with joy at the miracle of the birth, the promise of a life returned.

Mordecai straightened and kissed her sweaty forehead, then backed away from the bed. "Congratulations, Ziona." He swiped a hand across the corner of his eyes, tears of joy sparkling in their depths and leaking down his wrinkled cheeks.

The midwives placed the squalling infant in her arms.

She trailed a finger down the side of the ruddy face, bright green eyes staring back at her. She lightly touched a birthmark in the shape of an oak leaf, adorning his chubby cheek. The mark did not fade. Her face broke into a huge smile and she hugged him close.

"Caerwyn. Welcome, my child."

OTHER BOOKS BY SUSAN FAW

The Spirit Shield Saga:

Soul Survivor
Seer Of Souls
Soul Sanctuary
Soul Sacrifice

Coming Soon!

The Heart Of The Citadel

Sign up for my newsletter and be the first to know the release date for Heart of Destiny,

HEART OF DESTINY NEWSLETTER SIGN UP:
https://app.convertkit.com/landing_pages/151316?v=6

ABOUT THE AUTHOR: SUSAN FAW

Professional by day, book nerd and fantasy champion by night, Susan is a masked crusader for the fantastical world. Championing mythical rights, she quells uprisings and battles infidels who would slay the lifeblood of her pen. It's all in a night's work, for this whirlwind writer. Welcome to the quest.

VISIT SUSAN ONLINE:

http://susanfaw.com/

https://www.facebook.com/SusanFaw

https://twitter.com/susandfaw

https://www.pinterest.com/susandfaw

https://www.bookbub.com/authors/susan-faw

FIND OUT HOW IT ALL BEGAN! DOWNLOAD THE FREE PREQUEL, SOUL SURVIVOR AT THE LINK BELOW!

http://susanfaw.com/soul-survivor-prequel-free-download/

JOIN MY STREET TEAM FOR THE LATEST NEWS!
https://app.convertkit.com/landing_pages/98068?v=6